CROSSROADS
OF
TWILIGHT

ROBERT JORDAN

TOR®
fantasy

A TOM DOHERTY ASSOCIATES BOOK
NEW YORK

This is a work of fiction. All of the characters, organizations, and events portrayed in this novel are either products of the author's imagination or are used fictitiously.

CROSSROADS OF TWILIGHT

Copyright © 2003 by Bandersnatch Group, Inc.

Excerpt from *Knife of Dreams* copyright © 2005 by Bandersnatch Group, Inc.

The phrase "The Wheel of Time" and the snake-wheel symbol are trademarks of Bandersnatch Group, Inc.

All rights reserved.

Maps by Ellisa Mitchell
Interior illustration by Matthew C. Nielsen and Ellisa Mitchell

A Tor Book
Published by Tom Doherty Associates
120 Broadway
New York, NY 10271

www.tor-forge.com

Tor® is a registered trademark of Macmillan Publishing Group, LLC.

ISBN 978-1-250-25253-1

Our books may be purchased in bulk for promotional, educational, or business use. Please contact your local bookseller or the Macmillan Corporate and Premium Sales Department at 1-800-221-7945, extension 5442, or by email at MacmillanSpecialMarkets@macmillan.com.

First Edition: January 2003
First Premium Mass Market Edition: May 2020

Printed in the United States of America

0 9 8 7 6 5 4

Praise for
Robert Jordan and
The Wheel of Time®

"His huge, ambitious Wheel of Time series helped redefine the genre." —George R. R. Martin, internationally bestselling author of *A Game of Thrones*

"Anyone who's writing epic secondary world fantasy knows Robert Jordan isn't just a part of the landscape, he's a monolith within the landscape." —Patrick Rothfuss, internationally bestselling author of The Kingkiller Chronicle

"*The Eye of the World* was a turning point in my life. I read, I enjoyed. (Then continued on to write my larger fantasy novels.)" —Robin Hobb, *New York Times* bestselling author of The Farseer Trilogy

"Robert Jordan's work has been a formative influence and an inspiration for a generation of fantasy writers." —Brent Weeks, *New York Times* bestselling author of *The Way of Shadows*

"Jordan has come to dominate the world Tolkien began to reveal" —*The New York Times*

"One of fantasy's most acclaimed series." —*USA Today*

"Robert Jordan was a giant of fiction whose words helped a whole generation of fantasy writers, including myself, find our true voices. I thanked him then, but I didn't thank him enough." —Peter V. Brett, internationally bestselling author of The Demon Cycle

"[Robert Jordan's] impact on the place of fantasy in the culture is colossal. . . . He brought innumerable readers to fantasy. He became the *New York Times* Best Seller List's face of fantasy." —Guy Gavriel Kay, internationally bestselling author of *Tigana*

"Jordan's writing is so amazing! The characterization, the attention to detail!" —Clint McElroy, cocreator of the #1 podcast *The Adventure Zone*

"The Wheel of Time [is] rapidly becoming the definitive American fantasy saga. It is a fantasy tale seldom equaled and still less often surpassed in English."
—*Chicago Sun-Times*

"Hard to put down for even a moment. A fittingly epic conclusion to a fantasy series that many consider one of the best of all time." —*San Francisco Book Review* on *A Memory of Light*

The Wheel of Time®

By Robert Jordan

By Robert Jordan and Brandon Sanderson

By Robert Jordan and Teresa Patterson

By Robert Jordan, Harriet McDougal, Alan Romanczuk, and Maria Simons

For Harriet
Then, now, and always

CONTENTS

And it shall come to pass, in the days when the Dark Hunt rides, when the right hand falters and the left hand strays, that mankind shall come to the Crossroads of Twilight and all that is, all that was, and all that will be shall balance on the point of a sword, while the winds of the Shadow grow.

—From *The Prophecies of the Dragon,* translation believed done by Jain Charin, known as Jain Farstrider, shortly before his disappearance

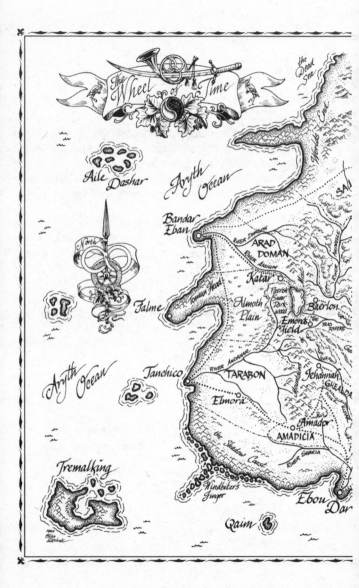

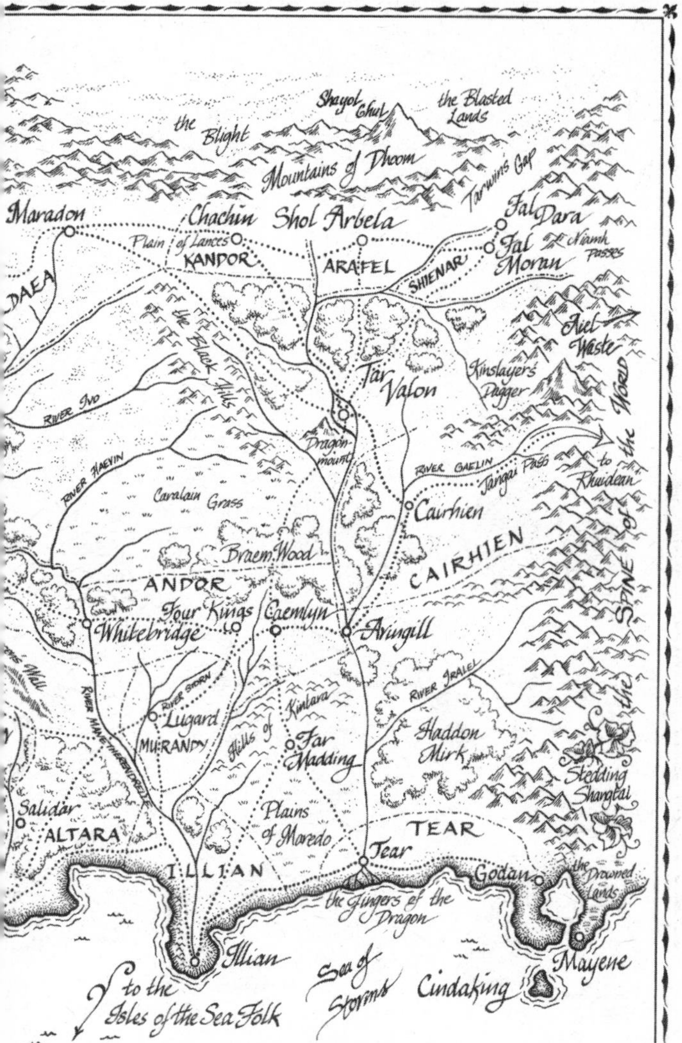

Shayol Ghul
the Blasted Lands
the Blight
Mountains of Dhoom
Tarwins Gap
Maradon
Chachin
Shol Arbela
Fal Dara
Fal Moran
Niamh Passes
Plain of Lances
KANDOR
ARAFEL
SHIENAR
DAEA
Aiel Waste
the Black Hills
Tar Valon
Kinslayer's Dagger
River Ivo
Dragonmount
River Haevin
River Gaelin
Jangai Pass
to Rhuidean
Caralain Grass
Cairhien
Braem Wood
CAIRHIEN
ANDOR
Four Kings
Caemlyn
Whitebridge
Aringill
Spine of the World
River Storn
River Iralell
Lugard
Kintara
Hills of
MURANDY
Far Madding
Haddon Mirk
Stedding Shangtai
River Manetherendrelle
Salidar
ALTARA
Plains of Maredo
TEAR
Tear
ILLIAN
Godan
the Drowned Lands
the Fingers of the Dragon
Illian
Mayene
Sea of Storms
Cindaking
to the Isles of the Sea Folk

PROLOGUE

Glimmers of the Pattern

R odel Ituralde hated waiting, though he well knew it was the largest part of being a soldier. Waiting for the next battle, for the enemy to move, to make a mistake. He watched the winter forest and was as still as the trees. The sun stood halfway to its peak, and gave no warmth. His breath misted white in front of his face, frosting his neatly trimmed mustache and the black fox fur lining his hood. He was glad that his helmet hung at his pommel. His breastplate held the cold and radiated it through his coat and all the layers of wool, silk and linen beneath. Even Dart's saddle felt cold, as though the white gelding were made of frozen milk. The helmet would have addled his brain.

Winter had come late to Arad Doman, very late, but with a vengeance. From summer heat that lingered unnaturally into fall, to winter's heart in less than a month. The leaves that had survived the long summer's drought had been frozen before they could change color, and now they glistened like strange, ice-covered emeralds in the morning sun. The horses of the twenty-odd armsmen around him occasionally stamped a hoof in the knee-deep snow. It had been a long ride this far, and they had farther to go whether this day turned out good or ill. Dark clouds roiled the sky to northward. He did not need his weather-wise there to tell him the temperature would plummet before nightfall. They had to be under shelter by then.

"Not as rough as winter before last, is it, my Lord?" Jaalam said quietly. The tall young officer had a way of reading Ituralde's mind, and his voice was pitched for the others to hear. "Even so, I suppose some men would be dreaming of mulled wine about now. Not this lot, of course. Remarkably abstemious. They all drink tea, I believe. Cold tea. If they had a few birch switches, they'd be stripping down for snow baths."

"They'll have to keep their clothes on for the time being," Ituralde replied dryly, "but they might get some cold tea tonight, if they're lucky." That brought a few chuckles. Quiet chuckles. He had chosen these men with care, and they knew about noise at the wrong time.

He himself could have done with a steaming cup of spiced wine, or even tea. But it was a long time since merchants had brought tea to Arad Doman. A long time since any outland merchant had ventured farther than the border with Saldaea. By the time news of the outside world reached him, it was as stale as last month's bread, if it was more than rumor to begin. That hardly mattered, though. If the White Tower truly was divided against itself, or men who could channel really were being called to Caemlyn . . . well, the world would have to do without Rodel Ituralde until Arad Doman was whole again. For the moment, Arad Doman was more than enough for any sane man to go on with.

Once again he reviewed the orders he had sent, carried by the fastest riders he had, to every noble loyal to the King. Divided as they were by bad blood and old feuds, they still shared that much. They would gather their armies and ride when orders came from the Wolf; at least, so long as he held the King's favor. They would even hide in the mountains and wait, at his order. Oh, they would chafe, and some would curse his name, but they would obey. They knew the Wolf won battles. More, they knew he won wars. The Little Wolf, they called him when they thought he could not hear, but he did not care whether they drew attention to his stature—well, not much—so long as they rode when and where he said.

Very soon they would be riding hard, moving to set a trap that would not spring for months. It was a long chance he was taking. Complex plans had many ways to fall apart, and this plan had layers inside layers. Everything would be ruined before it began if he failed to provide the bait. Or if someone ignored his order to evade couriers from the

King. They all knew his reasons, though, and even the most stiff-necked shared them, though few were willing to speak of the matter aloud. He himself had moved like a wraith racing on a storm since he received Alsalam's latest command. In his sleeve where the folded paper lay tucked above the pale lace that fell onto his steel-backed gauntlet. They had one last chance, one very small chance, to save Arad Doman. Perhaps even to save Alsalam from himself before the Council of Merchants decided to put another man on the throne in his place. He had been a good ruler, for over twenty years. The Light send that he could be again.

A loud crack to the south sent Ituralde's hand to the hilt of his longsword. There was a faint creak of leather and metal as others eased their weapons. For the rest, silence. The forest was as still as a frozen tomb. Only a limb breaking under the weight of snow. After a moment, he let himself relax—as much as he had relaxed since the tales came north of the Dragon Reborn appearing in the sky at Falme. Perhaps the man really was the Dragon Reborn, perhaps he really had appeared in the sky, but whatever the truth, those tales had set Arad Doman on fire.

Ituralde was sure he could have put out that fire, given a freer hand. It was not boasting to think so. He knew what he could do, with a battle, a campaign, or a war. But ever since the Council had decided the King would be safer smuggled out of Bandar Eban, Alsalam seemed to have taken into his head that he was the rebirth of Artur Hawkwing. His signature and seal had marked scores of battle orders since, flooding out from wherever the Council had him hidden. They would not say where that was, even to Ituralde himself. Every woman on the Council that he confronted went flat-eyed and evasive at any mention of the King. He could almost believe they did not know where Alsalam was. A ridiculous thought, of course. The Council kept an unblinking eye on the King. Ituralde had always believed the merchant Houses interfered too much, yet he wished they would interfere now. Why they remained silent was a mystery, for a king who damaged trade did not remain long on the throne.

He was loyal to his oaths, and Alsalam was a friend, besides, but the orders the King sent could not have been better written to achieve chaos. Nor could they be ignored.

Alsalam was the King. But he had commanded Ituralde to march north with all possible speed against a great gathering of Dragonsworn that Alsalam supposedly knew of from secret spies, then ten days later, with no Dragonsworn yet in sight, an order came to move south again, with all possible speed, against another gathering that never materialized. He had been commanded to concentrate his forces to defend Bandar Eban when a three-pronged attack might have ended it all and to divide them when a hammer blow could have done the same, to harry ground he knew the Dragonsworn had abandoned, and to march away from where he knew they camped. Worse, Alsalam's orders often had gone directly to the powerful nobles who were supposed to be following Ituralde, sending Machir in this direction, Teacal in that, Rahman in a third. Four times, pitched battles had resulted from parts of the army blundering into one another in the night while moving to the King's express command and expecting none but enemies ahead. And all the while the Dragonsworn gained numbers, and confidence. Ituralde had had his triumphs—at Solanje and Maseen, at Lake Somal and Kandelmar—the Lords of Katar had learned not to sell the products of their mines and forges to the enemies of Arad Doman—but always, Alsalam's orders wasted his gains.

This last order was different, though. For one thing, a Gray Man had killed Lady Tuva trying to stop it from reaching him. Why the Shadow might fear this order more than any other was a mystery, yet it was all the more reason to move swiftly. Before Alsalam reached him with another. This order opened many possibilities, and he had considered every last one he could see. But the good ones all started here, today. When small chances of success were all that remained, you had to seize them.

A snowjay's strident cry rang out in the distance, then a second time, a third. Cupping his hands around his mouth, Ituralde repeated the three harsh calls. Moments later a shaggy, pale dapple gelding appeared out of the trees, his rider in a white cloak streaked with black. Man and horse alike would have been hard to see in the snowy forest had they been standing still. The rider pulled up beside Ituralde. A stocky man, he wore only a single sword, with a short blade, and there were a cased bow and a quiver fastened to his saddle.

"Looks like they all came, my Lord," he said in his permanently hoarse voice, pushing his cowl back from his head. Someone had tried to hang Donjel when he was young, though the reason was lost in the years. What remained of his short-cropped hair was iron-gray. The dark leather patch covering the socket of his right eye was a remnant of another youthful scrape. One eye or two, though, he was the best scout Ituralde had ever known. "Most, anyways," he went on. "They put two rings of sentries around the lodge, one inside the other. You can see them a mile off, but nobody will get close without them at the lodge hearing of it in time to get away. By the tracks, they didn't bring no more men than you said they could, not enough to count. Course," he added wryly, "that still leaves you outnumbered a fair bit."

Ituralde nodded. He had offered the White Ribbon, and the men he was to meet had accepted. Three days when men pledged under the Light, by their souls and hope of salvation, not to draw a weapon against another or shed blood. The White Ribbon had not been tested in this war, however, and these days some men had strange ideas of where salvation lay. Those who called themselves Dragonsworn, for instance. He had always been called a gambler, though he was not. The trick was in knowing what risks you could take. And sometimes, in knowing which ones you had to take.

Pulling a packet sewn into oiled silk from his boot top, he handed it to Donjel. "If I don't reach Coron Ford in two days, take this to my wife."

The scout tucked the packet somewhere beneath his cloak, touched his forehead, and turned his horse west. He had carried its like for Ituralde before, usually on the eve of battle. The Light send this was not the time Tamsin would have to open that packet. She would come after him—she had told him so—the first incident ever of the living haunting the dead.

"Jaalam," Ituralde said, "let us see what waits at Lady Osana's hunting lodge." As he heeled Dart forward, the others fell in behind him.

The sun rose to its height and began again to descend as they rode. The dark clouds in the north moved closer, and the chill bit deeper. There was no sound but the crunch of hooves breaking through the snow crust. The forest seemed empty save for themselves. He did not see any of the sentries Donjel had spoken of. The man's opinion of what could be seen from a mile differed from that of most. They would be expecting him, of course. And watching to make sure he was not followed by an army, White Ribbon or no White Ribbon. A good many of them likely had reasons they felt sufficient to feather Rodel Ituralde with arrows. A lord might pledge the White Ribbon for his men, but would all of those feel bound? Sometimes, there were chances you just had to take.

About midafternoon, Osana's so-called hunting lodge loomed suddenly out of the trees, a mass of pale towers and slender, pointed domes that would have fitted well among the palaces of Bandar Eban itself. Her hunting had always been for men or power, her trophies numerous and noteworthy despite her relative youth, and the "hunts" that had taken place here would have raised eyebrows even in the capital. The lodge lay desolate, now. Broken windows gaped like mouths with jagged teeth. None showed a glimmer of light or movement. The snow covering the cleared ground around the lodge had been well trampled by horses, however. The ornate brass-bound gates of the main courtyard stood open, and he rode through without slowing, followed by his men. The horses' hooves clattered on the paving stones, where the snow had been beaten to slush.

No servants came out to greet him, not that he had expected any. Osana had vanished early in the troubles that now shook Arad Doman like a dog shaking a rat, and her servants had drifted quickly to others of her house, taking whatever places they could find. These days, the masterless starved, or turned bandit. Or Dragonsworn. Dismounting in front of the broad marble stairway at the end of the courtyard, he handed Dart's reins to one of his armsmen, and Jaalam ordered the men to take shelter where they could find it for themselves and the animals. Eyeing the marble balconies and wide windows that surrounded the courtyard, they moved as if expecting a crossbow bolt between the shoulder blades. One set of stable doors stood slightly ajar, but in spite of the cold, they divided themselves between the corners of the courtyard, huddling with the horses where they could keep watch in every direction. If the worst came, perhaps a few might make it out.

Removing his gauntlets, he tucked them behind his belt and checked his lace as he climbed the stairs with Jaalam. Snow that had been trodden underfoot and frozen again crackled beneath his boots. He refrained from looking anywhere but straight ahead. He must appear supremely assured, as though there were no possibility events should go other than as he expected. Confidence was one key to victory. The other side believing you were confident was sometimes almost as good as actually being confident. At the head of the stairs, Jaalam pulled open one of the tall, carved doors by its gilded ring. Ituralde touched his beauty spot with a finger to make sure it was in place—his cheeks were too cold to feel the black velvet star clinging—before he stepped inside. As self-assured as he would have been at a ball.

The cavernous entry hall was as icy as the outside. Their breath made feathered mists. Unlit, the space seemed already wreathed in twilight. The floor was a colorful mosaic of hunters and animals, the tiles chipped in places, as though heavy weights had been dragged over them, or perhaps dropped. Aside from a single toppled plinth that might once have held a large vase or a small statue, the hall was bare. What the servants had not taken when they fled had long since been looted by bandits. A single man awaited them, white-haired and more gaunt than when Ituralde had last seen him. His breastplate was battered, and his earring was just a small gold hoop, but his lace was immaculate, and the sparkling red quarter moon beside his left eye would have gone well at court, in better times.

"By the Light, be welcome under the White Ribbon, Lord Ituralde," he said formally, with a slight bow.

"By the Light, I come under the White Ribbon, Lord Shimron," Ituralde replied, making his courtesy in return. Shimron had been one of Alsalam's most trusted advisors. Until he joined the Dragonsworn, at least. Now he stood high in their councils. "My armsman is Jaalam Nishur, honor bound to House Ituralde, as are all who came with me."

There had been no House Ituralde before Rodel, but Shimron answered Jaalam's bow, hand to heart. "Honor be

to honor. Will you accompany me, Lord Ituralde?" he said
as he straightened.

The great doors to the ballroom were gone from their
hinges, though Ituralde could hardly imagine bandits looting those. They left a tall pointed arch wide enough for ten
men to pass. Within the windowless oval room, half a hundred lanterns of every size and sort beat at shadows, though
the light barely reached the domed ceiling. Separated by
a wide expanse of floor, two groups of men stood against
the painted walls, and if the White Ribbon had induced
them to leave off helmets, all two hundred or more were
armored otherwise, and certainly no one had put aside his
swords. To one side were a few Domani lords as powerful
as Shimron—Rajabi, Wakeda, Ankaer—each surrounded
by his cluster of lesser lords and sworn commoners and
smaller clusters, of few as two or three, many containing
no nobles at all. The Dragonsworn had councils, but no one
commander. Still, each of those men was a leader in his
own right, some counting their followers in scores, a few
in thousands. None appeared happy to be where he was,
and one or two shot glares across the floor, to where fifty or
sixty Taraboners stood in one solid mass and scowled back.
Dragonsworn they might all be, yet there was little love lost
between Domani and Taraboners. Ituralde almost smiled
at the sight of the outlanders, though. He had not dared to
count on half so many appearing today.

"Lord Rodel Ituralde comes under the White Ribbon."
Shimron's voice rang through the lantern shadows. "Let
whoever may think of violence search his heart, and consider his soul." And that was the end of formality.

"Why does Lord Ituralde offer the White Ribbon?"
Wakeda demanded, one hand gripping the hilt of his longsword and the other in a fist at his side. He was not a tall
man, though taller than Ituralde, but as haughty as if he
held the throne himself. Women had called him beautiful,
once. Now a slanting black scarf covered the socket of his
missing right eye, and his beauty spot was a black arrowhead pointing at the thick scar running from his cheek up
onto his forehead. "Does he intend to join us? Or ask us to
surrender? All know the Wolf is bold as well as devious. Is
he that bold?" A rumble rose among the men on his side of
the room, part mirth, part anger.

Ituralde clasped his hands behind his back to keep from fingering the ruby in his left ear. That was widely known as a sign that he was angry, and sometimes he did it on purpose, but he needed to present a calm face, now. Even while the man spoke past his ear! No. Calm. Duels were entered into in anger, but he was here to fight a duel, and that required calm. Words could be deadlier weapons than swords.

"Every man here knows we have another enemy to the south," he said in a steady voice. "The Seanchan have swallowed Tarabon." He ran his gaze over the Taraboners, and met flat stares. He never had been able to read Taraboners' faces. Between those preposterous mustaches—like hairy tusks; worse than a Saldaean's!—and those ridiculous veils, they might as well wear masks, and the poor light from the lanterns did not help. But he had seen them veiled in mail, and he needed them. "They have flooded onto Almoth Plain, and moved ever north. Their intent is clear. They mean to have Arad Doman, too. They mean to have the whole world, I fear."

"Does Lord Ituralde want to know who we will support if these Seanchan invade us?" Wakeda demanded.

"I have true faith you will fight for Arad Doman, Lord Wakeda," Ituralde said mildly. Wakeda went purple at having the direct insult flung in his teeth, and his oath-men's hands went to hilts.

"Refugees have brought word that there are Aiel on the plain, now," Shimron put in quickly, as though he feared Wakeda might break the White Ribbon. None of Wakeda's oath-men would draw steel unless he did, or commanded them to. "They fight for the Dragon Reborn, so say the reports. He must have sent them, perhaps as an aid to us. No one has ever defeated an Aiel army, not even Artur Hawkwing. You recall the Blood Snow, Lord Ituralde, when we were younger? I believe you agree with me that we did not defeat them there, whatever the histories may say, and I cannot believe the Seanchan have the numbers we did then. I myself have heard of Seanchan moving south, away from the border. No, I suspect the next we hear will be of them *retreating* from the plain, not advancing on us." He was not a bad commander in the field, but he had always been pedantic.

Ituralde smiled. Word came more swiftly from the south than from anywhere else, but he had been afraid he would have to bring up the Aiel, and they might have thought he was trying to trick them. He could hardly believe it himself, Aiel on Almoth Plain. He did not point out that Aiel sent to help the Dragonsworn were more likely to have appeared in Arad Doman itself. "I've questioned refugees, too, and they speak of Aiel raids, not armies. Whatever the Aiel are doing on the plain may have slowed the Seanchan, but it hasn't turned them back. Their flying beasts have begun scouting on our side of the border. That does not smack of retreat."

Producing the paper from his sleeve with a flourish, he held it up so all could see the Sword and Hand impressed in green-and-blue wax. As always of late, he had used a hot blade to separate the Royal Seal on one side while leaving it whole, so he could show it unbroken to doubters. There had been plenty of those, when they heard some of Alsalam's orders. "I have orders from King Alsalam to gather as many men as I can, from wherever I can find them, and strike as hard as I can at the Seanchan." He took a deep breath. Here, he took another chance, and Alsalam might have his head on the block unless the dice fell the right way. "I offer a truce. I pledge in the King's name not to move against you in any way so long as the Seanchan remain a threat to Arad Doman, if you will all pledge the same and fight beside me against them until they are beaten back."

A stunned silence answered him. Bull-necked Rajabi appeared poleaxed. Wakeda chewed his lip like a startled girl.

Then Shimron muttered, "Can they *be* beaten back, Lord Ituralde? I faced their . . . their chained Aes Sedai on Almoth Plain, as did you." Boots scraped the floor as men shifted their feet, and faces darkened in bleak anger. No man liked to think he was helpless before an enemy, but enough had been there in the early days, with Ituralde and Shimron, for all to know what this enemy was like.

"They can be defeated, Lord Shimron," Ituralde replied, "even with their . . . little surprises." A strange thing to call the earth erupting under your feet, and scouts that rode what looked like Shadowspawn, but he had to sound assured as well as look it. Besides, when you knew what the enemy could do, you adapted. That had been one core of warfare long before the Seanchan appeared. Darkness cut the Seanchan advantages, and so did storms, and a weather-wise could always tell you when a storm was coming. "A wise man stops chewing when he reaches bone," he continued, "but so far, the Seanchan have had their meat sliced thin before they reached for it. I intend to give them a tough shank to gnaw. More, I have a plan to make them snap so fast they'll break their teeth on bone before they have a mouthful of meat. Now. I have pledged. Will you?"

It was hard not to hold his breath. Each man seemed to be looking inward. He could all but see them mulling it over. The Wolf had a plan. The Seanchan had chained Aes Sedai and flying beasts and the Light alone knew what else. But the Wolf had a plan. The Seanchan. The Wolf.

"If any man can defeat them," Shimron said finally, "you can, Lord Ituralde. I will so pledge."

"I *do* so pledge!" Rajabi shouted. "We'll chase them back across the ocean where they came from!" He had a bull's temperament as well as its neck.

Surprisingly, Wakeda thundered his agreement with equal enthusiasm, and then a storm of voices broke, calling that they would match the King's pledge, that they would smash the Seanchan, even some that they would follow the Wolf into the Pit of Doom. All very gratifying, but not all Ituralde had come for.

"If you ask *us* to fight for Arad Doman," one voice shouted above the rest, "then ask *us!*" The men who had been calling their pledges fell to angry mutters and half-heard curses.

Hiding his pleasure behind a bland expression, Ituralde turned to face the speaker, on the other side of the room. The Taraboner was a lean man, with a sharp nose that made a tent of his veil. His eyes were hard, though, and keen. Some of the other Taraboners frowned as if displeased he had spoken, so it appeared they had no one leader any more than the Domani, but he had spoken. Ituralde had hoped for the pledges he had received, but they were not necessary to his plan. The Taraboners were. At least, they would make it a hundred times more likely to work. He addressed the man courteously, with a bow.

"I offer you the chance to fight for Tarabon, my good Lord. The Aiel are making some confusion on the plain; the refugees speak of it. Tell me, could a small company of your men—a hundred, perhaps two—cross the plain in that disorder and enter Tarabon, if their armor was marked with stripes, as those who ride for the Seanchan?"

It seemed impossible the Taraboner's face could grow any tighter, yet it did, and it was the turn of the men on his side of the room to mutter angrily and curse. Enough word had come north for them to know of a king and panarch put on their thrones by the Seanchan and swearing fealty to an empress on the other side of the Aryth Ocean. They could not like reminders of how many of their countrymen now rode for this empress. Most of the "Seanchan" on Almoth Plain were Taraboners.

"What good could one small company do?" the lean man growled, contemptuous.

"Little good," Ituralde replied. "But if there were fifty such companies? A hundred?" These Taraboners might have that many men behind them, all told. "If they all struck on the same day, all across Tarabon? I myself would ride with them, and as many of my men as can be outfitted in Taraboner armor. Just so you will know this is not simply a stratagem to get rid of you."

Behind him, the Domani began protesting loudly. Wakeda the loudest of all, if it could be believed! The Wolf's plan was all very well, but they wanted the Wolf himself at their head. Most of the Taraboners began arguing among themselves, over whether so many men could cross the plain without being discovered, even in such small bands, over what good if any they could do in Tarabon in small companies, over whether they were willing to wear armor marked with Seanchan stripes. Taraboners argued as easily as Saldaeans, and as hotly. Not the sharp-nosed man. He met Ituralde's gaze steadily. Then gave a slight nod. It was hard to tell, behind those thick mustaches, but Ituralde thought he smiled.

The last tension faded from Ituralde's shoulders. The fellow would not have agreed while the others argued if he were not more of a leader among them than he seemed. The others would come, too, he was certain. They would ride south with him into the heart of what the Seanchan considered their own, and slap them hard and full across the face. The Taraboners would want to stay afterward, of course, and continue the fight in their own homeland. He could not expect anything more. Which would leave him and the few thousand men he could take with him to be hounded back north again, all the long way across Almoth Plain. If the Light shone on him, hounded with fury.

He returned the Taraboner's smile, if smile it was. With any luck, furious generals would not see where he was leading them until it was too late. And if they did . . . Well, he had a second plan.

Eamon Valda held his cloak tight around himself as he tramped through the snow among the trees. Cold and steady, the wind sighed through the snow-laden branches, a deceptively quiet sound in the damp gray light. It sliced through the thick white wool as through gauze, chilling him to the bone. The camp sprawling around him through the forest was too quiet. Movement provided a little warmth, but in this, men huddled together unless driven to move.

Abruptly he stopped in his tracks, wrinkling his nose at a sudden stench, a gagging foulness like twenty midden heaps crawling with maggots. He did not gag; instead, he scowled. The camp lacked the precision he preferred. The tents were clustered haphazardly wherever the limbs overhead grew thickest, the horses tethered close by rather than properly picketed. It was the sort of slackness that led to filth. Unwatched, the men would bury horse dung under a few shovels of dirt to be done with it quicker, and dig latrines where they would not have to walk far in the cold. Any officer of his who allowed that would cease to be an officer, and learn firsthand how to use a shovel.

He was scanning the camp for the source of the smell, when suddenly there was no smell. The wind did not change; the stink just vanished. He was startled for only a moment. Walking on, he scowled all the harder. The stench had come from *some*where. He would find whoever thought discipline had slackened, and make examples of them. Discipline had to be tight, now; tighter than ever.

At the edge of a broad clearing, he paused again. The snow in the clearing was smooth and unmarked despite the camp hidden all around it. Staying back among the trees, he scanned the sky. Scudding gray clouds hid the noonday sun. A flicker of motion made his breath catch before he

realized it was just a bird, some small brown thing wary of
hawks and staying low. He barked a laugh that was more
than touched with bitterness. Little more than a month since
the Light-cursed Seanchan had swallowed Amador and
the Fortress of Light in one unbelievable gulp, but he had
learned new instincts. Wise men learned, while fools . . .

Ailron had been a fool, puffed up with old tales of glory
brightened by age and new hope of winning real power to
go with his crown. He refused to see the reality in front of
his eyes, and Ailron's Disaster had been the result. Valda
had heard it named the Battle of Jeramel, but only by some
of the bare handful of Amadician nobles who escaped,
dazed as poleaxed steers yet still trying mechanically to
put the best face on events. He wondered what Ailron had
called it when the Seanchan's tame witches began tearing
his orderly ranks to bloody rags. He could still see that in
his head, the earth turning to fountains of fire. He saw it
in his dreams. Well, Ailron was dead, cut down trying to
flee the field and his head displayed on a Taraboner's lance.
A suitable death for a fool. He, on the other hand, had over
nine thousand of the Children gathered around him. A man
who saw clearly could make much out of that in times like
these.

On the far side of the clearing, just inside the treeline,
was a rude house that had once belonged to a charcoal
burner, a single room with winter-brown weeds thick in the
gaps between the stones. By all appearances, the man had
abandoned the place some time ago; parts of the thatch roof
sagged dangerously, and whatever had once filled the narrow windows was long since gone, replaced now by dark
blankets. Two guards stood beside the ill-fitting wooden
door, big men with the scarlet shepherd's crook behind
the golden sunflare on their cloaks. They had their arms
wrapped around themselves and were stamping their boots
against the cold. Neither could have reached his sword in
time to do any good, had Valda been an enemy. Questioners
liked to work indoors.

Their faces might have been carved stone as they
watched him approach. Neither offered more than a half-
hearted salute. Not for a man without the shepherd's crook,
even if he was Lord Captain Commander of the Children.
One opened his mouth as if to question Valda's purpose,

but Valda walked by them and pushed open the rough door.
At least they did not try to stop him. He would have killed
them both, if they had.

At his entrance, Asunawa looked up from the crooked
table where he was perusing a small book, one bony hand
cupped around a steaming pewter cup that gave off the odor
of spices. His ladder-back chair, the only other piece of
furniture in the room, appeared rickety, but someone had
strengthened it with rawhide lashings. Valda tightened his
mouth to stop a sneer. The High Inquisitor of the Hand of
the Light demanded a real roof, not a tent, even if it was
thatch sorely in need of patching, and mulled wine when no
one else had tasted wine of any sort in a week. A small fire
burned on the stone hearth, too, giving a meager warmth.
Even cook fires had been banned since before the Disaster,
to prevent smoke giving them away. Still, although most
Children despised the Questioners, they held Asunawa in a
strange esteem, as if his gray hair and gaunt martyr's face
graced him with all the ideals of the Children of the Light.
That had been a surprise, when Valda first learned of it; he
was unsure whether Asunawa himself knew. In any case,
there were enough Questioners to make trouble. Nothing
he could not handle, but it was best to avoid that sort of
trouble. For now.

"It is almost time," he said, shutting the door behind him.
"Are you ready?"

Asunawa made no move to rise or reach for the white
cloak folded across the table beside him. There was no sunflare on that, just the scarlet crook. Instead, he folded his
hands over the book, hiding the pages. Valda thought it was
Mantelar's *The Way of the Light*. Odd reading for the High
Inquisitor. More suited to new recruits; those who could
not read when they swore were taught so they could study
Mantelar's words. "I have reports of an Andoran army in
Murandy, my son," Asunawa said. "Deep in Murandy, perhaps."

"Murandy is a long way from here," Valda said as though
he did not recognize an old argument starting anew. An argument that Asunawa often seemed to forget he had already
lost. But what were Andorans doing in Murandy? If the reports were true; so many were travelers' fantasies wrapped
in lies. Andor. The very name rankled in Valda's memory.

Morgase was dead, or else a servant to some Seanchan. They had little respect for titles other than their own. Dead or a servant, she was lost to him, and more importantly by far, his plans for Andor were lost. Galadedrid had gone from a useful lever to just another young officer, and one who was too popular with the common soldiers. Good officers were never popular. But Valda was a pragmatic man. The past was the past. New plans had replaced Andor.

"Not so far if we move east, across Altara, my son, across the north of Altara. The Seanchan cannot have moved far from Ebou Dar yet."

Spreading his hands to catch the hearthfire's small warmth, Valda sighed. They had spread like a plague in Tarabon, and here in Amadicia. Why did the man think Altara was different? "Are you forgetting the witches in Altara? With an army of their own, need I remind you? Unless they're into Murandy by now." Those reports he believed, of the witches on the move. In spite of himself, his voice rose. "Maybe this so-called Andoran army you've heard about is the witches, and their army! They gave Caemlyn to al'Thor, remember! And Illian, and half the east! Do you really believe the witches are divided? Do you?" Slowly he drew a deep breath, calming himself. Trying to. Every tale out of the east was worse than the last. A gust of wind down the chimney blew sparks into the room, and he stepped back with a curse. Bloody peasant hovel! Even the chimney was ill made!

Asunawa snapped the small book shut between his palms. His hands were folded as in prayer, but his deep-set eyes suddenly seemed hotter than the fire. "I believe the witches must be destroyed! That is what I believe!"

"I'd settle for knowing how the Seanchan tame them." With enough tame witches, he could drive al'Thor out of Andor, out of Illian and everywhere else he had settled like the Shadow itself. He could better Hawkwing himself!

"They must be destroyed," Asunawa asserted stubbornly.

"And us with them?" Valda demanded.

A knock came at the door, and at Asunawa's curt summons one of the guards from outside appeared in the doorway, standing rigidly erect, arm snapping across his chest in a crisp salute. "My Lord High Inquisitor," he said respectfully, "the Council of the Anointed is here."

Valda waited. Would the old fool continue to be stubborn with all ten surviving Lords Captain outside, mounted and ready to ride? What was done, was done. What had to be done.

"If it brings down the White Tower," Asunawa said finally, "I can be content. For now. I will come to this meeting."

Valda smiled thinly. "Then I am content. We will see the witches fall together." Certainly, he would see them fall. "I suggest you have your horse readied. We have a long way to ride by nightfall." Whether Asunawa would see it with him was another matter.

Gabrelle enjoyed her rides through the wintery woods with Logain and Toveine. He always let Toveine and her follow at their own pace in a semblance of privacy, so long as they did not lag too far behind. The two Aes Sedai seldom spoke more than absolutely necessary, though, even when they truly were private. They were far from friends. In fact, Gabrelle often wished Toveine would ask to stay behind when Logain offered these outings. It would have been very pleasant to be really alone.

Holding her reins in one green-gloved hand and keeping her fox-lined cloak shut with the other, she let herself feel the cold, just a little, just for the refreshing vigor of it. The snow was not deep, but the morning air was crisp. Dark gray clouds promised more snow, soon. High overhead flew a long-winged bird of some sort. An eagle, perhaps; birds were not her strong point. Plants and minerals stayed in one place while you studied them, and so did books and manuscripts, though those might crumble under her fingers, if they were old enough. She could barely make the bird out at that height, in any case, but an eagle fit the landscape. Woodland surrounded them, small dense thickets dotted among more widely spaced trees. Great oaks and towering pines and firs had killed off most of the undergrowth, though here and there the thick brown remains of a hardy vine, waiting for a still distant spring, clung to a boulder or a low gray ledge of stone. She carefully held that landscape in her mind like a novice exercise, chill and empty.

With no one in sight except her two companions, she could almost imagine she was somewhere other than the

Black Tower. That horrid name came all too easily to mind, now. A thing as real as the White Tower, and no longer "so-called" for anyone who laid eyes on the great stone bar-racks buildings that held hundreds of men in training, and the village that had grown up around them. She had lived in that village for nearly two weeks, and there were parts of the Black Tower she still had not seen. Its grounds cov-ered miles, surrounded by the beginnings of a wall of black stone. Still, she could almost forget, here in the woods.

Almost. Except for the bundle of sensation and emotion, the essence of Logain Ablar, that always rode in the back of her mind, a constant feel of controlled wariness, of muscles always on the edge of tensing. A hunting wolf might feel that way, or perhaps a lion. The man's head moved con-stantly; even here he watched his surroundings as though expecting attack.

She had never had a Warder—they were needless flam-boyance for Browns; a hired servant could do all she needed—and it felt peculiar to be not only part of a bond, but at the wrong end of it, so to speak. Worse than simply the wrong end; *this* bond required her to obey, and she was hedged about with prohibitions. So it was not the same as a Warder bond, really. Sisters did not *force* their Warders to obedience. Well, not very often. And sisters had not bonded men against their will for centuries. Still, it did provide a fascinating study. She had worked at interpreting what she sensed. At times, she could almost read his mind. Other times, it was like fumbling through a mineshaft with no lamp. She supposed she would try to study if her neck were stretched on the headsman's block. Which, in a very real way, it was. He could sense her as well as she could him.

She must always remember that. Some of the Asha'man might believe the Aes Sedai were resigned to their captiv-ity, but only a fool could think fifty-one sisters who had been forcibly bonded would all embrace resignation, and Logain was no fool. Besides, he knew they had been sent to destroy the Black Tower. Yet if he suspected that they were still trying to find a way to end the threat of hundreds of men who could channel . . . Light, constrained as they were, one order could halt them in their tracks! You will do nothing to harm the Black Tower. She could not understand why that command had not been given as a simple precaution. They must succeed. Fail, and the world was doomed.

Logain turned in his saddle, an imposing, broadshouldered figure in a well-fitting coat dark as pitch, without a touch of color save for the silver Sword and the red-and-gold Dragon on his high collar. His black cloak was thrown back, as though he were refusing to let the cold touch him. He might be; these men seemed to believe they had to fight everything, all the time. He smiled at her—reassuringly?—and she blinked. Had she let too much anxiety slip into her end of the bond? It was such a delicate dance, trying to control her emotions, to present just the right responses. It was almost like taking the test for the shawl, where every weave had to be made exactly so, without the slightest falter, despite every manner of distraction, only this test went on and on and on.

He turned his attention on Toveine, and Gabrelle exhaled softly. Just a smile, then. A companionable gesture. He was often congenial. He might have been likable if he were anything but what he was.

Toveine beamed back at him, and Gabrelle had to stop herself from shaking her head in wonderment, not for the first time. Pulling her hood a little forward as though against the cold, so it sheltered her face while giving her an edge to peek around, she studied the Red sister surreptitiously.

Everything she knew of the other woman said she buried her hates in shallow graves, if at all, and Toveine loathed men who could channel as deeply as any Red Gabrelle had ever met. *Any* Red must despise Logain Ablar, after the claims he had made, that the Red Ajah itself had set him up to become a false Dragon. He might be holding his silence now, but the damage was done. There were sisters captive with them who looked at Reds as though thinking they, at least, were caught in a trap of their making. Yet Toveine all but *simpered* at him. Gabrelle bit her underlip in perplexed thought. True, Desandre and Lemai had ordered everyone to achieve cordial relations with the Asha'man who held their bonds—the men must be lulled before the sisters could do anything useful—but Toveine bristled openly at every command from either sister. She had detested yielding to them, and might have refused if Lemai were not also Red, no matter that she had admitted it must be so. Or that no one had recognized her authority once she led them into captivity. She hated that, too. Yet that was when she had begun smiling at Logain.

For that matter, how could Logain sit at the other end of her bond and take that smile as anything but fraud? Gabrelle had picked at that knot before, too, without coming close to untying it. He knew too much about Toveine. Knowing her Ajah should have been enough. Yet Gabrelle felt as little suspicion in him when he looked at the Red sister as when he looked at her. He was hardly *free* of suspicion; the man was distrustful of everyone, it seemed. But less of *any* sister than of some Asha'man. That made no sense, either.

He's no fool, she reminded herself. *So, why? And why for Toveine, as well? What is she scheming at?*

Abruptly, Toveine flashed that seemingly warm smile at her, and spoke as if she had voiced at least one of her questions aloud. "With you near," she murmured in a mist of breath, "he's barely aware of me. You've made him *your* captive, sister."

Caught by surprise, Gabrelle flushed in spite of herself. Toveine never made conversation, and to say she disapproved of Gabrelle's situation with Logain was to understate drastically. Seducing him had seemed such an obvious way to get close enough to learn his plans, his weaknesses. After all, even if he *was* an Asha'man, she had been Aes Sedai long before he was born, and she was hardly a total innocent when it came to men. He had been so surprised when he realized what she was doing that she almost thought of *him* as the innocent. More fool, she. Playing the Domani turned out to hide many surprises, and a few pitfalls. Worst of all, a trap she could never reveal to anyone. Something she very much feared that Toveine knew, though, at least in part. But then, any sister who had followed her lead must know, too, and she thought several had. None had spoken of the problem, and none was likely to, of course. Logain could mask the bond, in a crude way she believed would still allow her to find him however well it hid his emotions, but sometimes when they shared a pillow, he let the masking slip. To say the least, the results were . . . devastating.

There was no calm restraint, then, no cool study. Not much of reason at all.

Hurriedly she summoned the image of the snowy landscape again and fixed it in her mind. Trees and boulders and smooth, white snow. Smooth, *cold* snow.

Logain did not look back at her, or give any outward sign, but the bond told her that he was aware of her momentary loss of control. The man brimmed with smugness! And *satisfaction!* It was all she could do not to seethe. But he would expect her to seethe, burn him! He *had* to know what she felt from him. Letting her anger rise, though, only filled the fellow with *amusement!* And he was not even attempting to hide it!

Toveine was wearing a small, satisfied smile, Gabrelle noticed, but she had only a moment to wonder why.

They had had the morning to themselves, but now another rider appeared through the trees, a cloakless man in black who angled his horse in their direction when he saw them, and dug his bootheels into his animal's flanks for speed despite the snow. Logain reined in to wait, the image of calm, and Gabrelle stiffened as she halted her mount beside him. The feelings carried by the bond had shifted. Now they were the tension of a wolf waiting to spring. She expected to see his gauntleted hands on his sword hilt rather than resting at ease on the tall pommel of his saddle.

The newcomer was almost as tall as Logain, with waves of golden hair to his wide shoulders and a winning smile. She suspected he knew it was a winning smile. He was too pretty not to know, much more beautiful than Logain. Life's forges had hardened Logain's face, and left edges. This young man was smooth, yet. Still, the Sword and the Dragon decorated his coat collar. He studied the two sisters with bright blue eyes. "Are you bedding both of them, Logain?" he said in a deep voice. "The plump one looks cold-eyed, to me, but the other appears warm enough."

Toveine hissed angrily, and Gabrelle's jaw clenched. She had made no real secret of what she did—she was no Cairhienin, to cloak in privacy what she was ashamed of in public—but that did not mean she expected to have it bantered about. Worse, the man spoke as though they were tavern lightskirts!

"Don't ever let me hear that again, Mishraile," Logain said quietly, and she realized the bond had changed again. It was cold, now; cold to make the snow seem warm. Cold to make a grave seem warm. She had heard that name before, Atal Mishraile, and felt distrust in Logain when he spoke it—certainly more than he felt for her or Toveine—but this was the feel of killing. It was almost laughable. The man held her prisoner, yet he was ready to do violence to defend her reputation? Part of her did want to laugh, but she tucked the information away. Any scrap might be useful.

The younger fellow gave no sign of hearing a threat. His smile never faltered. "The M'Hael says you can go, if you want. Can't see why you'd want to take on recruiting."

"Someone has to," Logain replied in a level tone.

Gabrelle exchanged puzzled glances with Toveine. Why *would* Logain want to go recruiting? They had seen parties of Asha'man return from that, and they were always tired from Traveling long distances, and usually dirty and snappish besides. Men beating the drum for the Dragon Reborn did not always get the warmest welcome, it seemed, even before anyone learned what they were really after. And why were she and Toveine just hearing of it? She would have *sworn* he told her everything when they were lying together.

Mishraile shrugged. "Plenty of Dedicated and Soldiers to do that sort of work. Of course, I suppose it bores you looking after training all the time. Teaching fools to sneak around in the woods and climb cliffs as if they couldn't channel a whisker. Even a fly-speck village might look better." His smile slid into a smirk, disdainful and not at all winning. "Maybe if you ask the M'Hael, he'll let you join his classes at the palace. You wouldn't be bored then."

Logain's face never changed, but Gabrelle felt one sharp bolt of fury through the bond. She had overheard tidbits about Mazrim Taim and his private classes, but all any of the sisters really knew was that Logain and his cronies did not trust Taim or any who attended his lessons, and Taim appeared not to trust Logain. Unfortunately, what the sisters could learn of the classes was limited; no one was bonded to a man of Taim's faction. Some thought the mistrust was because both men had claimed to be the Dragon Reborn, or even a sign of the madness that channeling brought to men. She had not detected any evidence of insanity in Logain, and she watched for it as hard as she watched for signs he was about to channel. If she were still bound to him when he went mad, it might seize her mind, too. Whatever caused a crack in the Asha'man's ranks must be exploited, though.

Mishraile's smile faded as Logain merely looked at him. "Enjoy your flyspecks," he said finally, pulling his horse around. A thud of his heel made the animal spring away as he called over his shoulder, "Glory waits for some of us, Logain."

"He may not enjoy his Dragon long," Logain murmured, watching the other man gallop off. "He's too free with his tongue." She did not think he meant the comment about her and Toveine, but what else could he mean? And why was he suddenly worried? Hiding it very well, especially considering the bond, but still, he was worried. Light, sometimes it seemed that knowing what was in a man's head made the confusion worse!

Abruptly, he turned his gaze on her and Toveine, studying. A new thread of concern slipped through the bond. About them? Or—an odd thought—*for* them?

"I fear we must cut short our ride," he said after a moment. "I have preparations to make."

He did not break into a gallop, but he still set a quicker pace back toward the village of the men in training than he had coming out. He was concentrating on something, now; thinking hard, Gabrelle suspected. The bond practically hummed with it. He must have been riding by instinct.

Before they had gone very far, Toveine moved her horse close to Gabrelle's. Leaning in her saddle, she tried to fix Gabrelle with an intent stare while darting quick glances at Logain as if afraid he might look back and see them talking. She never seemed to pay attention to what the bond told her. The divided effort made her bob about like a puppet, in danger of falling.

"We must go with him," the Red whispered. "Whatever it takes, you must see to it." Gabrelle raised her eyebrows, and Toveine had the grace to color, but she lost nothing of her insistence. "We cannot afford to be left behind," she breathed hurriedly. "The man didn't abandon his ambitions when he came here. Whatever vileness he plans, we can do nothing if we aren't right there when he tries."

"I can see what's in front of my nose," Gabrelle said

sharply, and felt relief when Toveine simply nodded and fell silent. It was all Gabrelle could do to control the fear that was rising in her. Did Toveine never *think* about what she must sense through the bond? Something that had always been there in the connection with Logain— determination—now lay hard and sharp as a knife. She thought she knew what it meant, this time, and knowing made her mouth dry. Against whom, she could not say, but she was sure that Logain Ablar was riding to war.

Slowly descending one of the wide hallways that spiraled gently through the White Tower, Yukiri felt prickly as a starved cat. She could barely make herself listen to what the sister gliding beside her was saying. The morning was still dim, first light darkened by the snow falling heavily on Tar Valon, and the middle levels of the Tower were as icy as a Borderland winter. Well, perhaps not so cold as that, she allowed after a moment. She had not been that far north in a number of years, and memory expanded what it did not shrink. That was the reason written records were so important. Except when you did not dare write down anything, at least. Still, it was chill enough. For all the ancient builders' cleverness and skill, heat from the great furnaces in the basement never reached this high. Drafts made the flames dance on the gilded stand-lamps, and some were strong enough to stir the heavy tapestries spaced along the white walls, spring flowers and woodlands and exotic animals and birds alternating with scenes of Tower triumphs that would never be displayed in the public areas below. Her own rooms, with their warm fireplaces, would once have been much more comfortable.

News from the outside world churned through her head despite her efforts to avoid it. Or rather, more often, the lack of solid news. What eyes-and-ears reported from Altara and Arad Doman was all confusion, and the few reports beginning to seep out of Tarabon again were frightening. Rumor put the Borderland rulers everywhere from the Blight to Andor to Amadicia to the Aiel Waste; the only confirmed fact was that none were where they were supposed to be, guarding the Blightborder. The Aiel *were* everywhere, and finally out of al'Thor's control, it appeared, if they had ever been in it. The latest news from Murandy made her want to grind her teeth and weep at the same time, while Cairhien . . . ! Sisters all over the Sun Palace, some suspected of being rebels and none known to be loyal, and still no word of Coiren and her embassy since they departed the city, though they should have been back in Tar Valon long since. And as if that were not enough, al'Thor himself had vanished like a soap bubble yet again. Could the tales that he had half-destroyed the Sun Palace be true? Light, the man *could* not go mad yet! Or had Elaida's witless offer of "protection" frightened him into hiding? Did *anything* frighten him? He frightened her. He frightened the rest of the Hall, too, let them put whatever face on it they wanted.

The only thing truly certain was that none of that mattered a spit in a rainstorm. Knowing so did not help her mood in the slightest. Worry over being caught in a tangle of roses, even if the thorns might kill you eventually, was a luxury when you had a knife point pressed to your ribs.

"Every time she's left the Tower in the last ten years, it has been on her own affairs, so there are no recent records to check," her companion murmured. "It's difficult to learn exactly when she *has* been out of the Tower and remain . . . discreet." Her dark golden hair held back by ivory combs, Meidani was tall, and slender enough to look overbalanced by her bosom, an effect emphasized by both the fit of her dark silver embroidered bodice and the way she walked in a stoop to put her mouth more on the level of Yukiri's ear. Her shawl was caught on her wrists, the long gray fringe dragging the floor tiles.

"Straighten your backbone," Yukiri growled quietly. "My ears aren't clogged with dirt."

The other woman jerked herself upright, faint splashes of color in her cheeks. Pulling her shawl higher on her arms, Meidani half glanced over her shoulder toward her Warder Leonin, who was following at a discreet distance. If they could barely hear the faint tinkle of the silver bells in the lean man's black braids, though, he could hear nothing said in a moderate tone. The man knew no more than necessary—precious little, in fact, except that his Aes Sedai wanted certain things of him; that was enough for any good Warder—and he might cause problems if he learned too much, but there was no need for whispering. People who saw whispering wanted to know what the secret was.

The other Gray was no more the source of her irritation than the outside world, however, even if the woman was a jackdaw in swan's feathers. Not the main source, anyway. A disgusting thing, a rebel pretending loyalty, yet Yukiri was actually glad that Saerin and Pevara had convinced her that they should not yet turn Meidani and her sister jackdaws over to Tower law. Their wings were clipped, now, and they were useful. They might even gain a measure of clemency, for when they did face justice. Of course, when the oath that had clipped Meidani's wings came out, Yukiri might easily find herself wishing for clemency herself. Rebels or not, what she and the others had done with Meidani and her confederates was as far outside the law as murder. Or treason. An oath of personal obedience—sworn on the Oath Rod itself; sworn under duress—was all too close to Compulsion, which was clearly prohibited if not really defined. Still, sometimes you had to smudge the plaster to smoke out hornets, and the Black Ajah were hornets with venomous stings. The law would have its course in due time—without the law, there was nothing—but she needed to be more concerned with whether she would survive the smoking out than with what penalties the law would exact. Corpses had no need to worry about punishment.

She motioned curtly for Meidani to go on, but no sooner had the other woman opened her mouth than three Browns rounded a corner from another hallway right in front of them, flaunting their shawls like Greens. Yukiri knew Marris Thornhill and Doraise Mesianos slightly, in the manner Sitters knew sisters from other Ajahs who spent long periods in the Tower, which was to say enough to attach names to faces and not much more. Mild and absorbed in their studies was how she would have described them, if pressed. Elin Warrel was so newly raised to the shawl, she still should have been bobbing curtsies on instinct. Instead of offering courtesies to a Sitter, though, all three stared at Yukiri and Meidani the way cats stared at strange dogs. Or maybe dogs at strange cats. No mildness, there.

"May I ask about a point of Arafellin law, Sitter?"

Meidani said, as smoothly as if that were what she had been intending to say all along.

Yukiri nodded, and Meidani began rambling about fishing rights on rivers versus lakes, hardly an inspired choice. A magistrate might ask an Aes Sedai to listen to a case of fishing rights, but only to bolster her own opinion if powerful people were involved and she was worried about an appeal to the throne.

A single Warder trailed the Browns—Yukiri could not recall whether he belonged to Marris or Doraise—a heavyset fellow with a hard round face and a dark top knot who eyed Leonin and the swords on his back with a distrust surely picked up from his sister. That pair stalked by up the slowly spiraling corridor with plump chins high, the skinny newling leaping anxiously to keep up. The Warder strode after them radiating the air of a man in hostile country.

Hostility was all too usual, nowadays. The invisible walls between the Ajahs, once barely thick enough to hide each Ajah's own mysteries, had become hard stone ramparts with moats. No, not moats; chasms, deep and wide. Sisters never left their own Ajah's quarters alone, often took their Warders even to the library and the dining rooms, and always wore their shawls, as though someone might mistake their Ajah, otherwise. Yukiri herself was wearing her best, embroidered in silver and thread-of-gold, with the long silk fringe that hung to her ankles. So she supposed she was flaunting her Ajah a bit, too. And lately, she had been considering that a dozen years was long enough to go without a Warder. A horrible thought, once she sifted out the source. No sister should have need of a Warder inside the White Tower.

Not for the first time, the thought hit her hard that someone had to mediate among the Ajahs, and soon, or the rebels would dance in through the front door, bold as thieves, and empty the house while the rest of them squabbled over who got Great Aunt Sumi's pewter. But the only end of the thread she could see to begin working out the snarl was to have Meidani and her friends publicly admit that they had been sent to the Tower by the rebels to spread rumors—tales they still insisted were true!—that the Red Ajah had created Logain as a false Dragon. *Could* it be true? Without

Pevara knowing? Impossible to think that a Sitter, especially Pevara, could have been fooled. In any case, that bit of the tangle had been overlaid with so many others by now that it scarcely could make any difference by itself. Besides, it would throw away the aid of ten out of the fourteen women she could be sure were not Black Ajah, not to mention likely exposing what the rest of them were doing, before the storm over it blew out.

She shivered, and it had nothing to do with drafts in the corridor. She and every other woman who might reveal the truth would die before that storm ended, by so-called accident or in bed. Or she might just vanish, apparently gone out of the Tower never to be seen again. She had no doubt of that. Any evidence would be buried so deep, an army with shovels could never dig it up. Even rumors would be plastered over. It had happened before. The world and most sisters still believed Tamra Ospenya had died in her bed. She had believed it. They had to have the Black Ajah wrapped up and tied, as near as possible, before they dared risk going public.

Meidani took up her report again once the Browns were safely past, but fell silent only moments later when, just ahead of them, a big hairy hand suddenly thrust aside a tapestry from behind. An icy draft swept out of the doorway that had been hidden by the tapestry's brightly colored birds from the Drowned Lands, and a heavy fellow in a thick brown workcoat backed into the corridor, pulling a handcart stacked high with split hickory that another serving man in a rough coat was pushing from behind. Common laborers: neither had the white Flame on his chest.

At sight of two Aes Sedai, the men hastily let the tapestry fall back into place and wrestled their cart out of the way against the wall while trying to make their bows, almost toppling the load, which set them grabbing at the sliding firewood frantically while still bobbing. No doubt they had expected to finish their work without encountering any sisters. Yukiri always felt sympathy for the people who had to haul wood and water and everything else up the servants' ramps all the way from the ground, but she strode past them with a scowl.

Talk while walking was never overheard, and the hallways in the common areas had seemed a good place to be private with Meidani. Much better than her own apartments, where any ward against eavesdropping would only announce to everyone in the Gray quarter that she was discussing secrets, and, far worse, with whom. There were only two hundred or so sisters in the Tower at the moment, a number the White Tower could swallow and seem vacant, and with everyone keeping to themselves, the common areas should have been empty. So she had thought.

She had taken into account the liveried servants rushing about to check lamp-wicks and oil levels and a dozen other things, and the plain-clad workers carrying wicker baskets of the Light knew what on their backs. They were always about in the early hours, readying the Tower for the day, but they made hasty bows and curtsies and scurried to get out of a sister's way. Out of hearing. Tower servants knew how to be tactful, especially since anyone eavesdropping on a sister would be shown the door. Given the present mood in the Tower, the servants were particularly quick to avoid so much as a chance of overhearing things they should not.

What she had failed to reckon on was how many sisters would choose to walk outside the quarters, by twos and threes, despite the hour and the cold, Reds trying to stare down anyone they encountered except other Reds, Greens and Yellows competing for the crown of haughty and Browns doing their best to outdo both. A few Whites, all but one Warderless, attempted to maintain a façade of cool reason while jumping at their own footfalls. One little group was not out of sight for more than minutes, it seemed, before another appeared, so Meidani spent nearly as much time chattering about points of law as she did giving her report.

Worst of all, twice Grays smiled in what looked like relief on seeing others of their Ajah, and would have joined them had Yukiri not shaken her head. Which infuriated her no end, because it let all who saw know she had special reason to be alone with Meidani. Even if the Black Ajah took no notice, and the Light send there was no reason they should, too many sisters spied on other Ajahs these days, and in spite of the Three Oaths, the tales they carried somehow grew in the carrying. With Elaida apparently trying to force the Ajahs into line by brute force, those tales too often resulted in penances, and the best to be hoped for was that you could pretend to have chosen to take it on for reasons of your own. Yukiri had already suffered through one such, and she had no desire to waste days scrubbing floors again, especially now that she had more on her plate than she knew what to do with. And taking the alternative, a private visit to Silviana, was no better, even if it did save the time! Elaida seemed fiercer than ever since she began summoning Silviana for her own supposedly private penances. The whole Tower was still buzzing with that.

As much as Yukiri hated admitting it, all that made her careful how she looked at the other sisters she saw. Look too long, and you might seem to be spying yourself. Shift your gaze away too fast, and you looked furtive, with the same result. Even so, she could barely keep her eyes from lingering on one pair of Yellows who glided along a crossing corridor like queens in their own palace.

The dark stocky Warder following just far enough behind to give them privacy must have belonged to Pritalle Nerbaijan, a green-eyed woman who had largely escaped the Saldaean nose, because Atuan Larisett had no Warder. Yukiri knew little about Pritalle, but she would learn more after seeing her in close conversation with Atuan. In high-necked gray slashed with yellow and a silk-fringed shawl, the Taraboner was striking. Her dark hair, in thin, brightly beaded braids that hung to her waist, framed a face that somehow seemed perfect as it was without being beautiful. She was even fairly modest, at least as Yellows went. But she was the woman Meidani and the others were trying to study without being caught out. The woman whose name they were afraid to speak aloud except behind strong wards. Atuan Larisett was one of only three Black sisters Talene knew. That was how they organized themselves, three women who knew each other, three women who formed one heart, with each woman knowing one more the other two did not. Atuan had been Talene's "one more," so there was some hope she could be followed to two others.

Just before the pair passed out of view beyond the corner, Atuan glanced up the spiral hallway. Her gaze only brushed by Yukiri, yet that was enough to make Yukiri's heart leap into her throat. She kept walking, holding her face calm with an effort, and risked a quick glance of her own when she reached the corner. Atuan and Pritalle were already well along the corridor, heading toward the outer ring. The Warder was in the way, but neither was looking back. Pritalle was shaking her head. To something Atuan was saying? They were too far for Yukiri to hear any sound other than the faint click of the dark Warder's bootheels on the floor tiles. It had just been a glance. Of course it had. She quickened her step to take her beyond sight if one of them did look over a shoulder, and let out a long breath she had not realized she was holding. Meidani echoed her faintly, her shoulders sagging.

Strange, how it takes us, Yukiri thought, squaring her own shoulders.

When they first learned Talene was a Darkfriend, Talene had been a shielded prisoner. *And she still scared us spitless,* she admitted to herself. Well, what they did to make her confess had scared them spitless first, but learning the truth turned their tongues to dust. Now Talene was tethered tighter than Meidani, closely guarded even if she did appear to walk free—how to keep a Sitter prisoner without anyone noticing had been beyond even Saerin—and she was pathetically eager to offer up every scrap she knew or even suspected in hope it might save her life, not that she had any choice. Hardly an object of fear. As for the rest . . .

Pevara had tried to maintain that Talene must be wrong about Galina Casban, and went into a rage that lasted a full day when she finally was convinced that her Red sister was really Black. She still spoke of strangling Galina with her own hands. Yukiri herself had felt a cold detachment when Temaile Kinderode was named. If there were Darkfriends in the Tower, it stood to reason some had to be Grays, though perhaps disliking Temaile helped. She remained cool even after she did the sums and realized that Temaile had left the Tower at the same time that three sisters were murdered. That provided more names for suspicion, other sisters who had gone then, too, but Galina and Temaile and the rest were out of the Tower, beyond reach for the moment, and only the two could be proven Darkfriends.

Atuan was right there, Black Ajah without doubt, walking the Tower as she wished, unrestrained and unbound of the Three Oaths. And until Doesine could arrange for her to be questioned in secret—a difficult matter, even for a Sitter of Atuan's Ajah, since it had to be secret from *every*one—

until then, all they could do was watch. A distant, carefully circumspect watching. It was like living with a red adder, never knowing when you would find yourself eye to eye with it, never knowing when it might bite. Like living in a den of red adders, and only being able to see one.

Suddenly, Yukiri realized that the wide, curving corridor was empty ahead as far as she could see, and a glance back showed only Leonin behind. The Tower might have been empty save for the three of them. Nothing in sight moved except the flickering flames on the stand lamps. Silence.

Meidani gave a small start. "Forgive me, Sitter. Seeing her so suddenly took me aback. Where was I? Oh, yes. I understand that Celestin and Annharid are trying to find out her close friends in the Yellow." Celestin and Annharid were Meidani's fellow conspirators, both Yellows. There were two from each Ajah—except the Red and the Blue, of course—which had proven very useful. "I fear that won't be much help. She has a wide circle of friends, or did before the . . . current situation rose between the Ajahs." A touch of satisfaction tinged her voice, however smooth her face; she was still a rebel, in spite of the added oath. "Investigating all of them will be difficult, if not impossible."

"Forget her for the moment." It took an effort for Yukiri not to crane her neck trying to look every way at once. A tapestry worked with large white flowers rippled slightly, and she hesitated until she was sure it was a draft and not another servant coming out of a servants' ramp. She never could recollect where they were located. Her new topic was as dangerous as discussing Atuan, in its own way. "Last night, I remembered you were a novice with Elaida, and close friends as I recall. It would be a good idea for you to renew that friendship."

"That was some years ago," the taller woman replied stiffly, lifting her shawl to her shoulders and wrapping it around herself as though she suddenly felt the cold. "Elaida very properly broke it off when she was raised Accepted. She might have been accused of favoritism if I were in a class she was given to teach."

"As well for you that you weren't a favorite," Yukiri said dryly. Elaida's current ferocity had its precedent. Before she went off to Andor years ago, she had pushed those she favored so hard that sisters had needed to step in more than once. Siuan Sanche had been one of them, strange to remember, though Siuan had never needed rescuing from standards she could not meet. Strange and sad. "Even so, you *will* do everything in your power to renew that friendship."

Meidani walked two dozen paces along the corridor opening and closing her mouth, adjusting and readjusting her shawl, twitching her shoulders as though trying to shrug off a horsefly, looking everywhere but at Yukiri. How had the woman ever functioned as a Gray, with so little self-control? "I did try," she said finally, in a breathy tone. She still avoided Yukiri's eye. "Several times. The Keeper . . . Alviarin always put me off. The Amyrlin was busy, she had appointments, she needed rest. There was always some excuse. I think Elaida just doesn't want to take up a friendship she dropped more than thirty years ago."

So the rebels had remembered that friendship, too. How had they thought to use it? Spying, most likely. She would have to find out how Meidani was supposed to pass on what she learned. In any case, the rebels had provided the tool, and Yukiri would use it. "Alviarin is out of your way. She left the Tower yesterday, or maybe the day before. No one is quite certain. But the maids say she took spare clothes, so it's unlikely she'll return for a few days at the soonest."

"Where could she have gone in this weather?" Meidani frowned. "It's been snowing since yesterday morning, and it was threatening before."

Yukiri stopped and used both hands to turn the other woman to face her. "The only thing that need concern you, Meidani, is that she's gone," she said firmly. Where *had* Alviarin gone in this? "You have a clear path to Elaida, and you will take it. And you will keep a close watch to see if anyone might be reading Elaida's papers. Just be sure no one sees you watching." Talene said the Black Ajah knew everything that came out of the Amyrlin's study before it was announced, and they needed someone close to Elaida if they were to find out how it was done. Of course, Alviarin saw everything before Elaida signed, and the woman had taken on more authority than any Keeper in memory, but that was no reason to accuse her of being a Darkfriend. No reason not to, either. Her past was being investigated, too. "Watch Alviarin, as well, as much as you can, but Elaida's papers are the important thing."

Meidani sighed and gave a reluctant nod. She might have to obey, but she knew the added danger she would be in if Alviarin did turn out a Darkfriend. Yet Elaida herself still might be Black, whatever Saerin and Pevara insisted. A Darkfriend as Amyrlin Seat. Now that was a thought to pickle your heart.

"Yukiri!" a woman's voice called from back up the hallway.

A Sitter in the Hall of the Tower did *not* jump like a startled goat at hearing her own name, but Yukiri did. If she had not been holding on to Meidani, she might have fallen, and as it was, the pair of them staggered like drunken farmers at a harvest dance.

Recovering, Yukiri jerked her shawl straight and set her face in a scowl that did not diminish when she saw who was hurrying toward her. Seaine was supposed to be keeping close to her own rooms, with as many White sisters around her as she could manage, when she was not with Yukiri or one of the other Sitters who knew about Talene and the Black Ajah, but here she was scurrying down the hallway with only Bernaile Gelbarn, a stocky Taraboner and another of Meidani's jackdaws, for company. Leonin stepped aside, and gave Seaine a formal bow, fingertips pressed to his heart. Meidani and Bernaile were foolish enough to exchange smiles. They were friends, but they should know better, when they could not tell who might see.

Yukiri was in no mood for smiles. "Taking the air, Seaine?" she said sharply. "Saerin won't be pleased, when I tell her. Not at *all* pleased. *I'm* not pleased, Seaine."

Meidani made a small sound in her throat, and Bernaile's head twitched, her multitude of narrow beaded braids rattling against one another. The pair of them took to studying a tapestry that supposedly showed the humbling of Queen Rhiannon, and for all their smooth faces, clearly they wished they were somewhere else. In their eyes, Sitters were supposed to be equals. And so they were. Normally. After a fashion. Leonin should not have been able to hear a word, but he could feel Meidani's mood, of course, and he moved a step farther away. While still keeping watch along the corridor, of course. A good man. A wise man.

Seaine had sense enough to look abashed. Unconsciously, she smoothed her dress, covered with snowy embroidery along the hem and across the bodice, but almost immediately her hands knotted in her shawl and her eyebrows drew down stubbornly. Seaine had been strong-willed from the day she first came to the Tower, a furniture-maker's daughter from Lugard who had talked her father into buying passage for her and her mother. Passage for two upriver, but only one down. Strong-willed and confident. And frequently as blind to the world around her as any Brown. Whites were often like that, all logic and no judgment. "There's no need for me to hide from the Black Ajah, Yukiri," she said.

Yukiri winced. Fool woman, naming the Black right out in the open. The corridor was still empty in both directions as far as the curve allowed sight, but carelessness led to more carelessness. She could be stubborn herself, when there was need, but at least she showed more brain than a goose about when and where. She opened her mouth to give Seaine a piece of her mind, a sharp piece, but the other woman rushed on before she could speak.

"Saerin told me I could find you." Seaine's mouth tightened and spots of color flared in her cheeks, at having asked permission or at having to ask. It was understandable for her to resent her situation, of course. Just witless for her not to accept it. "I need to talk to you alone, Yukiri. About the second mystery."

For a moment, Yukiri was as puzzled as Meidani and Bernaile looked. They could sham not listening, but that did not shut their ears. Second mystery? What did Seaine mean? Unless . . . Could she mean the thing that had brought Yukiri into the hunt for the Black Ajah in the first place? Wondering why the heads of the Ajahs were meeting in secret had lost its urgency compared to finding Darkfriends among the sisters.

"Very well, Seaine," Yukiri said, more calmly than she felt. "Meidani, take Leonin down the hall until you can just see Seaine and me around the curve. Keep a sharp eye for anyone coming this way. Bernaile, do the same up the hall." They were moving before she finished speaking, and as soon as they were out of earshot, she turned her attention to Seaine. "Well?"

To her surprise, the glow of *saidar* sprang up around the White Sitter, who wove a ward against eavesdropping around the pair of them. It was a clear sign of secrets to anyone who saw. This had better be important.

"Think about it logically." Seaine's voice was calm, but her hands still gripped her shawl in fists. She stood very straight, towering over Yukiri, though she was not much above average height herself. "It's more than a month, almost two, since Elaida came to me, and nearly two weeks since you found Pevara and me. If the Black Ajah knew about me, I would be dead by now. Pevara and I would have been dead before you and Doesine and Saerin ever walked in on us. Therefore, they don't know. About any of us. I admit I was frightened, at first, but I have control of myself, now. There's no reason for the rest of you to keep trying to treat me like a novice," a little heat invaded the calmness, "and a brainless one, at that."

"You'll have to talk to Saerin," Yukiri said curtly. Saerin had taken charge from the start—after forty years in the Hall for the Brown, Saerin was very good at taking charge—and Yukiri had no intention of going against her unless she must, not without the Sitter's privilege she could hardly claim in the circumstances. As well try to catch a falling boulder. If Saerin could be convinced, Pevara and Doesine would come around, and she herself would hardly try to stand in the way. "Now, what about this 'second secret'? You *do* mean the Ajah heads' meeting?"

Seaine's face took on a muley expression. Yukiri almost expected her ears to lie back. Then she exhaled. "Did the head of your Ajah have a hand in choosing Andaya for the Hall? More than usual, I mean?"

"She did," Yukiri replied carefully. Everyone had been sure Andaya would go into the Hall one day, perhaps in another forty or fifty years, yet Serancha had all but anointed her, when the customary method was discussion until a consensus could be reached on two or three candidates, then a secret ballot. That was Ajah business, though, as secret as Serancha's name and title.

"I knew it." Seaine nodded excitedly, not at all her normal manner. "Saerin says that Juilaine was handpicked for the Brown, too, apparently not their usual way, and Doesine says the same about Suana, though she was hesitant about saying anything. I think Suana may be head of the Yellow herself. In any case, she was a Sitter for forty years the first time, and you know it isn't common to take a chair after you were a Sitter that long. And Ferane stepped down for the White less than ten years ago; no one has ever entered the Hall again so soon. To cap it off, Talene says the Greens nominate choices and their Captain-General chooses one, but Adelorna chose Rina without any nominations."

Yukiri managed to stifle a grimace, but only by a hair. Everyone had their suspicions about who headed other Ajahs, else no one would ever have noticed the meetings in the first place, yet speaking those names aloud was rude at best. Anyone but a Sitter might face penance for it. Of course, she and Seaine both knew when it came to Adelorna. In her attempts to curry favor, Talene poured out all the secrets of the Green without being asked. It embarrassed all of them, except Talene herself. At least it explained why the Greens had been in such an outstanding rage when Adelorna was birched. Still, Captain-General was a ridiculous title, Battle Ajah or no Battle Ajah. At least Head Clerk really described what Serancha did, in a manner of speaking.

Down the corridor, Meidani and her Warder were standing just in sight on the curve, apparently taking quietly. One or the other always watched further down around the curve, though. In the opposite direction, Bernaile was just in sight, too. Her head was swiveling constantly as she tried to watch Yukiri and Seaine while keeping an eye out for anyone approaching. The way she kept shifting from one foot to the other would attract attention, too, but these days a sister alone outside her Ajah quarter was asking for trouble, and she knew it. This conversation had to end soon.

Yukiri raised one finger. "Five Ajahs had to choose new Sitters after women they had in the Hall joined the rebels." Seaine nodded, and Yukiri raised a second finger. "Each of those Ajahs chose a woman as Sitter who wasn't the . . . logical . . . choice." Seaine nodded again. A third finger joined the first two. "The Brown had to choose two new Sitters, but you didn't mention Shevan. Is there anything . . ." Yukiri smiled wryly, "odd . . . about her?"

"No; according to Saerin, Shevan would likely have been her replacement when she decided to step down, but—"

"Seaine, if you're actually implying the Ajah heads *conspired* over who would go into the Hall—and I never heard a more crack-brained notion!—if that's what you're suggesting, why would they choose five odd women and one who isn't?"

"Yes, I am suggesting it. With the rest of you keeping me practically under lock and key, I've had more time for thinking than I know what to do with. Juilaine and Rina and Andaya gave me a hint, and Ferane made me decide to check." What did Seaine mean about Andaya and the other two giving a hint? Oh. Of course: Rina and Andaya were not really old enough to be in the Hall yet, either. The custom of not talking about age soon enough became the habit of not thinking about it, either.

"Two might have been coincidence," Seaine went on, "even three, though that strains credulity, but five makes a pattern. Except for the Blue, the Brown was the only Ajah to have two Sitters join the rebels. Maybe there's a reason in that why they chose one odd sister and one not, if I can figure it out. But there is a pattern, Yukiri—a puzzle—and whether it's rational or not, something tells me we had better solve it before the rebels get here. It makes me feel as though somebody's hand is on my shoulder, but when I look, there isn't anyone there."

What strained credulity was the idea of the Ajah heads conspiring in the first place. *But then,* Yukiri thought, *a conspiracy of Sitters is beyond far-fetched, and I'm in the middle of one.* And there was the simple fact that no one outside an Ajah was supposed to know the Ajah's head, but the Ajah heads against all custom did. "If there's a puzzle," she said wearily, "you have a long time to solve it. The rebels can't leave Murandy before spring, whatever they've told people, and the march upriver will take months, if they hold their army together that long." She did not doubt they would, though, not any longer. "Go back to your rooms before someone sees us standing here warded, and think on your puzzle," she said, not unkindly, resting a hand on Seaine's sleeve. "You'll have to put up with being looked after until we're *all* sure you are safe."

The expression on Seaine's face would have been called

sullen on anyone but a Sitter. "I'll speak to Saerin again," she said, but the light of *saidar* around her vanished.

Watching her join Bernaile and the two of them glide up the curving hallway toward the Ajah quarters, both as wary as fawns when wolves were out, Yukiri felt a heavy heart. It was a pity the rebels could not get there before summer. At least that might make the Ajahs come together again, so sisters were not forced to slink about the White Tower. *As well wish for wings,* she thought sadly.

Determined to keep her mood in check, she went to gather up Meidani and Leonin. She had a Black sister to investigate, and at least investigation was a puzzle she knew how to work.

Gawyn's eyes popped open in the darkness as a new wave of cold rose into the hayloft. The barn's thick stone walls normally kept out the worst of the night's chill, if only the worst. Voices murmured below; no one sounded excited. He took his hand away from the sword lying beside him and tugged his gauntlets tighter. Like all the rest of the Younglings, he slept in every stitch he could put on. Probably it was just time to wake some of the men around him for their sentry turns, but he was fully awake now himself, and he doubted he would find sleep again soon. In any case, his sleep was always fretful, troubled by dark dreams, haunted by the woman he loved. He did not know where Egwene was, or whether she was alive. Or whether she could forgive him. He stood up, letting the loose hay he had pulled over himself slide off his cloak, and buckled on his sword belt.

As he picked his way among the shadowy mounds of men sleeping atop the stacked bales of hay, the faint scrape of boots on wooden rungs told him someone was climbing the ladder to the loft. A dim figure appeared at the top of the ladder, then stopped to wait for him.

"Lord Gawyn?" Rajar's deep voice said softly, in a Domani accent unaltered by six years' training in Tar Valon. The First Lieutenant's rumbling voice was always a surprise, coming from a slight man who stood barely higher than Gawyn's shoulder. Even so, had times been different, Rajar surely would have been a Warder by this time. "I thought I'd have to wake you. A sister just arrived, on foot. A messenger from the Tower. She wanted the sister in charge here. I told Tomil and his brother to take her to the Mayor's house before they turned in for the night."

Gawyn sighed. He should have gone home when he returned to Tar Valon and found the Younglings expelled from the city, instead of letting himself be caught here by winter. Especially when he was sure Elaida wanted them all dead. His sister Elayne would come to Caemlyn, eventually, if she was not already there. Certainly any Aes Sedai would see that the Daughter-Heir of Andor reached Caemlyn in time to claim the throne before someone else could. The White Tower would not give up the advantage of a queen who would also be Aes Sedai. On the other hand, Elayne could be on her way to Tar Valon, too, or residing in the White Tower right that minute. He did not know how she had become entangled with Siuan Sanche, or how deeply—she always dove into a pond without checking the depth—but Elaida and the Hall of the Tower might want to question her closely, Daughter-Heir or not. Queen or not. He was sure she could not be held accountable, though. She was still only one of the Accepted. He had to tell himself that frequently.

The newest problem was that an army lay between him and Tar Valon, now. At least twenty-five thousand soldiers on this side of the River Erinin and, he had to believe, as many on the west bank. They had to be supporting the Aes Sedai whom Elaida called rebels. Who else would dare besiege Tar Valon itself? The way that army had appeared, though, seeming to materialize out of nowhere in the middle of a snowstorm, was enough to raise prickles on his back still. Rumor and alarms always flew ahead of any large force under arms on the march. Always. This one had arrived like spirits, in silence. The army was as real as stone, however, so he could neither enter Tar Valon to find whether Elayne was in the Tower, nor ride south. Any army would take notice of upward of three hundred men on the move, and the rebels would have no goodwill toward the Younglings. Even if he went alone, travel in winter was very slow, and he could reach Caemlyn as quickly if he waited until spring. There was no hope of finding passage on a ship, either. The siege would mire river traffic in a hopeless snarl. *He* was mired in a hopeless snarl.

And now, an Aes Sedai had come in the middle of the night. She would not simplify matters any.

"Let's find out what news she brought," he said quietly, motioning Rajar down the ladder ahead of him.

Twenty horses and their stacked saddles crowded nearly every inch of the dark barn not taken by Mistress Millin's two dozen or so milkcows in their stalls, so he and Rajar had to thread their way to the wide doors. The only warmth came from the sleeping animals. The two men guarding the horses were silent shadows, but Gawyn could feel them watching Rajar and him slip out into the icy night. They would know about the messenger, and be wondering.

The sky was clear, and the waning moon still gave a fair light. The village of Dorlan shone with snow. Holding their cloaks close, the pair of them trudged knee-deep through the village in silence, along what had once been the road to Tar Valon from a city that had not existed for hundreds of years. Nowadays, nobody traveled in this direction from Tar Valon except to come to Dorlan, and there was no reason to come in winter. By tradition, the village supplied cheeses to the White Tower and to no one else. It was a tiny place, just fifteen slate-roofed, gray stone houses with drifts of snow piled up as high as the bottoms of the first-floor windows. A little distance behind each house stood its cowbarn, all crowded with men and horses now, as well as cows. Most of Tar Valon might well have forgotten Dorlan existed. Who thought about where cheese came from? It had seemed a very good place for keeping out of sight. Until now.

All the houses but one in the village were dark. Light leaked through the shutters on several windows of Master Burlow's dwelling, upstairs and down. Garon Burlow had the misfortune to own the largest house in Dorlan, in addition to being Mayor. Villagers who had shifted sleeping arrangements to find a bed for an Aes Sedai must be regretting it by now; Master Burlow had had two rooms already empty.

Stamping the snow from his boots on the stone step, Gawyn rapped at the Mayor's stout door with a gauntleted fist. No one answered, and after a moment he lifted the latch and led Rajar in.

The beam-ceilinged front room was fairly large for a farmhouse, and dominated by several tall open-front cabinets, full of pewter and glazed crockery, and a long, polished table lined with high-back chairs. All of the oil lamps had been lit, an extravagance in winter, when a few tallow candles would do, but the flames in the fireplace had made little impression on the split logs, yet, or on the temperature of the room. Even so, the two sisters who had rooms above were barefoot on the rugless wooden floor, with fur-lined cloaks flung hastily over their linen nightdresses. Katerine Alruddin and Tarna Feir were watching a small woman in a dark, yellow-slashed riding dress and cloak that were snow-damp to her hips. She stood as near the wide hearth as she would, tiredly warming her hands and shivering. Afoot in the snow, she could not have made the trip from Tar Valon in less than two or three days, and even Aes Sedai felt the cold eventually. She had to be the sister Rajar had spoken of, yet compared to the others, the agelessness was hardly noticeable in her. Compared to the other two, she was hardly noticeable at all.

The absence of the Mayor and his wife put an extra knot in Gawyn's middle, though he had half expected it. They would have been there making over the Aes Sedai, offering hot drinks and food, no matter the hour, unless they had been sent back to their bed to give Katerine and Tarna privacy with the messenger. Which likely meant he was a fool to want to know the message. But he had known that before he left the barn.

". . . boatman said he would stay where we landed until the siege lifted," the small woman was saying in weary tones as Gawyn entered, "but he was so frightened, he could be leagues downriver by now." As the cold from the doorway reached her, she looked around, and some of the fatigue drained from her square face. "Gawyn Trakand," she said. "I have orders for you from the Amyrlin Seat, Lord Gawyn."

"Orders?" Gawyn said, drawing off his gauntlets and tucking them behind his belt to gain time. Blunt truth might be in order for once, he decided. "Why would Elaida send me orders? Why should I obey if she did? She disowned me, and the Younglings." Rajar had taken a respectful stance for the sisters, hands folded behind his back, and he gave Gawyn a quick sidelong glance. He would not speak out of turn, whatever Gawyn said, but the Younglings did not share Gawyn's belief. Aes Sedai did what they did, and no man could know why until a sister told him. The Younglings had cast their lots with the White Tower wholeheartedly, embracing fate.

"That can wait, Narenwin," Katerine snapped, jerking her cloak tighter. Her black hair spilled around her shoulders half in tangles, as though she had taken a few hasty swipes with a comb and given up. There was an intensity about her that reminded Gawyn of a hunting lynx. Or maybe one wary of traps. She spared half a glance for him and Rajar; no more. "I have pressing business in the Tower. Tell me how to find this nameless fishing village. Whether or not your boatman is still there, I'll find someone to take me across."

"And me," Tarna put in, her strong jaw stubborn and her blue eyes sharp as spears. In contrast to Katerine, Tarna's long, pale yellow hair was as neat as if she had had a maid attending her before coming downstairs. She was every bit as focused, though, just more controlled. "I also have urgent reason to reach the Tower without any further delay." She gave Gawyn a nod and Rajar a lesser, cool as the marble she seemed carved from. Yet, more friendly than the face she showed Katerine or got in return. There was always a stiffness between the two women, though they shared the same Ajah. They did not like one another, perhaps even disliked each other. With Aes Sedai, it was hard to be sure.

Gawyn would not be sorry to see either leave. Tarna had ridden into Dorlan barely a day after the mysterious army arrived, and however Aes Sedai determined these things, she immediately displaced Lusonia Cole from her room upstairs and Covarla Baldene from command of the eleven other sisters already in the village. She might have been a Green from the way she took charge of everything, questioning the other sisters about the situation, inspecting the Younglings closely every day as though searching for possible Warders. Having a Red study them that way made the men start looking over their shoulders. Worse, Tarna spent long hours out riding, no matter the weather, trying to find some local who could show her a way into the city past the besiegers. Sooner or later, she would lead their scouts back to Dorlan. Katerine had come only yesterday, in a fury at having her path to Tar Valon blocked, and straightaway took command from Tarna and her room from Covarla. Not that she used her authority in the same way. She avoided the other sisters, refusing to tell anyone why she had disappeared at Dumai's Wells or where she had been. But she, too, had inspected the Younglings. With the air of a woman examining an axe she had a mind to use, and not a care how much blood was shed. He would not have been surprised if she had tried to bully him into cutting a way to the bridges into the city for her. He would be more than happy to see them go, in fact. But then, when they left, he would have to deal with Narenwin. And with Elaida's orders.

"It's hardly a village, Katerine," the shivering sister said, "just three or four squalid little fisherman's houses a full day downriver by land. More than that from here." Plucking at her damp skirts, she held them nearer the fire. "We may be able to find a way to send messages into the city, but you two are needed here. All that stopped Elaida sending fifty sisters, or more, rather than just me, was the difficulty of getting even one tiny boat across the river unseen, even in darkness. I must say, I was surprised to learn there were any sisters this close to Tar Valon. Under the circumstances, every sister who is outside the city must—"

Tarna cut her off firmly with a raised hand. "Elaida cannot even know I am here." Katerine closed her mouth and frowned, her chin lifting, but she let the other Red continue. "What were her orders to you regarding the sisters in Dorlan, Narenwin?" Rajar took to studying the floorboards in front of his boots. He had faced battle without flinching, yet only a fool wanted to be around Aes Sedai who were arguing.

The short woman fussed with her divided skirts a moment longer. "I was ordered to take charge of the sisters I found here," she said stuffily, "and do what I could." After a moment, she sighed, and amended herself reluctantly. "The sisters I found here under Covarla. But, surely—"

This time, Katerine broke in. "I was never under Covarla, Narenwin, so those orders cannot apply to me. In the morning, I will set out to find these three or four fisherman's huts."

"But—"

"Enough, Narenwin," Katerine said in an icy voice. "You can make your arrangements with Covarla." The black-haired woman gave her Ajah sister a glance from the corner of her eye. "I suppose you may accompany me, Tarna. A fishing boat should have room for two." Tarna bent her head the slightest fraction, possibly in thanks.

Their business concluded, the pair of Reds gathered their cloaks around them and glided toward the door deeper into the house. Narenwin shot a vexed look at their backs, and turned her attention to Gawyn, her face settling into the semblance of a calm mask.

"Have you any word of my sister?" he asked before she could open her mouth. "Do you know where she is?"

The woman really was tired. She blinked, and he could almost see her forming an answer that would tell him nothing.

Stopping halfway to the door, Tarna said, "Elayne was with the rebels when I saw her last." Every head jerked toward her. "But your sister is safe from retribution," she went on calmly, "so put that out of your mind. Accepted can't choose which sisters to obey. I give you my word; under the law, she can suffer no lasting harm of it." She seemed unaware of Katerine's frozen stare, or Narenwin's popping eyes.

"You could have told me before this," Gawyn said roughly. No one spoke roughly to Aes Sedai, not more than once, but he was past caring. Were the other two surprised that Tarna knew the answer, or surprised that she had given it? "What do you mean by 'no lasting harm'?"

The pale-haired sister barked a laugh. "I can hardly promise she won't suffer a few welts if she puts her feet too far wrong. Elayne *is* one of the Accepted, not Aes Sedai. Yet that protects her from greater harm if she is led astray by a sister. And you never asked. Besides, she doesn't need rescuing, even if you could manage it. She is with Aes Sedai. Now you know as much as I can tell you of her, and I am going to find a few hours' more sleep before daylight. I will leave you to Narenwin."

Katerine watched her go without altering her expression by an eyelash, a woman of ice with the eyes of a hunting cat, but then she herself strode from the room so quickly that her cloak flared behind her.

"Tarna is correct," Narenwin said once the door closed behind Katerine. The small woman might not make a good show of Aes Sedai serenity and mystery alongside the other two, but alone she managed very well. "Elayne is sealed to the White Tower. So are you, for all your talk of disowning. The history of Andor seals you to the Tower."

"The Younglings are all sealed to the Tower by our own choice, Narenwin Sedai," Rajar said, making a leg formally. Narenwin's gaze remained on Gawyn.

He closed his eyes, and it was all he could do not to scrub at them with the heels of his hands. The Younglings *were* sealed to the White Tower. No one would ever forget that they had fought, on the very grounds of the Tower, to stop the rescue of a deposed Amyrlin. For good or ill, the tale would follow them to their graves. He was marked by that, as well, and by his own secrets. After all that bloodshed, he was the man who had let Siuan Sanche walk free. More importantly, though, Elayne bound him to the White Tower, and so did Egwene al'Vere, and he did not know which tied the tighter knot, the love of his sister or the love of his heart. To abandon one was to abandon all three, and while he breathed, he could not abandon Elayne or Egwene.

"You have my word that I will do all I can," he said wearily. "What does Elaida want of me?"

The sky above Caemlyn was clear, the sun a pale golden ball near its noonday peak. It shed a brilliant light on the blanket of white covering the surrounding countryside, but gave no warmth. Still, the weather was warmer than Davram Bashere would have expected back home in Saldaea, though he did not regret the marten fur lining his new cloak. Cold enough in any case for his breath to have frosted his thick mustaches with more white than the years had put in them. Standing in ankle-deep snow among the leafless trees on a rise perhaps a league north of Caemlyn, he held a long, gold-mounted looking glass to his eye, studying the activity on lower ground about a mile south of him. Quick nosed his shoulder impatiently from behind, but he ignored the bay. Quick disliked standing still, but sometimes you had to, whatever you wanted.

A sprawling camp was going up down there among the scattered trees, astride the road to Tar Valon, soldiers unloading supply wagons, digging latrines, erecting tents and building lean-tos of brush and tree limbs scattered in clumps of varying size, each lord and lady keeping their own men close. They expected to be in place for some time. From the horselines and the general extent of the camp, he estimated close to five thousand men, give or take a few hundred. Fighting men; fletchers, farriers, armorers, laundresses, wagon drivers and other camp followers as good as doubled that, though as usual they were making their own camp on the fringes. Most of the camp followers spent more time staring toward the rise where Bashere stood than they did working. Here and there a soldier paused in his labors to peer toward the higher ground, too, but bannermen and squadmen quickly drove them back to their work. The nobles and officers riding about the rising camp never so much as glanced north, that Bashere saw. A fold of land hid them from the city, though he could see the silver-streaked gray walls from his rise. The city knew they were there, of course; they had announced themselves that morning with trumpets and banners in sight of the walls. Well out of bowshot, though.

Laying siege to a city with high, strong walls that stretched more than six leagues in circumference was no easy matter, and complicated in this instance by Low Caemlyn, the warren of brick and stone houses and shops, windowless warehouses and long markets, that lay outside Caemlyn's walls. Seven more like camps were being made, though, spaced around the city where they could cover every road, every gate that would allow a sizable sortie. They already had patrols out, and likely watchers lurked in the now-deserted buildings of Low Caemlyn. Small parties might get past into the city, maybe a few pack animals by night, but not near enough to feed one of the world's great cities. Hunger and disease ended more sieges than swords or siege engines ever did. The only question was whether they brought down besieged or besieger first.

The plan seemingly had all been well thought out by someone, but what confused him were the banners in the camp below. It was a strong looking glass, crafted by a Cairhienin named Tovere, a gift from Rand al'Thor, and he could make out most of the banners whenever a breeze straightened them. He knew enough of Andoran sigils to pick out the Oak and Axe of Dawlin Armaghn and the five

Silver Stars of Daerilla Raened and several more banners of lesser nobles who supported Naean Arawn's claim to the Lion Throne and Rose Crown of Andor. Yet Jailin Maran's cross-hatched Red Wall was down there, too, and Carlys Ankerin's paired White Leopards, and Eram Talkend's golden Winged Hand. By all reports, they were oathsworn to Naean's rival, Elenia Sarand. Seeing them with the others was like seeing wolves and wolfhounds sharing a meal. With a cask of good wine opened in the bargain.

Two other banners, gold-fringed and at least twice the size of any others, were on display as well, though both were too heavy for the occasional gust to make them more than stir. They shone with the glisten of thick silk. He had seen the pair clearly enough earlier, however, when the bannermen rode back and forth atop the rise that hid their camp, the banners spread out above them in the breeze of their gallop. One was the Lion of Andor, white on red, the same as flew from the tall round towers dotted along the city wall. In both cases it was a declaration of someone's right to the throne and crown. The second large banner below him proclaimed the woman throwing her claim against that of Elayne Trakand. Four silver moons on a field of twilight blue, the sign of House Marne. All this was in support of Arymilla Marne? A month ago, she would have been lucky if anyone except her own House or that half-witted Nasin Caeren gave her a bed for the night!

"They ignore us," Bael growled. "I could break them before sunset, and leave not one alive to see the sun rise again, yet they ignore us."

Bashere looked sideways at the Aielman. Sideways and up. The man towered above him by well over a foot. Only Bael's gray eyes and a strip of sun-dark skin were visible above the black veil drawn across his face. Bashere hoped the man was just shielding his mouth and nose from the cold. He was carrying his short spears and bull-hide buckler, and he had a cased bow on his back and a quiver at his hip, but only the veil mattered. This was no time for the Aiel to start killing. Twenty paces downslope toward the camp, thirty more Aielmen were squatting on their heels, holding their weapons casually. One in three had his face bare, so maybe it was the cold. With Aiel, you could never be sure, though.

Quickly considering several approaches, Bashere decided

on lightness. "Elayne Trakand would not like that, Bael, and if you've forgotten what it's like being a young man, that means Rand al'Thor won't like it."

Bael grunted sourly. "Melaine told me what Elayne Trakand said. We must do nothing on her part. That is simpleminded. When an enemy comes against you, you make use of whoever will dance the spears by your side. Do they play at war the way they play at their Game of Houses?"

"We are outlanders, Bael. That counts, in Andor."

The huge Aielman grunted again.

There seemed no point trying to explain the politics involved. Outland help could cost Elayne what she was trying to gain, and her enemies knew it and knew she knew it, so they had no fear of Bashere or Bael or the Legion of the Dragon, whatever their numbers. In fact, despite the siege, both sides would go to great effort to avoid pitched battle. It was a war, but of maneuver and skirmishes unless someone blundered, and the winner would be whoever gained an unassailable position or forced the other into one that could not be defended. Bael likely would see it as no different from *Daes Dae'mar*. In all truth, Bashere saw a great deal of similarity himself. With the Blight on its doorstep, Saldaea could not afford contests for the throne. Tyrants could be endured, and the Blight soon killed the stupid and the greedy, but even this peculiar sort of civil war would allow the Blight to kill Saldaea.

He returned to studying the camp through his looking glass, trying to puzzle out how an utter fool like Arymilla Marne could have gained the backing of Naean Arawn and Elenia Sarand. That pair was greedy and ambitious, each utterly convinced of her own right to the throne, and if he understood the tangled web Andorans used to decide these matters, each had far better claim than Arymilla. Wolves and wolfhounds were not in it. This was wolves deciding to follow a lapdog. Perhaps Elayne knew the reason, but she would barely even exchange notes with him, brief and uninformative. Too much chance someone would learn of it and think she was plotting with him. It was *very* like the Game of Houses.

"Someone is going to dance the spears, it seems," Bael said, and Bashere lowered the ornate tube long enough to find where the Aielman was pointing.

There had been a steady stream of people fleeing the city ahead of the siege for days, but someone had left it too late. Half a dozen canvas-topped wagons stood halted in the middle of the Tar Valon Road just outside the edge of Low Caemlyn, surrounded by fifty horsemen under a blue-and-white quartered banner that appeared to show a running bear, or maybe some sort of thick-bodied hound, when it rippled in a sudden wind. Dispirited folk huddled to one side, clutching cloaks around themselves, men with their heads down, children clinging to women's skirts. Some of the horsemen had dismounted to ransack the wagons; chests and boxes and even what looked to be clothes already dotted the snow. Likely they were searching for coin or drink, though any other valuable that turned up would go into someone's saddlebags, too. Soon enough someone would cut free the wagon teams, or perhaps they would just take the wagons. Wagons and horses were always useful for an army, and the peculiar rules of this very peculiar Andoran civil war did not appear to give much protection to those who were in the wrong place at the wrong time. But the city gates were swinging open, and as soon as the gap was wide enough, red-coated lancers poured out of the twenty-foot-high arch at a gallop, sunlight glittering on lance points and breastplates and helmets, thundering down the road between the long, empty markets. The Queen's Guards were coming out. Enough of them, anyway. Bashere swung his glass back to the wagons.

Apparently the officer under the bear, if bear it was, had done his sums already. Fifty against two hundred made very poor odds, with only a few wagons at stake. The men who had dismounted were back in their saddles, and even as Bashere found them, the lot of them galloped away north toward him, the blue-and-white banner streaming behind its staff. Most of the people huddled beside the road stared after the departing soldiers, their confusion as clear as if he had been able to make out their faces, but a few immediately rushed to begin gathering up their scattered belongings out of the snow and piling them back into the wagons.

The arrival of the Guardsmen, drawing rein around the wagons a few minutes later, put a quick end to that. Guardsmen quickly began herding people toward the wagons. Some still tried to dart past them for some prized belonging, and one man began waving his arms in protest at a Guardsman, an obvious officer with white plumes on his helmet and a red sash across his breastplate, but the officer leaned from the saddle and backhanded the protester in the face. The fellow went down on his back like a stone, and after one frozen moment, everyone who was not already scrambling onto the wagons went scurrying, except a pair of men who paused to pick up the fallen man by his shoulders and heels, and they hurried as best they could carrying his limp weight. A woman up on the last wagon in line was already lashing her reins to get her team turned around and headed back toward the city.

Bashere lowered the glass to study the camp, then pressed it back to his eye for a closer look. Men were still digging away with shovel and mattock, and others wrestling sacks and barrels down from wagons. Nobles and officers walked their horses about the camp, keeping an eye on the work. All calm as cattle in pasture. Finally, someone pointed toward the rise between them and the city, then another and another, and mounted men began to trot, plainly shouting orders. The bear-banner was just coming into sight of the camp on the height.

Tucking the glass beneath his arm, Bashere frowned. They had no guards on the high ground to warn them of what might be happening beyond their sight. Even in the certainty no one was going to offer battle, that was stupid. It might also be useful, if the other camps were as careless, and if no one corrected the mistake. He puffed irritably through his mustaches. If he had been going to fight the besiegers.

A glance showed him the wagons halfway back to the Tar Valon Gate with their escort of Guardsmen, the wagon drivers lashing their teams as if pursuit were breathing down their necks. Or maybe it was just the officer with the sash, who was waving his sword over his head for some reason. "There'll be no dancing today," he said.

"Then I have better to do with my day than watch wet-landers dig holes," Bael replied. "May you always find water and shade, Davram Bashere."

"At the moment, I'd rather have dry feet and a warm fire," Bashere muttered without thinking, then wished he had not. Step on a man's formality and he might try to kill you, and the Aiel were formal and strange besides.

But Bael threw back his head and laughed. "The wet-lands turn everything on its head, Davram Bashere." A curious gesture of his right hand brought the other Aiel to their feet, and they loped off eastward in long, easy strides. The snow did not seem to give them any difficulty.

Sliding his looking glass into the leather case hanging from Quick's saddlebow, Bashere mounted and turned the bay west. His own escort had been waiting on the reverse slope, and they fell in behind him with only the faint creak of leather and never a jingle of unsecured metal. They num-bered fewer than Bael's escort, but they were tough men from his estates at Tyr, and he had led them into the Blight many times before bringing them south. Every man had his assigned part of the trail to watch, ahead or behind, left or right, high or low, and their heads swiveled constantly. He hoped they were not just going through the motions. The forest was sparse here, every branch bare except on oak and leatherleaf, pine and fir, but the snow-covered land rolled so that a hundred mounted men could be fifty paces away and unseen. Not that he expected any such thing, but then, what killed you was always what you never expected. Un-consciously, he eased his sword in its scabbard. You just had to expect the unexpected.

Tumad had command of the escort, as he did most days Bashere did not have something more important for the young lieutenant to do. Bashere was grooming him. He could think clearly and see beyond what was in front of him; he was destined for higher rank, if he lived long enough. A tall man, if a couple of hands shorter than Bael, today he wore disgruntlement on his face like a second nose.

"What troubles you, Tumad?"

"The Aielman was right, my Lord." Tumad tugged an-grily at his thick black beard with a gauntleted fist. "These Andorans spit at our feet. I do not like having to ride away while they thumb an ear at us." Well, he was still young.

"You find our situation boring, perhaps?" Bashere laughed. "You need more excitement? Tenobia is only fifty leagues north of us, and if rumor can be believed, she brought Ethe-nielle of Kandor and Paitar of Arafel and even that Shien-aran Easar with her. All the might of the Borderlands come looking for us, Tumad. Those Andorans down in Murandy

don't like us being in Andor, either, so I hear, and if that
Aes Sedai army they're facing doesn't chop them to pieces,
or hasn't already, they may come looking for us. So may
the Aes Sedai, for that matter, sooner or later. We've ridden
for the Dragon Reborn, and I can't see any sister forgetting
that. And then there are the Seanchan, Tumad. Do you really think we've seen the last of them? They will come to
us, or we will have to go to them; one or the other is sure.
You young men don't know excitement when it's crawling
in your mustache!"

Quiet chuckles rippled through the men following, men
as old as Bashere himself for the most part, and even Tumad
flashed white teeth through his beard in a grin. They had
all been on campaign before, if never one so odd as this.
Straightening around, Bashere watched the way through
the trees, but with only half his attention.

In all truth, Tenobia did worry him. The Light only knew
why Easar and the others had decided to leave the Blightborder together, much less strip away as many soldiers as
hearsay said they had brought south. Even hearsay divided
by half. Doubtless they had reasons they considered good
and sufficient, and doubtless Tenobia shared them. But
he knew her; he had taught her to ride, watched her grow
up, presented her the Broken Crown when she took the
throne. She was a good ruler, neither too heavy-handed nor
too light, intelligent if not always wise, brave without being foolhardy, but impulsive was a mild description of her.
Sometimes, hotheaded was mild. And he was as sure as he
could be that she had her own goal aside from whatever the
others aimed at. The head of Davram Bashere. If that was
so, she was unlikely to settle for another period of exile,
after coming this far. The longer Tenobia worried a bone
in her teeth, the harder it was to convince her to give it up.
It was a neat problem. She should be in Saldaea guarding
the Blightborder, but so should he. She could convict him
of treason twice-over at least for what he had done since
coming south, but he still could see no other way to have
gone. Rebellion—Tenobia could define that loosely when
she chose—rebellion was horrible to contemplate, yet he
wanted his head firmly attached to his neck a while longer.
A neat and thorny problem.

The encampment containing the eight thousand–odd light cavalry he had left after Illian and fighting the Seanchan spread wider than the camp back on the Tar Valon Road, but it could not be said to sprawl. The horselines were uniform rows with a farrier's forge at either end, stretched between equally straight rows of large gray or shell-white tents, though those showed a good many patches, now. Every man could be mounted and ready to fight inside a count of fifty from a trumpet signal, and his sentries were placed to make sure they had that count and more. Even the camp followers' tents and wagons, a hundred paces south of the rest, were more orderly than the soldiers besieging the city, as though they had followed the example of the Saldaeans. Somewhat, at least.

As he rode in with his escort, men moved quickly and grimly among the horselines, almost as if the signal to mount had been sounded. More than one had his sword drawn. Voices called to him, but at the sight of a large crowd of men and women, mostly women, gathered in the center of the camp, he felt a sudden numbness inside. He dug in his heels, and Quick sprang forward at a gallop. He did not know whether anyone followed him or not. He heard nothing but the blood pounding in his ears, saw nothing but the crowd in front of his own sharp-peaked tent. The tent he shared with Deira.

He did not rein in on reaching the crowd, just threw himself out of the saddle and hit the ground running. He heard people speak without taking in what they were saying. They parted in front of him, opening a path to his tent, or he would have run over them.

Just inside the tentflaps, he halted. The tent, large enough for twenty soldiers to sleep in, was crowded to the walls with women, wives of nobles and officers, but his eyes quickly found his own wife, Deira, seated on a folding chair in the middle of the carpets that served for a floor, and the numbness faded. He knew she would die one day—they both would—but the only thing he feared was living without her. Then he realized that some of the women were helping her to lower her dress to her waist. Another was pressing a folded cloth to Deira's left arm, and the cloth was growing red as blood ran down her arm in a sheet and dripped from her fingers into a bowl set on the carpet. There was a considerable amount of dark blood already in the bowl.

She saw him at the same instant, and her eyes flashed in a face that was much too pale. "It comes from hiring outlanders, husband," she said fiercely, her right hand shaking a long dagger at him. As tall as most men, inches taller than he, and beautiful, her face framed with raven hair winged with white, she had a commanding presence that could become imperious when she was angry. Even when she obviously could barely sit upright. Most women would have been flustered at being bare to the waist in front of so many, with her husband present. Not Deira. "If you did not always insist on moving like the wind, we could have good men from our own estates to do whatever was needful."

"A dispute with servants, Deira?" he said, cocking an eyebrow. "I never thought you'd start taking knives to them." Several of the women gave him cool, sidelong glances. Not every man and wife dealt together as he and Deira did. Some thought them odd, since they seldom shouted.

Deira scowled at him, then grunted a short, involuntary laugh. "I will start at the beginning, Davram. And go slowly, so you can understand," she added with a small smile, pausing to thank the women who draped a white linen sheet around her bare torso. "I returned from my ride to find two strange men ransacking our tent. They drew daggers, so naturally, I hit one of them with a chair and stabbed the other." She directed a grimace at her cut arm. "Not well enough, since he managed to touch me. Then Zavion and some of the others came in, and the pair fled through a slit they had made in the rear of the tent."

Several of the women nodded grimly and gripped the hilts of the daggers they all wore. Until Deira said darkly, "I told them to give chase, but they insisted on tending my scratch." Hands dropped away from hilts, and faces colored, though none looked in the least apologetic for disobeying. They had been in a ticklish position. Deira was their liege lady as he was their liege lord, but whether or not she called it a scratch, she could have bled to death if they had left her to go chasing the thieves. "In any event," she went on, "I ordered a search. They won't be hard to find. One has a lump on his head, and the other is bleeding." She gave a sharp, satisfied nod.

Zavion, the sinewy, red-haired Lady of Gahaur, held up a threaded needle. "Unless you have taken up an interest in embroidery, my Lord," she said coolly, "may I suggest that you withdraw?"

Bashere acquiesced with a small bow of his head. Deira never liked him to watch her being sewn up. He never liked watching her being sewn up.

Outside the tent, he paused to announce in a loud voice that his lady wife was well and being tended, and that they should all go on about their business. The men departed with wishes for Deira's well being, but none of the women stirred a foot. He did not press them. They would remain until Deira herself appeared, whatever he said, and a wise man tried to avoid battles he would not only lose, but look foolish losing.

Tumad was waiting on the edge of the crowd, and he fell in beside Bashere, who walked with his hands clasped tightly behind his back. He had been expecting this, or something like, for a long time, but he had almost begun to think it would not happen. And he had never expected Deira to nearly die because of it.

"The two men have been found, my Lord," Tumad said. "At least, they apparently meet the description the Lady Deira gave." Bashere's head jerked around, murder on his face, and the younger man quickly added, "They were dead, my Lord, just outside the camp. Each got one thrust with a narrow blade." He stabbed a finger at the base of his skull, just behind the ear. "It had to be more than one did it, unless he was faster than a rock viper."

Bashere nodded. The price of failure often was death. Two to search, and how many to silence them? How many remained, and how long before they tried again? Worst of all, who was behind it? The White Tower? The Forsaken? It seemed a decision had been reached for him.

No one except Tumad was close enough to hear him, but he spoke softly anyway, and chose his words cautiously. Sometimes, the price of carelessness was death, too. "You know where to find the man who came to me yesterday?

Find him, and tell him I agree, but there will be a few more
than we talked about."

The light feathery snow falling on the city of Cairhien
dimmed the morning sunlight only a little, just muting the
brightness. From the tall narrow window in the Sun Palace,
fitted with a casement of good glass panes against the cold,
Samitsu could see clearly the wooden scaffolding erected
around the ruined section of the palace, broken cubes of
dark stone still littered with rubble and stepped towers that
stopped abruptly short of equaling the rest of the palace's
towers. One, the Tower of the Risen Sun, was simply no
longer there. Several of the city's fabled "topless" towers
loomed through the drifting white flakes, enormous square
spires with huge buttresses, much taller by far than any in
the palace despite its location on the highest hill in a city
of hills. They were wrapped in their own scaffolds and
still not completely rebuilt twenty years after the Aiel had
burned them; another twenty might see them done. There
were no workmen clambering along the planks on any of
the scaffolding, of course, not in this weather. She found
herself wishing the snow could give her a respite, too.

When Cadsuane departed a week past, leaving her in
charge, her task had appeared straightforward. Make sure
the Cairhienin pot did not begin to boil again. That had appeared a simple task at the time, though she had seldom
dabbled in politics to speak of. Only one noble retained sizable forces under arms, and Dobraine was cooperative, for
the most part, seeming to want everything kept quiet. Of
course, he had accepted that fool appointment as "Steward
of Cairhien for the Dragon Reborn." The boy had named
a "Steward" of Tear, too, a man who had been in rebellion against him a month gone! If he had done as much in
Illian . . . It seemed all too probable. Those appointments
would cause no end of trouble for sisters to sort out before
all was said and done! The boy brought *nothing* but trouble! Yet so far Dobraine seemed to be using his new post
only to run the city. And to quietly rally support for Elayne
Trakand's claim to the Sun Throne, if she ever made one.
Samitsu was satisfied to leave it at that, not caring one way

or another who took the Sun Throne. She did not care much
for Cairhien at all.

The falling snow beyond her window swirled in a gust
of wind like a white kaleidoscope. So . . . tranquil. Had she
ever valued tranquility before? She certainly could not recall it, if she had.

Neither the possibility of Elayne Trakand taking the
throne nor Dobraine's new title had brought nearly as much
consternation as the ridiculous, and ridiculously persistent,
rumors about the al'Thor boy going to Tar Valon to submit
to Elaida, though she had done nothing to quell those. That
tale had everyone from nobles to stablemen half afraid to
breathe, which was very well and good for maintaining the
peace. The Game of Houses had ground to a halt; well, compared to how matters normally were in Cairhien. The Aiel
who came into the city from their huge camp a few miles
east very likely helped, however much they were hated by
the general run of folk. Everyone knew they followed the
Dragon Reborn, and no one wanted to risk finding themselves on the wrong end of thousands of Aiel spears. Young
al'Thor was *much* more useful absent than present. Rumors
out of the west of Aiel raiding elsewhere—looting, burning,
killing indiscriminately, so merchants' hearsay claimed—
gave people another reason to step gingerly with those here.

In fact, there seemed to be no burrs to prick Cairhien out
of its quiet, aside from the occasional street brawl between
Foregaters and city folk who considered the noisy, brightly
clad Foregaters as alien as the Aiel and a good deal safer to
fight. The city was crowded to the attics, with people sleeping anywhere they could find shelter from the cold, yet food
supplies were more than adequate if not overabundant, and
trade was actually better than expected in winter. All in all,
she should have felt content that she was carrying out Cadsuane's instructions as well as the Green could wish for.
Except that Cadsuane would expect more. She always did.

"Are you listening to me, Samitsu?"

Sighing, Samitsu turned from the peaceful view through
the window, taking pains not to smooth her yellow-slashed
skirts. The Jakanda-made silver bells in her hair tinkled
faintly, but today the sound failed to soothe her. At the best
of times she did not feel entirely comfortable in her apartments in the palace, though a blazing fire in the wide marble

fireplace gave a good warmth and the bed in the next room had the best-quality feather mattresses and goose down pillows. All three of her rooms were overly ornate in the severe Cairhienin fashion, the white ceiling plaster worked in interlocking squares, the wide bar-cornices heavily gilded, and the wooden wall panels polished to a soft glow yet dark even so. The furnishings were darker still, and massively constructed, edged with thin lines of gold leaf and inlaid with patterned ivory wedges. The flowered Tairen carpet in this room seemed garishly disordered compared to everything else, and emphasized the surrounding stiffness. It all seemed too much like a cage, of late.

What really discomfited her, though, was the woman with her hair in ringlets to her shoulders standing in the middle of the carpet, fists on her hips, a belligerent set to her chin, and a frown narrowing her blue eyes. Sashalle wore the Great Serpent ring, of course, on her right hand, but also an Aiel necklace and bracelet, fat beads of silver and ivory intricately worked and carved, gaudy against her high-necked dress of brown wool, which was plain if fine and well cut. Not crude pieces, certainly, but . . . flamboyant, and hardly the sort a sister would wear. The oddity of that jewelry might hold the key to much, if Samitsu could ever find the reason behind it. The Wise Ones, especially Sorilea, looked at her as if she were a fool for not knowing without asking, and refused to be bothered with answering. They did that all too often. *Most* especially Sorilea. Samitsu was unused to being thought a fool, and she disliked it immensely.

Not for the first time, she found it difficult to meet the other sister's gaze. Sashalle was the major reason contentment eluded her, no matter how well everything was going otherwise. Most maddening, Sashalle was a Red, yet despite her Ajah, she was *oathsworn* to young al'Thor. How could any Aes Sedai swear fealty to anyone or anything other than the White Tower itself? How in the *Light* could a *Red* swear to a man who could channel? Maybe Verin had been right about *ta'veren* twisting chance. Samitsu could not begin to think of any other reason for thirty-one sisters, *five* of them Red, to take such an oath.

"The Lady Ailil has been approached by lords and ladies who represent most of House Riatin's strength," she replied, much more patiently than she felt. "They want her to take the High Seat of Riatin, and she wants White Tower approval. Aes Sedai approval, at least." For something to do besides match stares—and likely lose—she moved to a blackwood table where a gold-worked silver pitcher sitting on a silver tray still gave off the faint scent of spices. Filling a cup with mulled wine provided an excuse to break the fleeting eye contact. Needing an excuse made her replace the pitcher on the tray with a sharp clink. She found herself avoiding looking at Sashalle too often. Even now, she realized she was looking at the other woman sideways. To her frustration, she could not quite make herself turn completely to meet her stare.

"Tell her no, Sashalle. Her brother was still alive when last seen, and rebellion against the Dragon Reborn is nothing that need concern the Tower; certainly not now it's done with." The memory arose of Toram Riatin as last seen, running off into a strange fog that could take on solid form and kill, a fog that resisted the One Power. The Shadow had walked outside the walls of Cairhien that day. Samitsu's voice tightened from the effort to stop it short of trembling. Not with fear, but anger. That had been the day she failed at Healing young al'Thor. She hated failures, hated remembering them. And she should not have to explain herself. "Most of Riatin's strength is not all. Those still tied to Toram will oppose her, with force of arms if necessary, and in any case, fostering upheaval inside the Houses themselves is no way to maintain the peace. There is a precarious balance in Cairhien now, Sashalle, but it *is* a balance, and we mustn't disturb it." She managed to stop short of saying Cadsuane would be displeased if they did. That would hardly carry weight with Sashalle.

"Upheaval will come whether or not we foster it," the other sister said firmly. Her frown had faded as soon as Samitsu showed she had been listening, though the set of her jaw remained. Perhaps it was stubbornness rather than belligerence, yet that hardly mattered. The woman was not arguing or trying to convince her, just stating her own position. And most galling of all, plainly doing that much as a courtesy. "The Dragon Reborn is the herald of upheaval and change, Samitsu. The herald foretold. And if he weren't, this is Cairhien. Do you think they have really stopped playing at *Daes Dae'mar?* The surface of the water may be still, but the fish never stop swimming."

A *Red,* preaching the Dragon Reborn like a street-corner demagogue! Light! "And if you are wrong?" In spite of herself, Samitsu bit off the words. Sashalle—burn her!—maintained a perfect serenity.

"Ailil has forsworn any claim to the Sun Throne in favor of Elayne Trakand, which is what the Dragon Reborn desires, and she is ready to swear fealty to him, if I ask it. Toram led an army against Rand al'Thor. I say the change is worth making and the chance worth taking, and I will tell her so."

The bells in Samitsu's hair chimed at an irritated shake of her head, and she barely managed to stop herself from sighing again. Eighteen of those Dragonsworn sisters remained in Cairhien—Cadsuane had carried some away with her, then sent Alanna back to take off still more—and others of the eighteen besides Sashalle stood higher than she, but the Aiel Wise Ones kept them out of her way. In principle, she disapproved of how that was done—Aes Sedai *could* not be apprentices, not to anyone! It was outrageous!—but in practice, it did make her job easier. They could not meddle or try to take charge with Wise Ones running their lives and watching over their every hour. Unfortunately, for some reason she could not learn, the Wise Ones looked differently on Sashalle and the other two sisters who had been stilled at Dumai's Wells. Stilled. She felt a faint shiver at the thought, but only faint, and it would be less if she ever managed to work out how Damer Flinn had Healed what could not be Healed. At least *someone* could Heal stilling, even if it was a man. A man channeling. Light, how the horror of yesterday became merely the uneasiness of today, once you grew accustomed.

She was sure that Cadsuane would have arranged matters with the Wise Ones before leaving had she known about the difference with Sashalle and Irgain and Ronaille. At least, she thought she was sure. This was not the first time she had been pulled into one of the legendary Green's designs. Cadsuane could be more devious than a Blue, schemes inside plots wrapped in stratagems and all hidden behind still others. Some were planned to fail in order to help others succeed, and only Cadsuane knew which were which, not at all a comforting thought. In any case, those three sisters were free to come and go as they desired, do as they desired. And they certainly felt no need to follow the guidance Cadsuane had left behind or to follow the sister she had named to lead. Only their mad oath to al'Thor guided or constrained them.

Samitsu had never felt weak or ineffectual in her life except when her Talent failed her, yet she very much wished that Cadsuane would return and take matters out of her hands. A few words delivered in Ailil's ear would quench any desire the lady had to mount the High Seat, of course, yet it would come to nothing unless she found some way to deflect Sashalle from her purpose. No matter that Ailil feared having her silly secrets aired abroad, inconsistency in what Aes Sedai told her could well make her decide it was better to try vanishing to her country estates rather than risk offending a sister whatever she did. Cadsuane would be upset over losing Ailil. Samitsu herself would be upset. Ailil was a conduit into half the plots brewing among the nobles, a gauge to be sure those intrigues were all still petty and unlikely to bring any major disturbance. The cursed Red knew that. And once Sashalle gave Ailil this permission, it would be her the woman came running to with her news, not Samitsu Tamagowa.

While Samitsu was floundering in her quandary, the door to the hallway opened to admit a pale, stern-faced Cairhienin woman, a hand shorter than either Aes Sedai. Her hair was in a thick gray roll on the nape of her neck, and she wore an unadorned gray dress so dark it was nearly black, the current livery of a Sun Palace servant. Servants never announced themselves or asked admittance, of course, but Corgaide Marendevin was hardly just another servant; the heavy silvery ring of long keys at her waist was a badge of office. Whoever ruled Cairhien, the Holder of the Keys ruled the Sun Palace in simple fact, and there was nothing submissive in Corgaide's manner. She made a minimal curtsy carefully aimed halfway between Samitsu and Sashalle.

"I was asked to report anything unusual," she said to the air, though it had been Samitsu who asked. Very likely, she had known of the power struggle between them as soon as they did themselves. Little in the palace escaped her. "I am told there is an Ogier in the kitchens. He and a young man supposedly are looking after work as masons, but I have never heard of Ogier and human masons working together. And *Stedding* Tsofu sent word no masons would be available from any *stedding* for the foreseeable future, when we inquired after . . . the incident." The pause was barely perceptible, and her grave expression did not alter, but half the gossip about the attack on the Sun Palace laid it to al'Thor's doing, the other half to Aes Sedai. A few tales mentioned the Forsaken, but only to pair them with either al'Thor or the Aes Sedai.

Pursing her lips in thought, Samitsu set aside the cursed tangle Cairhienin made of everything they touched. Denials of Aes Sedai involvement did little good; the Three Oaths went only so far in a city where a simple yes or no could give rise to six contradictory rumors. But, Ogier . . . The palace kitchens scarcely took in stray passersby, yet the cooks very likely would give an Ogier a hot meal just for the strangeness of seeing him. Ogier were even more uncommon than usual, this last year or so. A few were still seen now and then, but walking as fast as only an Ogier could, and seldom stopping in one place more than long enough to sleep. They rarely traveled with humans, much less worked with them. The pairing tickled something in her mind, though. Hoping to tease whatever it was into the open, she opened her mouth to ask a few questions.

"Thank you, Corgaide," Sashalle said with a smile. "You've been most helpful. But if you will leave us, now?" Being abrupt with the Holder of the Keys was a good way to find yourself with dirty bed linens and poorly spiced meals, unemptied chamber pots and messages that went astray, a thousand annoyances that could make life a misery and leave you wading in mud trying to accomplish anything at all, yet somehow, that smile appeared to take the sting out of her words for Corgaide. The gray-haired woman bowed her head slightly in assent and again made the smallest possible curtsy. This time, obviously to Sashalle.

No sooner had the door closed behind the gray-haired woman than Samitsu thumped her silver cup back on the tray hard enough to splash warm wine over her wrist and rounded on the Red sister. She was on the brink of losing control of Ailil, and now the Sun Palace itself appeared to be slipping through her fingers! It was as likely Corgaide would sprout wings and fly as keep silent about what she had seen here, and whatever she said would flash through the palace and infect every servant down to the men who mucked out the stables. That final curtsy had made it quite clear what she thought. Light, but Samitsu hated Cairhien! The customs of civility between sisters were deeply ingrained, but Sashalle did not stand high enough to make her hold her tongue in the face of this disaster, and she intended to deliver the rough side of it.

Frowning at the other woman, though, she saw Sashalle's face—*really* saw it, perhaps for the first time—and suddenly she knew why it troubled her so, perhaps even why she had found it difficult to look directly at the Red sister. It was no longer an Aes Sedai face, outside of time and standing apart from age. Most people were unsure of the look until it was pointed out, but it was unmistakable to another sister. Perhaps some bits remained, scraps that made Sashalle appear closer to beautiful than she really was, yet anyone at all would put an age to her, somewhere short of her middle years. The realization froze Samitsu's tongue.

What was known about women who had been stilled was little better than rumor. They ran away and hid from other sisters; eventually, they died. Usually, they died soon rather than late. The loss of *saidar* was more than most women could bear for very long. But it was all really tittle-tattle; as far as she knew, no one in a very long time had had the nerve to try learning more. The rarely acknowledged fear in the darkest corner of every sister's head, that the same fate might come to her one day in a careless moment, kept anyone from wanting to know too much. Even Aes Sedai could hide their eyes when they did not want to see. There were always those rumors, though, almost never mentioned and so vague you could never recall where you heard them first, whispers on the edge of hearing, yet forever floating about. One that Samitsu had only half remembered, till now, said that a woman who was stilled grew young again, if she lived. It had always seemed ludicrous, till now. Regaining the ability to channel had not given Sashalle back everything. Once more she would have to work with the Power for years to gain the face that would proclaim her Aes Sedai to any sister who could see her clearly. Or . . . would she regain it? It seemed inevitable, yet this was unmapped terrain. And if her face was changed, was anything else about her changed as well? Samitsu shivered, harder than she had for the thought of stilling. Perhaps it was as well she had gone slow in trying to puzzle out Damer's way of Healing.

Fingering her Aiel necklace, Sashalle seemed unaware that Samitsu had any grievance, unaware of Samitsu's scrutiny. "This may be nothing, or it may warrant looking into," she said, "but Corgaide was only reporting what she heard. If we want to learn anything, we must go and see for ourselves." Without another word, she gathered her skirts and started out of the apartments, leaving Samitsu only a choice between following or remaining behind. It was intolerable! Yet remaining was unthinkable.

Sashalle was no taller than she, not to speak of, but she had to hurry to keep up as the Red glided swiftly along wide, square-vaulted corridors. Taking the lead was out of the question, unless she chose to run. She fumed in silence, though it required gritting her teeth. Arguing with another sister in public was improper at best. Worse, without any doubt, it would be futile. And that would only dig the hole she was in deeper. She felt a very great desire to kick something.

Stand-lamps at regular intervals gave plenty of light even in the darkest stretches of hallway, but there was little color or decoration beyond the occasional tapestry with everything in it arranged in orderly fashion, whether animals being hunted or nobles fighting gallantly in battle. A few niches in the walls held ornaments of gold or Sea Folk porcelain, and in some corridors the cornices were worked in friezes, most left unpainted. That was all. Cairhienin hid their opulence out of public view, as they did with so much. The serving men and women who hurried industriously along the halls like streams of ants wore livery the color of charcoal, except for those in service to nobles resident in the palace, who seemed bright beside the rest, with their House badges embroidered on their breasts, and their collars and sometimes sleeves marked in House colors. One or two even had a coat or dress all in House colors, and appeared almost an outlander among the others. But they all kept their eyes down and barely paused long enough to offer quick bows or curtsies to the two sisters as they passed.

The Sun Palace required countless hundreds of servants, and it seemed they were all scurrying about this morning tending their chores.

Nobles strolled in the hallways, too, offering their own cautious courtesies to the Aes Sedai as they passed, perhaps with a greeting carefully balanced between an illusion of equality and the true state of affairs, spoken in low voices that did not carry far. They proved the old saying that strange times make for strange traveling companions. Old enmities had been put away in the face of new dangers. For the moment. Here, two or three pale Cairhienin lords in dark silk coats with thin stripes of color across the front, some with the fronts of their heads shaved and powdered soldier-fashion, promenaded alongside an equal number of dark Tairens, taller in their bright coats with fat, striped sleeves. There, a Tairen noblewoman in a snug pearl-sewn cap, colorfully brocaded gown, and pale lace ruff walked arm-in-arm beside a shorter Cairhienin noble with her hair in an elaborate tower that reached well above her companion's head, smoky gray lace under her chin, and narrow stripes of her House colors cascading down the front of her wide-skirted dark silk. All like bosom friends and trusted confidants.

Some pairings did look odder than others. A number of women had begun wearing outlandish clothes of late, apparently never noticing how they drew men's eyes and made even the servants struggle not to stare. Tight breeches and a coat barely long enough to cover the hips were not suitable garments for a woman, no matter how much effort went into rich embroidery or patterning the coat with gemstones. Jeweled necklaces and bracelets and pins with sprays of colorful feathers only pointed up the oddity. And those brightly dyed boots, with their heels that added as much as a hand to a woman's height, made them appear in danger of falling down with every swaying step.

"Scandalous," Sashalle muttered, eyeing one such pair of women and twitching her skirts in displeasure.

"Scandalous," Samitsu murmured before she could stop herself, then snapped her mouth shut so hard her teeth clicked. She needed to control her tongue. Voicing agreement just because she agreed was a habit she could ill afford with Sashalle.

Still, she could not help glancing back at the pair in disapproval. And a bit of wonder. A year ago, Alaine Chuliandred and Fionnda Annariz would have been at each other's throats. Or rather have had their armsmen at one another's throats. But then, who would have expected to see Bertome Saighan walking peacefully with Weiramon Saniago, neither man reaching for the dagger at his belt? Strange times and strange traveling companions. Doubtless they were playing the Game of Houses, maneuvering for advantage as they always had, yet dividing lines that once were graven in stone now turned out to have been drawn on water instead. Very strange times.

The kitchens were on the lowest level of the Sun Palace above-ground, at the back, a cluster of stone-walled beamed-ceiling rooms centered around a long windowless room full of iron stoves and brick ovens and dressed-stone fireplaces, and the heat was enough to make anyone forget the snow outside, or even that it was winter. Normally, sweaty-faced cooks and under-cooks, as darkly clad as any other palace servants beneath their white aprons, would have been scurrying about getting ready to prepare the midday meal, kneading loaves on long flour-strewn tables topped with marble, basting the joints and fowl that were turning on spits in the fireplaces. Now, only the trotting spit-dogs were moving, eager to earn their bits from the joints. Baskets of turnips and carrots stood unpeeled and unchopped, and smells sweet and spicy came from untended pots of sauces. Even the scullions, boys and girls surreptitiously wiping their faces on their aprons, stood on the fringe of a group of women clustered around one of the tables. From the doorway, Samitsu could see the back of an Ogier's head rising above them where he was seated at the table, taller than most men would have been standing up, and broad with it. Of course, Cairhienin were short by and large, and that helped. She laid a hand on Sashalle's arm, and for a wonder, the woman stopped where they were without protest.

". . . vanished without leaving a clue where he was going?" the Ogier was asking in a deep rumble like the earth shifting. His long, tufted ears, sticking up through dark hair that hung to his high collar, flicked back and forth uneasily.

"Oh, do stop talking about him, Master Ledar," a woman's

voice answered in a quaver that seemed well-practiced. "Wicked, he was. Tore half the palace apart with the One Power, he did. He could turn your blood to ice just looking at you, and kill you as soon as look. Thousands have died by his own hand. Tens of thousands! Oh, I never like talking about him."

"For someone as never likes talking about something, Eldrid Methin," another woman said sharply, "you surely talk of little else." Stout and quite tall for a Cairhienin, nearly as tall as Samitsu herself, with a few strands of gray hair escaping her white plain-lace cap, she must have been the chief cook on duty, because everyone Samitsu could see quickly nodded agreement and twittered with laughter and said, "Oh, right you are, Mistress Beldair," in a particularly sycophantic way. Servants had their own hierarchies, as rigidly maintained as the Tower itself.

"But that sort of thing really is not for us to be gossiping over, Master Ledar," the stout woman went on. "Aes Sedai business, that is, and not for the likes of you and me. Tell us more about the Borderlands. Have you really seen Trollocs?"

"Aes Sedai," a man muttered. Hidden by the crowd around the table, he had to be Ledar's companion. Samitsu could see no grown men among the kitchen folk this morning. "Tell me, do you really think they bonded those men you were talking about, those Asha'man? As Warders? And what about the one who died? You never said how."

"Why, it was the Dragon Reborn as killed him," Eldrid piped up. "And what else would Aes Sedai bond a man as? Oh, terrible, they was, them Asha'man. Turn you to stone with a look, they could. You can tell one just by looking at him, you know. Frightful glowing eyes, they have."

"Be quiet, Eldrid," Mistress Beldair said firmly. "Maybe they was Asha'man and maybe not, Master Underhill. Maybe they was bonded and maybe not. All I or anyone else can say is they was with *him*," the emphasis in her voice made plain who she was talking about; Eldrid might consider Rand al'Thor fearful, but this woman did not want to so much as name him, "and soon after *he* left, suddenly the Aes Sedai was telling them what to do and they was doing it. Of course, any fool knows to do as an Aes Sedai says. Anyway, those fellows are all gone off, now. Why are you so interested in them, Master Underhill? Is that an Andoran name?"

Ledar threw back his head and laughed, a booming sound that filled the room. His ears twitched violently. "Oh, we want to know everything about the places we visit, Mistress Beldair. The Borderlands, you say? You might think it's cold here, but we've seen trees crack open like nuts on the fire from the cold in the Borderlands. You have blocks of ice in the river, floating down from upstream, but we've seen rivers as wide as the Alguenya frozen so merchants can drive loaded trains of wagons across them, and men fishing through holes cut in ice nearly a span thick. At night, there are sheets of light in the sky that seem to crackle, bright enough to dim the stars, and . . ."

Even Mistress Beldair was leaning toward the Ogier, caught up, but one of the young scullions, too short to see past the adults, glanced behind him, and his eyes went wide when they lit on Samitsu and Sashalle. His gaze stayed fixed on them as if trapped, but he fumbled with one hand till he could tug at Mistress Beldair's sleeve. The first time, she shook him off without looking around. At a second tug, she turned her head with a scowl that vanished in a blink when she, too, saw the Aes Sedai.

"Grace favor you, Aes Sedai," she said, hastily tucking stray hair back under her cap as she bobbed her curtsy. "How may I serve you?" Ledar broke off short in midsentence, and his ears stiffened for a moment. He did not look toward the doorway.

"We wish to speak with your visitors," Sashalle said, moving into the kitchen. "We won't disrupt your kitchen for long."

"Of course, Aes Sedai." If the stout woman felt any surprise at two sisters wanting to talk to kitchen visitors, she showed none. Head swinging from side to side to take in everyone, she clapped her plump hands and began spouting orders. "Eldrid, those turnips will never peel themselves. Who was watching the fig sauce? Dried figs are hard to come by! Where is your basting spoon, Kasi? Andil, run, fetch some. . . ." Cooks and scullions scattered in every direction, and a clatter of pots and spoons quickly filled the kitchen, though everyone was plainly making an effort to be as quiet as possible so as not to disturb the Aes Sedai.

They were plainly making an effort not to even look in their direction, though that involved some contortion.

The Ogier rose to his feet smoothly, his head coming near the thick ceiling beams. His clothing was what Samitsu remembered from meeting Ogier before, a long dark coat that flared over turned-down boots. Stains on his coat said he had been traveling hard; Ogier were a fastidious people. He only half turned to face her and Sashalle even as he made a bow, and he rubbed at his wide nose as if it itched, partially hiding his broad face, but he appeared young, for an Ogier. "Forgive us, Aes Sedai," he murmured, "but we really must be moving on." Bending to gather a huge leather scrip that had a large rolled blanket tied across the top and showed the impressions of several square shapes packed around whatever else was stuffed inside, he hoisted the broad strap over one shoulder. His capacious coat pockets bulged with angular shapes, too. "We have a long way to go before nightfall." His companion remained seated, though, his hands spread on the tabletop, a pale-haired young man with a week's growth of beard who seemed to have slept more than one night in his rumpled brown coat. He watched the Aes Sedai warily, with dark eyes that belonged on a cornered fox.

"Where are you going that you can reach by nightfall?" Sashalle did not stop until she was standing in front of the young Ogier, close enough to need to crane her neck to look up at him, though she made it seem graceful rather than awkward, as it should have been. "Are you on your way to the meeting we've heard about, in *Stedding* Shangtai? Master . . . Ledar, is it?"

His tall ears twitched violently, then were still, and his teacup-sized eyes narrowed almost as warily as the young man's, till the dangling ends of his eyebrows trailed onto his cheeks. "Ledar, son of Shandin son of Koimal, Aes Sedai," he said reluctantly. "But I'm certainly not going to the Great Stump. Why, the Elders wouldn't let me close enough to hear what was being said." He gave a deep bass chuckle that sounded forced. "We can't get where we're going tonight, Aes Sedai, but every league behind us is a league we don't have to walk tomorrow. We need to be on our way." The unshaven young man stood up, running a hand nervously along the long hilt of the sword belted at his waist, yet he made no move to pick up the scrip and blanket roll at his feet and follow as the Ogier started toward the door that led to the street, even when the Ogier said over his shoulder, "We need to go now, Karldin."

Sashalle glided fluidly into the Ogier's path, though she had to take three strides to his one. "You were asking after work as a mason, Master Ledar," she said in tones brooking no nonsense, "but your hands are not as callused as any mason's I've ever seen. It would be best for you to answer my questions."

Suppressing a triumphant smile, Samitsu moved up beside the Red sister. So Sashalle thought she could simply push her aside and ferret out what was going on, did she? The woman was in for a surprise. "You really must stay a while longer," she said to the Ogier in a low voice; the noise in the kitchen should keep anyone from overhearing, yet there was no need to take chances. "When I came to the Sun Palace, I had already heard of a young Ogier, a friend of Rand al'Thor. He left Cairhien some months past, in company with a young man named Karldin. Isn't that right, Loial?" The Ogier's ears wilted.

The young man bit off a coarse curse he should have known better than to mouth in front of sisters. "I leave when I want to leave, Aes Sedai," he said harshly, but in a low voice. For the most part, he divided his gaze between her and Sashalle, yet he was watchful for any of the kitchen workers who might come near. He did not wish to be overheard, either. "Before I do, *I* want some answers. What happened to . . . my friends? And *him*. Did he go mad?"

Loial sighed heavily, and made a pacifying gesture with one huge hand. "Be easy, Karldin," he murmured. "Rand wouldn't like you starting trouble with Aes Sedai. Be easy." Karldin's scowl only deepened.

Abruptly it occurred to Samitsu that she could have handled this better. Those were not the eyes of a cornered fox, but a wolf. She had grown too accustomed to Damer and Jahar and Eben, safely bonded and tamed. That might be an overstatement, though Merise was making an effort with Jahar—that was Merise's way—yet it seemed the horror of yesterday could become the complacency of today after long enough exposure. Karldin Manfor was an Asha'man, too, and neither bonded nor tame. Was he embracing the male half of the Power? She almost laughed. Did birds fly?

Sashalle was watching the young man with a studying frown, her hands much too still on her skirts, but Samitsu was glad not to see the light of *saidar* around her. Asha'man could feel it when a woman held the Power, and that might make him act . . . precipitately. Certainly she and Samitsu together could handle him—could they, if he already held the Power? Of course they could. Of course!—but it would be much better if they did not have to.

Sashalle certainly was making no move to take charge, now, so Samitsu laid a hand lightly on his left arm. Through his coatsleeve, it felt like a bar of iron. So he was as uneasy as she. As uneasy as she? Light, but Damer and those other two had spoiled all her instincts!

"*He* seemed sane as most men when I last saw him," she said softly, with just a slight emphasis. None of the kitchen folk were nearby, but a few had begun sneaking peeks toward the table. Loial exhaled heavily in relief, a sound like wind rushing across the mouth of a cave, but she kept her attention on Karldin. "I don't know where he is, but he was alive as of a few days ago." Alanna had been closemouthed as a mussel beyond that, and overbearing, too, with Cadsuane's note in her fist. "Fedwin Morr died of poison, I fear, but I have no idea who gave it to him." To her surprise, Karldin merely shook his head, with a rueful grimace, and muttered something incomprehensible about wine. "As for the others, they became Warders of their own free will." As much as any man did anything of his free will. Her Roshan certainly had not wanted to be a Warder, until she decided she wanted him for one. Even a woman who was not Aes Sedai could usually make a man decide the way she wanted. "They thought it a better choice, safer, than returning to . . . the others like you. You see, the damage here was done with *saidin*. You understand who must have been behind it? It was an attempt to kill the one whose sanity you fear for."

That did not seem to surprise him, either. What sort of men *were* these Asha'man? Was their so-called Black Tower a murder pit? The tightness went out of his arm, though, and suddenly he was just a road-weary young man who needed to shave. "Light!" he breathed. "What do we do now, Loial? Where do we go?"

"I . . . don't know," Loial replied, his shoulders sagging

tiredly and his long ears drooping. "I . . . We have to find him, Karldin. Somehow. We can't give up now. We have to let him know we did what he asked. As much as we could."

And what was it al'Thor had asked, Samitsu wondered. With a little luck, she could learn a great deal from these two. A tired man, or Ogier, feeling lost and alone, was ripe for answering questions.

Karldin gave a small jump, his hand tightening on his sword hilt, and she bit back a curse of her own as a palace serving woman came running into the room with her skirts gathered almost to her knees. "Lord Dobraine's been murdered!" the serving woman squealed. "We will all be killed in our beds! My own eyes have seen the dead walking, old Maringil himself, and my mam says spirits will kill you if there has been a murder done! They—" Her mouth froze open when she caught the presence of Aes Sedai, and she skidded to a halt still clutching her skirts. The kitchen folk seemed frozen, too, all watching the Aes Sedai from the corners of their eyes to see what they would do.

"Not Dobraine," Loial moaned, ears laying flat against his head. "Not him." He looked as much angry as saddened, his face stony. Samitsu did not think she had ever seen an Ogier angry.

"What is your name?" Sashalle demanded of the serving woman before Samitsu could even part her lips. "How do you know he was murdered? How do you even know he's dead?"

The woman swallowed, her eyes held by Sashalle's cool gaze. "Cera, Aes Sedai?" she said hesitantly, bending her knees in a curtsy and only then realizing that she still had her skirts gathered up. Hastily smoothing them down only seemed to fluster her more. "Cera Doinal? They say . . . Everybody says Lord Dobraine is . . . I mean, he was . . . I mean . . ." She swallowed again, hard. "They all say his rooms are covered with blood. He was found lying in a great pool of it. With his head cut off, they say."

"*They* say a great many things," Sashalle said grimly, "and usually they're wrong. Samitsu, you will come with me. If Lord Dobraine *has* been injured, you may be able to do something for him. Loial, Karldin, you come, too. I don't want you out of my sight before I have a chance to ask a few questions."

"Burn your questions!" the young Asha'man growled, shouldering his belongings. "I'm leaving!"

"No, Karldin," Loial said gently, laying a huge hand on his companion's shoulder. "We can't go before we know about Dobraine. He's a friend, Rand's friend, and mine. We can't. Anyway, where are we hurrying to?" Karldin looked away. He had no answer.

Samitsu squeezed her eyes shut, and took a deep breath, but there was no help for it. She found herself following Sashalle out of the kitchens, once more hurrying to keep up with the other woman's quick, gliding stride. In fact, she found herself half-running; Sashalle set an even more rapid pace than before.

The babbling of voices rose behind them as soon as they were out the door. The kitchen folk probably all were pressing the serving woman for particulars, details she very likely would invent where her knowledge failed. Ten different versions of events would find their way out of that kitchen, if not as many as there were kitchen folk. Worst of all, ten different versions of events *in* the kitchen would find their way out, every one adding to the rumors Corgaide doubtless was already starting. She could hardly recall a day that had gone so badly for her, so suddenly, like slipping on one patch of ice only to find another under her feet, then another. Cadsuane would have her hide to make gloves after this!

At least Loial and Karldin trailed after Sashalle as well. Whatever she learned from them might still be put to advantage, a way to salvage something. Scurrying along at Sashalle's side, she studied them in brief glances over her shoulder. Taking short strides to keep from over-running the Aes Sedai, the Ogier was frowning in worry. Over Dobraine, very likely, but also perhaps over only completing his mysterious task "as well as he could." That was a mystery she intended to solve. The young Asha'man had no difficulty keeping up, though he wore an expression of stubborn reluctance and his hand caressed his swordhilt. The danger in him did not lie in steel. He stared suspiciously at the backs of the Aes Sedai ahead, once meeting Samitsu's glance with a dark glower. He had the sense to keep his mouth shut, though. She would have to find a way to pry it open later for more than snarling.

Sashalle never glanced behind to make sure the pair were following, but then, she had to hear the thud of the Ogier's boots on the floor tiles. Her face was thoughtful, and Samitsu would have given a great deal to know what she was thinking. Sashalle might be oathsworn to Rand al'Thor, but what protection did that give to an Asha'man? She was Red, after all. *That* had not changed with her face. Light, this could be the worst patch of ice of all!

It was a long arduous climb from the kitchens to Lord Dobraine's apartments in the Tower of the Full Moon, which was usually set aside for visiting nobility of high rank, and all along the way, Samitsu saw the evidence that Cera had been far from the first to hear what the ever-anonymous *they* had to say. Rather than endless streams of servants flowing along the corridors, small excited knots stood whispering anxiously. At sight of the Aes Sedai, they sprang apart and scurried away. A handful did gape at seeing an Ogier striding through the palace, yet for the most part, they all but fled. The nobles who had been about before had all vanished, doubtless back to their own rooms to mull over what opportunities and hazards Dobraine's death afforded them. Whatever Sashalle thought, Samitsu no longer doubted. If Dobraine had been alive, his own servants would have put paid to the rumor already.

For further confirmation, the hallway outside Dobraine's rooms was crowded with ashen-faced servants, their sleeves ringed to the elbows in the blue-and-white of House Taborwin. Some wept, and others looked lost, their foundation stone pulled out from under them. At a word from Sashalle, they stood aside for the Aes Sedai, moving drunkenly or mechanically. Dazed eyes swept by the Ogier without actually registering what they saw. Few remembered to make even half-hearted courtesies.

Inside, the anteroom was almost as full of Dobraine's servants, most staring as if poleaxed. Dobraine himself lay motionless on a litter in the middle of the large room, his head still attached to his body but his eyes closed and a drying sheet of blood, from a long cut in his scalp, across his still features. A dark trickle had leaked from his slack mouth. Two serving men with tears streaming down their cheeks paused in the act of laying a white cloth over his face at the entrance of the Aes Sedai. Dobraine did not appear to be breathing, and there were bloodstained gashes in the chest of his coat, with its thin stripes of color that marched down to his knees. Beside the litter, a dark blot larger than a man's body marred the green-and-yellow Tairen maze of the fringed carpet. Anyone who lost that much blood had to be dead. Two other men lay sprawled on the floor, one with death-glazed eyes gazing at the ceiling, the other on his side, an ivory knife hilt sticking up from his ribs where the blade had surely reached his heart. Short, pale-skinned Cairhienin, both wore the livery of palace servants, but a servant never carried the long, wooden-handled dagger that lay beside each corpse. A House Taborwin man, his foot drawn back to kick one of the corpses, hesitated on seeing the two sisters, then planted his boot hard in the dead man's ribs anyway. Clearly, proper decorum lay far from anyone's mind at the moment.

"Move that cloth out of the way," Sashalle told the men by the litter. "Samitsu, see whether you can still help Lord Dobraine."

Whatever she believed, instinct had moved Samitsu toward Dobraine, but that command—it was *clearly* a command!—put a stutter in her step. Gritting her teeth, she kept moving, and knelt carefully beside the litter, on the side away from the still damp blot, to put her hands on Dobraine's blood-soaked head. She never minded getting blood on her hands, but bloodstains were impossible to get out of silk unless you channeled, and she still felt a pang of guilt at the waste when she used the Power for something so mundane.

The necessary weaves were second nature to her, so much so that she embraced the Source and delved the Cairhienin lord without a thought. And blinked in surprise. Instinct had made her go ahead, though she had been certain there were three corpses in the room, yet life still flickered in Dobraine. A tiny guttering flame that the shock of Healing might well extinguish. The shock of the Healing she knew.

Her eyes searched out the pale-haired Asha'man. He was crouched beside one of the dead servants, calmly searching the man, oblivious of the shocked stares of the living servants. One of the women suddenly noticed Loial, standing just inside the door, and goggled as if he had leapt out of thin air. With his arms folded across his chest and a grim expression on his broad face, the Ogier looked as though he were standing guard.

"Karldin, do you know the kind of Healing that Damer Flinn uses?" Samitsu asked. "The kind that uses all of the Five Powers?"

He paused for a moment, frowning at her. "Flinn? I don't even know what you're talking about. I don't have much Talent for Healing, anyway." Eyeing Dobraine, he added, "He looks dead to me, but I hope you can save him. He was at the Wells." And he bent back to rummaging though the dead servant's coat.

Samitsu licked her lips. The thrill of being filled with *saidar* always seemed diminished to her, in situations like this. Situations when all of her possible choices were bad. Carefully, she gathered flows of Air, Spirit and Water, weaving them just so, the basic weave of Healing that every sister knew. No one in living memory had the Talent for Healing as strongly as she, and most sisters were limited in what they could Heal, some to little more than bruises. By herself, she could Heal almost as well as a linked circle. Most sisters could not regulate the weave to any degree at all; most did not even try to learn. She had been able to from the start. Oh, she could not Heal one particular thing and leave everything else as it was, the way Damer could; what she did would affect everything from the stab wounds to the stuffed nose Dobraine was also suffering from. Delving had told her everything that ailed him. But she could wash away the worst injuries as if they had never been, or Heal so whoever she Healed appeared to have spent days recovering on her own, or anything in between. Each took no less of her strength, but they did require less from the patient. The smaller the amount of change in the body, the smaller the amount of the body's strength it drained. Only, except for the gash in his scalp, Dobraine's wounds were all serious, four deep punctures in his lungs, two of them gashing the heart as well. The strongest Healing would kill him before his wounds finished closing, while the weakest would revive him long enough to drown in his own blood. She had to choose somewhere in the middle and hope that she was right.

I am the best that ever has been, she thought firmly.

Cadsuane had told her that. *I am the best!* Altering the weave slightly, she let it sink into the motionless man.

Some of the servants cried out in alarm as Dobraine's body convulsed. He half sat up, deep-set eyes opening wide, long enough for what sounded all too much like a long death rattle to rush out of his mouth. Then his eyes rolled back in his head, and he slipped from her grasp, thudding back down onto the litter. Hastily, she readjusted the weave and delved him again, holding her breath. He lived. By a hair, and so weak he might yet die, but it would not be those stabs that killed him, except indirectly. Even through the drying blood that matted his hair, shaven away from his forehead, she could see the puckered pink line of a fresh, tender scar across his scalp. He would have the same beneath his coat, and he might be troubled by shortness of breath when he exerted himself, if he pulled through, yet for the moment, he did live, and that was all that mattered. For the moment. There was still the matter of who had wanted him dead, and why.

Releasing the Power, she stood unsteadily. *Saidar* draining out of her always made her feel tired. One of the serving men, gaping, hesitantly handed her the cloth he had been going to lay on his lord's face, and she used it to wipe her hands. "Take him to his bed," she said. "Get as much mild honey-water down him as you can. He needs to gain strength quickly. And find a Wise Woman . . . a Reader? Yes, a Reader. He will need her, too." He was out of her hands, now, and herbs might help. At least, they were unlikely to harm, coming from a Reader, and at worst the woman would make sure they gave him enough honey-water and not too much.

With much bowing and many murmurs of thanks, four of the serving men took up the litter and carried Dobraine deeper into the apartments. Most of the other servants followed hurriedly, wearing expressions of relief, and the rest dashed out into the corridor. An instant later, glad shouts and cheers broke out, and she heard her name nearly as often as Dobraine's. Very gratifying. It would have been more satisfying if Sashalle had not smiled and given her an approving nod. Approving! And why not a pat on the head, while she was about it?

Karldin had paid no mind at all to the Healing, insofar

as Samitsu had noticed. Finishing his search of the second corpse, he rose and crossed the room to Loial, attempting to show the Ogier something, shielded by his body, without letting the Aes Sedai notice. Loial plucked it—a sheet of cream-colored paper, creased from folding—out of the Asha'man's hand and held it up in front of his face opened out in his thick fingers, ignoring Karldin's scowl.

"But this makes no sense," the Ogier muttered, frowning as he read. "No sense at all. Unless—" He cut off abruptly, long ears flickering, and exchanged a tense look with the pale-haired fellow, who gave a curt nod. "Oh, this is very bad," Loial said. "If there were more than two, Karldin, if they found—" He choked off his words again at a frantic head shake from the young man.

"I will see that, please," Sashalle said, holding out her hand, and please or no please, it was not a request.

Karldin attempted to snatch the paper from Loial's hand, but the Ogier calmly handed it to Sashalle, who inspected it without any change of expression, then handed it to Samitsu. It was thick paper, smooth and expensive, and new-looking. Samitsu had to control her eyebrows' desire to climb as she read.

At my command, the bearers of this are to remove certain items, which they will know, from my apartments and take them out of the Sun Palace. Make them private of my rooms, give them whatever aid they require and keep silent on this matter, in the name of the Dragon Reborn and on pain of his displeasure.

Dobraine Taborwin

She had seen Dobraine's writing often enough to recognize the rounded hand as his. "Obviously, someone employs a very good forger," she said, earning a quick, contemptuous glance from Sashalle.

"It did seem unlikely he wrote it himself and was stabbed by his own men in mistake," the Red said in cutting tones. Her gaze swung to Loial and the Asha'man. "What is it they might have found?" she demanded. "What is it you are *afraid* they found?" Karldin stared back at her blandly.

"I just meant whatever they were looking for," Loial answered. "They had to be here to steal something." But his

tufted ears twitched so hard they almost vibrated before
he could master them. Most Ogier made very poor liars, at
least while young.

Sashalle's ringlets swung as she shook her head deliberately. "What you know is important. The pair of you are not
leaving until I know it, too."

"And how are you going to stop us?" The very quietness
of Karldin's words made them more dangerous. He met
Sashalle's gaze levelly, as if he had not a worry in the world.
Oh, yes; very much a wolf, not a fox.

"I thought I'd never find you," Rosara Medrano announced, marching into that moment of perilous silence
still wearing her red gloves and fur-lined cloak, with the
hood thrown back to reveal the carved ivory combs in her
black hair. There were damp patches on the shoulders of
the cloak from melted snow. A tall woman, as brown as a
sun-dark Aiel, she had gone out at first light to try finding
spices for some sort of fish stew from her native Tear. She
spared only the briefest glance for Loial and Karldin, and
did not waste a moment inquiring after Dobraine. "A party
of sisters has entered the city, Samitsu. I rode like a mad-
woman to get here ahead of them, but they could be riding
in at this moment. There are Asha'man with them, and one
of the Asha'man is Logain!"

Karldin barked a rough laugh, and suddenly Samitsu
wondered whether she was going to live long enough for
Cadsuane to have her hide.

CHAPTER
I

Time to Be Gone

The Wheel of Time turns, and Ages come and pass, leaving memories that become legend. Legend fades to myth, and even myth is long forgotten when the Age that gave it birth comes again. In one Age, called the Third Age by some, an Age yet to come, an Age long past, a wind rose in the Rhannon Hills. The wind was not the beginning. There are neither beginnings nor endings to the turning of the Wheel of Time. But it was *a* beginning.

Born among the groves and vineyards that covered much of the rugged hills, the olive trees in evergreen rows, the ordered vines leafless till spring, the cold wind blew west and north across the prosperous farms dotting the land between the hills and the great harbor of Ebou Dar. The land lay winter fallow still, but men and women were already oiling plowshares and tending harnesses, preparing for the planting to come. They paid little mind to the trains of heavily laden wagons moving east along the dirt roads carrying people who wore odd clothes and spoke with odd accents. Many of the strangers seemed to be farmers themselves, familiar implements lashed to their wagon boxes, and in their wagons unfamiliar saplings with roots balled in rough cloth, but they were heading on toward more distant land. Nothing to do with life here and now. The Seanchan hand lay lightly on those who did not contest Seanchan rule, and the farmers of the Rhannon Hills had seen no changes in their lives. For them, rain or the lack of it had always been the true ruler.

West and north the wind blew, across the broad blue-green expanse of the harbor, where hundreds of huge ships sat rocking at anchor on choppy swells, some bluff-bowed and rigged with ribbed sails, others long and sharp-prowed, with men laboring to match their sails and rigging to those of the wider vessels. Not nearly so many ships still floated there as had only a few days before, though. Many now lay in the shallows, charred wrecks heeled over on their sides, and burned frames settling in the deep gray mud like blackened skeletons. Smaller craft skittered about the harbor, slanting under triangular sails or crawling on oars like many-legged waterbugs, most carrying workers and supplies to the ships that still floated. Other small vessels and barges rode tethered to what appeared to be tree trunks shorn of branches, rising out of the blue-green water, and from those men dove holding stones to carry them down swiftly to sunken ships below, where they tied ropes to whatever could be hauled up for salvage. Six nights ago death had walked across the water here, the One Power killing men and women and ships in darkness split by silver lightnings and hurtling balls of fires. Now the rough rolling harbor, filled with furious activity, seemed at peace by comparison, the chop giving up spray to the wind that blew north and west across the mouth of the River Eldar, where it widened into the harbor, north and west and inland.

Sitting cross-legged atop a boulder covered with brown moss, on the reed-fringed bank of the river, Mat hunched his shoulders against the wind and cursed silently. There was no gold to be found here, no women or dancing, no fun. Plenty of discomfort, though. In short, it was the last sort of place he would choose, normally. The sun stood barely its own height above the horizon, the sky overhead was pale slate gray, and thick purple clouds moving in from the sea threatened rain. Winter hardly seemed winter without snow—he had yet to see a single flake in Ebou Dar—but a cold damp morning wind off the water could serve as well as snow to chill a man to the bone. Six nights since he had ridden out of the city in a storm, yet his throbbing hip seemed to think he was still soaked to the skin and clinging to a saddle. This was no weather or time of day for a man to be out by his own choice. He wished he had thought to bring a cloak. He wished he had stayed in bed.

Ripples in the land hid Ebou Dar, just over a mile to the south, and hid him from the city, as well, but there was not a tree or anything more than scrub brush in sight. Being in the open this way made him feel as though ants were crawling under his skin. He should be safe, though. His plain brown woolen coat and cap were nothing like the clothes he was known by in the city. Instead of black silk, a drab woolen scarf hid the scar around his neck, and the collar of his coat was turned up to hide that, as well. Not a bit of lace or a thread of embroidery. Dull enough for a farmer milking cows. No one he needed to avoid would know him to recognize if they saw him. Not unless they were close. Just the same, he tugged the cap a bit lower.

"You intend to stay out here much longer, Mat?" Noal's tattered dark blue coat had seen better days, but then so had he. Stooped and white-haired, the broken-nosed old fellow was squatting on his heels below the boulder, fishing off the riverbank with a bamboo pole. Most of his teeth were missing, and sometimes he felt at a gap with his tongue as though surprised to find the empty space. "It's cold, in case you haven't noticed. Everybody always thinks it's warm in Ebou Dar, but winter is cold everywhere, even places that make Ebou Dar feel like Shienar. My bones crave a fire. Or a blanket, anyway. A man can be snug with a blanket, if he's out of the wind. Are you going to do anything but stare downriver?"

When Mat only glanced at him, Noal shrugged and went back to peering at the tarred wooden float bobbing among the sparse reeds. Now and then he worked one gnarled hand as though his crooked fingers felt the chill particularly, but if so, it was his own fault. The old fool had gone wading in the shallows to scoop up minnows for bait with a basket that now sat half-submerged and anchored by a smooth stone at the edge of the water. Despite his complaints about the weather, Noal had come along to the river without urging or invitation. From things he had said, everyone he cared about was long years dead, and the truth of it was, he seemed almost desperate for any sort of company. Desperate, indeed, to choose Mat's company when he could be five days from Ebou Dar by now. A man could cover a lot of ground in five days if he had reason to and a good horse. Mat had thought on that very subject often enough himself.

On the far side of the Eldar, half-hidden by one of the marshy islands that dotted the river, a broad-beamed rowboat backed oars, and one of the crew stood up and fished in the reeds with a long boathook. Another oarsman helped him heave what he had caught into the boat. At this distance, it looked like a large sack. Mat winced and shifted his eyes downriver. They were still finding bodies, and he was responsible. The innocent died along with the guilty. And if you did nothing, then only the innocent died. Or as bad as died. Maybe worse than, depending on how you looked at it.

He scowled irritably. Blood and ashes, he was turning into a bloody philosopher! Taking responsibility drained all the joy out of life and dried a man to dust. What he wanted right then was a great deal of mulled wine in a snug common room full of music, and a plump, pretty serving maid on his knee, somewhere far from Ebou Dar. Very far. What he had were obligations he could not walk away from and a future he did not fancy. There seemed no help at all in being *ta'veren,* not if this was how the Pattern shaped itself to you. He still had his luck, anyway. At least, he was alive and not chained in a cell. Under the circumstances, that counted as luck.

From his perch, he had a fairly clear view down past the last low marshy river islands. Wind-caught spray drifted up the harbor like banks of fine mist, but not enough to hide what he needed to see. He was attempting to do sums in his head, counting ships afloat, trying to count wrecks. He kept losing his place, though, thinking he had counted vessels twice and starting over. The Sea Folk who had been recaptured intruded on his thoughts, too. He had heard that gibbets in the Rahad, across the harbor, displayed more than a hundred corpses, with placards listing "murder" and "rebellion" as their crimes. Normally, the Seanchan used the headsman's axe and the impaling stake, while the Blood got the strangling cord, but property had to settle for being hanged.

Burn me, I did what I could, he thought sourly. There was no use feeling guilty that that was all he could do. Not a bit of use. None! He had to concentrate on the people who escaped.

The Atha'an Miere who got away had taken ships in the harbor for their flight, and while they might have seized some smaller craft, anything they could board and overwhelm in the night, they had intended to carry off as many of their people as possible. With thousands of them laboring as prisoners in the Rahad, that would have meant big ships, by choice, and that meant Seanchan greatships. Many of the Sea Folk's own vessels were large enough, for certain, but they all had been stripped of their sails and rigging by that time, to be fitted out in the Seanchan fashion. If he could calculate how many greatships remained, he might have some notion of how many Atha'an Miere had actually reached freedom. Freeing the Sea Folk Windfinders had been the right thing to do, the only thing he could do, but aside from the hangings, hundreds and hundreds of bodies had been fished out of the harbor in the last five days, and the Light only knew how many had washed out to sea with the tides. The gravediggers labored from sunup to sundown, and the graveyards were filled with weeping women and children. Men, too. More than a few of those dead had been Atha'an Miere, with no one to weep while they were dumped into mass graves, and he wanted some idea of the number he had saved to balance his bleak suspicions of the number he had killed.

Estimating how many ships had made it out into the Sea of Storms was difficult, though, quite apart from losing the count. Unlike Aes Sedai, Windfinders had no strictures against using the Power as a weapon, not when the safety of their people was at stake, and they would have wanted to halt pursuit before it began. No one gave chase in a burning ship. The Seanchan, with their *damane,* had even less compunction against fighting back. *Lightning bolts lacing through the rain as numerous as blades of grass and balls of fire streaking across the sky, some the size of horses, and the harbor seemed aflame from one side to the other, till even in a storm the night made any Illuminator's show look stark.* Without turning his head he could count a dozen places where the charred ribs of a greatship stuck up out of shallow water or a huge bluff-bowed hull lay on its side with the harbor waves licking against the tilted deck, and twice as many where the lines of blackened timbers were finer, the remains of Sea Folk rakers. Apparently they had disliked leaving their own vessels to people who had put them in chains. Three dozen right in front of him, and that without adding in the sunken wrecks that had salvage boats working over them. Perhaps a seafarer could tell greatship from raker by the tops of masts sticking out of the water, but the task was beyond him.

Suddenly an old memory tugged at him, of lading ships

for an attack from the sea, and how many men could be crowded into how much space for how long. It was not his memory, really, from an ancient war between Fergansea and Moreina, yet it seemed his. Realizing that he had not actually lived one of those ancient bits of other men's lives that were stuck in his head always took him a little by surprise now, so maybe they were his, in a way. They were certainly sharper than some stretches of his own life. The vessels he recalled had been smaller than most in the harbor, yet the principles were the same.

"They don't have enough ships," he muttered. The Seanchan had even more in Tanchico than had come here, but the losses here were sufficient to make the difference.

"Enough ships for what?" Noal said. "I never saw so many in one place before." That was quite a statement, coming from him. To hear Noal tell it, he had seen everything, and nearly always bigger or grander than what was in front of his nose. Back home, they would have said he kept tight purse-strings on the truth.

Mat shook his head. "They don't have enough ships left to take them all back home."

"We don't have to go home," a woman drawled behind him. "We've come home."

He did not quite jump at the slurred Seanchan accent, but it was a near thing before he recognized who was speaking.

Egeanin was scowling, her eyes like blue daggers, but not for him. At least, he thought not. She was tall and lean, with a hard face that was pale-skinned despite a life at sea. Her green dress was bright enough for a Tinker, or close to it, and embroidered with a mass of tiny yellow and white blossoms on the high neck and down the sleeves. A flowered scarf tied tightly under her chin held a long black wig on her head, spilling halfway down her back and over her shoulders. She hated the scarf and the dress, which did not quite fit, but her hands checked every other minute to make sure the wig was straight. That concerned her more than her clothes, though concern was not nearly a strong enough word.

She had only sighed over cutting her long fingernails short, but she almost had a fit, red-faced and pop-eyed, when he told her she must shave her head completely. The way her hair had been cut before, shaved above her ears with only a bowl-like cap and a wide shoulder-length tail in the back remaining, shouted that she was of the Seanchan Blood, a lesser noble. Even someone who had never laid eyes on a Seanchan would have remembered seeing her. She had agreed, reluctantly, but afterward she was close to hysterical until she was able to cover her scalp. Not for the reasons most women would have gone over the moon, though. No, among the Seanchan, only the Imperial family shaved their heads. Men who went bald began wearing wigs as soon as their hair started falling out to any noticeable degree. Egeanin would have died before letting anyone think she was pretending to belong to the Imperial family, even people who would never have had the thought in their lives. Well, that sort of pretense did carry a death penalty among the Seanchan, but he would never have believed she would go on about it so. What was one more death penalty when your neck was already being stretched for the axe? The strangling cord, in her case. The noose would be for him.

Slipping the half-drawn knife back up his left sleeve, he slid down from the boulder. He landed poorly and almost fell, barely hiding a wince at the stabbing jar to his hip. He did hide it, though. She was a noblewoman *and* a ship captain, and she made enough tries at taking charge without him showing any more weakness to give her an opening than he had to. She had come to him for help, not the other way 'round, but that buttered no bread with her. Leaning against the boulder with his arms folded, he pretended he was lounging, idly kicking at tufts of dead grass to work the pain out. *That* was sharp enough to put sweat on his forehead despite the cold wind. Fleeing in that storm had cost him ground with his hip, and he had not made it up yet.

"Are you sure about the Sea Folk?" he asked her. No point in mentioning the lack of ships again. Too many Seanchan settlers had spread out from Ebou Dar anyway, and apparently even more from Tanchico. However many ships they had, no power on earth would ever root all the Seanchan out, now.

Reaching toward the wig again, she hesitated, frowning at her short fingernails, and instead tucked her hands under her arms. "What about them?" She knew he had been behind the Windfinders' break for freedom, but neither of them had mentioned it specifically. She always tried to avoid talking about the Atha'an Miere. Quite aside from all the sunken ships and dead, freeing *damane* was another death-penalty charge, and disgusting besides, in the Seanchan view, as bad as rape or molesting children. Of course, she had helped free some *damane* herself, though to her way of looking, that was among the least of her crimes. Still, she avoided that topic, too. There were quite a few subjects she held silent on.

"Are you *certain* about the Windfinders who were caught? I've heard talk about cutting off hands, or feet." Mat swallowed a sour taste. He had seen men die, had killed men with his own hands. The Light send him mercy, he had killed a woman, once! Not even the darkest of those other men's memories burned so hot as that, and a few of those were dark enough to need drowning in wine when they floated to the surface. But the thought of deliberately cutting off somebody's hands curdled his stomach.

Egeanin's head jerked, and for a moment he thought she would ignore his question. "Talk from Renna, I'll wager," she said, with a dismissive gesture. "Some *sul'dam* talk about that nonsense to frighten recalcitrant *damane* when they're new-leashed, but nobody's done it in, oh, six or seven hundred years. Not many, anyway, and people who can't control their property without . . . mutilation . . . are *sei'mosiev* to start." Her mouth twisted in loathing, though whether for mutilation or *sei'mosiev* was unclear.

"Shamed or not, they do it," he snapped. *Sei'mosiev* went beyond being shamed, to a Seanchan, but he doubted that anyone who deliberately cut off a woman's hand could be humiliated enough to kill themselves. "Is Suroth one of that 'not many'?"

The Seanchan woman glared to match his and planted her fists on her hips, leaning forward with her feet astride as though she were on the deck of a ship and about to berate a fumble-witted sailor. "The High Lady Suroth doesn't own these *damane,* you lump-brained farmer! They're property of the Empress, may she live forever. Suroth might as well slit her own wrists straightaway as order something like that for Imperial *damane.* That's even if she would; I've never heard of her mistreating her own. I'll try to put this in terms you can understand. If your dog runs away, you don't maim it. You switch the dog so it knows not to do that again, and you put it back in the kennel. Besides, *damane* are just too—"

"Too valuable," Mat finished for her dryly. He had heard that till he was sick of it.

She disregarded his sarcasm, or maybe did not notice. In his experience, if a woman did not want to hear something, she could ignore it till you yourself started to doubt you had spoken. "You're finally beginning to understand," she drawled, nodding. "Those *damane* you're so worried about probably don't even have welts left by this time." Her gaze went to the ships in the harbor, and slowly took on a look of loss, made deeper by the hardness of her face. Her thumbs ran across her fingertips. "You wouldn't believe what my *damane* cost me," she said in a quiet voice, "her and hiring the *sul'dam* for her. Worth every throne I paid, of course. Her name's Serrisa. Well-trained, responsive. She'll gorge herself on honeyed nuts, if you let her, but she never gets seasick or the sulks, the way some do. A pity I had to leave her in Cantorin. I suppose I'll never see her again." She sighed regretfully.

"I'm sure she misses you as much as you miss her," Noal said, flashing a gap-toothed smile, and for all the world, he sounded sincere. Maybe he was. He contended that he had seen worse than *damane* and *da'covale,* for what that was worth.

Egeanin's back stiffened, and she frowned as if she did not believe his sympathy. Or else she had just realized how she was staring at the ships in the harbor. Certainly, she turned away from the water very deliberately. "I gave orders that no one was to leave the wagons," she said firmly. Likely, crewmen on her ships had jumped at that tone. She jerked her head away from the river as though she expected Mat and Noal to jump where she indicated, too.

"Did you, now?" Mat grinned, showing teeth. He could manage an insolent grin that sent most puffed-up fools into apoplexy. Egeanin was far from a fool, most times, but puffed-up she was. Ship captain and noblewoman. He did not know which was worse. Bah for both! "Well, I was about ready to head that way. Unless you're not done fishing, Noal. We can wait here awhile, if you're not."

But the old man was already emptying the remaining silver-gray minnows out of his basket into the water. His hands had been broken badly, maybe more than once by their lumpy appearance, yet they were deft in winding his line around the bamboo pole. In the short time he had been fishing, he had caught nearly a dozen fish, the largest less than a foot long, strung through the gills on a looped reed, and he moved those to the basket before picking it up. He claimed that if he could find the right peppers, he was going to make a fish stew—from Shara, of all places! As well say from the moon!—a stew that would make Mat forget all about his hip. The way Noal went on about the peppers, Mat suspected any forgetting would be because he was focused on finding enough ale to cool his tongue.

Egeanin, waiting impatiently, was paying no attention to Mat's grin, either, so he slipped an arm around her. If they were heading back, they might as well get started. She knocked his hand away from her shoulder. The woman made some maiden aunts he had known look like tavern girls.

"We're supposed to be lovers, you and I," he reminded her.

"There's nobody here to see," she growled.

"How many times do I have to tell you, Leilwin?" That was the name she was using. She claimed it was Taraboner. At any rate, it did not sound Seanchan. "If we don't even hold hands unless we see somebody watching, we're going to look a pretty strange pair of lovers to anybody we don't see."

She snorted in derision, yet she let him put his arm back around her, and slipped hers around him. But she gave him a warning stare at the same time.

Mat shook his head. She was crazy as a spring hare if she thought he enjoyed this. Most women had a little padding over their muscles, at least the women he liked, but hugging Egeanin was like hugging a fence post. Almost as hard, and definitely as stiff. He could not puzzle out what Domon saw in her. Maybe she had not given the Illianer any choice. She had *bought* the man, after all, same as buying a horse. *Burn me, I'll never understand these Seanchan,* he thought. Not that he wanted to. The only thing was, he had to.

As they were turning away, he took one last glance back at the harbor, and almost wished he had not. Two small sailing craft broke through a wide wall of mist that was drifting slowly down the harbor. Drifting against the wind. Time to be gone and past time.

It was better than two miles from the river to the Great North Road, across rolling countryside covered in winter-brown grasses and weeds and dotted with clumps of vine-tangled bushes too thick to push through even with most of the leaves gone. The rises hardly deserved the name of hill, not for anyone who had climbed in the Sand Hills and the Mountains of Mist as a boy—there were gaps in his own memories, but Mat could remember some of that—yet before long, he was glad he had an arm around somebody. He had sat motionless on that bloody rock for too long. The throb in his hip had faded to a dull ache, but it still made him limp, and without some sort of support, he would have been staggering on the slopes. Not that he leaned on Egeanin, of course, but holding on helped steady him. The woman frowned at him as though she thought he was trying to take advantage.

"If you did as you were told," she growled, "I wouldn't need to carry you."

He showed his teeth again, this time not trying to disguise it as a smile. The way Noal scampered along beside them easily, never missing a step despite balancing his basket of fish on his hip with one hand and carrying his fishing pole in the other, was embarrassing. For all he looked hard-worn, the old man was spry enough. Too spry by half, at times.

Their route slanted north of the Circuit of Heaven, with its long, open-ended tiers of polished stone seats where, in warmer weather, wealthy patrons sat on cushions beneath colorful canvas awnings to watch their horses race. Now the awnings and poles were stowed away, the horses all in their country stables, those the Seanchan had not taken, and the seats were empty save for a handful of small boys darting up and down the tiers in a game of keep-away. Mat was fond of horses, and racing, but his eyes slid past the Circuit toward Ebou Dar. Whenever he topped a rise, the city's massive white ramparts were visible, deep enough that they supported a road encircling the city on top, and looking gave him an excuse to pause a moment. Fool woman! A scrap of a limp did not mean she was carrying him! He managed to keep a good temper, take the rough with the smooth and no complaining. Why could she not?

Inside the city white roofs and walls, white domes and spires, ringed in thin bands of color, gleamed in the gray morning light, a picture of serenity. He could not make out the gaps where buildings had burned to the ground. A long line of farmers' high-wheeled ox-carts was trundling through the wide arched gateway that opened on the Great North Road, men and women on their way to the city markets with whatever they had left to sell this late in winter, and in their midst a merchant's train of big, canvas-topped wagons behind six- and eight-horse teams, carrying goods from the Light knew where. Seven more trains, ranging from four wagons to ten, stood in line at the side of the road to wait for the gate guards to finish their inspections. Trade never stopped entirely while the sun shone, no matter who ruled a city, unless there was actual fighting. Sometimes it did not stop completely then. The stream of people flowing the other way was mostly Seanchan, soldiers in ordered ranks with their segmented armor painted in stripes and helmets that looked like the heads of huge insects, some marching and some mounted, nobles who were always mounted, wearing ornate cloaks, pleated riding dresses and lace veils, or voluminous trousers and long coats. Seanchan settlers were still departing the city, too, wagon upon wagon filled with farmers and craftsmen and the tools of their trades. The settlers had begun leaving as soon as they came off the ships, but it would be weeks before they were all gone. It was a peaceful scene, workaday and ordinary if you ignored what lay behind it, yet every time they reached a place where he could see the gates, his mind flashed back to six nights ago, and he was there again, at those same gates.

The storm had grown worse as they crossed the city from the Tarasin Palace. Rain fell by buckets, pounding the darkened city and slicking the paving stones under the horses' hooves, and wind howled off the Sea of Storms, driving the rain like stones from slings and jerking at cloaks so that keeping at all dry was a lost cause. Clouds hid the moon, and the deluge seemed to soak up the light of the pole-lanterns carried by Blaeric and Fen, on foot ahead of the rest. Then they entered the long passageway through the city wall, and gained a bit of shelter, at least from the rain. The wind made the high-ceilinged tunnel keen like a flute. The gate guards were waiting just inside the far end of the passage, four of them also bearing pole-lanterns. A dozen more, half of them Seanchan, carried halberds that could strike at a man in the saddle or pull him out of it. Two Sean-

chan with their helmets off were peering from the lighted
doorway of the guardhouse built into the white-plastered
wall, and shifting shadows behind them told of others inside. Too many to fight past quietly, maybe too many to
fight past at all. Not without everything going off like an
Illuminator's firework bursting in his hand.

The guards were not the danger, anyway, not the main
danger. A tall, plump-faced woman in dark blue, her divided ankle-length skirts bearing red panels worked with
silver lightning bolts, stepped past the men in the guardhouse door. A long silvery metal leash was coiled in the
sul'dam's left hand, the free end connecting her to the graying woman in a dark gray dress who followed her out with
an eager grin. Mat had known they would be there. The
Seanchan had *sul'dam* and *damane* at all the gates, now.
There could even be another pair inside, or two. They did
not mean to let one woman who could channel escape their
nets. The silver foxhead medallion beneath his shirt lay
cold against his chest; not the cold that signaled someone
embracing the Source nearby, just the accumulated chill of
the night and his flesh too icy to warm it, but he could not
stop waiting for the other. Light, he was *juggling* fireworks
tonight, with the fuses lit!

The guards might have been puzzled by a noblewoman
leaving Ebou Dar in the middle of the night and that
weather, with over a dozen servants and strings of packhorses indicating a journey of some distance, but Egeanin
was of the Blood, her cloak embroidered in an eagle with
spread black-and-white wings, and long fingers on her red
riding gloves to accommodate her fingernails. Ordinary
soldiers did not question what the Blood chose to do, even
the low Blood. Which did not mean there were no formali-
ties. Anyone was free to leave the city when they wished,
but the Seanchan recorded the movement of *damane,* and
three rode in the entourage, heads down and faces covered
by the hoods of their gray cloaks, each linked to a mounted
sul'dam by the silvery length of an *a'dam*.

The plump-faced *sul'dam* walked by them with barely a
glance, strolling down the tunnel. Her *damane* peered intently at every woman they passed, though, sensing whether
she could channel, and Mat held his breath when she paused
beside the last mounted *damane* with a slight frown. Even

with his luck, he would not bet against the Seanchan recognizing an Aes Sedai's ageless face if they looked inside that hood. There were Aes Sedai held as *damane,* but what were the odds that all three of Egeanin's would be? Light, what were the odds one of the low Blood would own three?

The plump-faced woman made a clicking sound, as you might to a pet dog, and twitched the *a'dam,* and the *damane* followed her on. They were looking for *marath'damane* trying to escape the leash, not *damane.* Mat still thought he might choke. The sound of dice rolling had started up again in his head, loud enough to rival the occasional rumble of distant thunder. Something was going to go wrong; he knew it.

The officer of the guards, a burly Seanchan with tilted eyes like a Saldaean but pale honey-brown skin, bowed courteously and invited Egeanin into the guardhouse, to have a cup of spiced wine while a clerk wrote down the information about the *damane.* Every guardhouse Mat had ever seen was a stark place, yet the lamplight glowing in the arrowslits made this one seem almost inviting. A pitcherplant probably looked inviting to a fly, too. He had been glad of the rain dripping from the hood of his cloak and running down his face. It disguised the sweat of nerves. He held one of his throwing knives, resting flat atop the long bundle draped in front of his saddle. With it lying flat like that, none of the soldiers should notice. He could feel the woman inside the cloth breathing under his hands, and his shoulders were knotted from waiting for her to cry out for help. Selucia kept her mount close to him, peering at him from the shelter of her hood with her golden braid tucked out of sight, never even glancing away when the *sul'dam* and *damane* walked by. A shout from Selucia would have put the weasel in the chicken run as much as one from Tuon. He thought the threat of the knife had held both women silent—they had to believe he was desperate enough or crazy enough to use it—but he still could not be sure. There was so much about night he could not be sure of, so much off-balance and askew.

He remembered holding his breath, wondering when someone would notice that the bundle he carried was richly embroidered and question why he was letting it get soaked with rain, wondering and cursing himself for grabbing a wall hanging because it had been close to hand. In memory, everything slowed. Egeanin stepped down, tossing her reins to Domon, who took them with a bow from his saddle. Domon's hood was pushed back just enough to show that his head was shaved on one side and his remaining hair gathered in a braid that hung to his shoulder. Raindrops dripped from the stocky Illianer's short beard, yet he managed the proper stiff-necked arrogance of a *so'jhin,* hereditary upper servant to one of the Blood and thus almost equal to the Blood. Definitely higher than any common soldier. Egeanin glanced back toward Mat and his burden, her face a frozen mask that could pass for hauteur if you did not know she was horrified by what they were doing. The tall *sul'dam* and her *damane* turned briskly back up the tunnel, finished with their inspection. Vanin, just behind Mat leading one of the strings of packhorses and as always sitting his horse like a sack of suet, leaned from his saddle and spat. Mat did not know why that hung in his memory, but it did. Vanin spat, and trumpets sounded, thin and sharp in the distance far behind them. From south of the city, where men had been planning to fire Seanchan supplies stored along the Bay Road.

The officer of the guard hesitated at the sound of the trumpets, but suddenly a bell pealed loudly in the city itself, then another, and then it seemed hundreds were clanging alarm in the night as the black sky split with more lightning than any storm had ever birthed, silver-blue streaks stabbing down inside the walls. They bathed the tunnel in flickering light. That was when the shouting started, amid the explosions back in the city, and the screaming.

For a moment, Mat had cursed the Windfinders for moving sooner than he had been promised. But the dice in his head had stopped, he realized. Why? It made him want to curse all over again, but there was no time for even that. In the next instant the officer was hurriedly urging Egeanin back into her saddle and on her way, hurriedly shouting orders to the men boiling out of the guardhouse, directing one into the city at a run to see what the alarm was while he arrayed the rest against any threat from inside or out. The plump-faced woman ran to place herself and her *damane* with the soldiers, along with another pair of women linked by an *a'dam,* who came running from the guardhouse. And Mat and the others galloped out into the storm, carrying with them three Aes Sedai, two of them escaped *damane,* and the kidnapped heir to the Seanchan Crystal Throne, while behind them a far worse storm broke over Ebou Dar. *Lightning bolts more numerous than blades of grass.* . . .

With a shiver, Mat pulled himself back to the present. Egeanin scowled at him, and gave him an exaggerated pull. "Lovers arm-in-arm don't hurry," he muttered. "They . . . stroll." She sneered. Domon had to be blinded by love. That, or he had taken too many thumps on the head.

The worst was over and done, in any case. Mat hoped that getting out of the city had been the worst. He had not felt the dice since. They were always a bad sign. His backtrail was as muddled as he could manage, and he was sure it would take someone as lucky as he to separate the gold from the dross. The Seekers had been on Egeanin's scent before that night, and she would be wanted on charges of stealing *damane* now, as well, but the authorities would expect her to be riding as hard as she could and already leagues from Ebou Dar, not sitting just outside the city. Nothing except a co-incidence of timing connected her to Tuon. Or to Mat, and that was important. Tylin certainly would have leveled her own charges against him—no woman was going to forgive a man tying her up and shoving her under a bed, even when she had suggested it—yet with any luck, he was beneath suspicion for anything else that had happened that night. With any luck, no one except Tylin had a thought for him at all. Trussing a queen like a pig for market would be enough to get a man dead usually, but it had to count for moldy on-ions alongside the Daughter of the Nine Moons disappear-ing, and what could Tylin's Toy have to do with that? It still irritated him that he had been seen as a hanger-on—worse, a pet!—but there were advantages.

He thought he was safe—from the Seanchan, anyway—yet one point worried him like a thorn buried in his heel. Well, several did, most growing out of Tuon herself, but this one had a particularly long point. Tuon's disappearance should have been as shocking as the sun vanishing at noon, but no alarm had been raised. None! No announcements of rewards or offers of ransom, no hot-eyed soldiers searching every wagon and cart within miles, galloping through the countryside to root out every cubbyhole and niche where a woman might be hidden. Those old memories told him something of hunting for kidnapped royalty, yet except for the hangings and the burned ships in the harbor, from the outside Ebou Dar seemed unchanged from the day before the kidnapping. Egeanin alleged that the search would be in utter secrecy, that many of the Seanchan themselves might still not know Tuon was missing. Her explanation involved the shock to the Empire and ill omens for the Return and the loss of *sei'taer,* and she sounded as if she believed every word, but Mat refused to buy a penny's worth. The Seanchan were strange folk, but no one could be that strange. The silence of Ebou Dar made his skin prickle. He felt a trap in that silence. When they reached the Great North Road, he was grateful that the city was hidden behind the low hills.

The road was a broad highway, a major avenue of trade, wide enough for five or six wagons abreast uncrowded, with a surface of dirt and clay that hundreds of years of use had packed nearly as hard as the occasional ancient paving stone that stuck an edge or corner inches into the air. Mat and Egeanin hurried across to the verge on the other side with Noal dogging their heels, between a merchant's train rumbling toward the city, guarded by a scar-faced woman and ten hard-eyed men in leather vests covered with metal discs, and a string of the settlers' oddly shaped wagons, rising to peaks at the ends, that were heading north, some pulled by horses or mules, others by oxen. Clustered between the wagons, barefoot boys used switches to herd four-horned goats with long black hair and big, dewlapped white cows. One man at the rear of the wagons, in baggy blue breeches and a round red cap, was leading a massive humpbacked bull by a thick cord tied to a ring in its nose. Except for his clothes, he could have been from the Two Rivers. He eyed Mat and the others, walking in the same direction, as if he might speak, then shook his head and plodded on without looking at them again. Contending with Mat's limp, they were not moving fast, and the settlers forged ahead slowly but steadily.

Hunch-shouldered and clutching the scarf beneath her chin with her free hand, Egeanin let out a breath and loosened fingers that had begun to grip Mat's side almost painfully. After a moment, she straightened and glared at the farmer's departing back as though she were ready to chase after him and box his ears and his bull's. If that were not bad enough, once the farmer was twenty or so paces away, she shifted her scowl to a company of Seanchan soldiers marching down the middle of the road at a pace that would soon overtake the settlers, perhaps two hundred men in a column four abreast followed by a motley collection of mule-drawn wagons covered with tightly lashed canvas. The middle of the road was left free for military traffic. Half a dozen well-mounted officers in thin-plumed helmets that hid all but their eyes rode at the column's head, looking neither left nor right, red cloaks spread neatly over their horses' cruppers. The banner following on the officers' heels was marked with what looked like a stylized silver arrowhead, or maybe an anchor, crossed by a long arrow and a jagged lightning bolt in gold, with script and numerals below that Mat could not make out as gusts swept the banner this way and that. The men on the supply wagons wore dark blue coats and breeches and square red-and-blue caps, but the soldiers were even more showy than most Seanchan, their segmented armor striped in blue banded at the bottom with silvery white and red banded with golden yellow, their helmets painted in all four colors so they resembled the faces of fearsome spiders. A large badge with the anchor—Mat thought it must be an anchor—and arrow and lightning was fastened to the front of each helmet, and every man except the officers carried a double-curve bow at his side, with a bristling quiver at his belt balancing a short-sword.

"Ship's archers," Egeanin grumbled, glowering at the soldiers. Her free hand had left her scarf, but it was still clenched in a fist. "Tavern brawlers. They always cause problems when they're left ashore too long."

They had a well-trained look, to Mat. Anyway, he had never heard of soldiers who did not get in fights, especially when they were drunk or bored, and bored soldiers tended to get drunk. A corner of his mind wondered how far those bows would carry, but it was an absent thought. He wanted nothing to do with any Seanchan soldiers. If he had his way, he would have nothing to do with any soldiers ever again. But his luck never ran that far, it seemed. Fate and luck were different, unfortunately. Two hundred paces at most, he decided. A good crossbow would outrange them, or any Two Rivers bow.

"We're not in a tavern," he said through his teeth, "and they're not brawling now. So let's not start one just because you were afraid a farmer would speak to you." Her jaw set, and she shot him a look hard enough to crack his skull. It was the truth, though. She was fearful of opening her mouth near anyone who might recognize her accent. A wise precaution, in his book, but everything seemed to grate at her. "We'll have a bannerman over here asking questions if you keep glaring at them. Women around Ebou Dar are famous for being demure," he lied. What could she know of local customs?

She gave him a sidelong frown—maybe she was trying to figure out what demure meant—but she stopped grimacing at the archers. She just looked ready to bite instead of hit.

"That fellow's dark as an Atha'an Miere," Noal muttered absently, staring at the passing soldiers. "Dark as a Sharan. But I'd swear he has blue eyes. I've seen the like before, but where?" Trying to rub his temples, he almost struck himself on the head with the bamboo fishing pole, and he took a step as though he meant to ask the fellow where he had been born.

With a lurch, Mat caught the old man's sleeve. "We're going back to the show, Noal. Now. We should never have left."

"I told you that," Egeanin said with a sharp nod.

Mat groaned, but there was nothing for it but to keep walking. Oh, it was way past time to be gone. He only hoped he had not left it too late.

CHAPTER
2

Two Captains

About two miles north of the city a wide blue banner stretched between two tall poles rippled in the wind, proclaiming Valan Luca's Grand Traveling Show and Magnificent Display of Marvels and Wonders in brilliant red letters large enough to be read from the road, perhaps a hundred paces east. For those unable to read, it at least indicated the location of something out of the ordinary. This was The Largest Traveling Show in the World, so the banner claimed. Luca claimed a great many things, but Mat thought he must be telling the truth about that. The show's canvas wall, ten feet high and tightly pegged at the bottom, enclosed as much ground as a good-sized village.

The people streaming by looked toward the banner curiously, but the farmers and merchants had their work ahead of them and the settlers their future, and none turned aside. Thick ropes fastened to posts set in the ground were meant to herd crowds to the wide, arched entrance just behind the banner, but there was no one waiting to get in, not at this hour. Of late, few came at any hour. The fall of Ebou Dar had brought only a slight drop in attendance, once people realized the city would not be looted and they did not have to flee for their lives, but with the Return, all those ships and settlers, nearly everyone decided to hold on to their coin against more pressing needs. Two bulky men, huddling in cloaks that might have come from a ragbag, were on duty beneath the banner to keep out anyone who wanted to peek around without paying, but even those were in short supply, nowadays. The pair, one with a crooked nose above

Two Captains   101

a thick mustache and the other missing an eye, were squatting on the dirt, tossing dice.

Surprisingly, Petra Anhill, the show's strongman, stood watching the two horse-handlers play, arms larger than most men's legs folded across his chest. He was shorter than Mat, but at least twice as wide, his shoulders straining the heavy blue coat his wife made him wear against the cold. Petra seemed engrossed in the dicing, but the man did not gamble, not so much as pitching pennies. He and his wife, Clarine, a dog trainer, saved every coin they could spare, and Petra needed small excuse to talk at length about the inn they intended to buy one day. Even more surprising, Clarine was at his side, enveloped in a dark cloak and apparently as absorbed in the gaming as he.

Petra glanced warily over his shoulder into the camp when he saw Mat and Egeanin approaching arm-in-arm, which made Mat frown. People looking over their shoulders was never good. Clarine's plump brown face broke into a warm smile, though. Like most women in the show, she thought he and Egeanin were romantic. The bent-nosed horse-handler, a heavy-shouldered Tairen named Col, leered as he scooped up the wager, a few coppers. No one but Domon could see Egeanin as pretty, but to some fools, nobility bestowed beauty. Or money did, and a noblewoman must be rich. A few thought any noblewoman who abandoned her husband for the likes of Mat Cauthon might be open to leaving him, too, and bringing her money with her. That was the story Mat and the others had put around to explain why they were hiding from the Seanchan: a cruel husband and a lovers' flight. Everyone had heard that sort of tale, from gleemen or books if seldom real life, often enough to accept it. Col kept his head down, though. Egeanin—Leilwin—had already drawn her belt knife on a sword-juggler, a too-handsome fellow who had been overly suggestive in asking her to share a cup of wine in his wagon, and no one doubted she would have used the blade if he had pressed his suit an inch further.

As soon as Mat reached the strongman, Petra said quietly, "There are Seanchan soldiers talking to Luca, about twenty of them. The officer's talking with him, leastwise." He did not sound frightened, but worry creased his forehead, and he laid a protective hand on his wife's shoulder. Clarine's smile faded, and she raised one hand to rest atop his. They trusted Luca's judgment, after a fashion, yet they knew the risk they were running. Or thought they did. The risk they believed in was bad enough.

"What do they want?" Egeanin demanded, pushing free of Mat, before he could crack his teeth. In fact, no one waited for him.

"Hold these for me," Noal said, handing his pole and basket to the one-eyed man, who gaped up at him. Straightening, Noal slipped a knobbly hand beneath his coat, where he kept two long-bladed knives. "Can we reach our horses?" he asked Petra. The strongman eyed him doubtfully. Mat was not the only one unsure whether Noal still possessed all his wits.

"They don't seem interested in searching," Clarine said hastily, making a hint of a curtsy to Egeanin. Everyone was supposed to pretend Mat and the others were part of the show, but few managed to carry it off with Egeanin. "The officer's been in Luca's wagon for a good half-hour, but the soldiers have been standing by their horses all that time."

"I don't think they're here about you," Petra added respectfully. Again, to Egeanin. Why should he be different? Probably practicing to welcome nobles to that inn. "We just didn't want you to be surprised or worried, seeing them. I'm sure Luca will send them off with no trouble." Despite his tone, the creases remained in his forehead. Most men became upset if their wives ran off, and a nobleman could make others bear the brunt of his ire. A traveling show, strangers just passing through, made a particularly easy target without added complications. "You don't have to worry about anybody talking out of turn, my Lady." Glancing at the horse handlers, Petra added, "Does she, Col?" Bent-nose shook his head, his eyes on the dice he was bouncing on his palm. He was a big man, but not as big as Petra, and the strongman could straighten horseshoes with his bare hands.

"Everybody likes a chance to spit on a noble's boots now and then," the one-eyed fellow mumbled, peering into the basket of fish. He was almost as tall and wide-shouldered as Col, but his face was all leathery wrinkles, and he had even fewer teeth than Noal. Glancing at Egeanin, he ducked his head and added, "Begging your pardon, Lady. 'Sides, this way we all get a little coin, which there ain't been much of lately. Right, Col? Anybody talks, them Seanchan'll take us all up, maybe hang us like they did them Sea Folk. Or put us to work cleaning them canals the other side of the harbor." Horse handlers did whatever needed doing around the show, from mucking the horselines and cleaning animals' cages to erecting and taking down the canvas wall, but he shuddered as though digging out silted canals in the Rahad was a worse prospect than hanging.

"Did I say anything about talking?" Col protested, spreading his hands. "I just asked how long we're going to sit here, that's all. I just asked when we're going to see some of this coin."

"We sit here as long as I say sit." It was remarkable how hard Egeanin could make that drawl sound without raising her voice, like a blade sliding free of the scabbard. "You see your coin when we reach our destination. There will be a little something extra for those who serve me faithfully. And a cold grave for anyone who thinks on betrayal." Col pulled his much-patched cloak tight and widened his eyes trying to look indignant, or maybe innocent, but he just appeared to be hoping she would come close enough for him to filch her purse.

Mat ground his teeth. For one thing, that was his gold she was promising with such a free hand. She had her own, but not near enough for this. More importantly, she was trying to take charge again. Light, except for him, she would still be in Ebou Dar scheming to avoid the Seekers, if not already being put to the question. Except for him, she would never have thought of staying close to Ebou Dar to throw off pursuit, or found a hiding place with Luca's show. But why were soldiers there? The Seanchan would have sent a hundred men, a thousand, for a vague suspicion of Tuon's presence. If they suspected the Aes Sedai . . . No; Petra and Clarine did not know they were helping hide Aes Sedai, but they would have mentioned *sul'dam* and *damane,* and the soldiers would not be hunting sisters without them. He fingered the foxhead through his coat. He wore that waking and sleeping, and it might give him a little warning.

He never considered trying for the horses, and not just because Col and a dozen more like him would go running

to the Seanchan before he was well out of sight. They had
no particular animosity toward him or Egeanin that he
knew—even Rumann, the sword-juggler, seemed to have
settled in happily with a contortionist named Adria—but
some folks would not resist the temptation of a little more
gold, either. In any case, no warning dice tumbled in his
head. And there were people inside those canvas walls he
could not leave behind.

"If they're not searching, then we have nothing to worry
about," he said confidently. "But thanks for the warning,
Petra. I've never liked surprises." The strongman made a
small gesture as if to say it was nothing, but Egeanin and
Clarine looked at Mat as though startled to find him there.
Even Col and the one-eyed lout blinked at him. It took an
effort to stop short of gritting his teeth again. "I'll just wander near Luca's wagon and see what I can see. Leilwin, you
and Noal find Olver and stay with him." They liked the boy,
everyone did, and that would keep them out of his hair. He
could eavesdrop better alone. And if they had to run, maybe
Egeanin and Noal could help get the boy out, at least. The
Light send it did not come to that. He could see nothing but
disaster in it.

"Well, I suppose nobody lives forever," Noal sighed,
retrieving his bamboo pole and basket. Burn him, but the
fellow could make a colicky goat seem cheerful! Petra's
frown certainly deepened. Married men always seemed to
be worried, one reason Mat was in no hurry himself. As
Noal vanished around the corner of the canvas wall, the
one-eyed man watched the fish go regretfully. He appeared
to be another without a full set of wits. He probably had a
wife somewhere.

Mat pulled his cap almost down to his eyes. Still no dice.
He tried not to think of how many times he had nearly had
his throat slit or his skull split without any dice. But surely
they would have been there if there was any real danger. Of
course they would.

He had not taken three steps inside the entrance before
Egeanin caught up to him and slipped her arm around his
waist. He stopped in his tracks, eyeing her balefully. She
resisted his orders the way a trout fought the hook, but
this went beyond stubborn. "What do you think you're doing? What if this Seanchan officer recognizes you?" That

seemed as likely as Tylin herself walking into the show, but anything that might make her leave was worth grabbing.

"What are the chances this fellow is anyone I know?" she scoffed. "I don't have . . ." her face twisted for an instant, "didn't have . . . many friends this side of the ocean, and none in Ebou Dar." She touched an end of the black wig over her bosom. "Anyway, in this, my own mother wouldn't recognize me." Her voice turned bleak toward the end.

He was going to chip a tooth if he kept on clenching his jaw. Standing there arguing with her would be worse than useless, but the way she had stared at those Seanchan soldiers was fresh in his mind. "Don't glare at anybody," he warned her. "Don't even look at anybody."

"I'm a demure Ebou Dari woman." She made it sound a challenge. "You can do all the talking." She made that into a warning. Light! When a woman was not making everything smooth, she made things very rough indeed, and Egeanin never made anything smooth. He was definitely in danger of chipping a tooth.

Beyond the entrance, the show's main street meandered among wagons like those the Tinkers used, little houses on wheels with the wagon shafts lifted against the drivers' seats, and walled tents often as large as small houses. Most of the wagons were brightly painted, every shade of red or green, yellow or blue, and many of the tents were just as colorful, a few even striped. Here and there wooden platforms, where entertainers could perform, stood beside the street, their colored bunting beginning to look a bit grubby. The broad expanse of dirt, near thirty paces wide and beaten flat by thousands of feet, really was a street, one of several that wound through the show. The wind whipped away faint gray streamers of smoke rising from the tin chimneys that stuck up from the roofs of the wagons, and from some tents. Most of the showfolk were probably at breakfast if not still in bed. They rose late, as a rule—a rule Mat approved—and no one would want to eat sitting around a cook fire outside in this cold. The only person he saw was Aludra, the sleeves of her dark green dress pushed up her forearms, grinding something with a bronze mortar and pestle on a table that folded down from the side of her vivid blue wagon, just around the corner on one of the narrower side streets.

Intent on her work, the slender Taraboner did not see Egeanin and Mat. He could not help looking at her, though. With her dark hair in thin, beaded braids that hung to her waist, Aludra was probably the most exotic of Luca's marvels. He advertised her as an Illuminator, and unlike many of the other performers and marvels, she really was what Luca claimed, though Luca probably did not believe it himself. Mat wondered what she was grinding. And whether it might explode. She had promised to reveal the secret of fireworks if he could answer a riddle, but he had not found a glimmer, so far. He would, though. One way or another.

Egeanin poked a hard finger into his ribs. "We're supposed to be lovers, as you keep reminding me," she growled. "Who's going to believe it if you stare at that woman as though you're hungry?"

Mat grinned lasciviously. "I always look at pretty women, haven't you noticed?" Adjusting her head scarf with a little more vigor than usual, she gave a disparaging grunt, and he was satisfied. Her prudish streak came in handy now and then. Egeanin was on the run for her life, but she was still Seanchan, and she already knew more about him than he liked. He was not about to trust her with all of his secrets. Even the ones he did not know yet.

Luca's wagon sat in the very middle of the show's camp, the most favored position, as far as possible from the smells of the animal cages and horselines situated along the canvas walls. The wagon was garish even compared to the others in the show, a red-and-blue thing that shone like the finest lacquerwork, every surface spotted with golden comets and stars. The phases of the moon, in silver, ran all the way around just below the roofline. Even the tin chimney was painted in red and blue rings. A Tinker would have blushed. To one side of the wagon two ranks of helmeted Seanchan soldiers stood stiffly beside their horses, green-tasseled lances slanted at exactly the same angle. One of the men held the reins of an extra mount, a fine dun gelding with strong haunches and good ankles. The soldiers' blue-and-green armor appeared drab alongside Luca's wagon.

Mat was unsurprised to see he was not the only one interested in the Seanchan. A dark stocking cap covering his shaved head, Bayle Domon was squatting on his heels with his back against one wheel of the green wagon that belonged to Petra and Clarine, about thirty paces beyond the soldiers. Clarine's dogs lay under the wagon, a motley collection of smallish animals sleeping huddled together. The thick-bodied Illianer was pretending to whittle, but all he had produced was a small pile of shavings at his feet. Mat wished the fellow would grow a mustache to hide his upper lip or else shave off the rest of his beard. Someone might connect an Illianer to Egeanin. Blaeric Negina, a tall fellow leaning against the wagon as though keeping Domon company, had not hesitated to remove his Shienaran top-knot to avoid Seanchan notice, though he ran a hand over the black bristle growing on his head about as often as Ege-anin checked her wig. Maybe he should wear a cap.

In their dark coats with frayed cuffs and well-traveled boots, both men could pass for showfolk, maybe horse-handlers, except to other showfolk. They were watching the Seanchan while trying to seem not to, but Blaeric was the more successful, as might be expected from a Warder. His full attention appeared to be on Domon, except for an occa-sional glance at the soldiers, as casual as could be. Domon scowled at the Seanchan when he was not glaring at the lump of wood in his hand, as though ordering it to turn into a neat carving. The man had taken being *so'jhin* entirely too much to heart.

Mat was trying to figure out how to sneak close to Luca's wagon and eavesdrop unseen by the soldiers when the door at the back of the wagon opened and a pale-haired Seanchan marched down the steps, planting a helmet with a thin blue plume on his head as his boot touched the ground. Luca ap-peared behind him, resplendent in scarlet embroidered with golden sunbursts, bowing with elaborate flourishes as he followed the officer. Luca owned at least two dozen coats, most red and each gaudier than the last. It was a good thing his wagon was the largest in the show, or he would not have had room for them all.

Ignoring Luca, the Seanchan officer stepped up onto his gelding, adjusted his sword, and barked orders that sent his men flowing into their saddles and forming a column of twos that moved off at a slow walk toward the entrance. Luca stood watching them leave with a fixed smile on his face, poised for another bow if any looked back.

Mat stayed well to the side of the street and let his mouth

hang open, affecting to gape in wonder as the soldiers rode by. Not that any of them so much as glanced his way—the officer stared straight ahead and so did the soldiers behind him—but no one ever paid any mind to a country yokel, or remembered one.

To his surprise, Egeanin studied the ground in front of her toes, clutching the scarf knotted beneath her chin, until the last horseman passed. Lifting her head to look after them, she pursed her lips for a moment. "It seems I do know that boy," she drawled softly. "I carried him to Falme on *Fearless*. His servant died, mid-voyage, and he thought he could use one of my crew. I had to put him straight. You'd have thought he was of the Blood, the fuss he put up."

"Blood and bloody ashes," Mat breathed. How many other people had she gotten crosswise, fixing her face in their minds? Egeanin being Egeanin, probably hundreds. And he had been letting her walk around with just a wig and a change of clothes for disguise! Hundreds? Thousands, more likely. She could irritate a brick.

In any case, the officer was gone now. Mat exhaled slowly. His luck really was still with him. At times he thought that was all that kept him from bawling like a baby. He headed for Luca to find out what the soldiers had wanted.

Domon and Blaeric reached Luca as quickly as he and Egeanin did, and the scowl on Domon's round face deepened as he stared at Mat's arm around Egeanin's shoulder. The Illianer understood the necessity for the pretense, or said he did, yet he seemed to believe they could carry it off without so much as touching hands. Mat removed his arm from her—there was nothing to carry off here; Luca knew the truth; of everything—and Egeanin started to release him, too, yet after a look at Domon, she tightened her grip on Mat's waist instead, all without the slightest change of expression. Domon continued to scowl, but at the ground, now. Mat decided he would understand the Seanchan long before he understood women. Or Illianers, for that matter.

"Horses," Luca growled almost before Mat stopped walking. His frown took in all of them, but he focused most of his anger on Mat. A little the taller, Luca stretched to stare down at Mat. "That's what he wanted. I showed him the warrant exempting me from the horse lottery, signed by the High Lady Suroth herself, but was he impressed?

It didn't matter to him that I rescued a high-ranking Sean-chan." The woman had not been high-ranking, and he had not so much rescued her as given her a way to travel as a hired performer, but Luca always exaggerated to his own advantage. "I don't know how long that exemption is really good for, anyway. The Seanchan are desperate for horses. They might take it back any day!" His face was turning almost as red as his coat, and he jabbed a finger at Mat repeatedly. "You're going to get my horses taken! How do I move my show with no horses? Answer me that, if you can. I was ready to leave as soon as I saw that madness in the harbor, until you twisted my arm. You're going to get my head cut off! I could be a hundred miles from here, if not for you, riding in out of the night and snaring me in your crazy schemes! I'm not earning a penny here! There haven't been enough patrons the last three days to pay for feeding the animals one day! Half a day! I should have left a month ago! More! I should have!"

Mat almost laughed as Luca ran down into splutters. Horses. That was all; just horses. Besides, the notion that the show's heavy-laden wagons could cover a hundred miles in five days was as ludicrous as Luca's wagon. The man could have gone a month ago, two months, except for wanting to eke every copper he could out of Ebou Dar and its Seanchan conquerors. And as for talking him into stay-ing, six nights past, that had been as easy as falling out of bed.

Instead of laughing, Mat put a hand on Luca's shoulder. The fellow was vain as a peacock, and greedy besides, but there was no point making him angrier than he already was. "If you'd left that night, Luca, you think nobody would have gotten suspicious? You would have had Seanchan tear-ing your wagons apart before you made two leagues. You could say I saved you from that." Luca glowered. Some people just could not see beyond their own noses. "Anyway, you can stop worrying. As soon as Thom returns from the city, we can put as many miles behind us as you want."

Luca leaped so suddenly that Mat stepped back in alarm, but all the man did was caper in a little circle laughing. Domon goggled at him, and even Blaeric stared. Some-times, Luca seemed a flat bull-goose fool.

Luca had barely begun his dance when Egeanin shoved

Mat away from her. "As soon as Merrilin returns? I gave orders no one was to leave!" Her glare swung between him and Luca in cold fury, a cold that burned. "I expect my orders to be obeyed!"

Luca stopped cavorting abruptly and eyed her sideways, then suddenly made her a bow with so many flourishes you could practically see the cloak. You could almost see the *embroidery* on the cloak! He thought he had a way with women, Luca did. "You command, my sweet Lady, and I leap to obey." Coming upright, he shrugged apologetically. "But Master Cauthon has gold, and I fear gold commands my first obedience." Mat's chest full of gold coins in this very wagon had been all the arm-twisting needed to convince him. Maybe Mat being *ta'veren* had helped, but for enough gold, Valan Luca would help kidnap the Dark One.

Egeanin drew a deep breath, ready to berate Luca further, but the man turned his back and went scampering up the steps into his wagon shouting, "Latelle! Latelle! We must roust everybody out immediately! We're leaving at last, the minute Merrilin returns! The Light be praised!"

A moment later, he was back again, dashing back down the short stair followed by his wife drawing a black velvet cloak, sewn with glittering spangles, around herself. A stern-faced woman, she wrinkled her nose at Mat as though he had a bad smell and gave Egeanin a look that likely made her trained bears climb trees. Latelle disliked the idea of a woman running away from her husband even when she knew it was a lie. Luckily, she seemed to worship Luca for some reason, and she liked gold nearly as well as he did. Luca ran to the nearest wagon and began pounding on the door, and Latelle did the same at the next.

Not waiting around to watch, Mat hurried off down one of the side streets. More of an alley compared to the main street, it wound among the same sort of wagons and tents, all shut up tight against the cold, with smoke streaming from the metal chimneys. There were no platforms for performers here, but lines for drying laundry hung between some of the wagons, and here and there wooden toys lay scattered on the ground. This street was for living only, the narrowness meant to discourage outsiders.

He moved quickly despite his hip—he had walked most of the ache out—but he had not gone ten steps before Egeanin

and Domon caught up to him. Blaeric had vanished, probably gone to tell the sisters they were still safe and could
finally leave. The Aes Sedai, masquerading as servants sick
with worry that their mistress's husband would catch them,
were fed up with being confined to their wagon, not to mention fed up with sharing with the *sul'dam*. Mat had made
them share, so the Aes Sedai could watch the *sul'dam* while
the *sul'dam* kept the Aes Sedai out of his hair. Still Mat was
glad Blaeric had taken away the necessity for him to visit
that wagon again. One or another of the sisters had summoned him four or five times a day since their escape from
the city, and he went when he could not avoid it, but it was
never a pleasant experience.

Egeanin did not put her arm around him this time. She
strode at his side staring straight ahead, not bothering to
check her wig, for once. Domon lumbered behind like a
bear, muttering under his breath in his heavy Illianer accent. The stocking cap exposed the fact that his dark beard
stopped abruptly at the middle of each ear, with only stubble
above. It made him look . . . unfinished.

"Two captains on one ship make sure course for disaster,"
Egeanin drawled with overdone patience. Her understanding
smile looked as if it hurt her face.

"We aren't on a ship," Mat replied.

"The principle's the same, Cauthon! You are a farmer.
I know you're a good man in a tight spot." Egeanin shot a
dark look over her shoulder at Domon. He was the one who
had brought her and Mat together, back when she thought
she was getting a hired man. "But this situation needs judgment and experience. We're in dangerous waters, and you
have no knowledge of command."

"More than you might think," he told her dryly. He could
have spun out a list of the battles he remembered commanding, but only an historian would recognize most of them,
and maybe not even an historian. No one would believe it,
anyway. He certainly would not if someone else had made
that claim. "Shouldn't you and Domon be getting ready?
You wouldn't want to leave anything behind." Everything
she owned was already stowed away in the wagon she and
Mat shared with Domon—not a comfortable arrangement,
that—but he quickened his step, hoping she would take the
hint. Besides, he saw his destination ahead.

The bright blue wall-tent, crowded between a virulent
yellow wagon and an emerald green one, was barely large
enough to hold three cots, but providing shelter for everyone he brought out of Ebou Dar had required bribes to
make people move and more bribes to make others let them
in. What he had been able to hire was what the owners were
willing to let him have. At rates suitable for a good inn. Juilin, a dark compact man with short black hair, was sitting
cross-legged on the ground in front of the tent with Olver, a
thin little boy, if not so skinny as when Mat first saw him,
and short for ten, the age he claimed. Both coatless despite
the wind, they were playing Snakes and Foxes on a board the
boy's dead father had drawn for him on a piece of red cloth.
Tossing the dice, Olver counted the pips carefully and considered his move along the spiderweb of black lines and
arrows. The Tairen thief-catcher was paying less attention
to the game. He sat up straight at the sight of Mat.

Abruptly, Noal darted around from the rear of the tent,
breathing hard as if he had been running. Juilin glanced up
in surprise at the old man, and Mat frowned. He had told
Noal to come straight here. Where had he gone instead?
Noal looked at him expectantly, not with any guilt or embarrassment, just eager to hear what Mat had to say.

"You know about the Seanchan?" Juilin asked, turning
his attention to Mat, too.

A shadow moved inside the tent's entry flaps, and a dark-
haired woman, seated on the end of one of the cots with
an old gray cloak wrapped around her, leaned forward to
rest a hand on Juilin's arm. And to give Mat a wary look.
Thera was pretty, if you liked a mouth that always seemed
to be pouting, and it seemed that Juilin did, from the way
he smiled at her reassuringly and patted her hand. She
was also Amathera Aelfdene Casmir Lounault, Panarch of
Tarabon and the next thing to a queen. At least, she had
been, once. Juilin had known that, and so had Thom, yet
no one thought to tell Mat until they reached the show. He
supposed it hardly mattered, alongside everything else. She
answered faster to Thera than to Amathera, she made no
demands, except on Juilin's time, and there seemed little
chance anyone would recognize her here. In any case, Mat
hoped she felt more than gratitude for being rescued, because Juilin certainly felt more for her. Who was to say

a dethroned panarch could not fall in love with a thief-catcher? Stranger things had happened. Though he was not sure he could name one, offhand.

"They just wanted to see the warrant for Luca's horses," he said, and Juilin nodded, visibly relaxing a little.

"As well they didn't count the horselines." The warrant listed the exact number of horses Luca was allowed to keep. The Seanchan could be generous with their rewards, but given their need for mounts and wagon teams, they were not about to hand anyone a license to set up horse trading. "At best, they would have taken the extra. At worst . . ." The thief-catcher shrugged. Another cheerful soul.

With a gasp, Thera suddenly pulled her cloak tighter and jerked back into the depths of the tent. Juilin looked behind Mat, his eyes going hard, and the Tairen could match the Warders when it came to hard. Egeanin did not seem to catch hints, and she was glaring at the tent. Domon stood beside her with his arms folded, sucking his teeth in thought or forced patience.

"Get your tent packed up, Sandar," Egeanin ordered. "The show is leaving as soon as Merrilin returns." Her jaw tightened, and she did not quite glare at Mat. Not quite. "Make sure your . . . woman . . . doesn't give any trouble." Most lately, Thera had been a servant, *da'covale*, the property of the High Lady Suroth, until Juilin stole her away. To Egeanin, stealing *da'covale* was almost as bad as freeing *damane*.

"Can I ride Wind?" Olver exclaimed, bounding to his feet. "Can I, Mat? Can I, Leilwin?" Egeanin actually smiled at him. Mat had yet to see her smile at anyone else, even Domon.

"Not yet," Mat said. Not until they were far enough from Ebou Dar that no one was likely to remember the gray winning races with a small boy on his back. "In a few days, maybe. Juilin, will you tell the others? Blaeric already knows, so the sisters are taken care of."

Juilin did not waste time, aside from ducking inside the tent to reassure Thera. She seemed to need reassuring frequently. When he came out, carrying a dark Tairen coat that was beginning to show wear, he told Olver to put the game away and help Thera with the packing until he returned, then settled his flat-topped conical red hat on his head and started off, shrugging into the coat. He never so much as glanced at Egeanin. She considered him a thief, offensive in itself to a thief-catcher, and the Tairen had no love for her, either.

Mat started to ask Noal where he had been, but the old man darted nimbly after Juilin, calling over his shoulder that he would help let the others know the show was leaving. Well, two could spread the word faster than one—Vanin and the four surviving Redarms shared a crowded tent on one side of the show, while Noal himself shared another with Thom and the two serving men, Lopin and Nerim, on the opposite side—and the question could wait. Probably, he had just delayed to put his precious fish somewhere safe. In any case, the question suddenly seemed unimportant.

The noise of people shouting for horse handlers to bring their teams, and others demanding at the top of their lungs to know what was happening, was beginning to fill the camp. Adria, a slim woman holding a flowered green robe around her, came running up in bare feet and vanished into the yellow wagon, where the other four contortionists lived. Somebody in the green wagon bellowed hoarsely that people were trying to sleep. A handful of performers' children, some performers themselves, dashed by, and Olver looked up from folding the game. That was his most prized possession, but if not for that, he plainly would have gone after them. It was going to take some time yet before the show was ready to travel, but that was not what made Mat groan. He had just heard those bloody dice start rattling in his head again.

CHAPTER

3

A Fan of Colors

Mat did not know whether to curse or weep. With the soldiers gone and Ebou Dar about to be left in his dust, there seemed no reason for the dice, but there never was a bloody reason he could see until it was too late. Whatever was coming might lie days in the future or only an hour, but he had never been able to figure it out ahead of time. The only certainties were that something important—or dire—was going to happen and that he would not be able to avoid it. Sometimes, like that night at the gate, he did not understand why the dice had been tumbling even after they stopped. All he really knew for sure was that however much the dice made him twitch like a goat with the itch, once they started, he did not want them to stop ever. But they did. Sooner or later, they always did.

"Are you all right, Mat?" Olver said. "Those Seanchan can't catch us." He attempted gruff conviction, but a hint of question hung in his voice.

Abruptly Mat realized he had been staring at nothing. Egeanin frowned at him while fiddling absentmindedly with her wig, plainly angry that he was ignoring her. Domon's eyes had a studious look; if he was not deciding whether to be upset on Egeanin's behalf, Mat would eat his cap. Even Thera was peeking at him past the tent's entry flap, and she always tried to keep out of Egeanin's sight. He could not explain. Only a man with porridge for brains would believe he got warnings from hearing dice no one could see. Or maybe a man marked by the Power. Or by the Dark One. He was not anxious to have any of those things suspected about him. And it might be that night at the gate all over again. No, this was not a secret he cared to reveal. It would do no good, anyway.

"They'll never catch us, Olver, not you and me." He ruffled the boy's hair, and Olver gave a wide-mouthed grin, confidence restored as easy as that. "Not so long as we keep our eyes open and our wits about us. Remember, you can find a way out of any difficulty if you keep your eyes and wits sharp, but if you don't, you'll trip over your own feet." Olver nodded gravely, but Mat meant the reminder for the others. Or maybe himself. Light, there was no way any of them could be more alert. Except for Olver, who thought it was all a great adventure, they had all been jumping out of their skins since before leaving the city. "Go help Thera like Juilin told you, Olver."

A sharp gust cut through Mat's coat, making him shiver. "And put your coat on; it's cold," he added as the boy ducked past Thera into the tent. Rustles and scraping sounds from inside said that Olver was setting to work, with or without his coat, but Thera remained crouched at the tent's entrance, peering at Mat. For all the care anybody but Mat Cauthon took, the boy could catch his death.

As soon as Olver disappeared, Egeanin stepped closer to Mat, her fists on her hips again, and he groaned under his breath. "We are going to settle matters now, Cauthon," she said in a hard voice. "Now! I won't have our journey wrecked by you countermanding my orders."

"There's nothing to settle," he told her. "I was never your hired hand, and that's that." Somehow, her face managed to grow harder, as good as shouting that she did not see matters like that. The woman was as tenacious as a snapping turtle, but there had to be some way to pry her jaws from his leg. Burn him if he wanted to be alone with the dice rolling in his head, yet that was better than having to listen to them while arguing with her. "I'm going to see Tuon before we leave." The words popped out of his mouth before they were clear in his head. He realized that they had been lying there for some time, though, murky and slowly solidifying.

The blood drained from Egeanin's cheeks as soon as Tuon's name left his mouth, and he heard a squeak from Thera followed by the snap of the tentflaps being jerked shut. The onetime panarch had absorbed a great many Seanchan ways while she was Suroth's property, and many of their taboos as well. Egeanin was made of harder stuff, however. "Why?" she demanded. In almost the same breath, she went on, anxious and furious all at once. "You mustn't call her that. You must show respect." Harder in some ways.

Mat grinned, but she did not seem to see the joke. Respect? There was precious little respect in stuffing a gag in someone's mouth and rolling them up in a wall hanging. Calling Tuon High Lady or anything else was not going to change that. Of course, Egeanin was more willing to talk about freeing *damane* than she was about Tuon. If she could have pretended the kidnapping never happened, she would have, and as it was, she tried. Light, she had tried to ignore it while it was happening. In her mind, any other crimes she might have committed paled to nothing beside that.

"Because I want to talk with her," he said. And why not? He had to, sooner or later. People had begun trotting up and down the narrow street, now, half-dressed men with their shirts hanging out and women with their hair still wrapped in night-kerchiefs, some leading horses and others just milling about as far as he could make out. A wiry boy a little bigger than Olver went past doing handsprings wherever the crowd gave him a pace of room, practicing or maybe playing. The sleepy fellow in the deep green wagon still had not appeared. Luca's Grand Traveling Show would not be traveling anywhere for hours yet. There was plenty of time. "You could come with me," he suggested in his most innocent voice. He should have thought of this before.

The invitation made Egeanin go fence-post stiff for true. It hardly seemed possible her face could grow any paler, but an extra scrap of color leached out. "You will show her fitting respect," she said hoarsely, clutching the knotted scarf with both hands as though trying to squeeze the black wig tighter onto her head. "Come, Bayle. I want to make sure my things are stowed properly."

Domon hesitated as she turned and hurried away into the crowd without looking back, and Mat watched him warily. He had vague memories of a flight on Domon's rivership, once, but vague was the best he could say of them. Thom was friendly with Domon, a point in the Illianer's favor, yet he was Egeanin's man to the knife, ready to back her on anything down to disliking Juilin, and Mat trusted him no further than he did her. Which was to say, not very far.

Egeanin and Domon had their own goals, and whether Mat Cauthon kept a whole hide did not factor in them. He doubted that the man really trusted him, for that matter, but then, neither of them had much choice at the moment.

"Fortune prick me," Domon muttered, scratching the bristles growing above his left ear, "whatever you do be up to, you may be in over your head. I think she do be tougher than you do suspect."

"Egeanin?" Mat said incredulously. He looked around quickly to see whether anyone in the alley had heard his slip. A few glanced at him and Domon as they brushed by, but nobody glanced twice. Luca was not the only one eager to be gone from a city where the flow of patrons for the show had dried up and night lightning setting the harbor on fire was a fresh memory. They might all have fled that first night, leaving Mat nowhere to hide, except for Luca arguing them out of it. That promised gold had made Luca very persuasive. "I know she's tougher than old boots, Domon, but old boots don't count with me. This isn't a bloody ship, and I'm not letting her take charge and ruin everything."

Domon grimaced as if Mat were goose-brained. "The girl, man. Do you believe you could be so calm if you did be carried off in the night? Whatever you be playing at, with that wild talk of her being your wife, have a care or she may shave your head at the shoulders."

"I was just cutting the fool," Mat muttered. "How many times do I have to say it? I was unnerved for a minute." Oh, he had been that. Learning who Tuon was, while he was wrestling with her, would have unnerved a bloody Trolloc.

Domon grunted in disbelief. Well, it was hardly the best story Mat had ever come up with. Except for Domon, everyone who had heard him babbling seemed to accept the tale, though. Mat thought they had, anyway. Egeanin might get a knot in her tongue at the very thought of Tuon, but she would have said plenty if she believed he had been serious. Likely she would have put her knife in him.

Peering in the direction Egeanin had gone, the Illianer shook his head. "Try to keep a grip on your tongue from now on. Eg— . . . Leilwin . . . do near have a fit whenever she do think about what you did say. I've heard her muttering under her breath, and you can wager the girl herself does take it no lighter. You 'cut the fool' with her, and you may get us all shortened." He slid a finger across his throat expressively and gave a curt nod before pushing through the crowd after Egeanin.

Watching him go, Mat shook his own head. Tuon, tough? True, she was the Daughter of the Nine Moons and all of that, and she had been able to get under his skin with a look back in the Tarasin Palace, when he thought she was just another Seanchan noblewoman with her nose in the air, but that was just because she kept turning up where he did not expect. No more than that. Tough? She looked like a doll made of black porcelain. How tough could she be?

It was all you could do to keep her from breaking your nose and maybe more, he reminded himself.

He had been careful not to repeat what Domon called "wild talk," but the truth of it was, he *was* going to marry Tuon. The thought made him sigh. He knew it as sure as prophecy, which it was, in a way. He could not imagine how such a marriage could come about; it seemed impossible, on the face of it, and he would not weep if that proved to be so. But he knew it would not. Why did he always find himself bloody lumbered with bloody women who pulled knives on him or tried to kick his head off? It was not fair.

He intended to go straight to the wagon where Tuon and Selucia were being kept, with Setalle Anan to watch—the innkeeper could make a stone seem soft; a pampered noblewoman and a lady's maid would give her no trouble, especially with a Redarm on duty outside. At least, they had not so far, or he would have heard—but he found his feet wandering, taking him along the winding streets that ran through the show. Bustle filled all of them, wide and narrow alike. Men rushed by leading horses that frisked and shied, too long without exercise. Other people were taking down tents and packing the storage wagons, or hauling cloth-wrapped bundles and brass-bound chests and casks and canisters of every size out of the house-like wagons that had been standing here for months, partially unloading so everything could be repacked for travel even while the teams were being harnessed. The din was constant: horses whickered, women shouted for children, children cried over lost toys or yelled for the pure pleasure of noise, men bellowed to know who had been at their harness or who had borrowed some tool. A troupe of acrobats, slender but muscular women who worked on ropes dangling from tall poles, had surrounded one of the horse handlers, all of them waving their arms and giving voice at the top of their lungs and nobody listening. Mat paused a moment trying to figure out what they were arguing over, but eventually he decided they were not sure themselves. Two fighting coat-less men rolled on the ground, watched closely by the likely cause, a willowy hot-eyed seamstress named Jameine, but Petra appeared and pulled them apart before Mat could even get a bet down.

He was not afraid of seeing Tuon again. Of course not. He had stayed away, after sticking her into that wagon, to give her time to settle down and collect herself. That was all. Only . . . Calm, Domon had called her, and it was true. Kidnapped in the middle of the night, snatched out into a storm by people who would as soon have cut her throat as look at her, as far as she knew, and she had been by far the coolest of them all. Light, she could have planned it herself, that was how upset she was! It had made him feel as if the point of a knife were tickling between his shoulder blades then, and the knife was back again just thinking about her. And those dice were rattling away inside his skull.

The woman's hardly likely to offer to exchange vows here and now, he thought with a chuckle, but it sounded forced even to him. Yet there was no reason under the sun for him to be afraid. He was just properly wary, not afraid.

The show might have equaled a fair-sized village for size, but there was only so long a man could wander about in that much space before he started doubling back on him-self. Soon enough, too soon, he found himself staring at a windowless wagon painted in faded purple, surrounded by canvas-topped storage wagons and in sight of the southern-most horselines. The dung carts had not gone out this morn-ing, and the odor was strong. The wind carried a heavy scent from the nearest animal cages, too, a musky smell of big cats and bears and the Light knew what else. Beyond the storage wagons and pickets, a section of the canvas wall fell and another began to shake as men loosened the guy ropes holding the poles. The sun, half-hidden by dark clouds now, had climbed halfway to its noonday peak or better, but it was still too soon.

Harnan and Metwyn, two of the Redarms, had already

hitched the first pair of horses to the shaft of the purple wagon and were almost done with the second pair. Soldiers well trained in the Band of the Red Hand, they would be ready to take the road while the showfolk were still figuring out which way the horses were supposed to face. Mat had taught the Band to move fast when there was need. His own feet dragged as though he were wading in mud.

Harnan, with that fool tattoo of a hawk on his cheek, was the first to see him. Buckling a trace, the heavy-jawed file-leader exchanged looks with Metwyn, a boyish-faced Cairhienin whose appearance belied his age and his weakness for tavern brawls. They had no call to look surprised.

"Everything going smoothly? I want to be away in good time." Rubbing his hands together against the cold, Mat eyed the purple wagon uneasily. He should have brought her a present, jewelry or flowers. Either worked as well, with most women.

"Smooth enough, my Lord," Harnan replied in a cautious tone. "No shouting, no screaming, no crying." He glanced at the wagon as if he did not credit it himself.

"Quiet suits me," Metwyn said, stringing one of the reins through a ring on a horse-collar. "Woman starts crying, the only thing to do is leave, if you value your hide, and we can hardly drop these off by the side of the road." But he glanced at the wagon, too, and shook his head in disbelief.

There really was nothing for Mat to do except go inside. So he did. It only took two tries, with a smile fixed on his face, to make himself climb the short flight of painted wooden steps at the back of the wagon. He was not afraid, but any fool would know enough to be nervous.

Despite the lack of windows, the interior of the wagon was well lighted, with four mirrored lamps burning, and the lamps held good oil, so there was no rancid smell. But then, with the stink from outside, it would have been hard to tell. He needed to find a better spot to park this wagon. A small brick stove with an iron door, and an iron top for cooking, made the space toasty compared with outside. It was not a large wagon, and every inch of wall that could be spared was covered with cabinets or shelves or pegs for hanging clothing and towels and the like, but the table that could be let down on ropes was snug against the ceiling, and the three women inside the wagon were hardly crowded.

They could not have been more different, those three. Mistress Anan was sitting on one of the two narrow beds built into the walls, a regal woman with touches of gray in her hair, seemingly intent on her embroidery hoop and not looking at all as if she were a guard. A large golden ring hung in each of her ears, and her marriage knife dangled from a close-fitting silver necklace, the hilt with its red and white stones snug in the cleavage exposed by the narrow plunging neckline of her Ebou Dari dress that had one side of the skirt sewn up to expose yellow petticoats. She wore another knife, with a long, curved blade, tucked behind her belt, but that was just the custom of Ebou Dar. Setalle had refused to take on any disguise, which seemed well enough. No one had reason to be hunting for her, and finding clothes for everyone else had been a big enough problem as it was. Selucia, a pretty woman with skin the color of buttery cream, was cross-legged on the floor between the beds, a dark scarf covering her shaven head and a sullen expression on her face, though normally she was dignified enough to make Mistress Anan look flighty. Her eyes were as blue as Egeanin's, and more piercing, and she had made more fuss than Egeanin over losing the rest of her hair. She disliked the dark blue Ebou Dari dress she had been given, too, claiming the deep neckline was indecent, but it hid her as effectively as a mask. Few men who glimpsed Selucia's impressive bosom would be able to focus long on her face. Mat might have enjoyed the view for a moment or two himself, but there was Tuon, seated on the wagon's only stool, a leather-bound book open on her lap, and he could barely make himself look at anything else. His wife-to-be. Light!

Tuon was tiny, not just short but almost slim as a boy, and a loose-fitting dress of brown wool, bought from one of the showfolk, made her seem a child wearing her older sister's clothes. Not at all the sort of woman he enjoyed, especially with only a few days' growth of black stubble covering her scalp. If you ignored that, she *was* pretty, though, in a reserved way, with her heart-shaped face and full lips, her eyes large dark liquid pools of serenity. That utter calmness almost unnerved him. Not even an Aes Sedai would be serene in her circumstances. The bloody dice in his head did not help matters.

"Setalle has been keeping me informed," she said in a

cool drawl as he pulled the door shut. He had gotten so he could tell a difference in Seanchan accents; Tuon's made Egeanin sound as if she had a mouthful of mush, but they all sounded slurred and slow. "She's told me the story you have put about concerning me, Toy." Tuon had persisted in calling him that, back in the Tarasin Palace. He had not cared, then. Well, not much.

"My name is Mat," he began. He never saw where the pottery cup in her hand came from, but he managed to drop to the floor in time for it to shatter against the door instead of his head.

"I am a *servant,* Toy?" If Tuon's tone had been cool before, now it was deep winter ice. She barely raised her voice, but it was hard as ice, too. Her expression would have made a hanging judge look giddy. "A *thieving* servant?" The book slid from her lap as she stood and bent to snatch up the lidded white chamber pot. "A *faithless* servant?"

"We will need that," Selucia said deferentially, slipping the bulbous pot out of Tuon's hands. Setting it carefully to one side, she crouched at Tuon's feet almost as if ready to hurl herself at Mat, laughable as that was. Though nothing much seemed laughable right then.

Mistress Anan reached up to one of the railed shelves above her head and handed Tuon another cup. "We have plenty of these," she murmured.

Mat shot her an indignant look, but her hazel eyes twinkled with amusement. Amusement! She was supposed to be *guarding* those two!

A fist thumped on the door. "Do you need help in there?" Harnan called uncertainly. Mat wondered which of them he was asking.

"We have everything well in hand," Setalle called back, calmly pushing her needle through the fabric stretched on her hoop. You would have thought that needlework was the most important thing. "Go on about your work. Don't dawdle." The woman was not Ebou Dari, but she certainly had soaked up Ebou Dari ways. After a moment, boots thumped back down the steps outside. It seemed Harnan had been too long in Ebou Dar, as well.

Tuon turned the new cup in her hands as though examining the flowers painted on it, and her lips quirked in a smile so small it almost might have been Mat's imagination. She was more than pretty when she smiled, but it was one of those smiles that said she knew things he did not. He was going to break out in hives if she kept doing that. "I will not be known as a servant, Toy."

"My name is Mat, not . . . that other thing," he said, climbing to his feet and cautiously testing his hip. To his surprise, it ached no worse after smacking the floorboards. Tuon arched an eyebrow and hefted the cup in one hand. "I could hardly tell the showfolk I'd kidnapped the Daughter of the Nine Moons," he said in exasperation.

"The High Lady Tuon, peasant!" Selucia said crisply. "She is under the veil!" Veil? Tuon had worn a veil in the palace, but not since.

The tiny woman gestured graciously, a queen granting license. "It is of no import, Selucia. He is ignorant, yet. We must educate him. But you will change this story, Toy. I will not be a servant."

"It's too late to change anything," Mat said, keeping an eye on that cup. Her hands looked frail, with those long fingernails cut short, but he remembered how quick they were. "Nobody's asking you to *be* a servant." Luca and his wife knew the truth, but there had to be some reason to give everyone else why Tuon and Selucia were kept confined to this wagon and guarded. The perfect solution had been a pair of serving girls, about to be dismissed for theft, who had intended to betray their mistress's flight with her lover. It seemed perfect to Mat, anyway. To the showfolk, it only added to the romance. He had thought Egeanin was going to swallow her tongue while he was explaining to Luca. Maybe she had known how Tuon would take it. Light, he almost wished the dice would stop. How could a man think with that in his head?

"I couldn't leave you behind to raise an alarm," he went on patiently. That was true, as far as it went. "I know Mistress Anan has explained it to you." He thought about saying he had been babbling from nerves when he said she was his wife—she must think him a complete looby!—but it seemed best not to bring it up again. If she was willing to let the matter lie, all the better. "I know she's already told you this, but I promise no one's going to hurt you. We're not after ransom, just getting away with our heads still at-

tached. As soon as I can figure out how to send you home
safe and sound, I will. I promise. I'll make you as comfortable as I can until then. You'll just have to put up with the
other."

Tuon's big dark eyes crackled, heat lightning in a night
sky, but she said, "It seems I will see what your promises
are worth, Toy." At her feet, Selucia hissed like a doused
cat, her head half-turning as if to object, but Tuon's left hand
wiggled, and the blue-eyed woman blushed and went silent.
The Blood used something like Maiden handtalk with their
upper servants. Mat wished he understood the signals.

"Answer me a question, Tuon," he said.

He thought he heard Setalle murmur, "Fool." Selucia's
jaw knotted, and a dangerous look kindled in Tuon's eyes,
but if she was going to call him "Toy," he would be burned
if he gave her any titles.

"How old are you?" He had heard that she was only a few
years younger than he, but looking at her in that sack of a
dress, it seemed impossible.

To his surprise, that dangerous spark burst into flame.
Not just heat lightning, this time. He should have been
fried on the spot. Tuon threw back her shoulders and drew
herself to her full height. Such as that was; he doubted
she could reach five feet with her heels flat however she
stretched. "My fourteenth true-name day will come in five
months," she said in a voice that was far from cold. In fact,
it could have heated the wagon better than the stove. He felt
a moment of hope, but she was not finished. "No; you keep
your birth names here, don't you. That will be my twentieth
naming day. Are you satisfied, Toy? Did you fear you had
stolen a . . . child?" She almost hissed the last word.

Mat waved his hands in front of him, frantically dismissing the suggestion. A woman started hissing at him like
a kettle, a man with any brains found a way to cool her
down fast. She was gripping the cup so tightly that tendons
stood out on the back of her hand, and he did not want to
try his hip with another fall to the floor. Come to think on
it, he was not sure how hard she had tried to hit him the
first time. Her hands were very fast. "I just wanted to know,
that's all," he said quickly. "I was curious, making conversation. I'm only a little older myself." Twenty. So much for

hoping she was too young to marry for another three or four years. Anything that came between him and his wedding day would have been welcome.

Tuon studied him suspiciously with her head tilted, then tossed the cup onto the bed beside Mistress Anan and seated herself on the stool again, taking as much care about arranging her voluminous woolen skirts as if they had belonged to a silk gown. But she continued to examine him through her long eyelashes. "Where is your ring?" she demanded.

Unconsciously, he thumbed the finger on his left hand where the long ring usually lay. "I don't wear it all the time." Not when everybody in the Tarasin Palace knew he wore it. The thing would have stood out, with his rough layabout's garb, in any case. It was not even his signet, anyway, just a carver's try-piece. Strange, how his hand felt noticeably lighter without it. Too light. Strange that she remarked on it, too. But then, why not? Light, those dice had him shying at shadows and jumping at sighs. Or maybe it was just her, a discomforting thought.

He moved to sit on the unoccupied bed, but Selucia swung herself up onto it so quickly any of the acrobats might have been jealous, and stretched out with her head propped on her hand. That pushed her scarf askew for a moment, but she hurriedly straightened it, all the while staring at him proud and cold as a queen. He looked at the other bed, and Mistress Anan set down her embroidery long enough to ostentatiously smooth her skirts, making it clear she did not intend to share an inch. Burn her, she was behaving as though she were guarding Tuon from him! Women always seemed to club together so a man never had a fair chance. Well, he had managed to keep Egeanin from taking charge so far, and he was not about to be bullied by Setalle Anan or a bosomy lady's maid or the high and mighty High Lady Daughter of the Nine bloody Moons! Only, he could hardly go shoving one of them out of the way to find a place to sit.

Leaning against a drawered cabinet at the foot of the bed Mistress Anan was seated on, he tried to think of what to say. He never had trouble thinking of what to say to women, but his brain seemed deafened by the sound of those dice. All three women gave him disapproving looks—he could all but hear one of them telling him not to slouch!—so he smiled. Most women thought his best smile very winning.

Tuon let out a long breath that did not sound won over in the slightest. "Do you remember Hawkwing's face, Toy?" Mistress Anan blinked in surprise, and Selucia sat up on the bed frowning. At him. Why would she frown at *him*? Tuon just continued to look at him, hands folded in her lap, as cool and collected as a Wisdom at Sunday.

Mat's smile felt frozen. Light, what did she know? How could she know anything? *He lay beneath the burning sun, holding his side with both hands, trying to keep the last of life from leaking out and wondering whether there was any reason to hold on. Aldeshar was finished, after this day's work. A shadow blotted the sun for an instant, and then a tall man in armor crouched beside him, helmet tucked under his arm, dark deep-set eyes framing a hooked nose. "You fought well against me today, Culain, and many days past," that memorable voice said. "Will you live with me in peace?" With his last breath, he laughed in Artur Hawkwing's face.* He *hated* to remember dying. A dozen other encounters skittered through his mind, too, ancient memories that were his, now. Artur Paendrag had been a difficult man to get along with even before the wars started.

Drawing a deep breath, he took care choosing his words. This was no time to go spouting the Old Tongue. "Of course I don't!" he lied. A man who could not lie convincingly got short shrift from women. "Light, Hawkwing died a thousand years ago! What kind of question is that?"

Her mouth opened slowly, and for a moment he was sure she meant to answer question with question. "A foolish one, Toy," she replied finally, instead. "I can't say why it popped into my head."

The stiffness in Mat's shoulders relaxed, a little. Of course. He was *ta'veren*. People did things and said things around him they never would elsewhere. Nonsense qualified. Still, a thing like that could become uncomfortable when it hit too close to home. "My name is Mat. Mat Cauthon." He might as well not have spoken.

"I cannot say what I will do after returning to Ebou Dar, Toy. I have not decided. I may have you made *da'covale*. You are not pretty enough for a cupbearer, but it might please me to have you for one. Still, you have represented certain promises to me, so it pleases me now to promise, as well. So long as you keep your promises, I will neither escape nor betray you in any way, nor will I cause dissension among your followers. I believe that covers everything necessary." This time, Mistress Anan gaped at her, and Selucia made a sound in her throat, but Tuon appeared not to notice either woman. She just looked at him expectantly, waiting on a response.

He made a sound in his throat, too. Not a whimper, just a sound. Tuon's face was as smooth as a stern mask of dark glass. Her calm was madness, but this made gibbering look sane! She would *have* to be insane to think he would believe that offer. Except, he thought she did mean it. That, or she was a better liar than he ever hoped to be. Again he had that queasy sense that she knew more than he did. Ridiculous, of course, but there it was. He swallowed a lump in his throat. A hard lump.

"Well, that does all right for you," he said, trying to buy time, "but what about Selucia?" Time for what? He could not think with those dice pounding in his skull.

"Selucia follows my wishes, Toy," Tuon said impatiently. The blue-eyed woman herself straightened and stared at him as though indignant that he had doubted that. For a lady's maid, she could look fierce when she tried.

Mat did not know what to say or do. Without thinking, he spat on his palm and offered his hand as if sealing a bargain on a horse.

"Your customs are . . . earthy," Tuon said in a dry voice, but she spat on her own palm and clasped his hand. "'Thus is our treaty written; thus is agreement made.' What does that writing on your spear mean, Toy?"

He did whimper this time, and not because she had read the Old Tongue inscription on his *ashandarei*. A bloody stone would have whimpered. The dice had stopped as soon as he touched her hand. Light, what had happened?

Knuckles rapped on the door, and he was so on edge that he moved without thought, spinning, a knife coming into either hand ready to throw at whatever came in. "Stay behind me," he snapped.

The door opened, and Thom stuck his head in. The hood of his cloak was up, and Mat realized it was raining outside.

Between Tuon and the dice, he had missed the sound of rain hitting the wagon's roof. "I trust I'm not interrupting anything?" Thom said, knuckling his long white mustaches.

Mat's face heated. Setalle had frozen with her embroidery needle trailing blue thread down to her work, and her eyebrows seemed to be trying to climb over the top of her head. Tensed on the edge of the other bed, Selucia watched him slip the knives back up his sleeves with considerable interest. He would not have thought she was the sort to like dangerous men. That kind of woman was worth avoiding; they tended to find ways to make a man need to be dangerous. He did not glance back at Tuon. She was probably staring at him as if he had been capering like Luca. Just because he did not want to get married did not mean he wanted his future wife to think him a fool.

"What did you find out, Thom?" he asked brusquely. *Something* had happened, or the dice would not have stopped. A thought came that made his hair want to stand on end. This was the second time they had stopped in Tuon's presence. The third, counting the gate leading out of Ebou Dar. Three bloody times, and all tied to her.

Limping slightly, the white-haired man came the rest of the way in, pushing back his hood, and pulled the door shut behind him. His limp came from an old injury, not trouble in the city. Tall and lean and leathery, with sharp blue eyes and snowy mustaches that hung below his chin, it seemed he would draw attention wherever he went, but he had practice at hiding in plain sight, and his dark bronze coat and brown wool cloak were suitable for a man with a little coin to spend but not too much. "The streets are full of rumors about her," he said, nodding toward Tuon, "but nothing about her disappearing. I bought drinks for a few Seanchan officers, and they seem to believe she's snug in the Tarasin Palace or off on an inspection trip. I didn't sense any dissembling, Mat. They didn't know."

"Did you expect public announcements, Toy?" Tuon said incredulously. "As it is, Suroth may be considering taking her own life for the shame. Do you expect her to spread such an ill omen for the Return about for everyone to see on top of that?"

So Egeanin had been right. It still seemed impossible. And it did not seem at all important compared to the dice stopping. What had *happened*? He had shaken hands with Tuon, that was all. Shaken hands and made a bargain. He meant to keep his side, but what had the dice told him? That she would keep hers? Or that she would not? For all he knew, Seanchan noblewomen were in the habit of marrying—what was it she had said she was going to make him?—a cupbearer—maybe they married cupbearers all the time.

"There's more, Mat," Thom said, eyeing Tuon thoughtfully, and with a hint of surprise. It came to Mat that she did not appear overly concerned that Suroth might kill herself. Maybe she was as tough as Domon thought. What *were* the bloody dice trying to tell him? That was what was important. Then Thom went on, and Mat forgot about how tough Tuon might be and even the dice. "Tylin's dead. They're keeping it quiet for fear of disturbances, but one of the Palace Guards, a young lieutenant who couldn't hold his brandy, told me they're planning her funeral feast and Beslan's coronation for the same day."

"How?" Mat demanded. She was older than he, but not that much older! Beslan's coronation. Light! How would Beslan cope with that, when he hated the Seanchan? It had been his plan to fire those supplies on the Bay Road. He would have tried an uprising if Mat had not convinced him it would only result in a slaughter, and not of Seanchan.

Thom hesitated, stroking his mustaches with a thumb. Finally, he sighed. "She was found in her bedchamber the morning after we left, Mat, still bound hand and foot. Her head . . . Her head had been torn off."

Mat did not realize his knees had given way until he found himself sitting on the floor with his head buzzing. He could hear her voice. *You'll get your head cut off yet if you're not careful, piglet, and I wouldn't like that.* Setalle leaned forward on the narrow bed to press a hand against his cheek in commiseration.

"The Windfinders?" he said hollowly. He did not have to say more.

"According to what that lieutenant said, the Seanchan have settled on Aes Sedai for the blame. Because Tylin had sworn the Seanchan oaths. That's what they'll announce at her funeral feast."

"Tylin dies the same night the Windfinders escape, and

the Seanchan believe Aes Sedai killed her?" He could not imagine Tylin dead. *I'm going to have you for supper, duckling.* "That doesn't make sense, Thom."

Thom hesitated, frowning as he considered. "It could be political, in part, but I think that's what they really believe, Mat. That lieutenant said they're sure the Windfinders were running too hard to stop or go out of their way, and the quickest path out of the palace from the *damane* kennels goes nowhere near Tylin's apartments."

Mat grunted. He was sure it was not so. And if it were, there was nothing in the world he could do about it.

"The *marath'damane* had reason to murder Tylin," Selucia said suddenly. "They must fear her example for others. What reason had the *damane* you speak of? None. The hand of justice requires motive and proof, even for *damane* and *da'covale*." She sounded as though she were reading the words off a page. And she was looking at Tuon from the corner of her eye.

Mat looked over his shoulder, but if the tiny woman had been using her hands to tell Selucia what to say, they were resting in her lap, now. She was watching him, a neutral expression on her face. "Did you care for Tylin so deeply?" she said in a cautious voice.

"Yes. No. Burn me, I *liked* her!" Turning away, he scrubbed fingers through his hair, pushing the cap off. He had never been so glad to get away from a woman in his life, but this . . . ! "And I left her tied up and gagged so she couldn't even call for help, easy prey for the *gholam*," he said bitterly. "It was looking for me. Don't shake your head. Thom. You know it as well as I do."

"What is a . . . *gholam*?" Tuon asked.

"Shadowspawn, my Lady," Thom said. He frowned worriedly. He did not take easily to worry, but anybody except a fool would worry about a *gholam*. "It looks like a man, but it can slip through a mousehole, or under a door, and it's strong enough to . . ." He harrumphed through his mustaches. "Well, enough of that. Mat, she could have had a hundred guards around her, and it wouldn't have stopped that thing." She would not have needed a hundred guards if she had not taken up with Mat Cauthon.

"A *gholam*," Tuon murmured wryly. Suddenly she rapped Mat hard on the top of the head with her knuckles. Clapping a hand to his scalp, he stared over his shoulder incredulously. "I'm very happy that you show loyalty to Tylin, Toy," she told him in a severe voice, "but I won't have superstition in you. I will not have it. It does Tylin no honor." Burn him, Tylin's death seemed to concern her as little as whether or not Suroth committed suicide. What kind of woman was he going to marry?

When a fist pounded on the door this time, he did not even bother to stand. He felt numb at the core and scraped raw on the surface. Blaeric pushed into the wagon without asking, his dark brown cloak dripping rain. It was an old cloak, worn thin in spots, but he appeared not to care whether rain leaked through. The Warder ignored everyone but Mat, or almost everyone. The man actually took a moment to consider Selucia's bosom! "Joline wants you, Cauthon," he said, still studying her. Light! This was all Mat needed to make it a fine day.

"Who is Joline?" Tuon demanded.

Mat ignored her. "Tell Joline I'll see her once we're on the road, Blaeric." The last thing he wanted was to be forced to listen to more of the Aes Sedai's grievances now.

"She wants you now, Cauthon."

With a sigh, Mat got to his feet and gathered his cap from the floor. Blaeric looked as if he might try to drag him, otherwise. In his own current mood, he thought he might put a knife in the man if he tried. And get his neck broken for his pains; a Warder would not take a knife in the ribs lightly. He was fairly sure he had already died the one time he was allowed, and not in an old memory. Sure enough not to take risks he could sidestep.

"Who is Joline, Toy?" If he had not known better, he would have said Tuon sounded jealous.

"A bloody Aes Sedai," he grumbled, tugging the cap on, and got one small pleasure for the day. Tuon's jaw dropped in shock. He shut the door behind him on the way out before she could find a word to say. A very small pleasure. One butterfly on a midden heap. Tylin dead, and the Windfinders might take the blame yet, whatever Thom said. And that was aside from Tuon and the bloody dice. A very tiny butterfly on a very large midden.

The sky was full of dark clouds, now, and the downpour steady. A soaking rain, they would have called it back home.

It began to slick his hair, cap or no, and seep through his coat as soon as he stepped outside. Blaeric hardly seemed to notice, barely gathering his cloak. There was nothing for it but for Mat to hunch his shoulders and splash through the widening puddles on the dirt streets. By the time he could reach his wagon for a cloak, he would be drenched to the skin anyway. Besides, the weather fit his spirits.

To his surprise, rain or no rain, an incredible amount of work had been done in the short time he was inside. The canvas wall was gone as far as he could see in either direction, and half the storage wagons that had been around Tuon's wagon were missing, too. So were most of the animals that had been picketed on the horselines. A large, iron-barred cage containing a black-maned lion trundled past toward the road behind a plodding team, the horses as unconcerned with the apparently sleeping lion behind them as they were with the shower. Performers were already taking to the road, too, though how they determined the order of leaving was a mystery. Most of the tents seemed to have vanished; in one place three of the brightly colored wagons together might be missing, another place every second wagon, while elsewhere the wagons standing and waiting still seemed a solid mass. The only thing that said the showfolk were not scattering was Luca himself, a bright red cloak gathered around him against the wet as he paraded along the street, stopping now and then to clap a man on the shoulder or murmur something to a woman that made her laugh. If the show had been breaking apart, Luca would have been out chasing down those who tried to leave. He held the show together as much by persuasion as anything else, and he never let anyone leave without talking himself hoarse trying to argue them out of it. Mat knew he should feel good about seeing Luca still there, though it had never occurred to him that the man would run out on the gold, but right at that moment, he doubted that anything could make him feel anything but numb and angry.

The wagon that Blaeric took him to was almost as large as Luca's, but it had been whitewashed rather than painted. The white had long since run and streaked and faded, and the rain was washing it a little more toward gray, where the wood was not already bare. The wagon belonged to a company of fools, four morose men who painted their faces for the show's patrons, dousing each other with water and hitting each other with inflated pig-bladders, and otherwise spent their time and money imbibing as much wine as they could buy. With what Mat had paid for rent, they might be drunk for months, and it had cost more than that to make anyone take them in.

Four shaggy, nondescript horses were already hitched to the wagon, and Fen Mizar, Joline's other Warder, was up on the driver's seat, swathed in an old gray cloak and reins in hand. His tilted eyes watched Mat the way a wolf might watch an impudent cur. The Warders had been unhappy with Mat's plan from the start, sure they could have gotten the sisters away safely once they were outside the city walls. Perhaps they could have, but the Seanchan hunted vigorously for women who could channel—the show itself apparently had been searched four times in the days after Ebou Dar fell—and all it would have taken was one slip to land all of them in the stewpot. From what Egeanin and Domon said, the Seekers could make a boulder tell everything it had ever seen. Luckily, not all the sisters were as sure as Joline's Warders. Aes Sedai tended to dither when they could not agree on what to do.

When Mat reached the steps at the back of the wagon, Blaeric stopped him with a hand to his chest. The Warder's face might have been carved, no more concerned than a piece of wood with the rain running down his cheeks. "Fen and I are grateful to you for getting her out of the city, Cauthon, but this can't continue. The sisters are crowded, sharing with those other women, and they don't get on. There is going to be trouble if we can't find another wagon."

"Is that what this is about?" Mat said crossly, tugging his collar tighter. Not that it did much good. He was already wet through on the back, and not much better in front. If Joline had pulled him here to whine about the accommodations again . . .

"She'll tell you what it's about, Cauthon. Just you remember what I said."

Grumbling under his breath, Mat climbed the dirt-streaked steps and went in, not quite slamming the door behind him.

The wagon was laid out much like the one Tuon was in, though with four beds, two of them folded flat against the walls above the other two. He had no idea how the six women arranged sleeping, but he suspected it was not done peacefully. The air in the wagon all but crackled like grease on a griddle. Three women sat on each of the lower beds, each variously watching or ignoring the women seated on the other bed. Joline, who had never been held as *damane,* behaved as though the three *sul'dam* did not exist. Reading a small wood-bound book, she was an Aes Sedai to the inch and arrogance on a stick despite her well-worn blue dress, lately owned by a woman who taught the lions to do tricks. The other two sisters knew firsthand what it was to be *damane,* though. Edesina watched the three *sul'dam* warily, one hand resting near her belt knife, while Teslyn's eyes shifted constantly, looking at anything except the *sul'dam,* and her hands kneaded her dark woolen skirts. He did not know how Egeanin had coerced the three *sul'dam* into helping *damane* escape, but even though they were being sought by the authorities as surely as Egeanin, they had not changed their attitudes toward women who could channel. Bethamin, tall and as dark as Tuon in an Ebou Dari dress with a very deep neckline and skirts sewn up above her knee on one side to show faded red petticoats, seemed a mother waiting for inevitable misbehavior by children, while yellow-haired Seta, in high-necked gray wool that covered her completely, appeared to be studying dangerous dogs that would need to be caged sooner or later. Renna, she of the talk about cutting off hands and feet, pretended to be reading, too, but every so often her deceptively mild brown eyes rose from the slim volume to study the Aes Sedai, and when they did, she smiled in an unpleasant way. Mat felt like cursing before one of them opened her mouth. A wise man kept clear when women were at odds, especially if there were Aes Sedai among them, but this was how it always was when he came to this wagon.

"This better be important, Joline." Unbuttoning his coat, he tried to shake some of the water off. He thought he would do better wringing the garment out. "I just learned that the *gholam* killed Tylin the night we left, and I'm in no mood for complaints."

Joline marked her place carefully with an embroidered marker and folded her hands on the book before speaking. Aes Sedai never hurried; they just expected everyone else to. Without him, she likely would have been wearing an *a'dam* by now herself, but he had never found Aes Sedai particularly noted for gratitude, either. She ignored what he had said about Tylin. "Blaeric tells me the show has already begun moving," she said coolly, "but you must stop it. Luca will only listen to you." Her mouth tightened slightly on the words. Aes Sedai also were unused to not being listened to, and Greens were not the best at hiding their displeasure. "We must abandon the idea of Lugard for the time being. We must take the ferry across the harbor and go to Illian."

That was about as bad a suggestion as he had heard out of her, though she did not mean it for a suggestion, of course; she was worse than Egeanin that way. With half the show already on the road, or near enough, it would take all day just to get everyone down to the ferry landing, and it would mean going into the city, besides. Heading for Lugard took the show away from the Seanchan as quickly as possible, while they had soldiers camped all the way to the Illian border and maybe beyond. Egeanin was reluctant to tell what she knew, but Thom had his ways of learning these things. Mat did not bother to crack his teeth, though. He did not need to.

"No," Teslyn said in a tight voice, her Illianer accent strong. Leaning past Edesina, she looked as though she chewed rocks three meals a day, hard-faced and set-jawed, but there was a nervousness in her eyes, put there by her weeks as a *damane*. "No, Joline. I have told you, we do no dare risk it! We do no dare!"

"Light!" Joline spat, slamming her book to the floor. "Take hold of yourself, Teslyn! Just because you were held prisoner for a little time is no reason to go to pieces!"

"Go to pieces? Go to pieces? Let them put that collar on you and then speak of going to pieces!" Teslyn's hand went to her throat as though she felt the *a'dam*'s collar still. "Help me convince her, Edesina. She will have us collared again, if we do let her!"

Edesina drew back on herself against the wall behind the bed—a slim, handsome woman with black hair spilling to her waist, she always went silent when the Red and the Green argued, as they did often—but Joline did not spare her so much as a glance. "You ask a *rebel* for help, Teslyn? We should have left her for the Seanchan! Listen to me. You can feel it as well as I. Would you really accept a greater danger to avoid a lesser?"

"Lesser!" Teslyn snarled. "You do know nothing of—!"

Renna held her book out at arm's length and let it drop to the floor with a bang. "If my Lord will excuse us a little while, we still have our *a'dam,* and we can teach these girls to behave again in short order." Her accent had a musical quality, but the smile on her lips never touched her brown eyes. "It never works to let them go slack this way." Seta nodded grimly and stood as if to fetch out the leashes.

"I think we're done with *a'dam,*" Bethamin said, ignoring the shocked looks from the other two *sul'dam,* "but there are other ways to settle these girls down. May I suggest my Lord return in an hour? They'll tell you what you want to know without any squabbling once they can't sit down." She sounded as though she meant exactly what she said. Joline was staring at the three *sul'dam* in outraged disbelief, but Edesina was sitting up straight, gripping her belt knife with a determined expression, while Teslyn was now the one shrinking back against the wall, her hands clasped tightly at her waist.

"That won't be necessary," Mat said after a moment. Only a moment. However satisfying it might be to have Joline "settled down," Edesina might draw that knife, and that would set the cat among the chickens no matter how it turned out. "What greater danger are you talking about, Joline? Joline? What danger is greater than the Seanchan right now?"

The Green decided her stare was making no impression on Bethamin and turned it on Mat, instead. Had she been other than Aes Sedai, he would have said she looked sulky. Joline disliked explaining. "If you must know, someone is channeling." Teslyn and Edesina nodded, the Red sister reluctantly, the Yellow emphatically.

"In the camp?" he said in alarm. His right hand rose on its own to press against the silver foxhead under his shirt, but the medallion had not turned cold.

"Far away," Joline replied, still unwilling. "To the north."

"Much farther than any of us should be able to sense channeling," Edesina put in, a touch of fear in her voice. "The amount of *saidar* being wielded must be immense, inconceivable." She fell silent at a sharp glance from Joline, who turned back to study Mat as though deciding how much she had to tell him.

"At that distance," she went on, "we wouldn't be able to feel every sister in the Tower channeling. It has to be the Forsaken, and whatever they're doing, we do not want to be any closer than we can avoid."

Mat was still for a moment; then finally, he said, "If it's far, then we stick with the plan."

Joline went on arguing, but he did not bother to listen. Whenever he thought of Rand or Perrin, colors swirled in his head. A part of being *ta'veren*, he supposed. This time, he had not thought of either of his friends, but the colors had suddenly been there, a fan of a thousand rainbows. This time, they had almost formed an image, a vague impression that might have been a man and a woman seated on the ground facing one another. It was gone in an instant, but he knew as surely as he knew his name. Not the Forsaken. Rand. And he could not help wondering, what had Rand been doing when the dice stopped?

CHAPTER
4

The Tale of a Doll

Furyk Karede sat staring at his writing table without seeing the papers and maps spread out in front of him. Both of his oil lamps were lit and sitting on the table, but he no longer had need of them. The sun must be rimming the horizon, yet since waking from a fitful sleep and saying his devotions to the Empress, might she live forever, he had only donned his robe, in the dark Imperial green that some insisted on calling black, and sat here without moving since. He had not even shaved. The rain had stopped, and he considered telling his servant Ajimbura to swing a window open for a little fresh air in his room at The Wandering Woman. Clean air might clear his head. But over the last five days there had been lulls in the rain that ended with sudden drenching downpours, and his bed was located between the windows. He had needed to have his mattress and bedding hung in the kitchen to dry once already.

A tiny squeal and a pleased grunt from Ajimbura made him look up to find the wiry little man displaying a limp rat half the size of a cat on the end of his long knife. It was not the first Ajimbura had killed in this room recently, something Karede believed would not have happened if Setalle Anan still owned the inn, though the number of rats in Ebou Dar seemed to be increasing well in advance of spring. Ajimbura looked a little like a wizened rat himself, his grin both satisfied and feral. After more than three hundred years under the Empire, the Kaensada hill tribes were only half civilized, and less than half tamed. The man wore his white-streaked dark red hair in a thick braid that hung to his waist, to make a good trophy if he ever found his way back to those near-mountains and fell in one of the endless feuds between families or tribes, and he insisted on drinking from a silver-mounted cup that anyone who looked closely could see was the top of someone's skull.

"If you are going to eat that," Karede said as though there were any question, "you will clean it in the stableyard out of anyone's sight." Ajimbura would eat anything except for lizards, which were forbidden to his tribe for some reason he would never make clear.

"But of course, high one," the man replied with the hunch of his shoulders that passed for a bow among his people. "I know well the ways of the townspeople, and I would not embarrass the high one." After close to twenty years in Karede's service, without a reminder he still would have skinned out the rat and roasted it over the flames in the small brick fireplace.

Scraping the carcass off the blade into a small canvas sack, Ajimbura tucked that into a corner for later and carefully wiped his knife clean before sheathing it and settling on his heels to await Karede's needs. He would wait like that all day, if necessary, as patiently as a *da'covale*. Karede had never puzzled out exactly why Ajimbura had left his hill fort home to follow one of the Deathwatch Guard. It was a much more circumscribed life than the man had known before, and besides, Karede had nearly killed him three times before he made that choice.

Dismissing thoughts of his servant, he returned to the display on his writing table, though he had no intention of taking up his pen for the moment. He had been raised to banner-general for achieving some small success in the battles with the Asha'man, in days when few had achieved any, and now, because he had commanded against men who could channel, some thought he must have wisdom to share about fighting *marath'damane*. No one had had to do that in centuries, and since the so-called Aes Sedai revealed their unknown weapon only a few leagues from where he sat, a great deal of thinking had gone into how to cripple their power. That was not the only request littering the tabletop. Aside from the usual run of requisitions and reports that needed his signature, his comments on the forces arrayed against them in Illian had been solicited by four lords and three ladies, and on the special Aiel problem by six ladies and five lords, but those questions would be decided elsewhere, very likely already had been decided. His observations would only be used in the infighting over who controlled what in the Return. In any event, war had always been a second calling for the Deathwatch Guard. Oh, the Guards were always there whenever a major battle was fought, the swordhand of the Empress, might she live forever, to strike at her enemies whether or not she herself was present, always to lead the way where the fight was hottest, but their first calling was to protect the lives and persons of the Imperial family. With their own lives, when necessary, and willingly given. And nine nights past, the High Lady Tuon had vanished as if swallowed by the storm. He did not think of her as the Daughter of the Nine Moons, could not until he knew she was no longer under the veil.

He had not considered taking his own life, either, though the shame cut him keenly. It was for the Blood to resort to the easy way to escape disgrace; the Deathwatch Guard fought to the last. Musenge commanded her personal body-guard, but as the highest-ranking member of the Guard this side of the Aryth Ocean, it was Karede's duty to return her safely. Every cranny in the city was being searched on one excuse or another, every vessel larger than a rowboat, but most often by men ignorant of what they were searching for, unaware that the fate of the Return might rest on their diligence. The duty was his. Of course, the Imperial family was given to even more complicated intrigues than the rest of the Blood, and the High Lady Tuon frequently played a very deep game indeed, with a sharp and deadly skill. Only a few were aware that she had vanished twice before, and had been reported dead, to the very arrangement of her funeral rites, all by her own contriving. Whatever the reasons for her disappearance, though, he had to find and protect her. So far he had no clue how. Swallowed by the storm. Or perhaps by the Lady of the Shadows. There had been countless attempts to kidnap or assassinate her, beginning on the day of her birth. If he found her dead, he must find who had killed her, who had given the ultimate commands, and avenge her whatever the cost. That was his duty, too.

A slender man slipped into the room from the hallway without knocking. He might have been one of the inn's stablemen from his rough coat, but no local had his pale hair or the blue eyes that slid across the room as though memorizing everything in it. His hand slipped under his coat, and Karede rehearsed two ways of killing him bare-handed in the brief moment before he produced a small, gold-bordered ivory plaque worked with the Raven and the Tower. Seekers for Truth did not have to knock. Killing them was frowned upon.

"Leave us," the Seeker told Ajimbura, tucking away the plaque once he was sure Karede had recognized it. The little man remained crouched on his heels, motionless, and the Seeker's eyebrows rose in surprise. Even in the Kaensada Hills everyone knew a Seeker's word was law. Well, perhaps not in some of the more remote hill forts, not if they believed no one knew the Seeker was there, but Ajimbura knew better than this.

"Wait outside," Karede commanded sharply, and Ajimbura rose with alacrity, murmuring, "I hear and obey, high one." He studied the Seeker openly, though, as if to make sure the Seeker knew he had marked his face, before leaving the room. He was going to get himself beheaded, one day.

"A precious thing, loyalty," the pale-haired man said, eyeing the tabletop, after Ajimbura pulled the door shut behind himself. "You are involved in Lord Yulan's plans, Banner-General Karede? I would not have expected the Deathwatch Guard to be part of that."

Karede moved two bronze map-weights shaped like lions and let the map of Tar Valon roll up on itself. The other had not been unrolled, yet. "You must ask Lord Yulan, Seeker. Loyalty to the Crystal Throne is precious above the breath of life, followed closely by knowing when to keep silent. The more who speak of a thing, the more will learn of it who should not."

No one short of the Imperial family rebuked a Seeker or whatever Hand guided him, but the fellow appeared unaffected. Then again, he seated himself in the room's cushioned armchair and made a tent of his fingers, peering over them at Karede, who had the choice of moving his own chair or leaving the man almost at his back. Most people would have been very nervous about having a Seeker behind them. Most would have been nervous having a Seeker in the same room. Karede hid a smile and did not move. He had only to turn his head a fraction, and he was trained at seeing clearly what lay in the corners of sight.

"You must be proud of your sons," the Seeker said, "two following you into the Deathwatch Guard, the third listed among the honored dead. Your wife would have been very proud."

"What is your name, Seeker?" The answering silence was deafening. More people rebuked Seekers than inquired after their names.

"Mor," the reply came finally. "Almurat Mor." So. Mor. He had an ancestor who had come with Luthair Paendrag, then, and was rightly proud. Without access to the breeding books, which no *da'covale* was allowed, Karede had no way of knowing whether any of the tales about his own ancestry were true—he also might have an ancestor who had once followed the great Hawkwing—but it did not matter. Men who tried to stand on their forebears' shoulders rather than their own feet often found themselves shorter by a head. Especially *da'covale*.

"Call me Furyk. We are both the property of the Crystal Throne. What do you want of me, Almurat? Not to discuss my family, I think." If his sons were in trouble, the fellow would never have mentioned them so soon, and Kalia was beyond any misery. From the corner of his eye, Karede could see the struggle on the Seeker's face, though he hid it almost well enough. The man had lost control of the interview—as he might have expected, flashing his plaque as though a Deathwatch Guard were not ready to thrust a dagger into his own heart on command.

"Listen to a story," Mor said slowly, "and tell me what you think." His gaze was fastened to Karede as if by tacks, studying, weighing, evaluating as though Karede were on the block at sale. "This came to us in the last few days." By us, he meant the Seekers. "It began among the local people, as near as we can tell, though we have not yet found the original source. Supposedly, a girl with a Seandar accent has been extorting gold and jewelry from merchants here in Ebou Dar. The title Daughter of the Nine Moons was mentioned." He grimaced with disgust, and for a moment, his fingertips turned white, they were pressing against each other so hard. "None of the locals seem to understand what that title means, but the description of the girl is remark-ably precise. Remarkably accurate. And no one can recall hearing this rumor before the night after . . . the night after Tylin's murder was discovered," he finished, choosing the least unpleasant event to fix the time.

"A Seandar accent," Karede said in a flat voice, and Mor nodded. "This rumor has passed to our own people." That was not a question, but Mor nodded again. A Seandar ac-cent and an accurate description, two things no local could invent. Someone was playing a very dangerous game. Dan-gerous for themselves, and for the Empire. "How does the Tarasin Palace take recent events?" There would be Listen-ers among the servants, likely among even the Ebou Dari servants by now, and what the Listeners heard soon passed to the Seekers.

Mor understood the question, of course. There was no need to mention what should not be mentioned. He replied in an indifferent tone. "The High Lady Tuon's entourage carries on as though nothing has happened, except that Anath, her Truth Speaker, has taken to seclusion, but I am told that is not unusual for her. Suroth herself is even more distraught in private than in public. She sleeps poorly, snaps at her favorites, and has her property beaten over trifles. She ordered the death of one Seeker each day until matters are rectified, and only rescinded the order this morning, when she realized she might run out of Seekers before she ran out of days." His shoulders moved in a small shrug, perhaps to indicate this was all in a day for Seekers, perhaps in relief at a near escape. "It's understandable. If she is called to ac-count, she will pray for the Death of Ten Thousand Tears. The other Blood who know what has happened are trying to grow eyes in the backs of their heads. A few have even qui-etly made funeral arrangements, to cover any eventuality."

Karede wanted a clearer look at the man's face. He was inured to insult—that was part of the training—but this . . . Pushing back his chair, he stood and sat at the edge of the writing table. Mor stared at him unblinking, tensed to de-fend against an attack, and Karede drew a deep breath to still his anger. "Why did you come to me if you believe the Deathwatch Guards are implicated in this?" The effort of keeping his voice level almost strangled him. Since the

first Deathwatch Guards swore on the corpse of Luthair
Paendrag to defend his son, there had never been treason
among the Guards! Never!

Mor relaxed by increments as he realized that Karede
did not intend to kill him, at least not right then, but there
was a haze of sweat on his forehead. "I have heard it said a
Deathwatch Guard can see a butterfly's breath. Do you have
anything to drink?"

Karede gestured curtly to the brick hearth, where a silver
cup and pitcher sat near the flames, to keep warm. They
had been there, untouched, since Ajimbura brought them
when Karede awoke. "The wine may be cool by now, but
be free of it. And when your throat is wet, you will answer
my question. Either you suspect Guardsmen, or you wish to
play me in some game of your own, and by my eyes, I will
know which, and why."

The fellow sidled to the hearth, watching him from
the corner of his eye, but as Mor bent for the pitcher, he
frowned and then gave a small start. What appeared to be a
silver-rimmed bowl with a ram's-horn-patterned silver base
sat beside the cup. Light of heaven, Ajimbura had been told
often enough to keep that thing out of sight! There was no
doubt that Mor recognized it for what it was.

The man considered treason possible for the Guards?
"Pour for me as well, if you will."

Mor blinked, showing a faint consternation—he held the
only obvious cup—and then a light of understanding appeared in his eyes. An uneasy light. He filled the bowl, too,
a trifle unsteadily, and wiped his hand on his coat before
taking it up. Every man had his limits, even a Seeker, and a
man pushed to them was especially dangerous, but he was
also off balance.

Accepting the skull-cup with both hands, Karede raised
it high and lowered his head. "To the Empress, may she
live forever in honor and glory. Death and shame to her enemies."

"To the Empress, may she live forever in honor and
glory," Mor echoed, bowing his head and lifting his cup.
"Death and shame to her enemies."

Putting Ajimbura's cup to his lips, Karede was aware of
the other man watching him drink. The wine was indeed

cool, the spices bitter, and there was a faint, acrid hint of
silver polish; he told himself the taste of dead man's dust
was his imagination.

Mor dashed off half his own wine in hurried gulps, then
stared at his cup, seemed to realize what he had done, and
made a visible effort to regain control of himself. "Furyk
Karede," he said briskly. "Born forty-two years ago to
weavers, the property of one Jalid Magonine, a craftsman
in Ancarid. Chosen at fifteen for training in the Deathwatch
Guards. Cited twice for heroism and mentioned in dispatches three times, then, as a seven-year veteran, named
to the bodyguard of the High Lady Tuon upon her birth."
That had not been her name then, of course, but mentioning her birth-name would have been an insult. "That same
year, as one of three survivors of the first known attempt
on her life, chosen for training as an officer. Service during the Muyami Uprising and the Jianmin Incident, more
citations for heroism, more mentions in dispatches, and assignment back to the High Lady's bodyguard just before her
first true-name day." Mor peered into his wine, then looked
up suddenly. "At your request. Unusual, that. The following year, you took three serious wounds shielding her with
your body against another set of assassins. She gave you her
most precious possession, a doll. After more distinguished
service, with further citations and mentions, you were selected for the bodyguard of the Empress herself, may she
live forever, and served there until named to accompany the
High Lord Turak to these lands with the *Hailene*. Times
change, and men change, but before going to guard the
throne, you made two other requests for assignment to the
High Lady Tuon's bodyguard. *Most* unusual. And you kept
the doll until it was destroyed in the Great Fire of Sohima,
a matter of ten years."

Not for the first time, Karede was glad of the training
that allowed him to maintain a smooth face no matter what.
Careless expressions gave away too much to an opponent.
He remembered the face of the small girl who had laid that
doll on his litter. He could hear her still. *You have protected
my life, so you must take Emela to watch over you in turn,*
she said. *She can't really protect you, of course; she's only
a doll. But keep her to remind you that I will always hear if
you speak my name. If I'm still alive, of course.*

"My honor is loyalty," he said, setting Ajimbura's cup on the writing table carefully, so as not to slop wine onto his papers. However often the fellow polished the silver, Karede did not think he bothered to wash the thing. "Loyalty to the throne. Why did you come to me?"

Mor moved slightly, so the armchair was between them. No doubt he thought he was standing casually, but he was clearly ready to throw the winecup. He had a knife under his coat in the small of his back, and probably at least one other. "Three requests to join the High Lady Tuon's bodyguard. And you kept the doll."

"That much, I understand," Karede told him dryly. The Guards were not supposed to form attachments to those they were sent to guard. The Deathwatch Guard served only the Crystal Throne, served *whoever* succeeded to the throne, with a whole heart and a whole faith. But he remembered that serious child's face, already aware she might not live to do her duty yet trying to do it anyway, and he had kept the doll. "But there's more to it than rumor of a girl, isn't there?"

"A butterfly's breath," the fellow murmured. "It is a pleasure to talk to someone who sees deeply. On the night that Tylin was murdered, two *damane* were taken from the Tarasin Palace kennels. Both were formerly Aes Sedai. Do you not find the coincidence too much?"

"I find any coincidence suspect, Almurat. But what has that to do with rumors and . . . other matters?"

"This web is more tangled than you imagine. Several others left the palace that night, among them a young man who was apparently Tylin's pet, four men who were certainly soldiers, and an older man, one Thom Merrilin, or so he called himself, who was supposedly a servant, but who displayed much more education than would be expected. At one time or another, they were all seen with Aes Sedai who were in the city before the Empire reclaimed it." Intent, the Seeker leaned forward slightly over the back of the armchair. "Perhaps Tylin was not murdered because she swore fealty, but because she had learned of things that were dangerous. She might have been careless in what she revealed to the boy on the pillows, and he carried word to Merrilin. We can call him that until we learn a better name. The more I learn of that one, the more intriguing he is: knowledgeable of the world, well-spoken, at ease with nobles and crowns. A courtier, in fact, if you didn't know he was a servant. If the White Tower had certain plans in Ebou Dar, they might send such a man to carry them out."

Plans. Unthinking, Karede picked up Ajimbura's cup and almost drank before he realized what he was doing. He continued to hold the cup, though, so as not to give away his turmoil. Everyone—those who knew, anyway—was sure the High Lady Tuon's disappearance was part of the contest to succeed the Empress, might she live forever. Such was life in the Imperial family. If the High Lady were dead, after all, a new heir must be named. If she were dead. And if not . . . The White Tower would have sent their best, if they planned to carry her away. If the Seeker was not playing him in some game of his own. Seekers could try to snare anyone short of the Empress herself, might she live forever. "You have taken this notion to your superiors, and they rejected it, or you would not come to me. That, or . . . You haven't mentioned it to them, have you? Why not?"

"Much more tangled than you can imagine," Mor said softly, eyeing the door as if suspecting eavesdroppers. Why did he grow cautious now? "There are many . . . complications. The two *damane* were removed by the Lady Egeanin Tamarath, who has had dealings with Aes Sedai before. Close dealings, in fact. Very close. Clearly, she released the other *damane* to cover her escape. Egeanin left the city that same night, with three *damane* in her entourage, and also, we believe, Merrilin and the others. We don't know who the third *damane* was—we suspect someone important among the Atha'an Miere, or perhaps an Aes Sedai who was hiding in the city—but we have identified the *sul'dam* she used, and two have close connections with Suroth. Who herself has many connections to Aes Sedai." For all his wariness, Mor said that as if it were not a lightning bolt. No wonder he was on edge.

So. Suroth plotted with Aes Sedai and had corrupted at least some of the Seekers above Mor, and the White Tower had placed men under one of their best to carry out certain actions. It was all believable. When Karede was sent with the Forerunners, he had been tasked to watch the Blood for over-ambition. There had always been a possibility, this far from the Empire, that they would try to set up their own kingdoms. And he himself had sent men into a city he knew would fall whatever was done to defend it, so they could harm the enemy from within.

"You have a direction, Almurat?"

Mor shook his head. "They went north, and Jehannah was mentioned in the palace stables, but that seems an obvious attempt at deception. They will have changed direction at the first opportunity. We have checked on boats large enough to have carried the party across the river, but vessels of that size come and go all the time. There is no order in this place, no control."

"This gives me a great deal to think on."

The Seeker grimaced, a slight twisting of his mouth, but he seemed to realize he had gotten as much commitment as Karede would make. He nodded once. "Whatever you choose to do, you should know this. You may wonder how the girl extorted anything from these merchants. It seems two or three soldiers always accompanied her. The description of their armor was also very precise." He half stretched out a hand as though to touch Karede's robe, but wisely let it fall back to his side. "Most people call that black. You understand me? Whatever you choose to do, do not delay." Mor raised his cup. "Your health, Banner-General. Furyk. Your health, and the health of the Empire."

Karede drained Ajimbura's cup without hesitation.

The Seeker departed as abruptly as he had entered, and moments after the door closed behind him, it opened to admit Ajimbura. The little man stared accusingly at the skull-cup in Karede's hands.

"You know this rumor, Ajimbura?" As well ask whether the sun rose in the morning as ask whether the fellow had been listening. He did not deny it, in any case.

"I would not soil my tongue with such filth, high one," he said, drawing himself up.

Karede permitted himself a sigh. Whether the High Lady Tuon's disappearance was her own doing or some other's, she was in great danger. And if the rumor was some ploy by Mor, the best way to defeat another's game was to make the game your own. "Lay out my razor." Sitting down, he reached for his pen, holding the sleeve of his robe clear of the ink with his left hand. "Then you will find Captain Musenge, when he is alone, and give him this. Return quickly; I will have more instructions for you."

Shortly after noon on the following day, he was crossing the harbor on the ferry that departed each hour, according to the strict ringing of bells. It was a lumbering barge that heaved as long sweeps propelled it across the harbor's choppy surface. The ropes lashing a merchant's half-dozen canvas-covered wagons to the cleats on the deck creaked with every shift, the horses stamped their hooves nervously, and the oarsmen had to fend off wagon drivers and hired guards who wanted to empty their bellies over the side. Some men had no stomach for the motion of water. The merchant herself, a plump-faced woman with a coppery skin, stood in the bow wrapped in her dark cloak, balancing easily with the ferry's movements, staring fixedly at the approaching landing and ignoring Karede beside her. She might know that he was Seanchan, from the saddle on his bay gelding if nothing else, but a plain gray cloak covered his red-trimmed green coat, so if she thought of him at all, it was as an ordinary soldier. Not a settler, with a sword on his hip. There might have been sharper eyes back in the city, despite all he had done to evade them, but there was nothing he could do about that. With luck, he had a day, perhaps two, before anyone realized he would not be returning to the inn any time soon.

Swinging into his saddle as soon as the ferry bumped hard against the landing dock's leather-padded posts, he was first off when the loading gate swung aside, the merchant was still chivvying her drivers to the wagons and the ferrymen unlashing wheels. He kept Aldazar to a slow walk across the stones, still slippery with the morning's rain, a litter of horse dung, and the leavings of a flock of sheep, and let the bay's pace increase only when he reached the Illian Road itself, though he kept short of a trot even then. Impatience was a vice when beginning a journey of unknown length.

Inns lined the road beyond the landing, flat-roofed buildings, covered in cracked and flaking white plaster and with faded signs out front or none at all. This road marked the northern edge of the Rahad, and roughly dressed men slouching on benches in front of the inns sullenly watched him pass. Not because he was Seanchan; he suspected they would have been no brighter for anyone on horseback. Anyone who had two coins to rub, for that matter. Soon he left them behind, though, and the next few hours took him past olive orchards and small farms where the workers were accustomed enough to passersby on the road that they did not look up from their labors. The traffic was sparse in any case, a handful of high-wheeled farmers' carts and twice a merchant's train rumbling toward Ebou Dar, surrounded by hired guards. Many of the drivers and both merchants wore those distinctive Illianer beards. It seemed strange that Illian continued to send its trade to Ebou Dar while fighting to resist the Empire, but people on this side of the Eastern Sea were often peculiar, with odd customs, and little like the stories told of the great Hawkwing's homeland. Often nothing like. They must be understood, of course, if they were to be brought into the Empire, but understanding was for others, higher than he. He had his duty.

The farms gave way to woodlands and fields of scrub, and his shadow was lengthening in front of him, the sun more than halfway to the horizon, by the time he saw what he was looking for. Just ahead, Ajimbura was squatting on the north side of the road, playing a reed flute, the image of an idler shirking. Before Karede reached him, he tucked the flute behind his belt, gathered his brown cloak and vanished into the brush and trees. Glancing behind to make sure the road was empty in that direction as well, Karede turned Aldazar into the woodland at the same point.

The little man was waiting just out of sight of the road, among a stand of some sort of large pine tree, the tallest easily a hundred feet. He made his hunch-shouldered bow and scrambled into the saddle of a lean chestnut with four white feet. He insisted that white feet on a horse were lucky. "This way, high one?" he said, and at Karede's gesture of permission, turned his mount deeper into the forest.

They had only a short way to ride, no more than half a mile, but no one passing on the road could have suspected what waited there in a large clearing. Musenge had brought a hundred of the Guard on good horses and twenty Ogier Gardeners, all in full armor, along with pack animals to carry supplies for two weeks. The packhorse Ajimbura had brought out yesterday, with Karede's armor, would be

among them. A cluster of *sul'dam* were standing beside
their own mounts, some petting the six leashed *damane*.
When Musenge rode forward to meet Karede with Hartha,
the First Gardener, striding grim-faced beside him with his
green-tasseled axe over his shoulder. One of the women,
Melitene, the High Lady Tuon's *der'sul'dam,* stepped into
her saddle and joined them.

Musenge and Hartha touched fists to heart, and Karede
returned their salute, but his eyes went to the *damane.* To
one in particular, a small woman whose hair was being
stroked by a dark, square-faced *sul'dam.* A *damane's* face
was always deceptive—they aged slowly and lived a very
long time—but this one had a difference he had learned to
recognize as belonging to those who called themselves Aes
Sedai. "What excuse did you use to get all of them out of
the city at once?" he asked.

"Exercise, Banner-General," Melitene replied with a wry
smile. "Everyone always believes exercise." It was said the
High Lady Tuon in truth needed no *der'sul'dam* to train
her property or her *sul'dam,* but Melitene, with less black
than gray in her long hair, was experienced in more than
her craft, and she knew what he was really asking. He had
requested that Musenge bring a pair of *damane,* if he could.
"None of us would be left behind, Banner-General. Never
for this. As for Mylen . . ." That must be the former Aes
Sedai. "After we left the city, we told the *damane* why we
were going. It's always best if they know what's expected.
We've been calming Mylen ever since. She loves the High
Lady. They all do, but Mylen worships her as though she
already sat on the Crystal Throne. If Mylen gets her hands
on one of these 'Aes Sedai,'" she chuckled, "we'll have to
be quick to keep the woman from being too battered to be
worth leashing."

"I see no cause for laughter," Hartha rumbled. The Ogier
was even more weathered and grizzled than Musenge,
with long gray mustaches and eyes like black stones staring out of his helmet. He had been a Gardener since before
Karede's father was born, maybe before his grandfather.
"We have no target. We are trying to catch the wind in a
net." Melitene sobered quickly, and Musenge began to look
grimmer than Hartha, if that was possible.

In ten days, the people they sought would have put many

miles behind them. The best the White Tower could send would not be so blatant as to head due east after trying the ruse of Jehannah, nor so stupid to as to head too close to north, yet that left a vast and ever expanding area to be searched. "Then we must begin spreading our nets without delay," Karede said, "and spread them finely."

Musenge and Hartha nodded. For the Deathwatch Guard, what must be done, would be done. Even to catching the wind.

CHAPTER
5

The Forging of a Hammer

*H**e ran easily through the night in spite of the snow that covered the ground. He was one with the shadows, slipping through the forest, the moonlight almost as clear to his eyes as the light of the sun. A cold wind ruffled his thick fur, and suddenly brought a scent that made his hackles stand and his heart race with a hatred greater than that for the Neverborn. Hatred, and a sure knowledge of death coming. There were no choices to be made, not now. He ran harder, toward death.*

Perrin woke abruptly in the deep darkness before dawn, beneath one of the high-wheeled supply carts. Cold had seeped into his bones from the ground despite his heavy fur-lined cloak and two blankets, and there was a fitful breeze, not strong or steady enough to be called a light wind, but icy. When he scrubbed at his face with gauntleted hands, frost crackled in his short beard. At least it seemed not to have snowed any more during the night. Too often he had awakened covered with a dusting despite the shelter of a cart, and snowfall made things difficult for the scouts. He wished he could speak with Elyas the same way he talked with wolves. Then he would not have to endure this endless waiting. Weariness clung to him like a second skin; he could not recall when he had last had a sound night's sleep. Sleep, or the lack of it, seemed unimportant anyway. These days, only the heat of anger gave him the strength to keep moving.

He did not think it was the dream that had wakened him. Every night he lay down expecting nightmares, and every night they came. In the worst, he found Faile dead, or never found her. Those woke him up in shivering sweats. Anything less horrible, he slept through, or only half-woke with Trollocs cutting him up alive for the cookpot or a Draghkar eating his soul. This dream was fading quickly, in the manner of dreams, yet he remembered being a wolf and smelling . . . What? Something wolves hated more than they did Myrddraal. Something a wolf knew would kill him. The knowledge he had had in the dream was gone; only vague impressions remained. He had not been in the wolf dream, that reflection of this world where dead wolves lived on and the living could go to consult them. The wolf dream always remained clear in his head after he left, whether he had gone there consciously or not. Yet this dream still seemed real, and somehow urgent.

Lying motionless on his back, he sent his mind questing, feeling for wolves. He had tried using wolves to help his hunt, to no avail. Convincing them to take an interest in the doings of two-legs was difficult, to say the least. They avoided large parties of men, and for them, half a dozen was large enough to stay clear of. Men chased away game, and most men tried to kill a wolf on sight. His thoughts found nothing, but then, after a time, he touched wolves, at a distance. How far, he could not be sure, but it was like catching a whisper almost on the edge of hearing. A long way. That was strange. Despite scattered villages and manors and even the occasional town, this was prime country for wolves, untouched forest for the most part, with plenty of deer and smaller game.

There was always a formality to speaking with a pack you were not part of. Politely, he sent his name among wolves, Young Bull, shared his scent, and received theirs in reply, Leafhunter and Tall Bear, White Tail and Feather and Thunder Mist, a cascade of others. It was a sizable pack, and Leafhunter, a female with a feel of quiet certainty, was their leader. Feather, clever and in his prime, was her mate. They had heard of Young Bull, were eager to speak with the friend of the fabled Long Tooth, the first two-legs who had learned to speak with wolves after a gap of time that carried the feel of Ages vanished into the mists of the past. It was all a torrent of images and memories of scents that his mind turned into words, as the words he thought somehow became images and scents they could understand.

There is something I want to learn, he thought, once the greetings were done. *What would a wolf hate more than the Neverborn?* He tried to recall the scent from the dream, to add that, but it was gone from his memory. *Something that a wolf knows means death.*

Silence answered him, and a thread of fear blended with hatred and determination and reluctance. He had felt fear from wolves before—above all things they feared the wild-fire that raced through a forest, or so he would have said—but this was the prickling sort of fear that made a man's skin crawl, made him shiver and jump at things unseen. Laced with the resolution to go on no matter what, it felt close to terror. Wolves never experienced that kind of dread. Except that these did.

One by one they faded from his consciousness, a deliberate act of shutting him out, until only Leafhunter remained. *The Last Hunt is coming,* she said at last, and then she also was gone.

Did I offend? he sent. *If I did, it was in ignorance.* But there was no reply. These wolves, at least, would not speak with him again, not any time soon.

The Last Hunt is coming. That was what wolves called the Last Battle, Tarmon Gai'don. They knew they would be there, at the final confrontation between the Light and the Shadow, though why was something they could not explain. Some things were fated, as sure as the rise and fall of the sun and the moon, and it was fated that many wolves would die in the Last Hunt. What they feared was something else. Perrin had a strong sense that he also had to be there, was meant to be at least, but if the Last Battle came soon, he would not be. He had a job of work in front of him that he could not shirk—would not!—even for Tarmon Gai'don.

Putting nameless fears and the Last Battle alike out of his mind, he fumbled his gauntlets off and felt in his coat pocket for the length of rawhide cord he kept there. In a morning ritual, his fingers made another knot mechanically, then slid down the cord, counting. Twenty-two knots. Twenty-two mornings since Faile was kidnapped.

At the start, he had not thought there was need to keep count. That first day, he had believed he was cold and numb but focused, yet looking back he could see he had been overwhelmed by unbound rage and a consuming need to find the Shaido as fast as possible. Men from other clans had been among the Aiel who had stolen Faile, yet on the evidence, most were Shaido, and that was how he thought of them. The need to rip Faile away from them, before she could be hurt, had gripped him by the throat till he almost choked. He would rescue the other women captured with her, of course, but sometimes he had to list their names in his head to make sure he did not forget them entirely. Alliandre Maritha Kigarin, Queen of Ghealdan, and his liege woman. It still seemed off-kilter to have anyone oathsworn to him, especially a queen—he was a blacksmith! He had been a blacksmith, once—but he had responsibilities toward Alliandre, and she would never have been in danger except for him. Bain of the Black Rock Shaarad and Chiad of the Stones River Goshien, Aiel Maidens of the Spear who had followed Faile to Ghealdan and Amadicia. They had faced Trollocs in the Two Rivers, as well, when Perrin needed every hand that could raise a weapon, and that earned them the right to call on him. Arrela Shiego and Lacile Aldorwin, two foolish young women who thought they could learn to be Aiel, or some strange version of Aiel. They were oathsworn to Faile, and so was Maighdin Dorlain, a penniless refugee Faile had taken under her wing as one of her maids. He could not abandon Faile's people. Faile ni Bashere t'Aybara.

The litany came back to her, his wife, the breath of his life. With a groan, he clutched the cord so tightly that the knots impressed themselves painfully on a hand hardened by long days swinging the hammer at a forge. Light, twenty-two days!

Working iron had taught him that haste ruined metal, but in the beginning, he had been hasty, Traveling southward through gateways created by Grady and Neald, the two Asha'man, to where the farthest traces of the Shaido had been found, then leaping south again, the direction their tracks went, as soon as the Asha'man could make more gateways. Fretting every hour it took them to rest from making the first and holding them open long enough for everyone to pass through, his mind was eaten up with freeing Faile at any cost. What he found were days of increasing pain as the scouts spread farther and farther through uninhabited wilderness without locating the slightest sign that anyone had been that way before, until he knew he had to retrace his path, frittering away more days to cover ground the Asha'man had taken him across in a step, searching for any indication of where the Shaido had turned aside.

He should have known they would turn. South took them toward warmer lands, without the snow that seemed so strange to Aiel, yet it took them closer to the Seanchan in Ebou Dar, as well. He knew about the Seanchan, and he should have expected the Shaido to learn! They were after pillage, not a fight with Seanchan and *damane*. Days of slow marching with the scouts fanning out ahead, days when falling snow blinded even the Aiel and forced them all to a chafing halt, until finally Jondyn Barran found a tree scraped by a wagon and Elyas dug a broken Aiel spear shaft from beneath the snow. And Perrin at last turned east, at most two days south of where he had Traveled to the first time. He had wanted to howl when he realized that, yet he kept a tight hold on himself. He could not give way, not so much as an inch, not when Faile was depending on him. That was when he began to husband his anger, began to forge it.

Her kidnappers had gained a long lead because he was hasty, but since then, he had been as careful as he had been in a smithy. His anger was hardened and shaped to a purpose. Since finding the Shaido's trail again, he had Traveled no farther in one jump than the scouts could go and come between sunrise and sunset, and it was well that he had been cautious, because the Shaido changed directions suddenly several times, zigzagging almost as though they could not decide on a destination. Or maybe they had turned to join others of their kind. All he had to go by were old traces, old camps buried by snow, yet all of the scouts agreed the Shaido's numbers had swollen. There had to be at least two or three septs together, maybe more, a formidable quarry to hunt. Slowly but surely, though, he had begun overtaking them. That was what was important.

The Shaido covered more ground on the march than he would have thought possible, given their numbers and the snow, yet they did not seem to care whether anyone was tracking them. Perhaps they believed no one dared. Sometimes they had camped several days in one spot. Anger forged to a purpose. Ruined villages and small towns and

estates littered the Shaido's path as if they were human lo-
custs, storehouses and valuables looted, men and women
carried off along with the livestock. Often no one remained
by the time he arrived, only empty houses, the people seeking somewhere for food to survive until spring. He had
crossed the Eldar into Altara where a small ferry used by
peddlers and local farmers, not merchants, once ran between two villages on the forested riverbanks. How the
Shaido had gotten across, he did not know, but he had the
Asha'man make gateways. All that remained of the ferry
were the rough stone landings on either bank, and the few
unburned structures were deserted except for three slat-
ribbed feral dogs that slunk away at the sight of humans.
Anger hardened and shaped for a hammer.

Yesterday morning, he had come to a tiny village where a
double handful of stunned, dirty-faced people had stared at
the hundreds of lancers and bowmen riding out of the forest
at first light behind the Red Eagle of Manetheren and the
crimson Wolfshead, the Silver Stars of Ghealdan and the
Golden Hawk of Mayene, followed by long lines of high-
wheeled carts and strings of remounts. At first sight of Gaul
and the other Aiel, those people overcame their paralysis
and began running for the trees in panic. Catching a few
to answer questions had been difficult; they were ready to
run themselves to death rather than let an Aiel near. Brytan
had consisted of only a dozen families, but the Shaido had
carried off nine young men and women from there, along
with all of their animals, only two days ago. Two days. A
hammer was a tool with a purpose, and a target.

He knew he had to be careful, or lose Faile forever, but
being too careful could lose her, too. Early yesterday he had
told those who were going ahead to scout that they were to
go farther than before, push on harder, returning only with
a full turn of the sun unless they found the Shaido sooner.
In a little while the sun would rise, and at most a few hours
after that, Elyas and Gaul and the others would return, the
Maidens and Two Rivers men he knew could track a shadow
across water. As fast as the Shaido moved, the scouts could
move faster. They were not encumbered with families and
wagons and captives. This time, they would be able to tell
him exactly where the Shaido were. They would. He knew
it in his bones. The certainty flowed in his veins. He would

find Faile and free her. That came before anything, even living, so long as he lived long enough to accomplish it, yet he *was* a hammer, now, and if there was any way to accomplish it, any way at all, he intended to hammer these Shaido into scrap.

Tossing the blankets aside, Perrin tugged his gauntlets back on, gathered his axe from where it lay beside him, a half-moon blade balanced by a heavy spike, and rolled out into the open, rising to his feet on trampled, frozen snow. Carts stood all around him in rows, in what had been Brytan's fields. The arrival of more strangers, so many, and armed, with their foreign banners, had been more than the survivors of the little village could absorb. As soon as Perrin would let them, the pitiful remnant had fled into the forest, carrying what they could on their backs and on dragsleds. They had run as hard as if Perrin was another Shaido, not looking back for fear he was following them.

As he slipped the axe haft through the thick loop on his belt, a deeper shadow beside a nearby cart grew taller and resolved into a man swathed in a cloak that seemed black in the darkness. Perrin was not surprised; the nearby horselines thickened the air with the smell of several thousand animals, mounts and remounts and cart horses, not to mention the sweet stink of horse dung, but he still had caught the other's scent on waking. Man smell always stood out. Besides, Aram was always there when Perrin woke, waiting. A waning sickle moon low in the sky still gave enough light for him to make out the other man's face, if not clearly, and the brass-pommeled hilt of his sword slanting up past his shoulder. Aram had been a Tinker once, but Perrin did not think he would be again, even if he did wear a brightly striped Tinker coat. There was a frowning hardness about Aram now that moon shadows could not hide. He stood as though ready to draw that sword, and since Faile was taken, anger seemed a permanent part of his scent. A great deal had changed when Faile was taken. Anyway, Perrin understood anger. He had not, not really, before Faile was taken.

"They want to see you, Lord Perrin," Aram said, jerking his head toward two dim forms farther away between the lines of carts. The words came out in a faint mist in the cold air. "I told them to let you sleep." It was a fault Aram had, looking after him too much, unasked.

Testing the air, Perrin separated out the scents of those two shadows from the masking smell of the horses. "I'll see them now. Have Stepper readied for me, Aram." He tried to be in the saddle before the rest of the camp woke. Partly that was because standing still for long seemed beyond him. Standing still was not catching the Shaido. Partly it was to avoid having to share anyone's company he could avoid. He would have gone out with the scouts himself if the men and women already doing that job were not so much better at it than he.

"Yes, my Lord." A jaggedness entered Aram's scent as he trudged away across the snow, but Perrin barely noted it. Only something important would make Sebban Balwer root himself out of his blankets in the dark, and as for Selande Darengil . . .

Balwer appeared skinny even in a bulky cloak, his pinched face all but hidden in the deep hood. Had he stood straight instead of hunching, he still would have been at most a hand taller than the Cairhienin woman, who was not tall. With his arms wrapped around himself, he was hopping from one foot to the other, trying to avoid the cold that must be soaking through his boots. Selande, in a man's dark coat and breeches, made a good effort at ignoring the temperature despite the feathery white that marked every breath. She was shivering, but managed to swagger standing still, with one side of her cloak thrown back and a gloved hand on the hilt of her sword. The hood of her cloak was lowered, too, exposing hair cut short except for the tail in the back that was tied at the nape of her neck with a dark ribbon. Selande was the leader of those fools who wanted to be imitation Aiel, Aiel who carried swords. Her scent was soft and thick, like a jelly. She was worried. Balwer smelled . . . intent . . . but then, he nearly always did, though there was never any heat to his intensity, only focus.

The skinny little man stopped hopping to make a stiff, hurried bow. "The Lady Selande has news I think you should hear from her lips, my Lord." Balwer's thin voice was dry and precise, just like its owner. He would sound the same with his neck on a headsman's block. "My Lady,

if you would?" He was only a secretary—Faile's secretary,
and Perrin's—a fussy self-effacing fellow for the most part,
and Selande was a noblewoman, but Balwer made that more
than a request.

She gave him a sharp sideways glance, shifting her sword,
and Perrin tensed to grab her. He did not think she would
actually draw on the man, but then again, he was not sure
enough of her, or any of her ridiculous friends, to put it out
of the question. Balwer merely watched her, his head tilted
to one side, and his smell carried impatience, not concern.

With a toss of her head, Selande turned her attention to
Perrin. "I see you, Lord Perrin Goldeneyes," she began in
the crisp accents of Cairhien, but, aware that he had little
patience for her pretend Aiel formality, she hurried on. "I
have learned three things tonight. First, the least important, Haviar reported that Masema sent another rider back
toward Amadicia yesterday. Nerion tried to follow, but lost
him."

"Tell Nerion I said he isn't to follow anybody," Perrin
told her sharply. "And tell Haviar the same. They should
know that! They are to watch, listen, and report what they
see and hear, no more. Do you understand me?" Selande
gave a quick nod, a thorn of fear entering her scent for a
moment. Fear of him, Perrin supposed, fear that he was angry with her. Yellow eyes on a man made some people uneasy. He took his hand from his axe and clasped both hands
behind his back.

Haviar and Nerion were more of Faile's two dozen young
fools, one Tairen, the other Cairhienin. Faile had used the
lot of them for eyes-and-ears, a fact that still irritated him
for some reason, though she had told him to his face that
spying was a wife's business. A man needed to listen hard
when he thought his wife was joking; she might not be. The
whole notion of spying made him uncomfortable, but if
Faile could use them so, then so could her husband, when
there was need. Just the two, though. Masema seemed convinced that everyone except Darkfriends were fated to follow him sooner or later, yet he might grow suspicious if too
many left Perrin's camp to join him.

"Don't call him Masema, not even here," he added
brusquely. Lately the man claimed Masema Dagar was actually dead and risen from the grave as the Prophet of the

Lord Dragon Reborn, and he was touchier than ever about mention of his former name. "You get careless with your tongue in the wrong place, and you might be lucky if he just has a few of his bullyboys flog you the next time they can find you alone." Selande nodded again, gravely, and this time without any fear smell. Light, those idiots of Faile's lacked the sense to recognize what they should be afraid of.

"It's almost dawn," Balwer murmured, shivering and pulling his cloak tighter. "All will be waking before long, and some matters are best discussed unseen. If my Lady will continue?" Once again, that was more than a suggestion. Selande and the rest of Faile's hangers-on had been good only for causing trouble, that Perrin could see, and Balwer looked to be trying to put a fly up her nose for some reason, but she actually gave an embarrassed start and murmured an apology.

The darkness truly was beginning to lessen, Perrin realized, at least to his eyes. The sky overhead still looked black, dusted with bright stars, yet he could almost make out the colors of the six thin stripes that crossed the front of Selande's coat. He could tell one from another, anyway. The realization that he had slept later than usual made him growl. He could not afford to give in to weariness, however tired he was! He needed to hear Selande's report—she would not be worried about Masema sending out riders; the man did that almost every day—yet he looked anxiously for Aram and Stepper. His ears picked up the sounds of activity among the horselines, but there was no sign of his horse yet.

"The second thing, my Lord," Selande said, "is that Haviar has seen casks of salt fish and salt beef branded with Altaran markings, a great many of them. He says there are Altarans among Mas . . . among the Prophet's people, too. Several appear to be craftsfolk, and one or two could be merchants or town officials. Established men and women, in any case, solid folk, and some seem unsure they made the right decision. A few questions might reveal from where the fish and beef came. And perhaps gain more eyes-and-ears for you."

"I know where the fish and beef came from and so do you," Perrin said irritably. His hands knotted into fists behind his back. He had hoped the speed with which he was moving would keep Masema from sending out raiding parties.

That was what they were, and as bad as the Shaido if not worse. They offered people a chance to swear to the Dragon Reborn, and those who refused, sometimes those who simply hesitated too long, died by fire and steel. In any case, whether or not they marched off to follow Masema, those who swore were expected to donate generously in support of the Prophet's cause, while those who died were plainly Darkfriends, their belongings forfeit. Thieves lost a hand, by Masema's laws, but none of what his raiders did was thieving, according to Masema. By his laws, murder and a whole host of other crimes merited hanging, yet a fair number of his followers seemed to prefer killing to receiving oaths. There was more loot, that way, and for some of them murder was a fine game to play before eating.

"Tell them to keep clear of these Altarans," Perrin went on. "All sorts drift into Masema's following, and even if they are having second thoughts, it won't take them long to stink of zeal like the rest. They wouldn't hesitate to gut a neighbor then, much less somebody who's asked the wrong questions. What I want to know is what Masema's doing, what he's planning."

That the man had some scheme seemed obvious. Masema claimed it was blasphemy for anyone except Rand to touch the One Power, claimed he wanted nothing more than to join Rand in the east. As always, thought of Rand brought colors whirling through Perrin's head, more vividly than usual this time, but anger melted them to vapor. Blasphemy or no, Masema had accepted Traveling, which was not just channeling but *men* channeling. And no matter what he claimed, he had done it to remain in the west as long as possible, not to help rescue Faile. Perrin tended to trust people until they proved unreliable, but one sniff of Masema had told him the fellow was as insane as a rabid animal and less trustworthy.

He had considered ways to stop that scheme, whatever it was. Ways to stop Masema's killing and burning. Masema had ten or twelve thousand men with him, maybe more—the man was not very forthcoming about numbers, and the way they camped in a squalid sprawl made counting impossible—while less than a quarter of that number followed Perrin, several hundred of them cart drivers and grooms and others who would be more hindrance than help in a fight, yet with three Aes Sedai and two Asha'man, not to mention six Aiel Wise Ones, he could halt Masema in his tracks. The Wise Ones and two of the Aes Sedai would be eager to take part. More than simply willing, at least. They wanted Masema dead. But dispersing Masema's army would only break it into hundreds of smaller bands that would scatter across Altara and beyond, still looting and killing, just for themselves instead of in the name of the Dragon Reborn. *Breaking the Shaido will do the same thing,* he thought, and pushed the thought away. Stopping Masema would take time he did not have. The man would have to keep until Faile was safe. Until the Shaido were smashed to kindling.

"What's the third thing you learned tonight, Selande?" he said roughly. To his surprise, the smell of worry coming from the woman thickened.

"Haviar saw someone," she said slowly. "He did not tell me at first." Her voice hardened for a moment. "I made sure that will not happen again!" Drawing a deep breath, she seemed to struggle with herself, then burst out, "Masuri Sedai has visited Masema . . . the Prophet. It is true, my Lord; believe me! Haviar has seen her more than once. She slips into their camp hooded and leaves the same way, but he has had a good look at her face twice. A man accompanies her each time, and sometimes another woman. Haviar has not seen the man well enough to be sure, but the description fits Rovair, Masuri's Warder, and Haviar is certain the second woman is Annoura Sedai."

She broke off abruptly, her eyes shining darkly in the moonlight as she watched him. Light, she was as worried about how he would take it as by what it meant! He forced his hands to unclench. Masema despised Aes Sedai as much as he did Darkfriends; he nearly considered them Darkfriends. So why would he receive two sisters? Why would they go to him? Annoura's opinion of Masema lay hidden behind Aes Sedai mystery and double-jointed comments that could mean anything, but Masuri had said straight out that the man needed to be put down like a mad dog.

"Make sure Haviar and Nerion keep a sharp eye for the sisters and see if they can eavesdrop on one of their meetings with Masema." Could Haviar be mistaken? No, there were few women in Masema's camp, relatively speaking, and it passed belief that the Tairen could mistake one of those unwashed murderous-eyed harridans for Masuri. The sort of women willing to march with Masema usually made the men look like Tinkers. "Tell them to take care, though. Better to let the chance pass than get caught at it. They're no good to anyone strung up on a tree." Perrin knew he sounded gruff, and tried to make his voice milder. That seemed harder since Faile was kidnapped. "You've done well, Selande." At least he did not sound as if he were barking at her. "You and Haviar and Nerion. Faile would be proud if she knew."

A smile lit up her face, and she stood a little straighter, if that was possible. Pride, clean and bright, the pride of accomplishment, almost overwhelmed any other scent from her! "Thank you, my Lord. Thank you!" You would have thought he had given her a prize. Maybe he had, come to think on it. Though come to think Faile might not be best pleased that he was using her eyes-and-ears, or even knew about them. Once, the thought of Faile displeased would have made him uneasy, but that was before he learned about her spies. And that little matter of the Broken Crown that Elyas had let slip. Everybody always said that wives kept their secrets close, but there were limits!

Adjusting his cloak on his narrow shoulders with one hand, Balwer coughed behind the other. "Well said, my Lord. Very well said. My Lady, I'm sure you want to pass on Lord Perrin's instructions as soon as possible. It wouldn't do for there to be any misunderstanding."

Selande nodded without taking her eyes off Perrin. Her mouth opened, and Perrin was sure she intended to say something about hoping he found water and shade. Light, water was the one thing they had in plenty, even if it was mostly frozen, and this time of year, nobody needed shade even at noon! She probably did intend it, because she hesitated before saying, "Grace favor you, my Lord. If I may be so bold, Grace has favored the Lady Faile in you."

Perrin jerked his head in a nod of thanks. There was a taste of ashes in his mouth. Grace had a funny way of favoring Faile, giving her a husband who still had not found her after more than two weeks of searching. The Maidens said she had been made *gai'shain,* that she would not be mistreated, but they had to admit these Shaido already had broken their customs a hundred different ways. In his book, being kidnapped was mistreatment enough. Bitter ashes.

"The lady will do very well, my Lord," Balwer said softly, watching Selande vanish into the darkness among the carts. This approval was a surprise; he had tried to talk Perrin out of using Selande and her friends on the grounds they were hotheaded and unreliable. "She has the necessary instincts. Cairhienin do, usually, and Tairens to some extent, at least the nobles, especially once—" He cut off abruptly, and eyed Perrin cautiously. If he were another man, Perrin would have believed he had said more than he intended, but he doubted Balwer slipped in that fashion. The man's scent remained steady, not jiggling the way it would in a man who was unsure. "May I offer one or two points on her report, my Lord?"

The crunch of hooves in the snow announced the approach of Aram, leading Perrin's dun stallion and his own rangy gray gelding. The two animals were trying to nip at one another, and Aram was keeping them well apart, though with some difficulty. Balwer sighed.

"You can say whatever you need to in front of Aram, Master Balwer," Perrin said. The little man bowed his head in acquiescence, but he sighed again, too. Everybody in the camp knew that Balwer had the skill of fitting together rumors and chance-heard comments and things people had done to form a picture of what had really happened or what might, and Balwer himself considered that part of his job as a secretary, but for some reason he liked to pretend he never did any such thing. It was a harmless pretense, and Perrin tended to humor him.

Taking Stepper's reins from Aram, he said, "Walk behind us awhile, Aram. I need to talk with Master Balwer in private." Balwer's sigh was so faint that Perrin barely heard it.

Aram fell in behind the two of them without a word as they began to walk, frozen snow cracking beneath their feet, but his scent grew spiky again, and quivery, a thin, sour smell. This time, Perrin recognized the scent, though he paid it no more mind than usual. Aram was jealous of anyone except Faile who spent time with him. Perrin saw no way to put a stop to it, and anyway, he was as used to Aram's possessiveness as he was to the way Balwer hopped along at his side, glancing over his shoulder to see whether

Aram was close enough to hear when he finally decided to speak. Balwer's razor-thin scent of suspicion, curiously dry and not even warm but still suspicion, provided a counterpoint to Aram's jealousy. You could not change men who did not want to change.

The horselines and supply carts were located in the middle of the camp, where thieves would have a hard time reaching them, and although the sky still looked black to most eyes, the cart drivers and grooms, who slept close to their charges, were already awake and folding their blankets, some tending shelters made of pine boughs and other small tree limbs harvested from the surrounding forest, in case they might be needed another night. Cook fires were being lit and small black kettles set over them, though there was little to eat except porridge or dried beans. Hunting and trapping added some meat, venison and rabbits, partridges and woodhens and the like, but that could only go so far with so many to feed, and there had been nowhere to buy supplies since before crossing the Eldar. A ripple of bows and curtsies and murmurs of "A good morning, my Lord" and "The Light favor you, my Lord" followed Perrin, but the men and women who saw him stopped trying to strengthen their shelters, and a few began to pull theirs down, as though they had sensed his determination from his stride. They should have known his resolve by now. Since the day he realized how badly he had blundered, he had not spent two nights in one place. He returned the greetings without slowing.

The rest of the camp made a thin ring around the horses and carts, facing the encircling forest, with the Two Rivers men divided into four groups and the lancers from Ghealdan and Mayene spaced between them. Whoever came at them, from whatever direction, would face Two Rivers longbows and trained cavalry. It was not a sudden appearance by the Shaido that Perrin feared, but rather Masema. The man seemed to be following him meekly enough, but aside from this news of raiding, nine Ghealdanin and eight Mayeners had vanished in the last two weeks, and no one believed they had deserted. Before that, on the day Faile was stolen, twenty Mayeners had been ambushed and killed, and no one believed it had been anyone but Masema's men who did the killing. So an uneasy peace existed, a strange thorny sort of peace, yet a copper wagered on it lasting forever was likely a copper lost. Masema pretended to be unaware of any danger to that peace, but his followers seemed not to care one way or the other, and whatever Masema pretended, they took their lead from him. Somehow, though, Perrin intended to see that it endured until Faile was free. Making his own camp too tough a nut to crack was one way of making the peace last.

The Aiel had insisted on having their own thin wedge of the strange pie, though there were fewer than fifty of them, counting the *gai'shain* who served the Wise Ones, and he paused to study their low dark tents. The only other tents erected anywhere in the camp were those of Berelain and her two serving women, on the other side of the camp, not far from Brytan's few houses. Fleas and lice in hordes made those uninhabitable, even for hardened soldiers seeking shelter from the cold, and the barns were putrid ramshackle affairs that let the wind howl through and harbored worse vermin than the houses. The Maidens and Gaul, the only man among the Aiel not *gai'shain,* were all out with the scouts, and the Aiel tents were silent and still, though the smell of smoke coming from some of the vent holes told him the *gai'shain* were preparing breakfast for the Wise Ones, or serving it. Annoura was Berelain's adviser, and usually shared her tent, but Masuri and Seonid would be with the Wise Ones, maybe even helping the *gai'shain* with breakfast. They still tried to hide the fact that the Wise Ones considered them apprentices, though everyone in camp must be aware of it by now. Anyone who saw an Aes Sedai actually carrying firewood or water, or heard one being switched, could make it out. The two Aes Sedai were oathsworn to Rand—again the colors whirled in his head, an explosion of hues; again they melted under his constant anger—but Edarra and the other Wise Ones had been sent to keep an eye on them.

Only the Aes Sedai themselves knew how tightly their oaths held them, or what room they saw to maneuver between the words, and neither was allowed to hop unless a Wise One said toad. Seonid and Masuri had *both* said Masema should be put down like a mad dog, and the Wise Ones agreed. Or so they said. They had no Three Oaths to hold them to the truth, though in truth, that particular

Oath held the Aes Sedai more in letter than spirit. And he seemed to recall one of the Wise Ones telling him that Masuri thought that the mad dog could be leashed. Not allowed to hop unless a Wise One said toad. It was like a blacksmith's puzzle with the edges of the metal pieces sharpened. He needed to solve it, but one mistake and he could cut himself to the bone.

From the corner of his eye, Perrin caught Balwer watching him, lips pursed in thought. A bird studying something unfamiliar, not afraid, not hungry, just curious. Gathering Stepper's reins, he walked on so quickly that the little man had to lengthen his stride into small jumps to catch up.

Two Rivers men had the segment of camp next to the Aiel, facing northeast, and Perrin considered walking a little north, to where Ghealdanin lancers were camped, or south to the nearest Mayener section, but taking a deep breath, he made himself lead his horse through his friends and neighbors from home. They were all awake, huddling in their cloaks and feeding the remnants of their shelters into the cook fires or cutting up the cold remains of last night's rabbit to add to the porridge in the kettles. Talk dwindled and the smell of wariness grew thick as heads lifted to watch him. Whetstones paused in sliding along steel, then resumed their sibilant whispering. The bow was their preferred weapon, but everyone carried a heavy dagger or a short-sword as well, or sometimes a longsword, and they had picked up spears and halberds and other polearms with strange blades and points that the Shaido had not thought worth carrying off with their pillage. Spears they were accustomed to, and hands used to wielding the quarterstaff at feastday competitions found the polearms not much different once the weight of metal on one end was accounted for. Their faces were hungry, tired and withdrawn.

Someone raised a halfhearted cry of "Goldeneyes!" but no one took it up, a thing that would have pleased Perrin a month gone. A great deal had changed since Faile was taken. Now their silence was leaden. Young Kenly Maerin, his cheeks still pale where he had scraped off his attempt at a beard, avoided meeting Perrin's eyes, and Jori Congar, lightfingered whenever he saw anything small and valuable and drunk whenever he could manage it, spat contemptuously as Perrin passed by. Ban Crawe punched Jori's shoulder for it, hard, but Ban did not look at Perrin either.

Dannil Lewin stood up, tugging nervously at the thick mustache that looked so ridiculous beneath his beak of a nose. "Orders, Lord Perrin?" The skinny man actually looked relieved when Perrin shook his head, and he sat down again quickly, staring at the nearest kettle as though he were anxious for the morning gruel. Maybe he was; nobody got a full belly lately, and Dannil had never had much spare flesh on his bones. Behind Perrin, Aram made a disgusted sound very like a growl.

There were others here besides Two Rivers folk, yet they were no better. Oh, Lamgwin Dorn, a hulking fellow with scars on his face, tugged his forelock and bobbed his head. Lamgwin looked like a shoulderthumper, a tavern tough, but he was Perrin's bodyservant now, when he had need of one, which was not often, and he might just want to keep in a good odor with his employer. But Basel Gill, the stout onetime innkeeper Faile had taken on as their *shambayan,* busied himself folding his blankets with exaggerated care, keeping his balding head down, and Faile's chief maid, Lini Eltring, a bony woman whose tight white bun made her face seem even narrower than it was, straightened from stirring a kettle, her thin lips compressed, and raised her long wooden spoon as if to fend Perrin off. Breane Taborwin, dark eyes fierce in her pale Cairhienin face, slapped Lamgwin's arm hard and frowned up at him. She was Lamgwin's woman, if not his wife, and the second of Faile's three maids. They would follow the Shaido till they dropped dead, if necessary, and fall on Faile's neck when they found her, but only Lamgwin had an ounce of welcome for Perrin. He might have gotten more from Jur Grady—the Asha'man were estranged from everyone else themselves, by who and what they were, and neither had shown any animosity toward Perrin—but despite the noise of people tramping about on the frozen snow and cursing when they slipped, Grady was still wrapped in his blankets, snoring away beneath a pine-branch lean-to. Perrin walked through his friends and neighbors and servants and felt alone. A man could only proclaim his faithfulness so long before he just gave up. The heart of his life lay somewhere to the northeast. Everything would return to normal once he had her back.

A thicket of sharpened stakes ten paces deep encircled the camp, and he went to the edge of the Ghealdanin lancers' section, where angled paths had been left for mounted men to ride out, though Balwer and Aram had to fall in behind him in the narrow way. In front of the Two Rivers men, a man afoot would have to twist and turn to make it through. The edge of the forest lay little more than a hundred paces distant, easy bowshot for Two Rivers men, huge trees thrusting a canopy high into the sky. Some of the trees here were strange to Perrin, but there were pines and leatherleaf and elms out there, some as much as three or four paces thick at the base, and oaks that were larger still. Trees that big killed anything larger than weeds or small bushes that tried to grow beneath them, leaving wide spaces between, but shadows darker than the night filled those spaces. An old forest, one that could swallow armies whole and never give up the bones.

Balwer followed him all the way through the stakes before deciding that this was as close to alone with Perrin as he was likely to get any time soon. "The riders Masema has sent out, my Lord," he said, and holding his cloak close he cast a suspicious look back at Aram, who met it with a flat stare.

"I know," Perrin said, "you think they're going to the Whitecloaks." He was eager to be moving, and that much farther from his friends. He put the hand holding his reins on the saddlebow, but refrained from putting a boot in the stirrup. Stepper tossed his head, also impatient. "Masema could be sending messages to the Seanchan just as easily."

"As you have said, my Lord. A viable possibility, to be sure. May I suggest once again, however, that Masema's view of Aes Sedai is very close to that of the Whitecloaks? In fact, identical. He would see every last sister dead, if he could. The Seanchan view is more . . . pragmatic, if I may be permitted to call it that. Less in accord with Masema, in any case."

"However much you hate Whitecloaks, Master Balwer, they aren't at the root of every evil. And Masema has dealt with the Seanchan before."

"As you say, my Lord." Balwer's face did not change,

but he reeked of doubt. Perrin could not prove Masema's meetings with the Seanchan, and telling anyone how he had learned of them would only add to his present difficulties. That gave Balwer problems; he was a man who liked evidence. "As for the Aes Sedai and the Wise Ones, my Lord. . . . Aes Sedai always seem to believe they know better than anyone else, except possibly another Aes Sedai. I believe the Wise Ones are much the same."

Perrin snorted brief white plumes in the air. "Tell me something I don't know. Like why Masuri would meet with Masema, and why the Wise Ones allowed it. I'll wager Stepper against a horseshoe nail she didn't do it without their permission." Annoura was another question, but she could be acting on her own. It certainly seemed unlikely she was acting at Berelain's behest.

Shifting his cloak on his shoulders, Balwer peered back across the rows of sharpened stakes into the camp, toward the Aiel tents, squinting as if he hoped to see through the tent walls. "There are many possibilities, my Lord," he said testily. "For some who swear an oath, whatever is not forbidden is permitted, and whatever is not commanded can be ignored. Others take actions they believe will help their liege without first asking permission. The Aes Sedai and the Wise Ones fall into one of those categories, it seems, but further than that, I can only speculate, as matters stand."

"I could just ask. Aes Sedai can't lie, and if I press hard enough, Masuri might actually tell me the truth."

Balwer grimaced as though at a sudden stomach pain. "Perhaps, my Lord. Perhaps. More likely is that she would tell you something that sounds like the truth. Aes Sedai are experienced in that, as you know. In any event, my Lord, Masuri would wonder how you knew to ask, and that line of thought might lead to Haviar and Nerion. Under the circumstances, who can say who she might tell? Straightforward is not always the best way. Sometimes, certain things must be done behind masks, for safety."

"I told you the Aes Sedai couldn't be trusted," Aram said abruptly. "I told you that, Lord Perrin." He fell silent when Perrin raised a hand, but the stink of fury from him was so strong that Perrin had to exhale to clear his lungs. Part of him wanted to draw the scent deep and let it consume him.

Perrin studied Balwer carefully. If Aes Sedai could twist

the truth till you could not tell up from down, and they could and did, how far could you trust? Trust was always the question. He had learned that in hard lessons. He took a firm check on his anger, though. A hammer had to be used with care, and he was working a forge where one slip would tear the heart out of his chest. "And might matters change if some of Selande's friends began spending more time among the Aiel? They want to be Aiel, after all. That ought to give them enough excuse. And maybe one of them can strike up a friendship with Berelain, and with her advisor."

"That should be possible, my Lord," Balwer said after the slightest hesitation. "Lady Medore's father is a High Lord of Tear, giving her sufficient rank to approach the First of Mayene, and also a reason. Possibly one or two of the Cairhienin stand high enough, as well. Finding those to live among the Aiel will be easier still."

Perrin nodded. Infinite care with the hammer, however much you wanted to smash whatever lay within reach. "Then do it. But, Master Balwer, you've been trying to . . . guide . . . me to this since Selande left us. From now on, if you have a suggestion to make, make it. Even if I say no to nine in a row, I'll always listen to a tenth. I'm not a clever man, but I'm willing to listen to people who are, and I think you are. Just don't try poking me in the direction you want me to go. I don't like that, Master Balwer."

Balwer blinked, then of all things, bowed with his hands folded at his waist. He smelled surprised. And gratified. Gratified? "As you say, my Lord. My previous employer disliked me suggesting actions unless I was asked. I won't make the same mistake again, I assure you." Eyeing Perrin, he seemed to reach a decision. "If I may say so," he said carefully, "I have found serving you . . . pleasant . . . in ways I did not expect. You are what you seem, my Lord, with no poisoned needles hidden away to catch the unwary. My previous employer was known widely for cleverness, but I believe you are equally clever, in a different way. I believe I would regret leaving your service. Any man might say these things to keep his place, but I mean them."

Poisoned needles? Before entering Perrin's service, Balwer's last employment had been as secretary to a Murandian noblewoman fallen into hard times who could no longer afford to keep him. Murandy must be a rougher place than

Perrin thought. "I see no reason for you to leave my employ. Just tell me what you want to do and let me decide, don't try to prod. And forget the flattery."

"I never flatter, my Lord. But I am adept at shaping myself to my master's needs; it is a requirement of my profession." The little man bowed once more. He had never been this formal before. "If you have no further questions, my Lord, may I go to find the Lady Medore?"

Perrin nodded. The little man bowed yet again, backing away, then went skittering toward the camp, his cloak fluttering behind him as he dodged through the sharpened stakes like a sparrow hopping across the snow. He was a strange fellow.

"I don't trust him," Aram muttered, staring after Balwer. "And I don't trust Selande and that lot. They'll throw in with the Aes Sedai, you mark my words."

"You have to trust somebody," Perrin said roughly. The question was, who? Swinging into Stepper's saddle, he booted the dun in the ribs. A hammer was useless lying at rest.

CHAPTER
6

The Scent of a Dream

The cold air seemed clean and fresh in Perrin's nose as he galloped into the forest, the breezes full of the crispness of the snow that fountained in sprays beneath Stepper's hooves. Out here, he could forget old friends who were willing to believe the worst on rumor. He could try to forget Masema, and the Aes Sedai, and the Wise Ones. The Shaido were welded to the inside of his skull, however, an iron puzzle that would not yield no matter how he twisted. He wanted to wrench it apart, but that never worked with a blacksmith's puzzle.

After one short burst of speed, he slowed the dun to a walk, feeling a touch of guilt. The darkness beneath the forest canopy was deep, and stone outcrops between the tall trees warned of more hidden beneath the snow, a hundred places that could break a running horse's leg, and that without counting gopher holes and fox dens and badger sets. There was no need to take the risk. A gallop would not free Faile an hour sooner, and no horse could maintain that pace for long in any case. The snow here was knee-deep in places where it had drifted, and deep enough elsewhere. He rode northeast, though. The scouts would be coming from the northeast, with news of Faile. News of the Shaido, at least, a location. He had hoped for that so often, prayed for it, but today, he knew it would come. Yet knowing only increased his anxiety. Finding them was only the first part of solving this puzzle. Anger made his mind flash from one thing to another, yet no matter what Balwer said, Perrin knew he was methodical at best. He did not do well trying to think quickly, and lacking cleverness, methodical was going to have to do. Somehow.

Aram caught up to him, running his gray hard, and slowed to ride just a little behind and to one side like a heeling hound. Perrin let him. Aram never smelled comfortable when Perrin made him ride alongside. The onetime Tinker did not speak, but eddies in the icy air brought his scent, a melange of anger and suspicion and disgruntlement. He sat his saddle as tense as an over-wound clockspring and watched the forest around them grimly, as though he expected Shaido to leap out from behind the nearest tree.

In truth, almost anything could have hidden from most men in these woods. Where the sky overhead could be seen through the canopy of branches, it held a definite tinge of dark grayness, but for the moment that cast the forest in shadows murkier than night, and the trees themselves were massive columns of darkness. Yet even the shift of a black-winged jackdaw on a snow-mounded branch, its feathers fluffed against the cold, caught Perrin's eyes, and a hunting pine martin, a deeper black than the darkness, cautiously raising its head on another. He caught the scent of both, too. A faint whiff of man scent came from up in a massive oak with dark spreading limbs as thick as a pony. The Ghealdanin and Mayeners had their mounted patrols circling the camp a few miles out, but he preferred to rely on Two Rivers men closer in. He did not have enough men to ring the camp completely, yet they were used to forests, and to hunting animals that might hunt them in turn, used to noticing movement that would escape a man thinking in terms of soldiers and war. Ridgecats down from the mountains after sheep could hide in plain sight, and bear and wild boar were known to double back on their pursuers and lie in ambush. From branches thirty and forty feet above the ground, the men could see anything that moved below in time to warn the camp, and with their longbows, they could exact a heavy price from anyone who tried to force a way past them. Yet the presence of the guard touched his mind as lightly as the presence of the jackdaw. He was focused ahead through the trees and the shadows, intent on picking out the first sign of the scouts returning.

Abruptly Stepper tossed his head and snorted in a spew

of mist, eyes rolling in fear as he stopped dead, and Aram's gray squealed and shied. Perrin leaned forward to pat the trembling stallion's neck, but his hand froze as he caught a trace of scent, a smell of burned sulphur faint in the air, that made the hair on the back of his neck try to stand. Almost burnt sulphur; that was only a pale imitation of this smell. It had a reek of . . . wrongness, of something that did not belong in this world. The scent was not new—you could not ever have called that stink "fresh"—but not old, either. An hour, perhaps less. Maybe about the time he had wakened. About the time he had dreamed of this scent.

"What is it, Lord Perrin?" Aram was having difficulty controlling his gray, which danced in circles fighting the reins and wanting to run in any direction so long as it was away, but even while sawing at his reins he had his wolfhead-pommeled sword out. He practiced with it daily, for hours on end when he could, and those who knew about such things said he was good. "You may be able to make out a black thread from a white in this, but it isn't day yet to me. I can't see anything well enough to matter."

"Put that away," Perrin told him. "It isn't needed. Swords wouldn't do any good, anyway." He had to coax his trembling mount to move forward, but he followed the rank smell, scanning the snow-covered ground ahead. He knew that smell, and not just from the dream.

It only took a little while to find what he was looking for, and Stepper gave a grateful whicker when Perrin reined him in well short of a slab-like crest of gray stone, two paces wide, that jutted up to his right. The snow all around was smooth and unmarked, but dog tracks covered the tilted span of stone, as though a pack had scrambled over it as they ran. Dimness and shadows or no, they were plain to Perrin's eyes. Footprints larger than the palm of his hand, pressed into the stone as though it had been mud. He patted Stepper's neck again. No wonder the animal was frightened.

"Go back to the camp and find Dannil, Aram. Tell him I said to let everyone know there were Darkhounds here, maybe an hour ago. And put your sword away. You wouldn't want to try killing a Darkhound with a sword, believe me."

"Darkhounds?" Aram exclaimed, peering around into the murky shadows between the trees. There was an anxious fear in his scent, now. Most men would have laughed about travelers' tales or stories for children. Tinkers roamed the countryside, and knew what could be found in the wilds. Aram sheathed the sword on his back with obvious reluctance, but his right hand remained raised, half-reaching for the hilt. "How do you kill a Darkhound? Can they be killed?" Then again, maybe he did not have much good sense at that.

"Just be glad you don't have to try, Aram. Now go do like I told you. Everyone needs to keep a sharp lookout in case they come back. Not much chance of that, I'd say, but better safe." Perrin remembered facing a pack of them once, and killing one. He thought he had killed one, after hitting it with three good broadhead arrows. Shadowspawn did not die easily. Moiraine had had to finish that pack, with balefire. "Make sure the Aes Sedai and Wise Ones learn of this, and the Asha'man." Small chance any of them knew how to make balefire—the women might not admit knowing a forbidden weave if they did, and maybe not the men either—but maybe they knew something else that could work.

Aram was reluctant to leave Perrin alone until Perrin snapped at him, and then he turned back toward the camp trailing smells of umbrage and hurt, as if two men would have been a whit safer than one. As soon as the other man was out of sight, Perrin reined Stepper southward, the direction the Darkhounds had been heading. He did not want company for this, even Aram's. Just because people sometimes noted his sharp eyesight was no reason to flaunt it, or his sense of smell. There were already reasons enough to shun him without adding more.

It might have been chance that the creatures had passed so near his camp, but the last few years had made him uneasy with coincidences. All too often, they were not coincidence at all, not the way other men counted such things. If this was another bit of his *ta'veren* tugging at the Pattern, it was a bit he could have done without. The thing seemed to have more disadvantages than advantages even when it appeared to be working in your favor. The chance that favored you one minute could turn on you in the next. And there was always another possibility. Being *ta'veren* made you stand out in the Pattern, and some of the Forsaken could use that to find you at times, or so he had been told. Maybe some Shadowspawn could, too.

The trail he followed was surely near an hour old, but Perrin felt a tightness between his shoulder blades, a prickling on his scalp. The sky was still a deep dark gray where it showed, even to his eyes. The sun had not yet crested the horizon. Just before sunrise was one of the worst times to meet the Wild Hunt, when darkness was changing to light but the light had not taken hold. At least there was no crossroads nearby, no graveyard, but the only hearthstones to touch lay back in Brytan, and he was not certain how much safety those hovels held. In his mind, he marked out the location of a nearby stream, where the camp got its water by chopping through the ice. It was no more than ten or twelve paces wide and only knee-deep, but putting running water between you and Darkhounds would stop them supposedly. But then, so would facing them, supposedly, and he had seen the results of that. His nose tested the breezes, searching for that old scent. And for any hint of a newer. Coming on those things unaware would be worse than unpleasant.

Stepper caught scents almost as easily as Perrin, and sometimes noticed what they were sooner, but whenever the dun balked, Perrin forced him forward. There were plenty of tracks scattered in the snow, hoofprints of the mounted patrols going out and coming back, occasional sign of rabbits and foxes, but the only marks left by the Darkhounds were where stone stuck up out of the snow. The burnt sulphur smell was always strongest there, yet enough trace lingered in between to lead him to the next place where their tracks showed. The huge pawprints overlapped one another, and there was no way to tell how many Darkhounds there had been, but whether a pace wide or six, every rock surface they had crossed was smothered in tracks from one side to the other. A larger pack than the ten he had seen outside Illian. Much larger. Was that why there were no wolves in the area? He was sure that the certainty of death he had felt in the dream was something real, and he had *been* a wolf in the dream.

As the trail began to curve to the west, he felt a growing suspicion that firmed into certainty as it continued to bend. The Darkhounds had circled the camp completely, running right across the place north of the camp where several huge trees lay half toppled and propped by their neighbors, each with a tall chunk sliced cleanly out of its splintered trunk.

The tracks covered a stone outcrop as smooth and flat as a polished marble floor except for one hair-thin gouge cut through it straight as a plumb line. Nothing resisted the opening of an Asha'man's gateway, and two had opened here. A thick pine that had fallen blocking one had a section four paces wide burned out of it, but the charred ends were as neat as if they had come from a sawmill. It seemed that evidence of the One Power did not interest Darkhounds, however. The pack had not paused there any more than anywhere else, or even slowed that he could tell. Darkhounds could run faster than horses, and for longer, and the stench of them hardly seemed to have faded more in one place than another. At two points in that circuit he had picked up a forking in the trail, but that was only the pack coming from the north and departing south. Once around the camp, and then on their way after whatever or whoever they were hunting.

Plainly, that was not him. Perhaps the pack had circled because they sensed him, sensed someone who was *ta'veren*, yet he doubted that Darkhounds would have hesitated one instant at coming into the camp, had they been after him. The pack he had faced before had entered the city of Illian, though it had not tried to kill him till later. But did Darkhounds report what they saw, the way rats and ravens did? The thought made his jaw clench. The Shadow's attention was something any sane man feared, the Shadow's attention might interfere with freeing Faile. That concerned him more than anything else. Yet there were ways to fight Shadowspawn, ways to fight the Forsaken, if it came to that. Whatever came between him and Faile, Darkhounds or the Forsaken or anything else, he would find a way to go around or through, whichever was necessary. A man could only have so much fear in him at one time, and all of his fear was centered on Faile. There just was no room for any more.

Before he reached his starting place again, the breezes brought him the smells of people and horses, sharp in the icy cold, and he reined Stepper to a slow walk, and then to a halt. He had spotted some fifty or sixty horses near a hundred paces ahead. The sun had finally peeked above the horizon and begun to send sharply slanted shafts of light through the forest canopy, reflecting off the snow and lessening the gloom a little, though deep, dappled shadows remained between the sun's slender fingers. Some of those shadows enveloped him. The mounted party was not far from where he had first seen the Darkhounds' tracks, and he could see Aram's sickly green cloak and red-striped coat, the Tinker garments jarring with the sword on his back. Most of the riders wore rimmed red helmets shaped like pots and dark cloaks over red breastplates, and the long red streamers on their lances stirred in the light airs as the soldiers tried to keep watch in every direction. The First of Mayene often rode out in the mornings, with a suitable bodyguard of the Winged Guards.

He started to slip away without having to meet Berelain, but then he saw three tall women afoot among the horses, long dark shawls wrapped around their heads and draped over their upper bodies, and he hesitated. Wise Ones rode when they had to, if unwillingly, but tramping a mile or two in the snow wearing heavy woolen skirts was insufficient reason to force them onto horseback. Almost certainly Seonid or Masuri was in that group, as well, though the Aiel women seemed to like Berelain for some reason he could not fathom.

He had no thought of joining the riders, no matter who was with them, but hesitation cost him his chance at evasion. One of the Wise Ones—he thought it was Carelle, a fire-haired woman who always had a challenge in her sharp blue eyes—raised a hand to point in his direction, and the whole party turned, the soldiers whipping their horses around and peering through the trees toward him, lances tipped with a foot of steel half lowered. It was unlikely they could make him out clearly through the deep pools of shadow and bright bars of sunlight. He was surprised the Wise One had, but then, Aiel generally had sharp eyes.

Masuri was there, a slim woman in a bronze-colored cloak riding a dapple mare, and Annoura as well, keeping her brown mare well back but marked by the dozens of thin dark braids that hung from the opening of her cowl. Berelain herself sat a sleek bay gelding at the forefront, a tall beautiful young woman with long black hair, in a red cloak lined with black fur. A simple flaw lessened her beauty, though; she was not Faile. A worse flaw ruined it, as far as he was concerned. He had learned of Faile's kidnapping from her, and of Masema's contact with the Seanchan, but nearly everyone in the camp believed that he had slept with Berelain on the very night Faile was taken, and she had done nothing to correct the tale. It was hardly the kind of story he could ask her to stand up and deny publicly, yet she could have said something, told her maids to deny it, anything. Instead, Berelain held her silence, and her maids, gossiping like magpies, actually fostered the tale. That sort of reputation stuck to a man, in the Two Rivers.

He had avoided Berelain since that night, and he would have ridden away now even after they saw him, but she took a hoop-handled basket from the maid accompanying her, a plump woman wrapped in a blue-and-gold cloak, then spoke to the others and started her sleek bay gelding toward him. Alone. Annoura raised a hand and called something after her, but Berelain never glanced back. Perrin did not doubt she would follow wherever he went, and the way things were, leaving would only make people believe he wanted to be private with her. He dug his heels into Stepper's flanks, meaning to join the others no matter how little he wanted to—let her follow him back to them if she wanted—but she urged the bay to a canter despite the rough ground and the snow, even leaping a stone outcrop, her red cloak flowing out behind her, and met him halfway. She was a good rider, he admitted grudgingly. Not as good as Faile, but better than most.

"Your scowl is quite fierce," she laughed softly as she halted right in front of Stepper. From the way she held her reins, she was ready to block him if he tried going around. The woman had no shame at all! "Smile, so people think we are flirting." She pushed the basket at him with one crimson-gloved hand. "This should make you smile, at least. I hear you forget to eat." Her nose wrinkled. "And to wash, it seems. Your beard needs trimming, too. A careworn, somewhat disheveled husband rescuing his wife is a romantic figure, but she might not think so well of a dirty ragamuffin. No woman will ever forgive you ruining her image of you."

Suddenly confused, Perrin took the basket, sitting it in front of him on the tall pommel of his saddle, and unconsciously rubbed at his nose. He was accustomed to certain smells from Berelain, usually those of a hunting she-wolf, and he was the intended prey, but today she gave off no hunting scent. Not a whisker of it. She smelled patient as stone, and amused, with undercurrents of fear. The woman certainly had never been afraid of him that he recalled. And what did she have to be patient about? For that matter, what did she have to be amused about? A ridge cat smelling like a lamb would not have confounded him more.

Confusion or no, his stomach rumbled at the aromas drifting from the lidded basket. Roasted woodhen, unless he was much mistaken, and bread still warm from the baking. Flour was in short supply, and bread almost as rare as meat. It was true that he missed eating some days. He really did forget, sometimes, and when he remembered, eating was a chore, for he had to run the gauntlet of Lini and Breane or be given the cold shoulder by people he had grown up with just to get a meal. Food right under his nose made his mouth water. Would it be disloyal to eat food brought by Berelain?

"Thank you for the loaf and the woodhen," he said roughly, "but the last thing on earth I want is for anyone to think we're flirting. And I wash when I can, if it's any of your business. It isn't easy in this weather. Besides, nobody else smells any better than I do." She did, he realized suddenly. There was no hint of sweat or dirt under her light, flowery perfume. It irritated him that he had noticed she was wearing perfume, or that she smelled clean. It seemed a betrayal.

Berelain's eyes widened momentarily in startlement—why?—but then she sighed through her smile, which was beginning to look fixed, and a thread of irritation entered her scent. "Have your tent set up. I know there's a good copper bathtub in one of your carts. You won't have thrown that out. People expect a noble to look like a noble, Perrin, and that includes being presentable, even when it takes extra effort. It's a bargain between you and them. You must give them what they expect as well as what they need or want, or they lose respect and start resenting you for making them lose it. Frankly, none of us can afford for you to let that happen. We're all far from our homes, surrounded by enemies, and I very much believe that you, Lord Perrin Goldeneyes, may be our only chance of living to reach our homes again. Without you, everything falls apart. Now smile, because if we're flirting, then we aren't talking about something else."

Perrin bared his teeth. The Mayeners and the Wise Ones were watching, but at fifty paces, in this gloom, it would be taken for a smile. Lose respect? Berelain had helped strip him of any respect he once had from the Two Rivers folk, not to mention Faile's servants. Worse, Faile had given him some version of that lecture about a noble's duty to give people what they expected more than once. What *he* resented was hearing this woman, of all people, echo his wife. "What are we talking about, then, that you don't trust your own people to know?"

Her face remained smooth and smiling, yet the undercurrent of fear in her scent strengthened. It was nowhere near panic, but she believed herself in danger. Her gloved hands were tight on the bay's reins. "I've had my thief-catchers nosing about in Masema's camp, making 'friends.' Not as good as having eyes-and-ears there, but they took wine they supposedly stole from me, and they learned a little by listening." For an instant she regarded him quizzically, tilting her head. Light! She knew Faile used Selande and those other idiots as spies! It had been Berelain who told him about them in the first place. Likely Gendar and Santes, her thief-catchers, had seen Haviar and Nerion in Masema's camp. Balwer would have to be warned before he tried to set Medore on Berelain and Annoura. That would certainly make a fine tangle.

When he said nothing, she went on. "I put something in that basket besides bread and a woodhen. A . . . document . . . that Santes found early yesterday, locked away in Masema's camp desk. The fool never saw a lock without wanting to know what it hid. If he had to meddle with what Masema kept under lock and key, he should have memorized the thing instead of taking it, but what's done is done. Don't let anyone see you reading it after I went to all this trouble to hide it!" she added sharply as he lifted the basket's lid, revealing a cloth-wrapped bundle and releasing stronger smells of roasted bird and warm bread. "I've seen Masema's men following you before. They could be watching now!"

"I'm not a fool," he growled. He knew about Masema's watchers. Most of the man's followers were townsmen, and most of the rest awkward enough in the woods to shame a ten-year-old back home. Which was not to say one or two might not be hiding somewhere among the trees close enough to spy from among the shadows. They always kept their distance, since his eyes made them believe he was some sort of half-tame Shadowspawn, so he seldom detected their scents, and he had had other things on his mind this morning.

Fingering the cloth aside to expose the woodhen, almost as large as a fair-sized chicken, with its skin crisply browned, he tore off one of the bird's legs while feeling under the bundle and sliding out a piece of heavy, cream-colored paper folded in four. Careless of grease spots, he unfolded the paper atop the bird, a little clumsily in his gauntlets, and read while nibbling on the leg. To everyone watching, he would appear to be studying what part of the woodhen to attack next. A thick green wax seal, cracked on one side, held an impression of what he decided were three hands, each with the forefinger and little finger raised and the others folded. The letters written on the paper in a flowing script were oddly formed, some unrecognizable, but the thing was readable with a little effort.

The bearer of this stands under my personal protection. In the name of the Empress, may she live forever, give him whatever aid he requires in service to the Empire and speak of it to none but me.

By her seal
Suroth Sabelle Meldarath
of Asinbayar and Barsabba
High Lady

"The Empress," he said softly, soft like iron brushing silk. Confirmation of Masema's dealings with the Seanchan, though for himself, he had needed none. It was not the sort of thing Berelain would have lied about. Suroth Sabelle Meldarath must be someone important, to be handing out this kind of document. "This will finish him, once Santes testified where he found it." Service to the Empire? Masema knew Rand had fought the Seanchan! That rainbow burst into his head, and was swept away. The man was a traitor!

Berelain laughed as if he had said something witty, but her smile definitely looked forced, now. "Santes told me no one saw him in the bustle of setting up camp, so I allowed him and Gendar to go back with my last cask of good Tunaighan. They were supposed to return by an hour after dark, but neither has. I suppose they could be sleeping it off, but they've never—"

She broke off with a startled sound, staring at him, and he realized that he had bitten the thighbone in half. Light, he had stripped all the flesh from the leg without noticing. "I'm hungrier than I thought," he muttered. Spitting the nub of bone into the palm of his gauntlet, he dropped the pieces to the ground. "It's safe to assume Masema knows you have this. I hope you're keeping a heavy guard around you all the time, not just when you ride out."

"Gallenne has fifty men sleeping around my tent as of last night," she said, still staring, and he sighed. You would think she had never seen anybody bite a bone in two before.

"What has Annoura told you?"

"She wanted me to give it to her to destroy, so if I was asked, I could say I didn't have it and didn't know where it was, and she could support my word. I doubt that would satisfy Masema, though."

"No, I doubt it would." Annoura had to know that, too. Aes Sedai could be wrongheaded, or even foolish upon occasion, but they were never stupid. "Did she say she would destroy it, or that if you gave it to her, she could?"

Berelain's brow furrowed in thought, and it took her a moment to say, "That she would." The bay danced a few impatient steps, but she brought him under control easily, without paying attention. "I can't think what else she would want it for," she said after another pause. "Masema is hardly likely to be susceptible to . . . pressure." Blackmail, she meant. Perrin could not see Masema standing still for that either. Especially blackmail by an Aes Sedai.

Under cover of tearing the other leg loose from the bird, he managed to refold the piece of paper and tuck it into his sleeve, where his gauntlet would keep it from falling out. It was still evidence. But of what? How could the man be both a fanatic for the Dragon Reborn and a traitor? Could he have taken the document from . . . ? Who? Some collaborator he had captured? But why would Masema keep it locked away unless it had been meant for him? He *had* met with Seanchan. And how had he intended to use it? Who could tell what a thing this would allow a man to call on? Perrin sighed heavily. He had too many questions, and no answers. Answers required a quicker mind than his. Maybe Balwer would have a notion.

With a taste of food in it, his stomach wanted him to devour the leg in his hand and the rest of the bird too, but he closed the lid firmly and tried to take measured bites. There was one thing he could find out for himself. "What else has Annoura said? About Masema."

"Nothing, besides that he's dangerous and I should avoid him, as if I didn't know that already. She dislikes him and talking about him." Another brief hesitation, and Berelain added, "Why?" The First of Mayene was used to intrigues, and she listened for what was not said.

Perrin took another bite to give himself a moment while he chewed and swallowed. He was *not* used to intrigues, yet he had been exposed to enough of them to know that saying too much could be dangerous. So could saying too little, no matter what Balwer thought. "Annoura has been meeting with Masema in secret. So has Masuri."

Berelain's fixed smile remained in place, but alarm entered her scent. She started to twist in her saddle as if to look back at the two Aes Sedai, and stopped herself, licking her lips with the tip of her tongue. "Aes Sedai always have their reasons" was all she said. So, was she alarmed over her advisor meeting Masema, or alarmed that Perrin knew, or . . . ? He hated all these complications. They just got in the way of what was important. Light, he had managed to clean the second leg already! Hoping Berelain had not noticed, he hastily tossed the bones aside. His belly growled for more.

Her people had maintained their distance, but Aram had ridden a short way toward Perrin and Berelain and was leaning forward to peer at them through the shadowed trees. The Wise Ones were standing to one side talking among themselves, seemingly unaware that they were over their ankles in snow or that the cold breezes had picked up enough to flap the dangling ends of their shawls. Every so often one or another of the three looked Perrin and Berelain's way, too. Notions of privacy never kept a Wise One from sticking her nose wherever she wanted. They were like Aes Sedai that way. Masuri and Annoura were watching, too, though they appeared to be keeping their distance from one another. Perrin would have wagered that without the Wise Ones there, both sisters would have been using the One Power to eavesdrop. Of course, the Wise Ones probably knew how to do that, too, and they had allowed Masuri's visits to Masema. Would either Aes Sedai crack her teeth if they saw the Wise Ones listening with the Power? Annoura seemed almost as careful with the Wise Ones as Masuri was. Light, he had no time for this briar thicket! He had to live in it, though.

"We've given tongues enough to wag over," he said. Not that they needed any more than they had. Hooking the basket's hoop-handles over his pommel, he heeled Stepper's flanks. It could hardly be disloyal just to eat a bird.

Berelain did not follow immediately, yet before he reached Aram, she caught up and slowed her bay beside him. "I'll find out what Annoura is up to," she said determinedly, looking straight ahead. Her eyes were hard. Perrin would have pitied Annoura, if he had not been ready to try shaking answers out of her himself. But then, Aes Sedai seldom needed pity, and they seldom gave answers they did not want to give. The next instant, Berelain was all smiles and gaiety again, though the scent of determination still hung about her, almost crushing the fear scent. "Young Aram has been telling us all about Heartsbane riding these woods with the Wild Hunt, Lord Perrin. Could it really be so, do you think? I remember hearing those tales in the nursery." Her voice was light and amused and carrying. Aram's cheeks turned red, and some of the men beyond him laughed.

They stopped laughing when Perrin showed them the tracks in the stone slab.

CHAPTER

7

Blacksmith's Puzzle

When the laughter cut off, Aram put on a smug grin, and with none of the fear scent he had given off earlier. Anyone would have thought he had already seen the tracks himself and knew everything there was to know. No one paid any mind to his smirk, however, or to much of anything except the huge dog tracks impressed in stone, even Perrin's explanation that the Darkhounds were long gone. Of course, he could not tell them how he knew that, yet no one seemed to notice the lack. One of the sharply slanting bars of early morning light was falling directly on the gray slab, illuminating it clearly. Stepper had grown accustomed to the fading burnt-sulphur smell—at least he only snorted and laid back his ears—but the other horses shied at the tilted stone. None of the humans except Perrin could detect that smell, and most growled over their mounts' fractious behavior and peered at the oddly marked stone as if it were a curiosity displayed by a traveling show.

Berelain's plump maid screamed when she saw the tracks, and swayed on the point of falling off her round-bellied, nervously dancing mare, but Berelain merely asked Annoura in an absent fashion to look after her and stared at the prints with as little expression as if she herself were Aes Sedai. Her hands tightened on her reins, though, until the thin red leather paled across her knuckles. Bertain Gallenne, the Lord Captain of the Winged Guards, his red helmet embossed with wings and bearing three thin crimson plumes, had personal command of Berelain's bodyguard this morning, and he forced his tall black gelding close to the stone, swinging down from his saddle in knee-deep snow and removing his helmet to frown at the stone slab with his one eye. A scarlet leather patch covered the empty socket of the other, the strap cutting through his shoulder-length gray hair. His grimace said he saw trouble, but he always saw the worst possibilities first. Perrin supposed that was better in a soldier than always seeing the best.

Masuri dismounted, too, but no sooner was she on the ground than she paused with her dapple's reins in one gloved hand, looking uncertainly toward the three sun-dark Aiel women. A few of the Mayener soldiers muttered un-easily at that, yet they should have been used to it by now. Annoura hid her face deeper in her gray hood as if she did not want to see the rock and gave Berelain's maid a brisk shake; the woman goggled at her in astonishment. Masuri, on the other hand, waited beside her mare with an appear-ance of patience, spoiled only by smoothing the russet skirts of her silk riding dress as though unaware of what she was doing. The Wise Ones exchanged silent glances, expressionless as sisters themselves. Carelle stood on one side of Nevarin, a skinny green-eyed woman, and on the other Marline, with eyes of twilight blue and dark hair, rare among Aiel, not covered completely with her shawl. All three were tall women, as tall as some men, and none looked more than a few years older than Perrin, but no one could have managed that calm self-assurance without more years than their faces claimed. Despite the long necklaces and heavy bracelets of gold and ivory that they wore, their dark heavy skirts and the dark shawls that almost hid their white blouses could have suited farm women, yet there was no doubt who was in command between them and the Aes Sedai. In truth, sometimes there seemed to be doubt who was in command between them and Perrin.

Finally, Nevarin nodded. And gave a warm and approv-ing smile. Perrin had never before seen a smile out of her. Nevarin did not walk around scowling, but she usually seemed to be searching for someone to upbraid.

Not until that nod did Masuri hand her reins up to one of the soldiers. Her Warder was nowhere to be seen, and that had to be the Wise Ones' doing. Rovair usually stuck to her like a burr. Lifting her divided skirts, she waded through the snow, deeper the closer to the stone she came, and began passing her hands above the footprints, obviously channeling, though nothing happened that Perrin could see. The Wise Ones watched her closely, but then, Masuri's weaves were visible to them. Annoura displayed no interest. The ends of the Gray sister's narrow braids twitched as if she were shaking her head inside her hood, and she moved her horse back from the maid, well out of the Wise Ones' line of sight, though that took her farther from Berelain, who anyone could think might want her advice now. Annoura really did avoid the Wise Ones as much as she could.

"Fireside stories walking," Gallenne muttered, drawing his gelding away from the stone with a sideways glance at Masuri. Aes Sedai, he honored, yet few men wanted to be close to an Aes Sedai who was channeling. "Though I don't know why I'm surprised anymore after what I've seen since leaving Mayene." Intent on the tracks, Masuri did not seem to notice him.

A stir rippled through the mounted lancers, as though they had not really believed their own eyes until their commander gave confirmation, and some of them began to smell of uneasy fear, as if expecting Darkhounds to leap out of the shadows. Perrin could not pick out individuals among so many with any ease, but the jittery rankness was strong enough that it had to come from more than a few.

Gallenne seemed to sense what Perrin smelled; he had his faults, but he had commanded soldiers for a long time. Hanging his helmet on his long sword hilt, he grinned. The eyepatch gave it a grim quality, a man who could see a joke in the face of death and expected others to see it, too. "If the Black Dogs bother us, we'll salt their ears," he announced in a loud and hearty voice. "That's what you do in the stories, isn't it? Sprinkle salt on their ears, and they vanish." A few of the lancers laughed, though the miasma of fear did not lessen appreciably. Stories told by the fire were one thing, those same stories walking in the flesh quite another.

Gallenne led his black to Berelain and rested a gauntleted hand on her bay's neck. He gave Perrin a considering look that Perrin returned levelly, refusing to take the hint. Whatever the man had to say, he could say in front of him and Aram. Gallenne sighed. "They will keep their nerve, my Lady," he said softly, "but the fact is, our position is precarious, with enemies on every side and our supplies running out. Shadowspawn can only make matters worse. My duty is to you and Mayene, my Lady, and with all respect to Lord Perrin, you may wish to alter your plans." Anger crackled in Perrin—the man would abandon Faile!—but Berelain spoke before he could suggest it.

"There will be no alteration, Lord Gallenne." Sometimes it was easy to forget that she was a ruler, small though Mayene was, but there was a regal note in her voice fit for the Queen of Andor. Back straight, she made her saddle seem a throne, and she spoke loudly enough to make sure everyone heard her decision, firmly enough that everyone knew the decision *had* been made. "If we have enemies all around, then going on is as safe as turning back or turning aside. Yet if turning back or turning aside were ten times safer, I would still go on. I intend to see the Lady Faile rescued if we must fight our way through a thousand Darkhounds, and Trollocs as well. That I have sworn to do!"

A roar of cheers answered her, Winged Guards shouting and thrusting their lances into the air so the red streamers danced. The smell of fear remained, but they sounded ready to cut their way through any number of Trollocs rather than appear less in Berelain's eyes. Gallenne commanded them, but they felt more than fondness for their ruler, despite her reputation with men. Maybe because of it, in part. Berelain had kept Tear from swallowing Mayene by playing one man who found her beautiful against another. For his part, Perrin found it hard not to gape in surprise. She sounded as determined as he was! She *smelled* as determined! Gallenne bowed his gray head in unwilling acceptance, and Berelain gave a small, satisfied nod before turning her attention to the Aes Sedai beside the stone slab.

Masuri had stopped waving her hands about and was staring at the footprints, tapping a finger against her lips thoughtfully. She was a pretty woman without being beautiful, though some of that might have been Aes Sedai agelessness, with a grace and elegance that might also have come from being Aes Sedai. It was often difficult to tell a sister who had been born on a hardscrabble farm from one born in a grand palace. Perrin had seen her red-faced and angry, worn down and on the end of her tether, yet despite hard travel and life in the Aiel tents, her dark hair and her clothing looked as though she had a maid attending her, too. She might have been standing in a library.

"What have you learned, Masuri?" Berelain asked. "Masuri, if you please? Masuri?"

The last came a little more sharply, and Masuri gave a start, as though surprised to realize she was not alone. Possibly she was startled; in many ways she seemed more of the Green Ajah than the Brown, more intent on action than on contemplation, straight to the point and never vague, yet she was still capable of losing herself completely in whatever captured her interest. Folding her hands at her waist, she opened her mouth, but rather than speaking, she hesitated and looked a question at the Wise Ones.

"Go on, girl," Nevarin said impatiently, planting her fists on her hips in a jangle of bracelets. A frown made her appear more her usual self, but neither of the other Wise Ones looked any more approving. Three frowns in a row like three pale-eyed crows on a fence. "We were not simply letting you exercise your curiosity. Get on with it. Tell us what you learned."

Masuri's face reddened, but she spoke up immediately, her eyes on Berelain. She could not like being called down in public, no matter what anyone knew of her relationship with the Wise Ones. "Relatively little is known of Darkhounds, but I've made something of a study of them, in a small way. Over the years, I have crossed the paths of seven packs, five of them twice and two others three times." The color began to fade from her cheeks, and slowly she began to sound as if she were lecturing. "Some ancient writers say there *are* only seven packs, others say nine, or thirteen, or some other number they believed had special significance, but during the Trolloc Wars, Sorelana Alsahhan wrote of 'the hundred packs of the Shadow's hounds that hunt the night,' and even earlier, Ivonell Bharatiya supposedly wrote of 'hounds born of the Shadow, in numbers like unto the nightmares of mankind.' Though in truth, Ivonell herself may be apocryphal. In any case, the—" She gestured as if groping for a word. "Smell is not the right word, and neither is flavor. The sense of each pack is unique, and I can say with certainty that I have never encountered this one before, so we know the number seven is wrong. Whether the correct number is nine or thirteen or something else, tales of Darkhounds are much more common than Darkhounds themselves, and they are extremely rare this far south of the Blight. A second rarity: there may have been as many as fifty in this pack. Ten or twelve is the usual limit. A useful maxim: two rarities combined call for close attention." Pausing, she raised a finger to emphasize the point, then nodded when she thought Berelain had taken it, and folded her hands again. A gusting breeze pushed her yellowish-brown cloak off one shoulder, yet she did not appear to notice the loss of warmth.

"There is always a feel of urgency about Darkhounds' trails, but it varies according to a number of factors, not all of which I can be certain of. This one has an intense admixture of . . . I suppose you could call it impatience. That isn't really strong enough, by far—as well call a stabwound a pinprick—but it will do. I would say their hunt has been going on for some time, and their prey is eluding them somehow. No matter what the stories say—by the way, Lord Gallenne, salt doesn't harm Darkhounds in the least." So she had not been entirely lost in thought after all. "Despite the stories, they never hunt at random, though they will kill if the opportunity presents itself and doesn't interfere with the hunt. With Darkhounds, the hunt is paramount. Their quarry is always important to the Shadow, though at times we cannot see why. They have been known to bypass the great and mighty to slay a farmwife or a craftsman, or to enter a town or village and leave without killing, though clearly they came for some reason. My first thought for what brought them here had to be discarded, since they moved on." Her gaze flickered toward Perrin, so quickly he was not sure anyone else noticed. "Given that, I strongly doubt they will return. Oh, yes; and they are an hour or more gone. That, I'm afraid, is really all I can tell you." Nevarin and the other Wise Ones nodded their approval as she finished, and a touch of color returned to her cheeks, though it vanished quickly as she assumed a mask of Aes Sedai serenity. A shift in the breeze brought her scent to Perrin, surprised and pleased, and upset at being pleased.

"Thank you, Masuri Sedai," Berelain said formally, making a small bow in her saddle that Masuri acknowledged with a slight motion of her head. "You have put our minds at rest."

Indeed, the fear smell among the soldiers began to fade, though Perrin heard Gallenne grumble under his breath, "She might have told those last bits first."

Perrin's ears caught something else, too, through the stamping of horses' hooves and men's quiet, relieved laughter. A bluetit's trill sounded to the south, beyond the hearing of anyone else there, followed closely by the buzzing call of a masked sparrow. Another bluetit sounded, closer, followed again by a masked sparrow, and then the same pair called again closer still. There might be bluetits and masked sparrows in Altara, but he knew these birds carried Two Rivers longbows. The bluetit meant men were coming, more than a few and maybe unfriendly. The masked sparrow, that some back home called the thiefbird for its habit of stealing bright objects, on the other hand . . . Perrin ran a thumb along the edge of his axe, but he waited for one more pair of calls, close enough that the others might have noticed.

"Did you hear that?" he said, looking south as if he had just heard. "My sentries have spotted Masema." That brought heads up, listening, and several men nodded when the calls were repeated, closer still. "He's coming this way."

Growling curses, Gallenne clapped his helmet onto his head and mounted. Annoura gathered her reins, and Masuri began floundering back toward her dapple. The lancers shifted in their saddles and began giving off smells of anger, once more touched with fear. The Winged Guards were owed a blood debt by Masema, in their eyes, but none was anxious to try collecting with only fifty men, not when Masema always rode with a hundred at his back.

"I will not run from him," Berelain announced. She stared south wearing a cold frown. "We will wait for him here."

Gallenne opened his mouth, and closed it again without speaking—to her, at least. Drawing a deep breath, he began to bellow orders arraying his Guardsmen. That was not an easy matter. No matter how far apart the trees stood, forests were poor places for lancers. Any charge would be disjointed at its start, and sticking a man with a lance was difficult when he could dodge behind a tree trunk and come out behind you. Gallenne tried to form them in front of Berelain, between her and the approaching men, but she gave him a sharp look, and the one-eyed man changed his commands, lining the lancers up in a single crooked rank, bulging around massive trees but centered on her. One soldier Gallenne sent racing back toward the camp, crouching low in his saddle with his lance low as if at the charge, riding as fast as he could in spite of the snow and terrain. Berelain raised an eyebrow at that, yet said nothing.

Annoura began guiding her brown mare toward Berelain, but stopped when Masuri called her name. The Brown sister had gathered her dapple but still stood in the snow with the Wise Ones around her, who were tall enough in comparison to make her seem less than full-grown. Annoura hesitated until Masuri summoned her again, more sharply, and then Perrin thought he heard Annoura sigh heavily before she rode to them and dismounted. Whatever the Aiel women had to say, in voices pitched too softly for Perrin to hear, clustering in front of Annoura with heads bent close to hers, the Taraboner sister did not like. Her face remained hidden in her hood, but her thin braids swung ever faster with the shaking of her head, and at last she turned away abruptly and put a foot in the stirrup of her saddle. Masuri had been standing quietly, letting the Wise Ones have their say, but now she laid a hand on Annoura's sleeve and said something in a low voice that made Annoura's shoulders slump and the Wise Ones nod. Pushing back her hood to fall down her back, Annoura waited for Masuri to climb onto her mare before mounting her own horse, and then the two sisters rode back to the line of lancers together, crowding in beside Berelain with the Wise Ones pushing in between them, on the other side from Perrin. Annoura's wide mouth was turned down in a glum curve, and she was rubbing her thumbs nervously.

"What is it you're planning?" Perrin asked, trying not to sound suspicious. Maybe the Wise Ones had let Masuri meet with Masema, yet they still claimed to think the man was better dead. The Aes Sedai could not use the Power as a weapon unless they were in danger, but the Wise Ones had no such prohibition. He wondered whether they were linked. He knew more than he wanted about the One Power, and enough about the Wise Ones to be sure that Nevarin would be in control if they had formed a circle.

Annoura opened her mouth, but snapped it shut at a

warning touch from Carelle and glared at Masuri. The Brown sister pursed her lips and shook her head slightly, which did not seem to mollify Annoura. Her gloved hands gripped her reins so tightly that they shook.

Nevarin looked up at Perrin past Berelain as if she read his mind. "We *plan* to see you safely back to the camp, Perrin Aybara," she said sharply, "you and Berelain Paeron. We *plan* to see that as many as possible survive this day, and the days to come. Do you have objections?"

"Just don't do anything unless I tell you," he said. An answer like that could mean a lot of things. "Not anything."

Nevarin shook her head in disgust, and Carelle laughed as if he had made a huge joke. None of the Wise Ones seemed to think any more response was needed. They had been commanded to obey him, but their notions of obedience failed to square with any he had ever learned. Pigs would grow wings before he got a better answer out of them.

He could have put a stop to it. He knew he should. No matter what the Wise Ones had planned, meeting Masema this far from the others in the camp, when the man had to know who had stolen his Seanchan paper, was like hoping to snatch your hand off the anvil before the hammer fell. Berelain was almost as bad as the Wise Ones when it came to following orders, but he thought she would listen if he gave an order to withdraw to the camp. He thought she would, for all that her smell said she had her heels dug in hard. Staying was a senseless risk. He was sure he could convince her of that. Yet he did not want to run from the man, either. Part of him said he was being a fool. The larger part smoldered with anger that he found hard to control. Aram crowded in beside him scowling, but at least he had not drawn his sword. Waving a sword might put a hot coal in the hayloft, and the time for a confrontation with Masema had not come yet. Perrin rested a hand on his axe. Not yet.

Despite the sharply angled rays of light that penetrated through the thick branches overhead, the forest as a whole lay wrapped in dim early-morning shadows. Even at noon, it would be dim here. Sounds came to him first, the muffled thud of hooves in snow, the heavy breath of horses pushed for speed, and then a mass of riders appeared, a disordered mob flowing north among the huge trees at a near-gallop in spite of snow and rough ground. Rather than a hundred, they numbered two or three times that. A horse went down with a scream and lay thrashing atop its rider, but none of the others so much as slowed until, some seventy or eighty paces away, the man at their head raised a hand, and they suddenly drew rein in sprays of snow, lathered horses blowing hard and steaming. Here and there, lances stuck up among the riders. Most wore no armor, and many just a breastplate or a helmet, yet their saddles were hung about with swords and axes and maces. Shafts of sunlight picked out a few faces, grim flat-eyed men who looked as though they never had smiled and never would.

It occurred to Perrin that he might have made a mistake not to overrule Berelain. That was what came of hasty decisions, of letting anger do his thinking. Everyone knew that she often rode out in the mornings, and Masema might be desperate to recover his Seanchan document. Even with the Aes Sedai and Wise Ones, a fight in these woods could turn bloody, a free-for-all where men, and women, could die without once seeing who killed them. If no witnesses lived, it could always be blamed on bandits or even the Shaido. That had happened before. And if there were witnesses left, Masema was not above hanging a few dozen of his own men and claiming the guilty had been punished. He likely wanted to keep Perrin Aybara alive for a while yet, though, and he would not have expected the Wise Ones, or a second Aes Sedai. Small points to hang fifty-odd lives on. Very small points to hang Faile's life on. Perrin eased his axe in its loop on his belt. Beside him, Berelain smelled of cool calm and stony determination. No fear, oddly. Not a whiff. Aram smelled . . . excited.

The two parties sat regarding one another in silence, until at last Masema rode forward, followed by just two men, all three pushing back their hoods. None wore a helmet, or any piece of armor. Like Masema, Nengar and Bartu were Shienaran, but like him, they had shaved off their topknots, leaving bare heads with a look of skulls. The coming of the Dragon Reborn had broken all bonds, including those that had pledged these men to fight the Shadow along the Blight. Nengar and Bartu each carried a sword on his back and had another hanging at his saddlebow, and Bartu, shorter than the other two, had a cased horsebow and a quiver fastened to his saddle, too. Masema wore no visible weapons. The Prophet of the Lord Dragon Reborn needed none. Perrin was glad to see Gallenne watching the men Masema had left behind, for there was something about Masema that drew the eye. Maybe it was only knowing who he was, but that was more than enough.

Masema stopped his rangy sorrel a few paces from Perrin. The Prophet was a dark frowning man of average size with a faded arrow-scar white on his cheek, in a worn brown woolen coat and a dark cloak with frayed edges. Masema cared nothing for appearances, least of all his own. At his back, Nengar and Bartu held a fever in their eyes, but Masema's deep-set, almost black eyes seemed as hot as coals in a forge, as though the breezes must soon fan them to a glow, and his smell was the jangled, darting sharpness of pure insanity. He ignored the Wise Ones and Aes Sedai with a scorn he did not bother to hide. Wise Ones were worse than Aes Sedai, in his view; they not only blasphemed by channeling the One Power, they were Aiel savages to boot, a double sin. The Winged Guards could have been just more shadows beneath the trees. "You are taking a picnic?" he said with a glance at the basket hanging from Perrin's saddle. Normally, Masema's voice was as intense as his eyes, but now it sounded wry, and his lip curled as his eyes traveled to Berelain. He had heard the rumors, of course.

A wave of rage shot through Perrin, but he seized onto it, forcing it back. Folding it in with the rest, folding it tight. His anger had one target, and he would not waste it striking at another. Catching his rider's mood, Stepper bared his teeth at Masema's gelding, and Perrin had to rein him in sharply. "There were Darkhounds here in the night," he said, not very smoothly, but it was the best he could manage. "They're gone, and Masuri doesn't think they'll come back, so there's no need to worry."

Masema did not smell worried. He never smelled of anything except madness. The sorrel thrust his head aggressively toward Stepper, but Masema pulled him up with a harsh jerk. He rode well, Masema did, but he treated his horses as he did people. For the first time, he looked at Masuri. Perhaps his gaze grew a little hotter, if that was possible. "The Shadow can be found everywhere," he said, a heated pronouncement of unquestionable truth. "No one need fear the Shadow who follows the Lord Dragon Reborn, may the Light illumine his name. Even in death they will find the final victory of the Light."

Masuri's mare shied as though burned by that gaze, yet Masuri controlled the animal with a touch on the reins and met Masema's stare with Aes Sedai inscrutability, as calm as a frozen pond. Nothing hinted that she had been meeting this man in secret. "Fear is a useful spur to the wits, and to determination, when well controlled. If we have no fear of our enemies, that leaves only contempt, and contempt leads to the enemy's victory." You could have thought she was speaking to a simple farmer she had never met before. Annoura, watching, looked a little ill. Was she afraid their secret would come out? That their plans for Masema could be spoiled?

Masema's lip curled again, in a smile, or a sneer. The Aes Sedai seemed to cease to exist for him as he turned his attention back to Perrin. "Some of those who follow the Lord Dragon have found a town called So Habor." That was how he always referred to his followers: they really followed the Dragon Reborn, not him. The fact that Masema told them what do and when and how was just a detail. "A tidy place of three or four thousand people, about a day back, or a little less, to the south and west. It seems they were out of the Aiel's path, and their crop was good last year despite the drought. They have storehouses full of barley, millet and oats, and other needful things, I should imagine. I know you are running short on fodder. For your men as well as your horses."

"Why would their storehouses be full this time of year?" Berelain leaned forward with a frown, her tone just short of a demand, and not far short of disbelief.

Scowling, Nengar put a hand to his saddle-sword. No one made demands of the Prophet of the Lord Dragon. No one doubted him, either. No one who wished to live. Leather creaked as lancers shifted their saddles, but Nengar ignored them. The smell of Masema's madness slithered and flailed in Perrin's nose. Masema studied Berelain. He seemed unaware of Nengar or the lancers or the possibility that men might start killing one another any moment.

"A matter of greed," he said finally. "Apparently the grain traders of So Habor thought to make larger profits by holding their stock until winter drove prices up. But they normally sell west, into Ghealdan and Amadicia, and events there and in Ebou Dar have made them fearful that anything they send out will be confiscated. Their greed has left them with full storehouses and empty purses." A note of satisfaction entered Masema's voice. He despised greed. But then, he despised any human weakness, great or small. "I think they will part with their grain very cheaply, now."

Perrin smelled a trap, and it did not take a wolf's nose. Masema had his own men and horses to feed, and no matter how thoroughly they had scoured the country they crossed, they could not be in much better shape than Perrin's own people. Why had Masema not sent a few thousand of his followers into this town and taken whatever it held? A day back. That would take him farther from Faile, and maybe give the Shaido time to gain ground again. Was that the reason for this peculiar offer? Or a further delay to keep Masema in the west, close to his Seanchan friends?

"Perhaps there will be time to visit this town after my wife is free." Once again, Perrin's ears caught the faint sound of men and horses moving through the forest before anyone else, coming from the west, this time, from the camp. Gallenne's messenger must have galloped the whole way.

"Your wife," Masema said in a flat voice, directing a look at Berelain that made Perrin's blood boil. Even Berelain colored, though her face remained smooth. "Do you really believe you will have word of her today?"

"I do." Perrin's voice was as flat as Masema's, and harder. He clutched the pommel of his saddle, atop the hoop-handles of Berelain's basket, to keep from reaching for his axe. "Freeing her comes first. Her and the others. We can fill our bellies to bursting once that's done, but that comes first."

The horses approaching were audible to everyone, now. A long line of lancers appeared to the west, sifting through the shadowed trees with another mounted line behind it, the red streamers and breastplates of Mayene interspersed with the green streamers and burnished breastplates of Ghealdan. The lines stretched from opposite Perrin down below the mass of horsemen who were waiting on Masema. Men afoot ghosted from tree to tree, carrying long Two

Rivers bows. Perrin found himself hoping that they had not stripped the camp too far. Stealing that Seanchan paper might have forced Masema's hand, and he was a veteran of fighting along the Blight and against the Aiel. He might have thought further ahead than simply riding out to find Berelain. It was like another blacksmith's puzzle. Move one piece to shift another just enough to let a third slip free. A camp with weakened defenders could be overrun, and in these woods, numbers could count for as much as who had people channeling. Did Masema want to keep his secret enough to try putting a seal to it here and now? Perrin realized that he had moved one hand to rest on his axe, but he left it there.

Among the mass of Masema's followers, horses moved nervously at tugs from their riders, men shouted and waved weapons, but Masema himself studied the oncoming lancers and bowmen with no change of expression, neither more dour nor less. They might have been birds hopping from branch to branch. The smell of him writhed madly, unchanging.

"What is done to serve the Light, must be done," he said when the newcomers halted, some two hundred paces away. That was easy range for a Two Rivers bowman, and Masema had seen demonstrations, but he gave no sign that broadhead shafts might be aimed at his heart. "All else is dross and trash. Remember that, Lord Perrin Goldeneyes. *Everything* else is dross and trash!"

Jerking his sorrel around without another word, he headed back toward his waiting men trailed by Nengar and Bartu, all three pushing their horses without a care for broken legs or broken heads. The waiting company fell in behind, a mob flowing south, now. A few men at the tail end stopped to drag a limp shape from under the injured horse and put the animal out of its misery with a quick slash of a dagger. Then they began gutting and butchering. That much meat could not be allowed to go to waste. The rider, they left where they had dropped him.

"He believes every word he says," Annoura breathed, "but where does his belief lead him?"

Perrin considered asking her straight out where she thought Masema's belief was leading him, where *she* wanted to lead him, but she suddenly put on that impenetrable Aes

Sedai calm. The tip of her sharp nose had turned red from the cold; she regarded him with a level stare. You could pry that Darkhound-marked stone out of the ground bare-handed as easily as get an answer from an Aes Sedai who wore that look. He would have to leave questions to Bere-lain.

The man who had brought the lancers suddenly spurred his horse forward. A short compact fellow in a silver-plated breastplate and a helmet with a barred faceguard and three short white plumes, Gerard Arganda was a tough man, a soldier who had worked his way up from the bottom, against all odds, to become the First Captain of Alliandre's bodyguard. He had no liking for Perrin, who had brought his queen south for no good reason and gotten her kid-napped, but Perrin expected him to stop and make his re-spects to Berelain, perhaps confer with Gallenne. Arganda had a great deal of respect for Gallenne, and often spent time with him both smoking their pipes. Instead, the roan floundered past Perrin and the others, Arganda digging his heels into the animal's sides, trying to force more speed. When Perrin saw where the man was heading, he under-stood. A single horseman on a mouse-colored animal was approaching from the east at a steady walk, and beside him, an Aiel shuffled along on snowshoes.

CHAPTER
8

Whirlpools of Color

P errin did not realize he had moved until he found
himself crouched over Stepper's neck, streaking after
Arganda. The snow was no less deep, the ground no
smoother, the light no better, but Stepper raced through
the shadows, unwilling to let the roan stay in the lead, and
Perrin urged him to run faster. The approaching rider was
Elyas, his beard fanned out over his chest, a broad-brimmed
hat casting his face in shadows and his fur-lined cloak hanging down his back. The Aiel was one of the Maidens, with
a dark *shoufa* wrapped around her head and a white cloak,
used for hiding against the snow, worn over her coat and
breeches of grays and browns and greens. Elyas and one
Maiden, without the others, meant Faile had been found.
It had to.

Arganda ran his horse without a care for whether he
broke the roan's neck or his own, leaping stone outcrops,
splashing through the snow at a near-gallop, but Stepper
overtook him just as he reached Elyas and demanded in a
harsh voice, "Did you see the queen, Machera? Is she alive?
Tell me, man!" The Maiden, Elienda, her sun-darkened
face expressionless, raised a hand to Perrin. It might have
been meant for a greeting, or sympathy, but she never broke
her skimming stride. With Elyas to make his report to Perrin, she would carry hers to the Wise Ones.

"You've found her?" Perrin's throat was suddenly dry
as sand. He had waited so long for this. Arganda snarled
soundlessly through the steel bars of his helmet's faceguard, knowing that Perrin was not asking after Alliandre.

"We found the Shaido we've been following," Elyas said

carefully, both hands on the pommel of his saddle. Even Elyas, the fabled Long Tooth who had lived and run with wolves, was showing the strain of too many miles and not enough sleep. His whole face sagged with a weariness emphasized by the golden-yellow glow of his eyes beneath his hat brim. Gray streaked his thick beard and the hair that he wore hanging to his waist and tied with a leather cord at the nape of his neck, and for the first time since Perrin had known him, he looked old. "They're camped around a fair-sized town they took, in ridge country near forty miles from here. They've got no sentries to speak of close in, and those further out seem to be watching for prisoners trying to escape more than anything else, so we got near enough for a good look. But Perrin, there are more of them than we thought. At least nine or ten septs, the Maidens say. Counting *gai'shain*—folks in white, anyway—there could be as many people in that camp as in Mayene or Ebou Dar. I don't know how many spear fighters, but ten thousand might be on the low side from what I saw."

Knots of desperation twisted and tightened in Perrin's stomach. His mouth was so dry he could not have spoken had Faile miraculously appeared in front of him. Ten thousand *algai'd'siswai,* and even weavers and silversmiths and old men who passed their days reminiscing in the shade would pick up a spear if they were attacked. He had fewer than two thousand lancers, and they would have been overmatched against an equal number of Aiel. Fewer than three hundred Two Rivers men, who could wreak havoc with their bows at a distance but not stop ten thousand. That many Shaido would shred Masema's murderous rabble like a cat slaughtering a nest of mice. Even counting the Asha'man and the Wise Ones and Aes Sedai. . . . Edarra and the other Wise Ones were hardly generous in what they told him about Wise Ones, but he knew ten septs might have fifty women who could channel, maybe more. Maybe fewer, too—there was no set number—but not enough fewer to make a difference.

With an effort, he strangled the despair welling up in him, squeezed until only writhing filaments remained for his anger to burn up. A hammer had no place in it for despair. Ten septs or the whole Shaido clan, they still had Faile, and he still had to find a way.

"What does it matter how many there are?" Aram demanded. "When Trollocs came to the Two Rivers, there were thousands, tens of thousands, but we killed them just the same. Shaido can't be worse than Trollocs."

Perrin blinked, surprised to find the man right behind him, not to mention Berelain and Gallenne and the Aes Sedai. In his haste to reach Elyas, he had shut out everything else. Dimly visible through the trees, the men Arganda had brought out to confront Masema still held their rough lines, but Berelain's bodyguard was forming a loose ring centered on Elyas and facing outward. The Wise Ones stood outside the circle, listening to Elienda with grave faces. She spoke in a low murmur, sometimes shaking her head. Her view of matters was no brighter than Elyas's. He must have lost the basket in his haste, or thrown it away, because it hung from Berelain's saddle now. There was a look of . . . could it be sympathy, on her face? Burn him, he was too tired to think straight. Only, now more than ever, he had to think straight. His next mistake might be the last, for Faile.

"Way I heard it, Tinker," Elyas said quietly, "the Trollocs came to you in the Two Rivers, and you managed to catch them in a vise. You have any fancy plans for catching the Shaido in a vise?" Aram glared at him sullenly. Elyas had known him before he picked up a sword, and Aram disliked being reminded of that time, despite his brightly colored clothes.

"Ten septs or fifty," Arganda growled, "there must be some way to free the Queen. And the others, of course. And the others." His hard-bitten face was creased in a scowl of anger, yet he smelled frantic, a fox ready to chew off its own leg to escape a trap. "Will . . . ? Will they accept a ransom?" The Ghealdanin looked around until he found Marline coming through the Winged Guards. She managed a steady stride in spite of the snow, not staggering in the least. The other Wise Ones were no longer anywhere to be seen among the trees, nor Elienda. "Will these Shaido take a ransom . . . Wise One?" Arganda's honorific had the sound of an afterthought. He no longer believed the Aiel with them had any knowledge of the kidnapping, but there was a taint in him regarding Aiel.

"I cannot say." Marline seemed not to notice his tone. Arms folded across her chest, she stood looking at Perrin rather than Arganda. It was one of those looks where a woman weighed and measured you till she could have sewn you a suit of clothes or told you when your smallclothes were last washed. It would have made him uncomfortable back when he had had time for such things. When she spoke again, there was nothing of offering advice in her tone, merely a setting out of the facts. She might even have meant it so. "Your wetlander paying of ransom goes against our custom. *Gai'shain* may be given as a gift, or traded for other *gai'shain,* but they are not animals to be sold. Yet it seems the Shaido no longer follow *ji'e'toh.* They make wetlanders *gai'shain* and take everything instead of only the fifth. They may set a price."

"My jewels are at your disposal, Perrin," Berelain put in, her voice steady and her face firm. "If necessary, Grady or Neald can fetch more from Mayene. Gold, as well."

Gallenne cleared his throat. "Altarans are used to marauders, my Lady, neighboring nobles and brigands alike," he said slowly, slapping his reins against his palm. Although reluctant to contradict Berelain, he clearly intended to anyway. "There's no law this far from Ebou Dar, except what the local lord or lady says. Noble or common, they're accustomed to paying off anyone they can't fight off, and quick to tell the difference. It goes against reason that none of them tried to buy safety, yet we've seen nothing but ruins in these Shaido's path, heard of nothing but pillage right down to the ground. They may accept an offer of ransom, and even take it, but can they be trusted to give anything in return? Just making the offer gives away our one real advantage, that they don't know we are here." Annoura shook her head slightly, the barest movement, but Gallenne's one eye caught it, and he frowned. "You disagree, Annoura Sedai?" he asked politely. And with a hint of surprise. The Gray was almost diffident at times, especially for a sister, but she never vacillated about speaking up when she disagreed with advice offered to Berelain.

This time Annoura hesitated, though, and covered by pulling her cloak around herself and arranging the folds with care. It was clumsy of her; Aes Sedai could ignore heat or cold when they chose, remaining untouched when everyone around them was drenched with sweat or fighting to stop their teeth chattering. An Aes Sedai who paid attention to the temperature was buying time to think, usually about how to hide what she was thinking. Glancing toward Marline with a small frown, she finally reached a decision, and the slight crease in her forehead vanished.

"Negotiation is always better than fighting," she said in cool Taraboner accents, "and in negotiation, trust is always a matter of the precautions, yes? We must consider with care the precautions that must be taken. There is also the question of who is to approach them. Wise Ones may no longer be sacrosanct, since they took part in the battle at Dumai's Wells. A sister, or a group of sisters, might be better, yet even that must have careful arrangement. I myself am willing to—"

"No ransom," Perrin said, and when everyone stared at him, most in consternation, Annoura with her face unreadable, he said it again, in a harder voice. "No ransom." He would not pay these Shaido for making Faile suffer. She would be afraid, and they had to pay for that, not profit from it. Besides, Gallenne had the right of it. Nothing Perrin had seen, in Altara or Amadicia or before that in Cairhien, so much as hinted that the Shaido could be trusted to keep any bargain. As well trust rats in the grain bins and cutworms with the harvest. "Elyas, I want to see their camp." When he was a boy he had known a blind man, Nat Torfinn with his wrinkled face and thin white hair, who could disassemble any blacksmith's puzzle by touch. For years Perrin tried to learn how to duplicate that feat, but he never could. He had to see how the pieces fit together before he could make sense of them. "Aram, find Grady and tell him to meet me as fast as he can, at the Traveling ground." That was what they had come to call the place where they arrived at the end of each jump, and departed from for the next. It was easier for the Asha'man to weave a gateway in a place already touched by one they had woven before.

Aram gave one short, purposeful nod, then wheeled his gray and sped toward camp, but Perrin could see arguments and questions and demands gathering on the faces around him. Marline was still examining him, as though suddenly not quite sure what he was, and Gallenne was frowning at the reins in his hands, no doubt seeing matters turn out badly whatever he did, but Berelain wore a perturbed expression, objections visible in her eyes, and Annoura's mouth had tightened to a thin line. Aes Sedai disliked being interrupted, and, diffident for an Aes Sedai or not, she looked ready to vent her displeasure. Arganda, his face growing red, opened his mouth with the clear intention of shouting. Arganda had shouted often since his queen was kidnapped. There was no point in waiting to listen.

Digging in his heels, Perrin sent Stepper lunging through the line of Winged Guards, heading back toward the sheared trees. Not at a run, but not dawdling, either—a quick trot through the towering forests, hands tight on the reins and eyes already searching the dappled gloom for Grady. Elyas followed on his gelding without a word. Perrin had been sure he had no room in him for another ounce of fear, yet Elyas' silence made the weight grow. The other man never saw an obstacle without seeing a way around. His silence shouted of impassable mountains. There had to be a way, though. When they reached the smooth stone outcrop, Perrin walked Stepper back and forth through the slanting bars of light, around the toppled trees and between the standing ones, unable to make himself stop. He had to keep moving. There had to be a way. His mind darted like a caged rat.

Elyas dismounted to squat and frown at the sliced stone, paying little heed to his gelding tugging at the reins and trying to back away. Beside the stone, the thick trunk of a pine that had stood a good fifty paces tall was propped up at one end by the splintered remains of its stump, high enough that Elyas could have walked beneath the tree trunk upright. Brilliant rays of sunlight piercing the forest canopy elsewhere seemed to deepen the shadow to near blackness around the track-marked outcrop but that troubled him no more than it did Perrin. His nose wrinkled at the burnt-sulphur smell that still hung in the air. "I thought I caught this stink on the way here. I expect you'd have mentioned this if you didn't have things on your mind. A big pack. Bigger than anything I've ever seen or heard of."

"That's what Masuri said," Perrin said absently. What was keeping Grady? How many people were there in Ebou Dar? That was the size of the Shaido camp. "She said she's crossed the paths of seven packs, and this isn't one she's seen before."

"Seven," Elyas murmured in surprise. "Even an Aes Sedai would have to go some to do that. Most tales of Darkhounds are just people frightened by the dark." Frowning at the tracks crossing the smoothed stone, he shook his head, and sadness entered his voice when he said, "They were wolves, once. The souls of wolves, anyway, caught and twisted by the Shadow. That was the core used to make Darkhounds, the Shadowbrothers. I think that's why the wolves have to be at the Last Battle. Or maybe Darkhounds were made because wolves will be there, to fight them. The Pattern makes Sovarra lace look like a piece of string, sometimes. Anyway, it was a long time ago, during the Trolloc Wars as near as I can make out, and the War of the Shadow before that. Wolves have long memories. What a wolf knows is never really forgotten while other wolves remain alive. They avoid talking about Darkhounds, though, and they avoid Darkhounds, too. A hundred wolves could die trying to kill one Shadowbrother. Worse, if they fail, the Darkhound can eat the souls of those that aren't quite dead yet, and in a year or so, there'd be a new pack of Shadowbrothers that didn't remember ever being wolves. I hope they don't remember, anyway."

Perrin reined in, though he itched to keep moving. Shadowbrothers. The wolves' name for Darkhounds had taken on a new grimness. "Can they eat a man's soul, Elyas? Say a man who can talk to wolves?" Elyas shrugged. Only a handful of people could do what they did, as far as either man knew. An answer to that question might come only at the point of death. More importantly right then, if they had been wolves, once, they must be intelligent enough to report what they found. Masuri had implied as much. Foolishness to hope otherwise. How long before they did? How long did he have to free Faile?

The sound of hooves crunching in snow announced riders coming, and he hurriedly told Elyas that the Darkhounds had circled the camp, that they would be carrying word of him to whomever they reported to.

"I wouldn't worry overmuch, boy," the older man replied, watching warily for sight of the oncoming horses. Moving away from the stone, he began to stretch, working muscles over-long in the saddle. Elyas was too careful to be caught studying what would be swallowed in shadows to other eyes. "Sounds like they're hunting something more important than you. They'll stay on that till they find it if it takes all year. Don't worry. We'll get your wife out before those Darkhounds report you were here. Not saying it'll be easy, but we'll do it." There was determination in his voice, and in his scent, but not much hope. Almost none at all, in fact.

Fighting despair, refusing to let it rise again, Perrin resumed walking Stepper as Berelain and her bodyguard appeared through the trees, with Marline astride behind Annoura. As soon as the Aes Sedai drew rein, the twilight-eyed Wise One slid to the ground, shaking down her thick skirts to cover her dark stockings. Another woman might have appeared flustered over having her legs exposed, but not Marline. She was merely straightening her clothes. Annoura was the one who looked upset, a sour-faced disgruntlement that made her nose seem more like a beak. She kept silent, but her mouth was set to bite. She must have been certain her offer to negotiate with the Shaido would be accepted, especially with Berelain supporting and Marline seemingly neutral at worst. Grays were negotiators and mediators, adjudicators and treaty makers. That might have been her motivation. What else could it have been? A problem that he had to set aside while keeping it in mind. He had to take into account anything that might interfere with freeing Faile, but the problem he had to solve lay forty miles to the northeast.

While the Winged Guards formed their protective circle among the towering trees around the Traveling ground, Berelain brought her bay alongside Stepper and paced him, trying to engage Perrin in talk, to entice him with the rest of the woodhen. She smelled uncertain, doubtful of his decision. Maybe she hoped to talk him into attempting the ransom. He kept Stepper moving and refused to listen. To make that attempt was to gamble everything on one toss of the dice. He could not gamble with Faile as the stake. Methodical as working at a forge, that was the way. Light, but he was tired. He folded himself in tighter around his anger, embracing the heat for energy.

Gallenne and Arganda arrived shortly after Berelain, with a double column of Ghealdanin lancers in burnished breastplates and bright conical helmets who interspersed themselves among the Mayeners between the trees. A trace of irritation entering her scent, Berelain left Perrin and rode to Gallenne. The pair of them sat their horses knee-to-knee, the one-eyed man bending his head to listen to what Berelain had to say. Her voice was low, but Perrin knew their subject, at least in part. Now and then one of them glanced at him as he walked Stepper back and forth, back and forth. Arganda planted his roan in one spot and stared south through the trees toward the camp, still as a statue yet radiating impatience as a fire radiated heat. He was the picture of a soldier, with his plumes and his sword and his silvered armor, his face as hard as stone, but he smelled on the brink of panic. Perrin wondered how he himself smelled. You could never catch your own scent unless you were in a closed space. He did not think he smelled of panic, just fear and anger. All would be well once he had Faile back. All would be well, then. Back and forth, back and forth.

At last Aram appeared, with a yawning Jur Grady on a dark bay gelding, dark enough that the white stripe on its nose made it seem almost a black. Dannil and a dozen Two Rivers men, spears and halberds abandoned for the moment in favor of their longbows, rode close behind, but not too close. A stocky fellow with a weathered face already beginning to show creases, though he was short of his middle years yet, Grady looked like a sleepy farmer despite of the long-hilted sword at his waist and his black coat with the silver sword pin on the high collar, but he had left the farm behind forever, and Dannil and the others always gave him room. They gave Perrin room, too, hanging back and peering at the ground, sometimes darting quick, embarrassed looks at him or Berelain. It did not matter. All would be well.

Aram tried to lead Grady to Perrin, but the Asha'man knew why he had been summoned. With a sigh, he climbed down beside Elyas, who squatted in a patch of sunlight to mark a map in the snow with his finger and speak of distance and direction, describing the place he wanted to go in detail, a clearing on a slope that faced almost south, with the ridge above notched in three places. Distance and direction

were enough, if the distance and direction were precise, but
the better the picture in an Asha'man's mind, the closer he
could come to an exact spot.

"There's no margin for error here, boy." Elyas's eyes
seemed to brighten with intensity. Whatever others thought
of Asha'man, they never intimidated him. "There's lots of
ridges in that country, and the main camp is only a mile or
so the other side of this one. There'll be sentries, little parties that camp in a different place every night, maybe less
than two miles the other way. You put us out off by much,
and we'll be seen for sure."

Grady met that stare, unblinking. Then he nodded and
scrubbed stubby fingers through his hair, drawing a deep
breath. He looked as weary as Elyas. As bone-tired as Perrin felt. Making gateways, holding them open long enough
for thousands of people and horses to pass through, was
wearing work.

"Are you rested enough?" Perrin asked him. Tired men
made mistakes, and mistakes with the One Power could be
deadly. "Should I send for Neald?"

Grady stared up at him blearily, then shook his head.
"Fager's no more rested than me. Less, maybe. I'm stronger than he is, a bit. Better if I do it." He turned to face
northeast, and with no more warning, a vertical slash of
silver-blue appeared beside the track-marked stone. Annoura jerked her mare out of the way with a loud gasp as
the line of light widened into an opening, a hole in the air
that showed a sunlit clearing on steep ground among trees
much smaller than those around Perrin and the others. The
already splintered pine shivered as it lost another thin slice,
groaned, and collapsed the rest of the way with a snow-
muffled crash that made the horses snort and dance. Annoura glared at the Asha'man, her face growing dark, but
Grady just blinked and said, "Does that look like the right
place?" Elyas adjusted his hat before nodding.

That nod was all Perrin waited for. He ducked his head
and rode Stepper through into snow that was over the dun's
fetlocks. It was a small clearing, but the sky full of white
clouds overhead made it seem vastly open after the forest
behind. The light was almost blinding compared to the forest,
though the sun was still hidden by the tree-covered ridge
above. The Shaido camp lay on the other side of that ridge.

He stared toward the height yearningly. It was all he could do to stay where he was rather than race ahead to finally see where Faile was. He made himself turn Stepper to face the gateway as Marline came out.

Still studying him, hardly taking her eyes away long enough to place her feet in the snow without tripping, she moved to one side to let Aram and the Two Rivers men ride through. Accustomed to Traveling if not to Asha'man by now, they barely bent their heads enough to clear the top of the opening, and only the tallest did even that. It struck Perrin that the gateway was larger than the first one of Grady's make that he had passed through. He had had to dismount, then. It was a vague thought, no more important than a fly buzzing. Aram rode straight to Perrin, tight-faced and smelling impatient and eager to be going on, and once Dannil and the others were out of the way, climbing down and calmly fitting arrows to bows while they watched the surrounding trees, Gallenne appeared, peering grimly at the trees around them as though he expected an enemy to come dashing out, followed by half a dozen Mayeners who had to lower their red-streamered lances to crowd through after him.

A long pause passed with the gateway empty, but just when Perrin had decided to go back and see what was holding Elyas up, the bearded man led his horse out, with Arganda and six Ghealdanin riding at his heels, discontent carved on their faces. Their shining helmets and breastplates were nowhere to be seen, and they scowled as though they had been made to leave off their breeches.

Perrin nodded to himself. Of course. The Shaido camp was on the other side of this ridge, and so was the sun. That gleaming armor would have been like mirrors. He should have thought of that. He was still letting fear goad him into impatience and cloud his thinking. He had to be clearheaded, now more than ever. The detail he missed now could kill him and leave Faile in Shaido hands. It was easier to say that he had to let go of fear than to do it, though. How could he not be afraid for Faile? It had to be managed, but how?

To his surprise, Annoura rode through the gateway just ahead of Grady, who was leading his dark bay. Just as every time he had seen her pass through a gateway, she lay as flat on her mare as her saddle's high pommel would allow, grimacing at the opening that had been made with the tainted male half of the Power, and as soon as she was clear of it, she urged her horse as far up the slope as she could without entering the trees. Grady let the gateway snap shut, leaving the purple afterimage of a vertical bar in Perrin's eyes, and Annoura flinched and looked away, glaring at Marline, at Perrin. If she had been anyone other than an Aes Sedai, he would have said she was simmering in a sullen fury. Berelain must have told her to come, but it was not Berelain she blamed for her having to be there.

"From here, we go afoot," Elyas announced in a quiet voice that barely carried over the occasional stamp of a horse's hoof. He had said the Shaido were careless and had no sentries, or almost none, but he spoke as if they could be within twenty paces. "A man on a horse stands out. The Shaido aren't blind, just blind for Aiel, which means they see twice as sharp as any of you, so don't go skylining yourselves when we reach the crest. And try not to make any more noise than you can help. They aren't deaf, either. They'll find our tracks, eventually—can't do much about that in snow—but we can't let them know we were here until after we're gone."

Already sour over being shorn of his armor and plumes, Arganda began to argue about Elyas giving orders. Not being a complete fool, he did it in a quiet voice that would not carry, but he had been a soldier since the age of fifteen, he had commanded soldiers fighting Whitecloaks, Altarans and Amadicians, and as he was fond of pointing out, he had fought in the Aiel War and lived through the Blood Snow, at Tar Valon. He knew about Aiel, and he did not need an unbarbered woodsman to tell him how to put his boots on. Perrin let it pass, since the man did his complaining in between telling off two men to hold the horses. He really was not a fool, just afraid for his queen. Gallenne left all of his men behind, muttering that lancers were worse than useless off their horses and would probably break their necks if he made them walk any distance. He was no fool, either, but he did see the black side first. Elyas took the lead, and Perrin waited only long enough to transfer the thick brass-bound tube of his looking glass from Stepper's saddlebags to his coat pocket before following.

The underbrush grew in clumps beneath the trees, which were mostly pine and fir, with clusters of others that were winter-gray and leafless, and the terrain, no steeper than the Sand Hills back home, if more rocky, presented no problems for Dannil and the other Two Rivers men, who ghosted up the slope with arrows nocked and eyes watchful, almost as silent as the mist of their breath. Aram, no stranger to the woods himself, stayed close to Perrin with his sword out. Once he started to chop a tangle of thick brown vines out of his way until Perrin stopped him with a hand on his arm, yet he made little more noise than Perrin, the faint crunch of boots in snow. It was no shock that Marline moved through the trees as if she had grown up in a forest instead of the Aiel Waste, where anything that could be called a tree was rare and snow unheard of, though it seemed that all of her necklaces and bracelets should have made some clatter as they swung, but Annoura climbed with almost as little effort, floundering a little with her skirts but deftly avoiding the sharp thorns of dead cat's-claw and wait-a-minute vines. Aes Sedai usually found a way to surprise you. She managed to keep a wary eye on Grady, too, though the Asha'man appeared to be focused on putting one foot in front of the other. Sometimes he sighed heavily and paused for a minute, frowning toward the crest ahead, but somehow he never fell behind. Gallenne and Arganda were not young men, nor accustomed to walking where they could ride, and their breathing began to grow heavier as they ascended, sometimes pulling themselves up from tree to tree, but they watched one another nearly as much as they did the ground, each unwilling to let the other outdo him. The four Ghealdanin lancers, on the other hand, slipped and slid, tripped over roots hidden beneath the snow, caught their scabbards on vines, and growled curses when they fell on rocks or were stabbed by thorns. Perrin began to consider sending them back to wait with the horses. That, or hitting them over the head and leaving them to be picked up when he returned.

Abruptly, two Aiel stepped out of the undergrowth in front of Elyas, dark veils hiding their faces to the eyes,

white cloaks hanging down their backs and spears and
bucklers in hand. They were Maidens of the Spear by
their height, which made them no less dangerous than any
other *algai'd'siswai,* and in an instant, nine longbows were
drawn, broadhead points aimed at their hearts.

"You could get hurt that way, Tuandha," Elyas muttered.
"You should know better, Sulin." Perrin motioned for the
Two Rivers men to lower their bows, and for Aram to lower
his sword. He had caught their scents as soon as Elyas had,
before they stepped into the open.

The Maidens exchanged startled looks, but they un-
veiled, letting the dark veils hang down their chests. "You
see closely, Elyas Machera," Sulin said. Wiry and leather-
faced, with a scar across one cheek, she had sharp blue eyes
that could pierce like awls, but they still looked surprised,
now. Tuandha was taller and younger, and she might have
been pretty before losing her right eye and gaining a thick
scar than ran from her chin up under her *shoufa.* It pulled
up one corner of her mouth in a half-smile, but that was the
only smile she ever gave.

"Your coats are different," Perrin said. Tuandha frowned
down at her coat, all gray and green and brown, then at
Sulin's identical garment. "Your cloaks, too." Elyas *was*
tired, to make that slip. "They haven't started moving, have
they?"

"No, Perrin Aybara," Sulin said. "The Shaido seem prepared to stay in one place for a time. They made the people
from the city leave and go north last night, those they would
let leave." She gave a small shake of her head, still perturbed by the Shaido forcing people to become *gai'shain*
who did not follow *ji'e'toh.* "Your friends Jondyn Barran
and Get Ayliah and Hu Marwin have gone after them to see
if they can learn anything. Our spear-sisters and Gaul are
making their way around the camp again. We waited here
for Elyas Machera to return with you." She seldom let emotion into her voice, and there was none there now, but she
smelled of sadness. "Come, I will show you."

The two Maidens turned up the slope, and he hurried
after them, forgetting anyone else. A little short of the
crest, they crouched, then went to hands and knees, and
he copied them, crawling the last spans through the snow

to peer past a tree over the top of the ridgeline. The forest ended there, fading into scattered brush and isolated saplings on the downslope. He was high enough to see for several leagues, across rolling ridges like long treeless hills to where a dark band of forest began again. He could see everything he wanted to see, and so much less than he needed.

He had tried to imagine the Shaido camp from Elyas' description, but the reality dwarfed his imaginings. A thousand paces below lay a mass of low Aiel tents and every other sort of tent, a mass of wagons and carts and people and horses. It spread for well over a mile in every direction from the gray stone walls of a city halfway to the next rise. He knew the sprawl must be the same on the other side. It was not one of the great cities, not like Caemlyn or Tar Valon, less than four hundred paces wide along the side he could see and narrower on the others, it seemed, but still a city with high walls and towers and what looked like a fortress at the northmost end. Yet the Shaido encampment swallowed it whole. Faile was somewhere in that great lake of people.

Fumbling his looking glass from his pocket, he remembered at the last instant to cup one hand for shade on the far end of the tube. The sun was a golden ball almost ahead of him, just shy of halfway to its noonday height. A stray reflection from the lens could ruin everything. Groups of people leapt up in the looking glass, their faces clear, at least to his eye. Long-haired women with dark shawls over their shoulders, draped in dozens of long necklaces, women with fewer necklaces milking goats, women wearing the *cadin'sor* and sometimes carrying spears and bucklers, women peeking from the deep cowls of heavy white robes as they scurried across snow already trampled halfway to mud. There were men and children, too, but his eye skipped past them hungrily, ignored them. Thousands upon thousands of women, just counting those in white.

"Too many," Marline whispered, and he lowered the glass to glare at her. The others had joined the Maidens and him, all lying in a row in the snow along the ridgeline. The Two Rivers men were taking pains to keep their bowstrings up out of the snow without raising their bows above the ridgeline. Arganda and Gallenne were using their own looking glasses to study the camp below, and Grady was staring down the slope with his chin propped on his hands, every bit as intent as the two soldiers. Maybe he was using the Power in some way. Marline and Annoura were staring at the camp, too, the Aes Sedai licking her lips and the Wise One frowning. Perrin did not think Marline had intended to speak aloud.

"If you think I'll walk away just because there are more Shaido than I expected," he began heatedly, but she broke in, meeting his scowl with a level look.

"Too many Wise Ones, Perrin Aybara. Wherever I look, I can see a woman channeling. Just for a moment here, a moment there—Wise Ones do not channel all the time— but they are everywhere I look. Too many to be the Wise Ones of ten septs."

He drew a deep breath. "How many do you think there are?"

"I think maybe all the Shaido Wise Ones are down there," Marline replied, as calm as if she were talking about the price of barley. "All who can channel."

All of them? That made no sense! How could they all be together here, when the Shaido seemed to be scattered everywhere? At least, he had heard tales of what had to be Shaido raids all across Ghealdan and Amadicia, tales of raids here in Altara long before Faile was taken and rumors from even farther. *Why* would they all be together? If the Shaido intended to gather here, the whole clan . . . No, he had to deal with what he knew for fact. That was bad enough. "How many?" he asked again, in a reasonable tone.

"Do not growl at me, Perrin Aybara. I cannot say exactly how many Shaido Wise Ones remain alive. Even Wise Ones die from sickness, snakebite, accident. Some died at Dumai's Wells. We found bodies left behind, and they must have carried away those they could for proper burial. Even Shaido cannot have abandoned all custom. If all who remain alive are below, and the apprentices who can channel, I would say perhaps four hundred. Perhaps more, but fewer than five hundred. There were fewer than five hundred Shaido Wise Ones who could channel before they crossed the Dragonwall, and perhaps fifty apprentices." Most farmers would have shown more emotion over the barley.

Still staring at the Shaido camp, Annoura made a strangled sound, half a sob. "Five hundred? Light! Half the
Tower from one clan? Oh, Light!"

"We could sneak in, in the night," Dannil murmured
from down the row, "the way you sneaked into that Whitecloak camp back home." Elyas gave a grunt that might have
meant anything but did not sound hopeful.

Sulin snorted derisively. "*We* could not sneak into that
camp, not with any real hope of getting out. *You* would be
trussed like a goat for the spit before you passed the first
tents."

Perrin nodded slowly. He had thought of slipping in under
cover of darkness and somehow spiriting Faile away. And
the others, of course. She would not go without the others.
He had never had any real belief that could work, though,
not against Aiel, and the size of the camp had quenched the
last glimmers. He could wander for days among that many
people without finding her.

Abruptly, he realized that he was not having to fight
down despair. The anger remained, but it was cold as steel
in winter, now, and he could not detect a single drop of
the hopelessness that had threatened to drown him before.
There were ten thousand *algai'd'siswai* in that camp, and
five hundred women who could channel—Gallenne had
the right of it; prepare for the worst, and all your surprises
were pleasant ones—five hundred women who would not
hesitate to use the Power as a weapon; Faile was hidden like
one snowflake in a meadow covered with snow, but when
you piled up so much, there just was no point in despair.
You had to buckle down or be plowed under. Besides, he
could see the puzzle, now. Nat Torfinn had always said any
puzzle could be solved, once you found out where to push
and where to pull.

To the north and south, the land had been cleared farther
from the city than the rise where he lay. Scattered farm-
houses, none with smoke rising from its chimney, dotted
the landscape, and rail fences marked out fields beneath the
snow, but more than a handful of men trying to approach
from either direction might as well carry torches and banners and blow trumpets. There seemed to be a road leading
roughly south through the farms and another roughly north.
Useless to him, probably, but you never could tell. Jondyn

might bring back some information about the city, though what good that would do when the city was in the middle of the Shaido, he could not begin to guess. Gaul and the Maidens who were making their way around the camp would be able to tell him what lay beyond the next ridge. A saddle in that ridge had the look of a road heading somewhere east. Oddly, a cluster of windmills stood maybe a mile north of the saddle, long white arms turning slowly, and there appeared to another group of windmills atop the next rise beyond. A row of arches, like a long narrow bridge, stretched down the slope from the nearest windmills all the way to the city walls.

"Does anybody know what that is?" he asked, pointing. Studying it through the looking glass told him nothing except that it seemed made of the same gray stone as the wall. The thing was much too narrow for a bridge. It lacked side walls, and there did not seem to be anything for a bridge to cross.

"It is for bringing water," Sulin replied. "It runs for five miles, to a lake. I do not know why they did not build their city closer, but most of the land around the lake looks as if it will be mud when the cold goes away." She no longer stumbled over unfamiliar words like mud, yet a touch of awe remained in "lake," in the idea of so much water in one place. "You think to stop their water supply? That will surely make them come out." She understood fighting over water. Most fighting in the Waste started with water. "But I do not think—"

The colors erupted inside Perrin's head, an explosion of hues so strong that sight and hearing vanished. All sight except for the colors themselves, at least. They were a vast tide, as if all the times he had pushed them out of his head had built a dam that they now smashed aside in a silent flood, swirling in soundless whirlpools that tried to suck him under. An image coalesced in the middle of it, Rand and Nynaeve sitting on the ground facing one another, as clear as if they were right in front of him. He had no time for Rand, not now. Not now! Clawing at the colors like a drowning man clawing for the surface, he—forced—them—out!

Sight and hearing, the world around, crashed in on him.

". . . it's madness," Grady was saying in worried tones. "Nobody can handle enough of *saidin* for me to feel that far off! Nobody!"

"No one can handle that much of *saidar,* either," Marline murmured. "But someone is."

"The Forsaken?" Annoura's voice shook. "The Forsaken, using some *sa'angreal* we never suspected. Or . . . or the Dark One himself."

They were all three peering back to the north and west, and if Marline looked calmer than Annoura or Grady, she smelled as frightened and worried. Except for Elyas, the others were watching those three with the look of men awaiting an announcement that a new Breaking of the World had begun. Elyas's face was accepting. A wolf would snap at a landslide carrying him to his death, but a wolf knew that death came sooner or later, and you could not fight death.

"It's Rand," Perrin muttered thickly. He shuddered as the colors tried to return, but he hammered them down. "His business. He'll take care of it, whatever it is." Everyone was staring at him, even Elyas. "I need prisoners, Sulin. They must send out hunting parties. Elyas says they have sentries out a few miles, small groups. Can you get me prisoners?"

"Listen to me carefully," Annoura said, the words rushing out of her. She rose up out of the snow enough to reach over Marline and seize a fistful of Perrin's cloak. "Something is happening, perhaps wonderful, perhaps terrible, but in any case momentous, more so than anything in recorded history! We must know what! Grady can take us there, close enough to see. *I* could take us if I knew the weaves. We must know!"

Meeting her gaze, Perrin raised his hand, and she stopped with her mouth open. Aes Sedai never shut up that easily, yet she did. "I told you what it is. Our work is right down there in front of us. Sulin?"

Sulin's head swung from him to the Aes Sedai to Marline. Finally, she shrugged. "You will learn little useful even if you put them to the question. They will embrace the pain and laugh at you. And shame will be slow—if these Shaido can still be shamed."

"Whatever I learn will be more than I know now," he replied. His work lay in front of him. A puzzle to solve, Faile to free, and the Shaido to destroy. That was all that mattered in the world.

CHAPTER

9

Traps

A nd she complained again that the other Wise Ones
are timid," Faile finished in her best meek voice,
shifting the tall basket she held balanced on one
shoulder, shifting from foot to foot in the muddy snow. The
basket was not heavy, though filled with dirty laundry, and
the wool of her white robe was thick and warm, with two
under-robes beneath, but her soft leather boots, themselves
bleached white, gave little protection from the cold slush. "I
was told to report what the Wise One Sevanna said exactly,"
she added quickly. Someryn was one of the "other" Wise
Ones, and her mouth had turned down at the word timid.

With her eyes lowered, that was all Faile could see of
Someryn's face. *Gai'shain* were required to maintain a
humble manner, especially the *gai'shain* who were not
Aiel, and though she looked up through her eyelashes to
read Someryn's expression, the other woman was taller than
most men, even Aiel men, a yellow-haired giant who towered over her. Most of what she could see was Someryn's
over-large bosom, plump sun-dark cleavage exposed by a
blouse unlaced halfway down her chest and covered mainly
by a massive collection of long necklaces, firedrops and
emeralds, rubies and opals, three-tiered strands of fat pearls
and intricately patterned chains of gold. Most of the Wise
Ones seemed to dislike Sevanna, who "spoke for the chief"
until a new Shaido clan chief could be chosen, an event unlikely to occur any time soon, and they tried to undercut her
authority whenever they were not squabbling among themselves or forming cliques, but many shared Sevanna's love
of wetlander jewelry, and some had even begun wearing

finger rings, like Sevanna. On her right hand Someryn wore a large white opal that flashed caverns of red whenever she adjusted her shawl, and a long blue sapphire surrounded by rubies on the left. She had not adopted silk clothing, however. Her blouse was plain white *algode,* from the Waste, and her skirt and shawl thick wool as dark as the folded scarf that held her waist-long yellow hair back from her face. The cold did not appear to discomfort her in the least.

The two of them stood just beyond what Faile thought of as the border between the Shaido camp and the *gai'shain* camp—the prisoners' camp—not that there really were two camps. A few *gai'shain* slept among the Shaido, but the rest were kept to the center of the camp unless doing their assigned work, cattle fenced off from the lure of freedom by a wall of Shaido. Most of the men and women who passed them wore white *gai'shain* robes, though few as finely woven as what she wore. With so many to clothe, the Shaido scooped up any sort of white cloth they could find. Some were garbed in layers of coarse linen or toweling or robes of rough tent cloth, and many of the robes were stained with mud or soot. Only now and then did one of the *gai'shain* show the height and pale eyes of an Aiel. The vast majority were ruddy-faced Amadicians, olive-skinned Altarans, and pale Cairhienin, along with occasional travelers or merchants from Illian or Tarabon or elsewhere who had found themselves in the worst place at the worst time. The Cairhienin were the longest held and most resigned to their situation aside from the handful of Aiel in white, but they all kept their eyes down and moved about their tasks as fast as the trampled mush of snow and mud would allow. *Gai'shain* were expected to display humility, obedience, and an eagerness to embrace both. Any less resulted in painful reminders.

Faile would very much have liked to hurry on herself. Cold feet were only a small part of it, and eagerness to do Sevanna's laundry less. Too many eyes could see her standing there in the open with Someryn, and even with her deep cowl hiding her face, the broad mesh belt of shiny golden links around her waist and a close-fitting collar to match marked her as one of Sevanna's servants. No one called them that—in Aiel eyes, being a servant was demeaning— but that was what they were, the wetlanders at least, just unpaid and with fewer rights and less freedom than any servant Faile had ever heard tell of. Sooner or later Sevanna herself was going to learn that Wise Ones were stopping her *gai'shain* to question them. Sevanna had well over a hundred servants and kept adding to them, and Faile was certain that every last one was repeating every word they heard Sevanna say to the Wise Ones.

It was a brutally efficient trap. Sevanna was a harsh mistress, in a rather casual way, never snapping, seldom openly angry, but the slightest infraction, the smallest slip in demeanor or behavior, was punished immediately with the switch or the strap, and every night the five *gai'shain* who had pleased her least that day were chosen out for further punishment, sometimes a night bound and gagged on top of a beating, just to encourage the rest. Faile did not want to think of what the woman would order for a spy. On the other hand, the Wise Ones had made it clear that anyone who did not talk freely of what they heard, anyone who tried to hold back or bargain, faced an uncertain future, possibly ending in a shallow grave. Harming a *gai'shain* beyond the permitted limits of discipline was a violation of *ji'e'toh,* the web of honor and obligation that governed the lives of Aiel, but wetlander *gai'shain* seemed to stand outside a number of the rules.

Sooner or later, one side or the other of that trap would snap shut. All that had held the jaws apart this long was that the Shaido seemed to see their wetlander *gai'shain* as no different from cart horses or pack animals, though in truth the animals received far better treatment. Now and then a *gai'shain* tried to run away, but aside from that, one simply gave them food and shelter, put them to work and punished them if they faltered. The Wise Ones no more expected them to disobey, Sevanna no more expected them to spy on her, than they expected a cart horse to sing. Sooner or later, though . . . And that was not the only trap Faile was caught in.

"Wise One, I have nothing more to tell," she murmured when Someryn said nothing. Unless you were addled in the head, you did not just walk away from a Wise One, not until she dismissed you. "The Wise One Sevanna talks freely in front of us, but she says little."

The tall woman remained silent, and after a long moment Faile dared to raise her eyes a little more. Someryn was staring over Faile's head, her mouth hanging open in stunned amazement. Frowning, Faile shifted the basket on her shoulder and looked behind her, but there was nothing to account for Someryn's expression, just the sprawl of the camp, dark low Aiel tents mingled with peaked tents and walled tents and every sort of tent, most in shades of dirty white or pale brown, others green or blue or red or even striped. The Shaido took everything valuable when they struck, everything that might prove useful, and they left behind nothing that resembled a tent.

As it was, they hardly had enough shelter to go around. There were ten septs gathered here, more than seventy thousand Shaido and nearly as many *gai'shain,* by her estimate, and everywhere she saw only the usual bustle, dark-clad Aiel going about their lives among scurrying white-clad captives. A smith was working the bellows on his forge in front of an open tent with his tools laid out on a tanned bull hide, children were herding flocks of bleating goats with switches, a trader was displaying her goods in an open pavilion of yellow canvas, everything from golden candlesticks and silver bowls to pots and kettles, all looted. A lean man with a horse on a lead stood talking with a gray-haired Wise One named Masalin, no doubt seeking a cure for some ailment the animal had, from the way he kept pointing at the horse's belly. Nothing to make Someryn gape.

Just as Faile was about to turn back around, she noticed a dark-haired Aiel woman facing the other way. Not just dark hair, but hair black as a raven's wing, a great rarity among Aiel. Even from behind, Faile thought she recognized Alarys, another of the Wise Ones. There were over four hundred Wise Ones in the camp, but she had learned quickly to know all of them on sight. Mistaking a Wise One for a weaver or a potter was a quick way to earn a switching.

It might have meant nothing that Alarys was standing stock-still and looking in the same direction as Someryn, or that she had let her shawl slide to the ground, except that just beyond her, Faile recognized still another Wise One, also looking off to the north and west, and slapping at people who walked in front of her. That had to be Jesain, a woman who would have been called short even if she were not Aiel, with a great mass of hair red enough to make fire look pale and a temper to match. Masalin was talking to the man with the horse and gesturing to the animal. She could not channel, but three Wise Ones who could were all staring in the same direction. Only one thing could account for it; they saw someone channeling up there on the forested ridgeline beyond the camp. A Wise One channeling surely would not make any of them stare. Could it be an Aes Sedai? Or more than one? Better not to get her hopes up. It was too soon.

A clout on the head staggered her, and she nearly dropped the basket.

"Why are you standing like a lump?" Someryn snarled. "Go on with your work. Go, before I . . . !"

Faile went, balancing the basket with one hand, lifting the skirts of her robe out of the muddy snow with the other, and moving as quickly as she could without slipping and falling in the muck. Someryn never hit anyone, and she never raised her voice. If she was doing both, it was best to be out of her way with no delay. Humbly and obediently.

Pride said to maintain a cool defiance, a quiet refusal to yield, yet sense said that was the way to find herself guarded twice as closely as she was. The Shaido might take the wetlander *gai'shain* for domesticated animals, but they were not completely blind. They must think that she had accepted her captivity as inescapable if she were to be able to escape, and that was very much on her mind. The sooner, the better. Certainly before Perrin caught up. She had never doubted that Perrin was following her, that he would find her somehow—the man would walk through a wall if he took it into his head!—but she had to escape before that. She was a soldier's daughter. She knew the Shaido's numbers, she knew the strength Perrin had to call on, and she knew she had to reach him before that clash could take place. There was just the little matter of getting free of the Shaido, first.

What had the Wise Ones been looking at—the Aes Sedai or Wise Ones with Perrin? Light, she hoped not, not yet! But other matters took precedence, the laundry not least. She carried the basket toward what remained of the city of Malden, weaving through a steady flow of *gai'shain*. Those leaving the city each carried a pair of heavy buckets balanced on the ends of a pole carried across the shoulders, while the buckets of those going in swayed, empty, on their poles. As many people as were in the camp required a great deal of water, and this was how it came to them, bucket by bucket. It was easy to tell the *gai'shain* who had been inhabitants of Malden. This far north in Altara, they were fair rather than olive-complected, and some even had blue eyes, but all stumbled along in a daze. Shaido climbing the city walls in the night had overwhelmed the defenses before most of the residents knew they were in danger, and they still seemed unable to believe what their lives had come to.

Faile searched for a particular face, though, someone she hoped would not be carrying water today. She had been looking ever since the Shaido made camp here, four days ago. Just outside the city gates, which stood open and shoved back against the granite walls, she found her, a white-clad woman taller than herself with a flat basket of bread on her hip and her hood pushed back just enough to show a bit of dark reddish hair. Chiad appeared to be studying the iron-strapped gates that had failed to protect Malden, but she turned away from them as soon as Faile approached. They paused side by side, not really looking at one another while they pretended to shift their baskets. There was no reason two *gai'shain* should not talk to one another, but no one should remember that they had been captured together. Bain and Chiad were not watched as closely as *gai'shain* serving Sevanna, but that might change if anyone remembered. Almost everyone in sight was *gai'shain,* and from west of the Dragonwall besides, yet too many had learned to curry favor by carrying tales and rumors. Most people did what they must to survive, and some always tried to feather their own nests, whatever the circumstances.

"They got away the first night here," Chiad murmured. "Bain and I led them out to the trees and obscured the tracks coming back. No one seems to realize they are gone, as far as I can see. With so many *gai'shain,* it seems a wonder these Shaido notice any who run away."

Faile heaved a small sigh of relief. Three days gone. The Shaido did notice runaways. Few managed a full day of freedom, but the chances of success increased with every day uncaught, and it seemed certain the Shaido would move on tomorrow, or the next day. They had not halted as long as this since Faile was captured. She suspected they might be trying to march back to the Dragonwall and recross into the Waste.

It had not been easy talking Lacile and Arrela into leaving without her. What finally convinced them had been the argument that they could carry word to Perrin of where Faile was, along with a warning of how many Shaido there were and a claim that Faile already had her own escape well in hand and any interference by him might endanger that and her. She was sure she had made them believe all of that—she did have her escape in hand, in a way; she had several plans, in fact, and one of them had to work—but until this minute she had been half convinced the two women would decide their oaths to her required them to stay. Water oaths were tighter than oaths of fealty in some ways, yet they left considerable room for stupidity in the name of honor. In truth, she did not know whether the pair could find Perrin, but either way, they were free and she had only two other women to worry about. Of course, the absence of three of Sevanna's servants would be noticed very quickly, within hours, and the best trackers would be sent to bring them back. Faile was accustomed to the woods, but she knew better than to pit herself against Aiel trackers. It was very unpleasant for "ordinary" *gai'shain* who ran away and were recaptured. For Sevanna's *gai'shain,* it might be better to die in the attempt. At best, they would never be allowed the opportunity for a second try.

"The rest of us would have a better chance if you and Bain came with us," she said in a low voice. The flow of men and women in white carrying water by them continued, no one seeming to more than glance their way, but wariness had become ingrained in her these last two weeks. Light, it seemed more like two years! "What difference can there be between helping Lacile and Arrela reach the forest and helping the rest of us get further?" That was despair talking. She knew the difference—Bain and Chiad were her friends and had taught her about Aiel ways, about *ji'e'toh* and even a little Maiden handtalk—and it did not surprise her when Chiad turned her head slightly to regard her with gray eyes that had nothing of *gai'shain* meekness in them. Nor did her voice, though she still spoke quietly.

"I will help you as far as I can because it is not right for the Shaido to hold you. You do not follow *ji'e'toh.* I do. If I cast aside my honor and my obligations just because the

Shaido have, then I allow them to decide how I will act. I will wear white for a year and a day and then they will release me, or I will walk away, but I will not throw away who I am." Without another word, Chiad strode off into the throngs of *gai'shain*.

Faile half-raised a hand to stop her, then let it fall. She had asked that question before, receiving a gentler answer, and in asking again, she had insulted her friend. She would have to apologize. Not to keep Chiad's help—the woman would not withdraw that—but because she had her own honor, even if she did not follow *ji'e'toh*. You did not insult friends and simply forget it, or expect them to. Apologies must wait, though. They dared not be seen talking too long.

Malden had been a prosperous city, a producer of good wool and great quantities of fair-quality wine, but an empty ruin inside the walls, now. As many of the slate-roofed houses were timber as were stone, and fire had gotten loose during the looting. The southern end of the city was half piles of blackened timbers decorated with icicles, half scorched, roofless walls. The streets everywhere, whether stone-paved or dirt, were gray with windblown ash trampled into the snow, and the whole city stank of charred wood. Water was one thing Malden apparently never ran short of, but like all Aiel, the Shaido placed a very high value on it, and they knew nothing of fighting fires. There was little in the Aiel Waste that *could* burn. They might have let the entire city be consumed had they been finished with stealing, and as it was, they dithered over the waste of water before forcing *gai'shain* into bucket lines at spearpoint and letting the men of Malden bring out their pumpwagons. Faile would have thought the Shaido would at least have rewarded those men by allowing them to leave with the people who had escaped being chosen for *gai'shain,* but the men who worked the pumps were young and fit, just the sort the Shaido wanted for their *gai'shain*. The Shaido kept some of the rules regarding *gai'shain*—women who were pregnant or had children under the age of ten had been let go, and youths under sixteen, and the city's blacksmiths, who had been both mystified and grateful—but gratitude never entered into it.

Furniture littered the streets, large overturned tables and ornate chests and chairs, and sometimes a crumpled wall hanging or broken dishes. Bits of clothing lay everywhere, coats and breeches and dresses, most sliced to tatters. The Shaido had seized anything made of gold or silver, anything that had gems, anything useful or edible, but the furnishings must have been hauled outside in the frenzy of looting, then abandoned when whoever was carrying them decided that a little gilded edging or fine carving did not make them worth the effort. Aiel did not use chairs in any case, except for chiefs, and there was no room on the carts and wagons for any of those heavy tables. A few Shaido still wandered through, searching the houses and inns and shops for anything they might have missed, yet most people she saw were *gai'shain* carrying buckets. Aiel had no interest in cities except as storehouses to be plundered. A pair of Maidens passed her, using the butts of their spears to drive a naked, wild-eyed man, his arms bound behind him, toward the gates. Doubtless he had thought he could hide in a basement or attic until the Shaido were gone. Doubtless the Maidens had thought to find a cache of coin or plate. When a huge man in the *cadin'sor* of an *algai'd'siswai* stepped in front of her, she swerved to go around him as smoothly as she could. A *gai'shain* always made way for any Shaido.

"You are very pretty," he said, putting himself in her way. He was the biggest man she had ever seen, perhaps seven feet tall and thick in proportion. Not fat—she had never seen a fat Aiel—but very wide. He belched, and she smelled wine fumes. Drunken Aiel she had seen, since they found all those casks of wine here in Malden. She felt no fear, though. *Gai'shain* might be punished for any number of infractions, often for transgressions few of the wetlanders understood, but the white robes gave a certain protection, too, and she had another layer besides.

"I am *gai'shain* to the Wise One Sevanna," she said in as obsequious a tone as she could manage. To her disgust, she had gotten so she could manage it very well. "Sevanna would be displeased if I shirked my duties to talk." She tried again to step around him, and gasped when he seized her arm in a hand that could have wrapped around it twice with inches to spare.

"Sevanna has hundreds of *gai'shain*. She will not miss one for an hour or two."

The basket fell to the street as he plucked her into the air as easily as picking up a pillow. Before she knew what was happening, he had her tucked beneath his arm, her own arms trapped at her sides. She opened her mouth to scream, and he used his free hand to press her face flat against his chest. The smell of sweaty wool filled her nose. All she could see was gray-brown wool. Where were those two Maidens? Maidens of the Spear would not let him do this! *Any* Aiel who saw would step in! She never expected help from any of the *gai'shain*. One or two might run for help, if she was lucky, but the very first lesson a *gai'shain* learned was that even a threat of violence got you hung up by the ankles and beaten till you howled. The first lesson wetlanders learned, at least; Aiel already knew: a *gai'shain* was forbidden to offer violence for any reason. *Any* reason. Which did not stop her from kicking at the man furiously. She might as well have been kicking a wall for all the impression it made. He was moving, carrying her somewhere. She bit down as hard as she could, and got a mouthful of coarse dirty wool for her pains, her teeth sliding over muscle with no slack to give her purchase. He seemed made of stone. She screamed, but her shriek sounded muffled even to her own ears.

Abruptly, the monster carrying her stopped.

"I made this one *gai'shain*, Nadric," another man's deep voice said.

Faile felt a rumble of laughter in the chest against her face even before she heard it. She did not stop her kicking, never stopped writhing or trying to shout, yet her captor seemed unaware of her efforts. "She belongs to Sevanna now, Brotherless," the huge man—Nadric?—said contemptuously. "Sevanna takes what she wants, and I take what I want. It is the new way."

"Sevanna took her," the other man replied calmly, "but I never gave her to Sevanna. I never offered to trade her to Sevanna. Do you abandon your honor because Sevanna abandons hers?"

There was a long silence broken only by the smothered noises Faile was making. She did not stop struggling, could not stop, but she might as well have been an infant in swaddling.

"She is not pretty enough to fight over," Nadric said finally. He did not sound frightened or even concerned.

His hands fell away from her, and Faile's teeth ripped loose from his coat so suddenly she thought one or two might be jerked out, but the ground smashed into her back and all of the air rushed out of her lungs along with most of the wits from her head. By the time she could gather enough breath to push up on her hands, the huge man was striding away down the alley, almost back to the street. It *was* an alley, a narrow track of dirt between two stone buildings. No one would have seen what he did back here. Shivering—she was not trembling, just shivering!—spitting out the taste of unwashed wool and Nadric's sweat, she glared at his back. If the knife she had hidden away had been within reach, she would have stabbed him. Not pretty enough to fight over, was she? Part of her knew that was ludicrous, but she was grabbing hold of anything that could feed her anger, just for the warmth of it. To help her stop shivering. She would have stabbed him and stabbed him, until she could not lift her arms.

Getting up on legs that wobbled, she explored her teeth with her tongue. They were all sound, nothing broken or missing. Her face had been scraped by the rough wool of Nadric's coat, and her lips were bruised, but she was unhurt. She reminded herself of that. She was unhurt, and free to walk out of the alley. As free as anyone in *gai'shain* robes could be, anyway. If there were many like Nadric who no longer saw the protection of those robes, then order was breaking down among the Shaido. The camp would be a more dangerous place, but disorder would bring more opportunities for escape. That was how she had to look at this. She had learned something that could aid her. If only she could stop shivering.

At last, reluctantly, she looked at her rescuer. She had recognized his voice. He stood well back from her, watching her calmly, making no move to offer sympathy. She thought she would have screamed if he touched her. Another absurdity, since he had rescued her, but a fact all the same. Rolan was no more than a hand shorter than Nadric, and almost as wide, and she had reason to want to stab him, too. He was not Shaido, but one of the Brotherless, the *Mera'din,*

men who had left their clans because they would not follow
Rand al'Thor, and he had indeed been the one to "make her
gai'shain." True, he had kept her from freezing to death the
night after she was captured by wrapping her in his own
coat, yet she would not have needed the covering if he had
not cut off every last stitch of her clothing in the first place.
The first part of being made *gai'shain* was always being
stripped, but that was no reason to forgive him for any of it.

"Thank you," she said, the words sour on her tongue.

"I do not ask for gratitude," he said mildly. "Do not look
at me as though you want to bite me just because you could
not bite Nadric."

She managed not to snarl at him—barely; she could not
have summoned meekness right then had she wanted to—
before she turned away and stalked back out to the street.
Well, she tried to stalk. Her legs were still shaking enough
that it was more of a lurch. The passing *gai'shain* barely
glanced in her direction as they trudged along the street
with their water buckets. Few of the captives wanted to
share anyone else's troubles. They had enough of their own.

Reaching the laundry basket, she gave a sigh. It lay on
its side, white silk blouses and dark silk skirts divided for
riding spilled out over the dirty ash-smeared pavement. At
least it seemed no one had trodden on them. Anyone who
had been carrying water all morning, and had a day of it to
look forward to, could have been forgiven if they failed to
step aside, with bits of clothing lying all around that had
been cut off the people of Malden who had been made
gai'shain. She would have tried to forgive them. Righting
the basket, she began gathering the clothes, shaking off the
dirt and ash that would come loose and careful not to grind
in the rest. Unlike Someryn, Sevanna had taken to silk. She
wore nothing else. She was as proud of her silks as she was
of her jewelry, and equally possessive of both. She would
not be pleased if any of these garments failed to be returned
clean.

As Faile laid the last blouse atop the rest, Rolan reached
past her and lifted the basket with one hand. On the brink of
snapping at him—she could carry her own burdens, thank
you very much!—she swallowed the words. Her brain was
the only real weapon she possessed, and she had to use it
instead of letting her temper have control. Rolan had not

been here by chance. That was straining credulity too far. She had seen him frequently since she was captured, much more often than chance could account for. He had been following her. What was it he had told Nadric? He had not given her to Sevanna or offered to trade her. For all that he had been the one to capture her, she thought he disapproved of making wetlanders *gai'shain*—most of the Brotherless did—but apparently he still claimed his rights to her.

She was sure she did not need to fear him trying to force her. Rolan had had his chance for that, when he had her naked and bound, and he could have been looking at a fence post then. Perhaps he did not like women in that way. In any case, the Brotherless were almost as much outsiders among the Shaido as the wetlanders. None of the Shaido really trusted them, and the Brotherless themselves often seemed like men holding their noses, accepting what they considered a lesser wrong rather than embrace a greater, but no longer truly sure that it was lesser. If she could make a friend of the man, perhaps he would be willing to help her. Not to escape, certainly—that would be asking too much— but . . . Or would it? The only way to find out was to try.

"Thank you," she said again, and this time she worked up a smile. Surprisingly, he smiled back. A small smile, barely there at all, but Aiel were not demonstrative. They could seem stone-faced till you became used to them.

For a few paces they walked along side by side in silence, him carrying the basket in one hand and her holding up the skirts of her robes. They might have been out for a stroll. If you squinted. Some of the passing *gai'shain* looked at them in surprise, but they always put their eyes down again quickly. She could not think of how to begin—she did not want him to think she was flirting; he might like women after all—but he took away the necessity.

"I have watched you," he said. "You are strong and fierce, and not afraid, I think. Most of the wetlanders are frightened half out of their heads. They bluster until they are punished, and then they weep and cower. I think you are a woman of much *ji*."

"I am frightened," she replied. "I just try not let it show. Crying never does any good." Most men believed that. Tears could get in your way if you let them, but a few tears shed at night could help you make it through the next day.

"There are times to weep and times to laugh. I would like to see you laugh."

She did laugh, a dry laugh. "There's little reason while I wear white, Rolan." She glanced at him out of the corner of her eye. Was she going too fast? But he only nodded.

"Still, I would like to see it. Smiles suit your face. Laughter would suit it even better. I have no wife, but I can make a woman laugh, sometimes. I have heard you have a husband?"

Startled, Faile tripped over her own feet and caught herself on his arm. Quickly, she snatched her hand away, studying him past the edge of her cowl. He paused long enough for her to steady herself, then walked on when she did. His expression was no more than mildly curious. Despite Nadric, Aiel custom was for a woman to do the asking, after a man attracted her interest. Giving her gifts was one way. Making her laugh was another. So much for his not liking women. "I do have a husband, Rolan, and I love him very much. Very much. I can't wait to return to him."

"What happens while you are *gai'shain* cannot be held against you when you put off white," he said calmly, "but perhaps you wetlanders do not see it that way. Still, it can be lonely when you are *gai'shain*. Perhaps we can talk sometimes."

The man wanted to see her laugh, and she did not know whether to laugh or cry. He was announcing that he did not intend to give up trying to attract her interest. Aiel women admired perseverance in a man. Still, if Chiad and Bain would not, could not, help beyond giving her aid in reaching the trees, Rolan was her best hope. She thought she could convince him, given time. Of course she could; faint hearts never succeeded! He was a scorned outcast, accepted only because the Shaido needed his spear. But she was going to have to give him a reason to persist.

"I would like that," she said carefully. A little flirting might be necessary after all, but she could not go from telling him how much she loved her husband straight to wide-eyed and breathless. Not that she had any intention of going that far—she was no Domani!—yet she might need to come close. For the time being, a little reminder that Sevanna had usurped his "right" would not go amiss. "I have work to do now, though, and I doubt Sevanna would be pleased if I spent the time talking to you instead."

Rolan nodded again, and Faile sighed. He might know how to make a woman laugh, as he claimed, but he certainly did not talk very much. She was going to have to work to draw him out if she intended to get anything more than jokes she did not understand. Even with Chiad and Bain's help, Aiel humor remained incomprehensible to her.

They had reached the broad square in front of the fortress at the north end of the city, a towered mass of gray stone walls that had protected its inhabitants no better than the city walls. Faile thought she had seen the lady who had ruled Malden and everything for twenty miles around, a handsome dignified widow in her middle years, among the *gai'shain* hauling water. White-clad men and women carrying buckets crowded the stone-paved square. At the eastern end of the square, what looked like a section of the city's outer wall, gray and thirty feet high, was actually the wall of a huge cistern fed by an aqueduct. Four pumps, each worked by a pair of men, gushed out water to fill the buckets, a good bit more splashing to the paving stones than the men would have dared allow if they had known Rolan was close enough to see. Faile had considered crawling through the tunnel-like aqueduct to escape, but they had no way to keep anything dry, and wherever it let them out, they would be soaking wet and more likely to freeze to death than make it more than a mile or two in the snow.

There were two other places in the city to get water, both fed by stone conduits underground, but here a long, lion-footed blackwood table had been placed at the foot of the cistern wall. Once it had been a banqueting table, the top inlaid with ivory, but the ivory wedges had been pried out and several wooden washtubs sat on the tabletop now. A pair of wooden buckets stood beside the table, and at one end a copper kettle steamed over a fire made from broken-up chairs. Faile doubted that Sevanna had her laundry carried into the city to save her *gai'shain* the labor of hauling water out to the tents, but whatever the reason, Faile was grateful. A basket of laundry was lighter than full water buckets. She had carried enough of them to know. Two baskets stood on the table, but only one woman wearing the golden belt and collar was at work, the sleeves of her white robe rolled up as high as they would go and her long dark hair tied with a strip of white cloth to keep it from falling into the washtub's water.

When Alliandre saw Faile approaching with Rolan, she straightened, drying her bare arms on her robe. Alliandre Maritha Kigarin, Queen of Ghealdan, Blessed of the Light, Defender of Garen's Wall and a dozen more titles, had been an elegant, reserved woman, poised and stately. Alliandre the *gai'shain* was still pretty, but she wore a perpetually harried expression. With damp patches on her robes and her hands wrinkled from long immersion in the water, she could have passed for a pretty washerwoman. Watching Rolan set down the basket and smile at Faile before striding away, watching Faile return the smile, she raised a quizzical eyebrow.

"He's the one who captured me," Faile said, setting pieces of clothing from the basket on the table. Even here among none but *gai'shain,* it was best to talk while working. "He's one of the Brotherless, and I think he doesn't really approve of making wetlanders *gai'shain.* I think he may help us."

"I see," Alliandre said. With one hand she brushed delicately at the back of Faile's robe.

Frowning, Faile twisted to look over her shoulder. For a moment she stared at the dirt and ash that covered her back from the shoulders down; then heat flooded her face. "I fell," she said quickly. She could not tell Alliandre what had happened with Nadric. She did not think she could tell anyone. "Rolan offered to carry my basket."

Alliandre shrugged. "If he helped me escape, I would marry him. Or not, as he wanted. He's not quite pretty, but it wouldn't be painful, and my husband, if I had one, would never have to know. If he had any sense, he would be overjoyed to have me back and ask no questions he didn't want to hear answers to."

Hands tightening on a silk blouse, Faile gritted her teeth. Alliandre was her liege woman, through Perrin, and she held to that well enough, at least insofar as obeying commands, but the nature of the relationship had become strained. They had agreed that they must try to think like servants, try to *be* servants, if they were to survive, yet that meant that each had seen the other curtsying and scurrying to obey. Sevanna's punishments were dealt out by the nearest *gai'shain* to hand when she made her decision, and once Faile had been ordered to switch Alliandre. Worse, Alliandre had been ordered to return the favor twice. Holding back only meant a taste of the same for yourself plus the other woman having to endure a double dose from someone who would not spare her arm. It had to make a difference when you had twice made your liege-lady kick and shriek.

Abruptly she realized that the blouse she was gripping was one of those that had picked up extra dirt when the basket fell. Loosening her grip, she examined the garment anxiously. It did not seem that she had ground the dirt in. For a moment, she felt relief, and then irritation at being relieved. Even more irritating, the relief did not go away.

"Arrela and Lacile escaped three days ago," she said in a low voice. "They should be well away by now. Where is Maighdin?"

A worried frown appeared on the other woman's face. "She is trying to sneak into Therava's tent. Therava passed us with a group of Wise Ones, and from what we overheard, they seemed to be on their way to meet with Sevanna. Maighdin shoved her basket at me and said she was going to try. I think . . . I think she's becoming desperate enough to take too many chances," she said with a touch of hopelessness in her own voice. "She should have been here by now."

Faile drew a deep breath and let it out slowly. They were all becoming desperate. They had gathered supplies for their escape—knives and food, boots and men's breeches and coats that fit near enough, all carefully hidden in the wagons; the white robes would serve as blankets, and as cloaks to hide them in the snow—but the chance to use all that preparation seemed no closer now than the day they were captured. Only two weeks. Twenty-two days to be exact. That should have not been long enough to change anything, but their pretense of being servants was changing them in spite of all they could do. Only two weeks, and they found themselves jumping to obey commands without thought, worrying over punishments and whether they were pleasing Sevanna. The worst of it was, they could see themselves doing these things, knew some part of them was being molded against their wills. For now, they could tell themselves they were just doing what was needed to avoid suspicion until they could escape, yet every day the reactions became more automatic. How long before escape was a pale dream dreamed in the night after a day of being a perfect *gai'shain* in thought as well as deed? No one had dared ask that question aloud, so far, and Faile knew that she herself tried not to think it, but the question was always on the edge of her consciousness. In a way, she was afraid of it leaving. When it did, would it already have been answered?

With an effort, she forced herself back from despondency. That was the second trap, and only willpower held it open. "Maighdin knows she has to be careful," she said in a firm voice. "She will be here soon, Alliandre."

"And if she is caught?"

"She won't be!" Faile said sharply. If she was . . . No. She had to think of victory, not defeat. Faint hearts never won.

Washing the silk was time-consuming. The buckets of water they fetched from the cistern pumps were icy cold, but hot water scooped from the copper kettle brought the temperature in the washtubs up to lukewarm. You could not wash silk in hot water. Sinking your hands into the washtubs felt wonderful in the cold, but you always had to take them out again, and then the cold was twice as bitter. There was no soap, not that was mild enough anyway, so each skirt and blouse had to be submersed one by one and delicately scrubbed against itself. Then it was laid on a piece of toweling and gently rolled up to squeeze out as much water as possible. The damp garment was dipped again, in another washtub that was filled with a mixture of vinegar and water—that reduced fading and enhanced the gloss of the silk—then rolled up in toweling again. The wet toweling was wrung out hard and spread in the sun to dry wherever there was room, while each piece of silk was hung on a horizontal pole, slung in the shade of a rough canvas pavilion erected at the edge of the square, and smoothed by hand to rub out wrinkles. With luck, nothing would need ironing. Both of them knew how silk had to be cared for, but ironing it needed experience neither of them had. None of Sevanna's *gai'shain* did, not even Maighdin, though she had been a lady's maid even before entering Faile's service, but Sevanna did not accept excuses. Every time Faile or Alliandre went to hang another garment, they checked those already there and smoothed any that seemed to need it.

Faile was adding hot water to a washtub when Alliandre said bitterly, "Here comes the Aes Sedai."

Galina was Aes Sedai, complete with the ageless face and a golden Great Serpent ring on her finger, but she wore white *gai'shain* robes, too—in silk as thick as anyone else's wool, no less!—along with a wide, elaborate belt of gold and firedrops that cinched her waist tightly and a tall matching collar around her neck, jewels fit for a monarch. She was Aes Sedai, and sometimes rode out from the camp alone, but she always returned, and she jumped when any Wise One crooked a finger, especially Therava, whose tent she often shared. In a way, that last was the strangest thing of all. Galina knew who Faile was, knew who her husband was and Perrin's connection to Rand al'Thor, and she threatened to reveal it to Sevanna unless Faile and her friends stole something from the very tent she slept in. That was the third trap lying in wait for them. Sevanna was obsessed with al'Thor, insanely convinced that she could somehow marry him, and if she learned about Perrin, Faile would never be allowed far enough out of her sight to think of escape. She would be staked out like a goat to draw a lion.

Faile had seen Galina slinking and cowering, but now the sister glided through the square like a queen disdaining the rabble around her, an Aes Sedai to the hilt. There were no Wise Ones here for her to simper at. Galina was pretty, but nowhere near beautiful, and Faile did not understand what Therava saw in her, unless it was simply the pleasure of dominating an Aes Sedai. That still left the question of why the woman remained when Therava seemed to take every opportunity to humiliate her.

Stopping a pace from the table, Galina surveyed them with a small smile that might have been called pitying. "You are not progressing very far in your work," she said. She was not speaking of the laundry.

It was Faile's place to do the talking, but Alliandre spoke up, even more bitterly than before. "Maighdin went to fetch your ivory rod this morning, Galina. When will we see some of the help you promised?" Help in their escape was the carrot Galina offered along with the stick of threatening

Faile's exposure. So far, however, they had seen only the stick.

"She went to Therava's tent this morning?" Galina whispered, the blood draining from her face.

It dawned on Faile that the sun was halfway down to the horizon in the west, and her heart began to thud painfully. Maighdin should have joined them long since.

The Aes Sedai seemed even more shaken than she. "This morning?" Galina repeated, looking over her shoulder. She gave a start and a cry when Maighdin suddenly appeared out of the throng of *gai'shain* crowding the square.

Unlike Alliandre, the golden-haired woman had grown tougher by the day since their capture. She was no less desperate, but she seemed to focus it all into determination. She always had a presence that belonged more to a queen than a lady's maid, though most lady's maids had it, but now she stumbled past them, dull-eyed, and plunged her hands into a water bucket, cupping a double handful to her mouth to drink thirstily, then scrubbing the back of a hand across her mouth.

"I want to kill Therava when we go," she said thickly. "I would like to kill her now." Her blue eyes took on life again, and heat. "You're safe, Galina. She thought I was there to steal. I hadn't started looking. Something . . . Something happened, and she left. After tying me up. For later." The heat faded from her gaze to be replaced by puzzlement. "What is it, Galina? Even I feel it, and I have so little ability these Aiel women decided I was no danger." Maighdin could channel. Not reliably, though and not very much— from what little Faile knew, the White Tower would have sent her away in a matter of weeks, and she claimed never to have gone—so her ability would not be of much use in aiding their escape. Faile would have asked what she was talking about, but she never got the chance.

Galina's face was still pale, but otherwise she was all Aes Sedai calm. Except that she seized a handful of Maighdin's cowl and the hair beneath and wrenched her head back. "Never you mind what it is," she said coolly. "Nothing to do with you. All you need worry about is getting me what I want. But you should worry about that very hard."

Before Faile could move to defend Maighdin, another woman wearing the wide golden belt over her white robes was there, pulling Galina away and slinging her to the ground. Plump and plain, Aravine had been weary-eyed and resigned the first time Faile saw her, the day the Amadician woman handed her the golden belt she wore and told her she was now in the service of "the Lady Sevanna." The intervening days had stiffened Aravine even more than they had Maighdin, though.

"Are you mad, to lay hands on an Aes Sedai?" Galina snapped, struggling to her feet. Brushing at the dirt staining her silk robes, she directed all her fury at the plump woman. "I will have you—"

"Shall I tell Therava you were manhandling one of Sevanna's *gai'shain*?" Aravine broke in coldly. Her accents were cultured. She might have been a merchant of some note, or perhaps even a noble, but she never spoke of what she had been before putting on white. "The last time Therava thought you'd poked your nose where she didn't want it, everybody inside a hundred paces could hear you squealing and begging."

Galina actually quivered with rage, the first time Faile had ever seen an Aes Sedai so outdone. With a visible effort, she gained control of herself. Just. Her voice dripped acid. "Aes Sedai do what we do for our own reasons, Aravine, reasons you could not possibly understand. You will regret incurring this debt when I decide to collect payment. You will regret it to your heart." Giving her robes a last brush, she stalked away, no longer the queen disdaining rabble but a leopard daring sheep to block her path.

Watching her go, Aravine seemed unimpressed, and uninclined to chat. "Sevanna wants you, Faile" was all she said.

Faile did not bother to ask why. She just dried her hands, rolled down her sleeves, and followed the Amadician woman, after promising Alliandre and Maighdin to return as soon as she could. Sevanna was fascinated with the three of them. Maighdin, the only true lady's maid among her *gai'shain*, seemed to interest her as much as Queen Alliandre, and Faile herself, a woman powerful enough to have a queen as her liege woman, and sometimes she summoned one of them by name to help her change clothes or bathe in the large copper bathtub that she used more often than the sweat tent, or just to pour her wine. The rest of the time they were given the same chores as her other servants, but she never asked whether they had already been assigned work or let them off because of it. Whatever Sevanna wanted, Faile knew she still would be held accountable for the laundry along with the other two. Sevanna wanted what she wanted when she wanted it, and she did not accept excuses.

There was no need for Faile to be shown the way to Sevanna's tent, but Aravine led the way through the throng of water carriers until they reached the first low Aiel tents, and then she pointed in the opposite direction to Sevanna's tent and said, "This way, first."

Faile stopped where she stood. "Why?" she asked suspiciously. There were actually men and women among Sevanna's servants who were jealous of the attentions she gave Faile, Alliandre and Maighdin, and though Faile had never detected that in Aravine, some of the rest might well try to get them in trouble by passing on false instructions.

"You will want to see this before you see Sevanna. Believe me."

Faile opened her mouth to demand more explanation, but Aravine simply turned and walked away. Faile gathered up the skirts of her robes and followed.

All sorts and sizes of carts and wagons stood among the tents, their wheels replaced by sleds. Most were piled high with bundles and wooden crates and barrels, with the wheels tied on top of the loads, but she did not have to follow Aravine far before she saw a flatbed cart that had been emptied. Except that the cart bed was not empty. Two women lay on the rough wooden planks, naked and cruelly hogtied, shivering in the cold yet panting as if they were running. Both women's heads hung tiredly, but as if they somehow knew Faile was there, both looked up. Arrela, a dark Tairen as tall as most Aiel women, averted her eyes in embarrassment. Lacile, slim and pale and Cairhienin, went bright red.

"They were brought back this morning," Aravine said, watching Faile's face. "They will be untied before dark, since it's the first time they've tried to escape, though I doubt they will be in any condition to walk before tomorrow."

"Why did you show me this?" Faile said. They had been so careful to keep the connection between them a secret.

"You forget, my Lady, I was there when you were all put in white." Aravine studied her a moment, then suddenly took Faile's hands and turned them so that her own hands

were between Faile's palms. Bending her knees just short
of kneeling, she said quickly, "Under the Light and by my
hope of rebirth, I, Aravine Carnel, do pledge my fealty and
obedience in all things to the Lady Faile t'Aybara."

Only Lacile appeared to have noticed; the Shaido walking past paid no mind to two *gai'shain* women. Faile jerked
her hands free. "How do you know that name?" She had
had to give more of her name than Faile, of course, but she
had chosen Faile Bashere once she realized that none of the
Shaido had a clue who Davram Bashere was. Aside from
Alliandre and the others, only Galina knew the truth. Or so
she had thought. "And who have you told?"

"I listen, my Lady. I overheard Galina speaking to you,
once." Anxiety touched Aravine's voice. "And I have told
no one." She did not sound surprised that Faile wanted to
hide her name, though clearly t'Aybara meant nothing to
her. Perhaps Aravine Carnel was not her true name, or not
all of it. "In this place, secrets must be held as closely as in
Amador. I knew these women were yours, but I told no one.
I know you intend to escape. I've been certain since the
second or third day, and nothing I've seen since convinces
me otherwise. Accept my oath, and take me with you. I can
help, and what is more, I can be trusted. I have proved it
by keeping your secrets. Please." The last word came out
strained, as if from someone unused to saying it. A noblewoman, then, rather than a merchant.

The woman had proven nothing beyond that she could
spy out secrets, but that in itself was a useful trait. On the
other hand, Faile knew of at least two *gai'shain* who had
tried to escape and been betrayed by others. Some people
really did try to feather their own nests no matter what the
circumstances. But Aravine already knew enough to ruin
everything. Faile thought about her hidden knife again. A
dead woman could betray nothing. But the knife was half a
mile away, she could think of no way to hide the body, and
besides, the woman *could* have curried favor with Sevanna
just by saying she thought Faile was planning escape.

Taking Aravine's hands between hers, she spoke as
quickly as the other woman had. "Under the Light, I do
accept your pledge and will defend and protect you and
yours through battle's wrack and winter's blast and all that
time may bring. Now. Do you know anyone else who can

be trusted? Not people you think you can trust, people you know you can."

"Not with this, my Lady," Aravine said grimly. Her face shone with relief, though. She had not been sure Faile would accept her. That it was relief rather that anything else made Faile tend to believe in her. Tend to, which was not to say completely. "Half would betray their own mothers in hopes of buying freedom, and the other half are too afraid to try or too stunned to be trusted not to panic. There must be some, and I have my eye on one or two, but I want to be very careful. One mistake is one more than I'll be allowed."

"Very careful," Faile agreed. "Did Sevanna really send for me? If she didn't—"

It seemed that she had, and Faile was quick about reaching Sevanna's tent—quicker than she would have liked, in truth; it was irritating to leap to avoid Sevanna's displeasure—but no one paid her the slightest heed when she walked in and stood meekly by the entry flaps.

Sevanna's tent was no low Aiel structure, but a wall-tent of red canvas large enough to need two center poles, lit by near a dozen mirrored stand-lamps. Two gilded braziers gave a little warmth, emitting thin tendrils of smoke that eddied out through the smoke holes in the roof, but the interior was little warmer than outside. Rich carpets, the snow carefully scraped away before they were laid, made a floor of reds and greens and blues, Tairen mazes and flowers and animals. Tasseled silk cushions lay strewn about the carpets, and one chair, a massive thing intricately carved and heavily gilded, sat in a corner. Faile had never seen anyone sit in it, but its presence was supposed to evoke the presence of a clan chief, she knew. She was just as happy to stand quietly with her eyes down. Three other *gai'shain* with golden belts and collars, one a bearded male, stood along one wall of the tent, in case some service was needed. Sevanna was there, and so was Therava.

Sevanna was a tall woman, a little taller than Faile herself, with pale green eyes and hair like spun gold. She might have been beautiful except for a strong hint of avarice around her plump mouth. Little about her really seemed Aiel, beyond her eyes and hair and sun-dark face. Her blouse was white silk, her skirt divided for riding and also silk, if a dark gray, and the scarf folded around her temples was a blaze of crimson and gold. Also silk. Red boots peeked out beneath the hem of her skirt when she moved. Jeweled rings decorated her every finger, and her necklaces and bracelets of fat pearls and cut diamonds and rubies as large as pigeon's eggs, sapphires and emeralds and firedrops, paled anything Someryn had. Not a single one was Aiel-made. Therava, on the other hand, was all Aiel, in dark wool and white *algode,* her hands bare and her necklaces and bracelets gold and ivory. No finger rings or gems for her. Taller than most men, her dark red hair touched with streaks of white, she was a blue-eyed eagle that it seemed must devour Sevanna like a crippled lamb. Faile would rather anger Sevanna ten times than Therava once, but the two women faced another across a table inlaid with ivory and turquoise, and Sevanna met Therava glare for glare.

"What is happening today means danger," Therava said with the air of someone tired of repeating herself. And perhaps about to draw the knife at her belt. She caressed the hilt as she spoke, and not entirely absently, Faile thought. "We need to put as much distance between ourselves and whatever it is as we possibly can, and as soon as we can. There are mountains to the east. Once we reach them, we can be safe until we gather all the septs together again. Septs that would never have been separated if you had not been so sure of yourself, Sevanna."

"You speak of safety?" Sevanna laughed. "Have you grown so old and toothless you need to be fed bread and milk? Look. These mountains of yours are how distant? How many days, or weeks, when we must crawl through this cursed snow?" She gestured to the table between them where a map lay spread out, weighted down with two thick golden bowls and a heavy three-pronged golden candlestick. Most Aiel disdained maps, but Sevanna had taken to them along with other wetland customs. "Whatever happened is far away, Therava. You agreed it is so, as did every Wise One. This city is full of food, enough to feed us for weeks, if we remain here. Who is there to challenge us, if we do? And if we do . . . You have heard the runners, the messages. In two or three weeks, four at the most, ten more septs will have joined me. Perhaps more! This snow will have melted by then, if these wetlanders from the city can be believed. We will travel quickly instead of having to drag everything on sleds." Faile wondered whether any of the city people had mentioned mud.

"Ten more septs will join *you*," Therava said, her voice flat except for the last word. Her hand tightened on the knife hilt. "You speak for the clan chief, Sevanna, and so I was chosen to advise you as a clan chief, who must listen to advice for the good of our clan. I advise you to move east and keep moving east. The other septs can join us as easily in those mountains as here, and if we must go a little hungry on the way, who among us is a stranger to privation?"

Sevanna fingered her necklaces, a large emerald on her right hand like green fire in the light of the stand-lamps. Her mouth tightened, and seemed hungrier for it. She might have known privation, but despite the lack of warmth in the tent, she no longer chose to. "I speak for the chief, and I say we will remain here." There was more than a hint of challenge in her voice, but she did not give Therava a chance to meet it. "Ah, I see that Faile has come. My good, obedient *gai'shain*." Taking something wrapped in a cloth from the table, she stripped away the cloth. "Do you recognize this, Faile Bashere?"

What Sevanna held was a knife with a single-edged blade a hand and a half long, a simple tool of the sort that thousands of farmers carried. Except that Faile recognized the pattern of rivets in the wooden handle, and the chip in the edge. It was the knife that she had stolen and hidden away with such care. She said nothing. There was nothing to say. *Gai'shain* were forbidden to possess any weapon, even a knife except when cutting meat or vegetables for cooking. She could not help jerking when Sevanna went on, though.

"As well Galina brought me this before you could use it. For whatever purpose. If you stabbed someone, I would have to be very angry with you."

Galina? Of course. The Aes Sedai would not allow them to escape before they did as she wanted.

"She is shocked, Therava." Sevanna's laughter was amused. "Galina knows what is required of *gai'shain*, Faile Bashere. What should I do with her, Therava? That is advice you can give me. Several wetlanders have been killed for hiding weapons, but I would hate to lose her."

Therava tipped Faile's chin up with a finger and stared into her eyes. Faile met that gaze without blinking, but she felt her knees tremble. She did not try telling herself it was only the cold. Faile knew she was not a coward, but when Therava looked at her, Faile saw herself as a rabbit in that eagle's talons, alive and waiting for the beak to descend. It had been Therava who first told her to spy on Sevanna, and however circumspect the other Wise Ones might have been, Faile had no doubt that Therava would slit her throat without the slightest qualm if she failed her. There was no use pretending the woman did not frighten her. She just had to control that fear. If she could.

"I think she was planning to run away, Sevanna. But I think she can learn to do as she is told."

The rough wooden table had been set out between the tents in the nearest open space to Sevanna's tent, a hundred paces away. At first, Faile thought that the shame of being naked would be the worst of it, that and the icy cold that pebbled her skin. The sun sat low in the sky; the air had grown colder, and it would get much colder before morning. She had to stay there till morning. The Shaido were good at learning what shamed wetlanders, and they used shame as a punishment. She thought she would die of blushing whenever anyone looked at her, but the Shaido who passed by did not even pause. In itself, nudity was no reason for shame among Aiel. Aravine appeared in front of her, but she stopped only long enough to whisper, "Keep your courage," and then she was gone. Faile understood. Whether or not the woman was loyal, she did not dare do anything to help.

After a very short time, Faile no longer worried about shame. Her wrists had been tied behind her, and then her ankles had been doubled back and tied to her elbows. She understood now why Lacile and Arrela had been panting. Breathing was an effort in this position. The cold bit deeper and deeper, until she was shivering uncontrollably, but even that soon seemed secondary. Cramps began to burn in her legs, her shoulders, her sides, bunching muscles that seemed on fire, twisting tighter and tighter and tighter. She focused on not screaming. That became the center of her existence. She—would—not—scream. But, oh, Light, she hurt!

"Sevanna ordered that you were to remain here till dawn,

Faile Bashere, but she did not say you could not have company."

She had to blink several times before she could see clearly. Sweat stung her eyes. How could she be sweating when she was frozen to the marrow? Rolan was standing in front of her, and strangely, he was carrying a pair of low bronze braziers full of glowing coals, with pieces of cloth wrapped around a leg of each to protect his hands from the heat. Seeing her stare at the braziers, he shrugged. "Once, a night in the cold would not have bothered me, but I have grown soft since I crossed the Dragonwall."

She almost gasped when he set the braziers beneath the table. Warmth flooded up through the cracks between the planks. Her muscles still shrieked with cramps, but oh, the blessed warmth. She did gasp when the man put an arm across her chest and the other across her bent knees. Suddenly she realized the pressure was gone from her elbows. He had . . . squeezed . . . her. One of his hands began working at her thigh, and she almost screamed as his fingers dug into knotted muscles, but she felt the knots begin to loosen. They still hurt, his massaging hurt, but the pain in that one thigh muscle was changing in kind. Not growing less, exactly, but she knew that it would, if he continued.

"You do not mind if I occupy myself while I try to think of a way to make you laugh, do you?" he asked.

Suddenly she realized that she was laughing, and not hysterically. Well, it was only partly hysteria. She was trussed like a goose for the oven and being saved from the cold for the second time by a man she thought maybe she would not stab after all, Sevanna would be watching her like a hawk from now on, and Therava might be trying to kill her as an example; but she knew she was going to escape. One door never closed but another opened. She was going to escape. She laughed until she cried.

CHAPTER

10

A Blazing Beacon

The wide-eyed maid was more used to kneading bread dough than doing up rows of tiny buttons, but eventually she finished buttoning Elayne into her dark green riding dress, curtsied and stepped back breathing heavily, though whether from the effort of concentration or just from being in the presence of the Daughter-Heir was hard to tell. The Great Serpent ring on Elayne's left hand might have had something to do with it, too. Just over twenty miles in a straight line would take you from the manor of House Matherin to the River Erinin and all its great commerce, but the distance was far greater in actual miles to be covered through the Chishen Mountains, and people here were more accustomed to cattle raids across the border from Murandy than any sort of visitor, especially a visitor who wrapped the Daughter-Heir and an Aes Sedai into one package. The honor seemed beyond what some of the servants could bear. Elsie had been painfully conscientious in folding the blue silk gown that Elayne had worn last night and packing it away in a large leather traveling chest, one of a pair in the apartment's dressing room, so conscientious that Elayne had nearly taken over the task herself. She had slept poorly at first, fitful and waking, then slept late when she could sleep, and she was beyond chafing to be on her way back to Caemlyn.

This was the fifth time she had spent a night out of Caemlyn since learning the city was threatened, and on each trip she had given a day to visiting three or four manors, once five, all the property of men and women bound to House Trakand by blood or oaths, and every visit took time. The

press of time weighed down her bones, yet presenting the
proper image was necessary. Riding clothes were needed to
travel from one manor to the next lest she arrived rumpled
and looking a fugitive, but she had to change before settling in whether it was for the night or just a few hours.
Half those hours might be taken up by shifting from riding
clothes to a gown and back again, but riding clothes spoke
of haste and need, perhaps of desperation, while the coronet
of the Daughter-Heir and an embroidered gown trimmed
with lace, unpacked from a set of traveling cases and
donned after washing, portrayed confidence and strength.
She would have brought her own maid to add to the impression if Essande had been up to keeping the pace in winter,
though she suspected the white-haired woman's slowness
would have had her chewing her tongue in frustration. Still,
Essande could not have been as slow as this goggled-eyed
young Elsie.

At last Elsie handed her her fur-lined crimson cloak with
a curtsy, and she slung the cloak around her shoulders hastily. A fire blazed on the stone hearth, but the room was
nowhere near warm, and recently she could not seem to
ignore the cold with any reliability. The girl bobbed as she
asked whether she could fetch men to carry down the chests
if it pleased Her Majesty. The first time she had done that,
Elayne had gently explained that she was not yet Queen, but
Elsie seemed horrified at the idea of addressing her simply
as my Lady, or even as Princess, though in truth the last
was considered very old-fashioned. Proper or not, it usually
pleased Elayne to hear someone acknowledge her right to
the throne, but this morning she was too tired to be anything but anxious to be on the road. Suppressing a yawn,
she told Elsie curtly to fetch the men and be quick about it,
and turned for the paneled door. The girl rushed to open it
for her, which took longer than if she had done it herself,
with a curtsy before opening and yet another after. Her divided silk skirts whispered furiously against each other as
she strode out of the room tugging on her red riding gloves.
If Elsie had delayed her one more second, she thought she
would have screamed.

It was the girl who shrieked, however, before Elayne had
gone three paces, a horrified howl that sounded ripped from
her throat. The cloak flared as Elayne spun around, embrac-

ing the True Source, feeling the richness of *saidar* flood through her. Elsie was standing on the strip of carpet that ran along the middle of the pale brown floor tiles, staring the other way down the hall with both hands pressed to her mouth. Two crossing corridors opened in that direction, but there was not another soul in sight.

"What is it, Elsie?" Elayne demanded. She had several weaves already on the edge of forming, ranging from a simple net of air to a fireball that would have demolished half the walls in front of her, and in her present humor, she wanted to use one of them, to strike out with the Power. Her moods were uncertain of late, to say the least.

The girl looked back over one shoulder, trembling, and if her eyes had been wide before, they bulged now. Her hands remained clamped to mouth as if to prevent another scream. Dark-haired and dark-eyed, tall and plump-bosomed in House Matherin's gray-and-blue livery, she was not really a girl—Elsie might be four or five years older than herself—but the way she behaved made it difficult to think of her any other way.

"What *is* it, Elsie? And *don't* tell me it was nothing. You look as if you'd seen a ghost."

The girl flinched. "I did," she said unsteadily. That she gave Elayne no title showed just how unsteady she was. "Lady Nelein, as was Lord Aedmun's grandmother. She died when I was little, but I remember even Lord Aedmun tiptoed around her temper, and the maids used to jump if she looked at them, and other ladies who visited, too, and the lords, as well. *Everybody* was afraid of her. She was right there in front of me, and she scowled so furious—" She broke off, blushing, when Elayne laughed.

It was more a laugh of relief than anything else. The Black Ajah had not somehow followed her to Lord Aedmun's manor. There were no assassins waiting with knives in their fists, no sisters loyal to Elaida wanting to whisk her back to Tar Valon. Sometimes she dreamed about those things, about all of them in the same dream. She released *saidar,* reluctantly as always, regretful as that fullness of joy and life drained out of her. Matherin supported her, but Aedmun might have taken it amiss if she had ruined half his home place.

"The dead cannot harm the living, Elsie," she said gently.

The more gently because she had laughed, not to mention
wanting to box the ninny's ears. "They're not of this world
anymore, and they can't touch anything in it, including
us." The girl nodded, and dropped another curtsy, but by
the size of her eyes and the trembling of her lips she was
unconvinced. Elayne had no time to cosset her, though.
"Fetch the men for my cases, Elsie," she said firmly, "and
don't worry about ghosts." With yet another curtsy the girl
dashed off, her head swiveling anxiously in case the Lady
Nelein leaped out of the paneled walls. Ghosts! The fool
girl *was* a ninny!

Matherin was an old House, if not large or strong, and
the main stairs, leading down to the entry hall, were broad
and trimmed with marble railings. The entry hall itself was
a generous space, with gray-and-blue floor tiles and mirrored oil lamps hanging on chains from the ceiling twenty
feet above. There was nothing in the way of gilding and
little inlay, but ornately carved chests and cabinets stood
along the sides of the hall, and two wall hangings were
displayed on one wall. One showed men hunting leopards
from horseback, a chancy business at best, and the other
women of House Matherin presenting a sword to the first
Queen of Andor, an event that Matherin treasured and that
might or might not have actually happened.

Aviendha was already down, pacing restlessly in the hall,
and Elayne sighed at the sight. They would have shared a
room, if not for the implication that Matherin could not provide adequately for two visitors of note, but Aviendha did
not really understand that the smaller the House, the loftier
the pride. Often, the smaller Houses possessed little more.
Pride, she should have understood, since a fierce pride and
strength all but shone from her. Straight-backed and even
taller than Elayne, a thick dark shawl draped over her pale
blouse and a folded gray head scarf holding back her long
reddish hair, she was the very picture of a Wise One despite being only a year older than Elayne. Wise Ones who
could channel often appeared to be much younger than they
were, and Aviendha had the dignity. At this moment she
did, anyway, though the pair of them had giggled together
often enough. Of course, her only jewelry was a long, silver Kandori necklace, an amber brooch in the shape of a
turtle and a wide ivory bracelet, and Wise Ones always wore

festoons of necklaces and bracelets, but Aviendha was not a Wise One yet, merely an apprentice. Elayne never thought of Aviendha as merely anything, but it did present problems now and then. Sometimes she thought the Wise Ones considered her an apprentice of some sort as well, or at least a student. A silly thought, to be sure, but sometimes . . .

As Elayne reached the foot of the stairs, Aviendha adjusted her shawl and asked, "Did you sleep well?" Her tone was untroubled, but anxiety nestled around her green eyes. "You did not send for wine to help you sleep, did you? I made sure your wine was watered when we ate, but I saw you looking at the wine pitcher."

"Yes, Mother," Elayne said in a sickly sweet voice. "No, Mother. I was wondering how Aedmun got his hands on such a fine vintage, Mother. It was a shame to water it. And I drank the goat's milk before I went to sleep." If anything brought her to birthing sickness, it would be goat's milk! And to think she used to like it.

Aviendha planted her fists on her hips, such an embodiment of indignation that Elayne had to laugh. There were inconveniences to being with child, ranging from abrupt swings in her temper to tenderness in her breasts to always being tired, but the coddling was the worst, in some ways. Everyone in the Royal Palace knew she was pregnant—a good many had known before she did, courtesy of Min's viewing and Min being too free with her tongue—and she did not think she could have been so mothered when she was an infant. Still, she put up with all the bother with as much grace as she could muster. Usually, she did. They were only trying to be helpful. She just wished every woman she knew did not believe that pregnancy had made her brainless. Nearly every woman she knew. Those who had never borne a child themselves were the worst.

Thinking of her baby—at times she wished Min had said whether it would be a boy or girl, or rather that Aviendha or Birgitte could recall exactly what Min actually had said; Min was always right, but the three of them had consumed a great deal of wine that night, and Min had been gone from the palace long before Elayne herself knew to ask—thinking of the child growing in her always made her think of Rand, just as thinking of him made her think of the babe. One followed the other as surely as cream rose in the milkpan. She missed Rand terribly, and yet she could not miss him. A part of him, the *sense* of him, rode always in the back of her head unless she masked the bond, right alongside her sense of Birgitte, her other Warder. The bond had its limits, however. He was somewhere to the west, far enough that she could tell little more than that he was alive. Nothing more, really, though she thought she would know if he had been badly injured. She was not sure she wanted to know what he was up to. He had been far to the south for a long time after leaving her, and now, just this morning, he had Traveled to the west. It was disconcerting, really, to feel him in one direction and then suddenly have him off in another, even farther away. He could be pursuing enemies or running from enemies or any one of a thousand things. She hoped very much it was something innocuous that made him Travel. He was going to die on her all too soon—men who could channel always died of it—but she wanted so very much to keep him alive as long as possible.

"He is well," Aviendha said almost as though she could read her mind. They had their own shared sense of one another since their mutual adoption as first-sisters, but it did not go as far as the Warder bond they and Min shared with Rand. "If he allows himself to be killed, I will cut off his ears."

Elayne blinked, then laughed again, and after a startled glance, Aviendha joined in. It was not that funny, except maybe to an Aiel—Aviendha's sense of humor was *very* odd—but Elayne could not stop laughing, and Aviendha seemed as helpless. Shaking with mirth, they hugged one another and hung on. Life was very strange. Had anyone told her a few years ago that she would share a man with another woman—with two other women!—she would have called them mad. The very idea would have been indecent. But she loved Aviendha every bit as much as she did Rand, only in a different way, and Aviendha loved Rand as much as she did. Denying that meant denying Aviendha, and she could as easily step out of her skin. Aiel women, sisters or close friends, often married the same man, and seldom gave him any say in the matter. She was going to marry Rand, and so was Aviendha, and so was Min. Whatever anyone said or thought, that was all there was to it. If he lived long enough.

Suddenly she became afraid that her laughter was edging toward tears. Please, Light, let her not be one of those women who became weepy when they were with child. It was bad enough not knowing whether she was going to be melancholy or furious from one minute to the next. Hours might pass when she felt perfectly normal, but then there were hours when she felt like a child's ball bouncing down an endless flight of stairs. This morning, she seemed to be on the stairs.

"He is well, and he will be well," Aviendha whispered fiercely, as if she intended to assure his survival by killing anything that threatened him.

With the tips of her fingers, Elayne brushed a tear from her sister's cheek. "He is well, and he will be well," she agreed softly. But they could not kill *saidin,* and the taint on the male half of the Power was what was going to kill him.

The lamps overhead flickered as one of the tall doors to the outside opened, letting in a gust of air even colder than that in the entry hall, and they quickly moved a little apart, just holding hands. Elayne schooled her face to a serene smoothness fully worthy of an Aes Sedai. She could not afford to let anyone see her apparently seeking comfort in a hug. A ruler, or one who sought to rule, was not allowed the slightest suggestion of weakness or tears, not in public. There were rumors enough about her as it was, as many bad as good. She was benevolent or cruel, fair-minded or arbitrary, generous or avaricious, all according to which tale you listened to. At least the tales balanced out one another, but anyone who could say they had actually seen the Daughter-Heir huddling in the arms of her companion might add a tale of fear to the blend, and if her enemies believed she was afraid, they would only grow bolder. And stronger. Cowardice was the sort of rumor that stuck like greasy mud; you never could wash it off completely. History recorded women who had lost their bids for the Lion Throne on no further discernible grounds. Capability was a requirement for a successful ruler and wisdom was to be hoped for, though women lacking both had gained the throne and muddled through somehow, but few would support a coward, and none of those people she wanted on her side.

The man who came in, turning to push the massive door shut behind him, had only one leg and used a crutch in place of the other. Even with fleece padding, the sleeve of his heavy woolen coat was worn from it. A heavy-shouldered former soldier, Fridwyn Ros managed Lord Aedmun's estate, with the aid of a fat clerk who had blinked at the Daughter-Heir in consternation, gaped at her Great Serpent ring with something near to awe, and scurried back to his ledgers in relief as soon as he realized she had no business with him. He had probably feared a levy on the manor's accounts. Master Ros had stared at her ring in amazement, to be sure, but he had grinned with delight at the Daughter-Heir and regretted that he could no longer ride for her with such sincerity that, had he been a liar, he would already have bilked Aedmun and the clerk of everything they owned between them. She did not fear him carrying the wrong tales.

His crutch made a rhythmic thump as he came up the hall, and he managed a credible bow in spite of it, including Aviendha in his courtesy. He had been startled by her at first, but surprisingly quick to catch their friendship, and if he did not entirely trust an Aiel, it meant he accepted her. You could not ask for everything.

"The men are strapping your cases to the pack animals, my Queen, and your escort is ready." He was one of those who refused to call her anything except "my Queen" or "Majesty," but a hint of doubt entered his voice at mention of her escort. He covered it hastily with a cough and hurried on. "The men we're sending with you are all mounted as well as I could manage. Young men, mainly, and a few more experienced, but they all know which end of a halberd has the point. I wish the manor could give you more, but I explained, when Lord Aedmun heard there were others claiming what's yours by right, he decided not to wait for spring, and he called in his armsmen and set out for Caemlyn. We've had a couple of bad snowfalls since, but he might be halfway there by now with luck in the passes." His gaze carried conviction, but he knew better than she that with the wrong luck Aedmun and his armsmen might be dead in those passes.

"Matherin has always maintained faith with Trakand," Elayne told him, "and I put my trust that it always will. I value Lord Aedmun's loyalty, Master Ros, and yours."

She did not insult Matherin, and him, by promising to remember or offering rewards, yet Master Ros' broad smile said she had already given him as much reward as he desired. Matherin would receive rewards, if they were earned, but they could not be held out as if offering to buy a horse.

Thumping along on his crutch, Master Ros bowed her to the door, and bowed her out onto the broad granite step where servants wearing heavy coats waited in the bitter cold with a stirrup cup of hot spiced wine that she rejected with a murmur. Until she had a chance to adjust to the sharp air, she wanted both hands to hold her cloak closed. Aviendha would probably have found a way to make her drop it anyway. *She* took a cup, after wrapping her shawl around her head and shoulders, the only concession she made to the icy morning. *She* was ignoring the cold, of course. Elayne was the one who had taught her how. Elayne tried again to push the cold away, and to her surprise, it receded. Not all the way—she still felt chilly—but it was better than freezing.

The sky was clear, the sun bright as it sat over the mountains, but storm clouds could come boiling across the surrounding peaks at any time. It would be best to reach their first destination today as quickly as possible. Unfortunately, Fireheart, her tall black gelding, was living up to his name, rearing and snorting gouts of steamy breath as if he had never worn a bridle before, and Aviendha's leggy arch-necked gray had taken it into her head to imitate him, dancing in the knee-deep snow and trying to go anywhere except where the groom tried to lead her. She was a more spirited animal than Elayne would have chosen for her sister, yet Aviendha herself had insisted after learning the mare's name. Siswai meant spear, in the Old Tongue. The grooms seemed capable women, but they appeared to think they needed to calm the animals before handing them over. It was all Elayne could do not to snap at them that she had managed Fireheart before they ever saw him.

Her escort was already mounted, to avoid standing in the snow, twenty-odd riders in the white-collared red coats and brightly burnished breastplates and helmets of the Queen's Guard. Master Ros' doubt might be explained by the fact that the riders' coats were silk, as were their red breeches with the white stripe up each leg, and by the pale lace they wore at neck and cuff. They certainly appeared more

ceremonial than effective. Or it might have been that they
were all women. Women were uncommon in jobs that required using weapons, just the occasional merchants' guard
or a rare woman who turned up in an army during time of
war, and Elayne had never heard of a group of all-female soldiers before she created one. Except the Maidens, of course,
but they were Aiel and a different matter. She hoped people
would think them an affectation on her part, and largely
decorative with all the lace and silk. Men tended to underes-
timate a woman carrying weapons until they faced one, and
even most other women tended to think her a brainless fool.
Bodyguards usually tried to appear so ferocious that no one
would dare trying to get past them, but her enemies would
just find a new way to attack if she stood the whole Queen's
Guard around her shoulder-to-shoulder. A bodyguard her
enemies would dismiss until it was too late for more than
regrets was her aim. She intended to make their uniforms
more elaborate, partly to feed those misconceptions and
partly to feed the women's pride as soldiers marked out from
the rest, but she herself had no doubts. Every one of them,
from merchants' guards to Hunters of the Horn, had been
carefully chosen for her skills, experience and courage. She
was ready to put her life in their hands. She already had.

A lean woman wearing a lieutenant's two golden knots
on the shoulder of her red cloak saluted Elayne with an
arm across her chest, and her roan gelding tossed his head,
making the silver bells in his mane chime faintly, as if he
too were saluting. "We are ready, my Lady, and the area is
clear." Caseille Raskovni was one of those who had been a
merchant's guard, and her Arafellin accents were not those
of an educated woman, but her voice was brisk and no-
nonsense. She used the proper form of address, and would
until Elayne was crowned, yet she was ready to fight to
gain that crown for Elayne. Very, very few, male or female,
signed the roster of the Queen's Guard these days unless
they were ready for that. "The men Master Ros handed over
are ready, too. As ready as they'll ever be." Clearing his
throat, the man shifted his crutch and took to studying the
snow in front of his boots.

Elayne could see what Caseille meant. Master Ros
had scraped together eleven men from the manor to send
to Caemlyn and outfitted them with halberds and short-

swords and what armor he could find, nine antique helmets without faceguards and seven breastplates with dents that made them vulnerable. Their mounts were not bad, though hairy with their winter coats, but even huddled as their riders were in thick cloaks, she could see that eight were unlikely to need to shave above once in a week, if that. The men Master Ros had described as being experienced had wrinkled faces and bony hands and probably not a full set of teeth between them. He had not been lying or trying to stint; Aedmun would have gathered all the fit men in the area to take with him and outfitted them in the best he had. The story had been the same everywhere. Apparently a great number of hale and hearty men scattered the length of Andor were trying to reach her in Caemlyn. And none of them likely to get into the city until all was decided, now. She could search every day without finding a single band. Still, this little bunch held their halberds as if they knew how to use them. Then again, that was not hard to do sitting a saddle at rest with the halberd's butt tucked in your stirrup. She could have managed that.

"We have visited nineteen of these manors, sister," Aviendha said softly, moving closer until their shoulders touched, "and counting these, we have gathered two hundred and five boys too young to be blooded and old men who should have laid down the spear long ago. I have not asked before. You know your people and your ways. Is this worth the time you give it?"

"Oh, yes, sister." Elayne kept her voice just as low, so the one-legged former soldier and the servants could not overhear. The best of people could turn muleheaded if they realized you wanted them to behave a certain way. Particularly if they realized that the help they had painfully gathered and offered, and you had accepted, was not what you were after at all. "Everyone in that village down by the river knows I'm here by now, and so do half the farms for miles. By noon, the other half will know, and by tomorrow, the next village over, and more farms. News travels slowly in winter, especially in this country. They *know* I've spoken my claim to the throne, yet if I gain the throne tomorrow or die tomorrow, they might not learn of it before the middle of spring, maybe not even until summer. But today they know that Elayne Trakand is alive that she visited the manor in silks and jewels and summoned men to her banner. People twenty miles from here will claim they saw me and touched my hand. Few people can say that without speaking in favor of whoever they claim to have seen, and when you speak in favor of someone, you convince yourself to favor them. There are men and women in nineteen places around Andor talking about how they saw the Daughter-Heir just this last week, and every day the area that talk covers spreads like an ink-blot.

"If I had time, I'd visit every village in Andor. It won't make a hair of difference in what happens in Caemlyn, but it may make all the difference after I win." She would not admit to any possibility other than winning. Especially not given who would take the throne if she failed. "Most Queens in our history spent the first years of their rule gathering the people solidly behind them, Aviendha, and some never did, but harder times than these are coming. I may not have one year before I need every Andoran to stand behind me. I can't wait until I have the throne. Harder times are coming, and I have to be ready. Andor has to be ready, and I must make it so," she finished firmly.

Smiling, Aviendha touched Elayne's cheek. "I think I will learn a great deal about being a Wise One from you."

To her mortification, Elayne blushed in embarrassment. Her cheeks felt on fire! Maybe the swings in humor were worse than the cosseting. Light, she had *months* of this to look forward to! Not for the first time, she found a kernel of resentment toward Rand. He had done this to her—all right, she had helped him, instigated the doing, in fact, but that was beside the point—he had done this and walked away with a smug grin on his face. She doubted his grin had really been smug, but she could picture it all too easily. Let *him* dart from giddy to weepy every other hour and see how he liked it! *I can't think in a straight line,* she thought irritably. That was his fault, too.

The grooms finally deemed Fireheart and Aviendha's Siswai meek enough to be mounted by ladies, and Aviendha climbed to her saddle from the stone mounting block with a good deal more grace than she once had shown, arranging her bulky undivided skirts to cover as much of her dark-stockinged legs as possible. She still believed that her own legs were superior to any horse, yet she had become a passable rider. Though she did have a tendency to look surprised when the horse did as she wanted. Fireheart tried to dance once Elayne was on his back, but she reined him in smartly, and a bit more sharply than she would have normally. Her teetering moods had taken her to a sudden sense of dread for Rand, and if she could not ensure his safety, there was one male at hand she could make certain did exactly as he was supposed to.

Six of the Guardswomen led the way down the road from the manor at a slow walk, all the depth of snow would allow, with the rest following her and Aviendha in smart columns, the last horsewomen in line leading the pack animals. The local men trailed behind raggedly with their own packhorse, a shaggy creature tied about with cookpots and rough bundles and even half a dozen live chickens. A few cheers greeted them as they rode through the thatch-roofed village and across the stone bridge that crossed a snake-curved frozen stream, loud cries of "Elayne of the Lily!" and "Trakand! Trakand!" and "Matherin stands!" But she saw a woman crying on her husband's chest, and tears on his face, too, and another woman who stood with her back to the riders and her head down, refusing even to look. Elayne hoped she would send their sons home to them. There should be little fighting at Caemlyn, unless she blundered badly, but there would be some, and once the Rose Crown was hers, battles lay ahead. To the south lay the Seanchan, and to the north, Myrddraal and Trollocs waiting to descend for Tarmon Gai'don. Andor would bleed sons in the days to come. Burn her, she was *not* going to cry!

Beyond the bridge, the road slanted up again, a steep climb through pine and fir and leatherleaf, but it was no more than a long mile to the mountain meadow they sought. The snow shining beneath the midmorning sun still bore the marks of hooves coming from where a gateway had left a deep furrow in the snow. It could have been nearer the manor, but the possibility of someone standing where your gateway opened was always the danger.

The glow of *saidar* surrounded Aviendha as they rode into the meadow. She had made the gateway to come here from their last stop yesterday afternoon, a manor a hundred miles north, so she would weave the gateway to go to Caemlyn, but the sight of Aviendha shining with the Power made

Elayne go broody. Whoever made the gateway to leave
Caemlyn always ended up making all the others until they
returned, since she learned the ground at each place her
gateway touched, but on each of their five trips, Aviendha
had asked to make that first gateway. She might simply have
wanted the practice, as she claimed, though Elayne hardly
had more practice than she did, but another possibility had
come to mind. Maybe Aviendha wanted to keep her from
channeling, in any considerable amount at least. Because
she was pregnant. The weave that had made them sisters of
the same mother could not have been used if either of them
had been with child, because the unborn child would have
shared in the bond, a thing it could not be strong enough
to survive, but surely one of the Aes Sedai in the palace
would have said something if channeling was to be avoided
in pregnancy. Then again, very few Aes Sedai ever bore
children. They might not know. She was aware there were
many things Aes Sedai did not know, however much they
might pretend otherwise to the rest of the world—she herself had taken advantage of that presumption from time to
time—but it seemed very strange that they might be ignorant of something so important to most women. It was as
though a bird knew how to eat every seed and grain except
barley, so supposedly knew, because if it did not know how
to eat barley, what else might it be ignorant of? Wise Ones
bore children, though, and they had said nothing about—

Abruptly concerns over her babe and channeling and
what Aes Sedai might or might not know were pushed right
out of her head. She could feel someone channeling *saidar*. Not Aviendha, not someone on one of the surrounding mountains, not anyone near as close as that. This was
distant, like a beacon blazing on a far mountaintop in the
night. A very distant mountain. She could not imagine how
much of the One Power was needed for her to feel channeling at that distance. Every woman in the world who could
channel must be able to sense this. To point straight to it.
And the beacon lay to the west. Nothing had changed in the
bond with Rand, she could not have said exactly where he
was within a hundred miles, but she knew.

"He's in danger," she said. "We must go to him, Aviendha."

Aviendha gave herself a shake and stopped staring west-

ward. The glow remained around her, and Elayne could feel
that she had drawn on the Source as deeply as she could.
But even as Aviendha turned to her, she felt the amount
of *saidar* the other woman held dwindle. "We must not,
Elayne."

Aghast, Elayne twisted in Fireheart's saddle to stare at
her. "You want to *abandon* him? To *that!*" No one could
handle so much of *saidar,* not the strongest circle, not
unaided. Supposedly a *sa'angreal* existed, greater than
anything else ever made, and if what she had heard was
correct, that might be able to handle this. Maybe. But from
what she had heard, no woman could use it and live, not
without *ter'angreal* made for the purpose, and no one had
ever seen one that she knew of. Surely no sister would try
even if she had found one. That much of the One Power
could level mountain ranges at a stroke! No sister would
try except perhaps one of the Black Ajah. Or worse, one of
the Forsaken. Maybe more than one. What else *could* it be?
And Aviendha simply wanted to *ignore* it, when she *must*
know that Rand was there?

The Guardswomen, unaware, were still waiting patiently
on their horses, keeping watch on the treeline around the
meadow and little concerned with that after their reception
at the manor, though Caseille was watching Elayne and
Aviendha, a slight frown visible behind the face-bars of her
helmet. She knew they never delayed at opening a gateway.
The men from the manor were gathered around their packhorse, pawing at the bundles and apparently arguing over
whether or not something had been included. Aviendha
still moved her gray closer to Elayne's black and spoke in a
voice that would not carry.

"We know nothing, Elayne. Not whether he is dancing
the spears or this is something else. If he dances the spears
and we rush in, will he attack us before he knows who we
are? Will we distract him because he does not expect us,
and allow his enemies to win? If he dies, we will find who
took his life and kill them, but if we go to him now, we go
blindly, and we may bring disaster on our backs."

"We could be careful," Elayne said sullenly. It infuriated her that she was feeling sullen, and showing it, but all
she could do was ride her moods and try not let them get
the upper hand completely. "We don't have to Travel right

to the spot." Gripping her pouch, feeling the small ivory carving of a seated woman that nestled inside, she looked pointedly at her sister's amber brooch. "Light, Aviendha, we have *angreal,* and neither of us is exactly helpless." Oh, Light, now she was sounding petulant. She knew very well that both of them together, *angreal* and all, would be flies battling a flame against what they could sense, but even so, a flybite at the right moment might make the difference. "And don't tell me I'll endanger the baby. Min said she will be born strong and healthy. You told me so yourself. That means I will live at least long enough for my daughter to be born." She hoped for a daughter.

Fireheart chose that moment to nip at the gray, and Siswai nipped back, and for a bit Elayne was occupied with getting her gelding under control and keeping Aviendha from being thrown and telling Caseille that they did not need any help, and by the end of it, she was not feeling sullen any longer. She wanted to smack Fireheart right between his ears.

Aside from making the animal obey the reins, Aviendha behaved as if nothing had happened at all. She did frown, a little uncertainly, her face framed by the dark wool of her shawl, but her uncertainty had nothing to do with the horse.

"I have told you about the rings in Rhuidean," she said slowly, and Elayne gave an impatient nod. Every woman who wanted to become a Wise One was sent through a *ter'angreal* before she began training. It was something like the *ter'angreal* used to test novices for being raised to Accepted in the White Tower, except that in this one, a woman saw her whole life. All of her possible lives, really, every decision made differently, an infinite fan of lives based on differing choices. "No one can remember all of that, Elayne, only bits and pieces. I knew I would love Rand al'Thor . . ." she was still uncomfortable sometimes about using just his first name in front of others, "and that I would find sister-wives. For most things, all you retain is a vague impression at best. A hint of warning, sometimes. I think if we go to him now, something very bad will happen. Maybe one of us will die, maybe both in spite of what Min said." That she said Min's name without fumbling was a measure of her concern. She did not know Min very well, and usually named her formally, as Min Farshaw. "Perhaps he will die. Perhaps something else. I do not know for sure—

maybe we will all survive, and we will sit around a fire with him roasting *pecara* when we find him—but the glimmer of a warning is there in my head."

Elayne opened her mouth angrily. Then she closed it again, anger draining away like water down a hole, and her shoulders slumped. Perhaps Aviendha's glimmer was true and perhaps not, but the fact was that her arguments had been good from the start. A great risk taken in ignorance, and taking it might bring disaster. The beacon had grown brighter still. And he was there, right where the beacon was. The bond did not tell her so, not at this distance, but she knew. And she knew she had to leave him to take care of himself while she took care of Andor.

"I don't have anything to teach you about being a Wise One, Aviendha," she said quietly. "You are already much wiser than I. Not to mention braver and more coolheaded. We return to Caemlyn."

Aviendha colored faintly under the praise—she could be very sensitive, at times—but she wasted no time in opening the gateway, a rotating view of a stableyard in the Royal Palace that widened into a hole in the air and let snow from the meadow fall onto the clean-swept paving stones as near three hundred miles away as made no difference. The sense of Birgitte, somewhere in the palace, sprang alive in Elayne's head. Birgitte had a headache and a sour stomach, not unusual occurrences of late, but they suited Elayne's mood all too well.

I must leave him to take care of himself, she thought as she rode through. Light, how often had she thought that? No matter. Rand was the love of her heart and the joy of her life, but Andor was her duty.

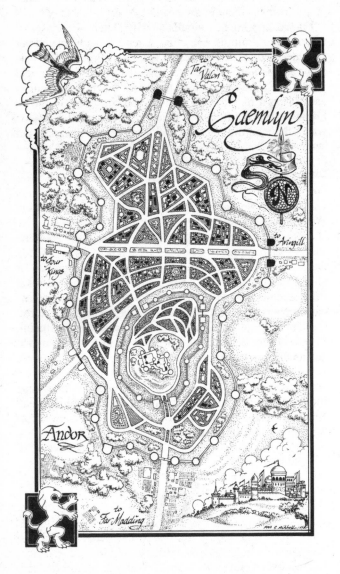

CHAPTER
11

Talk of Debts

The gateway was positioned so that Elayne seemed to be riding out of a hole in the wall against the street, into a square marked out for safety by sand-filled wine barrels standing on the paving stones. Oddly, she could not feel a single woman channeling anywhere in the palace, though it housed more than a hundred and fifty with the ability. Some would be stationed on the city's outer walls, of course, too far for her to sense anything short of a linked circle, and a few would be out of the city altogether, yet someone in the palace was almost always using *saidar,* whether to try forcing one of the captive *sul'dam* to admit that she really could see weaves of the One Power or simply to smooth the wrinkles from a shawl without heating an iron. Not this morning, though. Windfinder arrogance often matched the worst shown by any Aes Sedai, yet even that must be quashed by what they sensed. Elayne thought that if she climbed to a high window, she must be able to see the weaves of that great beacon, hundreds of leagues distant as they were. She felt like an ant that had just become aware of mountains, an ant comparing the Spine of the World to the hills it had always held in awe. Yes, even the Windfinders must be walking small in the face of that.

On the eastern side of the palace and fronted on north and south by two-story-high stables of pure white stone, the Queen's Stableyard traditionally was given over to the Queen's personal horses and carriages, and she had hesitated over using it before the Lion Throne was acknowledged hers. The steps that led to the throne were as delicate as any court dance, and if the dance sometimes came to resemble a tavern brawl, you still had to make your steps with grace and precision in order to gain your goal. Claiming the perquisites before being confirmed had cost some women their chance to rule. In the end, she had decided it was not a transgression that would make her seem over-proud. Besides, the Queen's Stableyard was relatively small and had no other use. There were fewer people to keep away from an opening gateway here. In fact, when she entered it, the stone-paved yard was empty apart from a single red-coated groom standing in one of the arched stable doorways, but he turned to give a shout inside, and dozens more came spilling out as she guided Fireheart clear of the marked-off square. After all, she might have returned with an entourage of powerful lords and ladies, or perhaps they just hoped she had.

Caseille brought the Guardswomen through the gateway, and ordered most to dismount and see to their animals. She and half a dozen more remained in their saddles, keeping watch over the heads of the people afoot. Even here, she would not leave Elayne unguarded. Particularly here, where she faced more danger than in any manor she had visited. The Matherin men milled about, getting in the way of grooms and Guards while gaping at the white stone balconies and colonnades that overlooked the yard and the spires and golden domes visible beyond. The cold seemed less here than in the mountains—refusing to let it touch her, as far as she could at present, did not make her totally unaware—but men and women and horses all still breathed faint plumes of mist. The odor of horse dung seemed strong, too, after the clean air of the mountains. A hot bath in front of a roaring fire would be welcome. Afterward, she would have to plunge back into the business of securing the throne, but right now a long soak would be just the thing.

A pair of grooms ran to Fireheart. One took his bridle with a hurried curtsy for Elayne, more concerned with seeing that the tall gelding made no bother while Elayne dismounted than with making courtesies herself, and another who made his bow and remained bent with his hands making a stirrup for Elayne. Neither gave more than a glance at the view of a snow-covered mountain meadow where they would normally see a stone wall. The stableworkers were accustomed to gateways by now. She had heard that they garnered drinks in the taverns by boasting of how often they saw the Power used and the things they supposedly had seen done with it. Elayne could imagine what those tales sounded like by the time they reached Arymilla. She rather enjoyed the thought of Arymilla chewing her fingernails.

As she set foot on the paving stones, a cluster of Guardswomen appeared around her, in crimson hats with white plumes lying flat on the broad brims, and lace-edged crimson sashes, embroidered with the White Lion, that slanted across their bright breastplates. Not until then did Caseille take the remainder of Elayne's escort to the stable. Their replacements were just as wary, eyes watching every direction, hands hovering near their sword hilts, except for Deni, a wide, placid-faced woman who carried a long brass-studded cudgel. They were only nine in number—*Only nine,* Elayne thought bitterly. *I need only nine bodyguards in the Royal Palace itself!*—yet every one who carried a sword was expert. Women who followed the "trade of the sword," as Caseille called it, had to be good, or else sooner or later they were cut down by some fellow whose only advantage was strength enough to batter her down. Deni possessed no facility with a sword at all, but the few men who had tested her cudgel regretted doing so. Despite her bulk, Deni was very quick, and she had no concept of fighting fair, or of practice, for that matter.

Rasoria, the stocky under-lieutenant in charge, seemed relieved when the grooms led Fireheart off. If Elayne's bodyguard had their way, no one except themselves would have been allowed within arm's reach. Well, maybe they were not quite *that* bad, but they looked with suspicion at almost everyone except Birgitte and Aviendha. Rasoria, a Tairen despite her blue eyes and the yellow hair she wore cut short, was among the worst in that regard, even insisting on watching the cooks make Elayne's meals and having everything tasted before it was brought up. Elayne had not protested, however over-zealous they might be. One experience of drugged wine was more than enough, even when she knew she would live at least long enough to bear her child. But it was neither the Guardswomen's mistrust nor the need for it that tightened her mouth. It was Birgitte, weaving her way through the crowded stableyard, but not toward her.

Aviendha was last to appear out of the gateway, of course,

after she was sure that everyone was through, and before she let the gateway wink out of existence, Elayne started in her direction, striding off so suddenly that her escort had to leap to maintain their guarding ring around her. As quickly as she moved, though, Birgitte, with her thick golden braid hanging to her waist, was there first, helping Aviendha down and handing the gray mare over to a long-faced groom who seemed almost as leggy as Siswai. Aviendha always had more difficulty getting off a horse than getting on, but Birgitte had more than assistance in mind. Elayne and her escort arrived just in time to hear the woman say to Aviendha in a low, hurried voice, "Did she drink her goat's milk? Did she get enough sleep? She feels . . ." Her voice trailed off at the end, and she drew a deep breath before turning to face Elayne, outwardly calm, and unsurprised to find her right there. The bond did work both ways.

Birgitte was not a big woman, though she stood taller than Elayne in her heeled boots, as tall as Aviendha, but she usually had a presence that was only heightened by the uniform of the Captain-General of the Queen's Guards, a short red coat with a high white collar worn over baggy blue trousers tucked into gleaming black boots, four golden knots on her left shoulder and four bands of gold on each white cuff. After all, she was Birgitte Silverbow, a hero out of legend. She remained wary of trying to live up to those legends; she claimed that the stories were grossly inflated where they were not complete fabrications. Yet she was still the same woman who had done every one of the things that formed the heart of those legends and more besides. Now, despite her apparent composure, unease tinged the concern for Elayne that flowed through the bond along with her headache and her sullen stomach. She knew very well that Elayne hated for them to check on her behind her back. That was not the whole reason for Elayne's irritation, but the bond let Birgitte know just how upset she was.

Aviendha, calmly unwrapping her shawl from around her head and draping it over her shoulders, attempted the gaze of a woman who had done nothing wrong and certainly was not involved with anyone else who had done anything wrong. She might have managed it if she had not widened her eyes for an added touch of innocence. Birgitte was a bad influence on her in some ways.

"I drank the goat's milk," Elayne said in a level voice, all too conscious of the Guardswomen ringing the three of them. Facing outward, eyes scanning the yard and the balconies and the rooftops, nearly every one was certainly listening. "I got enough sleep. Is there anything else you want to ask *me?*" Aviendha's cheeks colored faintly.

"I think I have all the answers I need for the moment," Birgitte replied without a hint of the blush Elayne had been hoping for. The woman *knew* she was tired, *knew* she had to be lying about the sleep.

The bond was decidedly inconvenient at times. *She* had drunk nothing but half a cup of extremely well watered wine last night, but she was beginning to *have* Birgitte's morning-after head *and* her sour stomach. None of the other Aes Sedai she had spoken to about the bond had mentioned anything of the kind, but she and Birgitte all too often mirrored one another, physically and emotionally. The last presented real problems when her moods were on a seesaw. Sometimes she managed to shrug it off, or fight it off, but today she knew she was going to have to suffer until Birgitte was Healed. She thought the mirroring must occur because they were both women. No one had heard of anyone bonding another woman before. Few had heard of it now, to tell the truth, and some of them seemed to believe it could not be true. A Warder was male as surely as a bull was male. Everyone knew that, and not many stopped to think that anything that "everyone knew" deserved close examination.

Being caught in a lie, when she was trying to follow Egwene's dictate about living as if she had already taken the Three Oaths, made Elayne defensive, and that made her blunt. "Is Dyelin back?"

"No," Birgitte said just as bluntly, and Elayne sighed. Dyelin had left the city days before Arymilla's army appeared, taking Reanne Corly with her to make gateways and speed her travel, and a great deal depended on Dyelin's return. On what news she brought back. On whether she brought anything besides news.

Choosing who would be Queen of Andor was quite simple, boiled down to essentials. There were over four hundred Houses in the realm, but only nineteen strong enough that others would follow where they led. Usually, all nineteen stood behind the Daughter-Heir, or most of them, unless she was plainly incompetent. House Mantear had lost the throne to Trakand when Mordrellen died only because Tigraine, the Daughter-Heir, had vanished and Mantear had begun running heavily to boy children. And because Morgase Trakand had gathered thirteen Houses in her support. Only ten of the nineteen were necessary to ascend the throne, by law and custom. Even claimants who still thought they should have the throne themselves usually fell in with the rest, or at least fell silent and gave up their pursuit, once another woman had ten Houses at her back.

Things had been bad enough when she had three declared rivals, but now Naean and Elenia were united behind Arymilla Marne, of all people, the least likely of the three to have succeeded, and that meant she had two Houses—two large enough to count; Matherin and those eighteen others she had visited were too small—her own Trakand and Dyelin's Taravin, to face six. Oh, Dyelin insisted that Carand, Coelan and Renshar would come to Elayne, and Norwelyn and Pendar and Traemane besides, but the first three wanted Dyelin herself on the throne, and the last three seemed to have gone into hibernation. Dyelin was firm in her loyalty, though, and tireless on Elayne's behalf. She persisted in her belief that some of the Houses that were keeping silent could be convinced to support Elayne. Of course, Elayne could not approach them herself, but Dyelin could. And now the situation verged on desperate. Six Houses supporting Arymilla, and only a fool would think she had not sent feelers out toward the others. Or that some might listen just because she did have six already.

Despite the fact that Caseille and her Guards had vacated the courtyard, Elayne and the others had to thread their way across the paving stones though a crowd. The men from Matherin were finally down off their horses, but they were still moiling about, dropping their halberds and picking them up only to drop them again, trying to unload their packhorse there in the stableyard. One of the boys was chasing a chicken that somehow had gotten loose and was scuttling between the horses' legs, while one of the wrinkled old men shouted encouragement, though whether for the boy or the chicken was unclear. A leather-faced bannerman with the merest fringe of white hair remaining, in a faded red coat that strained across his belly, was trying to establish order with the help of an only slightly younger Guardsman, both of them likely returned from their pensions, as a good many had, but another of the boys seemed about to lead his shaggy horse into the palace itself, and Birgitte had to order him out of the way before Elayne could enter. The boy, a fuzz-cheeked lad who could not have been above fourteen, gaped at Birgitte as widely as he had at the palace. She was certainly more picturesque in her uniform than the Daughter-Heir in a riding dress, and he had already seen the Daughter-Heir. Rasoria gave him a shove back toward the old bannerman, shaking her head.

"I don't flaming know what I can do with them," Birgitte grumbled as a maid liveried in red-and-white took Elayne's cloak and gloves in the small entry hall. Small in terms of the Royal Palace. With gilded stand-lamps flickering between narrow, fluted white columns, it was half again the size of Matherin's main entry hall, though the ceiling was not so high. Another maid with the White Lion on the left breast of her dress, a girl not that much older than the boy who had tried to bring his horse inside, offered a ropework silver tray with tall cups of steaming spiced wine before simultaneous frowns from Aviendha and Birgitte made her shy back. "The flaming boys fall asleep if they're put on guard," Birgitte went on, scowling at the retreating maid. "The old men stay awake, but half can't remember what they're flaming supposed to do if they see somebody trying to scale the bloody wall, and the other half together couldn't fight off six shepherds with a dog." Aviendha raised an eyebrow at Elayne and nodded.

"They aren't here to fight," Elayne reminded them as they started down a blue-tiled corridor lined with mirrored stand-lamps and inlaid chests, Birgitte and Aviendha on either side of her and the Guardswomen spreading out a few paces ahead of them and behind. *Light,* she thought, *I wouldn't have* taken *the wine!* Her head pounded in rhythm with Birgitte's, and she touched her temple, wondering whether she should order her Warder to go find Healing immediately.

Birgitte had other ideas, though. She eyed Rasoria and the others in front, then looked over her shoulder and motioned those following to fall back a little more. That was strange. She had handpicked every last woman in the

Guards, and she trusted them. Even so, when she spoke it was in a hurried near-whisper, bending her head close to Elayne. "Something happened just before you returned. I was asking Sumeko if she'd Heal me before you got back, and she suddenly fell over in a faint. Her eyes just rolled up in her head, and down she went. It isn't only her. Nobody will admit a flaming thing, not to me, but the other Kin I've seen have been jumping out of their bloody skins, and the Windfinders, too. Not one of them could spit if she had to. You were back before I could find a sister, but I suspect they'd give me the fish eye, too. They'll tell you, though."

The palace required the population of a large village to keep running, and servants had begun to appear, liveried men and women scurrying along the corridors, flattening themselves against the walls or ducking into crossing hallways to make room for Elayne's escort, so she explained the little she knew in as soft a voice and as few words as possible. Some rumors she did not mind reaching the streets, and inevitably Arymilla, but tales of Rand could be as bad as tales of the Forsaken by the time they were twisted through a few retellings. Worse, in a way. No one would believe the Forsaken were trying to put her on the throne as a puppet. "In any event," she finished, "it's nothing to do with us here."

She thought she sounded very convincing, very cool and detached, but Aviendha reached out to squeeze her hand, for an Aiel as much as a comforting hug with so many people to see, and Birgitte's sympathy flooded through the bond. It was more than commiseration; it was the shared feeling of a woman who had already suffered the loss she herself feared and more. Gaidal Cain was lost to Birgitte as surely as if he were dead, and on top of that, her memories of her past lives were fading. She remembered almost nothing clearly before the founding of the White Tower, and not all of that. Some nights, the fear that Gaidal would fade from her memory, too, that she would lose any remembrance of actually having known and loved him, left her unable to sleep until she drank as much brandy as she could hold. That was a poor solution, and Elayne wished she could offer a better, yet she knew her own memories of Rand would not die until she did, and she could not imagine the horror of knowing those memories might leave her. Still, she hoped someone Healed Birgitte's morning-after head soon, before her own split open like an over-ripe melon. Her ability with Healing fell short of the task, and Aviendha's was no stronger.

Despite the emotion she could feel in Birgitte, the other woman kept her face smooth and unconcerned. "The Forsaken," she muttered dryly. And softly. That was not a name to bandy about. "Well, as long as it has nothing to do with us, we're bloody all right." A grunt that might have been a laugh gave her the lie. But then, although Birgitte said she had never been a soldier before, she had a soldier's view. Long odds were usually the only odds you could find, but you still had to get the job done. "I wonder what they think of it?" she added, nodding toward the four Aes Sedai who had just stepped out of a crossing corridor down the hallway.

Vandene, Merilille, Sareitha and Careane had their heads together as they walked, or rather, the last three were clustered around Vandene, leaning toward her and talking with urgent gestures that made the fringes on their shawls sway. Vandene glided along slowly as if she were alone, paying no heed. She had always been slender, but her dark green dress, embroidered with flowers on the sleeves and shoulders, hung on her as though made for a stouter woman, and the white hair gathered at the nape of her neck seemed in need of a brush. Her expression was bleak, but that might have had nothing to do with whatever the other sisters were saying. She had been joyless ever since her sister's murder. Elayne would have wagered that dress had belonged to Adeleas. Since the murder, Vandene wore her sister's clothes more often than her own. Not that that accounted for the fit. The two women had been of a size, but Vandene's appetite for food had died with her sister. Her taste for most things seemed to have died then.

Sareitha, a Brown whose dark square face was not yet touched with agelessness, saw Elayne just then, and put a hand on Vandene's arm as if to draw her up the corridor. Vandene brushed the Tairen woman's hand away and glided on with the merest glance at Elayne, disappearing on along the hallway they had come out of. Two women in novice white, who had been following the others at a respectful distance, offered quick curtsies to the remaining sisters and hastened after Vandene. Merilille, a tiny woman in dark gray that made her Cairhienin paleness seem like ivory, stared as if she might follow. Careane adjusted her green-fringed shawl on shoulders wider than those of many men and exchanged quiet words with Sareitha. The pair of them turned to meet Elayne as she approached, making her curtsies almost as deep as the novices had given them. Merilille noticed the Guardswomen and blinked, then noticed Elayne and gave a start. *Her* curtsy matched the novices'.

Merilille had worn the shawl for over a hundred years, Careane for more than fifty, and even Sareitha had worn it longer than Elayne Trakand, but standing among Aes Sedai went with strength in the Power, and none of these three was more than middling strong among sisters. In Aes Sedai eyes, increased strength gave, if not increased wisdom, at least increased weight to your opinions. With a sufficient gap, those opinions became commands. Sometimes, Elayne thought the Kin's way was better.

"I don't know what it is," she said before any of the other Aes Sedai could speak, "but there is nothing we can do about it, so we might as well quit worrying. We have enough right in front of us without fretting over things we can't affect."

Rasoria half-turned her head, frowning and plainly wondering what she had missed, but the words smoothed the anxiety from Sareitha's dark eyes. Perhaps not from the rest of her, since her hands moved as if she wanted to smooth her brown skirts, yet she was willing to follow the lead of a sister who stood as high as Elayne. Sometimes, there were advantages to standing high enough that you could quell objections with a sentence. Careane had already regained serenity, if she had ever lost it. It sat easily on her, though she looked more like a wagon driver than an Aes Sedai despite her beryl-slashed silks and smooth, ageless coppery face. But then, Greens usually were made of tougher stuff than Browns. Merilille did not look at all serene. Wide eyes and half-parted lips gave her the appearance of startlement. That was usual for her, though.

Elayne continued along the hallway, hoping they would go about their business, but Merilille fell in beside Birgitte. The Gray should have taken primacy among the three, but she had developed a tendency to wait for someone to tell her what to do, and she shifted over without a word when Sareitha politely asked Birgitte to give her room. The sisters

were unfailingly courteous to Elayne's Warder when she
was acting as Captain-General. It was Birgitte as Warder
they tried to ignore. Aviendha received no such civility
from Careane, who elbowed in between her and Elayne.
Anyone not trained in the White Tower was a wilder by def-
inition, and Careane despised wilders. Aviendha pursed her
lips though she did not draw her belt knife or even suggest
that she might, for which Elayne was grateful. Her first-
sister could be . . . precipitate, at times. On second thought,
she would have forgiven a little hastiness from Aviendha
right then. Custom forbade rudeness toward another Aes
Sedai under any circumstances, but Aviendha could have
growled threats and waved her knife to her heart's content.
That might have been enough to make the threesome leave,
even if in a tizzy. Careane did not seem to notice the cool
green gaze marking her.

"I told Merilille and Sareitha it was nothing we could
do anything about," she said calmly. "But shouldn't we be
ready to flee if it comes closer? There's no shame flying
from that. Even linked, we would be moths fighting a forest
fire. Vandene wouldn't bother to listen."

"We really should make some sort of preparations,
Elayne," Sareitha murmured absently, as if making lists in
her head. "It's when you don't make plans that you wish you
had. There are a number of volumes in the library here that
mustn't be left behind. I believe several can't be found in
the Tower library."

"Yes." Merilille's voice was breathless, and as anxious
as her large dark eyes. "Yes, we really should be ready to
go. Perhaps . . . Perhaps we should not wait. Surely going
from necessity would not violate our agreement. I am sure
it would not." Only Birgitte as much as glanced at her, but
she flinched.

"If we do go," Careane said as if Merilille had not spoken, "we'll have to take all of the Kin with us. Allow them
to scatter, and the Light only knows what they'll do or when
we will ever catch them again, especially now that some
have learned to Travel." There was no bitterness in her
voice, though only Elayne among the sisters in the palace
could Travel. It seemed to make a difference to Careane
that the Kinswomen had begun in the White Tower, even
if most had been put out and a few had run away. She had

identified no fewer than four of them herself. At least they were not wilders.

Sareitha's mouth tightened, though. It weighed on her that several Kinswomen could weave gateways, and she had very different notions of the Kin. Normally, she limited her objections to the occasional frown or disparaging grimace, since Elayne had made her own views clear, but the stress of the morning seemed to have loosened her tongue. "We do indeed need to take them with us," she said in a cutting tone, "else they'll all be claiming to be Aes Sedai as soon as they're out of our sight. Any woman who maintains she was put out of the Tower over three hundred years ago will claim anything! They need to be kept under a close watch, if you ask me, instead of going about as they please, most *especially* those who can Travel. They may have gone where you told them and come back so far, Elayne, but how long before one of them doesn't return? Mark my words, once one of them escapes, others will follow, and we will have a mess on our hands we'll never clean up."

"There is no reason for us to go anywhere," Elayne said firmly, as much for the Guards as for the sisters. That distant beacon was still in the same spot where she had first sensed it, and if it did move, the chance seemed small that it would move toward Caemlyn, much less actually come there, but a rumor that Aes Sedai were planning flight might be enough to engender a stampede, mobs clawing to reach the gates ahead of whatever could frighten Aes Sedai. An army sacking the city would not kill as many. And these three chattered away as if there were no one to hear but the wall hangings! There was some excuse for Merilille, but not the others. "We will remain here, as the Amyrlin Seat has commanded, until the Amyrlin commands otherwise. The Kinswomen will continue to receive every courtesy until they are welcomed back into the Tower, and that is the Amyrlin's command, too, as you very well know. And you will continue teaching the Windfinders and go about your lives as Aes Sedai should. We are supposed to deal with people's fears and soothe them, not spread senseless gossip and panic."

Well, perhaps she had been a touch more than firm. Sareitha put her gaze on the floor tiles like a rebuked novice. Merilille flinched again at mention of the Windfinders, but that was to be expected. The others gave lessons, but the

Sea Folk held Merilille as tightly as they did one of their apprentices. She slept in their quarters and normally was not seen without two or three of them, and her trailing meekly at their heels. They refused to accept anything less than meekness from her.

"Of course, Elayne," Careane said hastily. "Of course. None of us would suggest disobeying the Amyrlin." Hesitating, she adjusted her green-fringed shawl over her arms, seemingly occupied with setting it just so. She did spare a pitying look for Merilille. "But speaking of the Sea Folk, could you tell Vandene to take her share of the lessons?" When Elayne said nothing, her voice took on an edge that would have been called sullen in anyone not Aes Sedai. "She says she's too busy with those two runaways, but she finds enough time to keep me talking some nights until I'm half asleep. That pair is already so cowed they wouldn't squeak if their dresses caught fire. They don't need her attention. She could take her portion of teaching those cursed wilders. Vandene needs to start behaving as an Aes Sedai, too!"

Standing or no, rebuke or no, she gave Elayne a baleful glare that took her a moment to smother. Elayne had been the one who made the bargain that led to Aes Sedai having to teach Windfinders, but so far she herself had managed to miss giving more than a handful of lessons, claiming the press of other, more important duties. Besides, the Sea Folk saw a shorebound teacher as a hireling, even an Aes Sedai, and a hireling with less standing than a scullion at that. A scullion who might try to cheat on her labor. She still thought Nynaeve had gone away just to avoid giving those lessons. Certainly no one expected to end up in Merilille's state, but even a few hours at a time was bad enough.

"Oh, no, Careane," Sareitha put in, still avoiding Elayne's eye. And Merilille's. In her opinion, the Gray had gotten herself into this fix and thus deserved what came of it, but she did try not to rub salt in the wounds. "Vandene is distraught over her sister, and Kirstian and Zarya help her occupy her mind." Whatever she thought of the other Kin, she accepted that Zarya was a runaway, as she had to, since Adeleas had recognized her, and if Kirstian must be a liar, her own lie would make her pay in full for that. Runaways were not treated kindly. "I spend hours with her, too, and she almost never talks of anything but Adeleas. It's as if she

wants to add my memories to her own. I think she needs to
be allowed as much time as she needs, and those two keep
her from being alone too often." Giving Elayne a sidelong
glance, she drew breath. "Still, teaching the Windfinders
is certainly . . . challenging. Perhaps an hour now and then
would help pull her out of despondency, if only by making
her angry. Don't you agree, Elayne? Just an hour or two,
now and then."

"Vandene will be allowed as much time to grieve for her
sister as she needs or wants," Elayne said in level tones.
"And there will be no more discussion of it."

Careane sighed heavily and rearranged her shawl again.
Sareitha sighed faintly and began twisting the Great Serpent ring on the forefinger of her left hand. Perhaps they had
sensed her mood, or perhaps it was just that neither looked
forward to another session with the Windfinders. Merilille's
permanently surprised expression did not change, but then,
her sessions with the Sea Folk lasted all day and all night
unless Elayne managed to pry her away, and the Windfinders were becoming less and less willing to let her go no
matter how Elayne pried.

At least she had managed to avoid being curt with the
three. It took an effort, especially with Aviendha there.
Elayne did not know what she would do if she ever lost her
sister. Vandene was not only grieving for a sister, she was
searching for Adeleas's murderer, and there could be no doubt
that the killer was Merilille Ceandevin, Careane Fransi or
Sareitha Tomares. One of them, or worse, more than one.
The charge was hard to believe of Merilille, in her present
condition, but it was not easy to believe of any sister. As
Birgitte had pointed out, one of the worst Darkfriends she
had ever met, during the Trolloc Wars, was a mild-as-milk
lad who jumped at loud noises. And poisoned an entire
city's water supply. Aviendha's suggestion was to put all
three to the question, which had horrified Birgitte, but Aviendha was considerably less in awe of Aes Sedai than she
once had been. The proper courtesies must be maintained,
until there was evidence to convict. Then there would be no
courtesy at all.

"Oh," Sareitha said, brightening suddenly. "Here's Captain Mellar. He was a hero again while you were gone,
Elayne."

Aviendha gripped the hilt of her belt knife, and Birgitte stiffened. Careane's face went very still, very cold, and even Merilille managed a disapproving hauteur. Neither sister made any secret of her dislike for Doilan Mellar.

With a narrow face, he was not pretty, or even handsome, yet he moved with a swordsman's lithe grace that spoke of physical strength. As Captain of Elayne's bodyguard, he rated three golden knots of rank, and he wore them soldered to each shoulder of his brightly burnished breastplate. An ignorant observer might have thought he outranked Birgitte. The falls of snow-white lace at his throat and wrists were twice as thick and twice as long as those worn by any of the Guardswomen, but he had left off the sash again, perhaps because it would have obscured one set of golden knots. He claimed that he wanted nothing more in life than to command her bodyguard, yet he frequently talked of battles he had fought as a mercenary. It seemed he had never been on the losing side, and victory had often come from his unsung efforts on the field. He swept off his white-plumed hat in a deep, flourishing bow, managing his sword deftly with one hand, then offered a slightly lesser to Birgitte with an arm across his chest in salute.

Elayne arranged a smile on her face. "Sareitha says you were a hero again, Captain Mellar. How so?"

"Nothing more than my duty to my queen." Despite a voice thick with self-deprecation, his answering smile was warmer than it should have been. Half the palace thought him the father of Elayne's child. That she had not crushed that rumor seemed to make him believe he had prospects. The smile never reached his dark eyes, though. They remained as cold as death. "My duty to you is my pleasure, my Queen."

"Captain Mellar led another sortie without orders yesterday," Birgitte said in a carefully even voice. "This time the fighting almost spilled into the Far Madding Gate, which he had ordered left open against his return." Elayne felt her face growing hard.

"Oh, no," Sareitha protested. "It wasn't like that at all. A hundred of Lord Luan's armsmen tried to reach the city in the night, but they left it too late, and sunrise caught them. So did three times their number of Lord Nasin's men. If Captain Mellar hadn't opened the gates and led a rescue, they'd have been cut to pieces in sight of the walls. As it was, he managed to save eighty for your cause." Smiling, Mellar basked in the Aes Sedai's praise as if he had not heard Birgitte's criticism. Of course, he seemed unaware of Careane and Merilille's disapproving stares, too. He always managed to ignore disapproval.

"How did you know they were Lord Luan's men, Captain?" Elayne asked quietly. A small smile that should have given Mellar warning appeared on Birgitte's face. But then, he was one of those who seemed not to believe she was a Warder. Even if he did, few except Warders and Aes Sedai knew what the bond entailed. If anything, Mellar's expression grew more smug.

"I didn't go by banners, my Queen. Anybody can carry a banner. I recognized Jurad Accan through my looking glass. Accan is Luan's man to his toenails. Once I knew that. . . ." He made a dismissive gesture in a flurry of lace. "The rest was no more than taking a little exercise."

"And did this Jurad Accan bring any message from Lord Luan? Anything signed and sealed, affirming House Norwelyn's support for Trakand?"

"Nothing in writing, my Queen, but as I said—"

"Lord Luan has not declared for me, Captain."

Mellar's smile faded somewhat. He was unused to being cut short. "But, my Queen, Lady Dyelin says that Luan is as good as in your camp right now. Accan showing up is proof of—"

"Of nothing, Captain," Elayne said coldly. "Perhaps Lord Luan will be in my camp eventually, Captain, but until he declares, you've given me eighty men who need to be watched." Eighty out of a hundred. And how many of hers had he lost? And he had risked Caemlyn doing it, burn him! "Since you can find time in your duties commanding my bodyguard to lead sorties, you can find time to arrange for watching them. I won't spare anyone from the walls for it. Set Master Accan and his fellows to drilling the men I've brought in from the manors. That will keep them all busy and out of trouble most of each day, but I leave it to you how to keep them away from the walls the rest of the time. And I do expect them kept away from the walls and out of trouble, Captain. You may see to it now."

Mellar stared at her, stunned. She had never taken him to task before, and he did not like it, particularly in front of so many witnesses. There were no over-warm smiles now. His mouth twitched, and a sullen heat grew in his eyes. But there was nothing for him to do except to jerk another bow, murmur "As my Queen commands" in a hoarse voice, and leave with as good a grace as he could muster. Before he had gone three paces he was striding down the hall as if to trample anyone who got in his way. She would have to tell Rasoria to take care. He might try to soothe his bile by taking it out on those who had seen and heard. Merilille and Careane gave almost identical nods; they would have seen Mellar called down, and preferably put out of the palace, long since.

"Even if he did wrong," Sareitha said carefully, "and I am not convinced that he did, Captain Mellar saved your life at risk to his own, Elayne, your life and that of the Lady Dyelin. Was there really need to embarrass him in front of the rest of us?"

"Never think I avoid paying my debts, Sareitha." Elayne felt Aviendha grip one of her hands, and Birgitte the other. She gave each of them a light squeeze. When you were surrounded by enemies, it was good to have a sister and a friend close by. "I am going to find a hot bath now, and unless one of you wishes to scrub my back . . . ?"

They could recognize a dismissal, and they departed more gracefully than Captain Mellar, Careane and Sareitha already discussing whether or not the Windfinders would actually want lessons today, Merilille trying to look every direction at once in hope of avoiding any Windfinders. What would they talk of later, though? Whether Elayne was having a spat with the father of her child? Whether they had successfully hidden their guilt in killing Adeleas?

I always pay my debts, Elayne thought, watching them go. *And I help my friends pay theirs.*

A Bargain

A bath was not hard to find, though Elayne had to wait in the hall frowning at the lion-carved doors of her apartments, drafts flickering the mirrored stand-lamps while Rasoria and two of the Guardswomen went in to search. Once they were sure there were no assassins lying in wait, and guards had been arrayed in the corridor and outer room, Elayne entered to find white-haired Essande waiting in the bedchamber with Naris and Sephanie, the two young tirewomen she was training. Essande was slim, with Elayne's Golden Lily embroidered over her left breast and a very great dignity emphasized by her deliberate way of moving, though some of that came from age and aching joints she refused to acknowledge. Naris and Sephanie were sisters, fresh-faced, sturdy and shy-eyed, proud of their livery and happy to have been chosen out for this rather than cleaning hallways but almost as much in awe of Essande as of Elayne. There were more experienced maids available, women who had worked years in the palace, but sadly, girls who had come seeking any sort of work they could find were safer.

Two copper bathtubs sat on thick layers of toweling laid atop the rose-colored floor tiles where one of the carpets had been rolled up, evidence that word of Elayne's arrival had flown ahead of her. Servants had a knack for learning what was happening that the Tower's eyes-and-ears might envy. A good blaze in the fireplace and tight casements in the windows made the room warm after the corridors, and Essande waited only to see Elayne enter the room before sending Sephanie off at a run to fetch the men with the hot water. That would be brought up in double-walled pails with lids to keep it from getting cold on the way from the kitchens, though it might be delayed a little by Guardswomen checking to make sure there were no knives hidden in the water.

Aviendha eyed the second bathtub almost as doubtfully as Essande eyed Birgitte, the one still uneasy about actually stepping into water and the other still not accepting that anyone more than necessary should be present during a bath, but the white-haired woman wasted no time before quietly bustling Elayne and Aviendha both into the dressing room, where another fire on a wide marble hearth had taken the chill from the air. It was a great relief to have Essande help her out of her riding clothes, knowing that she had more ahead of her than a hasty wash and a show of ease while worrying about how quickly she could move on to her next destination. Other pretenses awaited, the Light help her, and other worries, but she was home, and that counted for much. She could almost forget about that beacon shining in the west. Almost. Well, not at all, really, but she could manage to stop fretting over it as long as she did not dwell on the thing.

By the time they had been undressed—with Aviendha slapping Naris' hands away and removing her own jewelry, doing her best to pretend that Naris did not exist and her garments were somehow removing themselves—by the time they had been bundled into embroidered silk robes and had their hair tied up in white toweling—Aviendha tried to wrap the towel around her own head three times, and only after the construction collapsed down her neck for the third time did she allow Naris to do it, muttering about getting so soft that she soon would need someone to lace up her boots until Elayne began laughing and she joined in, throwing her head back so that Naris had to start over again—by the time all that was done and they had returned to the bedchamber, the bathtubs were full and the scent of the rose oil that had been added to the water filled the air. The men who had brought up the water were gone, of course, and Sephanie was waiting with her sleeves pushed above her elbows in case someone wanted her back scrubbed. Birgitte was sitting on the turquoise-inlaid chest at the foot of the bed, her elbows on her knees.

Elayne allowed Essande to help her off with her pale green, swallow-worked robe and sank into her tub immediately, submerging herself to her neck in water just a hair short of too hot. That left her knees poking up, but it immersed most of her in the warmth, and she sighed, feeling weariness leach out of her and languor creep in. Hot water might have been the greatest single gift of civilization.

Staring at the other tub, Aviendha gave a start when Naris attempted to remove her robe, lavender and embroidered with flowers on the wide sleeves. Grimacing, she finally allowed it, and stepped gingerly into the water, but she snatched the round soap out of Sephanie's hand and began washing herself vigorously. Vigorously, but very careful not to slop so much as a spoonful of water over the tub's rim. The Aiel did use water for washing, as well as in the sweat tents, especially for rinsing out the shampoo they made from a fat leaf that grew in the Waste, yet the dirty water was conserved and used for watering crops. Elayne had shown her two of the great cisterns beneath Caemlyn, fed by a pair of underground rivers and large enough that the far side of each was lost in a forest of thick columns and shadows, but the arid Waste was in Aviendha's bones.

Ignoring Essande's pointed looks—*she* seldom said two words more than necessary, and thought baths no time to say anything—Birgitte talked while they bathed, though she took care of what she said in front of Naris and Sephanie. It was unlikely they were in the pay of another House, but maids gossiped almost as freely as men—it seemed almost a tradition. Some rumors were worth fostering, nonetheless. Mostly Birgitte talked of two huge merchants' trains that had arrived yesterday from Tear, the wagons heavy with grain and salted beef, and another from Illian with oil and salt and smoked fish. It was always worthwhile reminding people that food continued to flow into the city. Few merchants braved the roads of Andor in winter, none carrying anything as cheap as food, but gateways meant that Arymilla could intercept all the merchants she wished and her forces still would starve long before Caemlyn felt the first pangs of hunger. The Windfinders, who were making most of those gateways, reported that the High Lord Darlin—claiming the title of Steward in Tear for the Dragon Reborn, of all things!—was besieged in the Stone of Tear by nobles who wanted the Dragon Reborn out of Tear completely, but even they were unlikely to try stopping a rich trade in grain, particularly since they believed the Kin who accompanied the Windfinders were Aes Sedai. Not that any real attempt was made at deception, but Great Serpent rings had been made for Kinswomen who had passed their tests for Accepted before being put out of the Tower, and if anyone drew the wrong conclusion, no one actually lied to them.

The water was going to shed its heat if she waited much longer, Elayne decided, so she took a rose-scented soap from Sephanie and allowed Naris to begin scrubbing her back with a long-handled brush. If there had been news of Gawyn or Galad, Birgitte would have mentioned it straight off. She was as eager to hear as Elayne, and she could not have held it back. Gawyn's return was one rumor they dearly wanted to reach the streets. Birgitte performed her duties well as Captain-General, and Elayne meant her to keep the position, if she could be convinced, but having Gawyn there would allow both women to relax a little. Most of the soldiers in the city were mercenaries, and only enough of them to man the gates strongly and make a display along the miles of wall surrounding the New City, but they still numbered more than thirty companies, each with its own captain who inevitably was full of pride, obsessed with precedence, and ready to squabble over any imagined slight from another captain at the drop of a straw. Gawyn had trained his whole life to command armies. He could deal with the squabblers, leaving her free to secure the throne.

Apart from that, she simply wanted him away from the White Tower. She prayed that one of her messengers had gotten through and that he was well downriver by this time. Egwene had been besieging Tar Valon with her army for more than a week, now, and it would be the cruelest spinning of fate for Gawyn to be caught between his oaths to defend the Tower and his love for Egwene. Worse, he had already broken that oath once, or at least bent it, for love of his sister and perhaps his love of Egwene. If Elaida ever suspected that Gawyn had aided Siuan's escape, whatever credit he had gained by helping her replace Siuan as Amyrlin would evaporate like a dewdrop, and if he was still within Elaida's reach when she learned, he would find himself in a cell, and lucky to avoid the headsman. Elayne did not resent his decision to aid Elaida; he could not have known enough then to make any other choice. A good many sisters had been confused over what was happening, too. A good many still seemed to be. How could she ask Gawyn to see what Aes Sedai could not?

As for Galad . . . She had grown up unable to like the man, sure he must resent her, and resent Gawyn most of all. Galad had to have thought he would be First Prince of the Sword one day, until Gawyn was born. Her earliest memories of him were of a boy, a young man, already behaving more like a father or uncle than a brother, giving Gawyn his first lessons with a sword. She remembered being afraid he would break open Gawyn's head with the practice blade. But he had never given more than the bruises any youth expected in learning swords. He knew what was right, Galad did, and he was willing to do what was right no matter the cost to anyone, including himself. Light, he had started a war to help her and Nynaeve escape from Samara, and it was likely he had known the risk from the start! Galad fancied Nynaeve, or had for a time—it was hard to imagine he still felt that way, with him a Whitecloak, the Light only knew where and doing what—but the truth was, he had started that war to rescue his sister. She could not condone him being a Child of the Light, she could not like him, yet she hoped that he was safe and well. She hoped he found his way home to Caemlyn, too. News of him would have been nearly as welcome as news of Gawyn. That surprised her, but it was true.

"Two more sisters came while you were away. They're at the Silver Swan." Birgitte made it sound as though they were merely stopping at an inn because every bed in the palace was taken. "A Green with two Warders and a Gray with one. They came separately. A Yellow and a Brown left the same day, so there are still ten altogether. The Yellow went south, toward Far Madding. The Brown was heading east."

Sephanie, waiting patiently beside Aviendha's tub with nothing to do, exchanged a glance with her sister over Elayne's head and grinned. Like many in the city, they knew for a fact that the presence of Aes Sedai at the Silver Swan signified White Tower support for Elayne and House Trakand. Watching the two girls like a hawk, Essande nodded;

she knew it, too. Every streetsweeper and ragpicker was aware that the Tower was divided against itself, but even so, the name still carried weight, and an image of strength that never failed. Everyone knew the White Tower had lent support to every rightful Queen of Andor. In truth, most sisters looked forward to a sitting monarch who was also Aes Sedai, the first in a thousand years and the first since the Breaking of the World to be openly known as Aes Sedai, but Elayne would not be surprised to find there was a sister in Arymilla's camp, keeping discreetly out of notice. The White Tower never placed all of its coin on one horse unless the race was fixed.

"That's enough of the brush," she said, irritably twisting away from the bristles. Well trained, the girl laid the brush down on a stool and handed her a large Illianer sponge that she used to begin sluicing off soap. She wished *she* knew what those sisters meant. They were like a grain of sand in her slipper, so tiny a thing that you could hardly imagine it being a discomfort, but the longer it remained, the larger it seemed. The sisters at the Silver Swan were becoming a sizable stone just by being there.

Since before she arrived in Caemlyn the number at the inn had been changed frequently, a few sisters leaving every week and a few coming to replace them. The siege had not changed anything; the soldiers surrounding Caemlyn were no more likely to try stopping an Aes Sedai from going where she wanted than were the rebellious nobles in Tear. There had been Reds in the city too, for a while, asking after men heading for the Black Tower, but the more they learned, the more they had let their disgruntlement show, and the last pair had ridden out of the city the day after Arymilla appeared before the walls. Every Aes Sedai who entered the city was carefully watched, and none of the Reds had gone near the Silver Swan, so it seemed unlikely the sisters there had been sent by Elaida to kidnap her. For some reason she imagined little groups of Aes Sedai scattered from the Blight to the Sea of Storms, and constant streams of sisters flowing between, gathering information, sharing information. A peculiar thought. Sisters used eyes-and-ears to watch the world, and rarely shared what they learned unless it was a threat to the Tower itself. Likely those at the Swan were among the sisters sitting out the Tower's troubles, waiting to see whether Egwene or Elaida would end with the Amyrlin Seat before they declared themselves. That was wrong—an Aes Sedai should stand for what she thought was right without worrying over whether she was choosing the winning side!—but these made her uneasy for another reason.

Recently one of her watchers at the Swan had overheard a disturbing name, murmured and quickly shushed, as if in fear of eavesdroppers. Cadsuane. Not a common name, that. And Cadsuane Melaidhrin had meshed herself closely with Rand while he was in Cairhien. Vandene did not think much of the woman, calling her opinionated and muleheaded, but Careane had almost fainted in awe at hearing her name. It seemed the stories surrounding Cadsuane amounted to legends. Trying to deal with the Dragon Reborn single-handed was just the sort of thing Cadsuane Melaidhrin might do. Not that Elayne had concerns about Rand and any Aes Sedai, except that he might outrage her beyond her control—the man was too pigheaded himself sometimes to see where his own good lay!—but why would a sister in Caemlyn mention her name? And why had another hushed her?

Despite the hot bathwater, she shivered, thinking of all the webs the White Tower had spun through the centuries, so fine that none could see them except the sisters who did the spinning, so convoluted that none but those sisters could have unraveled them. The Tower spun webs, the Ajahs spun webs, even individual sisters spun webs. Sometimes those schemes blended into one another as though guided by a single hand. Other times they had pulled one another apart. That was how the world had been shaped for three thousand years. Now the Tower had divided itself neatly into rough thirds, one third for Egwene, one for Elaida, and one that was standing aside. If those last were in contact with one another, exchanging information—forming plans?—the implications . . .

A sudden tumult of voices, dimmed by the closed door, made her sit up straight. Naris and Sephanie squealed and leaped to clutch one another, staring wide-eyed at the door.

"What in the bloody flaming . . . ?" Snarling, Birgitte hurled herself off the chest and out of the room, slamming the door behind her. The voices rose higher.

It did not sound as if the Guardswomen were fighting, just arguing at the tops of the lungs, and the bond carried mainly anger and frustration, along with her *bloody* head-ache, but Elayne climbed out of the bathtub, holding out her arms for Essande to slip her robe on. The white-haired woman's calmness, and perhaps Elayne's, soothed the two maids enough that they blushed when Essande looked at them, but Aviendha leaped from her tub, splashing water everywhere, and dashed dripping into the dressing room. Elayne expected her to return with her belt knife, but in-stead she came back surrounded by the glow of *saidar* and holding the amber turtle in one hand. With the other she handed Elayne the *angreal* that had been in her belt pouch, an aged ivory carving of a woman clothed only in her hair. Excepting the towel atop her head, Aviendha wore only a wet sheen, and she angrily waved Sephanie away when the woman tried to put her robe on her. Knife or no knife, Avi-endha still tended to think as if she were going to fight with a blade and might need to move suddenly.

"Put this back in the dressing room," Elayne said, hand-ing the ivory *angreal* to Essande. "Aviendha, I really don't think we need to—"

The door opened a crack, and Birgitte put her head in, scowling. Naris and Sephanie jumped, not so soothed as they had seemed.

"Zaida wants to see you," Birgitte growled at Elayne. "I told her she'd have to wait, but—" With a sudden yelp, she staggered into the room, catching her balance after two steps and whirling to face the woman who had pushed her.

The Wavemistress of Clan Catelar did not look as though she had pushed anyone. The ends of her intricately knot-ted red sash swirling about her knees, she entered the room calmly, followed by two Windfinders, one of whom shut the door in Rasoria's angry face. All three swayed when they moved nearly as much as Birgitte did in her heeled boots. Zaida was short, with streaks of gray in her tightly curled hair, but her dark face was one of those that grew more beautiful with the years, and her beauty only seemed magnified by the golden chain, heavy with small medal-lions, that connected one of her fat golden earrings to her nose ring. More importantly, her air was one of command. Not of arrogance, but of the knowledge that she would be obeyed. The Windfinders eyed Aviendha, still glowing with the Power, and Chanelle's angular face tightened, yet aside from a murmur from Shielyn that "the Aiel girl" was ready to weave, they remained silent and waited. The eight earrings in Shielyn's ears marked her as Windfinder to a Clan Wavemistress, and Chanelle's honor-chain carried nearly as many golden medallions as that of Zaida herself. Both were women of authority, and it was plain in the way they held themselves and moved, yet one needed to know nothing of the Atha'an Miere to know as soon as one saw them that Zaida din Parede held the first spot.

"Your boots must have tripped you, Captain-General," she murmured with a small smile on her full lips, one dark tattooed hand toying with the golden scent-box that dangled on her chest. "Clumsy things, boots." She and the two Windfinders were barefoot as always. The soles of the Atha'an Miere's feet were as tough as shoe soles, unbothered by rough decks or cold floor tiles. Strangely, in addition to their blouses and trousers of brightly colored silk brocades, each woman wore a wide stole of plain white that hung below her waist and almost hid her multitude of necklaces.

"I was taking a bath," Elayne said in a tight voice. As if they could not see that with her hair done up and her robe clinging to her damply. Essande was almost *quivering* with indignation, which meant she must be beside herself with fury. Elayne felt close to it herself. "I will be taking a bath again as soon as you go. I will speak with you when I have finished taking my bath. If it pleases the Light." There! If they were going to shove into her rooms, let them chew on that for ceremony!

"The grace of the Light be upon you also, Elayne Sedai," Zaida replied smoothly. She raised an eyebrow at Aviendha, though neither at the continuing light of *saidar,* since Zaida could not channel, nor at her nudity, since the Sea Folk were quite casual about that, at least out of sight of landmen. "You have never invited me to bathe with you, though it would have been courteous, but we will not speak of that. I have learned that Nesta din Reas Two Moons is dead, killed by the Seanchan. We mourn her loss." All three women touched their white stoles and touched fingertips to lips, yet Zaida seemed as impatient with formality as Elayne. Without raising her voice or speeding its pace, she merely pushed on, almost shockingly abrupt and to the point for one of the Sea Folk.

"The First Twelve of the Atha'an Miere must meet to choose another Mistress of the Ships. What is happening to the west makes it clear there can be no delay." Shielyn's mouth tightened, and Chanelle raised her pierced scent box to her nose as if to drown the smell of something. Its spicy perfume was sharp enough to slice through the scent of rose oil in the room. However they had described what they sensed to Zaida, she displayed no unease, or anything but certainty. Her gaze held steady on Elayne's face. "We must be ready for whatever comes, and for that we need a Mistress of the Ships. In the name of the White Tower, you promised twenty teachers. I cannot take Vandene in her grief, or you, but I will take the other three with me. The rest, the White Tower owes, and I will expect prompt payment. I have sent to the sisters at the Silver Swan to see whether some of them will meet the Tower's debt, but I cannot wait on their reply. If it pleases the Light, I will bathe with the other Wavemistresses tonight at the harbor of Illian."

Elayne fought very hard to keep her own face smooth. The woman just *announced* that she intended to scoop up every Aes Sedai lying around loose in Caemlyn and carry them off? And it sounded very much as if she did not intend to leave any of the Windfinders behind. That made Elayne's heart sink. Until Reanne returned, there were seven of the Kin with sufficient strength to weave a gateway, but two of those could not make one large enough to admit a horse cart. Without the Windfinders, plans for keeping Caemlyn supplied from Tear and Illian became problematical at best. The Silver Swan! Light, whoever Zaida had sent would reveal every line of the bargain she had made! Egwene was not going to thank her for spilling that mess out into the open. She did not think she had ever had so many problems dropped in her lap in the course of one short statement.

"I regret your loss, and the Atha'an Miere's loss," she said, thinking fast. "Nesta din Reas was a great woman." She had been a powerful woman, anyway, and a very strong personality. Elayne had felt happy to walk away with more than her shift after her one meeting with her. Speaking of shifts, she could not afford time to dress. Zaida might not wait. She belted her robe tighter. "We must talk. Have wine brought for our guests, Essande, and tea for me. Weak tea," she sighed at a burst of caution through the bond to Birgitte. "In the smaller sitting room. Will you join me, Wavemistress?"

To her surprise, Zaida merely nodded as if she had expected this. That started Elayne thinking about Zaida's side of the bargain between them. The bargains; there were two, really, and that might be a key point.

No one had expected the smaller sitting room to be used for some time, so the air held a chill even after Sephanie rushed with a spark-wheel to light the kindling laid beneath split oak on the wide white hearth and scurried out of the room. Flames leapt up from the fatwood, catching on the log atop the fire-irons as the women arrayed themselves in the lightly carved low-backed chairs arranged in a semi-circle in front of the fireplace. Well, Elayne and the Sea Folk women arrayed themselves, Elayne arranging her robe carefully over her knees and wishing Zaida had delayed just an hour so she could be properly dressed, the Wind-finders coolly waiting for the Wavemistress to take a chair, then sitting to either side of her. Birgitte stood in front of the writing table with her hands on her hips and her feet apart, her face a thunderhead. The bond carried a clear desire to wring an Atha'an Miere neck. Aviendha leaned casually against one of the sideboards, and even when Essande brought her robe and pointedly held it out for her, she merely put it on and resumed her pose with her arms folded beneath her breasts. She had released *saidar,* but the turtle was still in her hand, and Elayne suspected she was ready to embrace the Power again in an instant. Neither Aviendha's cold green-eyed stare nor Birgitte's scowl affected the Sea Folk in the least, however. They were who they were, and they knew who they were.

"The *Atha'an Miere* were promised twenty teachers," Elayne said, emphasizing slightly. Zaida had said that *she* had been promised, that *she* would collect payment, but that bargain had been made with Nesta din Reas. Of course, Zaida might believe she would become the new Mistress of the Ships herself. "Proper teachers, to be selected by the Amyrlin Seat. I know that the Atha'an Miere pride them-selves on meeting their bargains in full, and the Tower will meet its side, too. But you knew when sisters here agreed to teach, that it was temporary. And a bargain quite apart from that made with the Mistress of the Ships. You admitted as much when you agreed for Windfinders to weave gateways to bring supplies to Caemlyn from Illian and Tear. Surely you would not have gotten involved in the affairs of the shorebound for any reason other than paying off a bargain. But if you are leaving, your help is at an end, and so is our requirement to teach. I fear you will harvest no teachers at the Silver Swan, either. The Atha'an Miere will have to wait until the Amyrlin sends teachers. According to the bargain made with the Mistress of the Ships." A pity she could not demand they stay away from the inn, but it might already be too late for that, and every reason she could think of sounded hollow. An argument that shattered for lack of a center would only embolden Zaida. The Atha'an Miere were ferocious hagglers. Scrupulous, but ferocious. She had to go very slowly, very carefully.

"My sister has you by the ear, Zaida din Parede," Aviendha chortled, slapping her thigh. "Hung up by the ankles, in fact." That was a Sea Folk punishment that she found incredibly amusing, for some reason.

Elayne stifled a burst of irritation. Aviendha enjoyed chances to tweak the Sea Folk's noses—she had begun while they were fleeing Ebou Dar and never really stopped—but this was no time for it.

Chanelle stiffened, her calm face sinking into a glare. The lean woman had been the butt of Aviendha's nose-tweaking more than once, including a regrettable episode involving *oosquai*, a very potent Aiel drink. The glow of *saidar* actually surrounded her! Zaida could not see that, but she knew about the *oosquai* and Chanelle being carried to her bed, sicking up the whole way, and she raised a peremptory hand toward the Windfinder. The glow faded, and Chanelle's face darkened. It might have been a blush or anger.

"All that you say may be so," Zaida said, which was not far from insulting, especially said to an Aes Sedai. "In any event, Merilille was not part of that. She agreed to be one of the teachers long before she reached Caemlyn, and she will go with me to continue her teaching."

Elayne drew a long breath. She could not even try to

argue Zaida out of this. A great part of the White Tower's influence rested on the fact that the Tower kept its word as surely as the Sea Folk. That it was *known* to keep its word. Oh, people said you had to listen carefully to be sure an Aes Sedai had promised what you thought she had, and that was often true, but once the promise was clear, it was as good as an oath under the Light. At least the Windfinders were not likely to let Merilille get away. They hardly let her out of their sight. "You may have to return her to me, if I have particular need of her." If Vandene and the two helpers found proof that she was Black Ajah. "If that happens, I will arrange a replacement." And who that could be, she had no idea.

"She has the rest of her year to serve. At least a year, by the bargain." Zaida gestured as if making a concession. "But so long as you understand that her replacement must come before she leaves. I will not let her go without another in her place."

"I suppose that will do," Elayne replied calmly. It would bloody well have to, since she had no other choice!

Zaida smiled faintly and let the silence stretch. Chanelle shifted her feet, but more in impatience than as if to rise, and the Wavemistress did not stir. Plainly she wanted something more, intended another bargain, and plainly she wanted Elayne to speak first. Elayne set herself to outwait the other woman. The fire had begun to blaze and crackle, sending sparks up the chimney and radiating a fine warmth into the room, but her damp robe absorbed the chill in the air and transferred it to her skin. Ignoring the cold was all very well, but how were you supposed to ignore being cold *and* wet? She met Zaida's gaze levelly and matched her tiny smile. Essande returned, followed by Naris and Sephanie carring ropework trays, the one with a silver teapot in the shape of a lion and thin green cups of Sea Folk porcelain, the other hammered silver cups and a tall-necked wine pitcher that gave off the aroma of spices. Everyone took wine, except for Elayne, who was never offered the choice. Peering into her tea, she sighed. She could see the bottom of the cup quite clearly. If they made it any weaker, they might as well give her water!

After a moment, Aviendha strode across the room to set her winecup back on the tray atop one of the sideboards and pour herself a cup of tea. She gave Elayne a nod and a smile combining sympathy with a suggestion that she really preferred watery tea to wine. Elayne smiled back in spite of herself. First-sisters shared the bad as well as the good. Birgitte grinned over the top of her silver cup, and proceeded to empty half of it in a gulp. The bond carried her amusement at the grumpiness she felt from Elayne. And it still carried her headache, in no way reduced. Elayne rubbed her temple. She should have insisted that Merilille Heal the woman as soon as she had seen her. A number of the Kin outstripped Merilille when it came to Healing, but she was the only sister in the palace with a halfway decent ability.

"You have great need of women to make these gateways," Zaida said suddenly. Her full mouth was no longer smiling. She disliked having spoken first.

Elayne sipped her wretched excuse for tea and said nothing.

"It might please the Light that I could leave one or two Windfinders here," Zaida went on. "For a set time."

Elayne wrinkled her brow as though considering. She *needed* those bloody women, and more than one or two. "What would you ask in return?" she said finally.

"One square mile of land on the River Erinin. Good land, mind. Not marshy or boggy. It is to be Atha'an Miere land in perpetuity. Under our laws, not Andor's," she added as if that were a small afterthought hardly worth mentioning.

Elayne choked on her tea. The Atha'an Miere hated leaving the sea, hated being out of sight of it. And Zaida was asking for land a thousand miles from the nearest salt water? Asking for it to be ceded absolutely, at that. Cairhienin and Murandians and even Altarans had bled trying to take bits of Andor, and Andorans had bled to keep them out. Still, one square mile was a small bit, and a small price to keep Caemlyn supplied. Not that she would let Zaida know that. And if the Sea Folk began trading directly into Andor, then Andoran goods would be able to move in Sea Folk bottoms everywhere the Sea Folk sailed, and that was everywhere. Zaida surely knew that already, but there was no point in letting her know that Elayne had thought of it. The Warder bond urged caution, yet there were times for boldness, as Birgitte should know better than anyone.

"Sometimes tea goes down the wrong way." Not a lie; merely an evasion. "For a square mile of Andor, I deserve more than two Windfinders. The Atha'an Miere got twenty teachers and more for help using the Bowl of the Winds, and when they go you will have twenty to replace them. You have twenty-one Windfinders with you. For a mile of Andor, I should have all twenty-one, and twenty-one more in their places when they leave, for as long as Aes Sedai teach Sea Folk." Best not to let the woman think that was her way of rejecting the offer out of hand. "Of course, the normal customs duties would apply to any goods moving off this land into Andor."

Zaida raised her silver cup to her mouth, and when she lowered it, she wore the tiniest smile. Yet Elayne thought it was a smile of relief rather than triumph. "Goods moving into Andor, but not goods coming from the river onto our land. I might leave three Windfinders. For half a year, say. And they must not be used in fighting. I will not have my people die for you, and I will not have other Andorans angry at us because Sea Folk have killed some of them."

"They will be asked only to make gateways," Elayne said, "though they must make them wherever I require." Light! As if she intended using the One Power as a weapon! The Sea Folk did so without a second thought, but she was trying very hard to behave as Egwene demanded, as though she had already taken the Three Oaths. Besides, if she blasted those camps outside the walls with *saidar,* or allowed anyone else to, not a House in Andor would stand with her. "They must stay until my crown is secure, whether that is half a year or longer." The crown should be hers in much less time, but as her old nurse Lini used to say, you counted your plums in the basket, not on the tree. Once the crown was hers, though, she would not need Windfinders to supply the city, and in all truth, she would be happy to see their backs. "But three is not nearly enough. You will want Shielyn, since she is your Windfinder. I will keep the rest."

The medallions on Zaida's honor-chain swayed gently as she shook her head. "Talaan and Metarra are apprentices still. They must return to their training. The others have duties, too. Four might be spared until your crown is secure."

From there it was just a matter of bargaining. Elayne had never expected to keep the apprentices, and Windfinders to

Clan Wavemistresses could not be spared either, which she had expected. Most Wavemistresses used their Windfinders and Swordmasters as close advisors, and would be parted from one as easily as she would be parted from Birgitte. Zaida tried to exclude others as well, such as Windfinders who served on large vessels like rakers and skimmers, but that would have disqualified the greater number right there, and Elayne refused, and refused to come down in her demands unless Zaida came up in her offers. Which the woman did slowly, grudging every concession. But not so slowly as Elayne might have expected. Clearly, the Wavemistress needed this bargain as much as she herself needed women who could weave gateways.

"Under the Light, it is agreed," she was able to say at last, kissing the fingertips of her right hand and leaning forward to press them to Zaida's lips. Aviendha grinned, obviously impressed. Birgitte kept a smooth face, but the bond said she found it hard to believe Elayne had come out so well.

"It is agreed, under the Light," Zaida murmured. Her fingers on Elayne's lips were hard and callused, though she could not have hauled on a rope herself in many years. She looked quite satisfied for a woman who had yielded nine of the fourteen Windfinders who had been on the table. Elayne wondered how many of those nine would be women whose ships had been destroyed by the Seanchan in Ebou Dar. Losing a ship was a serious matter among the Atha'an Miere, whatever the reason, and maybe cause enough to want to stay away from home a little longer. No matter.

Chanelle looked glum, her tattooed hands tight on the knees of her red brocaded trousers, yet not so glum as might be expected from a Sea Folk woman who would have to remain ashore a while longer. She was to command the Windfinders who stayed, and she did not like it that Zaida had acceded to her being under Elayne's authority, and Birgitte's. There were to be no more Sea Folk striding about the palace as if they owned it and making demands left and right. But then, Elayne suspected that Zaida had come to this meeting knowing she would leave some of her party behind, and Chanelle had come knowing she would command them. That hardly mattered, either, nor did it matter what advantage Zaida hoped to gain toward becoming Mistress of the Ships. That she saw some was clear as good

glass. All that mattered was that Caemlyn would not go
hungry. That and the . . . the *bloody* beacon still blazing in
the west. No, she would be a queen, and she could not be
a moonstruck girl. Caemlyn and Andor were all that *could*
matter.

CHAPTER
13

High Seats

Zaida and the two Windfinders departed from Elayne's apartments, graceful and outwardly unhurried but with almost as little ceremony as they had entered, a bare wish that the Light illumine Elayne and see her safe. For Atha'an Miere, that was almost rushing off without a word. Elayne decided that if Zaida did indeed want to be the next Mistress of the Ships, the woman had a rival she hoped to steal a march on. It might be well for Andor if Zaida did attain the Atha'an Miere throne, or whatever the Sea Folk called it; bargain or no bargain, she would always be aware that Andor had helped her, and that had to be for the good. Though if she failed, her rival would be aware of where Andor's favor had gone, too. Still, it was all if and maybe. Here and now was another thing altogether.

"I do not expect anyone to manhandle an ambassador," she said quietly once the doors had closed behind them, "but in the future I do expect the privacy of my rooms. Even ambassadors are not to be allowed simply to wander in. Am I understood?"

Rasoria nodded, her face wooden, but by the color that flashed into her cheeks, she felt the mortification of having let the Sea Folk pass as keenly as Birgitte, and the bond . . . *writhed* . . . until Elayne felt her own face growing red with a stinging embarrassment. "You did nothing wrong, exactly, but don't let it happen again." Light, now she sounded a dolt! "We will speak no more of it," she said stiffly. Oh, *burn* Birgitte *and* the bond! They *would* have had to wrestle with Zaida to stop her, but adding bone-deep humiliation to the other woman's headache was piling insult on injury! And Aviendha had no call to grin in that . . . that *smarmy* way. Elayne did not know when or how her sister had learned that she and Birgitte sometimes reflected one another, but Aviendha found the whole thing vastly amusing. Her sense of humor could be rough at times.

"I think you two will make each other melt, one day," she said, laughing. "But then, you already played that joke, Birgitte Trahelion." Birgitte scowled at her, sudden alarm crushing embarrassment in the bond, and she returned such a look of innocence it seemed her eyes might fall out of her face.

Better not to ask, Elayne decided. When you ask questions, Lini used to say, then you have to hear the answers whether you want to or not. She did not want to hear, not with Rasoria studiously examining the floor tiles in front of her boots and the rest of the Guardswomen in the anteroom failing to pretend not to be listening. She had never realized how precious privacy was until she lost it completely. Near enough completely, anyway. "I am going to finish my bath now," she said calmly. Blood and ashes, what joke *had* Birgitte played on her? Something that made her . . . melt? It could not have been much if she still did not know what it was.

Unfortunately, the bath water had gone cold. Tepid, anyway. Hardly anything she wanted to sit in. A little while longer soaking would have been wonderful, but not at the expense of waiting while the tubs were emptied bucket by bucket and more hot water brought up. The entire palace must know she was back by now, and the First Maid and the First Clerk would be anxious to make their daily reports. Daily when she was in the city, and doubly anxious because she had been gone for a day. Duty came before pleasure, if you were going to rule a country. And that went doubly for trying to gain the throne in the first place.

Aviendha pulled the towel from her head and shook down her hair, appearing relieved that she would not have to climb into water again. She started for the dressing room, shedding her robe before she reached the door, and had donned most of her garments when Elayne and the maids entered. With only a few mutters, she let Naris complete the job, although little remained beyond stepping into her heavy woolen skirt. She slapped the maid's hands away and tightened the laces of her soft knee-high boots herself.

For Elayne, it was not so easy. Unless some emergency loomed, Essande felt slighted when she did not discuss her choice of dresses. With close servants, there was always a delicate balance to maintain. Without exception a bodyservant knew more of your secrets than you thought she did, and she saw you at your worst, grumpy, tired, weeping in your pillow, in rages and sulks. Respect had to go both ways, or the situation became impossible. So Aviendha was sitting on one of the padded benches, allowing Naris to comb out her hair, before Elayne could conclude on a simple gray in fine wool, embroidered in green on the high neck and the sleeves and trimmed with black fox. It was not so much that she had difficulty deciding, but that Essande kept putting forward silks sewn with pearls or sapphires or firedrops, each more ornately embroidered than the last. No matter that the throne was not yet hers, Essande wanted to dress her every day as a queen readying for an audience.

There had been a point to that, back when every day brought delegations of merchants to offer petitions or make their respects, especially outlanders hoping the troubles in Andor would not affect their trade. The old saying that who held Caemlyn held Andor had never really been true, and in merchant eyes, the chances she would actually gain the throne had diminished with the arrival of Arymilla's army outside the gates. They could count the Houses arrayed on either side as easily as they could count coin. Even Andoran merchants avoided the Royal Palace now, keeping out of the Inner City as much as possible so no one would think they had gone to the palace, and bankers came well hooded, in anonymous carriages. None wished her ill, that she knew, and certainly none wanted to anger her, but neither did they want to anger Arymilla, not now. Still, the bankers did come, and so far she had not heard of any merchants presenting petitions to Arymilla. That would be the first sign that her cause was lost.

Getting into the dress took twice as long as it should have, since Essande allowed Sephanie to help Elayne. The girl breathed heavily the whole time, unaccustomed as yet to dressing someone else and fearful of making a mistake under Essande's eye. Much more than of making one in front of her mistress, Elayne suspected. Apprehension made the sturdy young woman clumsy, clumsiness made her more painstaking, and taking pains made her worry more about mistakes, so the result was that she moved more slowly than the frail older woman ever had. Finally, however, Elayne found herself seated facing Aviendha, letting Essande draw an ivory comb through her curls. In Essande's view, allowing one of the girls to slip a shift over Elayne's head or fasten her buttons was one thing, but risking either of them making a tangle in her hair quite another.

Before the comb had made two dozen strokes, though, Birgitte appeared in the doorway. Essande sniffed, and Elayne could all but see the woman grimace behind her back. Essande had given way on Birgitte being present at baths, however reluctantly, but the dressing room was sacrosanct.

Surprisingly, Birgitte let the maid's disapproval slide past without so much as a placating look. Usually, she refrained from pushing Essande an inch further than Elayne required. "Dyelin has returned, Elayne. She's brought company. The High Seats of Mantear, Haevin, Gilyard and Northan." For some reason, the bond carried streaks of puzzlement and annoyance.

Shared headache or no, Elayne could have jumped for joy. If Essande had not had the comb deep in her hair, she might have. Four! She had never expected Dyelin to accomplish so much. Hoped for it, prayed for it, but never expected it, certainly not in one short week. In truth, she had been sure Dyelin would return empty-handed. Four gave her an equal footing with Arymilla. It was galling to think of being on "an equal footing" with that foolish woman, but truth was truth. Mantear, Haevin, Gilyard and Northan. Why not Candraed? That was the fifth House Dyelin had gone to approach. No. She had four more Houses, and she was *not* going to fret over the lack of one.

"Entertain them in the formal sitting room until I can come, Birgitte." The small sitting room had been sufficient for Zaida—she hoped the Wavemistress had not noticed the slight—but four High Seats required more. "And ask the First Maid to arrange apartments." Apartments. Light! The Atha'an Miere would have to be hurried out of theirs to make room. Until they left, most beds that did not have two occupants had three. "Essande, the green silk with the sapphires, I think. And sapphires for my hair, too. The large sapphires."

Birgitte left still feeling puzzled and upset. Why? Surely she could not think she should have left *Dyelin* cooling her heels because of Zaida? Oh, Light, now she was feeling puzzled over Birgitte feeling puzzled; if that was allowed to feed on itself, they would both end up dizzy! As the door closed, Essande moved to the nearest wardrobe wearing a smile that might have been called triumphant.

Looking at Aviendha, who had motioned Naris and her comb away and was folding a dark gray scarf to tie her hair back, Elayne smiled herself. She needed something to take her out of that spinning loop. "Maybe you should wear silks and gems just this once more, Aviendha," she said in a gently teasing tone. "Dyelin won't mind, of course, but the others aren't used to Aiel. They might think I'm entertaining a stablehand."

She meant it for a joke—they twitted one another about clothes all the time, and Dyelin looked askance at Aviendha whatever she wore—but her sister frowned at the wardrobes lining the wall, then nodded and set the scarf down beside her on the tufted cushion. "Just so these High Seats will be properly impressed. Do not think I will do this all the time. It is a favor to you."

For someone just doing a favor, she pored over the clothes that Essande pulled out with a great deal of interest before deciding on a dark blue velvet slashed with green, and a silver net to catch her hair. They were her clothes, made for her, but since reaching Caemlyn she had avoided them as if they were crawling with death's-head spiders. Stroking the sleeves, she hesitated as if she might change her mind, but finally she let Naris do up the tiny pearl buttons. She declined Elayne's offer of emeralds that would have suited the gown admirably, keeping her silver snowflake necklace and heavy ivory bracelet, but at the last minute she did pin the amber turtle to her shoulder.

"You can never tell when it might be needful," she said.

"Better safe than sorry," Elayne agreed. "Those colors look beautiful on you." It was true, but Aviendha blushed. Compliment her on how well she shot a bow or how fast she could run, and she took it as no more than her due, but she had difficulty coming to grips with the fact that she was beautiful. That was a part of herself she had managed to ignore, till recently.

Essande shook her head in disapproval, unaware that the brooch was an *angreal*. Amber did not go with blue velvet. Or maybe it was Aviendha's horn-hilted knife, which she tucked behind her green velvet belt. The white-haired woman made sure that Elayne wore a small dagger with sapphires on the scabbard and pommel, hanging from a belt of woven gold. Everything had to be just so to gain Essande's approbation.

Rasoria gave a start when Aviendha entered the anteroom in her high-necked velvets. The Guardswomen had never seen her in anything but Aiel garb before. Aviendha scowled as if they had laughed, and gripped her belt knife firmly, but luckily her attention was diverted by a cloth-covered tray sitting on the long side table against the wall. Elayne's midday meal had been delivered while they were dressing. Whisking the blue-striped cloth aside, Aviendha tried to interest Elayne in eating, smiling and pointing out how sweet the stew of dried plums would be and exclaiming over the pieces of pork in the grainy mush. Slivers, they looked like. Rasoria cleared her throat and mentioned that a fire was burning nicely in the apartment's larger sitting room. She would be more than happy to carry the tray in for the Lady Elayne. Everyone tried to make sure Elayne ate properly, however they saw "properly," but this was ridiculous. The tray had been sitting there some time. The mush was a congealed mass that would have stuck in the bowl if she turned it upside down!

She had the High Seats of four Houses waiting on her, and they had waited long enough. She pointed that out, but offered to let the two of them eat if they were hungry. In fact, she implied that she might insist on them eating. That was enough to make Aviendha drop the cloth back over the tray with a shudder, and Rasoria wasted no more time, either.

It was only a short walk down the icy hallway to the formal sitting room, and the only things that moved, aside from them, were the bright winter wall hangings that stirred in the corridor's drafts, but the Guardswomen formed a ring around Elayne and Aviendha and kept watch as if they expected Trollocs. It was only with an effort that Elayne convinced Rasoria there was no need to search the sitting room before she entered. The Guardswomen served her and obeyed her, but they also were pledged to keep her alive, and they could be as muley over that last duty as Birgitte was over deciding whether she was Warder, Captain-General or elder sister at any given moment. Likely, following on the heels of the incident with Zaida, Rasoria would have wanted the lords and ladies waiting inside to surrender their weapons! The threat with the mush might have had its part, too. After a short argument, however, Elayne and Aviendha swept in through the wide doorway together, and alone. Elayne's feeling of satisfaction did not last, though.

The sitting room was large, meant to accept dozens of people comfortably, a dark-paneled space with layered carpets covering the floor tiles and a horseshoe arch of high-back chairs in front of a tall fireplace of white marble with fine red veins. Here, important dignitaries could be received with more honor than an audience before the throne, because it was more intimate. The blaze dancing along the logs on the hearth had barely had time to take an edge off the chill in the air, but that certainly was not the reason Elayne felt as if she had been struck in the stomach. She understood Birgitte's puzzlement, now.

Dyelin turned from warming her hands at the fire as they entered. A strong-faced woman with fine lines at the corners of her eyes and hints of gray in her golden hair, she had not waited to change on reaching the palace, and still wore a riding dress of deep gray that showed a few travel stains on the hem. Her curtsy was the merest bend of her neck, the slightest dip of her knees, but she intended no discourtesy. Dyelin knew who she was as surely as Zaida did—her only jewelry was a small golden pin in the shape of Taravin's Owl and Oak on her shoulder, a clear statement that the High Seat of Taravin needed nothing more—yet she had almost died to prove her loyalty to Elayne. "My Lady Elayne," she said formally, "it gives me honor to present to you Lord Perival, High Seat of House Mantear."

A pretty, golden-haired boy in a plain blue coat jerked away from peering through the four-barreled kaleidoscope on a gilded stand taller than he was. He had a silver cup in his hand that Elayne hoped very much did not contain wine, or at least extremely well watered if it did. One of the side tables held several trays laden with pitchers and cups. And an ornate teapot she knew might as well be filled with water. "My pleasure, my Lady Elayne," he piped, blushing and managing a credible bow despite a little clumsiness in handling the sword belted to his waist. The weapon looked much too long for him. "House Mantear stands with House Trakand." She returned his courtesy in a daze, spreading her skirts mechanically.

"Lady Catalyn, High Seat of House Haevin," Dyelin continued.

"Elayne," a dark-eyed young woman at her side murmured, touching her dark green divided skirts and making a fractional dip that might possibly have been intended for a curtsy, though perhaps she just meant to imitate Dyelin. Or perhaps she wanted to avoid poking her chin against the large enameled brooch on the high neck of her dress, the Blue Bear of Haevin. Her hair was caught in a silver net worked with the Blue Bear, too, and she wore a long ring with the sigil as well. A touch too much pride of House, perhaps. Despite her cool haughtiness, she was a woman only by courtesy, her cheeks still round with baby fat. "Haevin stands with Trakand, obviously, or I would not be here."

Dyelin's mouth tightened slightly, and she gave the girl a hard glance that Catalyn seemed not to see. "Lord Branlet, High Seat of House Gilyard."

Another boy, this one with unruly black curls, in green embroidered with gold on the sleeves, who hastily set his winecup down on a side table as if uneasy at being seen with it. His blue eyes were too big for his face, and he nearly tripped himself with his sword, bowing. "It is my pleasure to say that House Gilyard stands for Trakand, Lady Elayne." Halfway through, his voice broke from treble to bass, and he blushed even harder than Perival.

"And Lord Conail, High Seat of House Northan."

Conail Northan grinned over the rim of his silver cup. Tall and lean, in a gray coat with sleeves just too short to cover his bony wrists, he had an engaging grin, merry brown eyes, and an eagle's beak for a nose. "We drew straws for the order to be introduced, and I drew short. Northan stands with Trakand. Can't let a ninny like Arymilla take the throne." He managed his sword smoothly, and he at

least had reached his majority, but if he was many months
past sixteen, Elayne would eat his turned-down boots *and*
his silver-knot spurs.

Their youth was no surprise, of course, but she had expected Conail to have a graying head at his side to advise
him and the others to have their guardians looking over
their shoulders. There was no one else in the room aside
from Birgitte, standing in front of the tall arched windows
with her arms folded beneath her breasts. Bright midday
sunlight flooding through the clear glass set in the casements made her a silhouette of displeasure.

"Trakand welcomes all of you, and I welcome all of you,"
Elayne said, suppressing her dismay. "I will not forget your
support, and Trakand will not forget." Something of her
consternation must have crept through, because Catalyn's
mouth compressed and her eyes glittered.

"I am past my guardianship, as you must know, Elayne,"
she said in a stiff voice. "My uncle, Lord Arendor, said at
the Feast of Lights that I was as ready as I would ever be
and might as well have free rein then as in a year. Truth,
I think he wanted more time to go hunting while he still
can. He has always loved hunting, and he's quite old." Once
again she failed to see Dyelin's frown. Arendor Haevin and
Dyelin were roughly of an age.

"I have no guardian either," Branlet said uncertainly, his
voice nearly as high-pitched as Catalyn's.

Dyelin gave him a sympathetic smile and smoothed his
hair back from his forehead. It promptly fell forward again.
"Mayv was riding alone, as she liked to do, and her horse
stepped into a gopher hole," she explained quietly. "By
the time anyone found her, it was too late. There has been
some . . . discussion . . . over who's to take her place."

"They've been arguing for three months," Branlet muttered. For a moment he looked younger than Perival, a boy
trying to find his way with no one to show him the path.
"I'm not supposed to tell anyone that, but I can tell you.
You're going to be the Queen."

Dyelin put a hand on Perival's shoulder, and he stood up
straighter, though he still was shorter than she. "Lord Willin would be here with Lord Perival, but the years have him
bedridden. Age creeps up on us all, eventually." She shot
another look at Catalyn, but the girl was studying Birgitte,

now, her lips pursed. "Willin said I was to tell you that he sends his good wishes and also one he considers a son."

"Uncle Willin told me to uphold the honor of Mantear and of Andor," Perival said, intent as only a child being serious could be. "I will try, Elayne. I will try very hard."

"I'm sure you will succeed," Elayne told him, managing to put at least a little warmth into her tone. She wanted to chase them all out and ask Dyelin some very pointed questions, but that could not be, not right away. Whatever their ages, they were all the High Seats of powerful Houses, and she had to offer refreshment and at least a modicum of conversation before they went to change from their journey.

"Is she really the Captain-General of the Queen's Guards?" Catalyn asked as Birgitte handed Elayne a thin blue porcelain cup of slightly darkened hot water. The girl spoke as though Birgitte was not there. Birgitte raised an eyebrow before leaving, but Catalyn seemed practiced in not seeing what she did not want to see. The winecup in her plump hand gave off the sharply sweet aroma of spices. There was not so much as a drop of honey in Elayne's miserable excuse for tea.

"Yes, and my Warder, too," she said. Politely. As ready as she would ever be! The girl probably thought it a compliment. She deserved a switching for pure rudeness, yet you could not switch a High Seat. Not when you needed her support.

Catalyn's eyes flashed to Elayne's hands, but the Great Serpent ring did nothing to alter the coolness of her expression. "They gave you that? I had not heard you had been raised Aes Sedai. I thought the White Tower had sent you home. When your mother died. Or perhaps because of the troubles in the Tower we hear about. Imagine, Aes Sedai squabbling like farmwives at market. But how can she be a general *or* a Warder without a sword? In any case, my aunt Evelle says a woman should leave swords to men. You don't shoe your own horse when you have a farrier, or grind your own grain when you have a miller." A quote from Lady Evelle, no doubt.

Elayne schooled her face, ignoring the only slightly buried insults. "An army *is* a general's sword, Catalyn. Gareth Bryne says a general who uses another blade is mistaking the job." The name seemed to make no impression on her, either. Miners' children in the Mountains of *Mist* knew Gareth Bryne's name!

Aviendha appeared at Elayne's side, smiling as though delighted at the opportunity to talk with the girl. "Swords are no use at all," she said sweetly. Sweetly! Aviendha! Elayne had never realized her sister could dissemble so skillfully. She had a cup of mulled wine, too. It would have been too much to expect her to continue drinking bitter tea out of sisterly affection. "You should learn the spear. Also the knife, and the bow. Birgitte Trahelion could shoot your eyes out at two hundred paces with her bow. Maybe at three hundred."

"The spear?" Catalyn said faintly. And then, in a slightly incredulous tone, "My *eyes*?"

"You have not met my sister," Elayne said. "Aviendha, Lady Catalyn Haevin. Catalyn, Aviendha of the Nine Valleys Taardad." Perhaps she should have done that the other way around, but Aviendha *was* her sister, and even a High Seat must settle for being introduced to the sister of the Daughter-Heir. "Aviendha is Aiel. She's studying to become a Wise One."

The fool girl's mouth dropped open at the start, her chin falling more and more with each pronouncement until she was gaping like a fish. Very satisfying. Aviendha gave Elayne a smaller smile, her green eyes sparkling with approbation above her winecup. Elayne kept her own face smooth, but she wanted to grin back.

The others were much more easily handled, much less infuriating. Perival and Branlet were shy their first time in Caemlyn much less in the Royal Palace, hardly saying two words unless someone drew them out. Conail did think the claim that Aviendha was Aiel must be a joke, and nearly got her belt knife in his brisket for laughing raucously, but luckily, he thought that was a joke as well. Aviendha adopted an icy composure that might have made her seem a Wise One in her usual clothes; in velvets, she appeared even more a lady of the court no matter how she fingered her knife. And Branlet did keep sneaking sidelong peeks at Birgitte. It took Elayne a little while to realize that he was watching her walk in her heeled boots—those wide trousers were actually quite snug over the hips—but she only sighed. Fortunately, Birgitte never noticed, and the bond would have let

Elayne know even if she tried to hide it. Birgitte liked having men look at her. Grown men. It would have done Elayne's cause no good if her Warder smacked young Branlet's bottom.

Mainly they wanted to know whether Reanne Corly was an Aes Sedai. None of the four had ever seen a sister before, but they thought she must be, since she could channel, and carry them and their armsmen across hundreds of miles in a step. It was a good opportunity to practice evasion without actually lying, helped by the Great Serpent ring on her own finger. A lie would taint her relations with these four at the start, but it would hardly do to hope that rumors of Aes Sedai aid would filter out to Arymilla while spreading the truth about freely. Of course, all four were eager to let her know how many armsmen they had brought, a total of just over three thousand, nearly half of them crossbowmen or halberdiers who would be especially useful on the walls. That was a sizable force for four Houses to have had ready to hand when Dyelin came calling, but then, no House wanted its High Seat unguarded in these times. Kidnapping was not unheard of when the throne sat in question. Conail said as much, with a laugh; he seemed to find everything worth a laugh. Branlet nodded and scrubbed a hand through his hair. Elayne wondered how many of his numerous aunts, uncles and cousins knew he was gone, and what they would do when they learned.

"If Dyelin had been willing to wait a few days," Catalyn said, "I could have brought more than twelve hundred men." That was the third time in as many sentences that she had managed to point out that she had brought the largest contingent by a considerable margin. "I have sent to all of the Houses pledged to Haevin."

"And I to every House pledged to Northan," Conail added. With a grin, of course. "Northan may not summon as many swords as Haevin or Trakand—or Mantear," he put in with a bow to Perival, "but whoever rides when the Eagles call will be riding for Caemlyn."

"They will not ride very fast in winter," Perival said quietly. And astonishingly, since no one had spoken to him. "I think that whatever we do, we will have to do it with who we have now."

Conail laughed and cuffed the lad's shoulder and told him to buck up his spirits, because every man with a heart was on his way to Caemlyn to support the Lady Elayne, but Elayne studied Perival more closely. His blue eyes met hers for a moment without blinking before he shyly lowered his gaze. A boy, but he knew what he had ridden into better than Conail or Catalyn, who proceeded to tell them yet again how many armsmen she had brought, *and* how many Haevin could call on, as if everyone there except Aviendha did not know *exactly* how many rode to each House's summons, in trained soldiers and farmers who had carried a halberd or pike in some war and village men who could be drafted at need. Close enough to exactly, anyway. Lord Willin had done good work with young Perival. Now she had to keep it from going to waste.

Eventually it was time to exchange kisses, with Branlet blushing to his hair, and Perival blinking bashfully when Elayne bent to him, and Conail vowing never to wash his cheek. Catalyn returned a surprisingly hesitant peck to Elayne's cheek, as if it had just occurred to her that she had consented to placing Elayne above her, but after a moment she nodded to herself, cool pride settling back on her like a mantle. Once the four were handed over to the maids and serving men who would take them to the apartments that Elayne hoped the First Maid had had time to ready, Dyelin refilled her winecup and settled herself in one of the tall, carved chairs with a weary sigh.

"As fine a week's work as I've ever done, if I do say so myself. I got Candraed out of the way straight off. I never thought Danine would be able to make up her mind, and it only took an hour to prove me right, though I had to stay three to keep from offending her. The woman must keep in bed till noon from being unable to decide to which side of the mattress to climb down from! The rest were ready to see sense with only a little convincing. No one with any sense wants to risk Arymilla gaining the throne."

For a moment, she frowned at her wine, then fixed Elayne with a steady look. She never hesitated to speak her mind, whether or not she thought Elayne would agree, and plainly she intended to do so now. "It may have been a mistake to pass these Kinswomen off as Aes Sedai, however side-mouthed we've been about it. The strain may be too much to ask of them, and it puts us all at risk. This morning, for no reason I could make out, Mistress Corly was staring and

gaping like a goose-girl come to the city. I think she almost
failed at weaving the gateway to bring us here. That would
have been wonderful, everyone lined up to ride through a
miraculous hole in the air that never materialized. Not to
mention that it would have stuck me in Catalyn's company
for the Light knows how long. Odious child! There's a good
mind there, if someone took her in hand for a few years, but
she has a double dose of the viperous Haevin tongue."

Elayne gritted her teeth. She knew how cutting Haevins
could be. The whole family took *pride* in it! Catalyn obviously did. And she was tired of explaining what on this
day could frighten any woman who could channel. She was
tired of being reminded of what she was trying to ignore.
That *bloody* beacon was still blazing in the west, an utter
impossibility both for its size and its duration. The thing
had been unchanging for hours! *Anyone* who channeled for
this long without a rest *must* have fallen over with exhaustion
by now. And Rand bloody al'Thor was right there, in the
heart of it. She was certain of that! He was alive, but that
only made her want to slap his face for putting her through
this. Well, *his* face was not there, but—

Birgitte slammed her silver cup down on a side table so
hard that wine flew everywhere. Some laundress was going
to sweat to take that stain out of her coatsleeve. A maid
would labor for *hours* to restore the side table's polish.
"Children!" she barked. "People are going to die because
of the decisions they make, and they're flaming children,
Conail worst of all! You heard him, Dyelin. He wants to
challenge Arymilla's *champion* like Artur bloody Hawkwing! Hawkwing never fought anybody's flaming champion, and he knew when he was younger than *Lord* Northan
that it was a fool's game to rest so much on a flaming duel,
but Conail thinks he can win Elayne the flaming throne
with his flaming sword!"

"Birgitte Trahelion is right," Aviendha said fiercely. Her
hands were fists gripping her skirts. "Conail Northan *is* a
fool! But how could anyone follow those children into the
dance of spears? How could anyone ask them to lead?"

Dyelin regarded them both, and chose to answer Aviendha first. She was plainly bemused by Aviendha's garb.
But then, she was bemused by Aviendha and Elayne adopt-
ing one another as sisters, by Elayne having an Aiel friend

in the first place. That Elayne chose to include that friend in their counsels was something she tolerated. Though not without letting her toleration show. "I became High Seat of Taravin at fifteen, when my father died in a skirmish on the Altaran Marches. My two younger brothers died fighting cattle raiders out of Murandy that same year. I listened to advisors, but I told Taravin riders where to strike, and we taught the Altarans and the Murandians to look elsewhere for their thieving. The times choose when children must grow up, Aviendha, not we, and in these times, a High Seat who is a child cannot *be* a child any longer.

"As for you, Lady Birgitte," she went on in a drier voice. "Your language is, as ever . . . pungent." She did not ask how Birgitte presumed to know so much of Artur Hawkwing, things no historian knew, but she studied her appraisingly. "Branlet and Perival will take guidance from me, and so will Catalyn, I think, much as I regret the time I'll have to spend with the girl. As for Conail, he's hardly the first young man to think he's invincible and immortal. If you can't keep him reined in as Captain-General, I suggest you try walking him. The way he was eyeing those breeches of yours, he'll follow anywhere you lead."

Elayne . . . shrugged off . . . the pure fury welling up in her. Not her fury, any more than it had been her anger at Dyelin in the first place, or her anger at Birgitte splashing wine about. It was Birgitte's. She did not want to slap Rand's face. Well, she did, but that was beside the point. Light, Conail had been looking at Birgitte, too? "They are the High Seats of their Houses, Aviendha. No one in their Houses would thank me for treating them as less; far from it. The men who ride for them will fight to keep them alive, but it is Perival and Branlet, Conail and Catalyn they ride for, not me. Because they *are* the High Seats." Aviendha frowned, and folded her arms as though pulling a shawl around herself, but she nodded. Abruptly, and reluctantly—no one rose to such prominence among the Aiel without years of experience, and the approval of the Wise Ones—but she nodded.

"Birgitte, you will have to deal with them, Captain-General to High Seat. White hair wouldn't necessarily make them any wiser, and it definitely wouldn't make them any easier to deal with. They'd still have their own opinions, and with years of experience to give them weight, most likely they'd be ten times as certain they knew what needs to be done better than you do. Or than I do." She made a great effort to keep her tone clear of sharpness, and no doubt Birgitte felt the effort. At least, the flow of rage through the bond suddenly diminished. It was only tamped down, not gone—Birgitte enjoyed having men look, at least when she wanted them to look, but she very much did *not* like anyone saying she was trying to attract their attention—yet even so, she knew the danger to both of them of letting their emotions run too free.

Dyelin had begun sipping at her wine, still studying Birgitte. Only a bare handful knew the truth that Birgitte desperately wanted to keep hidden, and Dyelin was not among them, yet Birgitte had been careless enough, a slip of the tongue here, a slip there, that the older woman was certain that some mystery hid behind Birgitte's blue eyes. The Light only knew what she would think if she solved that riddle. As it was, the two were oil and water. They could argue over which way was up, and certainly over everything else. This time, Dyelin clearly thought she had won, foot and horse.

"Be that as it may, Dyelin," Elayne continued, "I would have been more pleased if you had brought their advisors with them. What's done is done, but Branlet troubles me in particular. If Gilyard accuses me of kidnapping him, matters become worse than they were, not better."

Dyelin waved that away. "You don't know the Gilyards well, do you? The way they squabble among themselves, they may not notice the boy is gone before summer, and if they do, none will repudiate what he's done. None of them will admit they were so busy in arguing over who's to be his guardian that they forgot to keep an eye on him. And second, none of them will admit they weren't consulted beforehand. In any event, Gilyard would stand for Zaida before standing for Marne, and they don't like Arawn or Sarand much better."

"I hope you're right, Dyelin, because I'm appointing you to deal with any angry Gilyards who appear. And while you're advising the other three, you can keep a thumb on Conail so he doesn't do anything completely harebrained."

For all her talk, the first suggestion made Dyelin wince slightly. The second made her sigh.

It made Birgitte laugh out loud. "If you have any problems, I'll lend you a pair of breeches and some boots, and you can walk for him."

"Some women," Dyelin murmured into her wine, "can make a fish bite by crooking a finger, Lady Birgitte. Other women have to drag their bait all over the pond." Aviendha laughed at that, but Birgitte's anger began to edge upward in the bond.

A wave of cold air swept into the room as the door opened, and Rasoria entered, coming to a stiff attention. "The First Maid and the First Clerk have come, my Lady Elayne," she announced. Her voice faltered at the end, as she caught the mood in the room.

A blind goat could have caught it, with Dyelin smug as a cat in the creamery, and Birgitte scowling at her and Aviendha both, and Aviendha choosing this moment to remember that Birgitte *was* Birgitte Silverbow, which on this occasion made her stare at the floor, as abashed as if she had been laughing at a Wise One. Now and again Elayne wished her friends could all get on as well as she and Aviendha did, but somehow they managed to rub on together, and she supposed that was really all she could ask from real people. Perfection was a thing for books and gleemen's stories.

"Send them in," she told Rasoria. "And don't disturb us unless the city is under attack. Unless it is important," she amended. In stories, women who gave orders like that were always setting themselves up for disaster. Sometimes, there were lessons in stories, if you looked for them.

CHAPTER
14

What Wise Ones Know

Halwin Norry, the First Clerk, and Reene Harfor, the First Maid, entered together, him making a jerky, unpracticed bow, and her a graceful curtsy that was neither too low nor too shallow. They could not have been more different. Mistress Harfor was round-faced and regally dignified, her hair in a neat gray bun atop her head, Master Norry tall and gawky as a wading-bird, with his little remaining hair sticking up behind his ears like sprays of white feathers. Each carried an embossed leather folder stuffed with papers, but she held hers at her side as if not to rumple her formal scarlet tabard, unwrinkled as it always seemed to be, no matter the hour or how long she had been on her feet, while he clutched his folder to his narrow chest as if to hide old inkstains, of which several spotted his tabard, including a large blot that made the White Lion's tail end in a black tuft. Courtesies done, they immediately put a little distance between them, each not quite watching the other.

As soon as the door closed behind Rasoria, the glow of *saidar* sprung up around Aviendha, and she wove a ward against eavesdropping that clung to the walls of the room. What was said between them was now as safe as they could make it, and Aviendha would know if anyone even tried to listen with the Power. She was very good with this sort of weave.

"Mistress Harfor," Elayne said, "if you will begin." She did not offer wine or seats, of course. Master Norry would have been shocked to his toenails by such a lapse in the proprieties, and Mistress Harfor might well have been offended.

As it was, Norry twitched and glanced sideways at Reene, and her mouth thinned. Even after a week's meetings, their dislike for giving their reports where the other could hear was palpable. They were jealous of their fiefs, the more so since the First Maid had moved into territory that once might have been considered Master Norry's responsibility. Of course, running the Royal Palace had always been the First Maid's charge, and it might be said that her new duties were only an extension of that. It would not be said by Halwin Norry, though. The blazing logs settled in the fireplace with a loud crack, sending a shower of sparks up the chimney.

"I am convinced the Second Librarian is . . . a spy, my Lady," Mistress Harfor said finally, ignoring Norry as if to make him disappear. She had resisted letting *anyone* else know that she was searching out spies in the palace, yet the First Clerk knowing seemed to grate on her worst of all. His only authority over her, if such it was, came from paying the palace accounts, and he never questioned an expenditure, but even that little was more than she wished. "Every three or four days Master Harnder visits an inn called the Hoop and Arrow, supposedly for the ale made by the innkeeper, one Millis Fendry, but Mistress Fendry also keeps pigeons, and whenever Master Harnder visits, she sends off a pigeon that flies north. Yesterday, three of the Aes Sedai staying at the Silver Swan found reason to visit the Hoop and Arrow, though it caters to a much poorer crowd than the Swan. They came and went hooded, and were closeted with Mistress Fendry in private for over an hour. All three are Brown Ajah. I fear that indicates Master Harnder's employer."

"Hairdressers, footmen, cooks, the master cabinetmaker, no fewer than five of Master Norry's clerks, and now one of the librarians." Leaning back in her chair and crossing her legs, Dyelin glowered sourly. "Is there anyone we *won't* eventually learn is a spy, Mistress Harfor?" Norry stretched his neck uncomfortably; he took the malfeasance of his clerks as a personal affront.

"I have hopes I may be reaching the bottom of that barrel, my Lady," Mistress Harfor said complacently. Neither spies nor the High Seats of powerful Houses ruffled her. Spies were pests she intended to rid the palace of as surely as she kept it clear of fleas and rats—though she had been forced to accept Aes Sedai aid with rats recently—while powerful nobles were like rain or snow, facts of nature to be endured until they went away, but nothing to get flustered over. "There are only so many people who can be bought, and only so many can afford to buy, or want to."

Elayne tried to picture Master Harnder, but all she could bring up in her mind was vague, a chubby, balding man who blinked incessantly. He had served her mother, and as she recalled, Queen Mordrellen before that. No one commented on the fact that it seemed he also served the Brown Ajah. Every ruler's palace between the Spine of the World and the Aryth Ocean contained the Tower's eyes-and-ears. Any ruler with half a brain expected it. Doubtless the Seanchan would soon be living under the White Tower's gaze, too, if they were not already. Reene had discovered several spies for the Red Ajah, assuredly legacies of Elaida's time in Caemlyn, but this librarian was the first for another Ajah. Elaida would not have liked other Ajahs knowing what went on in the palace while she was advisor to the Queen.

"A pity we have no false stories we want the Brown Ajah to believe," she said lightly. A *great* pity they, and the Reds, knew about the Kin. At best, they had to know there were a large number of women in the palace who could channel, and it would not take them long to figure out who they were. That would create any number of problems down the road, yet those difficulties did lie somewhere in the future. Always plan ahead, Lini used to say, but worry too hard over next year, and you can trip over tomorrow. "Watch Master Harnder and try to find out his friends. That will have to suffice for the time being." Some spies depended on their ears, either to hear gossip or listen at doors; others lubricated tongues with a few friendly cups of wine. The first part of counteracting a spy was to find out how he learned what he sold.

Aviendha snorted loudly and, spreading her skirts, started to sit down on the carpet before realizing what she wore. With a warning glance at Dyelin, she perched stiffly on the front edge of a chair instead, the picture of a court lady with her eyes flashing. Except that a lady of the court would not have checked the edge of her belt knife with a thumb. Left to her own devices, Aviendha would slit every spy's throat as soon as it could be stretched for the knife. Spying was a vile business, in her view, no matter how often Elayne explained that every spy found was a tool that could be used to make her enemies believe what she wanted.

Not that every spy necessarily worked for an enemy. Most of those the First Maid had uncovered took money from more than one source, and among those she had identified were King Roedran of Murandy, various Tairen High Lords and Ladies, a handful of Cairhienin nobles, and a fair number of merchants. A good many people were interested in what happened in Caemlyn, whether for its effect on trade or other reasons. Sometimes it seemed that everyone spied on everyone else.

"Mistress Harfor," she said, "you haven't found any eyes-and-ears for the Black Tower."

Like most people who heard the Black Tower mentioned, Dyelin shivered, and took a deep drink of her wine, but Reene just grimaced faintly. She had decided to ignore the fact that they were men who could channel, since she could not change matters. To her, the Black Tower was . . . an annoyance. "They haven't had time, my Lady. Give them a year, and you'll find footmen and librarians taking their coin, too."

"I suppose I will." Dreadful thought. "What else do you have for us today?"

"I've had a word with Jon Skellit, my Lady. A man who turns his coat once is often amenable to turning it again, and Skellit is." Skellit, a barber, was in the pay of House Arawn, which for the present made him Arymilla's man.

Birgitte bit off an oath in midword—for some reason, she tried to watch her language around Reene Harfor—and spoke in a pained voice. "You had a *word* with him? Without asking anyone?"

Dyelin was under no compunctions regarding the First Maid, and she muttered, "Mother's milk in a cup!" Elayne had never heard her use an obscenity before. Master Norry blinked and almost dropped his folder, and busied himself with not looking at Dyelin. The First Maid, however, merely paused until sure she and Birgitte were done, then went on calmly.

"The time seemed ripe, and so did Skellit. One of the men he hands his reports to left the city and hasn't returned yet, while it appears the other broke his leg. The streets are always icy where a fire has been put out." She said that so blandly, it seemed more than likely she had engineered the man's fall somehow. Hard times uncovered hard talents in the most surprising people. "Skellit is quite agreeable to carrying his next communication out to the camps himself. He saw a gateway made, and he won't have to pretend terror." You would have thought she herself had been seeing merchants' wagons rumble out of holes in the air for her entire life.

"What's to stop this barber keeping on running once he's outside the fla . . . uh . . . the city?" Birgitte demanded irritably, beginning to pace in front of the fire with her hands clasped behind her. Her heavy golden braid should have been bristling. "If he goes, Arawn will hire somebody else, and you'll have to hunt him out all over again. Light, Arymilla must have heard of the gateways almost as soon as she arrived, and Skellit has to know it." It was not the thought of Skellit escaping that irritated her, or not only that. The mercenaries thought they had been hired to stop soldiers, but for a few silvers they would allow one or two to slip through the gates by night in either direction. One or two could do no harm, as they saw matters. Birgitte did not like being reminded of that.

"Greed will stop him, my Lady," Mistress Harfor replied calmly. "The thought of earning gold from the Lady Elayne as well as from Lady Naean is enough to make the man breathe hard. It's true, Lady Arymilla must already have heard of the gateways, but that only adds credit to Skellit's reason for going in person."

"And if his greed is great enough for him to try earning still more gold by turning his coat a third time?" Dyelin said. "He could cause a great deal of . . . mischief, Mistress Harfor."

Reene's tone became a little crisper. She would never step over the boundaries, but she disliked *anyone* thinking her careless. "Lady Naean would have him buried under the nearest snowdrift, my Lady, as I made certain he is aware. She has never been patient. As I am sure you are aware. In any case, the news we get from the camps is quite sparse, to say the least, and he might see a few things we would like to know."

"If Skellit can tell us which camp Arymilla, Elenia and Naean will be in and when, I'll give him his gold with my own hand," Elayne said deliberately. Elenia and Naean stayed close to Arymilla, or she kept them close, and Arymilla was much less patient than Naean, much less willing to believe that anything could function without her presence. She spent half of each day riding from camp to camp, and never slept in the same two nights running, as far as anyone could learn. "That is the only thing he can tell us of the camps that I want to know."

Reene inclined her head. "As you say, my Lady. I will see to it." She too often tried not to say things straight out in front of Norry, but she gave no sign that she had heard any reproof. Of course, Elayne was not sure she actually would rebuke the woman openly. Mistress Harfor would continue to perform her duties properly if she did, and she certainly would continue hunting spies with undiminished ardor, if for no other reason than their presence in the palace offended her, yet Elayne might find a dozen inconveniences in every day, a dozen small discomforts that added up to misery, and not a one that she could directly attribute to the First Maid. *We must follow the steps of the dance as surely as our servants,* her mother had told her once. *You can keep hiring new servants, and spend all your time training them and suffering till they learn, only to find yourself back where you started, or you can accept the rules as they do, and live comfortably while you use your time to rule.*

"Thank you, Mistress Harfor," she said, for which she received another precise curtsy. Reene Harfor was another who knew her own worth. "Master Norry?"

The heron-like man gave a start and stopped frowning at Reene. In some ways, he saw the gateways as his, and not to be trifled with. "Yes, my Lady. Of course." His voice was a dusty monotone. "I trust the lady Birgitte already has informed you of the merchants' trains from Illian and Tear. I believe that is . . . um . . . her usual custom when you return to the city." For a moment, his eyes rested reproachfully on Birgitte. He would never think of causing Elayne the smallest irritation even if she shouted at him, but he lived by his own set of rules, and, in a mild fashion, he resented Birgitte stealing his chance to enumerate the wagons and casks and barrels that had arrived. He did love his numbers. At least,

Elayne supposed it was in a mild fashion. There seemed to be very little heat in Mister Norry.

"She did," she told him, with just a hint of apology, not enough to embarrass him. "I fear some of the Sea Folk are leaving us. We'll only have half the number to make gateways after today."

His fingers spidered across the leather folder against his chest as though feeling the papers within. She had never seen him consult one. "Ah. Ah. We shall . . . cope, my Lady." Halwin Norry always coped. "To continue, there were nine arsons yesterday and last night, slightly more than usual. Three attempts were made to fire warehouses storing food. None successful, I hasten to add." He might hasten to add, yet he did it in that same drone. "If I may say so, the Guards patrolling the streets are having an effect—the number of assaults and thefts has declined to little more than normal for this time of year—but it seems evident that some hand is directing the arsons. Seventeen buildings were destroyed, all save one abandoned," his mouth narrowed in disapproval; it would take far more than a siege to make him leave Caemlyn, "and in my opinion, all of the fires were placed so as to draw the water-wagons as far as possible from the warehouses where attempts were made. I now believe that pattern holds for every fire we've seen these past weeks."

"Birgitte?" Elayne said.

"I can try plotting the warehouses on a map," Birgitte replied doubtfully, "and put extra Guards on the streets that seem to be farthest away, but it's still leaving a lot to fla . . . uh . . . to chance." She did not look toward Mistress Harfor, but Elayne *felt* a faint hint of a blush from her. "Anybody can have flint and steel in a belt pouch, and it only takes a minute with some dry straw to start a fire."

"Do what you can," Elayne told her. It would be *pure* luck if they caught an arsonist in the act, and beyond luck if the arsonist could say more than that she had been handed coin by someone with a hood hiding her face. Tracing that gold back to Arymilla or Elenia or Naean would require Mat Cauthon's luck. "Have you anything more, Master Norry?"

Knuckling his long nose, he avoided her gaze. "It has . . . uh . . . come to my attention," he said hesitantly, "that Marne, Arawn and Sarand have all recently taken very

large loans against the revenues of their estates." Mistress
Harfor's eyebrows climbed before she got them under control.

Peering into her teacup, Elayne discovered that she had
actually emptied it. Bankers never told anyone how much
they had loaned to whom, or against what, but she did not
ask how he knew. It would be . . . embarrassing. For both
of them. She smiled when her sister took the cup, then grimaced when Aviendha returned with it filled again. Aviendha seemed to think she should drink weak tea till her
eyes floated! Goat's milk was better, but dishwater for tea
would do. Well, she would hold the *bloody* cup, but she did
not have to drink.

"The mercenaries," Dyelin growled, the heat in her eyes
enough to make a bear back up. "I've said it before, and
I'll say it again; the trouble with sell-swords is they don't
always stay bought." She had opposed hiring mercenaries
to help defend the city from the start, though the fact was
that without them, Arymilla could have ridden in with her
army by any gate she picked, or near enough. There simply
had not been enough men to guard every gate properly otherwise, much less man the walls.

Birgitte had opposed the mercenaries, too, yet she had
accepted Elayne's reasons, if reluctantly. She still distrusted
them, but now she shook her head. Sitting on the arm of a
chair near the fire, she rested her spurred boot on the seat.
"Mercenaries have a concern for their reputations if not
their honor. Changing sides is one thing; actually betraying a gate is something else entirely. A company that did
that would never be hired again, anywhere. Arymilla would
have to offer enough for a captain to live the rest of his life
like a lord, and at least convince his men they'd be able to,
as well."

Norry cleared his throat. Even that sounded dusty, somehow. "It seems they may have borrowed against the same
revenues twice or even three times. The bankers, of course,
are . . . unaware . . . of this, as yet."

Birgitte began to curse, then cut herself off. Dyelin
scowled at her wine hard enough to make it turn sour.
Aviendha squeezed Elayne's hand, just a quick pressure
quickly released. The fire crackled in a shower of sparks,
some nearly reaching the carpets.

"The mercenary companies will have to be watched." Elayne raised a hand to forestall Birgitte. The other woman had not opened her mouth, but the bond shouted volumes. "You will have to find the men for it somewhere." Light! They seemed to be guarding against as many people inside the city as outside! "It shouldn't take that many, but we need to know if they start to act strangely, or secretively, Birgitte. That might be our only warning."

"I was thinking what to do if one of the companies does sell out," Birgitte said wryly. "Knowing won't be enough unless I have men to rush to any gate I think is going to be betrayed. And half the soldiers in the city are mercenaries. Half the rest are old men who were living on their pensions a few months gone. I'll shift the mercenaries' postings at irregular intervals. It will be harder for them to betray a gate if they can't be sure where they'll be tomorrow, but that doesn't make it impossible." Protest how she would that she was no general, she had seen more battles and sieges than any ten generals living, and she knew very well how these matters unfolded.

Elayne almost wished she had wine in her cup. Almost. "Is there any chance the bankers will learn what you have, Master Norry? Before the loans come due?" If they did, some might decide they preferred Arymilla on the throne. She could strip the country's coffers to repay those loans, then. She might even do it. Merchants rode the political winds, whichever way they blew. Bankers had been known to attempt to influence events.

"In my opinion, it is unlikely, my Lady. They would have to . . . um . . . ask the right questions of the right people, but bankers are normally . . . um . . . closemouthed . . . with one another. Yes, I think it unlikely. For the time being."

There was nothing to be done in any case. Except to tell Birgitte there might be a new source for assassins and kidnappers. Only given her hard expression and a sudden grimness in the bond, she had already realized that. There would be little chance of keeping the bodyguard under a hundred women, now. If there ever had been.

"Thank you, Master Norry," Elayne said. "You've done well, as always. Let me know immediately if you see any indications that the bankers have asked those questions."

"Of course, my Lady," he murmured, ducking his head like an egret darting after a fish. "My Lady is very kind."

When Reene and Norry left the room, him holding the door for her and making a bow that was a hair more graceful than usual and her giving him a slight bow of her head as she glided past him into the corridor, Aviendha did not release the ward she was holding. As soon as the door closed, its solid sound swallowed by the ward, she said, "Someone tried to listen."

Elayne shook her head. There was no way to tell who—a Black sister? A curious Kinswoman?—but at least the eavesdrop had failed. Not that there was much chance of anyone getting past one of Aviendha's wards, maybe not even the Forsaken, but she would have spoken up right away if someone had.

Dyelin took Aviendha's announcement with less aplomb, muttering about the Sea Folk. She had not turned a hair at hearing that half the Windfinders were leaving, not in front of Reene and Norry, but now she demanded to know the whole story. "I never did trust Zaida," she grumbled when Elayne finished. "This agreement sounds good for trade, I suppose, but it wouldn't surprise me if she had one of the Windfinders try to listen in. She struck me as a woman who wants to know everything, just in case it might be useful one day." There was very little hesitant about Dyelin, yet she hesitated now, rolling her winecup between her palms. "Are you certain this . . . this *beacon* . . . can't harm us, Elayne?"

"As certain as I can be, Dyelin. If it was going to crack open the world, I think it would have by now." Aviendha laughed, but Dyelin turned quite pale. Really! Sometimes you had to laugh if only to keep from crying.

"If we tarry much longer now that Norry and Mistress Harfor are gone," Birgitte said, "somebody might start wondering why." She waved a hand at the walls, indicating the ward she could not see. She knew it was still in place, though. The daily meetings with the First Maid and the First Clerk always concealed a little something more.

Everyone gathered around her as she moved a pair of golden Sea Folk porcelain bowls on one of the side tables and pulled a much-folded map from inside her short coat. It rode there always, except when she slept, and then it resided beneath her pillow. Spread out, with empty winecups at the corners to hold it flat, the map displayed Andor from the River Erinin to the border between Altara and Murandy. In truth, it could have been said to show all of Andor, since what lay farther west had been only half under Caemlyn's control for generations. It had hardly been a masterpiece of the mapmaker's art to begin with, and creases obscured much of the detail, but it showed the terrain well enough, and every town and village was marked, every road and bridge and ford. Elayne set her teacup down at arm's length from the map to avoid spilling on it and adding more stains. And to rid herself of the wretched excuse for tea.

"The Borderlanders are moving," Birgitte said, pointing to the forests north of Caemlyn, to a spot above Andor's northmost border, "but they haven't covered much ground. At this rate, they'll be well over a month getting close to Caemlyn."

Swirling her silver cup, Dyelin peered into the dark wine, then looked up suddenly. "I thought you northerners were used to snow, Lady Birgitte." Even now she had to probe, and telling her not to would only make her ten times as certain that Birgitte was hiding secrets, and twenty times as determined to learn them.

Aviendha scowled at the older woman—when she was not in awe of Birgitte, sometimes she became fiercely protective of Birgitte's secrets—but Birgitte herself met Dyelin's gaze levelly, with no hint of alarm in the bond. She had become quite comfortable with the lie about her origins. "I haven't been back to Kandor in a long time." That was simple truth, though it had been far longer than Dyelin could have imagined. The country had not even been called Kandor, then. "But no matter what you're used to, moving two hundred thousand soldiers, not to mention the Light alone knows how many camp followers, is slow going in winter. Worse, I sent Mistress Ocalin and Mistress Fote to visit some of the villages a few miles south of the border." Sabeine Ocalin and Julanya Fote were Kinswomen who could Travel. "They say the villagers think the Borderlanders are camped for the winter."

Elayne *tsked,* frowning at the map as she traced distances with a finger. She was counting on news of the Bor-

derlanders, if not on the Borderlanders themselves. Word of
an army that size entering Andor should be leaping ahead
of it like wildfire in dry grass. No one but a fool could believe they had marched all those hundreds of leagues to
try conquering Andor, but everyone who heard would be
speculating on their intentions and what to do about them,
a different opinion on every tongue. Once the news began
to spread, anyway. When it did, she had an advantage over
everyone else. She had arranged for the Borderlanders to
cross into Andor into the first place, and she had already
arranged for them to leave.

The choice had not been very difficult. Stopping them
would have been a bloody affair, if it could have been managed at all, and they wanted no more than the width of a
road to march onward into Murandy, where they thought
they would find the Dragon Reborn. That was her doing, as
well. They hid their reason for seeking Rand, and she was
not about to give them a true location, not when they had as
many as a dozen Aes Sedai with them and hid that fact, too.
But once news of them reached the High Seats . . .

"It should work," she said softly. "If necessary, we can
plant rumors of the Borderlanders ourselves."

"It should work," Dyelin agreed, then added in a dark
voice, "As long as Bashere and Bael keep a close rein on
their men. It's going to be a volatile mix, with Borderlanders, Aiel and the Legion of the Dragon all within a few
miles of one another. And I can't see how we can be sure
the Asha'man won't do something mad." She ended with a
sniff. In her book, a man had to be mad in the first place,
or he would never have chosen to become an Asha'man.
Aviendha nodded. She disagreed with Dyelin almost as frequently as Birgitte did, but for the most part, the Asha'man
were one thing they agreed on.

"I'll make sure the Borderlanders stay well clear of the
Black Tower," Elayne reassured them, though she had done
the same before. Even Dyelin knew that Bael and Bashere
would hold their forces in check—neither man wanted a
battle he did not need, and Davram Bashere certainly would
not fight his own countrymen—but anyone had a right to be
uneasy about the Asha'man and what they might do. She
slid her finger from the six-pointed star identifying Caemlyn across the few miles to the ground the Asha'man had

usurped. The Black Tower was not marked, but she knew all too well exactly where it lay. At least that was well away from the Lugard Road. Sending the Borderlanders south into Murandy without upsetting the Asha'man would not be difficult.

Her mouth compressed at the thought that she must not upset the Asha'man, but there was nothing to be done about it any time soon, so she mentally shifted the black-coated men to one side. What could not be dealt with now, had to be dealt with later.

"And the others?" She did not have to say more. Six major Houses remained uncommitted—at least to her or Arymilla. Dyelin claimed they would all come to Elayne eventually, but they showed no sign of it so far. Sabeine and Julanya had been looking for word of those six, too. Both women had spent the last twenty years as peddlers, accustomed to hard journeys, sleeping in stables or under the trees, and listening to what people did not say as much as to what they said. They made perfect scouts. It would be a great loss if they had to be shifted to helping keep the city supplied.

"Rumor has Lord Luan a dozen places, east and west." Frowning at the much-creased map as though Luan's position should have been marked on it, Birgitte muttered a curse, *much* viler than called for, now that Reene Harfor was absent. "Always the next village over, or the one beyond that. Lady Ellorien and Lord Abelle seem to have vanished completely, difficult as that has to be for a High Seat. At least, Mistress Ocalin and Mistress Fote haven't been able to find a whisper of them, or of any House Pendar or House Traemane armsmen, either. Not a man or a horse." *That* was very unusual. Someone was exerting great effort.

"Abelle was always a ghost when he wanted to be," Dyelin muttered, "always able to catch you wrong-footed. Ellorien . . ." Brushing fingers against her lips, she sighed. "The woman's too flamboyant to disappear. Unless she's with Abelle or Luan. Or both of them." She was not happy with that idea, no matter what she said.

"As for our other 'friends'," Birgitte said, "Lady Arathelle crossed out of Murandy five days ago, here." She touched the map lightly, some two hundred miles south of Caemlyn. "Four days ago, Lord Pelivar crossed about five or six miles west of that, and Lady Aemlyn here, another five or six miles."

"Not together," Dyelin said, nodding. "Did they bring any Murandians? No? Good. They could be moving to their estates, Elayne. If they move further apart, we'll know for certain." Those three Houses made her most anxious of all.

"They could be heading home," Birgitte agreed, reluctantly as always when agreeing with Dyelin. Drawing her intricate braid over her shoulder, she gripped it in a fist almost the way Nynaeve did. "The men and horses must be worn out, after marching into Murandy in winter. But all we can be sure of is that they're on the move."

Aviendha snorted. With her in elegant velvets, it was a startling sound. "Always assume your enemy will do what you do not want. Decide what you least want them to do, and plan on that."

"Aemlyn, Arathelle and Pelivar aren't enemies," Dyelin protested weakly. Wherever she believed their allegiance would fall in time, those three had announced their support of Dyelin herself for the throne.

Elayne had never read of any queen being *forced* onto the throne—that sort of thing might not have made it into the histories in any case—yet Aemlyn, Arathelle and Pelivar seemed willing to try, and not for hope of power for themselves. Dyelin did not want the throne, but she would hardly be a passive ruler. The simple fact was that Morgase Trakand's final year had been marred by blunder after blunder, and few knew or believed that she had been a captive of one of the Forsaken during that time. Some Houses wanted anyone except another Trakand on the throne. Or thought they did.

"What is the last thing we want them to do?" Elayne said. "If they disperse to their estates, then they are out of it until spring at the earliest, and everything will be decided by then." The Light willing, it would. "But if they continue on to Caemlyn?"

"Without the Murandians, they don't have enough armsmen to challenge Arymilla." Studying the map, Birgitte rubbed her chin. "If they don't know by now that the Aiel and the Legion of the Dragon are staying out of this, they'll have to learn of it soon, but they'll want to be careful. None of them seems foolish enough to provoke a fight they can't

win when they don't have to. I'd say they'll camp somewhere to the east or southeast, where they can keep an eye
on events and maybe influence what happens."

Downing the last of her wine, which must have been cold
by now, Dyelin exhaled heavily and walked over to fill her
cup again. "If they come to Caemlyn," she said in a leaden
tone, "then they are hoping that Luan or Abelle or Ellorien
will join them. Perhaps all three."

"Then we must figure out how to stop them reaching
Caemlyn before our plans come to fruit, without making
them permanent enemies." Elayne worked to make her
voice as sure and firm as Dyelin's was dull. "And we must
plan what to do in case they arrive here too early. If that
happens, Dyelin, you will have to convince them the choice
is between me and Arymilla. Otherwise, we'll be in a tangle
we may never straighten out, and all of Andor in it with us."

Dyelin grunted as if she had been punched. The last
time the great Houses split evenly among three claimants
for the Lion Throne had been nearly five hundred years
ago, and seven years of open war followed before a queen
was crowned. The original claimants were all dead by that
point.

Without thinking, Elayne picked up her teacup and took
a sip. The tea had gone cold, but honey exploded on her
tongue. Honey! She looked at Aviendha in astonishment,
and her sister's lips quirked in a small smile. A conspira-
torial smile, as if Birgitte did not know exactly what had
happened. Even their strangely enhanced bond did not ex-
tend to her tasting what Elayne did, yet she had surely felt
Elayne's surprise and pleasure on tasting the tea. Planting
fists on hips, she adopted a censorious look. Or rather, she
tried to; despite all she could do, a smile crept onto her face,
too. Abruptly, Elayne realized that Birgitte's headache was
gone. She did not know when it had vanished, but it certainly was not there any longer.

"Hope for the best and plan for the worst," she said.
"Sometimes, the best actually happens."

Dyelin, unaware of the honey or anything except that
they were all three grinning, harrumphed loudly. "And
sometimes it doesn't happen. If your clever scheme comes
off *exactly* as planned, Elayne, we won't have any need for

Aemlyn or Ellorien or the others, but it's a terrible gamble. All it takes to go wrong is—"

The left-hand door opened to admit a wave of cold and an apple-cheeked woman with icy eyes and the golden knot of an under-lieutenant on her shoulder. She might have knocked first, but if so, the ward had sealed off the sound. Like Rasoria, Tzigan Sokorin had been a Hunter for the Horn before joining Elayne's bodyguard. It seemed the guard had changed. "The Wise One Monaelle wishes to see the Lady Elayne," Tzigan announced, drawing herself up rigidly. "Mistress Karistovan is with her."

Sumeko could be put off, but not Monaelle. Arymilla's people would as soon interfere with Aes Sedai as with the Aiel, yet only something important would have brought a Wise One into the city. Birgitte knew that, too; she immediately began folding the map up again. Aviendha let the warding dissipate and released the Source.

"Ask them to come in," Elayne said.

Monaelle did not wait on Tzigan, gliding into the room as soon as the ward vanished, her multitude of gold and ivory bracelets rattling as she lowered her shawl from shoulders to elbows in the comparative warmth. Elayne did not know how old Monaelle was—Wise Ones were not as reticent about age as Aes Sedai, but they *were* oblique—yet she appeared not far into her middle years. There were hints of red in her waist-long yellow hair, but not a touch of gray. Short for an Aiel, shorter than Elayne, with a mild, motherly face, she was barely strong enough in the Power to have been accepted in the White Tower, but strength did not count among Wise Ones, and among them, she stood very high. More importantly for Elayne and Aviendha, she had been the midwife at their rebirth as first-sisters. Elayne offered her a curtsy, ignoring Dyelin's disapproving sniff, and Aviendha made a deep bow, folding herself over her hands. Aside from the duties owed to her midwife under Aiel customs, she was still only an apprentice Wise One, after all.

"I assume your need for privacy is ended, since you lowered the ward," Monaelle said, "and it is time I checked on your condition, Elayne Trakand. It should be done twice in the month until full term." Why was she frowning at Aviendha? Oh, Light, the velvets!

"And I have come to see what she does," Sumeko added, following the Wise One into the room. Sumeko was imposing, a stout woman with confident eyes, in well-cut red-belted yellow wool, with silver combs in her straight black hair, and a red-enameled silver circle-pin on the high neck of her dress. She might have been a noblewoman or a successful merchant. Once she had shown a certain diffidence, at least around Aes Sedai, but no longer. Not with Aes Sedai or soldiers of the Queen's Guards. "You may go," she told Tzigan. "This doesn't concern you." Or with nobles, for that matter. "You may leave, too, Lady Dyelin, and you, Lady Birgitte." She studied Aviendha as if considering adding her to the list.

"Aviendha may remain," Monaelle said. "She is missing a great many lessons, and she must learn this sooner or later." Sumeko nodded in acceptance of Aviendha, but she kept a coolly impatient gaze on Dyelin and Birgitte.

"Lady Dyelin and I have matters to discuss," Birgitte said, stuffing the folded map back under her red coat as she started for the door. "I'll tell you tonight what we've thought of, Elayne."

Dyelin gave her a sharp look, almost as sharp as the one she had given Sumeko, but she set her winecup on one of the trays and made her courtesies to Elayne, then waited with visible impatience while Birgitte bent to murmur at length in Monaelle's ear and the Wise One replied briefly, but just as quietly. What were they whispering about? Probably goat's milk.

Once the door closed behind Tzigan and the other two women, Elayne offered to send for more wine, since what was in the pitchers was cold, but Sumeko declined curtly, and Monaelle politely if rather absently. The Wise One was studying Aviendha with such intensity that the younger woman began to redden and looked away, gripping her skirts.

"You mustn't take Aviendha to task about her clothes, Monaelle," Elayne said. "I asked her to wear them, and she did as a favor to me."

Pursing her lips, Monaelle thought before answering. "First-sisters should give one another favors," she said finally. "You know your duty to our people, Aviendha. So far, you have done well at a difficult task. You must learn to live in two worlds, so it is fitting that you become comfortable in those clothes." Aviendha began to relax. Until Monaelle continued. "But not too comfortable. From now on, you will spend every third day and night in the tents. You can return with me tomorrow. You have a great deal to learn yet before you can become a Wise One, and that is as much your duty as is being a binding cord."

Elayne reached out and took her sister's hand, and when Aviendha tried to let go after one squeeze, she held on. After a brief hesitation, Aviendha clung, too. In a strange way, having Aviendha there had comforted Elayne for the loss of Rand; she was not only a sister but a sister who also loved him. They could share strength and make each other laugh when they wanted to cry, and they could cry together when that was needed. One night in three alone very likely meant one night in three weeping alone. Light, what was Rand *doing*? That awful beacon to the west was still blazing as strongly as ever, and she was certain that he was in the heart of it. Not one particle had changed in the bond with him, but she was certain.

Suddenly she realized that she had a crushing grasp on Aviendha's hand, and Aviendha was holding hers as fiercely. They loosened their grips at the same instant. Neither let go, however.

"Men cause trouble even when they are elsewhere," Aviendha said softly.

"They do," Elayne agreed.

Monaelle smiled at the exchange. She was among the few who knew about the bonding of Rand, and who the father of Elayne's baby was. None of the Kinswomen did, though.

"I'd think you've let a man cause you all the trouble he could, Elayne," Sumeko said primly. The Kin's Rule followed the rules for novices and Accepted, forbidding not only children but anything that might lead to them, and they held to it strictly. Once, a Kinswoman would have swallowed her tongue before suggesting an Aes Sedai fell short of their Rule. Much had changed since then, however. "I'm supposed to travel to Tear today so I can bring back a shipment of grain and oil tomorrow, and it is growing late, so if you are done talking about men, I suggest you let Monaelle get on with what she came for."

Monaelle positioned Elayne in front of the fireplace, close

enough that the heat from the nearly consumed logs was near to uncomfortable—it was best if the mother was very warm, she explained—then the glow of *saidar* surrounded her, and she began to weave threads of Spirit and Fire and Earth. Aviendha watched almost as avidly as Sumeko.

"What is this?" Elayne asked as the weave settled around her and sank into her. "Is it like Delving?" Every Aes Sedai in the palace had Delved her, though only Merilille had sufficient skill with Healing for it to be much use, but neither they nor Sumeko had been able to say much more than that she was with child. She felt a faint tingling, a sort of hum inside her flesh.

"Don't be silly, girl," Sumeko said absently. Elayne raised an eyebrow, and even thought of waving her Great Serpent ring under Sumeko's nose, but the round-faced woman did not appear to notice. She might not have noticed the ring, either. She was leaning forward, peering as though she could see the weave inside Elayne's body. "The Wise Ones learned about Healing from me. And from Nynaeve, I suppose," she allowed after a moment. Oh, Nynaeve would have gone up like an Illuminator's firework, hearing that. But then, Sumeko had outstripped Nynaeve long since. "And they did learn the simple form from Aes Sedai." A snort like ripping canvas showed what Sumeko thought of the "simple" form, the only sort of Healing Aes Sedai had known for thousands of years. "This is something of the Wise Ones' own."

"It is called Caressing the Child," Monaelle said in an abstracted voice. Most of her attention was focused on the weave. A simple Delving to learn what ailed someone—it *was* simple, come to think—would have been finished by now, but she altered the flows, and the hum inside Elayne changed pitch, sinking deeper. "It may be some part of Healing, a sort of Healing, but we have known this since before we were sent to the Three-fold Land. Some of the ways the flows are used are similar to what Sumeko Karistovan and Nynaeve al'Meara showed us. In Caressing the Child, you learn the health of mother and child, and by changing the weaves, you can cure some problems of either, but they will not work on a woman who is not with child. Or on a man, of course." The hum grew louder, until it seemed everyone must be able to hear it. Elayne thought her teeth were vibrating.

An earlier thought returned to her, and she said, "Will channeling hurt my child? If I channel, I mean."

"No more than breathing does." Monaelle let the weave vanish with a grin. "You have two. It is too early to say whether they are girls are boys, but they are healthy, and so are you."

Two! Elayne shared a wide smile with Aviendha. She could almost feel her sister's delight. She was going to have twins. Rand's babies. A boy and a girl, she hoped, or two boys. Twin girls would present all manner of difficulties for the succession. No one ever gained the Rose Crown with *everyone* behind her.

Sumeko made an urgent sound in her throat, gesturing toward Elayne, and Monaelle nodded. "Do exactly as I did, and you will see." Watching Sumeko embrace the Source and form the weave, she nodded again, and the round Kinswoman let it sink into Elayne, letting out a gasp as if she felt the humming herself. "You will not have to worry about birthing sickness," Monaelle went on, "but you will find that you have difficulty in channeling sometimes. The threads may slip away from you as though greased or fade like mist, so you will have to try again and again to make the simplest weave or hold it. This may grow worse as your pregnancy progresses, and you will not be able to channel at all while in labor or giving birth, but it will come right after the children are born. You soon will become moody, too, if that has not already started, weepy one minute and snarling the next. The father of your child will be wise to step warily and keep his distance as much as he can."

"I hear she's already snapped his head off once this morning," Sumeko muttered. Releasing the weave, she straightened and adjusted her red belt around her girth. "This is remarkable, Monaelle. I never thought of a weave that could only be used on a pregnant woman."

Elayne's mouth tightened, but what she said was "You can tell all of that with this weave, Monaelle?" It was best that people thought her babes were Doilan Mellar's. Rand al'Thor's children would be targets, stalked for fear or advantage or hatred, but no one would think twice about

Mellar's, perhaps not even Mellar. It *was* for the best, and that was that.

Monaelle threw back her head, laughing so hard that she had to wipe a corner of her eyes with her shawl. "I know this from bearing seven children and having three husbands, Elayne Trakand. The ability to channel shields you from the birthing sickness, but there are other prices to pay. Come, Aviendha, you must try, too. Carefully, now. Exactly as I did."

Eagerly, Aviendha embraced the Source, but before she had begun to weave a thread, she let *saidar* go and turned her head to stare toward the dark-paneled wall. Toward the west. So did Elayne, and Monaelle, and Sumeko. The beacon that had been burning for so long had just vanished. One instant it had been there, that raging blaze of *saidar,* and then it was gone as if it had never existed.

Sumeko's massive bosom heaved as she drew a deep breath. "I think something very wonderful or very terrible has happened today," she said softly. "And I think I am afraid to learn which."

"Wonderful," Elayne said. It was done, whatever *it* was, and Rand was alive. That was wonderful enough. Monaelle glanced at her quizzically. Knowing about the bond, she could puzzle out the rest, but she only fingered one of her necklaces in a thoughtful manner. In any case, she would pry it out of Aviendha soon enough.

A knock at the door made them all start. All but Monaelle, anyway. Pretending not to see the other women jump, she focused a little too intently on adjusting her shawl which made the contrast all the greater. Sumeko coughed to hide her embarrassment.

"Come," Elayne said loudly. A half-shout was necessary to be heard through the door even without a ward.

Caseille put her head into the room, plumed hat in hand, then came in the rest of the way and closed the door carefully behind her. The white lace at her neck and wrists was fresh, the lace and lions on her sash gleamed, and her breastplate sparkled as if freshly burnished, but obviously she had gone right back on duty after cleaning up from their overnight trip. "Forgive me for interrupting, my Lady, but I thought you should know right away. The Sea Folk are in a frenzy, those that are still here. It seems one of their apprentices has gone missing."

"What else?" Elayne said. A missing apprentice might be bad enough, but something in Caseille's face told her there *was* more.

"Guardswoman Azeri happened to tell me that she saw Merilille Sedai leaving the palace about three hours ago," Caseille said reluctantly. "Merilille and a woman who was cloaked and hooded. They took horses, and a loaded pack mule. Yurith said the second woman's hands were tattooed. My Lady, no one had any reason to be looking for—"

Elayne waved her to silence. "No one did anything wrong, Caseille. No one will be blamed." Not among the Guards, anyway. A fine pickle this was. Talaan and Metarra, the two apprentice Windfinders, were very strong in the Power, and if Merilille had been able to talk either one into trying to become Aes Sedai, she might have been able to convince herself that taking the girl where she could be entered into the novice book was reason enough to evade her own promise to teach the Windfinders. Who would be more than upset over losing Merilille, and more than furious over the apprentice. *They* would blame everyone in sight, and Elayne most of all.

"Is this general knowledge about Merilille?" she asked.

"Not yet, my Lady, but whoever saddled their horses and loaded that mule won't hold their tongues. Stablehands don't have much to gossip about." More of a brush fire than a pickle, then, and small chance of putting it out before it reached the barns.

"I hope you will dine with me later, Monaelle," Elayne said, "but you must forgive me, now." Duty to her midwife or no, she did not wait for the other woman's assent. Trying to douse the fire might be enough to stop the barns from catching. Maybe. "Caseille, inform Birgitte, and tell her I want an order sent to the gates immediately to watch for Merilille. I know; I know; she may be out of the city already, and the gate guards won't stop an Aes Sedai, anyway, but maybe they can delay her, or frighten her companion into scuttling back into the city to hide. Sumeko, would you ask Reanne to assign every Kinswoman who can't Travel to start searching through the city. It's a small hope, but

Merilille may have thought it was too late in the day to start out. Check every inn, including the Silver Swan, and . . ."

She hoped Rand had done something wonderful today, but she could not waste time even thinking about that now. She had a throne to gain and angry Atha'an Miere to deal with, before they could vent their anger on her, it was to be hoped. In short, it was a day like every other since she returned to Caemlyn, and that meant her hands were quite full enough.

CHAPTER
15

Gathering Darkness

The evening sun was a ball of blood on the treetops, casting a lurid light across the camp, a widely spaced sprawl of horselines and canvas-covered wagons and high-wheeled carts and tents in every size and sort with the snow between trampled to slush. Not the time of day or sort of place that Elenia wished to be on horseback. The smell of boiling beef wafting from the big black iron cookpots was enough to turn her stomach. The cold air frosted her breath and promised a bitter night to come, and the wind cut through her best red cloak without regard for the thick lining of plush white fur. Snowfox was supposed to be warmer than other furs, but she had never found it so.

Holding the cloak closed with one gloved hand, she rode slowly and tried very hard, if not very successfully, not to shiver. Given the hour, it seemed more than likely she would be spending the night here, but as yet, she had no idea where she would sleep. Doubtless in some lesser noble's tent, with the lord or lady shuffled off to find haven elsewhere and trying to put the best face on being evicted, but Arymilla liked leaving her on tenterhooks until the very last, about beds and everything else. One suspense was no sooner dispelled than another replaced it. Plainly the woman thought the constant uncertainty would make her squirm, perhaps even strive to please. That was far from the only miscalculation Arymilla had made, beginning with the belief that Elenia Sarand's claws had been clipped.

She had just four men with the two Golden Boars on their cloaks as escort—and her maid, Janny, of course, huddling in her cloak till she seemed a bundle of green wool piled on her saddle—and she had not seen a single fellow more in the camp who she could be sure held a scrap of loyalty to Sarand. Here and there one of the clumps of men huddled around the campfires with their laundresses and seamstresses displayed House Anshar's Red Fox, and a double column of horsemen wearing Baryn's Winged Hammer passed her heading in the opposite direction at a slow walk, hard-faced behind the bars of their helmets. They were of little real account, in the long run. Karind and Lir had gotten singed badly by being slow when Morgase took the throne. This time they would take Anshar and Baryn wherever the advantage lay the instant they saw it clearly, abandoning Arymilla with as great an alacrity as they had leapt to join her. When the time came.

Most of the men trudging through the muddy slush or peering hopefully into those disgusting cookpots were levies, farmers and villagers gathered up when their lord or lady marched, and few wore any sort of House badge on their shabby coats and patched cloaks. Even separating putative soldiers from farriers and fletchers and the like was near impossible, since nearly all had belted on a sword of some description, or an axe. Light, a fair number of the *women* wore knives large enough to be called short-swords, but there was no way to tell some conscripted farmer's wife from a wagon driver. They wore the same thick wool and had the same rough hands and weary faces. It did not really matter, in any case. This winter siege was a dire mistake— the armsmen would begin going hungry long before the city did—but it gave Elenia an opportunity, and when an opening presented itself, you struck. Keeping her hood back far enough to show her features clearly in spite of the freezing wind, she nodded graciously to every unwashed lout who so much as looked in her direction, and ignored the surprised starts that some gave at her condescension.

Most would remember her affability, remember the Golden Boars her escort wore, and know that Elenia Sarand had taken notice of them. On such a foundation power was built. A High Seat as much as a queen stood atop a tower built of people. True, those at the bottom were bricks of the basest clay, yet if those common bricks crumpled in their support, the tower fell. That was something Arymilla

appeared to have forgotten, if she had ever known. Elenia
doubted that Arymilla spoke to anyone lower than a steward or a personal servant. Had it been . . . prudent . . . she
herself would have passed a few words at every campfire,
perhaps grasping a grubby hand now and then, remembering people she had encountered before or at least dissembling well enough to make it seem she did. Pure and simple,
Arymilla lacked the wit to be queen.

The camp covered more ground than most towns, more
like a hundred clustered camps of varying sizes than one,
so she was free to wander without worrying too much about
straying close to the outer boundaries, but she took a care
anyway. The guards on sentry would be polite, unless they
were utter fools, yet without any doubt they had their orders. On principle, she approved of people doing as they
were told, but it would be best to avoid any embarrassing
incidents. Especially given the likely consequences if Arymilla actually thought she had been trying to leave. She had
already been forced to endure one frigid night sleeping in
some soldier's filthy tent, a shelter hardly worth the name,
complete with vermin and badly patched holes, not to mention the lack of Janny to help her with her clothes and add a
little warmth under the sorry excuse for blankets, and that
had been for no more than a perceived slight. Well, it had
been an actual slight, but she had not thought Arymilla
bright enough to catch it. Light, to think that *she* must step
warily around that . . . that pea-brained ninny! Pulling her
cloak closer, she tried to pretend that her shudder was just a
reaction to the wind. There were better things to dwell on.
More important things. She nodded to a wide-eyed young
man with a dark scarf wrapped around his head, and he
recoiled as though she had glared. Fool peasant!

It was grating to think that, only a few miles away, that
young chit Elayne sat snug and warm in the comfort of the
Royal Palace, attended by scores of well-trained servants
and likely without two thoughts in her head beyond what to
wear tonight at a supper prepared by the palace cooks. Rumor had the girl with child, possibly by some Guardsman.
It might be so. Elayne had never possessed any more sense
of decency than her mother. Dyelin was the brain there, a
sharp mind and dangerous notwithstanding her pathetic
lack of ambition, perhaps advised by an Aes Sedai. There

must be at least one real Aes Sedai among all those absurd rumors.

So many fabulations drifted out of the city that telling reality from nonsense became difficult—Sea Folk making holes in the *air*? Absolute drivel!—yet the White Tower clearly had an interest in putting one of its own on the throne. How could it not? Even so, Tar Valon seemed to be pragmatic when it came to these matters. History clearly showed that whoever reached the Lion Throne would soon find that she was the one the Tower actually had favored all along. The Aes Sedai would not lose their connection to Andor through a lack of nimbleness, particularly not with the Tower itself riven. Elenia was as certain of that as she was of her own name. In fact, if half what she heard of the Tower's situation was true, the next Queen of Andor might find herself able to demand whatever she wanted in return for keeping that connection intact. In any event, no one was going to rest the Rose Crown on her head before summer at the earliest, and a great deal could change before then. A very great deal.

She was making her second round of the camp when the sight of another small mounted party ahead of her, picking its slow way between the scattered campfires in the last light, made her scowl and draw rein sharply. The women were cloaked and deeply hooded, one in strong blue silk lined with black fur, the other in plain gray wool, but the silver Triple Keys worked large on the four armsmen's cloaks named them clearly enough. She could think of any number of people she would rather encounter than Naean Arawn. In any case, while Arymilla had not precisely forbidden them to meet without her—Elenia heard her teeth grind as much as felt them, and forced her face smooth—for the moment, it seemed wisest not to press matters. Especially when there seemed no possible advantage to such a meeting.

Unfortunately, Naean saw her before she could turn aside. The woman spoke hastily to her escort and, while armsmen and maid were still bowing in their saddles, spurred toward Elenia at a pace that sent clods of slush flying from her black gelding's hooves. The Light *burn* the fool! On the other hand, whatever was goading Naean to recklessness might be valuable to know, and dangerous not to. It might, but finding out presented its own dangers.

"Stay here and remember that you've seen nothing," Elenia snapped at her own meager retinue and dug her heels into Dawn Wind's flanks without waiting for any reply. She had no need for elaborate bows and courtesies every time she turned around, not beyond what seemliness demanded, and her people knew better than to do anything other than what she commanded. It was everyone else she had to worry about, burn them all! As the long-legged bay sprang forward, she lost her grip on her cloak, and it streamed behind her like the crimson banner of Sarand. She refused to gather the cloak under control, flailing around in front of farmers and the Light alone knew who, so the wind razored through her riding dress, another reason for irritation.

Naean at least had the sense to slow and meet her little more than halfway, beside a pair of heavily laden carts with their empty shafts lying in the muck. The nearest fire was almost twenty paces away, and the nearest tents farther, their entry flaps laced tight against the cold. The men at the fire were intent on the big iron pot steaming over the flames, and if the stench from it was enough to make Elenia want to empty her stomach, at least the wind that carried the stink would keep stray words from their ears. But they had better be important words.

With a face as pale as ivory in its frame of black fur, Naean might have been called beautiful by some despite more than a hint of harshness around her mouth and eyes as cold as blue ice. Straight-backed and outwardly quite calm, she seemed untouched by events. Her breath, making a white mist, was steady and even. "Do you know where we are sleeping tonight, Elenia?" she said coolly.

Elenia made no effort at all to stop from glaring. "Is *that* what you want?" Risking Arymilla's displeasure for a brainless question! The thought of risking Arymilla's displeasure, the thought that Arymilla's displeasure was something she needed to avoid, made her snarl. "You know as much as I, Naean." Tugging at her reins, she was already turning her mount away when Naean spoke again, with just a hint of heat.

"Don't play the simpleton with me, Elenia. And don't tell me you aren't as ready as I am to chew off your own foot to escape this trap. Now, can we at least pretend to civility?"

Elenia kept Dawn Wind half turned away from the other

woman and looked at her sideways, past the fur-trimmed
edge of her hood. That way, she could keep an eye on
the men crowding around the nearest fire, too. No House
badges displayed there. They could belong to anyone. Now
and then one fellow or another shielding bare hands in his
armpits glanced toward the two ladies on horseback, but
their real interest was on shuffling near enough the fire to
get warm. That, and how long it was going to take for the
beef to boil down to something approaching mush. That
sort seemed able to eat anything.

"Do you think you *can* escape?" she asked quietly. Civility was all very well, but not at the expense of remaining
here for all to see any longer than absolutely necessary. If
Naean saw a way out, though . . . "How? The pledge you
signed to support Marne has been posted across half of Andor by now. Besides, you can hardly think Arymilla will
just allow you to ride away." Naean flinched, and Elenia
could not help a tight smile. The woman was not so untouched as she feigned. She still managed to keep her voice
level, though.

"I saw Jarid yesterday, Elenia, and even at a distance
he looked like a thundercloud, galloping fit to break his
mount's neck and his own. If I know your husband, he's
already planning a way to cut you out of this. He would spit
in the Dark One's eye for you." That was true; he would.
"I'm sure you can see it would be best if I were part of those
plans."

"My husband signed the same pledge you did, Naean,
and he is an honorable man." He was too honorable for his
own good, in simple fact, but what Elenia wanted had been
his guide since before their wedding vows. Jarid had signed
the pledge because she wrote and told him to, not that she
had any choice as matters were, and he would even repudiate it, however reluctantly, if she were mad enough to ask
it. Of course, there was the difficulty in letting him know
what she did want at the moment. Arymilla was very careful not to let her within a mile of him. She had everything
in hand—as far as she could in the circumstances—but she
needed to let Jarid know, if only to stop him from "cutting
her a way out." Spit in the Dark One's eye? He could take
them both to ruin in the belief he was helping her, and he
might do it even knowing it meant their ruination.

It required a great effort not to allow the frustration and fury suddenly welling up inside her to show on her face, but she covered the strain with a smile. She took considerable pride in being able to produce a smile for any situation. This one held a touch of surprise. And a touch of disdain. "I'm not planning anything, Naean, and neither is Jarid, I'm sure. But if I were, why would I include you?"

"Because if I am not included in those plans," Naean said bluntly, "Arymilla might learn of them. She may be a blind fool, but she'll see once she's told where to look. And you might find yourself sharing a tent with your *betrothed* every night, not to mention *protected* by his armsmen."

Elenia's smile melted, but her voice turned to ice, matching the frozen ball that abruptly filled her stomach. "You want to be careful what you say, or Arymilla may ask her Taraboner to play cat's cradle with you again. In truth, I think I can guarantee as much."

It seemed impossible that Naean's face could grow any whiter, yet it did. She actually swayed in her saddle, and caught Elenia's arm as if to keep from falling. A gust of wind flung her cloak about, and she let it flail. Those once-cold eyes were quite wide, now. The woman made no effort to hide her fear. Perhaps she was too far gone to be capable of hiding it. Her voice came breathy and panicked. "I know you and Jarid are planning something, Elenia. I know it! Take me with you, and . . . and I will pledge Arawn to you as soon as I can be free of Arymilla." Oh, she *was* shaken, to offer that.

"Do you want to draw more attention than you already have?" Elenia snapped, pulling free of the other woman's grasp. Dawn Wind and the black gelding danced nervously, catching their riders' moods, and Elenia reined her bay hard to quiet him. Two of the men at the fire hurriedly put their heads down. No doubt they thought they saw two noblewomen arguing in the graying evening and wanted to attract no part of that anger on themselves. Yes; it must be only that. They might carry tales, but they knew better than to get mixed in their betters' arguments.

"I have no plans to . . . escape; none at all," she said in a quieter voice. Drawing her cloak close again, she calmly turned her head to check the carts, and the nearest tents. If Naean was frightened enough . . . When an opening presented itself . . . There was no one close enough to overhear, but she still kept her voice low. "Matters might change, of course. Who can say? If they do, I make you this promise, under the Light and by my hope of rebirth, I will not leave without you." A startled hope bloomed on Naean's face. Now to present the hook. "If, that is, I have in my possession a letter written in your own hand, signed and sealed, in which you explicitly repudiate your support of Marne, of your own free will, and swear the support of House Arawn to me for the throne. Under the Light and by *your* hope of rebirth. Nothing less will do."

Naean's head jerked back, and she touched her lips with her tongue. Her eyes shifted as though searching for a way out, for help. The black continued to snort and dance, but she barely tightened her reins enough to keep him from bolting, and even that seemed unconscious. Yes, she was frightened. But not too frightened to know what Elenia was demanding. The history of Andor contained too many examples for her not to know. A thousand possibilities remained so long as nothing was in writing, but the mere existence of such a letter would put a bit between Naean's teeth and the reins in Elenia's hands. Publication meant Naean's destruction, unless Elenia was fool enough to admit to coercion. She could try to hang on after that revelation, yet even a House with many fewer antagonisms between its members than Arawn, many fewer cousins and aunts and uncles ready to undercut one another in a heartbeat, would still break apart. The lesser Houses that had been tied to Arawn for generations would seek protection elsewhere. In a matter of years, if not sooner, Naean would be left as the High Seat of a minor and discredited remnant. Oh, yes; it had happened before.

"We've been together long enough." Elenia gathered her reins. "I wouldn't want to set tongues wagging. Perhaps we will have another chance to speak alone before Arymilla takes the throne." What a vile thought! "Perhaps."

The other woman exhaled as if all of the breath in her body were leaking out, but Elenia went on about turning her horse away, neither slowly nor in haste, not stopping until Naean said urgently, "Wait!"

Looking back over her shoulder, she did just that. Waited. Without speaking a word. What needed to be said had been said. All that remained was to see whether the woman was desperate enough to deliver herself into Elenia's hands. She should be. *She* had no Jarid to work for her. In fact, anyone in Arawn who suggested that Naean needed rescuing likely would find herself imprisoned for thwarting Naean's expressed will. Without Elenia, she could grow old in captivity. With the letter, though, her captivity would be of a different kind. With the letter, Elenia would be able to allow her every appearance of complete freedom. Apparently she was bright enough to see that. Or maybe just frightened enough of the Taraboner.

"I will get it to you as soon as I can," she said at last, in a resigned voice.

"I look forward to seeing it," Elenia murmured, barely bothering to mask her satisfaction. *But don't wait too long,* she almost added, and just stopped herself. Naean might be beaten, but a beaten foe could still put a knife in your back if goaded too far. Besides which, she feared Naean's threat as much as Naean feared hers. Perhaps more. So long as Naean did not know that, however, her blade had no point.

As she rode back to her armsmen, Elenia's mood was more buoyant than it had been since . . . Certainly since before her "rescuers" had turned out to be Arymilla's men. Perhaps since before Dyelin had imprisoned her in Aringill in the first place, though she had never lost hope there. Her prison had been the governor's house, quite comfortable, even if she had to share an apartment with Naean. Communicating with Jarid certainly had presented no problem, and she thought she had made some inroads with the Queen's Guards in Aringill. So many of them had been new-come out of Cairhien that they were . . . unsure . . . where their true loyalties lay.

Now, this wonderfully fortuitous encounter with Naean lifted her spirits so much that she smiled at Janny and promised her a bevy of new dresses once they were inside Caemlyn. Which produced a properly grateful smile from the plump-cheeked woman. Elenia always bought new dresses for her maid when she felt particularly good, every one fine enough for a successful merchant. It was one way to insure loyalty and discretion, and for twenty years, Janny had delivered both.

The sun was only a red rim above the trees now, and it was time to find Arymilla so she could be told where she was sleeping tonight. The Light send it was a decent bed, in a warm tent that was not too smoky, with a decent meal beforehand. She could not ask more, at present. Even that did not dent her mood, though. She not only nodded to the clusters of men and women they rode past, she smiled at them. She almost went so far as to wave. Matters were progressing better than they had in quite some time. Naean was not simply disposed of as a rival for the throne, she had been leashed and brought to heel, or as good as, and that might—would!—be sufficient to bring Karind and Lir. And there were those who would accept *anyone* other than another Trakand on the throne. Ellorien, for one. Morgase had had her *flogged*! Ellorien would never stand for any Trakand. Aemlyn, Arathelle and Abelle were possibilities, too, with their own grievances that could be exploited. Perhaps Pelivar or Luan, as well. She had her feelers out. And she would not squander the advantage of Caemlyn, as that hoyden Elayne had. Historically, holding Caemlyn was enough to gather the support of at least four or five Houses by itself.

The timing would be key, certainly, or all the advantage would fall to Arymilla, but Elenia could already see herself seated on the Lion Throne, with the High Seats kneeling to swear fealty. She already had her list of which High Seats would need to be replaced. No one who had opposed her was going to be allowed to cause her trouble later. A series of unfortunate accidents would see to that. A pity she could not choose their replacements, but accidents could happen with incredible frequency.

Her happy contemplation was shattered by the scrawny man who suddenly came up beside her on a stocky gray, his eyes feverishly bright in the fading light. For some reason, Nasin had sprigs of green fir stuck in his thin white hair. It made him look as if he had been climbing in a tree, and his red silk coat and cloak were so worked with brightly colored flowers they could have passed for Illianer carpets. He was ludicrous. He was also High Seat of the most powerful single House in Andor. And he was quite mad. "Elenia, my darling treasure," he brayed, spraying spittle, "how sweet the sight of you is to my eyes. You make honey seem stale and roses drab."

Without need for conscious thought, she hastily reined Dawn Wind back and to the right, putting Janny's brown

mare between her and him. "I am *not* your betrothed, Nasin," she snapped, seething at having to say that aloud for
everyone to hear. "I am *married,* you old fool! Wait!" she
added, flinging up a hand.

The imperative word and the gesture were for her armsmen, who had laid hands on sword hilts and were glaring
at Nasin. Some thirty or forty men wearing House Caeren's
Sword and Star were following the man, and they would not
hesitate to cut down anyone they thought was threatening
their High Seat. Some already had blades half-drawn. They
would not harm her, of course. Nasin would have them
hanged to a man if she was even bruised. Light, she did not
know whether to laugh or cry over that.

"Are you still afraid of that young oaf Jarid?" Nasin demanded, angling his mount to follow her. "He has no right
to keep bothering you. The better man won, and he should
acknowledge it. I'll challenge him!" One hand, plainly bony
even in its tight red glove, fumbled at a sword he probably
had not drawn in twenty years. "I will cut him down like a
dog for frightening you!"

Elenia moved Dawn Wind deftly, so they described a
circle around Janny, who murmured apologies to Nasin and
pretended to take her mare out of his way while getting in
it. Mentally, Elenia added a little embroidery to the dresses
she would buy. Addlepated as he was, Nasin could go in
a blink from honeyed words of courtly love to groping at
her as if she were the lowest sort of tavern maid. That, she
could not endure, not again, certainly not in public. Circling, she forced a worried smile onto her face, though in
truth, the smile took more effort than the worry. If this old
fool forced Jarid to kill him, it would ruin everything! "You
know I could not abide to have men fight over me, Nasin."
Her voice was breathy and anxious, but she did not try to
control it. Breathy and anxious suited well enough. "How
could I love a man with blood on his hands?"

The ridiculous man frowned down that long nose till
she began to wonder whether she had gone too far. He was
mad as a spring hare, but not in everything. Not always. "I
had not realized you were so . . . sensitive," he said finally.
Without stopping his effort to ride around Janny. His de-
crepit face brightened. "But I should have known. I will remember, from now on. Jarid may live. So long as he doesn't

pester you." Abruptly, he seemed to notice Janny for the first time, and with an irritated grimace, he raised his hand high, balling it into a fist. The plump woman visibly steeled herself for the blow without moving aside, and Elenia gritted her teeth. Silk embroidery. Definitely unsuitable for a maid, but Janny had earned it.

"Lord Nasin, I have been looking for you *everywhere*," a woman's simpering voice cried, and the circling stopped.

Elenia exhaled in relief as Arymilla rode up in the twilight with her entourage, and had to stifle a surge of fury at feeling relief. In over-elaborately embroidered green silk, with lace under her chin and at her wrists, Arymilla was plump verging on stout, with a vacuous smile and brown eyes that were always wide with affected interest even when there was nothing to be interested in. Lacking the brains to tell the difference, she possessed just enough cunning to know there were things that should interest her, and she did not want anyone to think she had missed them. The only real concern she had was her own comfort and the income to ensure it, and the only reason she wanted the throne was that the royal coffers could provide greater comfort than the revenues of any High Seat. Her entourage was larger than Nasin's, though only half were armsmen wearing the Four Moons of her House. For the most part, hangers-on and sycophants made up the rest, lesser lords and ladies of minor Houses and others willing to lick Arymilla's wrist for a place near power. She did love people to fawn over her. Naean was there, too, on the edge of the group with her armsmen and maid, apparently cool-eyed and in control of herself once more. But keeping well away from Jaq Lounalt, a lean man with one of those farcical Taraboner veils covering his huge mustaches and a conical cap pushing the hood of his cloak to a ridiculous height. The fellow smiled too much, as well. He hardly looked a man who could reduce someone to begging with just a few cords.

"Arymilla," Nasin said in a confused tone, then frowned at his fist as if surprised to find it raised. Lowering his hand to the pommel of his saddle, he beamed a smile at the silly woman. "Arymilla, my dear," he said warmly. Not with the sort of warmth he often directed at Elenia. Somehow, it seemed, he had become at least half-convinced that Arymilla was his daughter, and his favorite at that. Once, Elenia had heard him reminiscing at length with the woman about her "mother," his last wife, dead nearly thirty years now. Arymilla managed to hold her end of the conversation, too, though she had never met Miedelle Caeren as far as Elenia knew.

Still, despite all his fatherly smiles for Arymilla, his eyes sought through the shadowed crowd on horseback behind her, and his face relaxed when he found Sylvase, his grand-daughter and heir, a sturdy, placid young woman who met his gaze, unsmiling, then pulled her dark, fur-lined cowl well forward. She never smiled or frowned or showed any emotion at all that Elenia had ever detected, just kept an un-varying cowlike expression. Plainly, she had a cow's wits, too. Arymilla kept Sylvase closer than she did Elenia or Naean, and so long as she did, there was no chance that Na-sin would be forced to retire from his honors. He was mad, assuredly, but sly. "I hope you're taking good care of my little Sylvase, Arymilla," he murmured. "There are fortune hunters everywhere, and I want the darling girl kept safe."

"Of course, I am," Arymilla replied, brushing her over-fed mare past Elenia without so much as a glance. Her tone was honey-sweet, and sickeningly doting. "You know I'll keep her as safe as I keep myself." Smiling that empty-headed smile, she set about straightening Nasin's cloak on his shoulders and smoothing it with the air of someone set-tling a shawl on a beloved invalid. "It's much too cold out for you. I know what you need. A warm tent and some hot spiced wine. I'll be happy to have my maid prepare it for you. Arlene, accompany Lord Nasin to his tent and fix him some good spiced wine."

A slim woman in her entourage gave a violent twitch, then rode forward slowly, pushing back the hood of her plain blue cloak to reveal a pretty face and a tremulous smile. Suddenly all those lickspittles and toad-eaters were adjusting their cloaks against the wind or snugging their gloves, looking anywhere except at Arymilla's maid. Espe-cially the women. One of them could have been chosen as easily, and they knew it. Oddly, Sylvase did not look away. It was impossible to see her face in the shadows of her hood, but the opening turned to follow the slender woman.

Nasin's grin showed his teeth, making him look even more like a goat than usual. "Yes. Yes, mulled wine would be good. Arlene, is it? Come, Arlene, there's a good girl. Not too chill, are you?" The girl squeaked as he swept a corner of his cloak around her shoulders and gathered her so close she was leaning out of her saddle. "You'll be warm in my tent, I promise." Without so much as a glance back, he rode off at a walk, chortling and whispering at the young woman under his arm. His armsmen followed with the creak of leather and the slow, wet clop of hooves in the muck. One of them laughed, as if another had said something funny.

Elenia shook her head in disgust. Pushing a pretty woman in front of Nasin to distract him was one thing—she did not even have to be that pretty; any woman the old fool could corner was in danger—but using your own maid was revolting. Not as revolting as Nasin himself, though. "You promised to keep him away from me, Arymilla," she said in a low, tight voice. That lecherous old crackbrain might have forgotten her existence for the moment, but he would remember the next time he saw her. "You promised to keep him occupied."

Arymilla's face grew sullen, and she petulantly tugged her riding gloves tighter. She had not gotten what she wanted. That was a great sin, to her. "If you want to be safe from admirers, you ought to stay close to me instead of wandering about loose. Can I help it if you attract men? And I did rescue you. I haven't heard any thanks for that."

Elenia's jaw clenched so hard that it began to ache. Pretending that she supported this woman of her own choice was enough to make her want to bite something. Her choices had been made clear enough; write to Jarid or endure an extended honeymoon with her "betrothed." Light, she might have taken the choice if not for the certainty that Nasin would lock her up in some out-of-the-way manor and, after she had put up with his pawing, eventually forget she was there. And leave her there. Arymilla insisted on the pretense, though. She insisted on a great many things, some of them utterly insufferable. Yet they had to be suffered. For the time being. Perhaps, once matters were set straight, Master Lounalt could offer his attentions to Arymilla for a few days.

From somewhere she summoned an apologetic smile, and made herself bend her neck as if she were one of the boot-licking leeches who were watching her avidly. After all, if *she* crawled for Arymilla, it only proved they were right to. The feel of their eyes on her made her want to bathe. Doing this in front of Naean made her want to shriek. "I offer you all the gratitude that's in me, Arymilla." Well, that was no lie. All the gratitude that was in her came about equal to a desire to strangle the other woman. Very slowly. She had to inhale deeply before she could get the next part out, though. "You must forgive me for being slow, please." A *very* bitter word. "Nasin made me quite distraught. You know how Jarid would react if he learned of Nasin's behavior." Her own voice took on a honed edge at that last, but the fool woman giggled. She giggled!

"Of course you're forgiven, Elenia," she laughed, her face lightening. "All you need do is ask. Jarid is a hothead, isn't he? You must write to him and tell him how content you are. You are content, aren't you? You can dictate to my secretary. I do hate staining my fingers with ink, don't you?"

"Certainly I'm content, Arymilla. How could I not be?" Smiling required no effort at all, this time. The woman actually thought she was clever. Using Arymilla's secretary precluded any possibility of secret inks, but she could tell Jarid quite openly to do absolutely nothing without her counsel, and the brainless fluff would think she was only obeying.

Nodding with a smug self-satisfaction, Arymilla gathered her reins, imitated by her coterie. If she stuck a pot on her head and called it a hat, they would all wear pots, too. "It is getting late," she said, "and I want an early start in the morning. Aedelle Baryn's cook has an excellent repast waiting on us. You and Naean must ride with me, Elenia." She made it sound as though she were honoring them, and they had no choice except to behave as though she were, falling in on either side of her. "And Sylvase, of course. Come, Sylvase."

Nasin's granddaughter brought her mare closer, but not up beside Arymilla. She followed a little behind, with Arymilla's sycophants crowding on her heels since they had not been invited to ride with Arymilla. Despite the fitful, icy wind tugging at their cloaks, several of the women and two or three of the men tried unsuccessfully to engage the girl in conversation. She seldom said two words together. Still, with no High Seat in reach to fawn over, a High Seat's heir would do, and maybe one of the fellows hoped to marry well. Likely one or two were more in the nature of guards, or at least spies making sure she did not try to communicate with anyone in her House. This lot would find that exciting, touching on the edges of power. Elenia had her own plans for Sylvase.

Arymilla was another with no objections to nattering away when anyone with sense would be muffling herself in her cowl, and her chatter as they rode through the dying light flitted from what Lir's sister would offer at supper to the plans for her coronation. Elenia listened only enough to murmur approvingly at what seemed appropriate spots. If the fool wanted to offer a *sworn* amnesty to those who opposed her, far be it from Elenia Sarand to tell her she was a fool. It was painful enough having to . . . *simper* . . . at the woman without listening to her. Then one thing Arymilla said hit her ear like an awl.

"You and Naean won't mind sharing a bed, will you? It seems we are short of decent tents here."

She flitted on, but for a moment, Elenia could not hear a word. She felt as though her skin had been stuffed with snow. Turning her head slightly, she met Naean's shocked gaze. There was no possible way Arymilla could know about their chance meeting, not yet, and even if she did, why would she offer them a chance to plot together? A trap? Spies to listen to what they said? Naean's maid, or . . . Or Janny? The world seemed to spin. Black and silver flecks floated in front of Elenia's eyes. She thought she was about to faint.

Abruptly she realized that Arymilla had addressed something to her directly and was waiting on an answer with an increasingly impatient scowl. Frantically, she cast her mind about. Yes, she had it. "A gilded coach, Arymilla?" What a ridiculous notion. As well ride in a Tinker's wagon! "Oh, delightful! You do have such marvelous ideas!"

Arymilla's pleased simper put a little ease into Elenia's breathing. The woman *was* a brainless fool. Maybe there was a shortage of suitable tents. More likely she just thought they were safe, now. Tamed. Elenia turned her bared teeth into a simper of her own. But she put aside any idea of having the Taraboner "entertain" the woman, even for an hour.

With Jarid's signature on that pledge, there was only one way to clear her path to the throne. Everything was in hand and ready to go forward. The only question was whether Arymilla or Nasin should die first.

Night pressed down on Caemlyn with a hard cold driven deep by sharp winds. Here and there a glow of light spilling from an upper window spoke of people still awake, but most shutters were drawn, and a thin sliver of moon low in the sky only seemed to emphasize the darkness. Even the snow coating rooftops and piled along the fronts of buildings where it had escaped the day's traffic was a shadowy gray. The lone man muffled head to ankles in a dark cloak, striding through the frozen slush left on the paving stones, answered to Daved Hanlon or Doilan Mellar with equal ease; a name was no more than a coat, and a man changed his coat whenever needed. He had worn a number over the years. Given his wishes, he would have had his feet up in front of a roaring fire in the Royal Palace, a mug in his hand, a pitcher of brandy at his side, and a willing wench on his knee, but he had others' wishes to serve. At least the footing was better here in the New City. Not good, with this frozen muck underfoot that could turn a careless step into a sprawl, yet a man's boots were less likely to go out from under him here than back on the steeper hills of the Inner City. Besides, darkness suited him tonight.

There had been few people in the streets when he started out, and the number had dwindled away as darkness deepened. Wise people stayed indoors once night fell. Occasionally, dim shapes skulked in the deeper shadows, but after a brief study of Hanlon, they scuttled around corners ahead of him, or withdrew into alleys trying to muffle their curses as they floundered in snow that likely had not been touched by the sun. He was not bulky, and little taller than the average run of men, with his sword and breastplate hidden by his cloak to boot, but footpads looked for weakness or hesitation, and he moved with an obvious self-confidence, plainly unafraid of lurkers. An attitude helped by the long dagger concealed in his gauntleted right hand.

He kept an eye out for patrols of Guardsmen as he walked, but he did not expect to see any. The strongarms and prowlers would have sought other hunting grounds if the Guards were about. Of course, he could send nosy Guardsmen on their way with a word, yet he wanted no observers of any kind, and no questions why he was so far from the palace afoot. His step hesitated as two heavily cloaked women appeared at a crossing well ahead, but they moved on without glancing his way, and he breathed more easily. Very few women would venture out at this time of night without a man along to wield sword or cudgel, and even without seeing their faces he would have wagered a fistful of gold to a horse apple that pair were Aes Sedai. Or else some of those strange women who filled most of the beds in the palace.

The thought of that lot brought a scowl, and a prickling between his shoulder blades like the brush of nettles. Whatever was going on in the palace, it was enough to give him the grips. The Sea Folk women were bad enough, and not just because they went swaying along the halls in that seductive way, then pulled a knife on a man. He had not even thought of patting one on the bottom after he realized they and the Aes Sedai were staring at one another like strange cats in a box. And plainly, however impossibly, the Sea Folk were the larger cats. The others were worse, in a way. No matter what the rumors said, he knew the look of Aes Sedai, and it did not include wrinkles. Yet some of them could channel, and he had the disturbing notion that they all could. Which made no sense at all. Maybe the Sea Folk had some sort of peculiar dispensation, but as for these Kin, as Falion called them, everyone knew that if three women who could channel and were not Aes Sedai sat down at the same table, Aes Sedai would appear before they could finish a pitcher of wine and tell them to move on and never speak to one another again. And make sure they did it, besides. That was given. But there those women sat in the palace, over a hundred of them, holding their private meetings, walking around Aes Sedai without one frown between them. Until today, anyway, and whatever had set them huddling like frightened hens, the Aes Sedai had been every bit as anxious. There were too many oddities to suit him. When Aes Sedai behaved oddly, it was time for a man to look to the safety of his own skin.

With a curse he jerked himself out of his reverie. A man

needed to look out for his skin in the night, too, and letting his concentration drift was no way to do it. At least he had not stopped, or even slowed. After a few more steps, he smiled a thin smile and thumbed the blade of his dagger. The wind sighed down the street and fell, whistled across rooftops and fell, and in the brief silences between he could hear the faint crunch of the boots that had been following him since shortly after he left the palace.

At the next crossing street, he turned to his right at the same steady unhurried pace, then suddenly flattened his back against the front of a stable that stood hard on the corner. The wide stable doors were shut, and likely barred on the inside, but the smell of horse and horse dung hung in the icy air. The inn across the street was closed up tight, as well, its windows shuttered and dark, the only sound aside from the wind the creak of its swinging sign he could not make out in the night. No one to see what they should not.

He had a moment's warning, the sound of boots quickened in an effort not to let him out of sight too long, and then a cowled head was thrust cautiously around the corner. Not cautiously enough, of course. His left hand darted into the cowl to seize a throat at the same time his right made a practiced stop-thrust with the dagger. He half expected to find a breastplate, or a mail shirt under the man's coat, and he was ready if he did, but an inch of steel sank easily beneath the fellow's breastbone. He did not know why that seemed to paralyze a man's lungs, so he could not cry out, until he had drowned in his own blood, but he knew that it did. Still, tonight he had no time to wait. No Guards in sight at present did not mean matters would stay that way for long. With a quick wrench, he slammed the man's head against the stable's stone wall hard enough to crack a skull, then shoved his dagger to the hilt, feeling the blade grate as it dug through the fellow's spine.

His breathing remained steady—killing was just a thing that had to be done now and again, nothing to get excited over—but he hurriedly lowered the corpse to the snow against the wall and crouched beside it, wiping his blade on the dead man's dark coat while sticking his other hand into his armpit to tug off his steel-backed gauntlet. Head swiveling, he watched the street both ways as he felt quickly across the man's face in the darkness. A rasp of stubble under his fingers told him that it *was* a man, but no more. Man, woman or child made no difference to him—fools behaved as though children had no eyes to see or tongues to tell what they saw—yet he wished there had been a mustache or a bulbous nose, anything to spark a memory and tell him who this fellow had been. A squeeze at the dead man's sleeve found thick wool, neither fine nor particularly rough, and a sinewy arm that could have belonged to clerk or wagon driver or footman. To any man, in short, just like the coat. Searching down the body, he rifled through the fellow's pockets, finding a wooden comb and a ball of twine, which he tossed aside. At the man's belt, his hand paused. A leather sheath hung there, empty. No man on earth could have drawn a dagger after Hanlon's blade found his lungs. Of course, there was good cause for a man to carry his knife unsheathed when he walked out at night, but the reason that came most readily to mind right then was to stab someone in the back or cut a throat.

It was only a fleeting pause, though. Wasting no time on speculation, he sliced off the fellow's purse beneath the drawstrings. The weight of the coins he spilled into his hand and hastily stuffed into his own pocket told him there was no gold, likely not even a piece of silver, but a cut purse and no coins would make whoever found the body think him the prey of strongarms. Straightening, he tugged on his gauntlet, and only moments after driving his blade home, he was striding along the slush-covered pavement once more, dagger held close to his side beneath his cloak and eyes wary. He did not relax until he was a street away from the dead man, and then he did not relax very far.

Most people who heard of the killing would accept the tale of murder for theft that he had laid out for them, but not whoever had sent the fellow. Following all the way from the palace meant that he had been sent, but by whom? He was fairly sure that any of the Sea Folk who wanted a knife put in him would have done the deed herself. For all that the Kin troubled him just by being there, they seemed to keep quiet and walk small. True, people who practiced avoiding notice were the most likely to resort to a hired knife in the night, but he had never exchanged more than three words at a time with any of them, and he certainly had never tried to finger one. The Aes Sedai seemed more likely, yet he was sure he had done nothing to rouse their suspicions. Still, any one of them might have her own reasons for wanting him dead. You could never tell with Aes Sedai. Birgitte Trahelion was a silly bint who seemed to think she really was a character out of a story, maybe even the real Birgitte, if there had ever been a real Birgitte, but she could well think he was a threat to her position. She might be a strumpet, wiggling around the corridors in those trousers the way she did, yet she had a cold eye. That one could order a throat slit without blinking. The last possibility was the one that worried him most, though. His own masters were not the most trusting of people, and not always the most trustworthy. And the Lady Shiaine Avarhin, who currently gave him his orders, was the one who had sent a summons that had pulled him into the night. Where a fellow just happened to be waiting to follow him, knife in hand. He did not believe in coincidence, no matter what people said about this al'Thor.

Thoughts of turning back to the palace came and went in a flash. He had gold tucked away; he could bribe his way through the gates as easily as anyone else, or just order one opened long enough to let him ride out. But it would mean spending the rest of his life watching his back, and anyone who came inside arm's length of him might be the one sent to kill him. Not so different from the way he lived now. Except for the certainty that someone would put poison in his soup or a knife through his ribs sooner or later. Besides, that stone-eyed trull Birgitte was the most likely culprit. Or an Aes Sedai. Or maybe he had offended these Kin somehow. Still, it always paid to be careful. His fingers flexed around the dagger's hilt. Life was good at the moment, with plenty of comfort and plenty of women impressed or frightened into compliance by a Captain of the Guards, but life on the run was always preferable to death here and now.

Finding the correct street, much less the correct house, was not easy—one narrow side street looked very like another when darkness swathed both—but he took a care and eventually found himself pounding on the front doors of a tall, shadowed pile that could have belonged to a wealthy but discreet merchant. Except he knew now that it did not. Avarhin was a tiny House, extinct some said, but one daughter of it remained, and Shiaine possessed money.

One of the doors swung open, and he flung up a hand against the sudden glare of light. His left hand; the dagger in his right, he kept concealed and ready. Squinting through his spread fingers, he recognized the woman at the door, in the plain dark dress of a maid. Not that that eased his mind by a hair.

"Give us a kiss, Falion," he said as he stepped inside. Leering, he reached for her. Left-handed, of course.

The long-faced woman brushed his hand aside and shut the door firmly behind him. "Shiaine is closeted with a visitor in the front sitting room upstairs," she said calmly, "and the cook is in her bedchamber. There is no one else in the house. Hang your cloak on the rack. I will let her know you are here, but you may have to wait."

Hanlon let his leer vanish and his hand drop. For all of her ageless face, handsome was the best that Falion could be called, and even that might be stretching the truth, with her cold gaze and a colder manner in the bargain. She was hardly the sort of woman he would have chosen to fondle, but it seemed she was being punished by one of the Chosen and he was supposed to be part of the punishment, which altered matters. To some extent. Tumbling a woman who had no choice had never troubled him, and Falion certainly had none. Her maid's dress was simple truth; she did the work of four or five women by herself, maids and scullions and spit-girl, sleeping when she could and truckling whenever Shiaine frowned. Her hands were rough and red from doing laundry and scrubbing floors. Yet she was likely to survive her punishment, and the last thing he wanted was an Aes Sedai with a personal grudge against Daved Hanlon. Not when circumstances might well change before he had an opportunity to put a knife through her heart, anyway. Reaching an accommodation with her had been easy, though. She seemed to have a practical view. When others could see, he rumpled her every time she came in reach, and when there was time, he bundled her up to her tiny maid's room under the eaves. Where they mussed the bedclothes, then sat on the narrow bed in the cold and exchanged information. Though at her urging, he did give her a few bruises, just in case Shiaine chose to check. He hoped she remembered that it was at her urging.

"Where are the others?" he said, swinging his cloak off

and hanging it on the leopard-carved cloak rack. The sound of his boots on the floor tiles bounced from the entry hall's high ceiling. It was a fine space, with painted plaster cornices and several rich wall hangings on carved panels that were polished to a faint glow, well lit by mirrored standlamps with enough gilding for the Royal Palace itself, but burn him if it was much warmer than outside. Falion raised an eyebrow at the dagger in his hand, and he sheathed it with a tight smile. He could have it out again faster than anyone would believe, and his sword near as fast. "The streets are full of thieves at night." Despite the chill, he removed his gauntlets and tucked them behind his sword belt. Anything else might make it appear he thought himself in danger. The breastplate should be enough anyway, come the worst.

"I do not know where Marillin is," she said over her shoulder, already turning away and gathering her skirts for the stairsteps. "She went out before sunset. Murellin is in the stables with his pipe. We can talk after I inform Shiaine you've arrived."

Watching her climb the stairs, he grunted. Murellin, a hulking fellow Hanlon did not like at his back, was banished to the stables behind the house whenever he wanted to smoke his pipe, because Shiaine disliked the smell of the rough tabac he used, and since he usually took a pot of ale with him, or even a pitcher, he should not be coming in any time soon. Marillin worried him more. She was Aes Sedai, too, apparently as much under Shiaine's orders as Falion, or himself, but he had no agreements with her. No arguments, either, yet he distrusted any Aes Sedai on principle, Black Ajah or not. Where had she gone? To do what? What a man did not know could kill him, and Marillin Gemalphin spent entirely too much time off doing things he knew nothing about. He was coming to the conclusion that there were entirely too many things in Caemlyn he knew nothing about. Past time he learned, if he wanted to live.

With Falion gone, he went from the icy entry hall straight to the kitchen at the back of the house. The brick-walled room was empty, of course—the cook knew better than to poke her nose out of her room in the basement once she was sent away for the night—and the black iron stove and the ovens stood cold, but a small blaze on the long stone hearth made the kitchen one of the few rooms in the house that would be warm. Compared to the rest, at least. Shiaine was a stingy woman, except when it came to her own comforts. The fire here was only in case she happened to want mulled wine in the night, or a heated egg-milk.

He had been in this house above half a dozen times since coming to Caemlyn, and he knew which cabinets held the spices and which room off the kitchen always held a cask of wine. Always good wine. Shiaine never stinted there. Not with that she intended to drink herself, anyway. By the time Falion returned, he had the honeypot and a dish of ginger and cloves sitting on the wide kitchen table with a pitcher full of wine, and a poker thrust into the fire. Shiaine might say "come now" and mean "now," but when she wanted to make a man wait, it could be near daylight before she saw him. These calls always cost him sleep, burn the woman!

"Who is the visitor?" he asked.

"He gave no name, not to me," Falion said, propping the door to the hall open with a chair. That let some of the sparse warmth leak out, but she would want to be able to hear if Shiaine summoned her. Or maybe she wanted to make sure the other woman was not able to eavesdrop. "A lean man, tall and hard, with the look of a soldier. An officer of some rank, maybe a noble, by his manner, and Andoran by his accents. He seems intelligent and cautious. His clothes are quite plain, though costly, and he wears no rings or pins." Frowning at the table, she turned to one of the tall open-front cabinets beside the door to the hallway and added a second pewter cup to the one he had set out for himself. It had never occurred to him to set out two. Bad enough he had to fix his own wine. Aes Sedai or no Aes Sedai, she was the maid. But she took a chair at the table and pushed the dish of spices away from her for all the world as though she expected him to serve.

"Shiaine had two visitors yesterday, however, more careless than this fellow," she went on. "One, in the morning, had the Golden Boars of Sarand on the cuff of his gauntlets. He probably thought no one would notice small-work, if he thought at all. A plump, yellow-haired man in his middle years who looked down his nose at everything, complimented the wine as though surprised to find a decent vintage in the house, and wanted Shiaine to have me beaten for showing insufficient respect." She said even that in a cold, measured voice. The only time she had had any heat in her was when Shiaine put the strap to her. He had heard her howl right enough then. "A countryman who has seldom been to Caemlyn but believes he knows how his betters behave, I should say. You can mark him by a wart on his chin and a small half-moon scar beside his left eye. The fellow in the afternoon was short and dark, with a sharp nose and wary eyes, and no scars or marks I could see, though he wore a ring with a square garnet on his left hand. He was sparing with words, very mindful to give away nothing in the little I heard, but he carried a dagger with the Four Moons of House Marne on the pommel."

Folding his arms, Hanlon leaned against the side of the fireplace and kept his face smooth despite a desire to scowl. He had been sure that the plan was for Elayne to take the throne, though what came after remained a mystery. She had been promised to him as a queen. Whether or not she wore a crown when he took her mattered not a whit to him except for the spice it added—breaking that long-legged bit to saddle would be pure pleasure if she had been a farmer's daughter, especially after the chit cut a slice off him today in front of all those other women!—but dealings with Sarand and Marne said maybe Elayne was meant to die uncrowned. Maybe, in spite of all the promises that he could romp a queen, he had been placed where he was so he could kill her at some selected moment, when her death would bring some specific result sought by Shiaine. Or rather by the Chosen who had given her her orders. Moridin, the fellow was called, a name Hanlon had never heard before coming to this house. That did not trouble him. If a man had the nerve to call himself one of the Chosen, Hanlon was not fool enough to question it. The likelihood that he was no more than a dagger in this did trouble him. So long as a dagger did the job, what matter if it broke in the doing? Much better to be the fist on the hilt than the blade.

"Did you see any gold change hands?" he asked. "Did you hear anything?"

"I would have said," she replied thinly. "And by our agreement, it is my turn for a question."

He managed to mask his irritation behind an expectant look. The fool woman always asked about the Aes Sedai in the palace or those she called the Kin, or about the Sea Folk. Silly questions. Who was friendly with whom, and who unfriendly. Who exchanged private words and who avoided one another. What he had heard them say. As if he had nothing to do with his time but lurk around the hallways spying on them. He never lied to her—there was too much chance she might learn the truth, even mired here in this house as a maid; she was Aes Sedai, after all—but it was growing difficult to come up with something he had not already told her, and she was adamant that he give information if he expected to receive any. Still, he had a few tidbits to offer today, some of the Sea Folk going off, and the whole lot of them jumping for most of the day as if they had icicles shoved down their backs. She would have to settle for that. What he needed to know was important, not bloody gossip.

Before she could get her question out, though, the door to the outside opened. Murellin was large enough that he almost filled the doorway, yet icy cold still swirled in, a gust that made the small fire dance and sent sparks flying up the chimney until the big man pushed the door shut. He gave no sign that he felt the chill, but then, his brown coat looked thick as two cloaks. Besides, the man was not only the size of an ox, he had the wits of one. Setting a tall wooden mug down on the table with a thump, he tucked his thumbs behind his wide belt and eyed Hanlon resentfully. "You messing with my woman?" he muttered.

Hanlon gave a start. Not from any fear of Murellin, not with the oaf on the other side of the table. What startled him was the Aes Sedai leaping from her chair and snatching up the wine pitcher. Dumping in the ginger and cloves, she added a scoop of honey and swirled the pitcher around as if that was going to mix everything, then used a fold of her skirt to pull the poker from the fire and shove it into the wine without checking to see whether it was hot enough yet. She never looked in Murellin's direction at all.

"Your woman?" Hanlon said carefully. That earned a smirk from the other man.

"Near enough. The Lady figured I might as well use what you aren't. Anyway, Fally and me keep each other warm nights." Murellin started around the table, still grinning, but at the woman, now. A shout echoed in the hallway, and he stopped with a sigh, his grin fading.

"Falion!" Shiaine's distant voice called sharply. "Bring Hanlon up now and be quick about it!" Falion set the pitcher on the table hard enough to slop wine over the rim and was heading for the door before Shiaine finished. When the other woman spoke, Falion jumped.

Hanlon jumped too, if for a different reason. Catching up to her, he seized her arm as she took the first step on the stairs. A quick glance back showed the kitchen door closed. Maybe Murellin did feel the cold. He kept his voice low anyway. "What was that all about?"

"It is none of your business," she said curtly. "Can you get me something that will make him sleep? Something I can put in his ale or wine? He will drink anything, however it tastes."

"If Shiaine thinks I'm not obeying orders, it bloody well is my business, and you ought to see it that way, too, if you have two bloody thoughts to rub together."

She tilted her head, staring down that long nose at him, cold as a fish. "This has nothing to do with you. As far as Shiaine is concerned, I will still *belong* to you when you are here. You see, certain matters changed." Suddenly, something unseen grasped his wrist tightly and pulled his hand from her sleeve. Something else latched on to his throat, squeezing till he could not draw breath. Futilely, he scrabbled left-handed for his dagger. Her tone remained cool. "I thought certain other matters should change accordingly, but Shiaine does not see things logically. She says that when the Great Master Moridin wishes my punishment lessened, he will say so. Moridin *gave* me to her. Murellin is her way of making sure I understand that. Her way of making sure I know that I am her *dog* until she says otherwise." Abruptly she drew a deep breath, and the pressure vanished from his wrist and throat. Air had never tasted so sweet. "You can get what I ask for?" she said, as calm as if she had not just tried to kill him with the bloody Power. Just the thought that that had been touching him made his skin crawl.

"I can . . ." he began hoarsely, and stopped to swallow, rubbing at his throat. It felt as though it had been cinched in a hangman's noose. "I can get you something that will put him in a sleep he'll never wake from." As soon as it was safe, he was going to gut her like a goose.

She snorted derisively. "I would be the first Shiaine suspected, and I might as well cut my own wrists as object to anything she decided to do. It will be enough if he sleeps the nights through. Leave the thinking to me, and we will both be the better for it." Resting a hand on the carved newelpost, she glanced up the stairs. "Come. When she says now, she means now." A pity he could not hang her up like a goose to wait for the knife.

Following her, his boots thumped on the treads, sending a clatter through the entry hall, and it struck him that he had not heard the visitor leave. Unless the house had some secret way out he did not know, there was only the front door, the one in the kitchen, and a second at the back that could only be reached by passing the kitchen. So it seemed he was to meet this soldier. Maybe it was supposed to come as a surprise. Surreptitiously, he eased his dagger in its sheath.

As expected, the front sitting room had a fine blaze burning away in the wide fireplace of blue-veined marble. It was a room worth the looting, with Sea Folk porcelain vases on the gilt-edged side tables, and tapestries and carpets that would fetch a pretty price. Except that one of the carpets was likely worthless, now. A low blanket-covered mound lay near the middle of the room, and if the fellow that made it had not stained the carpet with his blood, Hanlon would eat the boots sticking out from one end.

Shiaine herself was sitting in a carved armchair, a pretty woman in gold-embroidered blue silk with an ornate belt of woven gold and a heavy gold necklace around her slim neck. Glossy brown hair hung below her shoulders even caught in a net of intricate lace. She looked delicate at first glance, but there was something vulpine about her face, and her smile never touched those big brown eyes. She was using a lace-edged handkerchief to clean a small dagger capped with a firedrop on the pommel. "Go tell Murellin that I will have a . . . bundle . . . for him to dispose of later, Falion," she said calmly.

Falion's face remained smooth as polished marble, but she made a curtsy that lacked little of cringing before she scuttled out of the room at a run.

Watching the woman and her dagger from the corner of

his eye, Hanlon moved to the covered mound and bent to lift a corner of the blanket. Glazed blue eyes stared out of a face that might have been hard, alive. The dead always looked softer. Apparently he had been neither as cautious nor as intelligent as Falion thought him. Hanlon let the blanket fall and straightened. "He said something you objected to, my Lady?" he said mildly. "Who was he?"

"He said several things I objected to." She held her dagger up, studying the small blade to be sure it was clean, then slid it into a gold-worked sheath at her waist. "Tell me, is Elayne's child yours?"

"I don't know who fathered the whelp," he said wryly. "Why, my Lady? Do you think I'd go soft? The last chit who claimed I'd gotten a child on her, I stuffed her down a well to cool her head and made sure she stayed there." There were a long-necked silver wine pitcher and two chased silver cups sitting on a tray on one of the side tables. "Is this safe?" he asked, peering into the cups. Both had wine in the bottom, but a little addition to one would have turned the dead man into easy prey.

"Catrelle Mosenain, an ironmonger's daughter from Maerone," the woman said, just as smoothly as if it were common knowledge, and he very nearly flinched in surprise. "You split her head open with a rock before you pitched her down, no doubt to spare her drowning." How did she know the wench's name, much less about the rock? He had not remembered her name himself. "No, I doubt you would go soft, but I would hate to think you were kissing the Lady Elayne without letting me know. I would purely hate that."

Suddenly she frowned at the bloodstained handkerchief in her hand and rose gracefully to glide to the fireplace and toss it into the flames. She stood there warming herself, never even glancing in his direction. "Can you arrange for some of the Seanchan women to escape? Best if it can be both those called *sul'dam* and the ones called *damane*," she stumbled a little over the strange words, "but if you can't do both, then a few of the *sul'dam* should do. They will free some of the others."

"Maybe." Blood and bloody ashes, she was dancing from one thing to another worse than Falion tonight. "It won't be easy, my Lady. They're all guarded close."

"I didn't ask whether it was easy," she said, staring into the flames. "Can you shift guards away from the food warehouses? It would please me if some of those actually burned. I am tired of attempts that always fail."

"That I cannot do," he muttered. "Not unless you expect me to go into hiding right after. They keep a record of orders that would make a Cairhienin wince. And it wouldn't do any good anyway, not with those bloody gateways bringing in more wagons every bloody day." In truth, he was not sorry for that. Queasy over the means used, certainly, but not sorry. He expected the palace would be the last place in Caemlyn to go hungry in any case, but he had lived out sieges on both sides of the lines, and he had no intention of ever boiling his boots for soup again. Shiaine wanted fires, though.

"Another answer I did not ask for." She shook her head, still looking into the fireplace, not at him. "But perhaps something can be done there. How close are you to actually . . . enjoying Elayne's affections?" she finished primly.

"Closer than the day I arrived in the palace," he growled, glowering at her back. He tried never to offend those the Chosen had set above him, but the chit was trying him. He could snap that slender neck like a twig! To keep his hands from her throat, he filled one of the cups and held it with no intention of drinking. In his left hand, of course. Just because there was one dead man in the room already did not mean she had no plans to make it two corpses. "But I have to go slow. It isn't as if I can back her into a corner and tickle her out of her shift."

"I suppose not," Shiaine said in a muffled voice. "She is hardly the sort of woman you are used to." Was she *laughing*? Was she *amused* at him? It was all he could do not to throw down the winecup and strangle the fox-faced bint.

Suddenly she turned around, and he blinked as she casually slipped her dagger back into its sheath. He had never seen her draw the bloody thing! He took a swallow of wine without thinking, and almost choked when he realized what he had done.

"How would you like to see Caemlyn looted?" she asked.

"Well enough, if I have a good company at my back and a clear path to the gates." The wine had to be safe. Two cups meant she had drunk, too, and if he had picked up the dead man's, there could not be enough poison left in it to sicken a mouse. "Is that what you want? I follow orders as well as the next man." He did when he seemed likely to survive them, or when they came from the Chosen. As well die for a fool as disobey the Chosen. "But sometimes it helps to know more than 'go there and do that.' If you told me what you're after here in Caemlyn, I might be able to help you reach it faster."

"Of course." She smiled a toothy smile while her eyes stayed as flat as brown stones. "But first, tell me why there is fresh blood on your gauntlet?"

He smiled back. "A footpad who got unlucky, my Lady." Maybe she had sent the man and maybe not, but he added her throat to the list of those he intended to slit. And he might as well add Marillin Gemalphin, too. After all, a lone survivor was the only one who could tell the tale of what had happened.

CHAPTER
16

The Subject of Negotiations

The morning sun sat on the horizon, leaving the nearer side of Tar Valon still wrapped in shadows, but the snow that covered everything gleamed brightly. The city itself seemed to shine behind its long white walls, all bravely towered and bannered, yet to Egwene, sitting her roan gelding on the riverbank above the city, it seemed even farther away than it really was. The Erinin widened to more than two miles here, and the Alindrelle Erinin and Osendrelle Erinin, flowing to either side of the island, were almost half that, so that Tar Valon appeared to sit in the middle of a great lake, unreachable despite the massive bridges that stood high above the waters so that ships could sail beneath them easily. The White Tower itself, a thick bone-white shaft rising to an impossible height from the city's heart, filled her own heart with a yearning for home. Not for the Two Rivers, but for the Tower. That was her home, now. A plume of smoke caught her eye, a faint black line rising from the far bank beyond the city, and she grimaced. Daishar stamped a hoof in the snow, but a pat on the neck sufficed to soothe the roan. It would take more to soothe his rider. Homesickness was the smallest part of it. Minuscule, compared to the rest.

With a sigh, she rested her reins on the high pommel of her saddle and raised the long brass-bound looking glass. Her cloak fell back, slipping off one shoulder, but she ignored the cold that misted her breath and placed a gloved hand to shield the front lens against the sun's glare. The city walls leaped closer in her sight. She focused on the tall curving arms of Northharbor that pushed out into the upstream currents. People moved purposefully atop the battlements that enfolded the harbor, but she could barely discern men from women at that distance. Still, she was glad that she was not wearing her seven-striped stole, and that her face was deep within her cowl, just in case someone there had a stronger glass than she. The wide mouth of the man-made harbor was blocked by a massive iron chain drawn taut a few feet above the water. Tiny dots on the water, diving birds fishing in front of the harbor, gave the chain scale. One single pace-long link would have required two men to lift it. A rowboat might slip under that barrier, but no vessel of any size would enter unless the White Tower allowed. Of course, the chain was only intended to keep out enemies.

"There they are, Mother," Lord Gareth murmured, and she lowered the glass. Her general was a stocky man in a plain breastplate worn over a plain brown coat, without any touch of gilt or embroidery anywhere. His face was bluff and weathered behind the bars of his helmet, and the years had given him a strange sort of comforting calmness. All you need do was look at Gareth Bryne to know that if the Pit of Doom opened in front of him, he would smother his fear and go about doing what needed doing. And other men would follow him. He had proved on battlefield after battlefield that following him was the path to victory. A good man to have following her. Her eyes followed his gauntleted hand, pointing upriver.

Just coming in sight around a point of land, five, six—no, seven—riverships were slicing furrows down the Erinin. Large vessels as such things were seen on the river, one with three masts, their triangular sails stood out tight, and their long sweeps cut hard through the blue-green water to add a little more speed. Everything about the craft spoke of a burning desire for speed, a desire to reach Tar Valon *now!* The river was deep enough here that ships could run within shouting distance of the banks in places, but these sailed in almost single file as close to the middle of the Erinin as the steersmen could manage and hold the wind. Sailors clinging to the mastheads kept watch along the shoreline, and not for mudbanks.

In fact, they had nothing at all to fear so long as they kept out of bowshot. True, from where she sat her horse, she could have set fire to every one of those ships, or simply cut holes through their hulls and let them sink. The work of moments. Yet doing so surely meant some of those aboard would drown. The currents were strong, the water like ice, and the swim to shore long, for those who actually could swim. Even one death would make what she did using the Power as a weapon. She was trying to live as though already bound by the Three Oaths, and the Oaths protected those vessels from her or any other sister. A sister who had sworn on the Oath Rod would not be able to *make* herself set those weaves, perhaps not even to form them, unless she could convince herself she was in immediate danger from the ships. But neither captains nor crews believed that, apparently.

As the riverships came closer, shouts thinned to threadbare by distance drifted across the water. The lookouts up on the masts pointed to her and Gareth, and it quickly became apparent they took her for an Aes Sedai with her Warder. Or at least, the captains were unwilling to take the chance she was not. After a moment, the beat of the sweeps increased. Only by a fraction, but the oarsmen labored to find that fraction. A woman on the quarterdeck of the lead vessel, likely the captain, waved her arms as if demanding still more effort, and a handful of men began running up and down the deck, tightening this line or loosening that to change the angle of the sails, though Egwene could not see that they achieved anything. There were men on those decks other than sailors, and most of those crowded to the railings, a handful raising looking glasses of their own. Some seemed to be measuring the distance left to cover before they reached the safety of the harbor.

She thought about weaving a flare, a starburst of light, perhaps with a loud bang, just above each of the vessels. That would certainly let anyone aboard with brains realize that neither speed nor distance kept them safe here, only a forbearance born of the Three Oaths. They *should* know that they were safe *because* of Aes Sedai. Exhaling heavily, she shook her head and mentally upbraided herself. That simple weave would also attract attention in the city, certainly more than the appearance of a single sister. Sisters often came to the riverbank to stare at Tar Valon and the Tower. Even if the only reaction to her flares was some sort of counterdisplay, once begun, that sort of contest could be very difficult to put a stop to. Once begun, matters might well escalate out of hand. There were too many opportunities for that, as it was, the more so these last five days.

"The harbormaster hasn't let above eight or nine ships in at one time since we arrived," Gareth said as the first vessel drew abreast of them, "but the captains seemed to have worked out the timing. Another clutch will appear soon, and reach the city about the time the Tower Guards are sure these fellows actually came to enlist. Jimar Chubain knows enough to guard against me sneaking men in aboard ships. He has more of the Guards crowded into the harbors than anywhere except at the bridge towers, and not many anywhere else, so far as I can learn. That will change, though. The flow of ships starts at first light and keeps up till near nightfall, here and at Southharbor too. This lot doesn't seem to be carrying as many soldiers as most do. Every plan is brilliant until the day comes, Mother, but then you must adapt to circumstances or be ridden down."

Egwene made a vexed sound. There must be two hundred or more passengers altogether on those seven ships. A few might be merchants or traders or some other sort of innocent traveler, but the low sun glittered off helmets and breastplates and steel discs sewn to leather jerkins. How many shiploads arrived each day? Whatever the number, a steady flow was pouring into the city to enlist under High Captain Chubain. "Why do men always rush so hard to kill or be killed?" she muttered irritably.

Lord Gareth looked at her calmly. He sat his horse, a big bay gelding with a white stripe down his nose, like a statue. Sometimes, she thought she knew one small part of how Siuan felt about the man. Sometimes she thought it would be worth whatever effort was needed to startle him, just to see him startled.

Unfortunately, she knew the answer to her own question as well as he did. At least as it applied to men going soldiering. Oh, there were men enough who rushed to support a cause or defend what they thought what was right, and some who sought adventure, whatever they believed that was, yet the simple fact was that for carrying a pike or spear, a man could earn twice each day what he would get for walking behind another man's plow, and half again

as much if he could ride well enough to join the cavalry.
Crossbowmen and archers fell in between. The man who
worked for another could dream of having his own farm
or shop one day, or a beginning toward one that his sons
could build on, but he surely had heard a thousand tales of
men soldiering for five years or ten and coming home with
enough gold to set themselves up in comfort, tales of ordinary men who rose to become generals, or lords. For a poor
man, Gareth had said bluntly, staring down the point of a
pike could be a better view than the hind end of somebody
else's plow horse. Even if he was far more likely to die from
the pike than earn fame or fortune. A bitter way to look at
it, yet she imagined that was how most of those men on
the ships saw matters, too. But then, that was how she had
gotten her own army. For every man who wanted to see the
usurper pulled from the Amyrlin Seat, for every man who
even knew for certain who Elaida was, ten if not a hundred
had joined for the pay. Some of the men on the ship were
raising their hands, to show the guards on the harbor walls
they were not holding weapons.

"No," she said, and Lord Gareth sighed. His voice remained calm, but his words were hardly comforting when
he spoke.

"Mother, so long as the harbors remain open, Tar Valon
will eat better than we do, and rather than growing weaker
with hunger, the Tower Guard will grow larger and stronger. I very much doubt that Elaida will let Chubain rush out
to attack us, as much as I wish he would. Every day you
wait only adds to the butcher's bill we'll have to pay sooner
or later. I've said from the start it will come to an assault,
in the end, and that hasn't changed, but everything else has.
Have the sisters put me and my men inside the walls now,
and I can take Tar Valon. It won't be clean. It never is. But
I can take the city for you. And fewer will die than if you
delay."

A knot formed in her belly, twisted tight till she could
hardly breathe. Carefully, step by step, she performed novice exercises to make it loosen. The bank contained the
river, guiding without controlling. Calm settled on her, in
her.

Too many people had begun seeing the uses of gateways,
and in a way, Gareth represented the worst. His business

was war, and he was very good at it. As soon as he learned
a gateway could take more than a small group of people at
one time, he had seen the implications. Even the great walls
of Tar Valon, beyond the range of any siege catapult not on
a barge, and worked with the Power till the largest catapult
could not mark them in any case, might as well be made of
paper against an army that could Travel. But whether Gareth Bryne had learned or not, other men would seize on
that idea. The Asha'man already had, it seemed. War had
always been ugly, yet it was going to grow uglier.

"No," she repeated. "I know people are going to die before this is over." The Light help her, she could see them
dying just by closing her eyes. Even more would die if she
made the wrong decisions, though, and not just here. "But
I have to keep the White Tower alive—against Tarmon
Gai'don—to stand between the world and the Asha'man—
and the Tower will die if this comes to sisters killing one
another in the streets of Tar Valon." That had already happened once. It could not be allowed a second time. "If the
White Tower dies, hope dies. I shouldn't have to tell you
that again."

Daishar snorted and tossed his head, lunging as though
he had sensed her irritation, but she reined him in firmly and
slipped the looking glass into the tooled leather case hanging from her saddle. The diving birds gave up their fishing and sprang into the air as the thick chain that blocked
Northharbor began to droop. It would dip beneath the surface well before the first ship reached the harbor mouth.
How long ago had it been that she reached Tar Valon by that
same route? Almost beyond memory, it seemed. An Age
gone. It had been another woman who came ashore and was
met by the Mistress of Novices.

Gareth shook his head with a quick grimace. But then, he
never gave up, did he? "You have to keep the White Tower
alive, Mother, but my job is to give it to you. Unless things
have changed that I don't know about. I can see sisters whispering and looking over their shoulders even if I don't know
what it means. If you still want the Tower, it will come to an
assault, better soon than late."

Suddenly the morning seemed darker, as though clouds
had obscured the sun. Whatever she did, the dead were going to pile up like cordwood, but she had to keep the White

Tower alive. She had to. When there were no good choices, you had to choose the one that seemed least wrong.

"I've seen enough here," she said quietly. With one last glance at that narrow line of smoke beyond the city, she turned Daishar toward the trees a hundred paces back from the river, where her escort waited among the evergreen leatherleaf and winter-bare beech and birch.

Two hundred light cavalry, in boiled leather breastplates or coats covered with metal discs, would certainly have attracted notice appearing on the riverbank, but Gareth had convinced her of the necessity of these men with their slender lances and short horsebows. Without any doubt, that smoke plume on the far bank rose from burning wagons or supplies. Pinpricks, yet those pinpricks came every night, sometimes one, sometimes two or three, till everyone looked for smoke first thing on rising. Hunting the raiders down had proved impossible, so far. Sudden snow squalls flared around the pursuers, or fierce freezing night winds, or the tracks simply vanished abruptly, the snow beyond the last hoofprint as smooth as fresh fallen. The residues of weavings made it plain enough they were being aided by Aes Sedai, and there was no point in taking a chance that Elaida had men and maybe sisters on this side of the river, too. Few things could please Elaida more than getting her hands on Egwene al'Vere.

They were not her whole escort, of course. Besides Sheriam, her Keeper, she had ridden out with six more Aes Sedai this morning, and those who had Warders had brought them, so behind the sister eight men waited in color-shifting cloaks that rippled in queasy-making fashion when a breeze caught them and otherwise made parts of riders and horses seem to vanish into the tree trunks. Aware of the dangers—from raiders, at least—aware that their Aes Sedai were wound tight to near breaking, they watched the surrounding copse as though the cavalrymen were not there. The safety of their own Aes Sedai was their primary concern, and that they trusted to no one else. Sarin, a black-bearded stump of a man, not that short but very wide, stayed so close to Nisao that he seemed to loom over the diminutive Yellow, and Jori managed to loom over Morvrin as well, though he was actually shorter than she. As broad as Sarin, but very short even for a Cairhienin.

Myrelle's three Warders, the three she dared acknowledge, clustered around her until she could not have moved her horse without pushing one of theirs out of her way. Anaiya's Setagana, lean and dark and as beautiful as she was plain, almost managed to surround her by himself, and Tervail, with his bold nose and scarred face, did the same with Beonin. Carlinya had no Warder, not unusual for a White, but she studied the men from the depths of her fur-lined cowl as if thinking about finding one.

Not too long ago, Egwene would have hesitated to be seen with those six women. They and Sheriam had all sworn fealty to her, for various reasons, and neither they nor she wanted the fact known or even suspected. They had been her way to influence events, to the extent that she could, when everyone thought her no more than a figurehead, a girl Amyrlin the Hall of the Tower could use as it wished and no one listened to. The Hall had lost that illusion when she brought them to declare war on Elaida, finally admitting what they had been about since the day they had fled the Tower in the first place, but that only made the Hall, and the Ajahs, worry over what she would do next and try to figure out how to make sure that whatever it was met with their approval. The Sitters had been very surprised when she accepted their suggestion of a council, one sister from each Ajah, to advise her with their wisdom and experience. Or perhaps they thought her success with the declaration of war had gone to her head. Of course, she had just told Morvrin and Anaiya and the others to make sure they were the sisters chosen, and they retained enough prestige within their Ajahs to manage it, just. She had been listening to their advice, if not always taking it, for weeks by that time, but now there was no longer any need to arrange furtive meetings or pass messages in secret.

It seemed, however, that there had been an addition to the party while Egwene was staring at the Tower.

Sheriam, wearing the narrow blue stole of her office outside her cloak, managed a very formal bow from her saddle. The flame-haired woman could be incredibly formal at times. "Mother, the Sitter Delana wishes to speak with you," she said as if Egwene could not see the stout Gray sister sitting there on a dappled mare almost as dark as Sheriam's black-footed mount. "On a matter of some importance, so she says." And the slight touch of asperity meant Delana had not told her what matter. Sheriam would not have liked that. She could be very jealous of her position.

"In private, if you please, Mother," Delana said, pushing back her dark hood to reveal hair nearly the color of silver. Her voice was deep for a woman's, but it hardly carried the urgency of someone with important matters to speak of.

Her presence was something of a surprise. Delana often supported Egwene in the Hall of the Tower, when Sitters were quibbling over whether a particular decision actually concerned the war against Elaida. That meant the Hall was required to support Egwene's commands as if they had stood with the greater consensus, and even the Sitters who had stood for war did not half like that little fact, which made for endless quibbling. They wanted to pull Elaida down, yet left to themselves, the Hall would have done nothing but argue. Truth to tell, though, Delana's support was not always welcome. One day she could be the very image of a Gray negotiator seeking consensus, and the next so strident in her arguments that every Sitter within hearing got her back up. She had been known to set the cat among the pigeons in other ways, too. No fewer than three times now, she had demanded the Hall make a formal declaration that Elaida was Black Ajah, which inevitably led to an awkward silence until someone called for the sitting to be adjourned. Few were willing to discuss the Black Ajah openly. Delana would discuss anything, from how they were to find proper clothes for nine hundred and eighty-seven novices to whether Elaida had secret supporters among the sisters, another topic that gave most sisters a case of the prickles. Which left the question of why she had ridden out so early, and by herself. She had never approached Egwene before without another Sitter or three for company. Delana's pale blue eyes gave away no more than did her smooth Aes Sedai face.

"While we ride," Egwene told her. "We will want a little privacy," she added when Sheriam opened her mouth. "Stay back with the others, please." The Keeper's green eyes tightened in what might almost have been anger. An efficient Keeper, and eager with it, she had pinned her hopes on Egwene and made little secret that she disliked being excluded from any meeting Egwene had. Upset or not, she bowed her head in acceptance with only a small hesitation. Sheriam had not always known which of them commanded, but she did now.

The land tended upward from the River Erinin, not in hills but simply rising toward the monstrous peak that loomed to the west, so massive it seemed to mock the name mountain. Dragonmount would have towered above everything else even in the Spine of the World; in the relatively flat country around Tar Valon, its white-capped crest seemed to reach the heavens, especially when a thin thread of smoke was streaming away from the jagged top as it was now. A thin thread at that height would be something else entirely, close at hand. Trees gave out less than halfway up Dragonmount, and no one had ever succeeded in reaching the crest or even coming close, though it was said the slopes were littered with the bones of those who had tried. Why anyone would try in the first place, no one could quite explain. Sometimes the long evening shadow of the mountain stretched all the way to the city. People who lived in the region were accustomed to Dragonmount dominating the sky, much as they were accustomed to the White Tower looming above the city walls and visible for miles. Both were unchanging fixtures that had always been there and always would be, but crops and crafts occupied the people's lives, not mountains or Aes Sedai.

In tiny hamlets of ten or a dozen stone houses roofed in thatch or slate, and the occasional village of a hundred, children playing in the snow or carrying buckets of water from the wells stopped to gape at the soldiers riding along the dirt tracks that passed for roads when not covered in snow. They carried no banners, but a few of the soldiers wore the Flame of Tar Valon worked on their cloaks or coatsleeves, and the Warders' strange cloaks named at least some of the women as Aes Sedai. Even this near the city, sisters had been an uncommon sight till recently, and they were still something to make a child's eyes gleam. But then, the soldiers themselves probably came close in the list of marvels. The farms that fed Tar Valon covered most of the land, stone-walled fields surrounding sprawling houses and tall barns of stone or brick, with copses and coppices and thickets of trees between, and groups of farm children often ran a little distance parallel to the line of travel, leaping across the snow like hares. Winter chores kept most older folk in-doors, but those who ventured out, heavily bundled against the cold, spared barely a glance for soldiers or Warders or Aes Sedai. Spring would be coming soon, and the plowing and planting, and what Aes Sedai did would not affect that. The Light willing, it would not.

There was no point to guards unless they rode as if ex-pecting an attack, and Lord Gareth had arranged a strong party of fore-riders and lines of flankers, with trailers rid-ing to the rear while he led the mass of the soldiers right behind the Warders who followed closely on the heels of Sheriam and the "council." They all made a large, lopsided ring around Egwene, and she could almost imagine she was riding through the countryside alone with Delana if she did not look around too closely. Or if she looked beyond. In-stead of pressing the Gray Sitter to speak—it was a long ride back to camp, and no one was allowed to weave a gate-way where the weave might be observed; there was plenty of time to hear what Delana had to say—Egwene compared the farms they passed to those in the Two Rivers.

Perhaps the realization that the Two Rivers was no longer home made her study them. Acknowledging the truth could never be a betrayal, yet she needed to remember the Two Rivers. You could forget who you were if you forgot where you came from, and sometimes the innkeeper's daughter from Emond's Field seemed a stranger to her. Any of these farms would have looked decidedly odd, set down near Emond's Field, though she could not put a finger on why, exactly. A different shape to the houses, a different slant to the roofs. And more often slate topped a house than thatch, here, when you could make out either through the snow that was often mounded on the rooftops. Of course, there was less thatch and more stone and brick in the Two Rivers now than there had been. She had seen it, in *Tel'aran'rhiod*. Change came so slowly you never noticed it creeping up on you, or far too fast for comfort, but it came. Nothing stayed the same, even when you thought it did. Or hoped it would.

"Some think you're going to bond him your Warder," Delana said suddenly in a quiet voice. She might have been engaging in casual conversation. Her whole attention seemed to be on arranging the hood of her cloak with green-gloved hands. She rode well, blending with the motion of her mare so effortlessly that she appeared unaware of the animal. "Some think perhaps you already have. I haven't had one myself for some time, but just knowing your Warder is there can be a comfort. If you choose the right one."

Egwene raised an eyebrow—she was proud that she did not gape at the woman; this was the very *last* topic she would have expected—and Delana added, "Lord Gareth. He spends a great deal of time with you. He's rather older than is usual, but Greens often choose a more experienced man for their first. I know you never actually had an Ajah, yet I often think of you as a Green. I wonder, will Siuan be relieved if you bond him, or upset? Sometimes I think one, sometimes the other. Their relationship, if it can be called that, is most peculiar, yet she seems completely unembarrassed."

"You must ask Siuan herself about that." Egwene's smile had some bite in it. So did her tone, for that matter. She did not entirely understand herself why Gareth Bryne had offered her his loyalty, but the Hall of the Tower had better uses for its time than gossiping like village women. "You can tell whoever you choose that I've bonded no one, Delana. Lord Gareth spends time with me, as you put it, because I am the Amyrlin and he is my general. You may remind them of that, as well." So Delana thought of her as a Green. That was the Ajah she would have chosen, though in truth, she wanted only one Warder. But Gawyn was either inside Tar Valon or else on his way to Caemlyn, and either way, she would not lay hands on him soon. She patted Daishar's neck unnecessarily and tried to keep her smile from becoming a glare. It had been pleasant to forget the Hall, among other things, for a while. The Hall made her understand why Siuan had so often looked like a bear with a sore tooth when she was Amyrlin.

"I wouldn't say it has become a matter for wide discussion," Delana murmured. "So far. Still, there is some interest in whether you will bond a Warder, and who. I doubt that Gareth Bryne would be considered a wise pick." She twisted in her saddle to look behind them. At Lord Gareth, Egwene thought, but when the Sitter turned back around, she said, very softly, "Sheriam was never your choice for Keeper, of course, but you must know that the Ajahs set the rest of that lot to watch you, as well." Her dappled gray mare was shorter than Daishar, so she had to look up at Egwene, which she tried to do without seeming to. Those watery blue eyes were suddenly quite sharp. "There was some thought that Siuan might be advising you . . . too well . . . after the way you brought about the declaration of war against Elaida. But she's still resentful over her changed circumstances, isn't she? Sheriam is seen as the most likely culprit, now. In any case, the Ajahs want a little warning if you decide to pull another surprise."

"I thank you for the warning," Egwene said politely. Culprit? She had proven to the Hall that she would not be their puppet, yet most insisted on thinking she had to be someone's. At least no one suspected the truth about her council. It was to be hoped no one did.

"There is another reason you should be wary," Delana went on, the intensity in her eyes belying the casualness of her voice. This was more important to her than she wanted Egwene to know. "You may be sure that any advice one of them gives you comes straight from the head of her Ajah, and as you know, the head of an Ajah and its Sitters don't always see eye to eye. Listening too closely could put you at odds with the Hall. Not every decision concerns the war, remember, but you will surely want some of those to go your way."

"An Amyrlin should listen to every side before making any decision," Egwene replied, "but I'll remember your warning when they advise me, Daughter." Did Delana think she was a fool? Or perhaps the woman was trying to make her angry. Anger made for hasty decisions and rash words that sometimes were hard to take back. She could not imagine what Delana was aiming at, but when Sitters could not manipulate her one way, they tried another. She had gotten a great deal of practice in sidestepping manipulation since being raised Amyrlin. Taking deep, regular breaths, she sought the balance of calm and found it. She had entirely too much practice at that, too, of late.

The Gray looked up at her past the edge of her hood, her face utterly smooth. But her pale blue eyes were *very* sharp, now, like augers. "You might inquire what they think on the subject of negotiations with Elaida, Mother."

Egwene almost smiled. The pause had been very deliberate. Apparently Delana disliked being called Daughter by a woman younger than most novices. Younger than most who had come from the Tower, let alone the newest. But then, Delana herself was too young to be a Sitter. And she could not hold her temper as well as the innkeeper's daughter. "And why would I ask that?"

"Because the subject has come up in the Hall in the last few days. Not as a proposal, but it has been mentioned, very quietly, by Varilin, and by Takima, and also by Magla. And Faiselle and Saroiya have appeared interested in what they have had to say."

Calm or no calm, a worm of anger suddenly writhed inside Egwene, and crushing it was no easy task. Those five had been Sitters before the Tower was broken, but more importantly, they were divided between the two major factions struggling for control of the Hall. In reality, they were divided between following Romanda or Lelaine, yet that pair would oppose one another if it meant they both drowned. They also kept an iron grip on their followers.

She might believe the others had been panicked by events, but not Romanda or Lelaine. For half a week now, talk of Elaida or retaking the Tower had been all but overwhelmed by worried conversations over that impossibly powerful, impossibly long eruption of the Power. Nearly everyone wanted to know what had caused it, and nearly everyone was afraid to learn. Only yesterday had Egwene been able to convince the Hall that it must be safe for a small party to Travel to where that eruption had been—even the memory was strong enough for everyone to pinpoint exactly where it had been—and most sisters still seemed to be holding their collective breath until Akarrin and the others returned. Every Ajah had wanted a representative, but Akarrin had been the only Aes Sedai to push forward.

Neither Lelaine nor Romanda seemed concerned, however. Violent and prolonged as the display had been, it also had been very far away, and no harm done that they could see; if it was the Forsaken's work, as seemed certain, the chance of learning anything was vanishingly small, and the possibility that they could do anything to counter it even smaller. Wasting time and effort on impossibilities was senseless when an important task lay right in front of them. So they said, gritting their teeth over finding themselves in agreement. They did agree that Elaida must be stripped of the stole and staff, though, Romanda with almost as much fervor as Lelaine, and if Elaida unseating a former Blue as Amyrlin had enraged Lelaine, Elaida's proclamation that the Blue Ajah was disbanded had made her near-rabid. If they were allowing talk of negotiation . . . It made no sense.

The last thing Egwene wanted was for Delana or anyone else to suspect that Sheriam and the others were more than a set of sheepdogs set to watch her, but she summoned them with a sharp call. They were smart enough to keep the secrets that needed keeping, since their own Ajahs would have their hides if even the half came out, and with no great haste, they came forward and rode in a cluster around her, their faces all masks of Aes Sedai serenity and patience. Then Egwene told Delana to repeat what she had said. For all her initial request for privacy, the Gray made only a perfunctory demurral before complying. And that was the end of calm and patience.

"That's madness," Sheriam said before anyone else could open her mouth. She sounded angry, and perhaps a little frightened. Well she might be. Her name was on a list of those marked for stilling. "None of them can really believe negotiation is possible."

"I should hardly think so," Anaiya put in dryly. Her plain face belonged on a farmwife rather than a Blue sister, and she dressed very simply, publicly at least, in good wool, but she handled her bay gelding as easily as Delana did her mare. Very little could ruffle Anaiya's calm. Of course, there was no Blue among the Sitters talking negotiation. Anaiya looked an unlikely soldier, but for Blues, this was war to the knife, no quarter asked or given. "Elaida has made the situation quite clear."

"Elaida is irrational," Carlinya said with a toss of her head that made her cowl fall to her shoulders and shook her short dark curls. She pulled the hood back into place irritably. Carlinya seldom showed any hint of emotion, yet her pale cheeks were nearly as flushed as Sheriam's, and heat filled her voice. "She cannot possibly believe that we will all come crawling back to her now. How can Saroiya believe she will accept anything less?"

"Crawling is what Elaida has demanded, though," Morvrin muttered acridly. Her usually placid round face wore a sour expression, too, and her plump hands were tight on

her reins. She scowled so hard at a flight of magpies, scattering from a stand of birch trees at the passage of horses,
that it seemed they should fall out of the sky. "Takima likes
the sound of her own voice, sometimes. She *must* be talking
to hear herself."

"Faiselle must, too," Myrelle said darkly, glaring at
Delana as though she were to blame. The olive-skinned
woman was known for her temper, even among Greens. "I
never expected to hear that sort of talk out of her. She's
never been a fool before."

"I can't believe Magla really means any such thing,"
Nisao insisted, peering at each of them in turn. "She just
can't. For one thing, as much as I hate to say it, Romanda
has Magla so tight under her thumb that Magla squeaks
whenever Romanda sneezes, and the only doubt Romanda
has is whether Elaida should be birched before she's ex-
iled."

Delana's expression was so bland, she had to be suppressing a smug smile. Plainly, this was exactly the reaction she
had hoped for. "Romanda holds Saroiya and Varilin just as
firmly, and Takima and Faiselle hardly put one foot in front
of the other without Lelaine's permission, but they still
said what they said. I think your advisors are closer to the
feelings of most sisters, though, Mother." Smoothing her
gloves, she gave Egwene a sidelong look. "You may be able
to nip this in the bud, if you move firmly. It seems you will
have the support you need from the Ajahs. And mine, of
course, in the Hall. Mine, and enough more to stop it dead."
As if Egwene needed support to accomplish that. Perhaps
she was trying to ingratiate herself. Or just to make it appear that support of Egwene was her only concern.

Beonin had been riding in silence, clutching her cloak
around her and peering at a spot between her brown mare's
ears, but suddenly she shook her head. Ordinarily, her large
blue-gray eyes made her appear startled, but they peered
from her hood in a blaze of anger as she glared from one of
her companions to another, including Egwene. "Why should
negotiations be out of the question?" Sheriam blinked at her
in surprise, and Morvrin opened her mouth with a scowl,
but Beonin plunged on, directing her ire at Delana, now, her
Taraboner accent stronger than usual. "We are Gray, you
and I. We negotiate, mediate. Elaida, she has stated the

conditions most onerous, but that is often the case in the beginning of negotiations. We can reunite the White Tower and assure the safety of everyone, if we only talk."

"We also judge," Delana snapped, "and Elaida has been judged." That was not precisely true, but she seemed more startled than anyone else by Beonin's outburst. Her voice dripped acid. "Perhaps you are willing to negotiate yourself into being birched. I am not, and I think you will find few others who are, either."

"The situation, it has altered," Beonin persisted. She stretched a hand toward Egwene, almost pleading. "Elaida would not have made the proclamation she did concerning the Dragon Reborn unless she had him in hand, one way or another. That flare of *saidar* was a warning. The Forsaken must be moving, and the White Tower, it must be—"

"Enough," Egwene cut in. "You are willing to open negotiations with Elaida? With the Sitters still in the Tower?" she amended. Elaida would never talk.

"Yes," Beonin said fervently. "Matters can be arranged to everyone's satisfaction. I know they can."

"Then you have my permission."

Immediately everyone but Beonin began talking frantically on top of one another, trying to dissuade her, telling her this was insanity. Anaiya shouted as loudly as Sheriam, gesturing emphatically, and Delana's eyes bulged in what looked like near terror. Some of the outriders began looking toward the sisters as much as they watched the farms they were riding past, and there was a stir among the Warders, who certainly had no need of their bonds at the moment to know their Aes Sedai were agitated, but they held their places. Wise men kept their noses out of the way when Aes Sedai began raising their voices.

Egwene ignored the shouts and arm-waving. She had considered every possibility she could think of for ending this struggle with the White Tower whole and united. She had talked for hours with Siuan, who had more reason than anyone to want to unseat Elaida. If it could have saved the Tower, Egwene would have surrendered to Elaida, forget whether the woman had come to the Amyrlin Seat legally. Siuan had nearly had apoplexy at the suggestion, yet she had agreed, reluctantly, that preserving the Tower superseded every other consideration. Beonin wore such a beautiful smile, it seemed a crime to quench it.

Egwene raised her voice just enough to be heard over the others. "You will approach Varilin and the others Delana named, and arrange to approach the White Tower. These are the terms I will accept: Elaida is to resign and go into exile." Because Elaida would never accept back the sisters who had rebelled against her. An Amyrlin had no say over how an Ajah governed itself, but Elaida had declared that the sisters who fled the Tower were no longer members of any Ajah. According to her, they would have to beg readmittance to their Ajahs, after serving a penance under her direct control. Elaida would not reunite the Tower, only shatter it worse than it already was. "Those are the only terms I will accept, Beonin. The *only* terms. Do you understand me?"

Beonin's eyes rolled up in her head, and she would have fallen from her horse if Morvrin had not caught her, muttering under her breath as she held the Gray upright and slapped her face, not lightly. Everyone else stared at Egwene as though they had never seen her before. Even Delana, who must have planned for something like this to happen from the first word she had said. They had come to a halt with Beonin's fainting fit, and the ring of soldiers around them drew up at a shouted command from Lord Gareth. Some stared toward the Aes Sedai, their anxiety plain even with their faces hidden behind the bars of their helmets.

"It's time to get back to camp," Egwene said. Calmly. What had to be done had to be done. Perhaps surrender would have healed the Tower, but she could not believe it. And now it might come down to Aes Sedai facing one another in the streets of Tar Valon, unless she could find a way to make her plan succeed. "We have work to do," she said, gathering her reins, "and there isn't much time left." She prayed there was enough.

CHAPTER
17

Secrets

Once Delana was sure that her noxious seed had taken root, she murmured that it might be best if they were not seen arriving back at the camp together and slipped away, pushing her mare to a quick trot through the snow and leaving the rest of them to ride on in uneasy silence except for the crunch of the horses' hooves. The Warders maintained their distance behind, and the escorting soldiers had their attention back on the farms and thickets, without so much as a glance toward the Aes Sedai that Egwene could see, now. Men never knew when to keep their mouths shut, though. Telling a man to be quiet only made him gossip all the harder, just to close friends he could trust, to be sure, as if they in turn would not tell everyone who would listen. The Warders might be different—Aes Sedai always insisted they were, those who had Warders—but no doubt the soldiers would talk of sisters arguing, and no doubt they would say Delana had been sent off with a flea in her ear. The woman had planned this very carefully. Worse than fireweed or stranglervine could grow if that seed was allowed to sprout, but the Gray Sitter had sheltered herself from blame very neatly. Truth almost always did come out in the end, but by the end, truth was often so wrapped around with rumors and speculation and absolute lies that most people never did believe it.

"I trust I don't have to ask whether any of you had heard about this before." Egwene said that quite casually, seemingly studying the countryside as they rode, but she was pleased when everyone denied it outright with considerable indignation, including Beonin, who was working her jaw and glaring at Morvrin. Egwene trusted them as far as she dared—they could not have given her their oaths without meaning to hold to every word; not unless they were Black Ajah, a niggling possibility that accounted for most of her caution—yet even oaths of fealty left room for the most loyal people doing the worst possible thing in the belief that it was in your best interest. And people who had been co-erced into their oaths could be adept at spotting the gaps and leeways.

"The real question," she continued, "is what was Delana after?" She had no need to explain, not for these women, every one experienced in the Game of Houses. If all Delana had wanted was to stop negotiations with Elaida while keeping her own name out of it, she could simply have spo-ken to Egwene alone at any time. Sitters needed no excuse to come to the Amyrlin's study. Or she could have used Halima, who slept on a pallet in Egwene's tent most nights despite being Delana's secretary. Egwene was troubled with headaches, and some nights only Halima's massages could soothe them so she could sleep. For that matter, an anony-mous note might have been sufficient to make her present the Hall with an edict forbidding negotiations. The touchi-est quibbler would have to admit that talks to end the war certainly touched on the war. But plainly Delana wanted Sheriam and the others to know, too. Her tale-bearing was an arrow aimed at another target.

"Strife between the Ajah heads and the Sitters," Car-linya said, as cool as the snow. "Perhaps strife between the Ajahs." Casually adjusting her cloak, intricately embroi-dered white-on-white but lined with dense black fur, she might have been discussing the price of a spool of thread. "Why she wants these things, I can't begin to say, but those will be the results, unless we are very careful, and she could not know we would be careful, or that we have any reason to be, so logically one or both must be her aim."

"The first answer that comes to mind isn't always correct, Carlinya," Morvrin said. "There's no saying that Delana thought her actions through as carefully as you have, or that she thought along the same lines." The stout Brown believed more in common sense than logic, or so she said, but in truth she seemed to blend the two, a combination that made her very hardheaded, and suspicious of quick or easy answers. Which was not a bad thing to be. "Delana may be trying to sway some among the Sitters on some issue that's important to her. Maybe she hopes to get Elaida declared Black Ajah after all. No matter the results, her goal may be something we don't even suspect. Sitters can be as petty as anyone else. For all we know, she might have a grudge against one of those she named dating back to when she was a novice and they taught her. Better to concentrate on what will come of it than to worry about why until we know more." Her tone was as placid as her broad face, but Carlinya's cool composure flickered to cool disdain for a moment. Her rationality made few concessions for human foibles. Or for anyone disagreeing with her.

Anaiya laughed, a sound of almost motherly amusement that made her bay dance a few steps before she reined him back to a walk. A motherly farmwife amused by the antics of others in the village. Even some sisters were foolish enough to dismiss her that easily. "Don't sulk, Carlinya. You are very probably right. No, Morvrin, she probably is. In any event, I believe we can squash any hopes she has for discord." That did not sound amused at all. No Blue was amused by anything that might hamper pulling Elaida down.

Myrelle gave a savage nod of agreement, then blinked in surprise when Nisao said, "Can you afford to stop this, Mother?" The tiny Yellow did not speak up often. "I don't mean whatever Delana is trying to do. If we can settle on what that is," she added quickly, making a gesture at Morvrin, who had opened her mouth again. Nisao looked a child alongside the other women, but it was a peremptory gesture. She was Yellow, after all, with all the self-assurance that implied, and unwilling to step back for anyone in most circumstances. "I mean the talk of parley with the Sitters in the Tower."

For a moment, everyone gaped at her, even Beonin.

"And why would we want to allow that?" Anaiya said finally, in a dangerous voice. "We didn't come all this way to *talk* to Elaida." She was a farmwife with a cleaver hidden behind her back and a mind to use it, now.

Nisao looked up at her and sniffed dismissively. "I didn't say we wanted it. I asked whether we dare stop it."

"I hardly see the difference." Sheriam's voice was icy, and

her face pale. With anger, Egwene thought, but it might have been fear.

"Then think for a while, and you might see it," Nisao said dryly. Dry the way a knife blade was dry, and equally cutting. "At present, talk of negotiations is limited to five Sitters, and very quiet, but will it remain so? Once word spreads that talks were proposed and rejected, how long before despair sets in? No, hear me out! We all set off full of righteous fury for justice, yet here we sit, staring at the walls of Tar Valon, while Elaida sits in the Tower. We've been here nearly two weeks, and for all anyone can see, we may be here two years, or twenty. The longer we sit with nothing happening, the more sisters will start making excuses for Elaida's crimes. The more they'll start thinking that we *have* to mend the Tower, never mind the cost. Do you want to wait until sisters start slipping back to Elaida one by one? I myself do not fancy standing on the riverbank defying the woman with just the Blue Ajah and the rest of you for company. Negotiations will at least let everyone see that *something* is happening."

"No one is going to return to Elaida," Anaiya protested, shifting on her saddle, but she wore a troubled frown, and she sounded as if she could see it happening. The Tower beckoned to every Aes Sedai. Very likely even Black sisters yearned for the Tower to be whole again. And there it stood, just a few miles away, but seemingly out of reach.

"Talk could buy time, Mother," Morvrin said reluctantly, and no one could put as much reluctance in her voice as she. Her frown was thoughtful, and not at all pleased. "A few more weeks, and Lord Gareth might be able to find the ships he needs to block the harbors. That will alter everything, in our favor. With no way for food to get in or mouths to get out, the city will be starving inside a month."

Egwene hung on to a smooth face with an effort. There was no real hope of ships to block the harbor, though none of them knew that. Gareth had made it plain enough to her, however, long before leaving Murandy. Originally, he had hoped to buy vessels while they marched north along the Erinin, using them to ferry supplies until they reached Tar Valon, then sinking them in the harbor mouths. Using gateways to reach Tar Valon had put paid to that in more ways than one. Word of the siege had left the city with the first ships sailing after the army arrived, and now, as far north and south as he had sent riders, ship captains were carrying out their business ashore by boat, from anchorages well out in the river. No captain was willing to risk the chance her ship would simply be seized. Gareth made his reports only to her, and his officers only to him, yet any sister could have known if she talked with a few soldiers.

Fortunately, even sisters looking for Warders rarely spoke to soldiers. They were generally accounted a thieving, un-lettered lot who only bathed by accident, when they had to wade a stream. Not the kind of man any sister spent time with except when compelled to. It made keeping secrets easier, and some secrets were essential. Including, some-times, secrets kept from those seemingly on your side. She could remember not thinking that way, but that was a part of the innkeeper's daughter she had been obliged to leave behind. This was another world, with very different rules from Emond's Field. A misstep there meant a summons to the Women's Circle. Here, a misstep meant death or worse, and for more than herself.

"The Sitters remaining in the Tower should be willing to talk," Carlinya put in, with a sigh. "They have to know that the longer the siege lasts, the more chance Lord Gareth will find his ships. I cannot think how long they will continue talking, though, when they realize we do not mean to sur-render."

"Elaida will insist on that," Myrelle muttered, yet she did not seem to be arguing, just talking to herself, and Sheriam shivered, drawing her cloak around her as though she had let the cold touch her.

Only Beonin looked happy, sitting eager and upright in her saddle, dark honey hair framing a wide smile inside her hood. She did not press her case, however. She was good at negotiation, so everyone said, and knew when to wait.

"I did say you could begin," Egwene said. Not that she had meant it for more than a setdown, yet if you were going to live by the Three Oaths, then you had to stand by what you said. She could not wait to hold the Oath Rod. It would be so much easier, then. "Just make sure you're very careful what you say. Unless they think we all grew wings to fly here, they must suspect we've rediscovered Traveling, but they can't be certain unless someone confirms it. It's better

SECRETS   399

for us if they stay uncertain. That must be one secret you hold as tightly as you hold the secret of our ferrets in the Tower."

Myrelle and Anaiya jerked at that, and Carlinya looked around as though fearful, though neither Warders nor soldiers were close enough to hear unless someone shouted. Morvrin merely took on an even more sour expression. Even Nisao looked a little ill, though she had had nothing to do with the decision to send sisters back to the Tower in secret, supposedly answering Elaida's summons. The Hall might be happy to learn that ten sisters were in the Tower trying to undermine Elaida however they could, even if the effort had borne no apparent fruit so far, but the Sitters would most definitely be *unhappy* at realizing that it had been kept secret because these women feared that some of the Sitters might actually be Black Ajah. As well for Sheriam and the others to reveal their oaths to Egwene as reveal that. The results for them might not be very different. The Hall had not ordered anyone birched yet, but the way most Sitters chafed at the bit over Egwene's control of the war, it could hardly come as a surprise if they jumped at the chance to show they still had some authority while simultaneously expressing their displeasure forcefully.

Beonin was apparently the only one who had opposed that decision—at least, until it became apparent the others were going ahead anyway—but she drew a shuddering breath, too, and a tightness settled around her eyes. In her case, the sudden realization of just what she had undertaken might have played its part, too. Just finding someone in the Tower who was willing to talk might prove a daunting task. Eyes-and-ears inside Tar Valon could offer only hearsay about events inside the Tower; news of the Tower itself came only in dribs and drabs, from sisters venturing into *Tel'aran'rhiod* to glimpse fleeting reflections of the waking world, but every last one of those scraps told of Elaida ruling by edict and caprice, with not even the Hall daring to stand against her. Beonin's face took on a grayish tinge, till she began to appear more sickly than Nisao. Anaiya and the others looked as bleak as death.

A wave of gloom rose in Egwene. These were among the strongest against Elaida, even the foot-dragging Beonin, who always wanted to talk rather than act. Well, Grays were noted for believing that anything could be solved with enough talk. They should try that on a Trolloc sometime, or just a footpad, and see how far they got! Without Sheriam and the rest, resistance to Elaida would have fallen apart before it ever had a chance to coalesce. It nearly had anyway. But Elaida was as firmly seated in the Tower as ever, and after all they had gone through, all they had done, it seemed that even Anaiya saw it all melting away into disaster.

No! Drawing a deep breath, Egwene straightened her shoulders and sat erect in her saddle. *She* was the lawful Amyrlin, no matter what the Hall had thought they were getting when they raised her, and she had to keep the rebellion against Elaida alive to have any hope of healing the Tower. If that required a pretense of negotiations, it would not be the first time Aes Sedai had pretended to aim at one thing while targeting another. Whatever was required to keep the rebellion alive and pull Elaida down, she would do. Whatever was required.

"Stretch the talks out as long as you can," she told Beonin. "You can talk about anything, so long as you keep the secrets that need keeping, but agree to nothing, and keep them talking." Swaying in her saddle, the Gray definitely looked sicker than Anaiya. She almost appeared ready to empty her stomach.

When the camp came into sight, with the sun nearly halfway to its noonday peak, the escort of lightly armored horsemen broke away back toward the river, leaving Egwene and the sisters to ride the last mile across the snow followed by the Warders. Lord Gareth paused as if he wanted to speak with her once more, but finally he turned his bay east after the cavalry, trotting to catch up as they vanished beyond a long, coppiced stand of trees. He would not bring up their disagreement, or their discussions, where anyone else could hear, and he believed that Beonin and the others were just what everyone else thought them, the Ajahs' watchdogs. She felt a little sad at holding things back from him, but the fewer who knew a secret, the more likely it would remain secret.

The camp was a sprawl of tents in every shape and size and color and state of repair that almost covered a broad tree-rimmed pasture, halfway between Tar Valon and Dragonmount, inside a ring of horselines and rows of wagons and carts in almost as many shapes as there were wagons and carts. Chimney smoke rose in several places a few miles beyond the treeline, but the local farmers stayed away except for selling eggs and milk and butter, or sometimes when one needed Healing from some accident, and there was no sign at all of the army Egwene had brought so far. Gareth had concentrated his forces along the river, part occupying the bridge towns on both banks and the rest in what he called reserve camps, placed where men could be rushed to help fight off any sortie in strength from the city, just in case he was wrong about High Captain Chubain. Always consider the possibility your assumptions are wrong, he had told her. No one objected to his placements, of course, not in general anyway. Any number of sisters were ready to nitpick the details, but holding the bridge towns was the only way to besiege Tar Valon, after all. By land, it was. And a good many Aes Sedai were pleased to have the soldiers out of sight if not out of mind.

Three Warders in color-shifting cloaks came riding out from the camp as Egwene and the others approached, one of them very tall and one quite short, so they seemed arranged in steps. Making their bows to Egwene and the sisters, nodding to the Warders behind, they all had that dangerous look of men so confident that they had no need to convince anyone how dangerous they were, which somehow made it all the more evident. A Warder at his ease and a lion resting on a hill, so went an old saying among Aes Sedai. The rest of it was lost in the years, but there really was no need to say more. The sisters were not entirely complacent about the safety of even a camp full of Aes Sedai, under the circumstances. Warders patrolled closely for miles in every direction, lions on the prowl.

Anaiya and the others, all but Sheriam, scattered as soon as they reached the first row of tents beyond the wagons. Each would be seeking out the head of her Ajah, ostensibly to report on Egwene's ride to the river with Lord Gareth, and more importantly, to make sure those Ajah heads knew that some of the Sitters were talking about negotiations with Elaida and that Egwene was being firm. It would have been easier if she knew who those women were, but even oaths of fealty did not stretch to revealing that. Myrelle had nearly swallowed her tongue when Egwene suggested it.

Being dropped into a job without training was hardly the best way to learn it, and Egwene knew she had oceans to learn yet about being Amyrlin. Oceans to learn, and a job of work to do at the same time.

"If you will forgive me, Mother," Sheriam said when Beonin, the last to go, vanished among the tents trailed by her scar-faced Warder, "I have a writing table piled high with paper." The lack of enthusiasm in her voice was understandable. The Keeper's stole came along with ever-growing stacks of reports to be sorted and documents to be prepared. Despite her zeal for the rest of the job, which in this case was to keep the camp running, Sheriam had been heard to mutter fervent wishes, when confronted by yet another mound of papers, that she was still Mistress of Novices.

Still, as soon as Egwene gave permission, she booted her black-footed dapple to a trot, scattering a covey of workmen in rough coats and mufflers wrapped around their heads, who were carrying large baskets on their backs. One fell flat on his face in the half-frozen muck that passed for a street. Sheriam's Arinvar, a slim Cairhienin with graying temples, paused long enough to make sure the fellow was getting to his feet, then spurred his dark bay stallion after her, leaving the workman to his curses, most of which seemed to be directed at his companions' laughter. Everyone knew that when an Aes Sedai wanted to go somewhere, you got out of the way.

What had spilled out of the fellow's basket onto the street caught Egwene's eye and made her shiver, a tall heap of meal crawling with weevils till it seemed there were as many moving black specks as meal. The men must all have been carrying ruined meal to the midden heaps. There was no use bothering to sift anything that infested—only someone who was starving could eat it—but too many baskets of meal and grain had to be disposed of every day. For that matter, half the barrels of salt pork and salt beef opened for use stank so that there was nothing to be done except bury them. For the servants and workmen, at least those who had experience of camp life, that was nothing new. A little worse than usual, but not unheard of. Weevils could appear any time, and merchants trying to stretch their profits always sold some rotting meat along with the good. Among the Aes Sedai, though, it was cause for deep worry.

Every barrel of meat, every sack of grain or flour or meal, had been surrounded by a Keeping as soon as bought, and whatever was woven into a Keeping could not change until the weave was removed. But still the meat rotted and the insects multiplied. It was as though *saidar* itself was failing. You could get a sister to make jokes about the Black Ajah before you could get her to talk about that.

One of the laughing men caught sight of Egwene watching them and nudged the mud-covered fellow, who moderated his language, though not very far. He even glowered as if blaming her for his fall. With her face half-hidden by her hood and the Amyrlin's stole folded in her belt pouch, they seemed to take her for one of the Accepted, not all of whom had enough proper clothing to always dress as they should, or perhaps a visitor. Women frequently slipped into the camp, often keeping their faces hidden in public until they left again whether they wore fine silks or threadbare wool, and showing a sour expression to a stranger or an Accepted was certainly safer than grimacing at an Aes Sedai. It seemed odd not to have everyone in sight bobbing and bowing.

She had been in the saddle since before first light, and if a hot bath was out of the question—water had to be carried in from the wells that had been dug half a mile west of the camp, which made all but the most fastidious or self-absorbed sisters limit themselves—if a long hot soak was not to be had, she still would have liked to put her feet back on the ground. Or better yet, put them up on a footstool. Besides, refusing to let the cold touch you was not at all the same as warming your hands at a toasty brazier. Her own writing table would have its pile of paper, too. Last night she had told Sheriam to give her the reports on the state of wagon repairs and the supply of fodder for the horses. They would be dry and boring, but she checked on different areas every day, so she could at least tell whether what people told her was based on fact or wishes. And there were always the eyes-and-ears' reports. What the Ajahs decided to pass along to the Amyrlin Seat made for fascinating reading when compared to what Siuan and Leane gave her from their agents. It was not so much that there were contradictions, yet what the Ajahs chose to keep to themselves could draw interesting pictures. Comfort and duty both pulled her toward her study—just another tent, really, though everyone called it the Amyrlin's study—but this was an opportunity to look around without having everything hastily made ready ahead of her arrival. Pulling her hood a little further forward to better conceal her face, she touched her heels lightly to Daishar's flanks.

There were few people mounted, mostly Warders, though the infrequent groom added to the traffic, leading a horse at as close to a trot as could be managed in the ankle-deep slush, but no one seemed to recognize her or her mount. In contrast to the nearly empty streets, the wooden walkways, no more than rough planks pegged atop sawn logs, shifted slightly under the weight of people. The handful of men, dotting the streams of women like raisins in a cheap cake, walked twice as fast as anyone else. Excepting Warders, men got their business among Aes Sedai done as quickly as possible. Nearly all the women had their faces hidden, their breath misting in the openings of their hoods, yet it was easy to pick out Aes Sedai from visitors whether their cloaks were plain or embroidered and lined with fur. The crowds parted in front of a sister. Anyone else had to weave her way through. Not that many sisters were about on this frigid midmorning. Most would be snug in their tents. Alone or in twos or threes, they would be reading, or writing letters, or questioning their visitors about whatever information those women had brought. Which might or might not be shared with the rest of a sister's Ajah, much less with anyone else.

The world saw Aes Sedai as a monolith, towering and solid, or it had before the current division in the Tower became common knowledge, yet the pure fact was that the Ajahs stood apart in all but name, the Hall their only true meeting point, and the sisters themselves were little more than a convocation of hermits, speaking three words beyond what was absolutely required only with a few friends. Or with another sister they had joined in some design. Whatever else changed about the Tower, Egwene was sure that never would. There was no point pretending that Aes Sedai had ever been anything but Aes Sedai or ever would be, a great river rolling onward, all its powerful currents hidden deep, altering its course with imperceptible slowness. She had built a few hasty dams in that river, diverting a stream here and a stream there for her own purposes, yet she knew they were temporary structures. Sooner or later those deep currents would undercut her dams. She could only pray they lasted long enough. Pray, and shore up as hard as she could.

Very occasionally one of the Accepted appeared in the throng, with the seven bands of color on the hood of her white cloak, but most by far were novices in unadorned white wool. Only a handful of the twenty-one Accepted in the camp actually possessed banded cloaks, and they saved their few banded dresses for teaching classes or attending sisters, yet great efforts had been made to see that every novice was dressed in white at all times, even if she only had one change. The Accepted inevitably tried to move with the swanlike glide of Aes Sedai, and one or two nearly managed despite the tilting of the walkways underfoot, but the novices darted along almost as quickly as the few men, scurrying on errands or hurrying to classes in groups of six or seven.

Aes Sedai had not had so many novices to teach in a very long time, not since before the Trolloc Wars, when there had been many more Aes Sedai as well, and the result of finding themselves with near a thousand students had been utter confusion until they were organized into these "families." The name was not strictly official, yet it was used even by Aes Sedai who still disliked taking any woman who asked. Now every novice knew where she was supposed to be and when, and every sister could at least find out. Not to mention that the number of runaways had declined. That was always a concern for Aes Sedai, and several hundred of these women might well attain the shawl. No sister wanted to lose one of those, or any, for that matter, not before the decision was made to send a woman away. Women still slipped off occasionally after realizing that the training was harder than they had expected and the road to an Aes Sedai's shawl longer, but quite apart from the families making it easier to keep track, running away seemed to be less attractive to women who had five or six cousins, as they were called, to lean on.

Well short of the big square pavilion that served as the Hall of the Tower, she turned Daishar down a side street. The walkway in front of the pale brown canvas pavilion was empty—the Hall was not a place anyone approached without business there—but the much-patched side curtains were kept down without a reason to make the workings of the Hall public, so there was no telling who might step out. Any Sitter would recognize Daishar at a glance, and some Sitters she would as soon avoid even more than others. Lelaine and Romanda, for example, who resisted her authority as instinctively as they opposed each other. Or any of those who had begun talking of negotiations. It was too much to believe that *they* were just hoping to rally spirits, or they would not have kept to whispers. The courtesies had to be maintained, though, no matter how often she wished she could box someone's ears, yet no one could think she was being snubbed if Egwene did not see her.

A faint silvery light flashed behind a tall canvas wall just ahead of her, surrounding one of the camp's two Traveling grounds, and a moment later two sisters emerged from behind one of the flaps. Neither Phaedrine nor Shemari was strong enough to weave a gateway by herself, but linked she thought they could just manage one big enough to walk through. Heads close together in deep conversation, strangely they were just pinning on their cloaks. Egwene kept her face averted anyway as she rode by. Both of the Browns had taught her as a novice, and Phaedrine still seemed surprised that Egwene was Amyrlin. Lean as a heron, she was quite capable of wading out into the muck to ask whether Egwene needed assistance. Shemari, a vigorous square-faced woman who looked more like a Green than a librarian, was always beyond proper in her behavior. Much beyond. Her deep curtsies, suitable for a novice, carried at least a suggestion of mockery no matter how smooth her expression, not least because she had been known to curtsy when she saw Egwene a hundred paces away.

Where had they been, she wondered. Somewhere indoors, perhaps, or at least warmer than the camp. No one really kept track of the sisters' comings and goings, of course, not even the Ajahs. Custom ruled everyone, and custom strongly discouraged direct questions about what a sister was doing or where she was going. Most likely, Phaedrine and Shemari had been to hear from some of their eyes-and-ears face to face. Or maybe to look at a book in some library. They *were* Brown. But she could not help thinking of Nisao's comment about sisters slipping away to

Elaida. It was quite possible to hire a boatman to make the crossing to the city, where dozens of tiny water gates gave entrance to anyone who wished it, but with a gateway, there was no need to risk exposure by riding to the river and asking after boats. Just one sister returning to the Tower with the knowledge of that weave would give away their largest advantage. And there was no way to stop it. Except to keep heart in the opposition to Elaida. Except to make the sisters believe there could be a quick end to this. If only there was a way to a quick end.

Not far beyond the Traveling ground, Egwene drew rein and frowned at a long wall-tent, even more patched than the Hall. An Aes Sedai came swanning down the walkway—she wore a plain dark blue cloak, and the cowl hid her face, but novices and others skipped out of her way as they never would have for a merchant, say—and paused in front of the tent, looking at it for a long moment before pushing aside the entry flap to go inside, her unwillingness as clear as if she had shouted. Egwene had never gone in there. She could feel *saidar* being channeled inside, though faintly. The amount necessary was surprisingly small. A quick visit from the Amyrlin should not draw too much attention, however. She very much wanted to see what she had set in motion.

Dismounting in front of the tent, though, she discovered a trifling difficulty. There was nowhere to tie Daishar. The Amyrlin always had someone rushing to hold her stirrup and take away her horse, but she stood there holding the gelding's reins, and clusters of novices bustled past with no more than a quick glance, dismissing her as one of the visitors. By this time, every novice knew all of the Accepted on sight, but few had seen the Amyrlin Seat close up. She did not even have the ageless face to tell them she was Aes Sedai. With a rueful laugh, she put a gloved hand into her belt pouch. The stole would tell them who she was, and then she could order one of them to hold her horse for a few minutes. Unless they thought it was a joke in bad taste, at least. Some of the novices from Emond's Field had tried to pull the stole from her neck, to keep her from getting in trouble. No, that was past and dealt with.

Abruptly, the entry flap was pushed open and Leane emerged, fastening her dark green cloak with a silver pin in the shape of a fish. The cloak was silk, and richly embroidered in silver and gold, as was the bodice of her riding dress. Her red gloves were embroidered on the backs, too. Leane paid minute attention to her clothes since joining the Green Ajah. Her eyes widened lightly at the sight of Egwene, but her coppery face smoothed immediately. Taking in the situation at a glance, she put out a hand to stop a novice who appeared to be by herself. Novices went to classes by family. "What's your name, child?" Much had changed about Leane, but not her briskness. Except when she wanted it to, anyway. Most men turned to putty when Leane's voice grew languorous, but she never wasted that on women. "Are you on an errand for a sister?"

The novice, a pale-eyed woman close to her middle years, with an unblemished skin that had never seen a day's work in the field, gaped openly before recovering enough to make her curtsy, a smoothly practiced spreading of her white skirts with mittened hands. As tall as most men but willowy and graceful and beautiful, Leane lacked the ageless look, too, yet hers was one of the two most well known faces in the camp. Novices pointed her out in awe, a sister who had once been Keeper, who had been stilled, and Healed so she could channel again, if not so strongly as before. And then she had changed Ajahs! The newest women in white already had learned that that just never happened, though the other was becoming a part of lore, unfortunately. It was harder to make a novice go slowly when you could not point out that she risked ending her quest for the shawl by burning herself out and losing the One Power forever.

"Letice Murow, Aes Sedai," the woman said respectfully, in a lilting Murandian accent. She sounded as if she wanted to say more, perhaps to give a title, but one of the first lessons on joining the Tower was that you had left behind who you used to be. It was a hard lesson, for some, especially those who possessed titles. "I'm going to visit my sister. I haven't seen her more than a minute since before we left Murandy." Relatives were always put in different novice families, as were women who had known each other before being entered in the novice book. It encouraged making new friends, and cut down on the inevitable tensions when one was learning faster than the other or had a higher potential. "She's free of classes, too, until the afternoon, and—"

"Your sister will have to wait a while longer, child," Leane broke in. "Hold the Amyrlin's horse for her."

Letice gave a start and stared at Egwene, who had finally managed to extract her stole. Handing Daishar's reins to the woman, she lowered her cowl and settled the long narrow strip of cloth onto her shoulders. Light as a feather in her pouch, the stole had real weight hanging around her neck. Siuan claimed that sometimes you could feel every woman who had ever worn the stole hanging from the ends of it, a constant reminder of responsibility and duty, and Egwene believed every word. The Murandian gaped at her harder than she had for Leane, and took longer to remember to curtsy. No doubt she had heard that the Amyrlin was young, but it seemed unlikely she had given a thought to how young.

"Thank you, child," Egwene said smoothly. There had been a time when she felt strange calling a woman ten years older than herself child. Everything changed, with time. "It won't be for long. Leane, would you ask someone to send a groom for Daishar? Now that I'm out of the saddle, I'd as soon stay out, and Letice should be allowed to see her sister."

"I will see to it myself, Mother."

Leane offered a fluid curtsy and moved away with never a hint that there was more between them than this chance encounter. Egwene trusted her far more than she did Anaiya or even Sheriam. She certainly kept no secrets from Leane, any more than from Siuan. But their friendship was yet another secret that had to be kept. For one thing, Leane had eyes-and-ears actually inside Tar Valon if not in the Tower itself, and their reports came to Egwene and Egwene alone. For another, Leane was much petted for accommodating so well to her reduced status, and every sister welcomed her, if only because she was living proof that stilling, the deepest dread of any Aes Sedai, could be reversed. They welcomed her with open arms, and because she *was* less, now, standing below at least half the sisters in the camp, they often spoke in front of her about matters they would never want the Amyrlin to know of. So Egwene did not so much as glance after her as she left. Instead, she offered Letice a smile—the woman reddened and bobbed another curtsy— then entered the tent, stripping off her gloves and tucking them behind her belt.

Inside, eight mirrored stand-lamps stood along the walls between low wooden chests. One with a bit of worn gilding and the rest of painted iron, no two of the lamps had the same number of arms, but they provided good illumination, if not so bright as outside. Assorted tables that seemed to have come from seven different farm kitchens made a row down the center of the canvas ground-cloth, the benches of the three farthest occupied by a half a dozen novices with their cloaks folded beside them, each woman surrounded by the glow of the Power. Tiana, the Mistress of Novices, hovered anxiously over them, walking between the tables, and surprisingly, so did Sharina Melloy, one of the novices acquired in Murandy.

Well, Sharina was not exactly hovering, just watching calmly, and perhaps it should not have been a surprise to find her there. A dignified, gray-haired grandmother with a tight bun on the back of her head, Sharina had run a very large family with a very firm hand, and she seemed to have adopted all of the other novices as granddaughters or grandnieces. She was the one who had organized them into those tiny families, completely on her own and apparently out of simple disgust at seeing everyone flounder around. Most Aes Sedai went more than a touch tight-mouthed if reminded of that, though they had accepted the form quickly enough once they realized how much easier it made keeping track and organizing classes. Tiana was inspecting the novices' work so closely that it seemed obvious she was attempting to ignore Sharina's presence. Short and slight, with large brown eyes and a dimple in her cheek, Tiana somehow looked young despite her ageless face, particularly alongside the taller novice's creased cheeks and broad hips.

The pair of Aes Sedai channeling at the table nearest the entrance, Kairen and Ashmanaille, had an audience of two as well, Janya Frende, a Sitter for the Brown, and Salita Toranes, a Sitter for the Yellow. The Aes Sedai and the novices were all performing the same task. In front of each woman, a close net woven of Earth, Fire and Air surrounded a small bowl or cup or the like, all made by the camp's blacksmiths, who were very puzzled at why the sisters wanted such things made of iron, not to mention having them made as finely as if they were silver. A second weave, Earth and Fire woven just so, penetrated each net to touch the object, which was slowly turning white. Very, very slowly, in every case.

Ability with the weave improved with practice, but of the Five Powers, strength in Earth was the key, and beside Egwene herself, only nine sisters in the camp—along with two of the Accepted and nearly two dozen novices—had sufficient of that to make the weaves work at all. Few among the sisters wanted to give any time to it, though. Ashmanaille, lean enough to make her seem taller than she really was, fingers tapping the tabletop on either side of the simple metal cup in front of her, was frowning impatiently as the edge of whiteness crept upward past halfway. Kairen's blue eyes were cold enough that it seemed her stare alone might shatter the tall goblet she was working on. That had only the smallest rim of white at the bottom. It must have been Kairen Egwene had seen going in.

Not everyone was unenthusiastic, though. Janya, slim in her pale bronze silks and wearing her brown-fringed shawl draped over her arms, studied what Kairen and Ashmanaille were doing with the eagerness of one who wished she could be doing the same. Janya wanted to know everything, to know how everything was done and why it happened that way. She had been extremely disappointed when she could not learn to make *ter'angreal*—only three sisters aside from Elayne had managed that, so far, with very spotty success—and she had made a concerted effort to learn this skill even after the testing showed she fell short of the required strength in using Earth.

Salita was the first to notice Egwene. Round-faced and almost as dark as charcoal, she eyed Egwene levelly, and the Yellow fringe of her shawl swayed slightly as she made a very precise curtsy, exact to the inch. Raised in Salidar, Salita was part of a disturbing pattern: too many Sitters who were too young for the position. Salita had only been Aes Sedai for thirty-five years, and rarely was a woman given a chair before wearing the shawl for a hundred or more. Siuan saw a pattern, anyway, and thought it disturbing, though she could not say why. Patterns she could not understand always disturbed Siuan. Still, Salita had stood for war against Elaida, and frequently supported Egwene in the Hall. But not always, and not in this. "Mother," she said coolly.

Janya's head jerked up, and she broke into a beaming smile. She also had stood for war, the only woman who had been a Sitter before the Tower divided to do so excepting Lelaine and Lyrelle, two of the Blues, and if her support for Egwene was not always unwavering, it was so here. As usual, words spilled out of her. "I will never get over this, Mother. It's simply amazing. I know we shouldn't be surprised any longer when you come up with something no one else has thought of—sometimes I think we've gotten too set in our ways, too sure what can and cannot be done—but to puzzle out how to make *cuendillar* . . . !" She paused for breath, and Salita moved into the gap smoothly. And coldly.

"I still say it is wrong," she said firmly. "I admit the discovery was a brilliant piece of work on your part, Mother, but Aes Sedai should not be making things for . . . sale." Salita invested that word with all the scorn of a woman who accepted the income from her estate in Tear without ever thinking how it had been come by. The attitude was not uncommon, though most sisters lived on the Tower's generous yearly allowance. Or had, before the Tower split apart. "On top of which," she went on, "nearly half the sisters forced into this are Yellow. I receive complaints every day. We, at least, have more important uses for our time than making . . . trinkets." That earned her a hard glare from Ashmanaille, a Gray, and a frigid stare from Kairen, who was Blue, but Salita ignored them. She was one of those Yellows who seemed to think the other Ajahs were only adjuncts to her own, which of course had the only truly useful purpose among them.

"And novices should not be doing weaves of this complexity at all," Tiana added, joining them. The Mistress of Novices was never shy about speaking up to Sitters, or to the Amyrlin, and she wore a disgruntled expression. She did not appear to realize that it deepened her dimple and made her look sulky. "It *is* a remarkable discovery, and I for one have no objections to trade, but some of these girls can barely manage to make a ball of fire change color with any surety. Letting them handle weaves like this will only make it more difficult to stop them from leaping to things they can't handle, and the Light knows, that's difficult enough already. They may even do themselves an injury."

"Nonsense, nonsense," Janya exclaimed, waving a slender hand as if to brush away the very idea. "Every girl who's been chosen can already make three balls of fire at once, and this requires very little more of the Power. There's no danger at all, so long as they're under a sister's supervision, and they always are. I've seen the roster. Besides, what we make in a day will bring enough to pay the army for a week or more, but the sisters alone can't produce near that much." Squinting slightly, she suddenly appeared to be looking through Tiana. The cascade from her tongue never slowed, yet she seemed to be talking at least half to herself. "We will have to take great care in the selling. The Sea Folk have a voracious appetite for *cuendillar,* and there are plenty of their ships still at Illian and Tear by all accounts—the nobles there are greedy for it, too—but even ravenous appetites have limits. I still cannot decide whether it will be best to appear with everything at once, or let it trickle out. Sooner or later, even the price of *cuendillar* will begin to drop." Abruptly she blinked and peered first at Tiana then at Salita, tilting her head to one side. "You do see my point, don't you?"

Salita glowered and hitched her shawl up on her shoulders. Tiana threw up her hands in exasperation. Egwene held her peace. For once, she felt no shame at being praised for one of her supposed discoveries. Unlike nearly everything else except Traveling, this one actually was hers, though Moghedien had pointed the way before she escaped. The woman did not know how to actually make anything—at least, she had not revealed any such knowledge however hard Egwene had pressed her, and she had pressed *very* hard—but Moghedien had a wide streak of greed, and even in the Age of Legends, *cuendillar* had been a prized luxury. She had known enough of how it was made for Egwene to puzzle out the rest. In any case, no matter who objected or how strenuously, the need for money meant the production of *cuendillar* would continue. Though as far as she was concerned, the longer before any of it was sold, the better.

Sharina slapping her hands together loudly in the back of

the tent jerked everyone's head that way. Kairen and Ash-manaille turned, too, the Blue even letting her weaves go so the goblet bounced on the tabletop with a metallic clatter. It was a sign of boredom. The process could be started over, though finding the precise point was very hard, and some sisters took every opportunity to do anything else during the hour they had to spend in the tent each day. An hour or until they completed one item start to finish, whichever came first. That was supposed to push them to try harder at increasing their skill, but few had progressed very far.

"Bodewhin, Nicola, off to your next class," Sharina announced. She did not speak loudly, but her voice had a strength that could have cut through a babble of voices much less the quiet of the tent. "You have just time to wash your hands and faces. Quickly, now. You don't want any bad reports."

Bode—Bodewhin—moved with efficient alacrity, releasing *saidar* and placing her half-made *cuendillar* bracelet in one of the chests along the wall for someone else to finish, then gathering her cloak. Plump-cheeked and pretty, she wore her hair in a long dark braid, though Egwene was not sure she had gotten permission from the Women's Circle. But then, that world was behind her, now. Tugging on her mittens as she hurried from the tent, Bode kept her eyes down and never glanced in Egwene's direction. Plainly, she still did not understand why a novice could not drop by to chat with the Amyrlin Seat whenever she wanted, even if they had grown up together.

Egwene would have loved to talk with Bode and some of the others, but an Amyrlin had lessons to learn, too. An Amyrlin had many duties, few friends, and no favorites. Be-sides, even the appearance of favoritism would mark the Two Rivers girls out and make their lives with the other novices a misery. *And it wouldn't do me much good with the Hall, either,* she thought wryly. She did wish the Two Rivers girls understood, though.

The other novice Sharina had named did not leave her bench or stop channeling. Nicola's black eyes flashed at Sharina. "I could be the best at this if I was ever allowed to really practice," she grumbled sullenly. "I'm getting better; I know I am. I can Foretell, you know." As if the one had anything to do with the other. "Tiana Sedai, tell her I can stay longer. I can finish this bowl before my next class, and I'm sure Adine Sedai won't mind if I'm just a little late." If her class was any time soon, she would be more than a little late if she tarried to complete the bowl; her hour's effort had turned only half of it white.

Tiana opened her mouth, but before she could utter a word, Sharina raised one finger, then a moment later, a second. It must have had some particular significance, because Nicola went pale and let go of her weaves on the instant, leaping up so quickly that she joggled the bench, earning quick frowns from the other two novices who shared it. They bent quickly back to their work, though, and Nicola almost ran to thrust the half-done bowl into a chest before snatching up her cloak. To Egwene's surprise, a woman she had not seen, dressed in a short brown coat and wide trousers, jumped up from where she had been sitting on the ground-cloth beyond the tables. Scowling blue-eyed daggers at everyone in sight, Areina ran out of the tent after Nicola, the two women mirror images of disgruntlement and discontent. Seeing the pair of them together made Egwene uneasy.

"I didn't know friends were allowed in here to watch," she said. "Is Nicola still causing problems?" Nicola and Areina had attempted to blackmail her, and Myrelle and Nisao, but that was not what she meant. That was still another secret.

"Better the girl's friendly with Areina than with one of the male grooms," Tiana said with a sniff. "We've had two get with child, you know, and ten more likely to. The girl needs more friends, though. Friends will do the trick with her."

She cut off as two more white-clad novices hurried into the tent, the pair of them squeaking and skidding to a halt when they found Aes Sedai standing right in front of them. Hastily dropping curtsies, they scuttled to the back of the tent at a gesture from Tiana and folded their cloaks on a bench before fetching a partly white goblet and an almost white cup from one of the chests.

Sharina saw them settled to work, then gathered her own cloak and swung it around her shoulders before coming up the tent. "If you will excuse me, Tiana Sedai," she said, making a curtsy that just came short of being to an equal,

"I've been told off to help with the midday meal today, and I wouldn't want to get crosswise with the cooks." Her dark eyes rested on Egwene for a brief moment, and she nodded to herself.

"Go on, then," Tiana said sharply. "I would hate to hear you had been switched for being late."

Without turning a hair, Sharina offered her courtesies again, neither in a hurry nor dragging it out, to Tiana, to the Sitters, to Egwene—with another glance that was penetrating but too short for offense—and when the tentflap swung shut behind her, Tiana blew out her cheeks in exasperation.

"Nicola causes less trouble than some," she said darkly, and Janya shook her head.

"Sharina doesn't cause problems, Tiana." She spoke as quickly as ever, but quietly, so her voice would not carry to the back of the tent. Disagreements between sisters were never aired in front of novices. Especially when the disagreement was over a novice. "She already knows the rules better than any Accepted, and never puts a toe over the line. She never shirks at even the dirtiest chores, either, and she's the first to lend a hand when another novice needs one. Sharina is simply who she is. Light, you can't allow a *novice* to intimidate you."

Tiana stiffened and opened her mouth angrily, but once Janya had the bit between her teeth, getting a word in edgewise was no easy matter. "Nicola, on the other hand, causes all sorts of problems, Mother," the Brown rushed on. "Ever since we found out she has the Foretelling, she's been Foretelling two or three times a day, to hear her tell it. Or rather, to hear Areina tell it. Nicola is smart enough to know everyone is aware she can't remember what she says when she Foretells, but Areina always seems to be there to hear and remember, and help her interpret. Some are the sort of thing anyone in the camp with half a brain and a credulous nature might think of—battles with the Seanchan or the Asha'man, an Amyrlin imprisoned, the Dragon Reborn doing nine impossible things, visions that might be Tarmon Gai'don or a bilious stomach—and the rest all just happen to indicate that Nicola ought to be allowed to go faster with her lessons. She's always too greedy for that. I think even most of the other novices have stopped believing her."

"She also pokes her nose everywhere," Salita put in the

moment Janya gave her an opening, "her and the groom, both." Her face remained smooth and cool, and she shifted her shawl as though that were the focus of her attention, but she rushed her words a little, perhaps fearing that the Brown would take over again. "They've both been switched for eavesdropping on sisters, and I myself caught Nicola trying to peek into one of the Traveling grounds. She said she just wanted to see a gateway open, but I think she was trying to learn the weave. Impatience, I can understand, but deceit cannot be tolerated. I no longer believe Nicola will attain the shawl, and frankly, I've begun to wonder whether she should be sent away soon rather than late. The novice book may be open to everyone," she finished with an expressionless glance at Egwene, "but we do not have to lower our standards completely."

Glaring, Tiana pursed her lips stubbornly, emphasizing her dimple again. You could almost forget she had worn the shawl for over thirty years and think her a novice herself. "As long as I am Mistress of Novices, the decision on whether to send a girl away is mine," she said heatedly, "and I do not intend to lose a girl of Nicola's potential." Nicola would be very strong in the Power, one day. "Or Sharina's," she added with a grimace, hands smoothing her skirts in irritation. Sharina's potential was nothing short of remarkable, far beyond anyone in living memory except for Nynaeve, and ahead of Nynaeve as well. Some thought she might become as strong as it was possible to be, though that was only speculation. "If Nicola has been bothering you, Mother, I will see to her."

"I was just curious," Egwene said carefully, swallowing a suggestion that the young woman and her friend both be watched closely. She did not want to talk about Nicola. It would be too easy to find herself with a choice between lying or revealing matters she dared not expose. A pity she had not allowed Siuan to arrange for two quiet deaths.

Her head jerked in shock at the thought. Had she gone that far from Emond's Field? She knew she would have to order men to die in battle sooner or later, and she thought she might be able to order a death if the need was great enough. If one death could stop the death of thousands, or even hundreds, was it not right to order it? But the danger presented by Nicola and Areina was simply that they might reveal secrets that could inconvenience Egwene al'Vere. Oh, Myrelle and the others might be lucky to get off with a birching, and they would certainly consider that more than inconvenient, but discomfort, however great, was *not* sufficient reason for killing.

Abruptly, Egwene realized that she was frowning, and Tiana and the two Sitters were watching her, Janya not bothering to hide her curiosity behind a mask of serenity. To cover herself, Egwene shifted her frown to the table where Kairen and Ashmanaille were once more at work. The white on Ashmanaille's cup had climbed a little farther, but in just that short time, Kairen had caught up. More than caught up, in fact, since her goblet stood twice as high as the cup.

"Your skill is improving, Kairen," Egwene said approvingly.

The Blue looked up at her, and drew a deep breath. Her oval face became an image of cool calm around those icy blue eyes. "There isn't much skill involved, Mother. All that's needed is to set the weave and wait." The last word held a touch of acridness, and for that matter, there had been a slight hesitation before Mother. Kairen had been sent off from Salidar on a very important mission only to see it collapse in a shambles, though from no fault of hers, and she had returned to them in Murandy to find everything she had left behind stood on its head and a girl she remembered as a novice wearing the Amyrlin's stole. Of late, Kairen had been spending a good deal of time with Lelaine.

"She is improving; in *some* things," Janya said with a pointed frown for the Blue sister. Janya might have been as sure as any other Sitter that the Hall was getting a puppet when they raised Egwene, but she seemed to have accepted that Egwene did wear the stole, and deserved the proper respect from everyone. "Of course, I doubt she'll catch Leane unless she applies herself, much less yourself, Mother. Young Bodewhin might catch her, in fact. I wouldn't want to be outdone by a novice, myself, but I suppose some don't feel that way." A stain of red crept into Kairen's cheeks, and her eyes dropped to the goblet.

Tiana sniffed. "Bodewhin's a good girl, but she spends more time giggling and playing with the other novices than applying herself if Sha—" She inhaled sharply. "If she isn't watched. Yesterday, she and Althyn Conly tried two items at once, just to see what would happen, and the things fused together in a solid lump. Useless for sale, of course, unless you find someone who wants a pair of half-iron, half-*cuendillar* cups joined at angles. And the Light knows what might have happened to the girls. They didn't seem to be harmed, but who can say about the next time?"

"Make sure there isn't a next time," Egwene said absently, her attention on Kairen's cup. The line of white crept upward steadily. When Leane did this weave, black iron turned to white *cuendillar* as if the iron were sinking quickly into milk. For Egwene herself, the change was faster than the blink of an eye, black to white in a flash. It would have to be Kairen and Leane, but even Leane was barely fast enough. Kairen needed time to improve. Days? Weeks? Whatever was necessary, because anything less meant disaster, for the women involved and for the men who would die fighting in the streets of Tar Valon and maybe for the Tower. Suddenly Egwene was glad she had approved Beonin's suggestion. Telling Kairen why she needed to try harder might have spurred her efforts, but this was another secret that had to be kept until the time came to unveil it to the world.

CHAPTER
18

A Chat with Siuan

Daishar had been taken away when Egwene left the tent, of course, but the seven-striped stole hanging from the opening of her cowl worked better than an Aes Sedai's face at making a way through the crowd. She moved in a ripple of curtsies, with the occasional bow thrown in from a Warder, or a craftsman who had some task among the sisters' tents. Some novices squeaked when they saw the Amyrlin's stole, and whole families stepped hurriedly off the walkway, making their deep curtsies in the mire of the street. Since she had been forced to order punishment for some of the Two Rivers women, word had spread among the novices that the Amyrlin was as hard as Sereille Bagand, and it was best to avoid incurring her temper, which could spring up like wildfire. Not that most of them knew enough history to have any real idea who Sereille had been, but her name had been a byword of iron-handed strictness in the Tower for a hundred years, and the Accepted made sure that novices absorbed tidbits like that. It was a good thing that Egwene's cowl hid her face. By the tenth time a novice family leaped out of her way like frightened hares, she was gritting her teeth so hard that seeing her face would have cemented her reputation for chewing iron and spitting nails. She had the horrible feeling that in a few hundred years, Accepted would be using her name to frighten novices the way they used Sereille's now. Of course, there was the little matter of securing the White Tower first. Small irritations had to wait. She thought she could have spit nails without the iron.

The crowds thinned to nothing around the Amyrlin's

study, which was just a peaked canvas tent with patched brown walls, despite the name. Like the Hall, it was a place to be avoided unless you had business there or were summoned. No one was simply asked to the Hall of the Tower or the Amyrlin's study. The most innocuous invitation to either *was* a summons, a fact that turned that simple tent into a haven. Sweeping through the entry flaps, she swung her cloak off with a feeling of relief. A pair of braziers made the tent deliciously warm after outside, and they gave off very little smoke. A touch of sweet scent lingered from the dried herbs that had been sprinkled on the glowing embers.

"The way those fool girls behave, you would think I—" she began in a growl, and cut off abruptly.

She was not surprised to see Siuan standing beside the writing table in plain blue wool, finely cut but simple, a wide tooled-leather folder held to her chest. Most sisters still seemed to believe, like Delana, that she was reduced to instructing Egwene in protocol and running errands, grudgingly in both cases, but she was always there bright and early, which seemed to have gone unnoticed so far. Siuan *had* been an Amyrlin who chewed iron, though no one would believe who did not already know. Novices pointed her out as often as they did Leane, but with an air of doubt that she really was who the sisters said. Pretty, if not quite beautiful, with a delicate mouth and dark glossy hair to her shoulders, Siuan looked even younger than Leane, only a few years older than Egwene. She could have been taken for one of the Accepted without the blue-fringed shawl draped across her arms. That was why she never went without the shawl, to avoid embarrassing mistakes. Her eyes had not changed any more than her spirit, however, and they were icy blue awls aimed at the woman whose presence was a surprise.

Halima was certainly welcome, yet Egwene had not expected to see her stretched out on the brightly colored cushions that were piled along one side of the tent, her head propped on one hand. Where Siuan was pretty, the sort of young woman—seemingly young, at least—who made men and women alike smile at her, Halima was stunning, with big green eyes in a perfect face and a full firm bosom, the sort who made men swallow and other women frown. Not that Egwene frowned, or believed the tales carried by women jealous of the way Halima attracted men just by being. She could not help the way she looked, after all. But even if her position as Delana's secretary was plainly a matter of charity by the Gray sister—a poorly educated country woman, Halima formed her letters with the awkwardness of a young child—Delana usually kept her busy all day with some sort of make-work. She seldom appeared before time for bed, and then it was nearly always because she had heard Egwene had one of her heads. Nisao could do nothing with those headaches, even using the new Healing, but Halima's massages worked wonders even when the pain had Egwene whimpering.

"I told her you wouldn't have time for visits this morning, Mother," Siuan said sharply, still glaring at the woman on the cushions as she took Egwene's cloak with her free hand, "but I might as well have played cat's cradle with myself as opened my mouth." Hanging the cloak on the rustic cloak stand, she snorted contemptuously. "Maybe if I wore breeches and had a mustache, she'd pay mind." Siuan seemed to believe every one of the rumors about Halima's supposed depredations among the prettier craftsmen and soldiers.

Strangely, Halima seemed amused by her reputation. She might even have enjoyed it. She laughed, low and throaty, and stretched on the cushions like a cat. She did have an unfortunate liking for low-cut bodices, incredible in this weather, and she nearly came out of her blue-slashed green silk. Silk was hardly the usual garb for a secretary, but Delana's charity ran deep, or her debt to Halima did.

"You seemed worried this morning, Mother," the green-eyed woman murmured, "and you slipped out so early for your ride, trying not to wake me. I thought you might like to talk. You wouldn't get so many headaches if you talked over your worries more. At least you know you can talk to me." Eyeing Siuan, who was peering down her nose disdainfully, Halima gave another smoky laugh. "And you know I don't want anything from you, unlike some." Siuan snorted again, and deliberately busied herself with placing the folder on the writing table just so between the stone inkwell and the sand jar. She even fiddled with the pen-rest.

With an effort, Egwene managed not to sigh. Just. Halima did ask for nothing beyond a pallet in Egwene's tent, so she could be on hand when one of Egwene's headaches came on, and sleeping there must have given difficulties with carrying out her duties for Delana. Besides, Egwene liked her earthy outspoken manner. It was very easy to talk to Halima and forget for a little while that she was the Amyrlin Seat, a relaxation she could not have even with Siuan. She had fought too hard for recognition as Aes Sedai and Amyrlin, and her grip on that recognition was too tenuous. Every slip from *being* Amyrlin would make the next slip easier, and the next, and the next after that, until she was back to being regarded as a child at play. That made Halima a luxury to be treasured quite apart from what her fingers could do to Egwene's headaches. To her annoyance, though, every other woman in the camp appeared to share Siuan's view, with the possible exception of Delana. The Gray seemed too prudish to employ a lightskirt, no matter what charity she thought she owed. In any case, whether the woman chased men, or even tripped them up, was beside the point now.

"I'm afraid I do have work, Halima," she said, tugging off her gloves. A mountain of work, most days. There was no sign of Sheriam's reports on the table yet, of course, but she would be sending them soon, along with a few petitions she thought merited Egwene's attention. Just a few; ten or twelve appeals for redress of grievances, with Egwene expected to pass the Amyrlin's judgment on each. You could not do that without study, and questions, not and hand down a just decision. "Perhaps you can have dinner with me." If she finished in time to do more than eat at her table right there in her study. It was getting on toward midday already. "We can talk then."

Halima sat up abruptly, eyes flashing and full lips compressed, but her scowl vanished as quickly as it had come. A smoldering remained in her eyes, though. Had she been a cat, she would have had her back arched and her tail like a bottle-brush. Rising gracefully to her feet on the layered carpets, she smoothed her dress over her hips. "Very well, then. If you're certain you don't want me to stay."

With remarkable timing, a dull throb began behind Egwene's eyes, an all too familiar precursor to a blinding headache, but she shook her head anyway and repeated that she had work to do. Halima hesitated a moment longer, her mouth going tight once more, hands fisting in her skirts, then she snatched her fur-lined silk cloak from the cloak stand and stalked out of the tent without bothering to pull the garment around her shoulders. She could do herself an injury going about like that in the cold.

"That fishwife temper will get her in trouble sooner or later," Siuan muttered before the entry flaps stopped swaying. Scowling after Halima, she twitched her shawl up onto her shoulders. "The woman holds it in around you, but she doesn't mind giving me the rough side of her tongue. Me or anybody else. She's been heard screaming at Delana. Who ever heard of a secretary screaming at her employer, and a sister at that? A Sitter! I don't understand why Delana puts up with her."

"That's Delana's business, surely." Questioning another sister's actions was just as forbidden as interfering with them. Only by custom, not law, yet some customs were as strong as law. Surely she did not have to remind *Siuan* of that.

Rubbing her temples, Egwene sat down carefully in the chair behind her writing table, but the chair wobbled anyway. Designed to fold for storage on a wagon, the legs had a habit of folding when they were not supposed to, and none of the carpenters had been able to fix them after repeated attempts. The table folded as well, but that held up more firmly. She wished she had taken the opportunity to acquire a new chair in Murandy, yet there had been so many things that needed buying and not enough coin to stretch when she already had a chair. At least she had acquired a pair of stand-lamps and a table-lamp, all three plain red-painted iron but with good mirrors that were free of bubbles. Good light did not seem to help her headaches, yet it was better than trying to read by a few tallow candles and a lantern.

If Siuan heard any rebuke, it did not slow her down. "It's more than just a temper. Once or twice, I've thought she was on the brink of trying to strike me. I suppose she has sense enough to hold back from that, but not everyone is Aes Sedai. I'm convinced she managed to break a wheelwright's arm somehow. He says he fell, but he looks to be lying to me, with his eyes shifting and his mouth twitching. He wouldn't like admitting a woman bent his elbow backwards, now would he?"

"Give over, Siuan," Egwene said wearily. "The man likely

tried to take liberties." He must have. She could not see how Halima could have broken a man's arm in any event. However you described the woman, muscular did not come into it.

Instead of opening the embossed folder that Siuan had laid on the table, she rested her hands on either side of it. That kept them away from her head. Maybe if she ignored the pain, it would go away this time. Besides, for a change, she had information to share with Siuan. "It seems that some of the Sitters are talking about negotiating with Elaida," she began.

Expressionless, Siuan balanced herself atop one of the two rickety three-legged stools in front of the table and listened attentively, only her fingers moving, lightly stroking against her skirts, until Egwene finished. Then she made fists and growled a set of curses that were pungent even for her, beginning with a wish for the lot of them to choke to death on week-old fish guts and sliding downhill fast from there. Coming from that young, pretty face only made them worse.

"I suppose you're right letting it go forward," she muttered once her invective ran down. "The talk will spread, now it's begun, and this way, you gain a jump on it. Beonin shouldn't surprise me, I suppose. Beonin's ambitious, but I always thought she'd have gone scurrying back to Elaida if Sheriam and the others hadn't stiffened her backbone." Voice quickening, Siuan fixed her eyes on Egwene as if to lend weight to her words. "I wish Varilin and that lot surprised me, Mother. Discounting the Blue, six Sitters from five Ajahs fled the Tower after Elaida carried out her coup," her mouth twisted slightly on the word, "and here we have one from each of those five. I was in *Tel'aran'rhiod* last night, in the Tower—"

"I hope you were careful," Egwene said sharply. Siuan hardly seemed to know the meaning of careful, sometimes. The few dream *ter'angreal* in their possession had lines of sisters panting to use them, mostly to visit the Tower, and while Siuan was not precisely forbidden one, it was the next thing to. She could have put her name down forever without the Hall granting her a single night. Quite aside from the sisters who blamed Siuan for the Tower being broken in the first place—she was not accepted back quite as warmly as Leane, on that account, nor cosseted by anyone—quite aside from that, too many remembered her rough teaching, when she was one of the few who knew how to use the dream *ter'angreal*. Siuan did not suffer fools gladly, and everyone was a fool their first few times in *Tel'aran'rhiod*, so now she had to borrow Leane's turn when she wanted to visit the World of Dreams, and if another sister saw her there, 'the next thing to' might become an outright ban. Or worse, set off a search for who had loaned her a *ter'angreal*, which might end by unmasking Leane.

"In *Tel'aran'rhiod*," Siuan said with a dismissive gesture, "I'm a different woman in a different dress every time I turn a corner." That was good to hear, though it seemed likely a lack of control had as much to do with it as intent. Siuan's belief in her own abilities was sometimes greater than warranted. "The point is, last night I saw a partial list of Sitters and managed to read most of the names before it changed to a tally of wines." That was a common occurrence in *Tel'aran'rhiod*, where nothing stayed the same for long unless it was a reflection of something permanent in the waking world. "Andaya Forae was raised for the Gray, Rina Hafden for the Green, and Juilaine Madome for the Brown. None has worn the shawl more than seventy years at most. Elaida has the same problem we do, Mother."

"I see," Egwene said slowly. She realized that she was massaging the side of her head. The throb behind her eyes beat on. It would grow stronger. It always did. By nightfall, she was going to regret having sent Halima away. Bringing her hand down firmly, she moved the leather folder in front of her a half inch to the left, then slid it back. "What of the rest? They had six Sitters to replace."

"Ferane Neheran was raised for the White," Siuan admitted, "and Suana Dragand for the Yellow. They've both been in the Hall before. It was only a partial list, and I didn't get to read it all." Her back straightened, and her chin shot out stubbornly. "One or two raised before time would be unusual enough—it happens, but not often—but this makes eleven—maybe twelve, but eleven for sure—between us and the Tower. I don't believe in coincidences that big. When the fishmongers are all buying at the same price, you can bet they were all drinking at the same inn last night."

"You don't have to convince me any more, Siuan." With a sigh, Egwene sat back, automatically catching the chair leg that always tried to fold when she did that. Clearly, something odd was happening, but what did it mean? And who could influence the choice of Sitters in *every* Ajah? Every Ajah except the Blue, at least; they had chosen one new Sitter, but Moria had been Aes Sedai well over a hundred years. And maybe the Red was not affected; no one knew what changes if any had been made in the Red Sitters. The Black might be behind it, but what could they gain, unless all of those too-young Sitters *were* Black? That seemed impossible in any case; if the Black Ajah had had that much influence, the Hall would have been all Darkfriends long ago. Yet if there was a pattern and coincidence would not hold, then *someone* had to be at the heart of it. Just thinking about the possibilities, the impossibilities, made the dull pain behind her eyes grow a little sharper.

"If this turns out to be happenstance after all, Siuan, you're going to regret ever thinking you saw a puzzle." She forced a smile saying that, to take out any sting. An Amyrlin had to be careful with her words. "Now that you've convinced me there is a puzzle, I want you to solve it. Who is responsible, and what are they after? Until we know that, we don't know anything."

"Is that all you want?" Siuan said dryly. "Before supper, or after?"

"After will have to do, I suppose," Egwene snapped, then took a deep breath at the abashed look on the other woman's face. There was no point taking her headache out on Siuan. An Amyrlin's words had power, and sometimes consequences; she had to remember that. "As soon as you can would be very good, though," she said in a milder voice. "I know you'll be as quick as you can."

Chagrined or not, Siuan seemed to understand that Egwene's outburst came from more than her own sarcasm. Despite her youthful appearance, she had years of practice at reading faces. "Shall I go find Halima?" she said, half rising. The lack of tartness attached to the woman's name was a measure of her concern. "It won't take a minute."

"If I give way for every ache, I'll never get anything done," Egwene said, opening the folder. "Now, what do you have for me today?" She kept her hands on the papers, though, to stop from rubbing her head.

One of Siuan's tasks each morning was to fetch what the

Ajahs were willing to share from their networks of eyes-and-ears, along with whatever individual sisters had passed on to their Ajahs and the Ajahs had decided to pass on to Egwene. It was a strange process of sieving, yet it still gave a fair picture of the world when added to what Siuan put in. She had managed to hold on to the agents that had been hers as Amyrlin by the simple expedient of refusing to tell anyone who they were despite every effort by the Hall, and in the end, no one could gainsay that those eyes-and-ears were the Amyrlin's, and that they should by rights report to Egwene. Oh, there had been no end of grumbling over it, and still was on occasion, but no one could deny the facts.

As usual, the first report came from neither the Ajahs nor Siuan, but Leane, written on thin sheets of paper in a flowing elegant hand. Egwene could not see exactly why, but you could never doubt that anything Leane wrote had been written by a woman. Those pages Egwene held to the table-lamp's flame one by one as soon as she read them, letting the paper burn almost to her fingers, then crumpling the ash. It would hardly do for her and Leane to behave like near-strangers in public then allow one of her reports to fall into the wrong hands.

Very few sisters were aware that Leane had eyes-and-ears inside Tar Valon itself. She might have been the only sister who did. It was a human failing to watch keenly what was happening down the street while ignoring what lay right at your feet, and the Light knew Aes Sedai had as many human failings as anyone else. Unfortunately, Leane had little new to communicate.

Her people in the city complained of filthy streets that were increasingly dangerous after dark and little safer by daylight. Once crime had been all but unknown in Tar Valon, but now the Tower Guards had abandoned the streets to patrol the harbors and the bridge towers. Except for collecting the customs duties and buying supplies, both done through intermediaries, the White Tower seemed to have shut itself off from the city completely. The great doors that allowed the public to enter the Tower remained shut and barred, and no one had seen a sister outside the Tower to know her as Aes Sedai since the siege began, if not earlier. All confirmation of what Leane had reported before. The last page made Egwene's eyebrows rise, though. Rumor in the streets said

Gareth Bryne had found a secret way into the city and would appear inside the walls with his whole army any day.

"Leane would have said if anyone had breathed a word that sounded like they meant gateways," Siuan said quickly when she saw Egwene's expression. She had read all of these reports already, of course, and knew what Egwene was seeing by which page she held. Shifting on the unsteady stool, Siuan almost fell off onto the carpets, she was paying so little heed. It did not slow her down a hair, though. "And you can be sure Gareth hasn't let anything slip," she went on while still righting herself. "Not that any of his soldiers are fool enough to desert to the city now, but he knows when to keep his mouth shut. He just has the reputation for attacking where he can't possibly be. He's done the impossible often enough that people expect him to. That's all."

Hiding a smile, Egwene held the paper mentioning Lord Gareth to the flame and watched it curl and blacken. A few months past, Siuan would have offered an acid comment about the man instead of praise. He would have been "Gareth bloody Bryne," not Gareth. She could not possibly miss doing his laundry and polishing his boots, but Egwene had seen her staring at him on those rare times when he came to the Aes Sedai camp. Staring, and then running away if he so much as glanced at her. Siuan! Running away! Siuan had been Aes Sedai for more than twenty years, and Amyrlin for ten, but she had no more idea how to deal with being in love than a duck had about shearing sheep.

Egwene crumbled the ash and dusted her hands together, her smile fading. She had no room to talk about Siuan. She was in love, too, but she did not even know where in the world Gawyn was, or what to do if she learned. He had his duty to Andor, and she hers to the Tower. And the one way to bridge that chasm, bonding him, might lead to his death. Better to let him go, forget him entirely. As easy as forgetting her own name. And she *would* bond him. She knew that. Of course, she could not bond the man without knowing where he was, without having her hands on him, so it all came full circle. Men were . . . a *bother*!

Pausing to press her fingers against her temples—it did nothing to lessen the pulsing pain—she put Gawyn out of her mind. As far out as she could. She thought she had a foretaste of what it was like having a Warder; there was always something of Gawyn in the back of her head. And liable to kick its way into her consciousness at the most inconvenient time. Concentrating on the business at hand, she picked up the next sheet.

Much of the world had vanished, as far as eyes-and-ears were concerned. Little news came from the lands held by the Seanchan, and that divided between fanciful descriptions of Seanchan beasts delivered as proof they were using Shadowspawn, horrifying tales of women being tested to see whether they should be collared as *damane,* and depressing stories of ... acceptance. The Seanchan, it seemed, were no worse rulers than any others and better than some—as long as you were not a woman who could channel—and all too many people appeared to have given up thoughts of resistance once it became clear the Seanchan would let them go on with their lives. Arad Doman was almost as bad, producing nothing but rumors, admitted as such by the sisters who wrote the reports but included just to show the state the country was in. King Alsalam was dead. No, he had begun channeling and gone mad. Rodel Ituralde, the Great Captain, also was dead, or he had usurped the throne, or was invading Saldaea. The Council of Merchants were all dead, as well, or had fled the country, or begun a civil war over who the next king was to be. Any of those might have been true. Or none. The Ajahs were accustomed to seeing everything, but now a third of the world had been enveloped in dense fog, with only the tiniest gaps. At least, if there were any clearer views, no Ajah had deigned to pass on what they saw there.

Another problem was that the Ajahs saw different things as having paramount importance, and largely ignored anything else. The Greens, for example, were particularly concerned over tales of Borderland armies near New Braem, hundreds of leagues from the Blight they were supposed to be guarding. Their report talked of the Borderlanders and only the Borderlanders, as if something had to be done and done now. Not that they suggested anything, or so much as hinted, yet frustrations came through in the cramped, hasty handwriting that spidered urgently across the page.

Egwene had the truth of that situation from Elayne, but she was content to let the Greens gnash their teeth for the moment, since Siuan had revealed why they were not rushing off to set matters straight. According to her agent in New Braem, the Borderlanders were accompanied by fifty or a hundred sisters, perhaps two hundred. The number of Aes Sedai might be uncertain, and it must be wildly inflated, of course, but their presence was a fact the Greens had to be aware of, though the reports they sent to Egwene never mentioned them. No Ajah had mentioned those sisters in their reports. In the end, though, there was little difference between two hundred sisters and two. No one could be certain who those sisters were or why they were there, yet poking a nose in would surely be seen as interfering. It seemed strange that they could be engaged in a war between Aes Sedai and still be held back from interfering with another sister by custom, but thankfully, it was so.

"At least they don't suggest sending anyone to Caemlyn." Egwene blinked, the pain behind her eyes sharpened by following the tight letters.

Siuan gave a derisive snort. "Why should they? As far as they know, Elayne is letting Merilille and Vandene guide her, so they're sure they'll get their Aes Sedai queen, and a Green at that. Besides, as long as the Asha'man stay out of Caemlyn, no one wants to take the chance of stirring them up. The way things stand, we might as well try pulling wasp-jellies out of the water with our bare hands, and even the Greens know it. Anyway, that won't stop some sister, Green or otherwise, from dropping into Caemlyn. Just a quiet visit to see one of her eyes-and-ears. Or to have a dress made, or buy a saddle, or the Light knows why else."

"*Even* the Greens?" Egwene said tartly. Everyone thought of Browns being this way and Whites that, even when it was demonstrably not so, yet sometimes she bristled a little at hearing Greens lumped together as if they were all the same woman. Maybe she did think of herself as a Green, or as having been one, which was silly. The Amyrlin was of all Ajahs and none—she adjusted the stole on her shoulders, reminding herself of the fact represented by those seven stripes—and she had never belonged to one in the first place. Yet she did feel a—not fondness; that was too strong—a sense of *sameness* between herself and Green sisters. "How many sisters are unaccounted for, Siuan? Even the weakest can Travel wherever they want, linked, and I wish I knew where they went."

For a moment, Siuan frowned in thought. "About twenty, I think," she said finally. "Maybe a few less. The number changes day to day. No one keeps track, really. No sister would stand still for it." She leaned forward, carefully balancing herself this time when the uneven legs made her stool lurch. "You've juggled matters beautifully, so far, Mother, but it can't last. Eventually, the Hall will find out everything that's going on in Caemlyn. They might accept keeping the Seanchan prisoners secret—that will be seen as Vandene's business, or Merilille's—but they already know there are Sea Folk in Caemlyn, and they'll learn about the bargain with them sooner or later. And the Kin, if not your plans for them." Siuan snorted again, though faintly. She was not certain how she herself felt about the idea of Aes Sedai retiring into the Kin, much less how other sisters would take to the notion. "My eyes-and-ears haven't picked up a glimmer, yet, but somebody's will, as sure as certain. You can't delay much longer, or we'll find ourselves wading through a school of silverpike."

"One of these days," Egwene muttered, "I'll have to see these silverpike you're always talking about." She held up a hand as the other woman opened her mouth. "One day. The agreement with the Sea Folk will cause problems," she confessed, "but when the Ajahs hear hints, they won't realize right away what they're hearing. Sisters teaching Sea Folk in Caemlyn? It's unheard of, but who is going to ask questions or interfere, against all custom? I'm sure there will be all sorts of grumbling, maybe some questions called in the Hall, but before it comes out that there *is* a bargain, I will have introduced my plan for the Kin."

"You think *that* won't sharpen their teeth?" Shifting her shawl, Siuan barely bothered to hide her incredulity. In fact, she scowled with it.

"It will cause argument," Egwene allowed judiciously. A considerable understatement. It would cause an uproar was what it would do, once the whole was known. Likely as close to a riot as had ever been seen among Aes Sedai. But the Tower had been dwindling for a thousand years now, if not more, and she planned to put an end to that. "But I do intend to go slowly. Aes Sedai may be reluctant to talk about age, Siuan, but they'll figure out soon enough that swearing on the Oath Rod shortens our lives by half at least. No one *wants* to die before they must."

"If they're convinced there really is a Kinswoman who's six hundred years old," Siuan said in grudging tones, and Egwene sighed with vexation. That was another thing the other woman was uncertain about, the Kin's claims of longevity. She valued Siuan's advice, valued that she did not just say what Egwene wanted to hear, but at times the woman seemed to drag her heels as hard as Romanda or Lelaine.

"If need be, Siuan," she said irritably, "I'll just let the sisters talk to a few women a hundred years or more older than any of them. They may try to dismiss them as wilders and liars, but Reanne Corly can prove she was in the Tower, and when. So can others. With luck, I'll convince the sisters to accept being freed of the Three Oaths so they can retire into the Kin before they ever learn there's a bargain with the Atha'an Miere. And once they accept *any* sister being freed of the Oaths, it won't be nearly as hard to convince them to let the Sea Folk sisters go. Beside that, the rest of that agreement is small turnips. As you keep saying, skill and a deft hand are necessary to get anything done in the Hall, but luck is absolutely required. Well, I'll be as skillful and deft as I can be, and as for luck, the odds seem to be in my favor for once."

Siuan grimaced and hemmed and hawed, but she had to agree in the end. She even agreed that Egwene might pull it off, with luck, and timing. Not that she was convinced about the Kin or the agreement with the Atha'an Miere either one, but what Egwene proposed was so unprecedented that it seemed the greater part of it might pass the Hall before they realized what was falling on them. Egwene was willing to settle for that. Whatever was laid before the Hall, almost always enough Sitters stood in opposition to make finding a consensus hard work at best, and nothing was done in the Hall without at least the lesser consensus and usually not without the greater. It seemed to her that most dealings with the Hall consisted of convincing them to do what they did not want to. There was certainly no reason for this to be any different.

While the Greens concentrated on the Borderlanders, the Grays focused south at present. Every Ajah was fascinated by the reports from Illian and Tear of large numbers of wilders among the Sea Folk, which they found interesting, if true, though there seemed strong doubt that it could be true, or else sisters would have known about it before this. After all, how could such a thing be hidden? No one mentioned that they had just accepted what they saw on the surface and never looked deeper. The Grays, though, were fascinated by the continued Seanchan threat to Illian and the recently begun siege of the Stone of Tear. Wars and threats of war always mesmerized Grays, since they were dedicated to ending strife. And to extending their influence, of course; every time the Grays stopped a war with a treaty, they increased the influence of all Aes Sedai, but of Grays most of all. The Seanchan seemed beyond negotiation, however, at least by Aes Sedai, and the Grays' outraged sense of being thwarted came through in curt words about Seanchan incursions across the border and the increasing forces being gathered by Lord Gregorin, the Steward in Illian for the Dragon Reborn, a title that was a matter of some concern in itself. Tear had its own Steward for the Dragon Reborn, the High Lord Darlin Sisnera, and he was besieged in the Stone by nobles who refused to accept Rand. It was a very strange siege. The Stone had its own docks and Darlin's enemies could not cut off supplies even holding the rest of the city as they did, and they seemed content to sit and wait in any event. Or perhaps they just could not see what to do next. Only the Aiel had ever taken the Stone by assault, and no one had ever starved it out. The Grays had some hopes in Tear.

Egwene's head came up as she read to the bottom of the page, and she hurriedly set that page down and picked up the next. The Grays had had some hopes. Apparently, a Gray sister had been recognized coming out of the Stone, and followed to a meeting with High Lord Tedosian and High Lady Estanda, two of the most prominent among the besiegers. "Merana," she breathed. "They say it was Merana Ambrey, Siuan." Unconsciously, she massaged her temple. The pain behind her eyes had ratcheted a little higher.

"She may do some good." Rising, Siuan crossed the carpets to a small table against the tent wall, where several mismatched cups and two pitchers sat on a tray. The silver pitcher held spiced wine, the blue-glazed pottery tea, both set there at first light against the Amyrlin's arrival and both long since gone cold. No one had expected Egwene to go riding off to the river. "As long as Tedosian and the others don't realize who she's really working for." Siuan's shawl slipped off one shoulder as she felt the side of the pottery pitcher, and the light of *saidar* surrounded her briefly as she channeled Fire, warming the contents. "They won't trust her to negotiate in good faith if they find out she's the Dragon Reborn's creature." Filling a polished pewter cup with tea, she added generous dollops from the honey jar, stirring it in well, and brought the cup back to Egwene. "This might help your head. It's some sort of herb concoction Chesa found, but honey cuts the taste."

Egwene took a cautious sip, and set the cup down with a shudder. If it tasted that sharp with honey, she did not want to imagine it without. The headache might be better. "How can you take this so calmly, Siuan? Merana turning up in Tear is the first real proof we've had. I'll take your Sitters as coincidence before that."

In the beginning, there had only been whispers, from the Ajahs or from Siuan's eyes-and-ears. There were Aes Sedai in Cairhien, and they seemed to move freely in and out of the Sun Palace while the Dragon Reborn was there. Then the whispers grew hoarse and uneasy, hesitant. The eyes-and-ears in Cairhien did not want to say it. No one wanted to repeat what their agents said. There were Aes Sedai in Cairhien, and they seemed to be following the orders of the Dragon Reborn. Worse were the names that trickled out. Some were women who had been in Salidar, among the first to resist Elaida, while others were women known to be loyal to Elaida. No one had mentioned Compulsion aloud that Egwene knew of, but they had to be thinking it.

"No use pulling your hair when the wind isn't blowing the way you want," Siuan replied, taking her stool again. She started to cross her knees, but hastily put both feet back on the carpet when her stool tilted. Muttering under her breath, she adjusted her shawl with a twitch of her shoulders. And was forced to balance against another lurch. "You have to trim your sails to take advantage of how the wind *is* blowing. Think coolly, and you make it back to shore. Get your neck hot, and you'll drown." Sometimes, Siuan could sound as if she still worked a fishing boat. "I believe you need more than one sip for that to do any good, Mother."

With a grimace, Egwene pushed the cup a little farther from her. The taste clinging to her tongue was at least as bad as her headache. "Siuan, if you see a way to make use of this, I wish you'd tell me. I don't even want to think about *using* the fact that Rand may have Compelled sisters. I don't want to think about the possibility that he could have." Neither about the possibility that he knew such a repulsive weave, or that he could lay that weave on anyone. She knew it—another little gift from Moghedien—and she very much wished she could forget how to make it.

"In this case, it isn't so much a matter of using as figuring out the effects. He'll have to be dealt with eventually, and maybe taught a lesson, but you don't want sisters flying off after him now, and these tales out of Cairhien make everyone cautious." Siuan's voice was calm enough, but she fidgeted, clearly agitated inwardly. It was nothing any Aes Sedai could speak of *too* calmly. "At the same time, once everyone thinks it through, they'll realize this makes nonsense out of those stories about him submitting to Elaida. She might have sent sisters to watch over him, but they wouldn't accept sisters who want to pull Elaida down. Realizing that will put a little backbone in those who've started thinking maybe Elaida has him on a lead. That's one less reason for anyone to consider yielding to her."

"What about Cadsuane?" Egwene said. Of all the names coming out of Cairhien, that one had sent the most shock through the sisters. Cadsuane Melaidhrin was a legend, and there were as many disapproving versions of the legend as approving. Some sisters had been sure it must be a mistake; Cadsuane must be dead by now. Others just appeared to wish she were dead. "Are you certain she remained in Cairhien after Rand disappeared?"

"I made sure my people kept an eye on her as soon as I heard her name," Siuan said, no longer sounding at all calm. "I don't know she's a Darkfriend, I just suspect, but I can guarantee that she was in the Sun Palace a week after he vanished."

Squeezing her eyes shut, Egwene pressed the heels of her palms against her lids. That hardly seemed to affect the pulsing needle in her head. Maybe Rand was in company with a Black sister, or had been. Maybe he had used Compulsion on Aes Sedai. Bad enough on anyone, but somehow worse used on Aes Sedai, more ominous. What was dared against Aes Sedai was ten times, a hundred times, as likely to be used against those who could not defend themselves. Eventually they would have to deal with him, somehow. She had grown up with Rand, yet she could not allow that to influence her. He was the Dragon Reborn, now, the hope of the world and at the same time maybe the single greatest threat the world faced. Maybe? The Seanchan could not do as much damage as the Dragon Reborn. And she was going to *use* the possibility that he had Compelled sisters. The Amyrlin Seat really was a different woman from that innkeeper's daughter.

Scowling at the pewter cup of so-called tea, she picked it up and made herself drink the vile stuff down, gagging and spluttering the whole way. Perhaps the taste would take her mind off her headache, at least.

As she set the cup down with a sharp clink of metal on wood, Anaiya pushed into the tent, mouth turned down and a frown creasing her plain face.

"Akarrin and the others have returned, Mother," she said. "Moria told me to inform you she has called the Hall to hear their report."

"So have Escaralde and Malind," Morvrin announced, coming in behind Anaiya with Myrelle. The Green seemed an image of serene fury, if that was possible, her olive face smooth and her eyes like dark embers, but Morvrin wore a scowl to make Anaiya look pleased. "They're sending novices and Accepted running to find all the Sitters," the Brown said. "We can't catch a whisper of what Akarrin found, but I think Escaralde and the others intend to use it to prod the Hall toward something."

Peering at the dark dregs floating in a few drops in the bottom of the pewter cup, Egwene sighed. She would have to be there, too, and now she would have to face the Sitters with a headache *and* that awful taste in her mouth. Perhaps she could call it a penance for what she was going to do to the Hall.

CHAPTER
19

Surprises

By custom, the Amyrlin was informed of the Hall sitting, yet nothing said they had to wait for her before starting the session, which meant that time might be short. Egwene wanted to leap to her feet and march straight to the big pavilion before Moria and the other two could spring whatever surprise they intended. Surprises in the Hall were seldom good. Surprises you learned about late were worse. Still, protocols that were law, not custom, had to be followed for the Amyrlin entering the Hall, so she remained where she was and sent Siuan to fetch Sheriam so she could be announced properly by the Keeper of the Chronicles. Siuan had told her that was really a matter of warning the Sitters of her presence—there were always matters they might want to discuss without the Amyrlin knowing—and she had not sounded entirely as if she were making a joke.

In any case, there was no point in going to the Hall until she could enter. Tamping down her impatience, she propped her head on her hands and massaged her temples as she tried to read a little more of the Ajah reports. Despite the vile "tea," or perhaps because of it, her headache made the words shimmer on the page every time she blinked, and Anaiya and the other two did not help.

No sooner did Siuan depart than Anaiya tossed back her cloak, settling on the stool Siuan had vacated—it did not seem to lurch under her, uneven legs or no—and began to speculate on what Moria and the others were after. She was not a flighty woman, so her ventures were quite constrained given the circumstances. Constrained, but no less upsetting for that.

"Frightened people do silly things, Mother, even Aes Sedai," she murmured, placing her hands on her knees, "but at least you can be sure Moria will be firm about Elaida, at least in the long run. She lays every sister who died after Siuan was deposed right at Elaida's feet. Moria wants Elaida birched for every single death before she goes to the headsman. A hard woman, harder than Lelaine in some ways. Tougher, anyway. She won't scruple at things that might make Lelaine balk. I'm very much afraid she will press for an assault on the city as soon as possible. If the Forsaken are moving so openly, on such a scale, then better a wounded Tower that's whole than a Tower divided. At least, I fear that's how Moria may see things. After all, however much we want to avoid sisters killing sisters, it wouldn't be the first time. The Tower has lasted a long time, and healed from many wounds. We can heal from this one, too."

Anaiya's voice suited her face, warm and patient and comforting, but making those remarks it seemed like fingernails screeching down a slat. Light, for all Anaiya saying this was what she feared out of Moria, she seemed much in accord with the sentiments. She was deliberate, unflappable, and never careless with words. If she favored an assault, how many others did, too?

As usual, Myrelle was anything but constrained. Mercurial and fiery described her best. She would not know patience if it bit her on the nose. She paced back and forth, as much as the confines of the tent allowed, kicking her deep-green skirts and sometimes kicking one of the bright cushions piled against the wall before turning to make another round. "If Moria is frightened enough to press for an assault, then she's frightened out of her wits. A Tower too wounded to stand alone won't be able to face the Forsaken or anyone else. Malind is who should concern you. She's always pointing out that Tarmon Gai'don could be upon us any day. I've heard her say that what we felt could well have been the opening blows of the Last Battle. *And* that it might happen here, next. Where better for the Shadow to strike than Tar Valon? Malind has never been afraid to make hard choices, or to retreat when she thought it necessary.

She would abandon Tar Valon *and* the Tower at once if she thought it would preserve at least some of us for Tarmon Gai'don. *She* will propose lifting the siege, fleeing somewhere the Forsaken can't find us until we're ready to strike back. If she puts the question to the Hall in the right way, she might even get the greater consensus in support." The very thought made the words dance harder on the page in front of Egwene.

Morvrin, her round face unrelenting, simply planted fists on ample hips and met each suggestion with a curt answer. "We don't know enough yet to be sure it was the Forsaken," and "You can't know until she says." "Perhaps it was, and perhaps not," and "Supposition isn't evidence." It was said she would not believe it was morning till she saw the sun for herself. Her firm voice brooked no nonsense, especially jumps to conclusions. It was not soothing to an aching head, either. She was not opposing the suggestions, really, just keeping an open mind. An open mind could go either way when it came down to the sticking point.

Egwene slapped the embossed folder shut on the reports with a loud smack. Between the disgusting taste on her tongue and the sharp throb in her head—not to mention their incessant voices!—she could not keep her place to read anyway. The three sisters looked at her in surprise. She had made it clear long ago that she was in charge, but she tried not to show temper. Oaths of fealty or no oaths of fealty, a young woman displaying temper was too easy to dismiss as sulky. Which only made her angrier, which made her head hurt more, which . . .

"I've waited long enough," she said, making an effort to keep her voice smooth. Her head gave it a slight edge of sharpness anyway. Perhaps Sheriam thought she was supposed to meet her at the Hall.

Gathering her cloak, she strode out into the cold while still swinging it around her shoulders, and Morvrin and the other two hesitated only a moment before following in her wake. Accompanying her to the Hall might seem a little like they were her entourage, but they *were* supposed to be watching her, and she suspected that even Morvrin was eager to hear what Akarrin had to report and what Moria and the rest intended to fashion from it.

Nothing too difficult to deal with, Egwene hoped, nothing like what Anaiya and Myrelle thought. If necessary, she could try applying the Law of War, but even if that was successful, ruling by edict had its disadvantages. When people *had* to obey you in one thing, they always found ways to wriggle away on others, and the more they were forced to obey, the more places they found for wriggling away. It was a natural balance you could not escape. Worse, she had learned just how addictive it was to have people jump when she spoke. You came to take it as the natural way of things, and then when they failed to jump, you were caught on the wrong foot. Besides, with her head pounding—it *was* pounding, now, not throbbing, though perhaps not as sharply—with her head, she was ready to snap at anyone who looked at her crosswise, and even when people had to swallow it, that never went down well.

The sun stood straight overhead, a golden ball in a blue sky with a scattering of white clouds, but it gave no warmth, only wan shadows and a glitter to the snow wherever it remained untrampled. The air felt as chill as it had by the river. Egwene ignored the cold, refused to let it touch her, but only the dead could have been unaware, with everyone's breath misting white in front of their faces. It was time for the midday meal, yet there was no possibility of feeding so many novices at once, so Egwene and her escort still moved through a wave of white-clad women leaping out of their way and starting to curtsy in the street. She set such a pace that they were usually past before the knots of novices could more than spread their skirts.

It was not a long way, with only four places that they needed to wade across the muddy streets. There had been talk of wooden bridges, tall enough to ride under, but bridges suggested a permanence to the camp that no one wanted. Even the sisters who spoke of them never pressed to have them built. Which left wading slowly, and taking care to keep your skirts and cloak high if you were not to arrive filthy to your knees. At least the remaining crowds vanished as they approached the Hall. That stood alone as always, or nearly so.

Nisao and Carlinya were already waiting in front of the big canvas pavilion with its patched side curtains, the tiny Yellow fretting her underlip with her teeth and eyeing Egwene anxiously. Carlinya was calmness itself, cool-eyed, hands folded at her waist. Except that she had forgotten her cloak, mud stained the scroll-embroidered hem of her pale skirt, and her cap of dark curls badly needed a comb. Making their courtesies, the pair joined Anaiya and the other two, a little distance behind Egwene. The lot of them murmured softly, the snatches that Egwene caught innocuous, about the weather, or how long they might have to wait. This was no place for them to seem too closely associated with her.

Beonin came down the walk at a run, her hurried breath misting, and skidded to a halt, staring at Egwene before joining the others. The strain around her blue-gray eyes was even more apparent than earlier. Perhaps she thought this would affect her negotiations. But she *knew* the talks would be a sham, just a ploy to gain time. Egwene controlled her breathing and practiced novice exercises, yet none of it helped her head. It never did.

There was no sign of Sheriam among the tents in any direction, but they were not precisely alone on the walkway outside the pavilion. Akarrin and the five other sisters who had gone with her, one from each Ajah, were waiting in a cluster on the other side of the entrance. Most offered curtsies to Egwene distractedly, yet kept their distance. Perhaps they had been warned to say nothing to anyone until they spoke before the Hall. Egwene could simply have demanded their report on the spot, of course. They might even have given it, to the Amyrlin. Likely they would have. On the other hand, an Amyrlin's relations with the Ajahs were always delicate, often including the Ajah she had been raised from. Nearly as delicate as relations with the Hall. Egwene made herself smile and bow her head graciously. If she gritted her teeth behind that smile, well, that helped keep her mouth shut.

Not all of the sisters seemed aware of her presence. Akarrin, slender in plain brown wool and a cloak with surprisingly elaborate green embroidery, was staring at nothing, nodding to herself now and then. Apparently she was practicing what she would say inside. Akarrin was not strong in the Power, little more than Siuan if at all, but only one other of the six, Therva, a slim woman in yellow-slashed riding skirts and a cloak edged with yellow, stood even as high as she. That was a distressing measure of just how frightened the sisters were by that strange beacon of *saidar*. The strongest should have stepped forward for the task that had been given to these, but except for Akarrin herself, zeal had been notably lacking. Her companions still appeared less than enthusiastic. Shana normally maintained a deep reserve despite eyes that made her appear constantly startled, but now they seemed ready to come out of her head with worry. She peered at the entrance to the Hall, closed off by heavy flaps, and her hands fiddled with her cloak as if she could not keep them still. Reiko, a stout Arafellin Blue, kept her eyes down, but the silver bells in her long dark hair chimed faintly as if she were shaking her head inside her cowl. Only Therva's long-nosed face wore a look of absolute serenity, completely unperturbed and unshakable, yet that in itself was a bad sign. The Yellow sister was excitable by nature. What had they seen? What *were* Moria and the other two Sitters after?

Egwene controlled her impatience; the Hall plainly was not sitting yet. It was gathering, but several Sitters strolled past her and into the big pavilion, none hurrying. Salita hesitated as if she might speak, but then only dipped her knees before raising her yellow-fringed shawl onto her shoulders and sweeping inside. Kwamesa peered down her sharp nose at Egwene while making her curtsy, and peered down her nose while studying Anaiya and the others briefly, but then, the slim Gray peered down her nose at everyone. She was not tall, but she tried to seem so. Berana, face a mask of haughtiness and big brown eyes as cold as the snow, paused to offer cool courtesies to Egwene and frown at Akarrin. After a long moment, perhaps realizing that Akarrin did not even see her, she smoothed her silver-embroidered white skirts, which did not need it, adjusted her shawl along her arms so the white fringe hung just so, and glided through the entry flaps as though she just happened to be going in that direction. All three were among the Sitters Siuan had pointed out as too young. As were Malind and Escaralde. But Moria had been Aes Sedai for a hundred and thirty years. Light, Siuan had her looking for conspiracies in everything!

Just as Egwene began to think that her head would explode from frustration if not from her headache, Sheriam suddenly appeared, hiking her cloak and skirts while half-running across the dirty slush of the street. "I'm terribly sorry, Mother," she said breathlessly, channeling hurriedly to clean off the mud she had splashed on herself. It fell to the walkway in a dry powder when she twitched her skirts. "I . . . I heard that the Hall was sitting, and I knew you would be looking for me, so I came as fast as I could. I'm very sorry." So Siuan was still searching for her.

"You're here now," Egwene said firmly. The woman must have been truly upset to offer apologies in front of the others, Akarrin and her companions more than Anaiya and the rest. Even when people knew better, they tended to take you for what you appeared to be, and the Keeper should not be seen apologizing and wringing her hands. Surely she knew that. "Go ahead and announce me."

Drawing a deep breath, Sheriam pushed back the hood of her cloak, adjusted her narrow blue stole, and stepped through the entry flaps. Her voice rang out clearly in the ritual phrases. "She comes, she comes. . . ."

Egwene barely waited for her to finish with ". . . the Flame of Tar Valon, the Amyrlin Seat," before striding in through the ring of braziers and stand-lamps that rimmed the pavilion's walls. The stand-lamps gave a good light, and the braziers, giving off a scent of lavender today, warmed the whole space. No one wished to have to ignore the cold when she could feel real warmth.

The arrangement of the pavilion followed ancient rules, modified only slightly to allow for the fact that they were not meeting in the White Tower, in the great circular chamber called the Hall of the Tower. At the far end, a simple if well polished bench stood atop a box-like platform covered with cloth striped in the seven colors of the Ajahs. That and the stole around Egwene's neck were surely the only places in the camp where the Red Ajah had any representation. Some Blues had wanted the color removed, since Elaida apparently had had the actual throne called the Amyrlin Seat repainted and a stole woven without blue, but Egwene had dug in her heels. If she was to be of all Ajahs and none, then she would be of *all* Ajahs. Down the bright layered carpets that served as a ground-cloth, two lines of benches slanted away from the entrance in groups of three, sitting atop cloth-covered boxes in the colors of the Ajahs. Well, six of the Ajahs. By tradition, the two oldest Sitters could claim the places closest to the Amyrlin Seat for their Ajahs, so Yellow and Blue held those spots here. After that, it was a matter of who came first and wished to be seated where, the first arrival always choosing her Ajah's place.

There were only nine Sitters present, too few for the Hall to be sitting yet, legally speaking, but an oddity in the seating struck Egwene right away. Unsurprisingly, Romanda was already in place, an empty bench between her and Salita, and Lelaine and Moria occupied the end benches of the Blue. Romanda, her hair in a tight gray bun on the nape of her neck, was the oldest Sitter, and almost always the first to reach her place when the Hall sat. Lelaine, next oldest despite her dark glossy hair, seemed unable to let the other woman gain a jump on her even in something so small. The men who had shifted the boxes—they were stored along the walls until the Hall was called to sit—must have just left through the back, because Kwamesa, already seated on her bench, was the only Gray Sitter in evidence, and Berana, just climbing to hers, the only White. But Malind, a round-faced Kandori with an eagle's eyes, and the lone Green, obviously had entered ahead of them, yet strangely, she had chosen to seat the Greens near the pavilion's entrance. The nearer the Amyrlin Seat the better, was the usual thing. And directly opposite her, Escaralde stood in front of the brown-covered boxes, in hushed argument with Takima. Almost as short as Nisao, Takima was a quiet bird-like woman, but she could be forceful when she wished, and with her fists on her hips she looked a sparrow in a temper, feathers all puffed out to make her seem larger. By the way she kept darting sharp looks toward Berana, the seating was what upset her. It was too late for anything to be changed for this sitting, of course, but in any case, Escaralde loomed back at Takima as if she expected to have to fight for her choice. It amazed Egwene how Escaralde could do that. Loom, that was. She stood inches shorter even than Nisao. It must have been sheer force of will. Escaralde never backed down when she thought she was in the right. And she always did think she was in the right. If Moria really did want an immediate assault on Tar Valon, and Malind really wanted to retreat, what did Escaralde want?

For all Siuan's talk of Sitters wanting to be warned, Egwene's entrance caused no great stir. For whatever reasons

Malind and the others had called the Hall to hear Akarrin's report, they had not considered the matter so sensitive that it needed to be held for Sitters' ears alone, so little clusters of four or five Aes Sedai were standing behind the benches of their Ajah's Sitters, and they made their curtsies as Egwene walked down the carpets toward her own seat. The Sitters themselves merely watched her, or perhaps inclined a head briefly. Lelaine eyed her coolly, then returned to frowning faintly at Moria, a quite ordinary-appearing woman in plain blue wool. So ordinary, in fact, that you could miss the ageless quality in her face at first glance. She sat staring straight ahead, absorbed in her own thoughts. Romanda was one of those to tilt her head a fraction. Inside the Hall, the Amyrlin Seat was still the Amyrlin Seat, but a little less so than outside it. Inside the Hall, Sitters felt their power. In a way, the Amyrlin could be said to be only the first among equals, inside the Hall. Well, perhaps a little more than that, but not by much. Siuan said as many Amyrlins had failed by believing the Sitters were fully her equals as by believing the difference was wider than really existed. It was like running along the top of a narrow wall with fierce mastiffs on either side. You maintained a careful balance and tried to watch your feet more than the dogs. But you were always aware of the dogs.

Unpinning her cloak as she stepped up onto the striped box, Egwene folded it across her bench before sitting. The benches were hard, and some Sitters brought cushions when they thought the sitting would be long. Egwene preferred not to. The prohibition on speeches seldom stopped at least one or two women from drawing their comments out at length, and a hard seat could help you remain awake through the worst. Sheriam took the Keeper's place standing to Egwene's left, and there was nothing to do but wait. Maybe she *should* have brought a cushion.

The other benches were beginning to fill, though slowly. Aledrin and Saroiya had joined Berana, Aledrin plump enough to make the other two appear slim. Of course, the vertical lines of white scrollwork running down Saroiya's skirts had that effect anyway, while Aledrin's wide white sleeves and the snowy panel running down the front of her dress did just the opposite. Each apparently was trying to find out whether the others knew what was afoot, from the way they were shaking their heads at each other and shooting glances toward the Blues, the Browns and the Greens. Varilin, a red-haired stork of a woman and taller than most men, had taken her seat beside Kwamesa, too. Adjusting and readjusting her shawl restlessly, Varilin darted her eyes from Moria to Escaralde to Malind and back. Magla, yellow-fringed shawl wrapped tightly around her broad shoulders, and Faiselle, a square-faced Domani in silks covered with dense green embroidery, were just entering the pavilion, each ignoring the other even when their skirts brushed. Magla was firmly in Romanda's camp and Faiselle in Lelaine's, and the two groups did not mix. Other sisters were trickling in by spurts, as well, Nisao and Myrelle among half a dozen or so who slipped in behind Magla and Faiselle. Morvrin was already among the Browns behind Takima and Escaralde, and Beonin stood on the edge of the Grays behind Varilin and Kwamesa. At this rate, half the Aes Sedai in the camp would be crowded into the pavilion before long.

While Magla was still walking down the carpets toward the Yellow seats, Romanda rose to her feet. "We are more than eleven now, so we may as well begin." Her voice was surprisingly high-pitched. You might have thought she had a beautiful singing voice, if you could imagine Romanda singing. Her face always seemed more set for scolding, at least slightly disapproving. "I don't think we need make this a formal session," she added when Kwamesa stood. "I hardly see why this need be done in session at all, but if it must, let us get it over and out of the way. Some of us have more important matters to deal with. As I'm sure you do, Mother."

That last was said with a deep bow of her head, in a tone perhaps a hair *too* respectful. Not far enough over the line to be called sarcasm, of course. She was too intelligent to place herself in jeopardy; fools seldom attained a Sitter's chair, or held it long, and Romanda had held a seat in the Hall for almost eighty years. This was her second time as a Sitter. Egwene inclined her own head slightly, eyes cool. An acknowledgment that she had been addressed and that she had marked the tone. A very careful balance.

Kwamesa was left looking around with her mouth open, uncertain whether she was to speak the phrases, always uttered by the youngest Sitter present, that opened a formal sitting of the Hall. Romanda's place gave her considerable influence and some measure of authority, yet others could override her in this. A number of Sitters frowned or shifted on their benches, but no one spoke.

Lyrelle glided into the pavilion, glided toward the Blue benches. Tall for a Cairhienin woman, which made her of average height for almost anywhere else, she was elegant in blue-slashed silk embroidered on the bodice with red and gold, her movements flowing. Some said she had been a dancer before coming to the Tower as a novice. By comparison, Samalin, the fox-faced Green who entered on her heels, seemed to stride mannishly, though there was nothing at all awkward about the Murandian woman. They both seemed surprised to see Kwamesa on her feet, and hurried to their respective benches. In any case, Varilin began plucking at Kwamesa's sleeve, until the Arafellin woman finally sat down. Kwamesa's face was a mask of cool calmness, yet she managed to radiate displeasure. She put a great store in ceremony.

"Perhaps there *is* reason for formal session." Lelaine's voice seemed low, after Romanda's. Arranging her shawl as though she had all the time in the world, she rose gracefully, very deliberately not looking at Egwene. A beautiful woman, Lelaine still was dignity incarnate. "It seems that talks with Elaida have been licensed," she said coolly. "I do understand that under the Law of War, we need not be consulted on this, but I also believe we should discuss it in session, especially since many of us face the possibility of being stilled if Elaida retains any power."

That word, "stilled," no longer carried quite the chill it had before Siuan and Leane were Healed from stilling, but murmurs rose among the watching Aes Sedai crowded behind the benches. It seemed that news of negotiations had not spread as quickly as Egwene expected. She could not tell whether the sisters were excited or dismayed, but clearly they were surprised. Including some of the Sitters. Janya, who had entered while Lelaine was speaking, stopped dead in her tracks, so that another knot of sisters coming in nearly walked into her. She stared at the Blue, then longer and harder at Egwene herself. Romanda plainly had not heard either, from the way her mouth hardened, and expressions among the too-young Sitters ranged from Berana's icy calm to amazed on Samalin's part and openly appalled on Salita's. For that matter, Sheriam swayed on her feet for a moment. Egwene hoped the woman would not sick up in front of the entire Hall.

More interesting, though, were the reactions of those Delana had reported as speaking of negotiation. Varilin sat very still and seemed to be suppressing a smile as she studied her skirts, but Magla licked her lips hesitantly and cast glances at Romanda from the corner of her eye. Saroiya had her eyes closed, and her mouth moved as though she might be uttering a prayer. Faiselle and Takima gazed at Egwene wearing almost identical tiny frowns. Then each noticed the other and gave a start, quickly assuming such regal serenity that they seemed to be mocking one another. It was very strange. Surely by now Beonin had informed all of them what Egwene had said, yet except for Varilin, they seemed upset. They could not possibly have thought they might really negotiate an end. Every woman sitting in this Hall risked stilling and execution just by being there. If there ever had been any path back except to remove Elaida, it had washed away months ago, when this Hall was chosen. There *was* no going back from that.

Lelaine appeared satisfied with the reactions to her words—smug as a cat in the milkbarn, in fact—but before she finished settling back onto her bench, Moria bounded to her feet. That caught every eye and caused a few more murmurs. No one called Moria particularly graceful, but the Illianer was not a woman who bounded. "That do need discussion," she said, "but it must come later. This Hall did be called by three Sitters asking the same question. That question must be addressed before any other. What did Akarrin and her party find? I do ask they be brought in to make their report before the Hall."

Lelaine scowled at her fellow Blue, and she could scowl with the best, her eyes as sharp as awls, yet Tower law was quite plain on the subject, for once, and well known to everyone. Often enough, it was neither. In an unsteady voice, Sheriam asked Aledrin, the youngest after Kwamesa, to go and escort Akarrin and the others before the Hall. Egwene decided she had best talk to the fire-haired woman as soon as this sitting was done. If Sheriam kept on this way, she would soon become worse than useless as Keeper.

Delana darted into the pavilion amid a cluster of sisters, the last Sitter to arrive, and was on her bench draping her shawl across her elbows by the time the plump White Sitter returned with the six sisters and led them to stand before Egwene. They must have left their cloaks on the walkway outside, because none was wearing one now. Delana peered at them, an uncertain frown drawing her eyebrows down. She seemed out of breath, as though she had run to get there.

Apparently, Aledrin felt that whether or not the sitting was formal, she, at least, should carry on with proper formality. "You have been called before the Hall of the Tower to relate what you have seen," she said in a strong Taraboner accent. Her combination of dark golden hair and brown eyes was not unusual in Tarabon, though she wore her shoulder-length hair caught in a lacy white net rather than in beaded braids. "I charge you to speak of these things without the evasion or holding back, and to answer all questions in complete fullness, leaving out nothing. Say now that you will do so, under the Light and by your hope of the rebirth and salvation, or suffer the consequences." Those ancient sisters who made this part of the Hall's ceremony had been well aware of how much leeway the Three Oaths gave. A little left out here, a touch of vagueness there, and the whole meaning of what you said could be stood on its head, all while you spoke only the truth.

Akarrin spoke the assurance loudly and somewhat impatiently, the other five with varying levels of formality and self-consciousness. Many sisters had lived their entire lives without being called to testify in front of the Hall. Aledrin waited until the last had repeated every word before marching back toward her bench.

"Tell us what you did see, Akarrin," Moria said as soon as the White Sitter turned away. Aledrin stiffened visibly, and when she took her seat, her face was utterly expressionless, but bright spots of color highlighted her cheeks. Moria should have waited. She must have been very anxious.

By tradition—there were many more traditions and customs than laws, and the Light knew there were more laws than anyone really knew, often contradictory layers of law laid down over the centuries, but tradition and custom ruled Aes Sedai as much as Tower law ever had, perhaps more so—by tradition, Akarrin addressed her response to the Amyrlin Seat.

"What we saw, Mother, was a roughly circular hole in the ground," she said, nodding for emphasis at nearly every other word. She seemed to choose those words carefully, as if to make sure she was absolutely clear to everyone. "It may have been a precise circle, originally, shaped like half of a ball, but the sides have collapsed in some places. The hole is approximately three miles across and perhaps a mile and a half deep." Someone gasped loudly, and Akarrin frowned as though whoever it was had tried to interrupt. She went on without pausing, however. "We could not be entirely certain of the depth. The bottom is covered with water and ice. We believe it may become a lake, eventually. In any event, we were able to ascertain our exact location without too much difficulty, and we are prepared to say that the hole is located where the city called Shadar Logoth once stood." She fell silent, and for a long moment the only sound was the rustle of skirts as Aes Sedai shifted uneasily.

Egwene wanted to shift, too. Light, a hole that size would cover half of Tar Valon! "Do you have any idea how this . . . hole . . . was created, Akarrin?" she asked finally. She was quite proud of how steady her voice was. Sheriam was actually trembling! Egwene hoped no one else noticed. A Keeper's actions always reflected on the Amyrlin. If the Keeper showed fear, a good many sisters would think that Egwene was afraid. That was hardly something she wanted anyone to suspect.

"Each of us was chosen because we have some ability at reading residues, Mother. Better than most, in truth." So they had *not* been chosen simply because no one stronger was interested. There was a lesson in that. What Aes Sedai did was seldom as simple as it appeared on the surface. Egwene wished she could stop having to relearn lessons she had thought already learned. "Nisain is the best of us at that," Akarrin went on. "With your permission, Mother, I will let her answer."

Nisain smoothed her dark woolen skirts nervously and cleared her throat. A gangly Gray with a strong chin and startlingly blue eyes, she had some small repute in matters of law and treaties, but she was obviously uneasy about speaking before the Hall. She looked straight at Egwene with the air of someone who did not want to actually see all the Sitters assembled. "Given the amount of *saidar* used there, Mother, it was no surprise to find the residues near as thick as the snow." More than a hint of Murandy clung to her tongue, a lilting sound. "Even after so long, I should have been able to grasp some idea of what was woven, if it was at all like anything I'm familiar with, but I have none. I could all but trace the weave, Mother, and it made no sense at all. None. In fact, it seemed so alien, it might not have been. . . ." Clearing her throat again, she swallowed. Her face grew a little paler. "It might not have been woven by a woman. We thought it must have been the Forsaken, of course, so I tested for resonance. We all did." Half-turning to gesture to her companions, she hurriedly turned back. She definitely preferred looking at Egwene to the Sitters, all leaning forward intently. "I can't say what was done, beyond scooping three miles out of the earth, or how it was done, but *saidin* was definitely used, too. The resonance was so strong, we should have been able to smell it. There was more *saidin* used than *saidar,* much more, Dragonmount beside a foothill. And that is all I can say, Mother." A sound fluttered through the pavilion, the sound of sisters letting out the breath they had been holding. Sheriam's exhalation seemed the loudest, but perhaps that was just because she was nearest.

Egwene schooled her face to stillness. The Forsaken, and a weave that could tear away half of Tar Valon. If Malind did propose flight, could she try to make the sisters remain and face that? Could she abandon Tar Valon, and the Tower, and the Light knew how many tens of thousands of lives? "Does anyone else have a question?" she asked.

"I have one," Romanda said in a dry tone. *Her* calm had not cracked by a hair. "But not for these sisters. If no one has any further questions for them, I'm sure they would like to be away from having the Hall stare at them."

It was not precisely her place to suggest that, but neither was it precisely not, so Egwene let it pass. No one else had questions for Akarrin or her companions, as it turned out, and Romanda offered them surprisingly warm thanks for their efforts. Again, not precisely her place.

"Who is your question for?" Egwene asked as Akarrin and the other five scattered to join the growing numbers of sisters crowding among the stand-lamps and braziers. They were eager, as Romanda had said, to get out from under the Hall's eyes, but they did want to hear what came of their work. It was very difficult for Egwene to keep asperity out of her voice. Romanda affected not to notice. Or perhaps did not notice.

"For Moria," she said. "We suspected the Forsaken from the start. We knew that whatever happened was powerful, and far away. All we've learned, really, is that Shadar Logoth is gone, and of that I can only say, the world is better off without that sinkhole of the Shadow." She fixed the Blue Sitter with a frown that had made many an Aes Sedai squirm like a novice. "My question is this. Has anything changed for us?"

"It should," Moria replied, meeting the other woman's stare levelly. She might not have been in the Hall as long as Romanda, but Sitters were at least supposedly on an equal footing. "We have long had preparations in case the Forsaken do come against us. Every sister does know to form a circle if she be able, or join one she does find forming, until every circle does reach thirteen. Everyone is to be brought in, even the novices, even the newest." Lelaine looked up at her sharply, but however much she wanted to chide Moria, they were of the same Ajah. They must give at least the appearance of a common front. The effort of keeping her mouth shut thinned Lelaine's lips, though.

Romanda was under no such constraint. "Must you explain what everyone here already knows? We are the ones who *made* those arrangements. Perhaps you have forgotten?" This time, her voice was cutting. Open displays of anger were forbidden in the Hall, but not goading.

If Moria felt the prick, though, she gave no outward sign beyond adjusting her shawl. "I must explain from the beginning, because we have no thought far enough. Malind, can our circles stand against what Akarrin and Nisain described?"

Despite her fierce eyes, Malind's full mouth always

looked ready to smile, but she was quite stern as she stood, and she stared at each Sitter in turn as if to impress her words on them. "They cannot. Even if we rearrange matters so the strongest sisters are always in the same circle—and that means they must live, eat and sleep together, if they're to link on the moment—even then, we would be mice facing a cat. Enough mice can overwhelm even a large hungry cat, but not before many mice are dead. If enough of these mice die, though, the White Tower dies." Again that ripple of sighs ran though the pavilion like an unsteady breeze.

Egwene managed to keep her face calm, but she had to force her fists to relax their grip on her skirt. Which would they propose, an assault or flight? Light, how *could* she oppose them?

Same Ajah or not, Lelaine could take the strain no longer. "What are you suggesting, Moria?" she snapped. "Even if we reunite the Tower this very day, that won't change the facts."

Moria smiled slightly, as if the other Blue had said just what she was hoping someone would say. "But we must change the facts. The fact at present do be that our strongest circles be too weak. We do have no *angreal,* much less *sa'angreal,* so we might as well ignore them. I'm no certain there be anything even in the Tower that would make a large enough difference, anyway. How, then, do we make our circles stronger? Strong enough, we must hope, to face what happened at Shadar Logoth and stop it. Escaralde, what have you to say on the matter?"

Startled, Egwene leaned forward. They *were* working together. But to what end?

She was not the only one to realize that the three Sitters who had called the Hall were all on their feet. By remaining standing, Moria and Malind had made a clear declaration. Escaralde stood like a queen, yet the tiny Brown seemed all too aware of the eyes sliding between her and Malind and Moria, the thoughtful frowns and too-still faces. She shifted her shawl twice before speaking. She sounded as though she were lecturing a class, her voice thin yet forceful.

"The ancient literature is quite clear, though little studied, I fear. It gathers dust rather than readers. Writings collected in the earliest years of the Tower make it plain that circles were not limited to thirteen, in the Age of Legends. The precise mechanism—I should say, the precise balance—is unknown, but it should not be too difficult to work out. For those of you who have not spent the time you should have in the Tower library, the *manner* of increasing the size of a circle involves . . ." For the first time, she faltered, and visibly forced herself to continue. ". . . involves the inclusion of men who can channel."

Faiselle popped to her feet. "What are you suggesting?" she demanded and sat down immediately, as though someone might think she was standing in support.

"I do ask that the Hall be cleared!" Magla said, rising. Like Moria, she was Illianer, and agitation thickened her accent markedly. "This do no be a matter for discussion before any save the Hall in closed sitting." She, too, dropped back onto her bench as soon as she finished, and sat glowering, wide shoulders hunched and hands opening and closing on her skirts.

"I do fear it be too late for that," Moria said loudly. She had to speak loudly, to be heard over the murmur of sisters talking excitedly behind the benches, a hum like a huge beehive. "What has been said has been said, and heard by too many sisters for anyone to try shutting the words away now." Her bosom rose as she pulled in a deep breath, and she raised her voice a notch louder. "I do put before the Hall the proposal that we do enter into an agreement with the Black Tower, that we may bring men into our circles at need." If she sounded a trifle strangled at the end, it was no wonder. Few Aes Sedai could say that name without emotion, disgust if not outright hatred. It struck against the buzz of voices—and produced absolute silence for the space of three heartbeats.

"That is madness!" Sheriam's shriek shattered the stillness in more ways than one. The Keeper did not enter discussions in the Hall. She could not even enter the Hall itself without the Amyrlin. Face flooding with red, Sheriam drew herself up, perhaps to face the inevitable rebuke, perhaps to defend herself. The Hall had other things on its mind than rebuking her, though.

Leaping up from their benches just long enough to get their words out, Sitters began to speak, to shout, sometimes on top of one another.

"Madness hardly begins to describe it!" Faiselle shouted, at the same time that Varilin cried, "How can we *ally* ourselves with men who can channel?"

"These so-called Asha'man are tainted!" Saroiya called out with no sign of the vaunted White Ajah reserve. Hands knotted in her shawl, she trembled so hard that the long snowy fringe swayed. "Tainted with the Dark One's touch!"

"Even suggesting such a thing puts us against all the White Tower stands for," Takima said roughly. "We would be despised by every woman who calls herself Aes Sedai, by Aes Sedai long in their graves!"

Magla went so far as to shake a fist, with a fury she did not attempt to mask. "Only a Darkfriend could suggest this! Only a Darkfriend!" Moria paled at the accusation, then went bright red with anger of her own.

Egwene did not know where she stood on this. The Black Tower was Rand's creation, and perhaps necessary, if there was to be any hope of winning the Last Battle, yet the Asha'man *were* men who could channel, a thing feared for three thousand years, and they channeled Shadow-stained *saidin*. Rand himself was a man who could channel, yet without him, the Shadow would win at Tarmon Gai'don. The Light help her for seeing it so coldly, but it was hard truth. Wherever she stood on the matter, matters were getting out of hand there and then. Escaralde was exchanging insults with Faiselle, both at the tops of their lungs. Open insults! In the Hall! Saroiya had abandoned the last shreds of White Ajah coolness and was screaming at Malind, who screamed back, neither waiting on the other. It would have been a wonder if either could understand what the other was saying, and perhaps a blessing if they could not. Surprisingly, neither Romanda nor Lelaine had opened her mouth since the beginning. They sat staring at one another, unblinking. Likely each was trying to read how the other would stand just so she could stand in opposition. Magla got down from her bench and stalked toward Moria with the glare of someone eager to come to blows. Not words, but fists. Magla's were clenched at her sides. Her vine-worked shawl slid off onto the carpets, unnoticed.

Standing, Egwene embraced the Source. Except for certain exactly prescribed functions, channeling was forbidden in the Hall—another of the customs that pointed to darker

days in the Hall's history—but she made a simple weave of
Air and Fire. "A proposal has been laid before the Hall,"
she said, and released *saidar*. That was not as hard as it
once had been. Not easy, not close to easy, but not as hard.
A memory of the Power's sweetness remained, enough to
sustain her until the next time.

Magnified by the weave, her words boomed in the pavilion like thunder. Aes Sedai shrank back, wincing and
covering their ears. The silence after seemed incredibly
loud. Magla gaped at her in astonishment, then gave a
start at realizing that she was standing halfway to the Blue
benches. Hastily unloosing her fists, she paused to snatch
up her shawl and hurried back to her own seat. Sheriam
stood weeping openly. Surely it had not been that loud.

"A proposal has been laid before the Hall," Egwene repeated into the silence. After that Power-magnified blare,
her voice rang in her own ears. Perhaps it *had* been louder
than she thought. That weave had never been intended for
use inside walls, even patched canvas walls. "How speak
you in support of an alliance with the Black Tower, Moria?"
She sat down as soon as she finished. How *did* she stand on
this? What difficulties would it present her? How could it be
used to advantage? The Light help her, indeed. Those were
the first two things to come to mind. She wished Sheriam
would dry her eyes and straighten her backbone. She was
the Amyrlin Seat, and she needed a Keeper, not a milksop.

It took a few minutes for order to restore itself, Sitters
straightening clothes and smoothing skirts unnecessarily,
avoiding each other's eyes and especially not looking at the
watching sisters crowded behind the benches. Some Sitters'
faces became stained with red that had nothing to do with
anger. Sitters did not shriek at one another like farmhands
at shearing. *Most* especially not in front of other sisters.

"We do be faced with two seemingly insurmountable difficulties," Moria said finally. Her voice was composed and
cool once more, but a hint of flush still hung in her cheeks.
"The Forsaken have discovered a weapon—discovered or
uncovered; they surely would have used it before now, had
they possessed it—a weapon we can no counter. A weapon
we can no match, though the Light do know why we would
wish to, but most importantly, a weapon we can neither survive nor stop. At the same time, the . . . Asha'man . . . have

grown like weeds. Reliable reports do put their numbers at nearly equal to all the Aes Sedai living. Even if that number do be inflated, we can no afford to believe it exaggerated far. And more men come every day. The eyes-and-ears do be too consistent to believe anything else. We should take these men and gentle them, of course, but we have ignored them because of the Dragon Reborn. We have put them off, to be dealt with later. The bitter truth do be that it be too late to try taking them. They do be too many. Maybe it did be too late when we did first learned what they were doing.

"If we can no gentle these men, then we must control them somehow. An agreement with the Black Tower—*alliance* be too strong a word—with a carefully worded agreement, we can take the first steps toward protecting the world from them. We also can bring them into our circles." Raising a cautionary finger, Moria ran her gaze along the benches, but her voice remained cool and composed. And firm. "We must make it clear that a sister will always meld the flows—I do *not* suggest letting a man control a linked circle!—but with men in the circles, we can expand them. With the blessings of the Light, perhaps we can expand the circles far enough to counter this weapon of the Forsaken. We do kill two hares with one stone. But these hares do be lions, and if we do no cast that stone, one of them will surely kill us. It is as simple as that."

Silence fell. Excepting Sheriam, at least. Standing hunched in on herself a few feet from Egwene, shoulders shaking, she still had not mastered her weeping.

Then Romanda sighed heavily. "Perhaps we can expand the circles enough to counter the Forsaken," she said in a quiet voice. In a way, that gave her words more weight than if she had shouted. "Perhaps we can control the Asha'man. A thin word, perhaps, in either context."

"When you do be drowning," Moria replied, equally quiet, "you do grab at whatever branch floats by, even when you can no be sure it will support your weight until you have hold. The water has no closed over our heads yet, Romanda, but we be drowning. We do be drowning."

Again there was silence, but for Sheriam's sniveling. Had she forgotten all self-control? But then, no one among the Sitters wore a pleasant expression, not even Moria or Malind or Escaralde. It was not a pleasant prospect that lay in

front of them. Delana's face had turned decidedly greenish.
She looked as if she might be the one to sick up rather than
Sheriam.

Egwene stood once more, long enough to ask the required question. Even when the unthinkable was proposed,
the rituals must be followed. Perhaps more so then than
ever. "Who speaks against this proposal?"

There was no shortage of speakers there, though everyone had regained herself enough for them to follow protocol. Several Sitters moved at once, but Magla was first
on her feet, and the others sat back with no outward displays of impatience. Faiselle followed Magla, and Varilin
followed Faiselle. Then came Saroiya, and finally Takima.
Each spoke at length, Varilin and Saroiya coming very near
making the forbidden speeches, and each spoke with all
the eloquence she could summon. No one reached a Sitter's
chair lacking eloquence at need. Even so, it soon became
clear that they were repeating themselves and each other,
just in different words.

The Forsaken and their weapon were never mentioned.
The Black Tower was the Sitters' topic, the Black Tower and
the Asha'man. The Black Tower was a blight on the face of
the earth, as great a threat to the world as the Last Battle
itself. The very name suggested connections to the Shadow,
not to mention being a direct slap at the White Tower. The
so-called Asha'man—no one used the name without adding
"so-called," or saying it with a sneer; "guardians" it meant
in the Old Tongue, and they were *anything* but guardians—
the so-called Asha'man were men who could *channel*!
Men doomed to go insane if the male half of the Power
did not kill them first. Madmen wielding the One Power.
From Magla to Takima, every one of them invested that with
every scrap of horror in them. Three thousand years of the
world's horror, and the Breaking of the World before that.
Men like this had *destroyed* the world, destroyed the Age
of Legends and changed the face of the world to desolation.
This was who they were being asked to make *alliance* with.
If they did so, they would be anathema in every nation, and
rightly. They would be scorned by every Aes Sedai, and
rightly. It could not be. It *could* not.

When Takima finally sat, arranging her shawl carefully
along her arms, she wore a small but quite satisfied smile.

Together they had managed to make the Asha'man seem more fearsome, more dangerous, than the Forsaken and the Last Battle combined. Maybe even a match for the Dark One himself.

Since Egwene had begun the ritual questions, it was for her to finish, and she rose long enough to say, "Who stands for an agreement with the Black Tower?" She had only thought there was silence in the pavilion before. Sheriam had finally governed her weeping, though tears glistened on her cheeks still, but her gulp sounded like shouts in the quiet that followed that question.

Takima's smile slid sideways when Janya stood as soon as the question left Egwene's mouth. "Even a slim branch is better than no branch when you're drowning," Janya said. "I'd rather try than trust to hope until I go under." She had the habit of speaking when she was not supposed to.

Samalin rose to stand beside Malind, and suddenly there was a rush, Salita and Berana and Aledrin together, with Kwamesa only a tick behind. Nine Sitters on their feet, and there it hung as the moments stretched out. Egwene realized she was biting her lip and stopped hurriedly, hoping no one had noticed. She could still feel the impression of her teeth. She hoped she had not drawn blood. Not that anyone was looking at her. Everyone seemed to be holding their breath.

Romanda sat frowning up at Salita, who was staring straight ahead, her face gray and her lips trembling. The Tairen sister might not be able to hide her fear, but she was going ahead. Romanda nodded slowly and then, shockingly, stood. She, too, decided to violate custom. "Sometimes," she said, looking straight at Lelaine, "we must do things we would rather not."

Lelaine met the gray-haired Yellow's eyes without blinking. Her face might have been cast in porcelain. Her chin rose by slow increments. And suddenly, she stood, glancing down impatiently at Lyrelle, who gaped at her a moment before coming to her feet.

Everyone stared. No one made a sound. It was done.

Almost done, anyway. Egwene cleared her throat, trying to catch Sheriam's attention. The next part was the Keeper's, but Sheriam stood scrubbing the tears from her cheeks with her fingers and running her eyes along the benches as if counting how many Sitters were standing and hoping to find she had miscounted. Egwene cleared her throat more loudly, and the green-eyed woman gave a start and turned to stare at her. Even then, it seemed to take forever before she recalled herself to her duty.

"The lesser consensus standing," she announced in an unsteady voice, "an agreement will be sought with . . . with the Black Tower." Inhaling deeply, she straightened to her full height, and her voice gained strength. She was back onto familiar ground. "In the interest of unity, I ask for the greater consensus to stand."

That was a powerful call. Even on matters that could be decided by the lesser consensus, unanimity was always preferred, always strived for. Hours of discussion, days, might go into reaching it, but the effort would not stop until every Sitter agreed or it was clear as well water that there could be no agreement. A powerful call, one that tugged at every sister. Delana rose like a puppet drawn up against her will, looking around uncertainly.

"I cannot stand for this," Takima said, against all decorum. "No matter what anyone says, no matter how long we sit, I cannot and I will not! I—will—*not*!"

No one else stood, either. Oh, Faiselle shifted on her bench, half moved as if to stand, adjusted her shawl, twitched again as if she might stand. That was as close as anyone came. Saroiya was biting her knuckle with an expression of horror, and Varilin wore the look of a woman who had been hit between the eyes with a hammer. Magla gripped the ends of her bench, holding herself in place and staring bleakly at the carpets in front of her. Plainly, she was aware of the scowl Romanda was aiming at the back of her neck, but her only response was to hunch her shoulders.

Takima should have been the end of it. There was no point in seeking the greater consensus when someone made it plain she would not stand. But Egwene decided to make her own break with decorum and protocol. "Is there anyone who feels she must leave her chair over this?" she asked in a loud, clear voice.

Gasps filled the pavilion, but she was holding her breath. This could shatter them, but better to have it out in the open now, if that was what was to come of it. Saroiya looked at her wildly, but no one moved.

"Then we will go forward," she said. "Carefully. It will take time to plan exactly who is to approach the Black Tower, and what they are to say." Time for her to plant a few safeguards, it was to be hoped. Light, she was going to have to scramble to deal with this. "First, are there suggestions for our . . . embassy?"

Chapter
20

In the Night

L ong before the sitting ended, in spite of the cloak folded beneath her, Egwene's bottom was quite numb from the hard wooden bench. After listening to endless discussion, she wished her ears were numb, as well. Sheriam, forced to stand, had begun shifting her feet as if wishing for a chair. Or maybe just to sit down on the carpets. Egwene could have left, freeing herself and Sheriam. Nothing required the Amyrlin to stay, and at best her comments were listened to politely. After which the Hall galloped off in its own direction. This had nothing to do with the war, and with the bit between their teeth, the Hall was not about to let her get a hand on the reins. She could have walked out at any time—with a slight interruption in the discussions for the required ceremonies—but if she did, she feared that first thing in the morning she might be handed a fully fledged plan, one the Sitters were already carrying out, and her with no idea what was coming until she read it. At least, that was her fear in the beginning.

Who spoke at the greatest length was no surprise, not any longer. Magla and Saroiya, Takima and Faiselle and Varilin, each fretting visibly when another Sitter had the floor. Oh, they accepted the decision of the Hall, at least on the surface. There was nothing else for them to do except resign their chairs; however hard the Hall might be willing to struggle for consensus if need be, once a course of action was decided, by whatever consensus, then *everyone* was expected to follow, or at the very least not hinder. That was the rub. What, exactly, constituted hindrance? None of the five spoke against a Sitter from her own Ajah, of course, but the other four leaped to their feet when any Sitter took her bench again, and all five if the Sitter was Blue. And whoever got the floor spoke very persuasively as to why the previous speaker's suggestions were utterly wrong and perhaps a recipe for disaster. Not that there was any real sign of collusion that Egwene could see. They eyed each other as warily as they did anyone else, frowned at each other as hard if not harder and, plainly, trusted none of the others to make her arguments.

In any event, little of what was suggested came close to conformity. The Sitters disagreed on how many sisters should be sent to the Black Tower and how many from each Ajah, on when those sisters were to be sent, what they must demand, what they should be allowed to agree to and what ordered to refuse entirely. In a matter this delicate, any error could lead to disaster. On top of which, every Ajah except the Yellow considered itself uniquely qualified to provide the leadership of the mission, from Kwamesa's insistence that the goal was negotiating a treaty, of sorts, to Escaralde's claim that historical knowledge was a necessity for such an unprecedented undertaking. Berana even pointed out that an agreement of this nature must be reached by absolute rationality; dealing with the Asha'man was sure to inflame passions, and anything except cold logic would surely lead to disaster on the spot. She grew rather heated about it, in fact. Romanda did want the party led by a Yellow, yet since it hardly seemed there would be any great need for Healing, she was reduced to a stubborn insistence that anyone else might be swayed by her Ajah's special interests and forget the point of what they were doing.

Sitters of the same Ajah supported one another only to the extent of not openly opposing, and no two Ajahs were willing to stand together on much beyond the fact that they had agreed to send an embassy to the Black Tower. Whether it should be called an embassy remained in dispute, even by some who had stood in its favor at the start. Moria herself seemed taken aback by the very idea.

Egwene was not the only one who found the constant argument and counterargument wearing, the points chopped so fine that nothing remained and everything had to begin over. Sisters drifted away from behind the benches. Others replaced them and then drifted away in turn after a few hours. By the time Sheriam uttered the ritual "Depart now in the Light," night had descended, and only a few dozen remained besides Egwene and the Sitters, several of whom sagged as though they had been run through a mangle like damp bed-linens. And nothing at all had been decided except that more talk was necessary before anything could be decided.

Outside, a pale half-moon hung in a velvet-black sky dusted with glittering stars, and the air was bitter cold. Her breath curling a pale mist in the darkness, Egwene walked away from the Hall smiling as she listened to the Sitters scattering behind her, some still arguing. Romanda and Lelaine were walking together, but the Yellow's clear high voice rose perilously close to shouting, and the Blue's was not far behind. They usually argued when forced into one another's company, but this was the first time Egwene had seen them choose it when they did not have to. Sheriam half-heartedly offered to fetch the reports on wagon repairs and fodder that she had asked for that morning, but the weary-eyed woman did not attempt to hide her relief when Egwene sent her off to her bed. With a hurried curtsy, she went scurrying away into the night clutching her cloak around her. Most of the tents stood dark, shadows in the moonlight. Few sisters remained awake long after nightfall. Lamp-oil and candles were never in generous supply.

For the moment, delay suited Egwene perfectly, but that was not the only reason for her smile. Somewhere in all that argument, her headache had gone away entirely. She would have no difficulty at all going to sleep this night. Halima always remedied that, yet her dreams were always troubled after one of Halima's massages. Well, few of her dreams were light, but these were darker than any others, and, strangely, she could never remember anything except that they *were* dark and troubled. Doubtless both things came from some remnant of the pains that Halima's fingers would not reach, yet the last was disturbing in itself. She had learned to remember every dream. She had to remember every dream. Still, with no headache tonight, she should have no problems, and dreaming was the least of what she had to do.

Like the Hall and her study, her tent stood in a little clearing with its own strip of wooden walkway, the nearest tents a dozen spans off to give the Amyrlin a bit of privacy. At least, that was how the spacing was explained. It might even have been the truth, now. Egwene al'Vere was certainly not irrelevant anymore. The tent was not large, short of four paces on a side, and crowded inside, with four brass-bound chests full of clothing stacked against one wall, two cots and a tiny round table, a bronze brazier, a washstand, a stand-mirror and one of the few real chairs in the camp. A simple piece with a little plain carving, it took up entirely too much room, but it was comfortable, and a great luxury when she wanted to curl her feet beneath her and read. When she had time to read anything for pleasure. The second cot was Halima's, and she was surprised to see the woman was not already there waiting on her. The tent was not unoccupied, however.

"You had nothing but bread for breakfast, Mother," Chesa said in a mildly accusing voice as Egwene ducked through the entry flaps. Not far from stout in her plain gray dress, Egwene's maid was sitting on the tent's stool, darning stockings by the light of an oil lamp. She was a pretty woman, without a touch of gray in her hair, yet sometimes it seemed that Chesa had been in her employ forever rather than just since Salidar. She certainly took all the liberties of an old servant, including the right to scold. "You ate nothing at all midday, as far as I can learn," she went on, holding up a snowy silk stocking to study the patch she was making in the heel, "and your dinner's gone cold there on the table an hour ago at least. Nobody's asked me, but if they did, I'd say those heads of yours come from not eating. You're much too skinny."

With that, she finally put the stocking down atop her mending basket and rose to take Egwene's cloak. And to exclaim that Egwene was cold as ice. That was another cause of headaches, in her book. Aes Sedai went around ignoring freezing cold or steaming heat, but your body knew whether you did or not. Best to bundle up warm. And wear red shifts. Everyone knew red was warmest. Eating helped, too. An empty belly always led to shivering. You never saw her shivering, now did you?

"Thank you, Mother," Egwene said lightly, which earned a soft snort of laughter. And a shocked look. For all her liberties, Chesa was a stickler for the proprieties to make Aledrin seem lax. The spirit, anyway, if often not the letter. "I don't have a headache tonight, thanks to that tea of yours." Maybe it had been the tea. Vile as that tasted, as a cure, it was no worse than sitting through a session of the Hall lasting more than half a day. "And I'm not very hungry, really. A roll will be enough."

Of course, it was not quite so simple as that. The relationship between mistress and servant was never simple. You lived in one another's sleeve, and she saw you at your worst, knew all your faults and foibles. There was no such thing as privacy from your maid. Chesa muttered and grumbled under her breath the whole time she was helping Egwene undress, and in the end, wrapped in a robe—red silk, to be sure, edged with frothy Murandian lace and embroidered with summery flowers; a gift from Anaiya—Egwene let her remove the linen cloth covering the tray on the little round table.

The lentil stew was a congealed mass in the bowl, but a little channeling fixed that, and with the first spoonful, Egwene discovered she did have some appetite. She ate every scrap, and the piece of blue-veined white cheese, and the somewhat shriveled olives, and the two crusty brown rolls, though she had to pick weevils out of both. Since she did not want to fall asleep too quickly, she drank only one cup of the spiced wine, which needed reheating, too, and had a slight bitterness for it, but Chesa beamed with approval as if she had cleaned the tray. Peering at the dishes, empty except for the olive pits and a few crumbs, she realized she had, at that.

Once she was in her narrow cot, two soft woolen blankets and a goose-down comforter pulled to her chin, Chesa took up the dinner tray, but she paused at the tent's entrance. "Do you want me to come back, Mother? If you get one of your heads . . . Well, that woman's found company, or she'd be here by now." There was open scorn in "that woman." "I could brew another pot of tea. I got it from a peddler who said it was sovereign for aching heads. And joints, and belly upsets, too."

"Do you really think she's a lightskirt, Chesa?" Egwene murmured. Already warm under her covers, she felt drowsy. She wanted sleep, but not just yet. Heads *and* joints *and* bellies? Nynaeve would laugh herself sick to hear that.

Perhaps it had been all those chattering Sitters who chased her headache away after all. "Halima does flirt, I suppose, but I don't think it's ever gone beyond flirting."

For a moment Chesa was silent, pursing her lips. "She makes me . . . uneasy, Mother," she said finally. "There's something just not right about that Halima. I feel it every time she's around. It's like feeling somebody sneaking up behind me, or realizing there's a man watching me bathe, or . . ." She laughed, but it was an uncomfortable sound. "I don't know how to describe it. Just, not right."

Egwene sighed and snuggled deeper under the covers. "Good night, Chesa." Channeling briefly, she extinguished the lamp, plunging the tent into pitch blackness. "You go sleep in your own bed tonight." Halima might be upset to come and find someone else on her cot. Had the woman *really* broken a man's arm? The man *must* have provoked her somehow.

She wanted dreams tonight, untroubled dreams—at least, dreams she could recall; few of her dreams were what anyone would call untroubled—but she had another sort of dream to enter first, and for that, it had been some time since she needed to be asleep. Nor did she need one of the *ter'angreal* the Hall guarded so closely. Slipping into a light trance was no harder than deciding to do so, especially as tired as she was, and . . .

. . . bodiless, she floated in an endless blackness, surrounded by an endless sea of lights, an immense swirl of tiny pinpoints glittering more sharply than stars on the clearest night, more numerous than the stars. Those were the dreams of all the people in the world, of people in all the worlds that were or could be, worlds so strange she could not begin to comprehend them, all visible here in the tiny gap between *Tel'aran'rhiod* and waking, the infinite space between reality and dreams. Some of those dreams, she recognized at a glance. They all looked the same, yet she knew them as surely as she did the faces of her sisters. Some, she avoided. Rand's dreams were always shielded, and she feared he might know when she tried to peek in. The shield would keep her from seeing anything, anyway. A pity she could not tell where someone was from their dreams; two points of light could be side-by-side here, and the dreamers a thousand miles apart. Gawyn's dreams tugged at her, and she fled. His dreams held their own dangers, not least because part of her wanted very much to sink into them. Nynaeve's dreams gave her pause, and the desire to put the fear of the Light into the fool woman, but Nynaeve had managed to ignore her so far, and Egwene would not sink to pulling her into *Tel'aran'rhiod* against her will. That was the sort of thing the Forsaken did. It was a temptation, though.

Moving without moving, she searched for one particular dreamer. One of two, at least; either would do. The lights seemed to spin around her, to sweep past so fast that they blurred into streaks while she floated motionless in that starry sea. She hoped that at least one of those she hunted was asleep already. The Light knew, it was late enough for anyone. Vaguely aware of her body in the waking world, she felt herself yawn and curl her legs up beneath her covers.

Then she saw the point of light she sought, and it swelled in her sight as it rushed toward her, from a star in the sky to a full moon to a shimmering wall that filled her vision, pulsing like a breathing thing. She did not touch it, of course; that could lead to all sorts of complications even with this dreamer. Besides, it would be embarrassing to slide into someone's dream accidentally. Reaching out with her will across the hair-fine space that remained between her and the dream, she spoke cautiously, so she would not be heard in a shout. She had no body, no mouth, but she spoke.

ELAYNE, IT'S EGWENE. MEET ME AT THE USUAL PLACE. She did not think anyone could eavesdrop, not without her knowing, yet there was no point in taking unneeded chances.

The pinprick winked out. Elayne had wakened. But she would remember, and know the voice had not been just part of a dream.

Egwene moved . . . sideways. Or perhaps it was more like completing a step that she had paused halfway through. It felt like both. She moved, and . . .

. . . she was standing in a small room, empty save for a scarred wooden table and three straight-back chairs. The two windows showed deep night outside, yet there was light of an odd sort, different from moonlight or lamplight or sunlight. It did not seem to come from anywhere; it just was. But it was more than enough to see that sad, sorry little

room clearly. The dusty wall-panels were riddled by bee-
tles, and broken panes in the windows had allowed snow to
drift in atop a litter of twigs and dead leaves. At least, there
was snow on the floor sometimes, and twigs and leaves
sometimes. The table and chairs remained where they
stood, but whenever she glanced away, the snow might be
gone when she looked back, the twigs and brown leaves in
different places as if scattered by a wind. They even shifted
while she was looking, simply here then there. That no longer seemed any odder to her than the feel of unseen eyes
watching. Neither was truly real, just the way things were
in *Tel'aran'rhiod*. A reflection of reality and a dream, all
jumbled together.

Everywhere in the World of Dreams felt empty, but this
room had the hollow emptiness that only came from a place
that was truly abandoned in the waking world. Not so many
months past, this little room had been the Amyrlin's study,
the inn that held it was called the Little Tower, and the
village of Salidar, reclaimed from the encroaching forest
had bustled, the heart of resistance to Elaida. Now, if she
walked outside, she would see saplings thrusting through
the snow in the middle of those streets that had been so
painfully cleared. Sisters did Travel to Salidar still, to visit
the dovecotes, all jealous that a pigeon sent by one of their
eyes-and-ears might fall into another's hands, but only in
the waking world. Going to the dovecotes here would be as
useless as wishing for the pigeons to find you by a miracle.
Tame animals seemed to have no reflections in the World
of Dreams, and nothing done here could touch the waking world. Sisters with access to the dream *ter'angreal* had
other places to visit than a deserted village in Altara, and
certainly no one else had reason to come here in the dream,
either. This was one of the places in the world Egwene
could be sure no one would catch her by surprise. Too many
others turned out to have eavesdroppers. Or bone-deep sadness. She hated seeing what had become of the Two Rivers
since she left.

Waiting for Elayne to appear, she tried to quell her impatience. Elayne was not a dreamwalker; she needed to use
a *ter'angreal*. And she would want to tell Aviendha where
she was going, no doubt. Still, as the minutes stretched out,
Egwene found herself pacing the rough floorboards irrita-

bly. Time flowed differently here. An hour in *Tel'aran'rhiod*
could be minutes in the waking world, or the other way
around. Elayne could be moving like the wind. Egwene
checked her clothing, a gray riding dress with elaborate
green embroidery on the bodice and in broad bands on
the divided skirts—had she been thinking of the Green
Ajah?—a simple silver net to catch her hair. Sure enough,
the Amyrlin's long narrow stole hung around her neck. She
made the stole vanish, then after a moment, allowed it to return. It was a matter of letting it come back, not consciously
thinking of it. The stole was part of how she thought of herself, now, and it was as Amyrlin that she needed to speak
to Elayne.

The woman who finally appeared in the room, though,
just flashing into existence, was not Elayne but Aviendha,
surprisingly garbed in silver-embroidered blue silk, with
pale lace at her wrists and throat. The heavy bracelet of
carved ivory she wore seemed as much out of place with
that dress as the dream *ter'angreal* that dangled from a
leather cord around her neck, a strangely twisted stone ring
flecked with color.

"Where is Elayne?" Egwene asked anxiously. "Is she all
right?"

The Aiel woman gave a startled glance at herself, and
abruptly she was in a dark bulky skirt and white blouse,
with a dark shawl draped over her shoulders and a dark
kerchief folded around her temples to hold the reddish hair
that now hung to her waist, longer than in life, Egwene suspected. Everything was mutable in the World of Dreams.
A silver necklace appeared around her neck, complicated
strands of intricately worked discs that the Kandori called
snowflakes, a gift from Egwene herself what seemed a very
long time ago. "She could not make this work," Aviendha
said, the ivory bracelet sliding on her wrist as she touched
the twisted ring that still hung from its strip of leather,
above the necklace now. "It is the babes." Suddenly, she
grinned. Her emerald eyes seemed almost to shine. "She
has a wonderful temper, sometimes. She threw the ring
down and jumped up and down on it."

Egwene sniffed. Babes? So there was to be more than
one. Oddly, Aviendha took it in stride that Elayne was with
child, though Egwene was convinced the woman loved

Rand, too. Aiel ways were peculiar, to say the least. Egwene would not have thought it of Elayne, though! And Rand! No one had actually said he was the father, and she could hardly ask something like that, but she could count, and she *very* much doubted that Elayne would lie with another man. She realized that she was wearing stout woolens, dark and heavy, and a shawl much thicker than Aviendha's. Good Two Rivers garments. The sort of clothes a woman would wear to sit in the Women's Circle. Say, when some fool woman had let herself get with child and showed no sign of marrying. A deep, relaxing breath, and she was back in her green-embroidered riding dress. The rest of the world was not the same as the Two Rivers. Light, she had come far enough to know that much. She did not have to like it, but she had to live with it.

"As long as she and the . . . babes . . . are well." Light, how many? More than one could present difficulties. No; she was not going to ask. Elayne surely had the best midwife in Caemlyn. Best just to change the subject quickly. "Have you heard from Rand? Or Nynaeve? I have some words for her, running off with him that way."

"We have heard from neither," Aviendha replied, adjusting her shawl as carefully as any Aes Sedai avoiding her Amyrlin's eyes. Was her tone careful, too?

Egwene clicked her tongue, vexed with herself. She really was beginning to see conspiracies everywhere and suspicions in everything. Rand had gone into hiding, and that was that. Nynaeve was Aes Sedai, free to do as she wished. Even when the Amyrlin commanded, Aes Sedai often found a way to do exactly as they wished anyway. But the Amyrlin was still going to set Nynaeve al'Meara down hard, once she laid hands on her. As for Rand . . . "I'm afraid trouble is heading your way," she said.

A fine silver teapot appeared on the table, on a hammered silver tray with two delicate green porcelain cups. A thread of steam rose from the spout. She could have made the tea appear already in the cups, yet pouring seemed part of offering someone tea, even ephemeral tea with no more reality than a dream. You could die of thirst trying to drink what you found in *Tel'aran'rhiod,* much less what you made, but this tea tasted as if the leaves had come from a new cask and she had put in just the right amount of honey.

Taking a seat on one of the chairs, she sipped hers as she explained what had happened in the Hall and why.

After the first words, Aviendha held her cup on her finger-tips without drinking and watched Egwene without blinking. Her dark skirts and pale blouse became the *cadin'sor,* coat and trousers of gray and brown that would fade into shadows. Her long hair was suddenly short, and hidden by a *shoufa,* the black veil hanging down her chest. Incongruously, the ivory bracelet still hung from her wrist although Maidens of the Spear did not wear jewelry.

"All of this because of the beacon we felt," she muttered, half to herself, when Egwene finished. "Because they think the Shadowsouled have a weapon." An odd way to put it.

"What else can it be?" Egwene asked, curious. "Did one of the Wise Ones say something?" It had been a long time since she believed that Aes Sedai possessed all knowledge, and sometimes the Wise Ones revealed pockets of information that could startle the most stolid sister.

Aviendha frowned, and her clothing changed back to the skirt and blouse and shawl, then after a moment to the blue silk and lace, this time with both the Kandori necklace and the ivory bracelet. The dream ring remained on its cord, of course. A shawl appeared around her shoulders. The room was winter cold, yet it hardly seemed that gauzy layer of pale blue lace could provide any warmth. "The Wise Ones are as uncertain as your Aes Sedai. Not as frightened, though, I think. Life is a dream, and everyone wakes eventually. We dance the spears with Leafblighter," that name for the Dark One had always seemed strange to Egwene, coming as it did from the treeless Waste, "but no one enters the dance certain they will live, or win. I do not think the Wise Ones would consider any alliance with the Asha'man. Is this wise?" she added cautiously. "From what you said, I cannot be certain whether you wish it."

"I don't see any other choice," Egwene said reluctantly. "That hole is three *miles* across. This is the only hope we have that I can see."

Aviendha peered into her tea. "And if the Shadowsouled possessed no weapon?"

Suddenly, Egwene realized what the other woman was doing. Aviendha was in training to be a Wise One, and garments or no, she was *being* a Wise One. Likely that was the reason for the shawl. Part of Egwene wanted to smile. Her friend was changing from the often hotheaded Maiden of the Spear she had first come to know. Another part of her remembered that the Wise Ones did not always have the same goals as Aes Sedai. What sisters valued deeply sometimes meant nothing to the Wise Ones. It made her sad, that she must think of Aviendha as a Wise One instead of just a friend. A Wise One who would see what was good for the Aiel rather than what was good for the White Tower. Still, the question was a good one.

"We do have to deal with the Black Tower sooner or later, Aviendha, and Moria was right; there are already too many Asha'man for any thought of gentling them all. And that's if we dared think of gentling them before the last Battle. Maybe a dream will show me another way, but none has so far." None of her dreams had showed her *anything* useful, so far. Well, not really. "This does give us at least the beginning of a way to handle them. In any case, it's going to happen. If the Sitters can agree on anything besides the fact they have to try for an agreement. So we must live with it. It might even be for the best, in the long run."

Aviendha smiled into her teacup. Not an amused smile; she seemed relieved, for some reason. Her voice was serious, though. "You Aes Sedai always think men are fools. Quite often, they are not. More often than you think, at least. Take a care with these Asha'man. Mazrim Taim is far from a fool, and I think he is a very dangerous man."

"The Hall is aware of that," Egwene said dryly. That he was dangerous, certainly. The other might be worth pointing out. "I don't know why we're even discussing this. It's out of my hands. The important thing is that eventually sisters will decide the Black Tower is no longer any reason to stay away from Caemlyn, if we're going to talk with them anyway. Next week or tomorrow, you'll find sisters popping in just to look in on Elayne and see how the siege is going. What we have to decide is how to keep what we want hidden, hidden. I have a few suggestions, and I hope you have more."

The notion of strange Aes Sedai appearing in the Royal Palace agitated Aviendha to the point that she flashed from blue silk to *cadin'sor* to woolen skirt and *algode* blouse and back again as they talked, though she appeared not to notice. Her face remained smooth enough to suit any sister. She certainly had nothing to worry about if the visiting Aes Sedai uncovered the Kinswomen, or the captive *sul'dam* and *damane,* or the bargain with the Sea Folk, but likely she was concerned about the repercussions on Elayne.

The Sea Folk not only made the *cadin'sor* appear, but a round bull-hide buckler lying beside her chair with three short Aiel spears. Egwene considered asking whether there was any special problem with the Windfinders— any problem beyond the usual, that was—yet she held her tongue. If Aviendha did not mention it, then the matter was something she and Elayne wanted to handle themselves. Surely she would have said something if it was anything Egwene should know about. Or would she?

Sighing, Egwene set her cup on the table, where it promptly disappeared, and rubbed her eyes with her fingers. Suspicion truly was part of her bones, now. And she was unlikely to survive long without it. At least she did not always have to act on her suspicions, not with a friend.

"You are tired," Aviendha said, once again in the white blouse and dark skirt and shawl, a concerned Wise One with sharp green eyes. "You do not sleep well?"

"I sleep well," Egwene lied, managing a smile. Aviendha and Elayne had their own worries without letting them know about her headaches. "I can't think of anything more," she said, rising. "Can you? Then we're done," she went on when the other woman shook her head. "Tell Elayne to take care of herself. You take care of her. And her babes."

"I will," Aviendha said, now in the blue silk. "But you must take care of yourself. I think you use yourself too hard. Sleep well and wake," she said gently, the Aiel way of saying good night, and she was gone.

Egwene frowned at the spot where her friend had vanished. She was not using herself too hard. Only as hard as she needed to. She slipped back to her body and discovered that it was sound asleep.

That did not mean that *she* was asleep, or not exactly. Her body slumbered, breathing slow and deep, but she let herself slip only far enough under for dreams to come. She could just have waited until she woke and recalled the dreams then as she wrote them into the little leather-bound book that she kept at the bottom of one of her clothing chests, tucked under thin linen shifts that would not be taken out till well into spring. But observing the dreams as they came saved time. She thought it might help her decipher what they meant. At least, those that were more than ordinary night fancies.

There were plenty of those, often featuring Gawyn, a tall beautiful man who took her in his arms and danced with her and made love with her. Once, even in her dreams, she had shied away from thoughts of making love with him. She had blushed to think about it awake. That seemed so foolish, now, so childish. She *would* bond him as her Warder one day, somehow, and she would marry him, and make love to him until he cried for mercy. Even in her sleep, she giggled at that. Other dreams were not so pleasant. Wading through waist-deep snow with trees thick all around her, knowing she had to reach the edge of the forest. But even when she glimpsed the end of the trees ahead, one blink and it receded into the distance, leaving her to flounder on. Or she was pushing a great millstone up a steep hill, but every time she was almost to the top, she slipped and fell and watched the huge stone roll back to the bottom, so she had to trudge back down and begin again, only every time, the hill was higher than before. She knew enough of dreams to know where those came from even if they had no special meaning. None beyond the fact that she was tired and had a seemingly endless task in front of her, anyway. There was no help for it, though. She felt her body jerking at the laborious dreams, and tried to soothe her muscles, make them relax. This sort of half-sleep was little better than none, and less if she spent the whole night thrashing around on her cot. Her efforts worked, a little. At least she only twitched through a dream of being forced to pull a cart jammed full of Aes Sedai down a muddy road.

Other dreams came, betwixt and between.

Mat stood on a village green, playing at bowls. The thatch-roofed houses were vague, in the manner of dreams—sometimes the roofs were slate; sometimes the houses seemed of stone, sometimes wood—but he was sharp and clear, dressed in a fine green coat and that wide-brimmed black hat, just as he had been the day he rode into Salidar. There was not another human being in sight. Rubbing the ball between his hands, he took a short run and casually rolled it across the smooth grass. All nine pins fell, scattered as if they had been kicked. Mat turned and picked up another ball, and the pins were back upright. No, there was a fresh set of pins. The old still lay where they had fallen. He hurled the ball again, a lazy underhanded bowl. And Egwene wanted to scream. The pins were not turned pieces of wood. They were men, standing there watching the ball roll toward them. None moved until the ball sent them flying. Mat turned to pick up another ball, and there were more new pins, new men, standing in orderly formation among the men lying sprawled on the ground as if dead. No, they were dead. Unconcerned, Mat bowled.

It was a true dream; she knew that long before it faded. A glimpse of a future that might come to pass, a warning of what should be watched for. True dreams were always possibilities, not certainties—she often had to remind herself of that; Dreaming was not Foretelling—but this was a dire possibility. Every one of those human pins had represented thousands of men. Of that, she *was* certain. And an Illuminator was part of it. Mat had met an Illuminator once, but that was long ago. This was something more recent. The Illuminators were scattered, their guildhouses gone. One was even working her craft with a traveling show that Elayne and Nynaeve had traveled with for a time. Mat might find an Illuminator anywhere. Still, it was only a possible future. Bleak and bloodstained, but only possible. Yet she had dreamed of it at least twice. Not the same dream, exactly, but always the same meaning. Did that make it more likely to come to pass? She would have to ask the Wise Ones to find out, and she was increasingly reluctant to do that. Every question she asked revealed something to them, and their goals were not hers. To save what they could of the Aiel, they would let the White Tower be ground to dust. She had more than any one people, any one nation, to think of.

More dreams.

She was struggling up a narrow, rocky path along the face of a towering cliff. Clouds surrounded her, hiding the ground below and the crest above, yet she knew that both were very far away. She had to place her feet very carefully. The path was a cracked ledge barely wide enough for her to stand on with one shoulder pressed against the cliff, a ledge littered with stones as large as her fist that could turn

under a misplaced step and send her hurtling over the edge.
It almost seemed this was like the dreams of pushing mill-
stones and pulling carts, yet she knew it was a true dream.

Abruptly, the ledge dropped away from under her with
the crack of crumbling stone, and she caught frantically at
the cliff, fingers scrabbling to find a hold. Her fingertips
slid into a tiny crevice, and her fall stopped with a jolt that
wrenched her arms. Feet dangling into the clouds, she listened to the falling stone crash against the cliff until the
sound faded to nothing without the stone ever hitting the
ground. Dimly, she could see the broken ledge to her left.
Ten feet away, it might as well have been a mile off for all
the chance she had of reaching it. In the other direction, the
mists hid whatever remained of the path, but she thought it
had to be farther away still. There was no strength in her
arms. She could not pull herself up, only hang there by her
fingertips until she fell. The edge of the crevice seemed as
sharp as a knife under her fingers.

Suddenly a woman appeared, clambering down the
sheer side of the cliff out of the clouds, making her way
as deftly as if she were walking down stairs. There was a
sword strapped to her back. Her face wavered, never settling clearly, but the sword seemed as solid as the stone.
The woman reached Egwene's level and held out one hand.
"We can reach the top together," she said in a familiar
drawling accent.

Egwene pushed the dream away as she would have a
viper. She felt her body thrash, heard herself groan in her
sleep, but for a moment she could do nothing. She had
dreamed of the Seanchan before, of a Seanchan woman
somehow tied to her, but this was a Seanchan who would
save her. No! They had put a leash on her, made her *damane*. She would as soon die as be saved by a Seanchan! A
very long time passed before she could address herself to
calming her sleeping body. Or maybe it only seemed a long
time. Not a Seanchan; never that!

Slowly, the dreams returned.

She was climbing another path along a cliff shrouded in
clouds, but this was a broad ledge of smoothly paved white
stone, and there were no rocks underfoot. The cliff itself
was chalky white and as smooth as if polished. Despite the

clouds, the pale stone almost gleamed. She climbed quickly
and soon realized that the ledge was spiraling around. The
cliff was actually a spire. No sooner did that thought occur
than she was standing on the top of it, a flat polished disc
walled by mist. Not quite flat, though. A small white plinth
stood centered in that circle, supporting an oil-lamp made
of clear glass. The flame on that lamp burned bright and
steady, without flickering. It was white, too.

Suddenly a pair of birds flashed out of the mist, two ravens black as night. Streaking across the spire-top, they
struck the lamp and flew on without so much as a pause. The
lamp spun and wobbled, dancing around atop the plinth,
flinging off droplets of oil. Some of those drops caught fire
in midair and vanished. Others fell around the short column, each supporting a tiny, flickering white flame. And
the lamp continued to wobble on the edge of falling.

Egwene woke in darkness with a jolt. She knew. For the
first time, she knew exactly what a dream meant. But why
would she dream of a Seanchan woman saving her, and
then of the Seanchan attacking the White Tower? An attack that would shake the Aes Sedai to their core and threaten
the Tower itself. Of course, it was only a possibility. But
the events seen in true dreams were more likely than other
possibilities.

She thought she was considering calmly, but at a rough
rustle of canvas from the entry flaps, she very nearly embraced the True Source. Hastily she ran through novice
exercises to compose herself, water flowing over smooth
stones, wind blowing through high grass. Light, she *had*
been frightened. It took two to achieve any sort of calm.
She opened her mouth to ask who was there.

"Asleep?" Halima's voice muttered softly. She sounded
wound up tight, almost excited. "Well, I wouldn't mind a
good night's sleep myself."

Listening to the woman undress for bed in the dark,
Egwene lay very still. If she let her know she was awake,
she would have to talk with her, and at the moment, that
would be embarrassing. She was fairly certain that Halima
had found herself company, if not for the whole night.
Halima could do as she wished, of course, but Egwene was
still disappointed. Wishing that she had remained asleep,

she found herself slipping under once more, and this time, she did not try to stop halfway. She would remember any dreams that came, and she did need some actual sleep.

Chesa came bright and early to bring her breakfast on a tray and help her dress. Actually, it was early and not bright at all. There was only the merest hint of sunlight, and the lamps' light was necessary to see anything. The embers in the brazier had died down during the night, of course, and the cold that hung in the air felt gray. There might be a chance of more snow today. Halima wriggled into her silk shift and dress, making laughing jokes about how she would like to have a maid while Chesa was doing up the rows of buttons that ran down Egwene's back. The plump woman wore a set face, ignoring Halima altogether. Egwene said nothing. She said nothing very determinedly. Halima was not her servant. She had no right to set standards for the woman.

Just as Chesa finished the last of the tiny buttons and gave Egwene's arm a pat, Nisao ducked into the tent, letting in a fresh wave of cold air. The brief glimpse afforded before the flaps fell behind her showed that it was still gray outside. Definitely a chance of snow.

"I must speak to the Mother alone," she said, holding her cloak around her as if she already felt the snow. Such a firm tone was unusual from the small woman.

Egwene nodded to Chesa, who curtsied, but still cautioned, "Now don't let your breakfast get cold," on her way out of the tent.

Halima paused, eyeing Nisao and Egwene both, before scooping up her cloak from where it lay in an untidy heap at the foot of her cot. "I suppose Delana has work for me," she said, sounding irritated.

Nisao frowned at the woman's back as she left, but without saying anything she embraced *saidar* and wove a ward against eavesdropping around her and Egwene. Without asking permission. "Anaiya and her Warder are dead," she said. "Some of the workmen bringing in sacks of coals last night heard a noise, like someone thrashing around, and for a wonder, they all went running to see what it was. They found Anaiya and Setagana lying in the snow, dead."

Egwene sat down slowly on her chair, which did not feel

particularly comfortable at the moment. Anaiya, dead. She had had no beauty except her smile, but when she smiled, it warmed everything around her. A plain-faced woman who loved lace on her robes. Egwene knew she should feel sadness for Setagana, too, but he had been a Warder. If he had survived Anaiya, it was unlikely he would have lived long. "How?" she said. Nisao would not have woven that ward just to tell her Anaiya was dead.

Nisao's face tightened, and despite the ward, she looked over her shoulder as if she feared someone might be listening at the entry flaps. "The workmen thought they had eaten badly preserved mushrooms. Some farmers are careless in gathering what they intend to sell, and the wrong sort can paralyze your lungs or make your throat swell up, so you die struggling for air." Egwene nodded impatiently. She had grown up in a country village, after all. "Everyone seemed willing to accept that," Nisao went on, but she did not hurry. Hands twisting and flexing on the edges of her cloak, she appeared reluctant to reach her conclusion. "There were no wounds, no injuries of any sort. No reason to think it was anything but a greedy farmer selling bad mushrooms. But . . ." She sighed, glancing over her shoulder again, and lowered her voice. "I suppose it was all the talk of the Black Tower in the Hall today. I tested for resonance. They were killed with *saidin*." A grimace of disgust crossed her face. "I think someone just wove solid flows of Air around their heads and let them smother." Shuddering, she drew her cloak closer.

Egwene wanted to shudder, too. She was surprised she did not. Anaiya, dead. Smothered. A deliberately cruel way of killing, used by someone who had hoped to leave no traces. "Have you told anyone, yet?"

"Of course not," Nisao said indignantly. "I came to you straightaway. As soon as I knew you'd be awake, at least."

"A pity. You will have to explain why you delayed. We can't keep this secret." Well, Amyrlins had kept darker secrets, for the good of the Tower as they saw it. "If we have a man who can channel among us, then the sisters need to be on their guard." A man who could channel hiding among the workmen or soldiers seemed unlikely, but less so than one coming there just to kill a single sister and her Warder.

Which raised another question. "Why Anaiya? Was she just in the wrong place at the wrong time, Nisao? Where did they die?"

"Near the wagons on the south side of camp. I don't know why they were there that time of night. Unless Anaiya was going to the privies and Setagana thought she need guarding even there."

"Then you're going to find out for me, Nisao. What were Anaiya and Setagana doing out when everybody else was asleep? Why were they killed? This, you will keep secret. Until you can give me reasons, no one but the two of us is to know you're looking for any."

Nisao's mouth opened and closed. "If I must, I must," she muttered only half under her breath. She was not really suited to keeping deep secrets, and she knew it. The last she had tried to keep had led directly to her having to swear fealty to Egwene. "Will this put a stop to talk about an agreement with the Black Tower?"

"I doubt it," Egwene said wearily. Light, how could she be weary already? The sun was not fully up yet. "Either way, I think it is going to be another very long day." And the best she could find to hope for in it was that she could make it to another night without a headache.

CHAPTER
21

A Mark

Alviarin stepped through the gateway, letting it snap shut behind her in a fading slash of brilliant blue-white, and almost immediately sneezed from the dust kicked up by her shoes. At once another sneeze racked her, and then another that brought tears to her eyes. Lit only by the glowing globe that floated in front of her, the rough-walled storeroom hewn out of the bedrock three levels below the Tower Library was empty except for centuries worth of dust. She would much rather have returned straight to her apartments in the Tower itself, but there was always the chance of walking in to find a servant cleaning, and then she would have to get rid of the body and hope that no one remembered that the servant had last been seen going into her rooms. Remain hidden and rouse not even the slightest hint of suspicion, Mesaana had commanded. That seemed over-timid when the Black Ajah had walked the Tower with impunity since its founding, but when one of the Chosen commanded, only a fool disobeyed. At least, if there was any chance of being found out.

Irritably, Alviarin channeled to force the dust out of the air, slamming it down so hard that the stone floor should have shaken. She would not have to go through this every time if she simply swept all the dust into a corner rather than leaving it spread out. No one else had come this far into the Library basements in years; no one would notice the room was clean. But someone was always doing what no one ever did. She often did so herself, and she did not intend to be caught through a foolish mistake. Still, she grumbled under her breath as she channeled the reddish mud from her shoes and the hem of her skirts and cloak. It seemed unlikely that anyone would recognize it as coming from Tremalking, the largest of the Sea Folk islands, but someone might wonder where she had been to get muddy. The Tower grounds would be buried in snow except where they had been shoveled clear and the dirt frozen hard. Still muttering to herself, she channeled again to muffle the squeal of rusted hinges as she pushed open the rough wooden door. There was a way to make a weave and hide it, so she would not have to soften that creak every time— she was certain there was—but Mesaana refused to teach it to her.

Mesaana was the real source of her annoyance. The Chosen taught what she wished and nothing more, hinted at wonders then withheld them. And Mesaana used her like an errand girl. She sat at the head of the Supreme Council and knew the names of every Black sister in every heart, which was more than Mesaana could say. The woman showed little interest in who would carry out her orders, so long as they *were* carried out, and to the absolute letter. All too often, she wanted them carried out by Alviarin herself, forcing her to deal with women and men who thought themselves her equals just because they also served the Great Lord. Too many of the Friends thought themselves equal to Aes Sedai, or even superior. Worse, Mesaana forbade her to make an object lesson of even one. Repellent little rodents, none able to channel, and Alviarin had to be polite just because some of them might be serving another of the Chosen! It was obvious that Mesaana did not know for sure. She was one of the Chosen, and she made Alviarin smile at the dust of the street for her uncertainty.

The ball of pale light floating ahead of her for illumination, Alviarin glided down the rough stone corridor, smoothing the dust behind with feathery brushes of Air so it would seem undisturbed and rehearsing several choice things she would like to say to Mesaana. She would actually say none of them, of course, which only honed her irritation. Criticizing one of the Chosen in even the mildest terms was a short path to pain, perhaps to death. Almost surely both, in truth. With the Chosen, grovel and obey was the only way to survive, and the first was as important as the second. The prize of immortality was worth a little groveling. With that, she could gain all the power she wished, much more than any Amyrlin had ever wielded. First, though, it was necessary to survive.

Once she reached the top of the first ramp leading upward, she no longer bothered hiding her traces. There was not nearly so much dust here, and that marked by the wheels of handcarts and scuffs from shoes; another set of faint footprints would never be noticed. She still walked quickly, though. Usually, the thought of living forever brightened her, the thought of eventually wielding power through Mesaana as she now did through Elaida. Well, almost the same; expecting to bring Mesaana to Elaida's state of compliance was too ambitious, but she could still tie strings to the woman that would assure her own rise. Today, her mind kept returning to the fact that she had been out of the Tower for almost a month. Mesaana would not have bothered to keep Elaida under control during her absence, though the Chosen would surely lay the fault at Alviarin's feet if anything had gone amiss. Of course, Elaida was properly cowed after the last time. The woman had *begged* for release from taking private penances from the Mistress of Novices. Of course she was too cowed to have stepped out of line. Of course. Alviarin pushed Elaida firmly to the back of her head, but she did not slow her steps.

A second ramp took her to the highest basement, where she let the glowing ball vanish and released *saidar*. The shadows here were dotted with pools of wan light that nearly touched one another, cast by lamps sitting in iron brackets along stone walls that were neatly dressed on this level. Nothing moved except for a rat that went scuttling away with a faint click of claws on the floorstones. That almost made her smile. Almost. The Great Lord's eyes riddled the Tower, now, though no one seemed to have noticed that the wardings had failed. She did not think it was anything Mesaana had done; the wards simply no longer worked as they were supposed to. There were . . . gaps. She certainly did not care whether the animal saw her, or reported what it had seen, but she still ducked quickly into a narrow circular staircase. There might be people about on this level, and people were not to be trusted the same as rats.

Perhaps, she thought as she climbed, she could probe Mesaana about that impossible flare in the Power, so long as she was . . . delicate. The Chosen would think she was hiding something if she never mentioned it. Every woman who could channel in the whole world had to be wondering what had happened. She would just have to be careful not to let slip anything that suggested that she had actually visited the site. Long after the flare vanished, of course—she was not stupid enough to simply stroll into *that!*—but Mesaana seemed to think Alviarin should carry out her *chores* without taking a moment for herself. Could the woman really believe that she had no affairs of her own to see to? It was best to behave as if she did have none. For the moment it was, at least.

In the shadows at the top of the stairs, she stopped in front of the small plain door, roughly finished on this side, in order to take hold of herself as she folded her cloak over her arm. Mesaana was one of the Chosen, but still human. Mesaana made mistakes. And she would kill Alviarin in a heartbeat if *she* made one. Grovel, obey and survive. And always be wary. She had known that long before meeting one of the Chosen. Retrieving the white Keeper's stole from her belt pouch, she settled it around her neck and cracked the door carefully to listen. Silence, as expected. She stepped out into the Ninth Depository and closed the door behind her. On the inner side, the door was no less plain, but polished to a soft glow.

The Tower Library was divided into twelve depositories, at least insofar as the world knew, and the Ninth was the smallest, given over to texts on various forms of arithmetic, yet it was still a large chamber, a long oval with a flattened dome for a ceiling, filled with row on row of tall wooden shelves, each surrounded by a narrow walkway four paces above the seven-colored floor tiles. Tall ladders stood alongside the shelves, on wheels so they could be moved easily, both on the floor and on the walkways, and mirrored brass stand-lamps with bases so heavy that each took three or four men to move. Fire was a constant concern in the Library. The stand-lamps all burned brightly, ready to light the way for any sister who wanted to find a book or boxed manuscript, but a shelved handcart holding three large leather-cased volumes to be replaced was still in the middle of one aisle exactly where she remembered it from the last time she walked through. She did not understand why there was any need for different forms of arithmetic or why so many books had been written on them, and for all the Tower prided itself on having the greatest collection of books in the world, covering every possible topic, it seemed that most Aes Sedai agreed with her. She had never seen another sister in the Ninth Depository, the reason she used it for her entryway. At the wide arched doors, standing invitingly open, she listened until she was satisfied that the corridor beyond was empty before slipping out. Anyone would have thought it strange that she had developed an interest for the books in there.

As she hurried along the main corridors, where the floor tiles were laid in repeating rows of the Ajah colors, it came to her that the Library was more silent than usual, even counting how few Aes Sedai remained in the Tower at present. There was always a sister or two to be seen, if only the librarians—some Browns actually maintained apartments in the upper levels in addition to their rooms in the Tower—yet the huge figures carved into the corridors' walls, fancifully garbed people and strange animals ten feet tall or more, might have been the Library's only inhabitants. Drafts made the intricately carved lamp wheels hanging ten paces overhead creak faintly on their chains. Her footsteps seemed unnaturally loud, casting soft echoes from the vaulted ceiling.

"May I help you?" a woman's voice said quietly behind her.

Startled, Alviarin spun around, almost dropping her cloak, before she could catch herself. "I just wanted to walk through the Library, Zemaille," she said, and immediately felt a stab of irritation. If she was jumpy enough to explain herself to a librarian, then she really did need to take a grip before she reported to Mesaana. She almost wanted to tell Zemaille what was happening on Tremalking, just to see whether the woman would flinch.

The bland expression on the Brown sister's dark face did not change, but a touch of some unreadable emotion altered the pitch of her voice. Tall and very lean, Zemaille always held that outer mask of reserve and distance, but Alviarin suspected she was less shy than she pretended, and less pleasant. "That's quite understandable. The Library is restful, and it's a sad time for us all. And sadder still for you, of course."

"Of course," Alviarin repeated as if by rote. A sad time? For her in particular? She considered drawing the woman to some secluded corner where she could be questioned and disposed of, but then she noticed another Brown, a round woman even darker than Zemaille, watching them from farther down the hall. Aiden and Zemaille were weak in the Power, yet overcoming both at once would be difficult if it was possible at all. Why were they both down here on the ground floor? The pair was seldom seen, shuttling between the rooms on the upper levels they shared with Nyein, the third Sea Folk sister, and the so-called Thirteenth Depository, where the secret records were kept. All three worked there, willingly immersed to their necks in their labors. She walked on and tried to tell herself she was being skittish without reason, but that did nothing to soothe the prickling between her shoulder blades.

The lack of librarians guarding the front entrance only made the prickles grow. Librarians always stood at *every* entrance, to make sure not a scrap of paper left the library without their knowledge. Alviarin channeled to shove one of the tall carved doors open before she reached it and left it standing agape on its bronze hinges as she hurried down the wide marble stairs. The broad, oak-lined stone path that led toward the tall white shaft of the Tower had been shoveled clear, but if it had not been, she would have used the Power to melt the snow away ahead of her, let anyone think of it what they would. Mesaana had made crystal clear the price of taking the risk that anyone might learn the weave for Traveling, or even that she knew it, else she would have Traveled from the spot. With the Tower in sight, looming over the trees and gleaming in the pale morning sunlight, she could have been there in a step. Instead, she fought the urge to run.

It was no surprise to find the Tower's wide, tall corridors empty. A few scurrying servants with the white Flame of Tar Valon on their breasts bobbed their bows and curtsies as she passed, but they were no more use, no more important, than the drafts that made the gilded stand-lamps flicker and rippled the bright tapestries hanging on the snowy white walls. Sisters kept to their own Ajah quarters as much as possible these days, of course, and unless she encountered a member of her own heart, even seeing an Aes Sedai she knew was Black Ajah would have been useless. She knew them, but they did not know her. Besides, she was not about to reveal herself to anyone she did not have to. Perhaps some of those marvelous instruments from the Age of Legends that Mesaana talked about would allow her to question any sister immediately one day, if the woman ever actually produced them, but now it was still a matter of ciphered orders left on pillows or in secret spots. What had once seemed almost instantaneous responses now seemed interminably delayed. A stocky bald-headed serving man making his bow gulped audibly, and she smoothed her features. She prided herself on her icy detachment, always presenting a cool unruffled surface. In any event, scowling her way though the Tower was going to get her exactly nowhere.

There was one person in the Tower she was sure she knew exactly where to find, someone she could demand answers from with no fear of what the woman thought. A little caution was needed even there, of course—careless questions revealed more than most answers were worth—but Elaida would tell her anything. With a sigh, she began to climb.

Mesaana had told her of another marvel of the Age of Legends that she wished very much to see, a thing called a "lift." The flying machines sounded much grander, of course, but it was far easier to envision a mechanical contrivance that whisked you from floor to floor. She was not really certain that buildings several times as high as the White Tower could really have existed, either—in the whole world, not even the Stone of Tear rivaled the Tower's height—but just knowing about "lifts" made climbing up spiraling hallways and sweeping flights of stairs seem laborious.

She did pause at the Amyrlin's study, only three levels up, but as expected, both rooms were empty, the bare writing tables polished till they shone. The rooms themselves seemed bare, with no wall hangings, no ornaments, nothing at all but the tables and chairs and unlit stand-lamps. Elaida rarely came down from her apartments near the Tower's peak anymore. That had seemed acceptable at one time, since it isolated the woman even more from the rest of the Tower. Few sisters made that climb willingly. Today, though, by the time Alviarin had climbed close to eighty spans, she was seriously considering making Elaida move back down.

Elaida's waiting room was empty, of course, though a folder of papers sitting atop the writing table said someone had been there. Seeing what they contained, and deciding whether Elaida needed to be punished for having it, could wait, though. Alviarin tossed her cloak down on the writing table and pushed open the door, newly carved with the Flame of Tar Valon and awaiting the gilder, that led deeper into the apartments.

She was surprised at the surge of relief she felt at seeing Elaida sitting behind the starkly carved and gilded writing table, the seven-striped—no, six-striped, now—stole around her neck and the Flame of Tar Valon picked out in moonstones among the gold-work on the high chairback above her head. A niggling worry that she had not let surface until now had been the possibility that the woman was dead in some fool accident. That would have explained Zemaille's comment. Choosing a new Amyrlin could have taken months, even with the rebels and everything else confronting them, but her days as Keeper would have been numbered. What surprised her more than her relief, though, was the presence of more than half the Sitters in the Hall standing in front of the writing table in their fringed shawls. Elaida *knew* better than to entertain this sort of delegation without her present. The huge gilded case clock against the wall, a vulgarly over-ornamented piece, chimed twice for High, small enameled figures of Aes Sedai popping out of tiny doors in its front as she opened her mouth to tell the Sitters that she needed to confer with the Amyrlin privately. They would leave with little hemming or hawing. A Keeper had no authority to order them out, but they knew that her authority extended beyond that her stole conferred even if they did not begin to suspect how that could be.

"Alviarin," Elaida said, sounding surprised, before she could get a word out. The hardness of Elaida's face softened in what almost seemed pleasure. Her mouth quirked close to a smile. Elaida had had no reasons to smile in some time. "Stand over there and be quiet until I have time to deal with you," she said, waving an imperious hand toward a corner of the room. The Sitters shifted their feet and adjusted their shawls. Suana, a beefy woman, gave Alviarin a tight glance, and Shevan, tall as a man and angular, stared straight at her with no expression, but the others avoided meeting her eye.

Stunned, she stood stock-still on the brightly patterned silk carpet, gaping. This could not be mere rebellion on Elaida's part—the woman would have to be insane!—but what in the name of the Great Lord had happened to give her the nerve? What?

Elaida's hand slapped the tabletop with a loud crack, a blow that made one of the lacquered boxes there rattle. "When I tell you to stand in the corner, Daughter," she said in a low, dangerous voice, "I expect you to obey." Her eyes glittered. "Or shall I summon the Mistress of Novices so these sisters can witness your 'private' penance?"

Heat suffused Alviarin's face, part humiliation and part anger. To have anyone *hear* such things said, and to her face! Fear bubbled in her, too, turning her stomach to acid. A few words from her, and Elaida would stand accused of sending sisters to disaster and captivity, not once but twice. Rumors had already begun swirling about events in Cairhien; murky rumors, but growing more certain by the day. And once it was learned that on top of that, Elaida had sent fifty sisters to try to defeat hundreds of men who could channel, not even the existence of the rebel sisters wintering in Murandy with their army would keep the Amyrlin's stole on her shoulders, or her head. She could not dare to do this. Unless . . . Unless she could discredit Alviarin as Black Ajah. That might gain her a little time. Only a little, surely, once the facts about Dumai's Wells and the Black Tower were known, but Elaida might be ready to grasp at straws. No, it was not possible, could not *be* possible. Flight certainly was impossible. For one thing, if Elaida was ready to lay charges, flight would only confirm them. For another, Mesaana would find her and kill her if she fled. All that flashed through her head as she moved on leaden feet to stand in the corner like a penitent novice.

There had to be a way to recover from this, whatever had happened. There was always a way to recover. Listening might find it for her. She would have prayed, if the Dark Lord listened to prayers.

Elaida studied her for a moment, then gave a satisfied nod. The woman's eyes still shone with emotion, though. Lifting the lid of one of the three lacquered boxes on her table, she took out a small, age-darkened ivory carving of a turtle and stroked it between her fingers. Fondling the carvings in that box was a habit she had when she wanted to soothe her nerves. "Now," she said. "You were explaining to me why I should enter negotiations."

"We were not asking permission, Mother," Suana said sharply, thrusting her chin out. She had too much chin, a square stone of it, and the arrogance to thrust it at anyone. "A decision of this sort belongs to the Hall. There is strong feeling in favor of it in the Yellow Ajah." Which meant she had strong feelings. She was the head of the Yellow Ajah, the First Weaver, something Alviarin knew because the Black Ajah knew all the Ajah secrets, or nearly all, and in Suana's view, her opinions *were* her Ajah's opinions.

Doesine, the other Yellow present, eyed Suana sideways, but said nothing. Pale and boyishly slim, Doesine looked as if she did not really want to be there, a pretty, sulky boy who had been dragged somewhere by his ear. Sitters often balked at arm-twisting from their Ajah's head, yet it was not beyond possibility that Suana had found some way.

"Many Whites also support talks," Ferane said, frowning distractedly at an ink stain on one plump finger. "It is the logical thing to do, under the present circumstances." She was First Reasoner, head of the White Ajah, but less likely than Suana to take her own views for those of the entire Ajah. A little less likely. Ferane often seemed as vague as the worst of the Browns—the long black hair that framed her round face needed a brush, and part of the fringe on her shawl appeared to have been dipped carelessly in her breakfast tea—but she could catch the slightest crack in the logic of an argument. She might well have been there by herself because she simply did not believe she needed any assistance from the other White Sitters.

Leaning back in her tall chair, Elaida began to glower,

her fingers stroking faster on the turtle, and Andaya spoke up quickly, not quite looking at Elaida while pretending to adjust the set of her gray-fringed shawl along her arms.

"The point, Mother, is that we must find a way to end this peacefully," she said, the Taraboner accent strong in her speech as it was when she felt uneasy. Frequently diffident around Elaida, she glanced at Yukiri as though hoping for support, but the slender little woman turned her head aside slightly. Yukiri was remarkably stubborn for such a tiny woman; unlike Doesine, she would not have responded to arm-twisting. So why was she here if she did not want to be? Realizing that she was on her own, Andaya rushed on. "It must not be allowed to come to fighting in the streets of Tar Valon. Or in the Tower; especially not that; not again. So far, the rebels seem content to sit and watch the city, but that cannot last. They have rediscovered how to Travel, Mother, and have used it to carry an army across hundreds of leagues. We must begin talks before they decide to use Traveling to bring that army into Tar Valon, or all is lost even if we win."

Fists knotted in her skirts, Alviarin swallowed hard. She thought her eyes might pop out of her head. The rebels knew how to Travel? They were here at Tar Valon already? And these fools wanted to *talk*? She could see carefully laid plans, carefully arranged designs, evaporating like mist in a summer sun. Perhaps the Dark Lord would listen, if she prayed very hard.

Elaida's scowl did not diminish, but she set the ivory turtle down very carefully, and her voice came close to normal. The old normal, before Alviarin reined her in, with a steel core beneath the softness of the words. "Do the Brown and the Green also support talks?"

"The Brown," Shevan began, then pursed her lips in thought and visibly changed what she had intended to say. Outwardly, she seemed utterly composed, yet she was rubbing her long thumbs against her bony forefingers unconsciously. "The Brown is quite clear on the historical precedents. You have all read the secret histories, or should have. Whenever the Tower has been divided against itself, disaster has struck the world. With the Last Battle looming, in a world that contains the Black Tower, we can no longer afford to remain divided a day longer than need be."

It hardly seemed that Elaida's face could grow darker, but mention of the Black Tower did it. "And the Green?" Her voice was still controlled.

All three Green Sitters were there, indicating very strong support among their Ajah, or heavy pressure from the head of the Green. As senior, Talene should have answered Elaida—Greens stuck to their hierarchies in everything—but the tall, golden-haired woman glanced at Yukiri for some reason, then just as oddly, at Doesine, and put her eyes on the carpet and stood plucking at her green silk skirts. Rina frowned faintly, wrinkling her upturned nose in puzzlement, but she had worn the shawl for fewer than fifty years, so it was left to Rubinde to reply. A sturdy woman, Rubinde appeared short and stocky alongside Talene, and almost plain despite eyes the color of sapphires.

"I am instructed to make the same points as Shevan," she said, ignoring the startled look that Rina gave her. Plainly there had been pressure from Adelorna, the Green 'Captain-General,' and plainly Rubinde disagreed if she was willing to make it public. "Tarmon Gai'don is coming, the Black Tower is almost as great a threat, and the Dragon Reborn is missing, if he isn't dead. We can no longer afford to be divided. If Andaya can talk the rebels back into the Tower, then we must let her try."

"I see," Elaida said in a flat tone. But strangely, her color improved, and the hint of a smile even touched her mouth. "Then by all means, talk them back, if you can. But my edicts stand. The Blue Ajah no longer exists, and every sister who follows that child Egwene al'Vere must serve penance under my guidance before she can be readmitted to *any* Ajah. I intend to *weld* the White Tower into a weapon to use at Tarmon Gai'don."

Ferane and Suana opened their mouths, protest painted on their faces, but Elaida cut them off with a raised hand. "I have spoken, daughters. Leave me now. And see to your . . . talks."

There was nothing the Sitters could do short of open defiance. What was the Hall's right was theirs, but the Hall seldom dared infringe far on the Amyrlin Seat's authority. Not

unless the Hall was united against the Amyrlin, and this
Hall was anything but united on any point. Alviarin had
helped insure that herself. They left, Ferane and Suana, stiff-
backed and tight-lipped, Andaya almost scurrying. None of
them so much as glanced in Alviarin's direction.

She barely waited for the door to close behind the last.
"This really changes nothing, Elaida, surely you see that. You
must think clearly, not trip over a momentary aberration."
She knew she was babbling, but she could not seem to stop.
"The disaster at Dumai's Wells, the certain disaster at the
Black Tower, these can still unseat you. You need me to hold
on to the staff and stole. You need me, Elaida. You . . ." She
clamped her teeth shut before her tongue threw everything
away. There still had to be a way.

"I'm surprised you returned," Elaida said, rising and
smoothing her red-slashed skirts. She had never given up
her way of dressing as a Red. Strangely, she was smiling
as she came around the table. Not a hint at a smile, but a
full, pleased curve of her lips. "Have you been hiding somewhere in the city since the rebels arrived? I thought you'd
have taken ship as soon as you learned they were here.
Who would have thought they would rediscover Traveling?
Imagine what we can do once we know that." Smiling, she
glided across the carpet.

"Now let me see. What do I have to fear from you? The
stories out of Cairhien are the talk of the Tower, but even
if sisters really were obeying the al'Thor boy, which I for
one cannot believe, everyone blames Coiren. She had the
responsibility of bringing him here, and she has as good
as been tried and convicted, in the minds of the sisters."
Elaida stopped in front of Alviarin, hemming her into the
corner. That smile never touched her eyes. She smiled, and
her eyes glittered. Alviarin could not break away from that
gaze. "In the last week, we've heard a good many things
about the 'Black Tower,' as well." Elaida's lips twisted in
disgust around the name. "It seems there are even more
men than you supposed. But everyone thinks Toveine must
have had the sense to learn that before she attacked. There
has been a good deal of discussion over it. If she comes
dragging back here defeated, she will harvest the blame. So
your threats . . ."

Alviarin staggered into the wall, blinking away spots, before she even realized that the other woman had slapped her. Her cheek already felt swollen. The glow of *saidar* had surrounded Elaida, and the shield settled on Alviarin before she could twitch, cutting her off from the Power. But Elaida did not intend to use the Power. She drew back a fist. Still smiling.

Slowly, the woman drew a deep breath and let her hand fall. She did not remove the shield, however. "Would you really use that?" she asked in an almost mild tone.

Alviarin's hand sprang away from the hilt of her belt knife. Grabbing it had been a reflex, but even if Elaida had not been holding the Power, killing her when so many Sitters knew they were together would have been as good as killing herself. Still, her face burned when Elaida sniffed contemptuously.

"I look forward to seeing your neck stretched on the headsman's block for treason, Alviarin, but until I have the proof I need, there are still a few things I can do. Do you remember how many times you had Silviana come to give me private penance? I hope you do, because you are going to take ten for every day I suffered. And, oh, yes." With a jerk, she pulled the Keeper's stole roughly from Alviarin's neck. "Since no one could find you when the rebels arrived, I asked the Hall to remove you as Keeper. Not the full Hall, of course. You may still have a little influence there. But it was surprisingly easy to gain the consensus from those who were sitting that day. A Keeper is supposed to be with her Amyrlin, not wandering off on her own. On second thought, you may not have any influence at all, since it turns out you were hiding in the city all along. Or did you sail back to find disaster, and actually think you could recover something from the ruins?

"No matter. It might have been better for you to leap on the first ship you could find leaving Tar Valon. But I must admit, the thought of you scuttling from village to village ashamed to show your face to another sister pales beside the pleasure I'll take seeing you suffer. Now get out of my sight before I decide it should be the birch rather than Silviana's strap." Tossing the white stole to the floor, she turned her back and released *saidar,* gliding toward her chair as if Alviarin had ceased to exist.

Alviarin did not leave, she fled, running with the feel of the Darkhounds' breath on the back of her neck. She had barely been able to think since she heard the word *treason*. That word, echoing in her head, made her want to howl. Treason could only mean one thing. Elaida knew, and she was searching for proof. The Dark Lord have mercy. But he never did. Mercy was for those afraid to be strong. She was not afraid. She was a skin stuffed to bursting with terror.

Back down through the Tower she fled, and if there was so much as a servant in the hallways, she did not see him. Horror blinded her eyes to anything not directly in her path. All the way back down to the sixth level she ran, to her own apartments. At least, she supposed they were still hers for the moment. The rooms with their balcony over-looking the great square in front of the Tower went with the office of Keeper. For the moment, it was enough that she still had rooms. And a chance to live.

The furnishings were still the Domani pieces left by the previous occupant, all pale striped wood inlaid with pearl-shell and amber. In the bedchamber, she threw open one of the wardrobes and fell to her knees, pushing aside dresses to rummage in the back for a small chest, a box less than two hands square, that had been hers for many years. The carving on the box was intricate but clumsy, rows of varied knots apparently done by a carver with more ambition than skill. Her hands shook as she carried it to a table, and she set it down to wipe clammy palms on her dress. The trick to opening the box was simply a matter of spreading her fingers as wide as they would go to press simultaneously at four knots in the carving, no two alike. The lid lifted slightly, and she threw it back, revealing her most precious possession wrapped in a small bundle of brown cloth to keep it from rattling if a maid shook the box. Most Tower servants would not risk stealing, but most did not mean all.

For a moment, Alviarin only stared at the package. Her most precious possession, a thing from the Age of Legends, but she had never dared use it before. Only in the worst emergency, Mesaana had said, the most desperate need, yet what need could be more dire than this? Mesaana said the thing could take hammer blows without breaking, but she undid the wrappings with the care she would have used with a piece of fine blown glass, revealing a *ter'angreal,* a brilliant red rod no larger than her forefinger, utterly smooth except for a few fine lines worked into the surface in a sinuous interconnecting pattern. Embracing the Source, she touched that pattern with hair-thin flows of Fire and Earth at two of the interconnections. That would not have been necessary in the Age of Legends, but something called the "standing flows" no longer existed. A world where almost any *ter'angreal* could be used by people unable to channel seemed odd beyond comprehension. Why had it been allowed?

Pressing one end of the rod hard with her thumb—the One Power was not enough, by itself—she sat down heavily and leaned against the chair's low back, staring at the thing in her hand. It was done. She felt hollow, now, a vast empty space with fears fluttering through the darkness like enormous bats.

Instead of rewrapping the *ter'angreal,* she tucked it into her belt pouch and got up long enough to stuff the box back into the wardrobe. Until she knew she was safe, she did not intend to let that rod out of her possession. But then all she could do was sit and wait, rocking back and forth with her hands clasped between her knees. She could not stop rocking any more than she could stop the low moans that trickled between her teeth. Since the founding of the Tower, no sister had ever been charged with being Black Ajah. Oh, there had been suspicions by individual sisters, and from time to time Aes Sedai had died to make sure those suspicions never went further, but never had it come to official charges. If Elaida was willing to speak openly of the headsman's block, she must be close to bringing charges. Very close. Black sisters had been made to disappear, too, when suspicions grew too great. The Black Ajah remained hidden whatever the cost. She wished she could stop moaning.

Suddenly the light in the room dimmed, enveloping the chamber in swirling twilight shadows. The sunlight at the casements seemed unable to penetrate beyond the glass panes. Alviarin was on her knees in a breath, eyes down. She trembled with wanting to pour out her fears, but with the Chosen, the forms must be followed. "I live to serve, Great Mistress," she said, and nothing more. She could not waste a moment, much less an hour screaming in pain. Her hands were clutched together to keep them from shaking.

"What is your grave emergency, child?" It was a woman's voice, but a voice of crystal chimes. Displeased chimes. Only displeased. Angry chimes might have meant death on the spot. "If you think I will raise a finger to get the Keeper's stole back for you, you are sadly mistaken. You can still do what I wish done, with a little extra effort. And you may consider your penances with the Mistress of Novices a small punishment from me. I did warn you about pushing Elaida quite so hard."

Alviarin swallowed her protests. Elaida was not a woman to bend without hard pushing. Mesaana had to know that. But protests could be dangerous, with the Chosen. Many things were dangerous, with the Chosen. In any case, Silviana's strap was a trifle compared to the headsman's axe.

"Elaida knows, Great Mistress," she breathed, raising her eyes. In front of her stood a woman of light-and-shadow, clothed in light-and-shadow, all stark blacks and silvery whites that flowed from one to the other and back. Silver eyes frowned from a face of smoke, with silver lips drawn in a tight line. It was only Illusion, and really not done any better than Alviarin could have. A flash of green silk skirt embroidered with elaborate bands of bronze showed as Mesaana glided across the Domani carpet. But Alviarin could not see the weaves that made the Illusion any more than she had felt those the woman had used to arrive or cast the room in shadows. For all she could sense, Mesaana could not channel at all! The lust for those two secrets usually cut at her, but today she hardly noticed. "She knows I am Black Ajah, Great Mistress. If she has uncovered me, then she has had someone digging deep. Dozens of us may be at risk, perhaps all of us." Best to make a threat as large as possible if you wanted to be sure of a response. It might even be so.

But Mesaana's response was a dismissive wave of one now-silver hand. Her face glowed like a moon around eyes blacker than coals. "That is ridiculous. Elaida cannot decide from one day to the next whether she even believes the Black Ajah exists. You are just trying to save yourself a little pain. Perhaps a little more will instruct you in your error." Alviarin began to plead as Mesaana raised that hand higher, and a weave she remembered much too well formed in the air. She had to make the woman understand!

Abruptly, the shadows in the room lurched. Everything

seemed to shift sideways as the darkness thickened in midnight lumps. And then the darkness was gone. Startled, Alviarin found herself with her begging hands stretched up toward a blue-eyed woman of flesh and blood, garbed in bronze-embroidered green. A tantalizingly familiar woman who looked just short of her middle years. She had known Mesaana walked the Tower disguised as one of the sisters, though no Chosen she had met showed any sign of agelessness, but she could not match that face to any name. And she realized something else, as well. That face was afraid. Hiding it, but afraid.

"She's been very useful," Mesaana said, not sounding afraid at all, in a voice that tugged the edge of recognition, "and now I will have to kill her."

"You were always . . . overly wasteful," replied a harsh voice, like rotten bone crumbling underfoot.

Alviarin fell over in shock at the tall shape of a man in sinuous black armor, all overlapping plates like the scales of a snake, standing in front of one window. It was not a man, though. That bloodless face had no eyes, just smooth dead white skin where they should have been. She had encountered Myrddraal before, in the service of the Dark Lord, and even managed to meet their eyeless gazes without giving way to the terror those stares engendered, but this one made her scrabble back across the floor until her back jarred a leg of the table. Lurks were alike as two raindrops, tall and lean and identical, but this one stood a head taller, and fear seemed to radiate from it, soaking into her bones. Unthinking, she reached for the Source. And nearly screamed. The Source was gone! She was not shielded; there was simply nothing there for her to embrace! The Myrddraal looked at her and smiled. Lurks never smiled. Never. Her breath came in ragged panting.

"She can be useful," the Myrddraal rasped. "I would not want the Black Ajah destroyed."

"Who are you to challenge one of the Chosen?" Mesaana demanded contemptuously, then ruined the effect by licking her lips.

"Do you think Hand of the Shadow is just a name?" The Myrddraal's voice no longer grated. Hollow, it seemed to boom down caverns from some unimaginable distance.

The creature grew as it spoke, swelling in size till its head brushed the ceiling, over two spans up. "You were summoned, and you did not come. My hand reaches far, Mesaana."

Shaking visibly, the Chosen opened her mouth, perhaps to plead, but suddenly black fire flashed around her, and she screamed as her clothing fell away in dust. Bands of black flame bound her arms to her sides, wrapped tight around her legs, and a seething ball of black appeared in her mouth, forcing her jaws wide. She writhed there, standing naked and helpless, and the look in her rolling eyes made Alviarin want to soil herself.

"Do you want to know why one of the Chosen must be punished?" The voice was a bone-grating rasp once more, the Myrddraal seemingly only a too-tall Lurk, but Alviarin was not fooled. "Do you want to watch?" it asked.

She should go facedown on the floor, grovel for her life, but she could not move. She could not look away from that eyeless stare. "No, Great Lord," she managed with a mouth as dry as dust. She knew. It could not be, but she knew. Tears were rolling down her cheeks, she realized.

The Myrddraal smiled again. "Many have fallen from great heights for wanting to know too much."

It flowed toward her—no; not it—the Great Lord, clothed in the skin of a Myrddraal, flowed toward her. He walked on legs, yet there was no other description for the way he moved. The pale, black-clad shape bent toward her, and she would have shrieked when he touched a finger to her forehead. She would have shrieked if she could have summoned any sound at all. Her lungs were airless sacks. The touch burned like red-hot iron. Vaguely, she wondered why she did not smell her own flesh burning. The Great Lord straightened, and the searing pain dwindled, vanished. Her terror did not lessen in the slightest, though.

"You are marked as mine," the Great Lord rasped. "Mesaana will not harm you, now. Unless I give her permission. You will find who threatens my creatures here and deliver them to me." He turned away from her, and the dark armor fell from his body. She was startled when it hit the carpeted floor tiles with a crash of steel rather than simply vanishing. He was clothed in black, and she could not have said whether it was silk or leather or something else. The darkness of it seemed to drink the light from the room. Mesaana began to thrash in her bonds, keening shrilly past the gag in her mouth. "Go now," he said, "if you wish to live another hour." The sound coming from Mesaana rose to a despairing scream.

Alviarin did not know how she got out of her rooms—she could not understand how she was upright when her legs felt like water—but she found herself running through the corridors, skirts pulled to her knees and running as hard as she could. Suddenly the head of a wide staircase loomed in front of her, and she barely managed to stop from running right out into the air. Sagging against the wall, shaking, she stared down the curving flight of white marble steps. In her mind, she could see her body breaking as it crashed down the stairway.

Breathing raggedly, in hoarse, raw-throated pants, she put a trembling hand to her forehead. Her thoughts tumbled one over another, as she would have down the stairs. The Great Lord had marked her as his. Her fingers slid across smooth unblemished skin. She had always prized knowledge—power grew from knowledge—but she did not want to know what was happening in the rooms she had left. She wished she did not know that anything was happening. The Great Lord had marked her, but Mesaana would find a way to kill her, for knowing that. The Great Lord had marked her and given her a command. She could live, if she found who was hunting the Black Ajah. Straightening her back with an effort, she hurriedly scrubbed at the tears on her cheeks with the heels of her palms. She could not pull her eyes away from the stairs falling away in front of her. Elaida surely suspected her, but if there was no more to it than that, she could always manufacture a hunt. It just had to include Elaida herself as a threat to be extinguished. Delivered to the Great Lord. Her fingers fluttered to her forehead again. She had the Black Ajah at her command. Smooth, unblemished skin. Talene had been there, in Elaida's rooms. Why had she looked at Yukiri and Doesine that way? Talene was Black, though she did not know that Alviarin was, of course. Would any mark show in a mirror? Was there something that others could see? If she had to manufacture a scheme for Elaida's supposed hunters,

Talene might be a place to start. She tried to trace the route any message would have taken from heart to heart before it reached Talene, but she could not stop staring down the stairs, seeing her body bounce and break its way to the bottom. The Great Lord had marked her.

CHAPTER

22

One Answer

Pevara waited with a touch of impatience while the slim little Accepted placed the rimmed silver tray on a side table and uncovered the dish of cakes. A short woman with a serious face, Pedra was not being laggard, or resentful over having to spend the morning fetching and carrying for a Sitter, just precise and careful. Those were useful qualities, to be encouraged. Still, when the Accepted asked whether she should pour the wine, Pevara said crisply, "We will do for ourselves, child. You may wait in the anteroom." She almost told the young woman to go back to her studies.

Pedra spread her banded white skirts in a graceful curtsy without any sign of being flustered the way Accepted often were when a Sitter showed snappishness. All too frequently, Accepted took any bite in a Sitter's tone as an opinion on their fitness for the shawl, as if Sitters had no other concerns.

Pevara waited until the door closed behind Pedra and the latch clicked before nodding approvingly. "That one will be raised Aes Sedai soon," she said. It was satisfying when any woman attained the shawl, but especially when the woman had appeared unpromising to begin with. Small pleasures seemed the only ones available, these days.

"Not one of ours, though, I think" was the reply from her surprising guest, who turned from a study of the row of painted miniatures of Pevara's dead family that stood in a line on the wave-carved marble mantel above the fireplace. "She's uncertain about men. I believe they make her nervous."

Tarna certainly had never been nervous about men or very much of anything else, at least not since she reached the shawl just over twenty years ago. Pevara could remember a very jumpy novice, but the pale-haired woman's blue eyes were steady as stones, now. And about as warm as stones in winter. Even so, there was something in that cool prideful face, something in the set of her mouth, that made her seem uneasy this morning. Pevara could hardly imagine what might make Tarna Feir nervous.

The real question, though, was why the woman had come to see her. It bordered on impropriety for her to visit any Sitter privately, particularly a Red. Tarna still maintained her rooms here in the Red quarter, but so long as she held her new position, she was no longer part of the Red Ajah despite the crimson embroidery on her dark gray dress. Delaying the move to her new apartment might be taken as a show of delicacy, by those who did not know her.

Anything out of the ordinary made Pevara wary since Seaine had pulled her into hunting the Black Ajah. And Elaida trusted Tarna, just as she had trusted Galina; it was wise to be very cautious with *anyone* Elaida trusted. Just thinking of Galina—the Light burn the woman forever!— still set Pevara's teeth on edge, but there was a second connection. Galina had taken a special interest in Tarna as a novice, too. True, Galina had taken an interest in any novice or Accepted she thought might join the Red, but it was another reason for caution.

Not that Pevara let anything show on her face, of course. She had been Aes Sedai too long for that. Smiling, she reached for the long-necked silver pitcher that sat on the tray giving off the sweet scent of spices. "Will you take wine, Tarna, in congratulation for being raised?"

Silver goblets in hand, they settled on spiral-worked armchairs, a style that had gone out of fashion in Kandor near a hundred years ago, but one that Pevara liked. She saw no reason to change her furniture or anything else according to the whims of the moment. The chairs had served her since they were new-made, and they were comfortable with the addition of a few cushions. Tarna sat stiffly, however, on the edge of her seat. No one had ever called her languid, but clearly she *was* uneasy.

"I am not certain congratulations are in order," she said,

fingering the narrow red stole draped around her neck. The exact shade was not prescribed, except that anyone who saw it must call the color red, and she had chosen a brilliant scarlet that nearly shone. "Elaida insisted, and I could not refuse. Much has changed since I left the Tower, inside as well as out. Alviarin made everyone . . . watchful . . . of the Keeper. I suspect some will want her birched, when she finally returns. And Elaida . . ." She paused to sip at her wine, but when she lowered the goblet, she went on in a different vein. "I have often heard you called unconventional. I have even heard that you once said you would like to have a Warder."

"I've been called worse than unconventional," Pevara said dryly. What had the woman been about to say concerning Elaida? She sounded as though she would have refused the Keeper's stole, given her wishes. Strange. Tarna was hardly shy or shrinking. Silence seemed best. Especially about Warders. She had been talking too much if *that* was general gossip. Besides, keep silent long enough, and the other woman always spoke if only to fill up the gap. You could learn a great deal through silence. She sipped her own wine slowly. There was too much honey in it for her taste, and not enough ginger.

Still stiff, Tarna rose and strode to the fireplace, where she stood staring at the miniatures sitting on their white lacquered stands. She raised a hand to touch one of the ivory ovals, and Pevara felt her own shoulders tighten in spite of herself. Georg, her youngest brother, had been only twelve when he died, when all of the people in those paintings died, in an uprising by Darkfriends. They had not been a family who could afford ivory miniatures, but once she had the coin, she found a painter who could capture her memories. A beautiful boy, Georg, tall for his years and utterly fearless. Long after the event, she had learned how her baby brother died. With a knife in his hand, standing over their father's body and trying to keep the mob from their mother. So many years ago, now. They would all have been long dead in any case, and their children's children's children, as well. But some hatreds never died.

"The Dragon Reborn is *ta'veren,* so I have heard," Tarna said finally, still staring at Georg's picture. "Do you think he alters chance everywhere? Or do we change the future

by ourselves, one step following another until we find ourselves somewhere we never expected?"

"What do you mean?" Pevara said, a trifle more curtly
than she could have wished. She did not like the other
woman peering at her brother's image so intently while
talking of a man who could channel, even if he was the
Dragon Reborn. She bit her lip so as not to tell Tarna to turn
around and look at her. You could not read someone's back
the way you could a face.

"I anticipated no great difficulty in Salidar. No great success, either, but what I found . . ." Was that a shake of her
head, or had she merely changed the angle at which she
was peering at the miniature? She spoke slowly, but with
an undercurrent of remembered urgency. "I left a pigeon-
handler a day outside the village, yet it took me less than
half a day to get back to her, and after I loosed the birds
with copies of my report, I pressed on so hard I had to pay
the woman off because she could not keep up. I can hardly
say how many horses I went through. Sometimes, the animal was spent to the point I had to show my ring to make a
stable take it in trade, even with silver added. And because
I pressed so hard, I happened to reach a village in Murandy
while a . . . recruiting party . . . was there. If I had not been
frightened out of my wits for the Tower by what I saw in
Salidar, I would have ridden to Ebou Dar and taken ship
for Illian and then upriver, but the thought of going south
instead of north, the thought of waiting for a vessel, sent me
like an arrow toward Tar Valon. So I was in that village to
see them."

"Who, Tarna?"

"Asha'man." The woman did turn then. Her eyes were
still blue ice, but tight. She held her goblet in both hands
as if trying to soak in the warmth. "I did not know what
they were then, of course, but they were openly recruiting
men to follow the Dragon Reborn, and it seemed wisest to
listen before I spoke. Well for me that I did. There were six
of them, Pevara, six men in black coats. Two with silver
swords on their collars were feeling men out about whether
they might like to learn to channel. Oh, they did not say
so right out. Wield the lightnings, they called it. Wield the
lightnings and ride the thunder. But it was clear enough to
me, if not to the fools they were talking to."

"Yes; very well for you that you kept silent," Pevara said quietly. "Six men who can channel would be more than merely dangerous for a sister by herself. Our eyes-and-ears are full of talk about these recruiting parties—they appear everywhere from Saldaea to Tear—but no one seems to have an idea of how to stop them. If it isn't too late for that already." She very nearly bit her lip again. That was the trouble with talking. Sometimes, you said more than you wanted.

Oddly, the comment took some of the stiffness out of Tarna. She resumed her seat, leaning back, though a hint of wariness still clung to the way she held herself. She chose her words carefully, pausing to touch the wine to her lips, but she did not actually drink, that Pevara saw. "I had a long time to think on the rivership coming north. Longer, after the fool captain ran us aground so hard he broke a mast and put a hole in the hull. Days trying to hail another ship, after we got ashore, and days finding a horse. Six of those men sent to one village convinced me, finally. Oh, the district around, as well, but it was not very populous. I . . . I believe it is too late."

"Elaida thinks they can all be gentled," Pevara said non-committally. She had already exposed herself too much.

"When they can send six to one small village, and Travel? There is only one answer I can see. We . . ." Tarna took a deep breath, fingering the bright red stole again, but now it seemed more in regret than to play for time. "Red sisters must take them as Warders, Pevara."

That was so startling that Pevara blinked. A hair less self-control, and she would have gaped. "Are you serious?"

Those icy blue eyes met her gaze steadily. The worst was past—the unthinkable spoken aloud—and Tarna was a woman of stone once more. "This is hardly a matter for joking. The only other choice is to let them run loose. Who else can do it? Red sisters are used to facing men like this, and ready to take the necessary risks. Anyone else will flinch. Each sister will have to take more than one, but Greens appear to manage well enough with that. I think the Greens will faint if this is suggested to them, though. We . . . Red sisters . . . must do what needs to be done."

"Have you broached this to Elaida?" Pevara asked, and Tarna shook her head impatiently.

"Elaida believes as you said. She . . ." The yellow-haired woman frowned into her wine before going on. "Elaida often believes what she wants to believe and sees what she wants to see. I tried to bring up the Asha'man the first day I was back. Not to suggest bonding; not to her. I am not a fool. She forbade me to mention them to her. But you are . . . unconventional."

"And do you believe they can be gentled *after* they're bonded? I have no idea what that would do to the sister holding the bond, and in truth, I don't want to learn." She was the one playing for time, Pevara realized. She had had no idea where this interview was headed when it began, but she would have wagered everything she owned against it coming to this.

"That might be the end, and it might prove impossible," the other woman replied coolly. The woman *was* stone. "Either way, I can see no other way to handle these Asha'man. Red sisters must bond them as Warders. If there is any way, I will be among the first, but it *must* be done."

She sat there, calmly sipping her wine, and for a long time, Pevara could only stare at her in consternation. Nothing Tarna had said proved she was not Black Ajah, yet she could not distrust every sister unable to prove that. Well, she could and did, when it came to matters of the Black, but there were other matters she had to deal with. She was a Sitter, not simply a hunting dog. She had the White Tower to think of, and Aes Sedai far from the Tower. And the future.

Dipping her fingers into her embroidered belt pouch, she drew out a small piece of paper rolled into a thin tube. It seemed to her that it should glow with letters of fire. So far, she was one of two women in the Tower who knew what was written there. Even once she had it out, she hesitated before handing it to Tarna. "This came from one of our agents in Cairhien, but it was sent by Toveine Gazal."

Tarna's eyes jerked to Pevara's face at the mention of Toveine's name, then fell to reading again. Her stony face did not change even after she finished and let the paper roll back into a tube in her hand. "This changes nothing," she

said flatly. Coldly. "It only makes what I suggest more urgent."

"On the contrary," Pevara sighed. "That changes everything. It changes the whole world."

CHAPTER

23

Ornaments

The air in the room was just sufficiently warmer than outside to put a mist on the glass panes set in the red-painted casements, and the glass contained bubbles besides, but Cadsuane stood peering out as if she could see the dreary landscape clearly. She could see with more than enough clarity, in any case. A few hapless folk, bundled and hatted and only shapeless skirts or baggy breeches distinguishing men from women, were trudging the muddy fields that surrounded the manor house, sometimes stooping to feel a handful of the soil. It would not be long before they could begin their plowing and manuring, but only their inspection indicated the coming of spring any time soon. Beyond the fields, the forest was all dark bare branches against a washed-out gray morning sky. A good coating of snow would have made the view much less bleak, but it snowed lightly and seldom here, with traces of one fall rarely lasting until the next. Still, she could think of few places better for her purposes, with the Spine of the World little more than a day's hard ride to the east. Who would think to look inside the borders of Tear? Had convincing the boy to stay here been too easy, though? With a sigh, she turned from the window, feeling the golden ornaments hanging in her hair sway, the small moons and stars, birds and fish. She was very aware of them, of late. Aware? Phaw! Of late, she had considered sleeping with them in place.

The sitting room was large but not ornate, like the manor house itself, with cornices of carved wood, painted red. The furniture was bright with paint but not a touch of gilding,

the two long fireplaces plain stone if well made, the and-
irons sturdy wrought metal made for long service rather
than appearances. The fires on the hearths were small, at
her insistence, the flames flickering low on half-consumed
splits, but either was enough to warm her hands, which was
all she wanted. Left to his own devices, Algarin would have
surrounded her with blazing warmth and smothered her
in servants, few as he still employed. A lesser Lord of the
Land, he was far from wealthy, yet he paid his debts in letter and spirit, even when most other men would have seen
quite the reverse of a debt.

The uncarved door to the hall creaked open—most of
Algarin's servants were nearly as old as he, and though they
kept everything dusted and neat, the lamps topped with
oil and the wicks trimmed, hinges in the manor seemed
to escape regular oiling—the door creaked open to admit
Verin, still dressed for a journey in simple brown wool with
divided skirts and carrying her cloak over her arm, still
patting her gray-streaked hair into place. The stout little
sister's square face wore a vexed expression, and she was
shaking her head. "Well, the Sea Folk are delivered to Tear,
Cadsuane. I didn't go near the Stone, but I heard that High
Lord Astoril stopped complaining about his creaking joints
and mustered inside with Darlin. Who'd have thought Astoril would stir himself, and on Darlin's side? The streets
are full of armsmen, most getting drunk and picking fights
with each other when they're not fighting Atha'an Miere.
There are as many Sea Folk in the city as everyone else
put together. Harine was aghast. She went rushing out to
the ships as soon as she could hire a boat, expecting to be
declared Mistress of the Ships and set everything to rights.
There seems no doubt that Nesta din Reas is dead."

Cadsuane was content to let the round little woman chatter on. Verin was not nearly so vague as she pretended.
Some Browns really were capable of tripping over their
own feet from not noticing them, but Verin was one of
those who wore an assumed cloak of unworldliness. She
seemed to believe that Cadsuane accepted the cloak for reality, yet if there was a point to be made, she would make
it. And what she left out might be revealing, too. Cadsuane
was less sure of the other sister than she might have wished.

Uncertainty was a fact of life, but she was uncertain about entirely too many things to suit her.

Unfortunately, Min must have been listening at the door, and that young woman had little patience. "I told Harine it wouldn't be like that," she protested, bursting into the room. "I told her she'd be punished for the bargain she made with Rand. Only after that will she become Mistress of the Ships, and I can't say if it will be ten days from now or ten years." Slim and pretty, and tall in her red-heeled boots, with dark ringlets hanging to her shoulders, Min had a low womanly voice, but she wore a boy's red coat and blue breeches. The coat was embroidered with colorful flowers on the lapels and up the sleeves, and the breeches in bands down the outsides of the legs, but they were still coat and breeches.

"You may come in, Min," Cadsuane said quietly. It was a tone that usually made people sit up and take notice. Those who knew her at all, anyway. Spots of color appeared in Min's cheeks. "The Wavemistress has already learned all she is going to from your viewing, I fear. But from your urgency, perhaps you've read someone else's auras and wish to tell me what you saw?" The girl's peculiar ability had proved helpful in the past and doubtless could again. Perhaps. As far as Cadsuane could tell, she did not lie about what she saw in the images and auras that she perceived floating around people, but she was not always forthcoming, either. Particularly not when it came to the one person Cadsuane would have liked to know about above all others.

Red cheeks or no red cheeks, Min raised her chin stubbornly. She had changed since Shadar Logoth, or perhaps it had begun earlier, but either way, the change was not for the better. "Rand wants you to come see him. He said to ask, so you needn't get snippy over it."

Cadsuane merely looked at her and let the silence stretch. Snippy? Definitely not for the better. "Tell him I will come when I am able," she said finally. "Close the door firmly behind you, Min." The young woman opened her mouth as if to say something more, but at least she retained sense enough to leave it unsaid. She even made a passable curtsy, in spite of those ridiculous boots, and shut the door firmly behind her. Just barely short of slamming it, in fact.

Verin shook her head again, giving a laugh that sounded only slightly amused. "She's in love with the young man, Cadsuane, and she's tucked her heart in his pocket. She'll follow that before her head, whatever you say or do. I think she's afraid he almost died on her, and you know how that can make a woman determined to hang on."

Cadsuane's lips thinned. Verin knew more about that sort of relations with men than she did—she had never believed in indulging with her own Warders, as some Greens did, and other men had always been out of the question—but the Brown had hit close to a truth without knowing. At least, Cadsuane did not think the other sister knew Min was bonded to the al'Thor boy. She herself only knew because the girl had let too much slip in a careless moment. Even the tightest mussel eventually yielded its meat once you got that first small crack in the shell. Sometimes it gave up an unexpected pearl, as well. Yes, Min would want to keep the lad alive whether she loved him or not, but no more than Cadsuane did.

Draping her cloak on the tall back of a chair, Verin moved to the nearest fireplace and stretched out her hands to warm them in front of the low flames. You could not say that Verin glided, but she was more graceful than her bulk suggested. How much of her was deception? Every Aes Sedai hid behind various masks, over time. It became habit after a while. "I believe the situation in Tear may be resolved peacefully yet," she said, peering into the fire. She might have been talking to herself. Or wanted Cadsuane to think it. "Hearne and Simaan are growing quite desperate, afraid the other High Lords will return from Illian and trap them in the city. They may be amenable to accepting Darlin, given their other choices. Estanda is made of sterner stuff, but if she can be convinced there's advantage for her in it—"

"I told you not to go near them," Cadsuane broke in sternly.

The stout woman blinked at her in surprise. "I didn't. The streets are always full of rumors, and I do know how to piece rumors together and sift out a little truth. I did see Alanna and Rafela, but I ducked behind a fellow hawking meat pies from a barrow before they saw me. I'm sure they didn't." She paused, clearly waiting for Cadsuane to explain why she had been told to avoid the sisters as well.

"I have to go to the boy now, Verin," Cadsuane said instead. That was the trouble with agreeing to advise someone. Even when you managed to set all the conditions you could wish for—most of them, anyway—you still had to come sooner or later when they called. Eventually. But it did give her a reason to evade Verin's curiosity. The answer was simple. If you tried to solve every problem yourself, you ended by solving none. And with some problems, how they were solved really did not matter in the long run. But not answering left Verin with a puzzle to ponder, a little butter for her paws. When Cadsuane was unsure of someone, she wanted them unsure of her, too.

Verin gathered up her cloak and left the room with her. Did the other woman mean to accompany her? But outside the sitting room, they encountered Nesune walking briskly down the hall. She came to a sudden halt. No more than a handful of people had ever managed to ignore Cadsuane, yet Nesune did a credible job, her nearly black eyes latching on to Verin.

"You're back then, are you?" The best of Browns did have a way of stating the obvious. "You wrote a paper on animals of the Drowned Lands, as I recall." Which meant that Verin had; Nesune recalled everything she had ever seen—a useful skill, if Cadsuane had been sure enough of her to make use of it. "Lord Algarin showed me the skin of a large snake he claims came from the Drowned Lands, but I'm convinced it is the same as I observed. . . ." Verin glanced helplessly at Cadsuane over her shoulder as the taller woman drew her away by her sleeve, but before they were three steps along the corridor, she was deep in discussion over this fool snake.

It was a remarkable sight, and troubling in a way. Nesune was loyal to Elaida, or had been, while Verin was one of those who wanted to pull Elaida down. Or had been. Now they talked amiably about snakes. That both had sworn fealty to the al'Thor boy could be laid to his being *ta'veren*, winding the Pattern around himself unconsciously, but was that oath sufficient to make them ignore their opposition over who held the Amyrlin Seat? Or were they affected by having a *ta'veren* in close proximity? She would have liked very much to know that. None of her ornaments protected against *ta'veren*. Of course, she did not know what two of the fish and one of the moons did, but it seemed unlikely they did that. It could have been as simple as Verin and Nesune both being Brown. Browns could forget everything else when they settled to study something. Snakes. Phaw! The small ornaments swayed as she shook her head before turning away, having the two receding Browns behind. What did the boy want? She had never liked being an advisor, necessary or not.

Drafts along the corridors rippled the few tapestries on the walls, all in old styles and showing the wear of having been taken down and rehung many times. The manor house had grown like a rambling farmhouse rather than being built large, with additions added whenever the family's fortunes and numbers waxed. House Pendaloan had never been wealthy, but there had been times they were numerous. The results showed in more than worn, old-fashioned wall hangings. The cornices were brightly painted, red or blue or yellow, but the hallways varied in width and height, and sometimes met at a slight skew. Windows that once had looked to the fields now looked down on courtyards, usually bare except for a few benches and placed purely to provide light. Sometimes there was no choice in getting from here to there except to take a roofed colonnade overlooking one of those courtyards. The columns were wooden more often than not, though bravely painted even where not carved.

On one of those walkways, with fat green columns, two sisters were standing together watching the activity in the courtyard below. At least, they were watching together when Cadsuane opened the door to the colonnade. Beldeine saw her step out, and stiffened, twitching at the green-fringed shawl she had worn fewer than five years. Pretty, with her high cheekbones and a slight tilt to her brown eyes, she had not yet achieved agelessness, and looked younger than Min, particularly when she shot Cadsuane a frosty stare and hurried from the colonnade in the other direction.

Merise, her companion, smiled after her in amusement, shifting her own green-fringed shawl slightly. Tall and usually quite serious, with her hair drawn back tightly from her pale face, Merise was not a woman who smiled often. "Beldeine, she is becoming concerned that she has no Warder yet," she said in the accents of Tarabon as Cadsuane stopped beside her, though her blue eyes returned to the courtyard. "She seems to be considering an Asha'man, if she can find one. I told her to talk to Daigian. If it does not help her, it will help Daigian."

All of the Warders they had with them were gathered in the stone-paved yard, in their shirtsleeves despite the cold, most seated on painted wooden benches watching two of their number work with wooden practice swords. Jahar, one of Merise's three, was a pretty, sun-dark young man. The silver bells fastened to the ends of his two long braids chimed with the fury of his attack. He moved like a striking blacklance. Not a breath of breeze stirred, but the eight-pointed star, like a golden compass rose, seemed to shift against Cadsuane's hair. Had it been held in her hand, she could have felt it vibrating clearly. But then, she already knew that Jahar was an Asha'man, and the star would not have pointed him out, merely told her that a man who could channel was nearby. The more men who could channel, the harder the star quivered, she had learned. Jahar's opponent, a very tall, broad-shouldered fellow with a stone face and a braided leather cord around his graying temples to hold back shoulder-length hair, was not the second Asha'man down there, but he was as deadly in his own way. Lan did not really seem to move that fast, but he . . . flowed. His blade of bundled laths was always there to deflect Jahar's, always moving the younger man just a touch more out of his line.

Suddenly, Lan's wooden blade struck Jahar's side with a resounding crack, a killing blow given with steel. While the younger man was still flinching from the force of the strike, Lan flowed back into a ready stance, long blade upright in his hands. Nethan, another of Merise's, rose to his feet, a lean fellow with wings of white at his temples and tall, if still a hand or more shorter than Lan. Jahar waved him away and raised his practice blade again, loudly demanding another go.

"Is Daigian still bearing up?" Cadsuane asked.

"Better than I expected," Merise admitted. "She stays in her room too much, but she keeps her weeping private." Her gaze shifted from the men dancing their swords to a

green-painted bench where Verin's stocky gray-haired Tomas sat next to a grizzled fellow with only a fringe of white
hair remaining. "Damer, he wanted to try his Healing on
her, but Daigian refused. She may never have had a Warder
before, but she knows that the grieving over a dead Warder
is part of remembering him. I am surprised that Corele
would consider allowing it."

With a shake of her head, the Taraboner sister returned
to studying Jahar. Other sisters' Warders did not really interest her, at least not like her own. "Asha'man, they grieve
as Warders do. I thought perhaps Jahar and Damer merely
followed the lead of the others, but Jahar, he says it is their
way, too. I did not intrude, of course, but I watched them
drink in memory of Daigian's young Eben. They never
mentioned his name, but they had a full winecup sitting for
him. Bassane and Nethan, they know they can die on any
day, and they accept that. Jahar *expects* to die; every day he
expects it. To him, every hour is most assuredly his last."

Cadsuane barely refrained from glancing at the other
woman. Merise did not often go on at such length. The
other woman's face was smooth, her manner unruffled, but
something had upset her. "I know you practice linking with
him," she said delicately, peering down into the courtyard.
Delicacy was required in talking to another sister about
her Warder. That was part of the reason she stared into the
courtyard, frowning. "Have you decided yet whether the
al'Thor boy succeeded at Shadar Logoth? Did he really
manage to cleanse the male half of the Source?"

Corele practiced linking with Damer, too, but the Yellow
was so focused on her futile efforts to reason out how to do
with *saidar* what he did with *saidin* that she would not have
noticed the Dark One's taint sliding down her throat. A pity
she herself had not come to the shawl fifty years later than
she had, or she would have bonded one of the men herself
and had no need to ask. But fifty years would have meant
that Norla died in her little house in the Black Hills before
Cadsuane Melaidhrin ever went to the White Tower. That
would have altered a great deal of history. For one thing,
it would have been unlikely that she would be in anything
approaching her present circumstances. So she asked, delicately, and waited.

Merise was quiet, and still, for a long moment, and then she sighed. "I do not know, Cadsuane. *Saidar* is a calm ocean that will take you wherever you want so long as you know the currents and let them carry you. *Saidin . . .* An avalanche of burning stone. Collapsing mountains of ice. It *feels* cleaner than when I first linked with Jahar, but anything could hide in that chaos. Anything."

Cadsuane nodded. She was not sure she had expected any other answer. Why should she find any certainty about one of the two most important questions in the world when she could find none on so many simpler matters? In the courtyard, Lan's wooden blade stopped, not with a crack this time, just touching Jahar's throat, and the bigger man flowed back to his waiting stance. Nethan stood again, and again Jahar waved him back, angrily raising his sword and setting himself. Merise's third, Bassane, a short wide fellow nearly as sun-dark as Jahar for all he was Cairhienin, laughed and made a rude comment about over-ambitious men tripping on their own blades. Tomas and Damer exchanged glances and shook their heads; men of that age usually had given up taunting long ago. The clack of wood on wood began once more.

The other four Warders were not the only audience for Lan and Jahar in the courtyard. The slim girl with her dark hair in a long braid, watching anxiously from a red bench, was the focus of Cadsuane's frown. The child would need to flash her Great Serpent ring under people's noses to be taken for Aes Sedai, which she was, if just technically. It was not only because Nynaeve's face was a girl's face; Beldeine still seemed as young. Nynaeve bounced on the bench, always on the point of leaping up. Occasionally her mouth moved as if she were silently shouting encouragement, and sometimes her hands twisted as though demonstrating how Lan should have moved his sword. A frivolous girl, full of passions, who only rarely demonstrated that she had a brain. Min was not the only one to have thrown her heart and head both down the well over a man. By the customs of dead Malkier, the red dot painted on Nynaeve's forehead indicated her marriage to Lan, though Yellows seldom married their Warders. Very few sisters did, for that matter. And of course, Lan was not Nynaeve's Warder, however much he and the girl pretended otherwise. Who he did belong to was a matter they evaded like thieves slipping through the night.

More interesting, more disturbing, was the jewelry Nynaeve wore, a long gold necklace and slim gold belt, with matching bracelets and finger rings, the gaudy red and green and blue gems that studded them clashing with her yellow-slashed dress. And she wore that peculiar piece as well, on her left hand, golden rings attached to a golden bracelet by flat chains. That was an *angreal,* much stronger than Cadsuane's shrike hair ornament. The others were much like her own decorations, too, *ter'angreal* and plainly made at the same time, during the Breaking of the World, when an Aes Sedai might find many hands turned against her, most especially those of men who could channel. Strange to think that they had been called Aes Sedai, too. It would be like meeting a man called Cadsuane.

The question—her morning seemed filled with questions, and the sun not halfway to noon yet—the question was, did the girl wear her jewelry because of the al'Thor boy, or the Asha'man? Or because of Cadsuane Melaidhrin? Nynaeve had demonstrated her loyalty to a young man from her own village, and she had shown her wariness of him as well. She did have a brain, when she chose to use it. Until that question was answered, however, trusting the girl too far was dangerous. The trouble was, little these days did not seem dangerous.

"Jahar is growing stronger," Merise said abruptly.

For an instant, Cadsuane frowned at the other Green. Stronger? The young man's shirt was beginning to cling damply to his back, while Lan appeared not to have broken his first sweat. Then she understood. Merise meant in the Power. Cadsuane only raised a questioning eyebrow, though. She could not recall the last time she had let shock reach her face. It might have been all those years ago, in the Black Hills, when she began earning the ornaments she now wore.

"At first, I thought the way these Asha'man train, the forcing, had pushed him to his full strength already," Merise said, frowning down at the two men working their practice blades. No; it was at Jahar she was frowning. Just a faint crinkle of her eyes, but she reserved her frowns for those who could see and know her displeasure. "At Shadar Logoth, I thought I must be imagining it. Three or four days ago, I was half convinced I was mistaken. Now, I am sure I am correct. If men gain strength by fits and starts, there is no saying how strong he will become."

She did not voice her obvious worry, of course: that he might grow stronger than she. Saying such a thing would have been unthinkable on many different levels, and while Merise had become somewhat accustomed to doing the unthinkable—most sisters would faint at the very idea of bonding a man who could channel—she was never comfortable giving them voice. Cadsuane was, yet she kept her voice neutral. Light, but she hated being delicate. Hated the necessity, anyway.

"He seems content, Merise." Merise's Warders always seemed content; she handled them well.

"He is in a fury of . . ." The other woman touched the side of her head as though fingering the bundle of sensations she felt through the bond. She really *was* upset! "Not rage. Frustration." Reaching into her green worked-leather belt pouch, she took out a small enameled pin, a sinuous figure in red and gold, like a snake with legs and a lion's mane. "I do not know where the al'Thor lad got this, but he gave it to Jahar. Apparently, for Asha'man, it is akin to attaining the shawl. I had to take it away, of course; Jahar, he is still at the stage where he has to learn to accept only what I say he can. But he is so agitated over the thing. . . . Should I give it back to him? In a way, it would come from my hand, then."

Cadsuane's eyebrows began to climb before she could control them. Merise was asking advice about one of her *Warders?* Of course, Cadsuane had suggested she sound the man out in the first place, but this degree of intimacy was . . . Unthinkable? Phaw! "I'm sure whatever you decide will be correct."

With one last glance at Nynaeve, she left the taller woman stroking the enameled pin with her thumb and frowning down into the courtyard. Lan had just defeated Jahar once more, but the young man was squaring up again, demanding yet another match. Whatever Merise decided, she had already learned one thing she did not like. The boundaries between Aes Sedai and Warders had always been as clear as the connections; Aes Sedai commanded, and Warders obeyed. But if Merise, of all people, was dithering over a collar pin—Merise, who managed her Warders with a firm hand—then new boundaries would have to be worked out, at least with Warders who could channel. It seemed unlikely that bonding them would stop now; Beldeine was evidence for that. People never really changed, yet the world did, with disturbing regularity. You just had to live with it, or at least live through it. Now and then, with luck, you could affect the direction of the changes, but even if you stopped one, you only set another in motion.

As expected, she did not find the door to the al'Thor boy's rooms unguarded. Alivia was there, of course, seated on a bench to one side of the door with her hands folded patiently in her lap. The pale-haired Seanchan woman had appointed herself the boy's protector, of sorts. Alivia credited him with freeing her from a *damane*'s collar, but there was more to it than that. Min disliked her, for one thing, and it was not the usual sort of jealousy. Alivia hardly seemed to know what men and women did together. But there was a connection between her and the boy, a connection revealed in glances that carried determination on her side and on his, hope, hard as that was to believe. Until Cadsuane knew what that was all about, she intended to do nothing to separate them. Alivia's sharp blue eyes regarded Cadsuane with a respectful wariness, but she did not see an enemy. Alivia had a short way with those she considered the al'Thor boy's enemies.

The other woman on guard was much of a size with Alivia, but the two could not have been more different, and not just because Elza's eyes were brown and she had the smooth, ageless look of Aes Sedai, where Alivia had fine lines at the corners of her eyes and threads of white almost hidden in her hair. Elza leaped to her feet as soon as she saw Cadsuane, drawing herself up in front of the door and wrapping herself tight in her shawl. "He is not alone," she said, frost riming her voice.

"Do you mean to stand in my way?" Cadsuane asked, just as coldly. The Andoran Green should have moved aside. Elza stood far enough below her in the Power that she should not have hesitated, much less waited, for a command, but the woman planted her feet, and her gaze actually grew heated.

It was a quandary. Five other sisters in the manor house had sworn fealty to the boy, and those who had been loyal to Elaida all stared at Cadsuane as if suspicious of her intentions toward him. Which raised the question of why Verin did not, of course. But only Elza tried to keep her away from him. The woman's attitude reeked of jealousy, which made no sense. She could not possibly believe herself better suited to advise him, and if there had been any suggestion that Elza desired the boy, as a man or a Warder, Min would have been snarling. The girl had finely honed instincts, there. Cadsuane would have ground her teeth, had she been the sort of woman to grind her teeth.

At the point when she thought she would have to order Elza to step aside, Alivia leaned forward. "He did send for her, Elza," she drawled. "He'll be upset if we keep her out. Upset with us, not her. Let her in."

Elza glanced at the Seanchan woman from the corner of her eye, and her lip curled in contempt. Alivia stood far above her in the Power—Alivia stood well above Cadsuane, for that matter—but she was a wilder, and a liar in Elza's view. The dark-haired woman hardly seemed to accept that Alivia had been *damane,* much less the rest of her story. Still, Elza darted a look at Cadsuane, then at the door behind her, and shifted her shawl. Plainly, she did not want the boy upset. Not with her.

"I'll see whether he's ready for you," she said, very near to sullen. "Keep her here," she added to Alivia, more sharply, before turning to knock lightly at the door. A male voice called from the other side, and she opened the door just wide enough to slip in, pulling it shut behind her.

"You'll have to forgive her," Alivia said in that irritatingly slow, soft Seanchan accent. "I think it's just that she takes her oath very seriously. She isn't used to serving anyone."

"Aes Sedai keep their word," Cadsuane replied dryly. The woman made her feel as if her own way of talking were as quick and crisp as a Cairhienin's! "We must."

"I think you do. Just so you know, I keep my word, too. I owe him anything he wants of me."

A fascinating comment, and an opening, but before she could take advantage of it, Elza came out. Behind her came Algarin, white beard trimmed to a neat point. He offered Cadsuane a bow, with a smile that deepened the wrinkles of his face. His plain coat of dark wool, made in his younger days, hung loosely on him now, and the hair on his head provided a thin covering. There was no chance to find out why he had been visiting the al'Thor boy.

"He will see you now," Elza said sharply.

Cadsuane very nearly did grind her teeth. Alivia would have to wait. And Algarin.

The boy was on his feet when Cadsuane entered, almost as tall and broad-shouldered as Lan in a black coat worked with gold on the sleeves and the high collar. It was too much like an Asha'man's coat with embroidery added to suit her, but she said nothing. He made a courteous bow, ushering her to a chair with a tasseled cushion in front of the fireplace and asking whether she would like wine. That in the pitcher sitting on a side table with two winecups had gone cold, but he could send for more. She had worked hard enough to force him into civility; he could wear any coat he wanted. There were more important matters he had to be guided in. Or prodded, or pulled as need be. She was not going to waste time or talk on his clothing.

Inclining her head politely, she declined the wine. A winecup offered many opportunities—to sip when you needed a moment's thought; to peer into when you wished to hide your eyes—yet this young man needed watching every moment. His face gave away almost as little as a sister's. With that dark reddish hair and those blue-gray eyes, he could have passed for Aiel, but few Aiel had eyes that cold. They made the morning sky she had been staring at earlier seem warm. Colder than they had been before Shadar Logoth. Harder, too, unfortunately. They also looked . . . weary.

"Algarin had a brother who could channel," he said, turning toward a facing chair. Halfway into the turn, he staggered. He caught himself on an arm of the chair with a barked laugh, pretending he had tripped over his own boots, but there had been no tripping. And he had not seized *saidin*—she had seen him stagger, doing that—or her ornaments would have warned her. Corele said he only needed a little more sleep to recover from Shadar Logoth. Light, she needed to keep the boy alive, or it had all been for nothing!

"I know," she said. And since it seemed Algarin might have told him everything, she added, "I was the one who captured Emarin and took him to Tar Valon." A strange thing for Algarin to be grateful for, in some eyes, but his younger brother survived being gentled for more than ten years after she had helped him reconcile to it. The brothers had been close.

The boy's eyebrows twitched as he settled into his chair. He had *not* known. "Algarin wants to be tested," he said.

She met his gaze levelly, serenely, and held her tongue. Algarin's children were married, those who still lived. Maybe he was ready to turn this piece of land over to his descendants. In any case, one man more or less who could channel hardly made any difference at this point. Unless it was the boy who was staring at her.

After a moment, his chin moved, the vestige of a nod. Had he been testing her? "Never fear that I'll fail to tell you when you're being a fool, boy." Most people remembered that after one meeting she had a sharp tongue. This young man required reminding from time to time. He grunted. It might have been a laugh. It might have been rueful. She reminded herself that he wanted her to teach him something, though he did not seem to know what. No matter. She had a list to choose from, and she had only begun on it.

His face might have been carved from stone for all the expression he showed, but he bounded to his feet and began to pace back and forth between the fireplace and the door. His hands were clenched in fists behind his back. "I've been talking with Alivia, about the Seanchan," he said. "They call their army the Ever Victorious Army for a reason. It's never lost a war. Battles, yes, but never a war. When they lose a battle, they sit down and work out what they did wrong, or what the enemy did right. Then they change what needs changing for them to win."

"A wise way," she said when the flow of words paused. Plainly, he expected some comment. "I know men who do the same. Davram Bashere, for one. Gareth Bryne, Rodel Ituralde, Agelmar Jagad. Even Pedron Niall did, when he was alive. All judged great captains."

"Yes," he said, still pacing. He did not look at her, perhaps did not see her, but he was listening. It was to be hoped that he actually heard, as well. "Five men, all great captains. The Seanchan *all* do it. That's been their way for a thousand years. They change what they have to change, but they don't give up."

"Are you considering the possibility they can't *be* defeated?" she asked calmly. Calmness always suited until you knew the facts, and usually after, too.

The boy rounded on her, stiff-necked and eyes like ice. "I can defeat them eventually," he said, struggling to keep his tone civil. That much was to the good. The less often she had to prove that she could and would punish transgressions of her rules, the better. "But—" He cut off with a growl as the sounds of argument in the hallway penetrated the door.

A moment later the door swung open, and Elza backed into the room, still arguing in a loud voice and trying to hold back two other sisters with her spread arms. Erian, her pale face flushed with color, was pushing the other Green ahead of her physically. Sarene, a woman so beautiful she made Erian look almost ordinary, wore a cooler expression, as might be expected from a White, but she was shaking her head in exasperation, and hard enough to make the colorful beads in her thin braids click together. Sarene possessed a temper, though she normally kept it sealed away tightly.

"Bartol and Rashan do be coming," Erian announced loudly, agitation thickening Illian in her speech. Those were her two Warders, left behind in Cairhien. "I did no send for them, but someone did Travel with them. An hour ago, I felt them suddenly closer, and just now, closer again. They are coming toward us now."

"My Vitalien, he also is coming closer," Sarene said. "He will be here in a few hours, I think."

Elza let her arms drop, though from the stiffness of her back, she was still glaring at the two sisters. "My Fearil will be here shortly as well," she muttered. He was her only Warder; it was said they were married, and Greens who married seldom took another another Warder at the same time. Cadsuane wondered whether she would have spoken if the others had not.

"I didn't expect it so soon," the boy said softly. Softly, but there was steel in his voice. "But I shouldn't have expected events to wait on me, should I, Cadsuane?"

"Events never wait on anyone," she said, standing. Erian flinched as if she had just noticed her, though Cadsuane was sure her face was as smooth as the boy's. And maybe as stony, at that. What had brought those Warders from Cairhien, and who had Traveled with them, might be problems enough to go on with, but she thought she had gotten another answer from the boy, and she was going to have to consider very carefully how to advise him on it. Sometimes, the answers were thornier than the questions.

CHAPTER

24

A Strengthening Storm

Midafternoon sunlight should have been slanting through the windows of Rand's bedchamber, but a hard rain was falling outside, and all the lamps were lit to hold off a twilight darkness. Thunder rattled the glass-filled casements in the windows. It was a fierce storm that had rolled down out of the Dragonwall faster than a running horse and brought a deeper cold, almost deep enough for snow. The raindrops pelting the house were half-frozen slush, and despite blazing logs on the hearthstone, a chill clung to the room.

Lying on his bed with his booted feet propped one atop the other on the coverlet, he stared up at the canopy and tried to put his thoughts in order. He could disregard the thunderstorm outside, but Min, snuggling under his arm, was another matter. She did not try to distract him; she just did it without trying. What was he to do about her? About Elayne, and Aviendha. Those two were only vague presences in his head, at this distance from Caemlyn. At least, he assumed they were still in Caemlyn. Assuming was dangerous when it came to those two. All he had of them at the moment was a general sense of direction and the knowledge they were alive. Min's body was pressed tight against his side, though, and the bond made her as vibrant inside his head as she was in the flesh. Was it too late to keep Min safe, to keep Elayne and Aviendha safe?

What makes you think you can keep anyone safe? Lews Therin whispered in his head. The dead madman was an old friend, now. *We are* all *going to die. Just hope that you aren't the one who kills them.* Not a welcome friend, just one he could not rid himself of. He no longer feared killing Min or Elayne or Aviendha any more than he feared going mad. Madder than he already was, at least, with a dead man in his head, and sometimes a foggy face he could almost recognize. Did he dare ask Cadsuane about either one?

Trust no one, Lews Therin murmured, then gave a wry laugh. *Including me.*

Without warning, Min punched him in the ribs hard enough to make him grunt. "You're getting melancholy, sheepherder," she growled. "If you're worrying about me again, I swear, I'll . . ." She had so many different ways of growling, Min did, each matched to very different sensations through the bond. There was the light irritation he felt from her now, this time touched with worry, and sometimes there was a sharp edge as if she were refraining from snapping his head off. There was a growl that almost made him laugh from the amusement in her head, or as close to laughing as he had come in what seemed a very long time, and a throaty growl that would have heated his blood even without the bond.

"None of that, now," she said warningly, before he could move the hand resting on her back, and rolled off the bed to her feet, tugging her embroidered coat straight with a reproving look. Since bonding him, she was even better at reading his mind, and she had been good enough before. "What are you going to do about them, Rand? What is Cadsuane going to do?" Lightning flashed in the windows, almost bright enough to wash out the lamps, and thunder boomed against the window glass.

"I haven't yet been able to see what she was going to do ahead of time, Min. Why should today be different?"

The thick feather mattress sagged beneath him as he swung his legs over the side and sat up facing her. He almost pressed a hand to the old wounds in his side without thinking, then caught himself and changed the movement to buttoning up his coat. Half-healed and never healing, those two overlapping wounds hurt since Shadar Logoth. Or maybe he was just more aware of how they throbbed, the heat of them a furnace of fever trapped in an area smaller than the palm of his hand. One, at least, he hoped, would begin to heal with Shadar Logoth gone. Maybe there had just not been enough time yet for him to feel any difference. It was not the same side that Min had fisted—she was always gentle with that, if not always with the rest of him—but he thought he had kept the pain hidden from her. No point in giving her something more to worry over. The concern in her eyes, and in her head, must be about Cadsuane. Or the others.

The manor house and all of its outlying buildings were crowded, now. It had seemed inevitable that sooner or later someone would try using the Warders left in Cairhien; their Aes Sedai had not blared that they were going off to find the Dragon Reborn, but neither had they been particularly secretive. Even so, he had never anticipated those who arrived with them. Davram Bashere with a hundred of his Saldaean light horse, dismounting in a wind-driven soaking rain and muttering about ruined saddles. Over half a dozen black-coated Asha'man who for some reason had not shielded themselves from the downpour. They rode with Bashere, but it had been like two parties arriving, a little distance between them always, a strong whiff of watchful wariness. And one of the Asha'man was Logain Ablar. Logain! An Asha'man, wearing the Sword and Dragon on his collar! Bashere and Logain both wanted to talk to him, but not in front of anyone, especially each other it seemed. Unexpected or not, though, they were hardly the most surprising of the visitors. He had thought the eight Aes Sedai must be more friends of Cadsuane, yet he would swear she had been as surprised as he to see most of them. Odder, all but one seemed to be with the Asha'man! Not prisoners, and certainly not guards, but Logain had been reluctant to explain with Bashere present, and Bashere reluctant to leave Logain the first chance to talk to Rand alone. Now they were all drying off and settling into their rooms, leaving him to try to put his thoughts in order. To the extent that he could, with Min close by. What *would* Cadsuane do? Well, he had tried to ask her advice. Events had outrun both of them, though. The decision had been made, whatever Cadsuane thought. Lightning flashed again in the windows. Lightning seemed to suit Cadsuane. You could never tell where it would strike.

Alivia would finish her, Lews Therin muttered. *She's going to help us die; she'd remove Cadsuane for us, if you tell her to.*

I don't want to kill her, Rand thought at the dead man. *I can't afford for her to die.* Lews Therin knew that as well as he, but the man grumbled under his breath anyway. Since Shadar Logoth, he seemed a touch less mad, sometimes. Or maybe Rand was a touch more. After all, he took talking to a dead man in his head as a matter of every day, and that was hardly sane.

"You have to do *something*," Min muttered, folding her arms beneath her breasts. "Logain's aura still speaks of glory, stronger than ever. Maybe he still thinks he's the real Dragon Reborn. And there's something . . . dark . . . in the images I saw around Lord Davram. If he turns against you, or dies . . . I heard one of the soldiers say Lord Dobraine might die. Losing even one of them would be a blow. Lose all three, and it might take you a year to recover."

"If you've seen it, then it's going to happen. I have to do what I can, Min, not worry over what I can't." She gave him one of those looks women had in great store, as if he were trying to start an argument.

A scratching at the door brought his head around and made Min shift her stance. He suspected she had slipped a throwing knife out of her sleeve and was hiding it behind her wrist. The woman carried more knives tucked about her than Thom Merrilin had. Or Mat. Colors whirled in his head, almost resolving into . . . what? A man on a wagon seat? Not the face that sometimes appeared in his thoughts, anyway, and the scene was gone in an instant, without any of the dizziness that accompanied the face.

"Come," he called, standing up.

Elza spread her dark green skirts in an elegant curtsy when she entered, her eyes bright on his face. A pleasant-appearing woman, and coolly complacent as a cat, she hardly seemed to see Min. Of all the sisters who had sworn to him, Elza was the most eager. The only eager one, really. The others had their reasons for swearing, their explanations, and of course Verin and the sisters who came to find him at Dumai's Wells had no real choice facing a *ta'veren,* but for all Elza's outer coolness, she seemed to burn inside with a passion to see he reached Tarmon Gai'don. "You said to let you know when the Ogier came," she said, never taking her eyes from his face.

"Loial!" Min shouted gleefully, tucking the knife back

up her sleeve as she rushed past Elza, who blinked at the sight of the blade. "I could have killed Rand for letting you get off to your room before I saw you!" The bond said she did not mean it. Not exactly.

"Thank you," Rand told Elza, listening to the sounds of merriment from the sitting room, Min's light laughter and Loial's quake of Ogier mirth, like the earth laughing. Thunder rolled across the sky.

Perhaps the Aes Sedai's passion extended to wanting to know what he said to Loial, because her lips thinned, and she hesitated before making another curtsy and sweeping out of the bedchamber. A brief pause in the sounds of pleasure announced her passage across the sitting room, and their resumption her departure. Only then did he seize the Power. He tried never to let anyone see him do that.

Fire flooded into him, hotter than the sun, and cold to make the worst blizzard seem spring, all a swirling rage that dwarfed the storm outside, threatening to scour him away for a moment's inattention. Seizing *saidin* was a war for survival. But the green of the cornices was suddenly greener, the black of his coat blacker, the gold of its embroidery more golden. He could see the grain of the vine-carved bedposts, see faint marks left by the craftsman's sanding all those years ago. *Saidin* made him feel as if he had been half-blind and numb without it. That was a part of what he felt.

Clean, Lews Therin whispered. *Pure and clean again.*

It was. The foulness that had marked the male half of the Power since the Breaking was gone. That did not stop nausea from rising in Rand, though, the violent urge to bend double and empty himself on the floor. The room seemed to spin for an instant, and he had to put a hand on the nearest bedpost to steady himself. He did not know why he should still feel this sickness, with the taint gone. Lews Therin did not know, or would not tell. But the sickness was the reason he could not let anyone see him take hold of *saidin,* if he could help it. Elza might burn to see him reach the Last Battle, but too many others wanted to see him fall, not all of them Darkfriends.

In that moment of weakness, the dead man reached for *saidin.* Rand could feel him clawing for it greedily. Was it harder than it had been to push him away? In some ways,

Lews Therin seemed more solidly part of him since Shadar Logoth. It did not matter. He had only so far left to go before he could die. He just had to last that far. Drawing a deep breath, he ignored the lingering traces of sickness in his belly and strode into the sitting room to the crash of thunder.

Min stood in the middle of the room holding one of Loial's hands in both of hers and smiling up at him. It took both of her hands to hold one of Loial's, and the pair did not come close to covering it. The top of his head missed the plaster ceiling by little more than a foot. He had donned a fresh coat of dark blue wool, the bottom flaring over baggy trousers to the tops of his knee-high boots, but for once his pockets did not bulge with the angular shapes of books. Eyes the size of teacups lit up at the sight of Rand, and the grin on his wide mouth really did split his face in two. The tufted ears sticking up through his shaggy hair quivered with pleasure.

"Lord Algarin has Ogier guest rooms, Rand," he boomed in a voice like a deep drum. "Can you imagine it? Six of them! Of course, they haven't been used in some time, but they're aired out every week, so there isn't any mustiness, and the bedsheets are very good linen. I thought I'd be back to doubling myself up in a human-sized bed. Umm. We aren't staying here long, are we?" His long ears sagged a little, then began to twitch uneasily. "I don't think we should. I mean, I might get used to having a real bed, and that wouldn't do if I'm going to stay with you. I mean . . . Well, you know what I mean."

"I know," Rand said softly. He could have laughed at the Ogier's consternation. He should have laughed. Laughter just seemed to have escaped him, lately. Spinning a web against eavesdropping around the room, he knotted it so he could release *saidin*. The last traces of nausea began to fade immediately. He could control the sickness, usually, with an effort, but there was no point when he did not have to. "Did any of your books get wet?" Loial's main concern coming in had been to check on his books.

Suddenly it struck him that he had thought of what he had done as spinning a web. That was how Lews Therin would put it. That sort of thing happened too often, the other man's turns of phrase drifting into his head, the other man's memories mingling with his. He was Rand al'Thor, not Lews Therin Telamon. He had woven a ward and tied off the weave, not spun a web and knotted it. But the one came to him as easily as the other.

"My *Essays of Willim of Maneches* got damp," Loial said disgustedly, rubbing his upper lip with a finger the thickness of a sausage. Had he been careless shaving, or was that the beginning of a mustache beneath his wide nose? "The pages may spot. I shouldn't have been so careless, not with a book. And my book of notes took some wet, too. But the ink didn't run. Everything is still readable, but I really need to make a case to protect . . ." Slowly, a frown crept onto his face, dangling the long ends of his eyebrows onto his cheeks. "You look tired, Rand. He looks tired, Min."

"He's been doing too much, but he's resting now," Min said defensively, and Rand did smile. A little. Min would always defend him, even to his friends. "You *are* resting, sheepherder," she added, letting go of Loial's huge hand and planting her fists on her hips. "Sit down and rest. Oh, sit down, Loial. I'll put a crick in my neck if I keep staring up at you."

Loial chuckled, the bellowing of a bull muted in his throat, as he examined one of the straight-back chairs dubiously. Compared to him, it seemed a chair made for a child. "Sheepherder. You don't know how good it is to hear you calling him sheepherder, Min." He sat down cautiously. The plain-carved chair creaked under his weight, and his knees stuck up in front of him. "I am sorry, Rand, but it is funny, and I haven't heard much to laugh at these past months." The chair was holding. With a quick glance toward the hall door, he added, a little too loudly, "Karldin doesn't have much sense of humor."

"You can speak freely," Rand told him. "We're safe behind a . . . a ward." He had almost said behind a shield, which was not the same thing. Except that he knew it was.

He was too weary to sit, just as he was too tired to find sleep easily most nights—his bones ached with it—so he went to stand in front of the fireplace. Winds gusting across the chimney top made the flames dance on the split logs and sometimes let a small puff of smoke into the room, and he could hear the rain drumming away at the windows, but the thunder seemed to have moved on. Maybe the storm was ending. Clasping his hands behind his back, he turned away from the fire. "What did the Elders say, Loial?"

Instead of answering straightaway, Loial looked at Min as if seeking encouragement or support. Perched on the edge of a blue armchair with her knees crossed, she smiled at the Ogier and nodded, and he sighed heavily, a wind gusting through deep caverns. "Karldin and I visited every *stedding*, Rand. All but *Stedding* Shangtai, of course. I couldn't go there, but I left a message everywhere we went, and Daiting isn't far from Shangtai. Someone will carry it there. The Great Stump is meeting in Shangtai, and that will attract crowds. This is the first time a Great Stump has been called in a thousand years, not since you humans fought the War of the Hundred Years, and it was Shangtai's turn. They must be considering something very important, but no one would tell me why it was called. They won't tell you about any Stump until you have a beard," he muttered, fingering a narrow patch of stubble on his broad chin. Apparently, he intended to remedy his lack, though it was not certain that he could. Loial was over ninety years old, now, yet for an Ogier, that was still a boy.

"The Elders?" Rand asked patiently. You had to be patient with Loial, with any Ogier. They did not see time the way humans did—who among humans would think of whose *turn* it was after a thousand years?—and Loial tended to go on at length, given half a chance. Great length.

Loial's ears twitched, and he gave Min another look, received another encouraging smile in return. "Well, as I said, I visited all the *stedding* but Shangtai. Karldin wouldn't go inside. He'd rather sleep every night under a bush than be cut off from the Source for a minute." Rand did not say a word, but Loial raised his hands from his knees, palms out. "I am getting to the point, Rand. I am. I did what I could, but I don't know whether it was enough. The *stedding* in the Borderlands told me to go home and leave matters to older and wiser heads. So did Shadoon and Mardoon, in the mountains on the Shadow Coast. The other *stedding* agreed to guard the Waygates. I don't think they really believe there's any danger, but they agreed, so you know they will keep a close guard. And I'm sure someone will take word to Shangtai. The Elders in Shangtai never liked having a Waygate right outside the *stedding*. I must have heard Elder

Haman say a hundred times that it was dangerous. I know they'll agree to have it watched."

Rand nodded slowly. Ogier never lied, or at least the few who made the attempt were so poor at it that they seldom tried a second time. An Ogier's word was taken as seriously as anyone else's sworn oath. The Waygates would be guarded closely. Except for those in the Borderlands, and in the mountains south of Amadicia and Tarabon. From gate to gate, a man could journey from the Spine of the World to the Aryth Ocean, from the Borderlands to the Sea of Storms, all in a strange world somehow outside of time, or maybe alongside it. Two days walking along the Ways could carry you a hundred miles, or five hundred, depending on the paths you chose. And if you were willing to risk the dangers. You could die very easily in the Ways, or worse. The Ways had turned dark and corrupted long ago. Trollocs did not care about that, though, at least not when they had Myrddraal driving them. Trollocs cared only for killing, especially when they had Myrddraal driving them. And nine Waygates would remain unwatched, with the danger that any of them might open up to let out Trollocs by the tens of thousands. Setting any sort of guard without the *stedding*'s cooperation might be impossible. Many people did not believe Ogier existed, and few of those who did wanted to meddle without leave. Maybe the Asha'man, if he had enough he could trust.

Suddenly, he realized that he was not the only one who was tired. Loial looked worn and gaunt. His coat was rumpled and hung loosely on him. It was dangerous for an Ogier to be outside the *stedding* too long, and Loial had left his home a good five years ago. Maybe those brief visits over the last few months had not been enough for him. "Maybe you should go home now, Loial. *Stedding* Shangtai is a only a few days from here."

Loial's chair creaked alarmingly as he sat bolt upright. His ears shot upright, too, in alarm. "My mother will be there, Rand. She's a famous Speaker. She would never miss a Great Stump."

"She can't have come all the way back from the Two Rivers already," Rand told him. Loial's mother was supposedly a famous walker, too, yet there were limits, even for Ogier.

"You don't know my mother," Loial muttered, a drum

booming darkly. "She'll still have Erith in tow, too. She will."

Min leaned toward the Ogier, a dangerous light in her eyes. "The way you talk about Erith, I know you want to marry her, so why do you keep running from her?"

Rand studied her from the fireplace. Marriage. Aviendha assumed that he would marry her, and Elayne and Min as well, in the Aiel fashion. Elayne appeared to think so, too, strange as that seemed. He thought she did. What did Min think? She had never said. He should never have let them bond him. The bond would smother them in grief when he died.

Loial's ears trembled with caution, now. Those ears were one reason Ogier made poor liars. He made placating gestures as though Min were the larger of them. "Well, I do want to, Min. Of course, I do. Erith is beautiful, and very perceptive. Did I ever tell you how carefully she listened to me explain about . . . ? Of course, I did. I tell everybody I meet. I do want to marry her. But not yet. It isn't like with you humans, Min. You do everything Rand asks. Erith will expect me to settle down and stay home. Wives never let a husband go anywhere or do anything, if it means leaving the *stedding* for more than a few days. I have my book to finish, and how can I do that if I don't see everything Rand does? I'm sure he's done all sorts of things since I left Cairhien, and I know I'll never get it all down right. Erith just wouldn't understand. Min? Min, are you angry with me?"

"What makes you think I'm angry?" she said coolly.

Loial sighed heavily, and so clearly in relief that Rand almost stared. Light, the Ogier actually thought she meant she was not angry! Rand knew he was feeling his way in the dark when it came to women, even Min—maybe especially Min—but Loial had better learn a lot more than he already knew before he married his Erith. Otherwise, she would skin him out like a sick goat. Best to get him out of the room before Min did Erith's job for her. Rand cleared his throat.

"Think on it overnight, Loial," he said. "Maybe you'll change your mind by morning." Part of him hoped Loial would. The Ogier had been too long from home. Another part of him, though . . . He could use Loial, if what Alivia had told him about the Seanchan was true. Sometimes, he disgusted himself. "In any case, I need to talk to Bashere, now. And Logain." His mouth tightened around the name. What *was* Logain doing in Asha'man black?

Loial did not stand. Indeed, his expression grew more troubled, ears slanting back and eyebrows drooping. "Rand, there's something I need to tell you. About the Aes Sedai who came with us."

Lightnings flared anew outside the windows as he went on, and the thunder crashed overhead harder than ever. With some storms, a lull only meant the worst was coming.

I told you to kill them all when you had the chance, Lews Therin laughed. *I told you.*

"Are you *positive* they've been bonded, Samitsu?" Cadsuane asked firmly. And loudly enough to be heard over the thunder booming on the manor house's rooftop. Thunder and lightning fit her mood. She would have liked to snarl. It required a goodly measure of her training and experience to sit calmly and sip hot ginger tea. She had not let emotion get the upper hand in a very long time, but she wanted to bite something. Or someone.

Samitsu held a porcelain cup of tea, too, but she had yet to swallow a drop, and she had ignored Cadsuane's offer of a chair. The slender sister turned from peering into the flames of the left-hand fireplace, the bells in her dark hair jingling as she shook her head. She had not bothered to dry her hair properly, and it hung damp and heavy down her back. Her hazel eyes were uneasy. "It's hardly the sort of question I could ask a sister, now is it, Cadsuane, and they certainly didn't tell me. As who would? At first, I thought maybe they had done like Merise and Corele. And poor Daigian." A brief wince of sympathy crossed her face. She knew in full the pain that was gnawing at Daigian over her loss. Any sister beyond her first Warder knew that too well. "But it's plain Toveine and Gabrelle are both with Logain. I think Gabrelle is bedding him. If there's bonding been done, it was the men who did it."

"Turnabout," Cadsuane muttered into her tea. Some said that turnabout was fair play, but she had never believed in fighting fair. Either you fought, or you did not, and it was never a game. Fairness was for people standing safely to one side, talking while others bled. Unfortunately, there was little she could do beyond trying to find a way to balance events. Balance was not at all the same as fairness. What a dog's dinner this was turning into. "I'm glad you gave me at least a little warning before I have to face Toveine and the others, but I want you to return to Cairhien the first thing tomorrow."

"There was nothing I could do, Cadsuane," Samitsu said bitterly. "Half the people I gave an order had begun checking with Sashalle to see if it was right, and the other half told me to my face she'd already said different. Lord Bashere talked her into turning the Warders loose—I have no idea how he found out about them in the first place—and she talked Sorilea into it, and there wasn't the least thing I could do to stop it. Sorilea was behaving as if I had just abdicated! She doesn't understand, and she made it plain she thinks I'm a fool. There's no point at all in me going back, unless you expect me to carry Sashalle's gloves for her."

"I expect you to watch her, Samitsu. No more than that. I want to know what one of these Dragonsworn sisters does when neither I nor the Wise Ones are looking over their shoulders and holding a switch. You've always been very observant." Patience was not always her strongest trait, but sometimes it was required with Samitsu. The Yellow *was* observant, and intelligent, and strong-willed most of the time, not to mention the best alive at Healing—at least until the appearance of Damer Flinn—but she could suffer the most astonishing collapses in her confidence. The stick never worked with Samitsu, but pats on the back did, and it was ridiculous not to use what worked. As Cadsuane reminded her how intelligent she was, how skilled at Healing—that was always necessary, with Samitsu; she could go into a depression over failing to Heal a dead man—how clever, the Arafellin sister began to draw up her composure. And her self-assurance.

"You can be assured Sashalle won't change her stockings without I know it," she said crisply. In truth, Cadsuane expected no less. "But if you don't mind me asking," with her confidence restored, Samitsu's tone made that the merest courtesy; she was no shrinking flower except when her self-assurance weakened, "why are you here, at the back end of

Tear? What's young al'Thor going to do? Or should I say, what are you going to have him do?"

"He intends something very dangerous," Cadsuane replied. Lightning flashed outside the windows, sharp silver forks in a sky near as dark as night. She knew exactly what he intended. She just did not know whether to stop it.

"It has to end!" Rand thundered, echoed by the crashes in the sky. He had doffed his coat before this interview, and rolled up his shirtsleeves to bare the Dragons twined around his forearms in scarlet and gold, the golden-maned heads resting on the backs of his hands. He wanted the man in front of him reminded with every look that he was facing the Dragon Reborn. But his hands were fists, to keep him from giving in to Lews Therin's urgings and throttling bloody Logain Ablar. "I don't need a war with the White Tower, and you bloody Asha'man bloody well won't give me a war with the White Tower! Do I make myself understood?"

Logain, hands resting easily atop the long hilt of his sword, did not flinch. He was a big man, if smaller than Rand, with a steady gaze that gave no sign that he had been dressed down or called to account. The silver sword and red-and-gold Dragon glittered brightly in the lamplight on the high collar of his black coat, and that itself looked freshly ironed. "Are you saying release them?" he asked calmly. "Will the Aes Sedai release those of ours they've taken?"

"No!" Rand said curtly. And sourly. "What's done can't be undone." Merise had been so shocked when he suggested she release Narishma, you would have thought he was asking her to abandon a puppy by the side of the road. And he suspected Flinn would fight as hard to hang on to Corele as she to him; he was fairly certain there was more between those two than the bond, now. Well, if an Aes Sedai could bond a man who channeled, what was to say a pretty woman could not fix on a gimpy old man? "You realize the mess you've created, though, don't you? As it is, the only man who can channel that Elaida wants alive is me, and that only till the Last Battle is done. Once she learns of this, she'll be twice as hot to see you all dead any way she can manage it. I don't know how the other lot will react, but Egwene was always a sharp bargainer. I may have to tell off Asha'man for Aes Sedai to bond until they have as many of you as you do of them. That's if they don't just decide you all have to die as soon as they can arrange it, too. What's done is done, but there cannot be any more!"

Logain stiffened a little more with every word, but his gaze held on Rand's. It was plain as horns on a ram that he was ignoring the others in the sitting room. Min had wanted no part of this meeting and taken herself off to read; Rand could not make up from down in Herid Fel's books, but she found them fascinating. He had insisted Loial remain, though, and the Ogier was pretending to study the flames in the fireplace. Except when he glanced at the door, tufted ears twitching, as if wondering whether he could slip out unnoticed under cover of the storm. Davram Bashere appeared even shorter than he really was alongside the Ogier, a graying man with dark tilted eyes, a beak of a nose, and thick mustaches curving down around his mouth. He had worn his sword, too, a shorter blade than Logain's, and serpentine. Bashere spent more time peering into his wine-cup than looking at anything else, but whenever his eyes touched Logain, he unconsciously ran a thumb along his sword hilt. Rand thought it was unconscious.

"Taim gave the order," Logain said, coldly uncomfortable explaining himself in front of an audience. Sudden lightning close to the house cast his face in lurid shadows for an instant, a bleak mask of darkness. "I assumed it came from you." His eyes moved slightly in Bashere's direction, and his mouth tightened. "Taim does a great many things people think are at your direction," he went on reluctantly, "but he has his own plans. Flinn and Narishma and Manfor are on the deserters' list, like every Asha'man you kept with you. And he has a coterie of twenty or thirty he keeps close and trains privately. Every man who wears the Dragon is one of that group except me, and he'd have kept the Dragon from me, if he dared. No matter what you've done, it is time to turn your eyes to the Black Tower before Taim splits it worse than the White Tower is. If he does, you'll find the larger part is loyal to him, not you. They know him. Most have never even seen you."

Irritably, Rand pushed his sleeves down and dropped into

a chair. What he had done made no matter to Logain. The man knew *saidin* was clean, but he could not believe Rand or any man had actually done the cleansing. Did he think the Creator had decided to stretch out a merciful hand after three thousand years of suffering? The Creator had made the world and then left humankind to make of it what they would, a heaven or the Pit of Doom by their choosing. The Creator had made many worlds, watched each flower or die, and gone on to make endless worlds beyond. A gardener did not weep for each blossom that fell.

For an instant, he thought those must have been Lews Therin's reflections. He had never gone on that way about the Creator or anything else that he recalled. But he could *feel* Lews Therin nodding in approval, a man listening to someone else. Still, it was not the kind of thing he would have considered before Lews Therin. How much space remained between them?

"Taim will have to wait," he said wearily. How long could Taim wait? He was surprised not to hear Lews Therin raging for him to kill the man. He wished that made him feel easier. "Did you just come to see that Logain reached me safely, Bashere, or to tell me somebody stabbed Dobraine? Or do you have an urgent task for me, too?"

Bashere raised an eyebrow at Rand's tone, and his jaw tightened as he glanced at Logain, but after a moment, he snorted so hard his thick mustaches should have shaken. "Two men ransacked my tent," he said, setting his winecup down on a carved blue table against the wall, "one carrying a note I could swear I wrote myself if I didn't know better. An order to carry away 'certain items.' Loial tells me the fellows who knifed Dobraine had the same sort of note, apparently in Dobraine's hand. A blind man could see what they were after, with a little thought. Dobraine and I are the most likely candidates to be guarding the seals for you. You have three, and you say three are broken. Maybe the Shadow knows where the last is."

Loial had turned from the fireplace as the Saldaean spoke, his ears rigid, and now he burst out, "That *is* serious, Rand. If someone breaks all the seals on the Dark One's prison, or maybe even just one or two more, the Dark One could break free. Even you can't face the Dark One! I mean, I know the Prophecies say you will, but that has to be just a way of speaking." Even Logain looked concerned, his eyes studying Rand as if measuring him against the Dark One.

Rand leaned back in his chair, careful not to let his tiredness show. The seals on the Dark One's prison on one hand, Taim splitting the Asha'man on the other. Was the seventh seal already broken? Was the Shadow beginning the opening moves of the Last Battle? "You told me something once, Bashere. If your enemy offers you two targets . . ."

"Strike at a third," Bashere finished promptly, and Rand nodded. He had already decided, anyway. Thunder rattled the windows till the casements shook. The storm was strengthening.

"I can't fight the Shadow and the Seanchan at the same time. I am sending the three of you to arrange a truce with the Seanchan."

Bashere and Logain seemed stunned into silence. Until they began to argue, one on top of the other. Loial just looked ready to faint.

Elza fidgeted, listening to Fearil report what had occurred since she left him in Cairhien. It was not the man's harsh voice that irritated her. She hated lightning, and wished she could ward away the violent lights flashing in the windows as she had warded her room against eavesdropping. No one would think her wish for privacy strange, since she had spent twenty years convincing everyone that she was married to the pale-haired man. Despite his voice, Fearil looked the sort a woman would marry, tall and lean and quite pretty. The hard edge to his mouth only made his face more so, really. Of course, some might think it peculiar that she had never had more than one Warder at a time, if they stopped to think about it. A man with just the right qualifications was difficult to find, but perhaps she should start looking. Lightning lit up the windows again.

"Yes, yes, enough," she broke in finally. "You did the right thing, Fearil. It would have been taken as odd if you were the only one to refuse to find your Aes Sedai." A sense of relief flashed through the bond. She was strict about obedience to her orders, and while he knew she could not kill him—would not, at least—punishment only required her to mask the bond so she did not share his pain. That, and a

ward to muffle his screams. She disliked screaming almost
as much as she disliked lightning.

"It is just as well you're with me," she went on. A pity
that the Aiel savages were still holding Fera, though she
would have to quiz the White on exactly why she had sworn
before she could be trusted. Until the journey to Cairhien,
she had not known she shared anything with Fera. A very
great pity that none of her own heart was with her, but only
she had been sent to Cairhien, and she did not question the
orders she received any more than Fearil questioned those
she gave. "I think a few people are going to have to die
soon." As soon as she decided which ones. Fearil bowed his
head, and a jolt of pleasure came through the bond. He did
like killing. "In the meanwhile, you will kill anyone who
threatens the Dragon Reborn. Anyone." After all, it had become perfectly clear to her, while she herself was a captive
of the savages. The Dragon Reborn had to reach Tarmon
Gai'don, or how could the Great Lord defeat him there?

CHAPTER
25

When to Wear Jewels

Perrin strode impatiently up and down the flowered carpets that floored the tent, shrugging with discomfort in the dark green silk coat he had seldom worn since Faile had had it made. She said the elaborate silver embroidery suited his shoulders, but the wide leather belt supporting his axe at his side, the one as plain as the other, only pointed up that he was a fool pretending to be more than he was. Sometimes he tugged his gauntlets tighter, or glared at his fur-lined cloak, lying across the back of a chair ready for him to put on. Twice, he pulled a sheet of paper from his sleeve and unfolded it to study the sketched map of Malden while he paced. That was the town where Faile was being held.

Jondyn and Get and Hu had caught up to the fleeing inhabitants of Malden, but the only useful thing they had gotten was this map, and making anyone pause long enough to provide that had been a chore. Those strong enough to fight were dead or wearing *gai'shain* white for the Shaido; those who remained to flee were the old and the very young, the sick and the lame. According to Jondyn, the thought that someone might force them to return and fight the Shaido had quickened their steps north toward Andor and safety. The map was a puzzle, with its maze of streets and the lady's fortress and the great cistern in the northeast corner. It tantalized him with possibilities. But they were possibilities only if he found a solution to the greater puzzle that was not shown on the map, the huge mass of Shaido surrounding the walled town, not to mention four or five hundred Shaido

Wise Ones who could channel. So the map went back into his sleeve, and he continued to pace.

The red-striped tent itself made him chafe as much as the map, and so did the furnishings, the gilt-edged chairs that folded for storage and the mosaic-topped table that did not, the stand-mirror and the mirrored washstand and even the brass-bound chests standing in a row along an outer wall. It was barely light outside, and all twelve of the lamps were lit, mirrors sparkling. The braziers that had held off the night's freezing cold still contained a few embers. He had even had Faile's two silk hangings, worked with lines of birds and flowers, brought out and hung from the roof poles. He had let Lamgwin trim his beard and shave his cheeks and neck; he had washed and donned clean clothes. He had had the tent set up as if Faile were going to return any moment from a ride. All so everyone would look at him and see a bloody lord, look at him and feel confident. And every bit of it reminded him that Faile was not out riding. Tugging off one of his gauntlets, he felt in his coat pocket and ran his fingers along the rawhide cord tucked in there. Thirty-two knots, now. He did not need reminding of that, but sometimes he lay awake a whole night in the bedding that did not have Faile in it, counting those knots. Somehow, they had become a connection to her. Anyway, wakefulness was better than nightmares.

"If you don't sit down, you are going to be too tired to ride to So Habor even with Neald's help," Berelain said, sounding faintly amused. "Just watching you is exhausting me."

He managed not to glare at her. In a dark blue silk riding dress, a wide golden necklace studded with firedrops tight around her neck and the narrow crown of Mayene holding a golden hawk in flight above her brows, the First of Mayene was seated atop her crimson cloak on one of the folding chairs with her hands folded around red gloves in her lap. She looked as composed as an Aes Sedai, and she smelled . . . patient. He did not understand why she had stopped smelling as if he were a fat lamb caught in brambles for her meal, but he almost felt grateful to her. It was good to have someone he could talk to about missing Faile. She listened, and smelled of sympathy.

"I want to be here if . . . when Gaul and the Maidens bring in some prisoners." The slip made him grimace as much as the delay. It was as if he doubted. Sooner or later they would capture some of the Shaido, yet apparently that was no easy matter. Taking prisoners did no good unless they could be brought away, and the Shaido were only careless compared to other Aiel. Sulin had been patient, too, explaining it to him. It was getting so hard for him to be patient, though. "What's keeping Arganda?" he growled.

As if the Ghealdanin's name had summoned him at last, Arganda pushed through the entry flaps, his face like stone and his eyes sunken. He looked as though he slept as little as Perrin. The short man wore his silvery breastplate, but no helmet. He had not shaved yet this morning, and graying stubble grizzled his chin. Dangling from one gauntleted hand, a fat leather purse clinked as he set it on the table alongside two already there. "From the Queen's strongbox," he said sourly. He had said little the last ten days that was not sour. "Enough to cover our share and more. I had to break open the lock and put three men to guard the chest. It's a temptation to the best of them, with the lock broken."

"Good, good," Perrin said, trying not to sound too impatient. He did not care whether Arganda had to set a hundred men guarding his queen's strongbox. His own purse was the smallest of the three, and he had gleaned every bit of gold or silver he could find to make it up. Slinging his cloak around his shoulders, he picked up the purses and brushed past the man out into the gray morning.

To his disgust, the camp had taken a more permanent air, though it was not by design, and there was nothing he could do about it. Many of the Two Rivers men slept under tents now, pale brown patched canvas rather than striped red like his, but big enough for eight or ten men each, with their ill-assorted polearms stacked at the front, and the others had turned their temporary brush shelters into sturdy little huts of woven evergreen branches. The tents and huts made at best meandering rows, not at all like the rigid lines seen among the Ghealdanin and Mayeners, yet it still looked a little like a village, with paths and lanes through the snow trampled down to bare, frozen earth. A neat stone fire-ring surrounded each of the cookfires, where clusters of men stood cloaked and hooded against the cold, waiting for their breakfast.

It was what was in those black iron cookpots that had

Perrin moving this morning. With so many men hunting, game was growing thin on the ground, and everything else was running out. They were down to searching for squirrels' hoards of acorns to grind for stretching the oatmeal, and this late in the winter, what they found were old and dried out at best. The sour mixture filled the belly after a fashion, but you had to be hungry to get it down. Most of the faces Perrin could see were watching the cookpots eagerly. The last of the carts were rattling though a gap made in the ring of sharpened stakes around the camp, the Cairhienin drivers swathed to their ears and hunched on their seats like dark sacks of wool. Everything the carts had held was stacked in the center of the camp. Empty, they lurched in the ruts left by the carts ahead, a single file disappearing into the surrounding forest.

Perrin's appearance with Berelain and Arganda at his heels caused a stir, although not among the hungry Two Rivers men. Oh, a few made cautious nods in his direction—one or two fools gave rough bows!—but most still tried not to look at him when Berelain was in the vicinity. Idiots. Stone-brained idiots! There were plenty of other people, though, gathered a little way from the red-striped tent, crowding into the lanes between the other tents. An unarmored Mayener soldier in a gray coat came running with Berelain's white mare, bowing and bending to hold her stirrup. Annoura was already up on a sleek mare almost as dark as Berelain's mount was pale. Thin beaded braids hanging down her chest from the cowl of her cloak, the Aes Sedai barely seemed to notice the woman she was supposed to advise. Back stiff, she peered fixedly toward the low Aiel tents, where nothing moved but the thin wavering lines of smoke rising from the smoke holes. One-eyed Gallenne, in his red helmet and breastplate and eyepatch, made up for the Taraboner sister's inattention, though. As soon as Berelain appeared, he barked an order that stiffened fifty of the Winged Guards to statues, long, red-streamered steel-tipped lances upright at their sides, and when she mounted, Gallenne snapped another command that put them on their horses so smoothly they seemed to move as one.

Arganda directed a frown toward the Aiel tents, frowned at the Mayeners, then stalked over to where as many Ghealdanin lancers waited, in shining armor and conical green helmets, and spoke softly to the fellow who would be commanding them, a lean man named Kireyin who Perrin suspected was nobly born from the haughty gaze visible behind the face-bars of his silvered helmet. Arganda was short enough that Kireyin had to bend to listen to what he had to say, and the necessity frosted the taller man's face even more. One of the men behind Kireyin was carrying a staff with a red banner bearing the three six-pointed Silver Stars of Ghealdan instead of a green-streamered lance, and one of the Winged Guards carried Mayene's Golden Hawk on blue.

Aram was there, too, though off to one side and not ready to ride. Wrapped in his putrid green cloak, sword hilt rising behind his shoulder, he shared his jealous scowls between the Mayeners and the Ghealdanin. When he saw Perrin, the man's scowl turned sullen, and he hurried off, blundering through the Two Rivers men waiting for their breakfast. He did not pause to offer apologies when he bumped someone. Aram had grown increasingly touchy, snapping and sneering at everyone but Perrin as the days passed and they sat and waited. Yesterday, he had almost come to blows with a pair of Ghealdanin over something none of them could quite recall once they were separated, except that Aram said the Ghealdanin had no respect and they said he had a bad mouth. That was why the former Tinker was staying behind this morning. Things were likely to be touchy enough in So Habor without Aram starting a fight when Perrin was not looking.

"Keep an eye on Aram," he said quietly when Dannil brought up his bay. "And keep a close eye on Arganda," he added, stuffing the purses into his saddlebags and buckling the flaps down tight. The weight of Berelain's contribution balanced his and Arganda's together very nicely. Well, she had cause to be generous. Her men were as hungry as anyone else. "Arganda looks a man ready to do something stupid, to me." Stayer frisked a little and tossed his head as Perrin took the reins, but the stallion settled quickly under a firm, gentle hand.

Dannil rubbed his tusk-like mustaches with a cold-reddened knuckle and eyed Arganda sideways, then exhaled heavily in a mist. "I'll watch him, Lord Perrin," he muttered, giving his cloak a hitch, "but no matter what you said about me being in charge, as soon as you're out of sight, he won't listen to a thing I say."

Unfortunately, that was true. Perrin would rather have taken Arganda with him and left Gallenne here, but neither had been willing to accept that. The Ghealdanin did accept that men and horses would begin starving soon unless food and fodder were found somewhere, but he could not make himself spend a day farther from his queen than he already was. In some ways, he seemed even more frantic than Perrin, or maybe just more ready to give in to it. Left to himself, Arganda would have been edging a little nearer the Shaido every day until he was right under their noses. Perrin was ready to die to free Faile. Arganda just seemed ready to die.

"Do what you can to keep him from doing anything stupid, Dannil." After a moment, he added, "As long as it doesn't come to blows." There was only so far he could expect Dannil to restrain the fellow, after all. There were three Ghealdanin for every Two Rivers man, and Faile would never be freed if it came to them killing each other. Perrin very nearly rested his head on Stayer's flank. Light, but he was tired, and he could not see any place ahead of him anywhere.

A slow clop of hooves announced the arrival of Masuri and Seonid, with their three Warders riding close behind wrapped in cloaks that made most of each man vanish, along with part of his horse. Both Aes Sedai wore shimmering silk, and a heavy gold necklace, layers of thick strands, showed under the edge of Masuri's dark cloak. A small white jewel dangled onto Seonid's forehead from a fine golden chain fastened in her hair. Annoura relaxed, settling more easily in her saddle. Back among the Aiel tents, the Wise Ones stood in a line watching, six tall women with their heads wrapped in dark shawls. The people of So Habor might be about as welcoming to Aiel as the people of Malden would have been, but Perrin had not been sure the Wise Ones would let either sister come alone. They had been the last reason for waiting. The sun was a red-gold rim on the treetops.

"The sooner there, the sooner back," he said, climbing into the bay's saddle. As he rode through the gap that had been made to let the carts out, Two Rivers men were already beginning to replace the missing stakes. No one lacked for wariness with Masema's people nearby.

It was a hundred paces to the treeline, but his eye caught movement, someone on a horse slipping away into the deeper shadows beneath the towering trees. One of Masema's watchers, no doubt, racing to tell the Prophet that Perrin and Berelain had left the camp. No matter how fast he rode, though, he could not be in time. If Masema wanted Berelain or Perrin dead, as seemed likely, he would have to wait on another opportunity.

Gallenne was not about to take any chances, though. No one had seen hide nor toenails of Santes or Gendar, Berelain's two thief-catchers, since the day they failed to return from Masema's camp, and to Gallenne that was as sure a message as their heads in a sack. He had his lancers spread in a sharp-eyed ring around Berelain before they reached the trees. And around Perrin, too, but that was only incidental. Given his wishes, Gallenne would have brought all nine hundred or so of his Winged Guards, or better yet, in his view, talked Berelain out of going. Perrin had tried that, as well, with no better luck. The woman had a way of listening, then doing exactly as she wished. Faile was like that, too. Sometimes a man just had to live with it. Most of the time, since there was nothing else to do.

The huge trees and stone outcrops sticking out of the snow broke up the formation, of course, but it was still a colorful sight even in the dim light of the forest, red streamers floating on light airs in slanted beams of sunlight, red-armored riders vanishing momentarily behind massive oaks and leatherleafs. The three Aes Sedai rode behind Perrin and Berelain, followed by their Warders, all watching the woods around them, and then the man with Berelain's banner. Kireyin and the banner of Ghealdan came a little behind, his men dressed in neat, shining lines, or as near as they could manage. The forest's openness was a deception, and ill suited to neat lines and bright banners, but add in embroidered silks and gems and a crown and Warders in those color-shifting cloaks, and it was a most impressive sight. Perrin could have laughed, though without much mirth.

Berelain seemed to sense his thoughts. "When you go to buy a sack of flour," she said, "wear plain wool so the seller

thinks you can't afford to pay any more than you must.
When you're after flour by the wagonload, wear jewels so
she thinks you can afford to come back for all she can lay
hands on."

Perrin snorted a laugh in spite of himself. It sounded very
much like something Master Luhhan had told him, once,
with a nudge in the ribs to say it was a joke and a look in his
eye that said it was a little more. Dress poor when you want
a small favor, and fine when you want a large one. He was
very glad Berelain no longer smelled like a hunting wolf. At
least that took one worry off his mind.

They soon caught up to the tail end of the carts, a line
that was no longer moving by the time they reached the
Traveling ground. Axework and sweat had removed the
trees sheared off by gateways and made a little clearing,
but it was crowded even before Gallenne spread his ring
of lancers around it facing outward. Fager Neald was there
already, a foppish Murandian with his mustache waxed to
points, on a dapple gelding. His coat would do for anyone
who had not seen an Asha'man before; the only other one
he had was black as well, and at least he had no collar pins
to mark him out. The snow was not deep, but the twenty
Two Rivers men led by Wil al'Seen were on their horses,
too, rather than standing and waiting for their feet to freeze
in their boots. They looked a harder lot than the fellows
who had left the Two Rivers with him, longbows slung
across their backs, bristling quivers and swords of various
descriptions at their belts. Perrin hoped he could send them
home soon, or better, take them home.

Most were balancing a polearm over their saddles, but
Tod al'Caar and Flann Barstere carried banners, Perrin's
own Red Wolfhead and the Red Eagle of Manetheren. Tod's
heavy jaw was set stubbornly, and Flann, a tall skinny fellow from up to Watch Hill, looked sullen. Likely he had not
wanted the job. Maybe Tod had not, either. Wil gave Perrin
one of those open, innocent looks that fooled so many girls
back home—Wil liked too much embroidery on his coat at
feastdays, and he purely loved riding ahead of those banners, probably in the hope some woman would think they
were his—but Perrin let it pass. He had not expected the
other three people in the clearing any more than he had the
banners.

Holding his cloak around him as if the mild breeze were a gale, Balwer clumsily heeled his blunt-nosed roan forward to meet Perrin. Two of Faile's hangers-on trailed after him with defiant expressions. Medore's blue eyes looked odd in her dark Tairen face, but then, her coat, with its puffy green-striped sleeves, looked odd on her bosomy frame. The daughter of a High Lord, she was every inch a noblewoman, and men's clothing just did not suit her. Latian, Cairhienin and pale in a coat almost as dark as Neald's, though marked with four slashes of red and blue across the chest, was not much taller than she, and the way he sniffled with a cold and rubbed at his sharp nose made him look much less competent. Neither wore a sword, another surprise.

"My Lord; my Lady First," Balwer said in that dry voice, ducking a bow in his saddle, a sparrow bobbing on a branch. His eyes flickered toward the Aes Sedai behind them, but that was the only sign he gave that he was aware of the sisters. "My Lord, I recalled that I have an acquaintance in this So Habor. A cutler who travels with his wares, but he may be at home, and I've not seen him in several years." This was the first time he had ever mentioned having a friend anywhere, and a town buried in the north of Altara seemed a peculiar place for it, but Perrin nodded. He suspected there was more to this friend than Balwer was letting on. He was beginning to suspect there was more to Balwer than the man let on.

"And your companions, Master Balwer?" Berelain's face stayed smooth inside her fur-lined cowl, but she smelled amused. She knew very well that Faile had used her young followers as spies and was sure that Perrin made the same use of them.

"They wanted an outing, my Lady First," the bony little man replied blandly. "I will vouch for them, my Lord. They've promised to cause no trouble, and they may learn something." He smelled amused, too—a musty smell, of course, coming from him—though with a touch of irritation. Balwer knew she knew, which did not please him, but she never made open reference to the fact, which did. There definitely was more to Balwer than he let on.

The man must have his reasons for taking them along. He had managed to take up all of Faile's young followers one way and another, and had them eavesdropping and watching among the Ghealdanin and the Mayeners and even the Aiel. According to him, what your friends said and did could be as interesting as what your enemies planned, and that was when you were sure they were your friends. Of course, Berelain knew that her people were being spied on. And Balwer knew she knew that, too. And she knew that he . . . It was all too sophisticated for a country blacksmith.

"We're wasting time," Perrin said. "Open the gateway, Neald."

The Asha'man grinned at him and stroked his waxed mustaches—Neald grinned too much since the Shaido were found; maybe he was eager to come to grips with them—he grinned and gestured grandly with one hand. "As you command," he said in a cheerful voice, and the familiar silvery slash of light appeared, widening into a hole in the air.

Without waiting for anyone else, Perrin rode through into a snow-covered field, surrounded by a low stone wall, in rolling country that seemed almost treeless compared with the forest he had left behind, just a few miles from So Habor unless Neald had made a substantial error. If he had, Perrin thought he might pull those fool mustaches right off the man's face. How could the fellow be *cheerful*?

Soon, though, he was riding west beneath a gray cloudy sky, along a snowy road with the high-wheeled carts trundling along in a line after him and early-morning shadows stretching ahead. Stayer tugged at the reins, wanting to run, but Perrin held him to a steady walk, no faster than the carthorses could manage. Gallenne's Mayeners had to cross fields beside the road to maintain their ring around him and Berelain, and that meant getting past the low walls of rough stone that divided field from field. Some had gates from one farmer's property to the next, probably to allow sharing plow-teams, and others they jumped flamboyantly with the streamers on their lances flying, risking their animal's legs and their necks. Perrin cared the less about their necks, in truth.

Wil and the two fools carrying the Wolfhead and the Red Eagle joined the Mayener bannerman behind the Aes Sedai and Warders, but the other Two Rivers men strung themselves out flanking the line of carts. There were far too many carts for fewer than twenty men to guard, yet the

cart drivers would feel easier seeing them. Not that anyone expected brigands, or Shaido for that matter, but no one
felt comfortable outside the protection of the camp. In any
case, here they would be able to see any threat well before
it reached them.

The low rolling hills did not really allow a very long
view, but it was farm country, with sturdy thatch-roofed
stone houses and barns scattered among the fields, and
nothing of wildness about it anywhere. Even most of the
small thickets clinging to the slopes were coppiced for firewood. But it struck Perrin suddenly that the snow on the
road ahead of him was not fresh; yet the only tracks were
those made by Gallenne's foreriders. No one moved around
any of those dark houses and barns; no smoke rose from
any of the thick chimneys. The countryside seemed absolutely still and absolutely empty. The hair on the back of his
neck stirred, trying to stand.

An exclamation from one of the Aes Sedai made him
look over his shoulder, and he followed Masuri's pointing
finger north to a shape flying through the air. It might have
been taken for a large bat at first glance, sweeping eastward
on long ribbed wings, a strange bat with a long neck and a
long thin tail trailing behind. Gallenne barked an oath and
pressed his looking glass to his eye. Perrin could see it well
enough unaided, and even make out the figure of a human
being clinging to the creature's back, riding it like a horse.

"Seanchan," Berelain breathed, both her voice and the
smell of her worried.

Perrin twisted in his saddle to watch the thing's flight until
the glare of the sunrise made him turn away. "Nothing to
do with us," he said. If Neald had made a mistake, he would
strangle the man.

CHAPTER
26

In So Habor

As it happened, Neald, who had had to remain to hold the gateway open till Kireyin and the Ghealdanin were through, had placed the hole in the air very close to where he aimed. He and Kireyin caught up at a gallop just as Perrin topped a rise and drew rein with the town of So Habor in front of him, on the other side of a small river crossed by a pair of arching timber bridges. Perrin was no soldier, but he knew right away why Masema had left this place alone. Hard against the river, the town had two massive stone walls dotted with towers around it, the inner rising taller than the outer. A pair of barges were tied to a long wharf that ran along the river wall from bridge to bridge, yet the wide bridge gates, iron-strapped and closed tight, seemed to be the only openings in that expanse of rough gray stone, and battlements topped the whole length of it. Built to hold off greedy neighboring nobles, So Habor would have had little fear of the Prophet's rabble even if they came by thousands. Anyone wanting to break into this town would need siege engines and patience, and Masema was more comfortable terrorizing villages and towns without walls or defenses.

"Well, it's glad I am to see people on the walls over there," Neald said. "I was beginning to think everyone in this country was dead and buried." He sounded only half joking, and his grin looked forced.

"As long as they're alive enough to sell grain," Kireyin murmured in his nasal, bored voice. Unbuckling his silvery, white-plumed helmet, he lifted it down to the tall pommel of his saddle. His eyes swept past Perrin and paused briefly on Berelain before he twisted around to address the Aes Sedai in the same weary tone. "Are we going to sit here, or go down?" Berelain arched an eyebrow at him, a dangerous look, as a man with any brains would see. Kireyin did not see.

Perrin's hackles were still trying to stand, the more so since seeing the town. Maybe it was just the part of him that was wolf, disliking walls. But he did not think so. The people atop the walls pointed toward them, and some held looking glasses. Those, at least, would be able to make out the banners clearly. Everyone would be able to see the soldiers, with the streamers on their lances floating on a morning breeze. And the first few carts of the line that stretched down the road out of their sight. Maybe everyone from the farms was crowded into the town. "We didn't come here to sit," he said.

Berelain and Annoura between them had laid out how to approach So Habor. The local lord or lady had surely heard of Shaido depredations not many miles to the north of them, and they might have heard of the Prophet's presence in Altara, too. Either thing was enough to make anyone wary; together, they might be enough to make people loose arrows and wait till after to ask who they had shot. In any case, it was highly unlikely they would welcome outland soldiers through their gates at the moment. The lancers remained spread along the rise, a show that these visitors possessed some armed might even if they chose not to employ it. Not that So Habor would be overly impressed by a hundred men, but the burnished armor of the Ghealdanin and the red armor of the Winged Guards said the visitors were not wandering tricksters. The Two Rivers men would impress no one until they used their bows, so they remained back with the carts, to hold up the cart drivers' spirits. It was all an elaborate bit of nonsense, fluff and feathers, but Perrin was a country blacksmith no matter who called him lord. The First of Mayene and an Aes Sedai should know what they were about in a thing like this.

Gallenne led the way down to the river at a slow walk, bright crimson helmet resting on his saddle, his back straight. Perrin and Berelain rode a little way behind, with Seonid between them and Masuri and Annoura to either side, the Aes Sedai with their hoods thrown back so anyone on those walls who could recognize an Aes Sedai face would have the opportunity to see three. Aes Sedai were welcomed most places, even where people really would rather not. At their backs came all four bannermen, with the Warders spaced among them in their eye-wrenching cloaks. And Kireyin with his shining helmet balanced on his thigh, sour-mouthed at being relegated to riding with the Warders and now and then glaring coldly down his nose at Balwer, who trailed at the rear with his two companions. No one had told Balwer he could come, yet no one had said he could not. He bobbed a bow whenever the nobleman looked at him, then went back to studying the town walls ahead.

Perrin could not shake his uneasiness as they drew nearer the town. The horses' hooves clattered hollowly on the southernmost bridge, a wide structure that rose high enough above the swift-flowing river to let a barge like those tied to the wharf pass easily underneath on sweeps. Neither of the broad bluff-bowed craft had any provision for stepping a mast. One of those barges had settled deep in the water, slanting against taut mooring ropes, and the other somehow looked abandoned, too. A rank, sour smell in the air made him rub at his nose. No one else seemed to notice.

Near the foot of the bridge, Gallenne drew up. The closed gates, covered with black iron straps a foot wide, would have forced a pause anyway. "We have heard of the troubles plaguing this land," he bellowed at the men atop the wall, managing formality at the top of his lungs, "but we are merely passing through, and we come for trade, not trouble; to buy grain and other needful things, not to fight. I have the honor to announce Berelain sur Paendrag Paeron, First of Mayene, Blessed of the Light, Defender of the Waves, High Seat of House Paeron, come to speak with the lord or lady of this land. I have the honor to announce Perrin t'Bashere Aybara . . ." He tossed in Lord of the Two Rivers for Perrin, and several other titles that Perrin had no more right to and had never heard before, then went on for the Aes Sedai, giving each the full honorific and adding her Ajah, as well. It was a very impressive recital. When he fell silent, there was . . . silence.

In the crenelations above, dirty-faced men exchanged bleak looks and fierce whispers, shifting crossbows and polearms nervously. Only a few wore helmets or any sort of armor. Most were in rough coats, but on one man Perrin thought he saw what might have been silk under a layer of grime. It was hard to tell, with so much caked dirt. Even his ears could not make out what they were saying.

"How do we know you're alive?" a hoarse voice shouted down at last.

Berelain blinked in surprise, but no one laughed. It was fool talk, yet Perrin thought the hair on the back of his neck really was standing stiff. Something was very wrong, here. The Aes Sedai seemed not to sense it. Then again, Aes Sedai could hide anything behind those smooth masks of cool serenity. The beads in Annoura's thin braids clicked faintly as she shook her head. Masuri ran an icy gaze along the men on the wall.

"If I must prove I am alive, you will regret it," Seonid announced loudly in crisp Cairhienin accents, a little more heated than her face suggested. "If you continue to point that crossbow at me, you will regret it even more." Several of the men hastily raised their crossbows to point at the sky. Not all, though.

More whispers rustled along the top of the wall, but someone must have recognized Aes Sedai. At last, the gates squealed open on massive rusty hinges. A gagging stench swept out of the town, the stink Perrin had been smelling, only stronger. Old dirt and old sweat, decaying middens and chamber pots too long unemptied. Perrin's ears tried to lie back. Gallenne half-lifted his red helmet as if to replace it on his head before urging his dun through the gates. Perrin booted Stayer to follow, easing his axe in its belt loop.

Just inside the gate, a filthy man in a torn coat poked Perrin's leg with a finger, then darted back when Stayer snapped at him. The fellow had been fat, once, but his coat sagged and his skin hung loose. "Just wanted to be sure," he muttered, scratching his side absently. "My Lord," he added, a tick late. His eyes seemed to focus on Perrin's face for the first time, and his scratching fingers froze. Golden yellow eyes were not a common sight, after all.

"Do you see many dead men walking?" Perrin asked wryly, trying to make a joke of it, as he patted the bay's neck. A trained warhorse wanted to be rewarded for protecting his rider.

The fellow flinched as if the horse had bared teeth at him again; his mouth twitched into a rictus smile, and he edged sideways. Until he bumped solidly into Berelain's mare. Gallenne was right behind her, still looking ready to don his helmet, his one eye trying to watch six ways at once.

"Where can I find your lord or lady?" she demanded impatiently. Mayene was a small nation, but Berelain was unaccustomed to being ignored. "Everyone else seems to have gone mute, but I heard you use your tongue. Well, man? Speak up."

The fellow stared up at her, licking his lips. "Lord Cowlin . . . Lord Cowlin is . . . away. My Lady." His eyes darted toward Perrin, then flickered away. "The grain merchants. . . . They're who you want. They can always be found at the Golden Barge. That way." He thrust out a hand pointing vaguely deeper into the town, then suddenly scrambled away, looking back over his shoulder at them as though fearful of pursuit.

"I think we should find somewhere else," Perrin said. That fellow had been afraid of more than yellow eyes. This place felt . . . askew.

"We are already here, and there is nowhere else," Berelain replied in a very practical voice. In all that stink, he could not catch her scent; he would have to go by what he heard and saw, and her face was calm enough for an Aes Sedai. "I've been in towns that smelled worse than this, Perrin. I'm sure I have. And if this Lord Cowlin is gone, it won't be the first time I've dealt with merchants. You don't really believe they've seen the dead walking, do you?" What was a man to say to that without sounding a pure wool head?

In any case, the others were already crowding through the gates, though not in any neat array, now. Wynter and Alharra heeled Seonid like mismatched guard dogs, the one fair, the other dark, and both ready to rip out throats at the blink of an eye. They certainly had the feel of So Habor. Kirklin, riding beside Masuri, looked unwilling to wait for that eye to blink; his hand rested on the hilt of his sword. Kireyin had a hand to his nose, and a glare in his eye that said someone was going to pay for making him smell this. Medore and Latian looked ill, too, but Balwer merely peered about, tilting his head, then drew the pair of them off into a narrow side street leading north. As Berelain said, they were there already.

The colorful banners looked decidedly out of place as Perrin rode through the cramped winding streets of the town. Some of the streets were actually quite wide for the size of So Habor, but they felt close, as if the stone buildings on either side somehow loomed higher than their two or three stories and were about to topple on his head, to boot. Imagination made the streets seem dim, too. It had to be imagination. The sky was not that gray. People filled the dirty stone paving, but not enough to account for all the farms in the area being abandoned, and everyone scurried, heads down. Not hurrying toward something; hurrying away. No one looked at anyone else. With a river practically on their doorsteps, they had forgotten how to wash, too. He did not see a face without a coating of grime or a garment that did not look to have been worn for a week, and hard work in muck with it. The stink only worsened the deeper into the town they rode. He supposed you could get used to anything, in time. Worst of all was the quiet, though. Villages were quiet sometimes, if not so still as the woods, but a town always held a faint murmur, the sound of shopkeepers bargaining and people going about their lives. So Habor did not even whisper. It barely seemed to breathe.

Getting better directions was difficult, since most people darted away if spoken to, but eventually they dismounted in front of a prosperous-appearing inn, three stories of neatly dressed gray stone under a slate roof, with a sign hanging out front announcing the Golden Barge. The sign even had a touch of gilt on the lettering, and on the grain mounded high in the barge and uncovered as it never would be for shipping. No grooms appeared from the stableyard beside the inn, so the bannermen had to serve as horse holders, a task that did not make them happy. Tod put so much attention into peering at the flow of dirty people that scurried by and fondling the hilt of his short-sword that Stayer very nearly got a couple of his fingers when he took the stallion's reins. The Mayener and the Ghealdanin seemed to be wishing they had lances rather than banners. Flann just looked wild-eyed. In spite of the morning sun, the light did seem . . . shadowy. Going inside did not make things any better.

At first glance, the common room bore out the inn's prosperity, with polished round tables and proper chairs instead of benches, standing beneath a high, stout-beamed ceiling. The walls were painted with fields of barley and oats and millet, ripening under a bright sun, and a colorfully painted clock stood on the carved mantel above a wide fireplace of white stone. The fireplace was cold, though, the air nearly as icy as outside. The clock had run down and the polish dulled. Dust lay on everything. The only people in the room were six men and five women huddling over their drinks around an oval table, larger than the rest, that stood in the middle of the floor.

One of the men leaped to his feet with an oath, face paling underneath the dirt, when Perrin and the others entered. A plump woman with lank greasy hair shoved her pewter cup to her mouth and tried to gulp so fast that wine spilled over her chin. Maybe it was his eyes. Maybe.

"What happened in this town?" Annoura said firmly, tossing back her cloak as though a fire blazed on the hearth. The calm gaze she ran across the people at the table froze every one of them. Abruptly Perrin realized that neither Masuri nor Seonid had followed him inside. He doubted very much that they were waiting in the street with the horses. What they and their Warders *were* doing was any man's guess.

The man who had jumped up tugged at his coat collar with a finger. The coat had been fine blue wool once, with a row of gilded buttons to his neck, but he appeared to have been spilling food down the front of it for some time. Maybe more than had gone into him. He was another whose skin hung slack. "H-happened, Aes Sedai?" he stammered.

"Be quiet, Mycal!" a haggard woman said quickly. Her dark dress was embroidered on the high neck and along the sleeves, but dirt made the colors uncertain. Her eyes were sunken pits. "What makes you think something happened, Aes Sedai?"

Annoura would have continued, but Berelain stepped in as the Aes Sedai opened her mouth again. "We are looking for the grain merchants." Annoura's expression never changed, but her mouth snapped shut with an audible click.

Long looks passed between the people around the table. The haggard woman studied Annoura for a moment, quickly passing on to Berelain and obviously taking in the silks and firedrops. And the diadem. She spread her skirts in a curtsy. "We are the merchant's guild of So Habor, my Lady. What's left of—" Breaking off, she took a deep, shuddering breath. "I am Rahema Arnon, my Lady. How may we serve you?"

The merchants seemed to brighten a little on learning that their visitors had come for grain and other things that they could supply, oil for lamps and cooking, beans and needles and horseshoe nails, cloth and candles and a dozen things more that the camp needed. At least, they grew a little less fearful. Any ordinary merchant hearing the list Berelain gave would have been hard-pressed not to smile greedily, but this lot . . .

Mistress Arnon shouted for the innkeeper to bring wine—"the best wine; quickly, now; quickly"—but when a long-nosed woman stuck her head hesitantly into the common room, Mistress Arnon had to rush over and catch her soiled sleeve to keep her from vanishing again. The fellow in the food-stained coat called for someone named Speral to bring the sample jars, but after shouting three times with no response, he gave a nervous laugh and darted into a back room to return a moment later, his arms around three large cylindrical wooden containers that he sat on the table, still laughing nervously. The others wore a collection of twitching smiles as they bowed and curtsied Berelain to a seat at the head of the oval table, greasy-faced men and women scratching at themselves without appearing to notice what they were doing. Perrin tucked his gauntlets behind his belt and stood against a painted wall, watching.

They had agreed to leave the bargaining to Berelain. She was willing to admit, reluctantly, that he knew more of horseflesh than she, but she had negotiated treaties covering the sale of years' worth of the oilfish harvest. Annoura had smiled thinly at the suggestion that a jumped-up country lad might take a hand. She did not call him that—she could "my Lord" him as smoothly as Masuri or Seonid—yet it was clear she thought some things clearly above his ability. She was not smiling now, standing behind Berelain and studying the merchants as if to memorize their faces.

The innkeeper brought wine, in pewter cups that had last seen a polishing cloth weeks ago if not months, but Perrin only peered into his and swirled it in the cup. Mistress Vadere, the innkeeper, had dirt under her fingernails and embedded in her knuckles like part of her skin. He noticed that Gallenne, standing with his back to the opposite wall and one hand on his sword hilt, only held his cup, too, and Berelain never touched hers. Kireyin sniffed at his, then drank deeply and called for Mistress Vadere to bring him a pitcher.

"Thin stuff, to be called your best," he told the woman through his nose, and looking down it, "but it might wash away the stink." She stared at him blankly, then fetched a tall pewter pitcher to his table without saying a word. Kireyin apparently took her silence for respect.

Master Crossin, the fellow in the food-stained coat, unscrewed the tops of the wooden containers and spilled out hulled samples of the grain they had to offer in piles on the table, yellow millet and brown oats, the barley only a little darker brown. There would have been no rain before the harvest. "The finest quality, as you can see," he said.

"Yes, the finest." The smile slid off Mistress Arnon's face, and she jerked it back. "We sell only the finest."

For people touting their wares as the finest, they did not seem to bargain very hard. Perrin had watched men and women back home selling the wool clip and the tabac to merchants down from Baerlon, and they always disparaged the buyers' offers, sometimes complaining the merchants were trying to beggar them when the price was twice what it had been the year before or even suggesting they might wait till next year to sell at all. It was a dance as intricate as any at a feastday.

"I suppose we might lower the price further for such a large quantity," a balding man told Berelain, scratching at his gray-streaked beard. It was cut short, and greasy enough to cling close to his chin. Perrin wanted to scratch his own beard just watching the fellow.

"It's been a hard winter," a round-faced woman muttered. Only two of the other merchants bothered to frown at her.

Perrin set his winecup down on a nearby table and walked over to the gathering in the middle of the room. Annoura gave him one sharp, warning glance, but several of the merchants looked at him curiously. And cautiously. Gallenne had made his introductions all over again, but these folk were not entirely clear where Mayene was, exactly, or how powerful, and the Two Rivers only meant good tabac, to them. Two Rivers tabac was known everywhere. If not for the presence of an Aes Sedai, his eyes might have set them running. Everyone fell silent as Perrin scooped up a handful of millet, the tiny spheres smooth and vivid yellow on his palm. This grain was the first clean thing he had seen in the town. Letting the grain spill back onto the table, he picked up the lid of one of the containers. The threads cut into the wood were sharp and unworn. The lid would fit tightly. Mistress Arnon's eyes slid away from his, and she licked her lips.

"I want to see the grain in the warehouses," he said. Half the people around the table twitched.

Mistress Arnon drew herself up, blustering. "We don't sell what we don't have. You can watch our laborers load every sack on your carts, if you wish to spend hours in the cold."

"I was about to suggest a visit to a warehouse," Berelain put in. Rising, she drew her red gloves from behind her belt and began tugging them on. "I would never buy grain without seeing the warehouse."

Mistress Arnon sagged. The bald-headed man put his head down on the table. No one said anything, though.

The dispirited merchants did not bother to fetch their cloaks before leading them into the street. The breeze had picked up to a wind, cold as only a late winter wind could be, when people were already thinking ahead to spring, but they did not seem to notice. The hunch of their shoulders had nothing to do with cold.

"Can we go now, Lord Perrin?" Flann asked anxiously when Perrin and the others appeared. "This place makes me want a bath." Annoura gave him a frown in passing that made him flinch like one of the merchants. Flann tried a placating smile on her, but it was a sickly effort, and too late for anything but her back.

"As soon as I can arrange it," Perrin said. The merchants were already scurrying down the street, heads down and not looking at anyone. Berelain and Annoura managed to follow without appearing to rush, gliding along, one as composed as the other, two fine ladies out for a stroll and never mind the filth underfoot, or the stink in the air, or the dirty people who started at the sight of them and sometimes all but ran away as fast as they could. Gallenne had finally donned his helmet, and openly held his sword hilt with both hands, ready to draw. Kireyin was carrying his helmet on his hip, his other hand occupied with his winecup. Contemptuously eyeing the grimy-faced folk who hurried by, he sniffed at the wine as if it were a pomander to fight off the stench of the town.

The warehouses were located on a stone-paved street barely wider than a wagon, between the town's two walls. The smell was better there, close to the river, but the windblown street was empty except for Perrin and the others. There was not even a stray dog to be seen. Dogs disappeared when a town grew hungry, but why would a town with enough grain to sell be hungry? Perrin pointed to a two-story warehouse chosen at random, no different from any other, a windowless stone building with a wide pair of wooden doors held shut by a wooden bar that could have done for a ceiling beam at the Golden Barge.

The merchants suddenly recalled that they had forgotten to bring men to lift the bars. They offered to go back for them. The Lady Berelain and Annoura Sedai could rest in front of the fire at the Golden Barge while workmen were fetched. They were sure Mistress Vadere would lay a fire. Their tongues went still when Perrin placed his hand beneath the thick beam and shoved it up out of the wooden brackets. The thing was heavy, but he backed up with it to give him room to turn and toss it down on the street with a crash. The merchants stared. This might have been the first time they had ever seen a man in a silk coat do anything that could be called work. Kireyin rolled his eyes and took another sniff at his wine.

"Lanterns," Mistress Arnon said weakly. "We'll need lanterns, or torches. If . . ."

A ball of light appeared floating above Annoura's hand, glowing bright enough in the gray morning to cast everyone in faint shadows on the paving and the stone walls. Some of the merchants put hands up to shield their eyes. After a moment, Master Crossin tugged one of the doors open by an iron ring.

The smell inside was the familiar sharp scent of barley, almost strong enough to overcome the stench of the town, and something more. Small dim shapes slunk away into the shadows ahead of Annoura's light. He could have seen better without it, or at least deeper into the darkness. The glowing ball cast a large pool of light, and walled off what lay beyond. He smelled cat, closer to feral than not. And rat, too. A sudden squeal in the black depths of the warehouse, suddenly cut off, spoke of cat meeting rat. There were always rats in grain barns, and cats to hunt them. It was comforting, and normal. Almost enough to soothe his uneasiness. Almost. He smelled something else, a smell he should know. A fierce yowl deep in the warehouse turned to rising cries of pain that died abruptly. Apparently the rats of So Habor sometimes hunted back. Perrin's hackles stirred again, but surely there was nothing here the Dark One would want to spy on. Most rats were just rats.

There was no need to go very far in. Coarse sacks filled the darkness, in high slant-sided stacks on low wooden platforms to keep the sacks off the stone floor. Rows and rows of stacks piled nearly to the ceiling, and likely the same on the floor above. If not, this building still held enough grain to feed his people for weeks. Walking to the nearest stack, he drove his belt knife into a pale brown sack and sliced down through the tough jute fibers. A flood of barleycorns spilled out. And, clear in the glow of Annoura's brilliant light, wriggling black specks. Weevils, almost as many as there were barleycorns. Their scent was sharper than that of the barley. Weevils. He wished the hair on his neck would stop trying to rise. The cold should have been enough to kill weevils.

That one sack was proof, and his nose knew the smell of weevils, now, but he moved to another stack, then another, and another, each time slicing open one sack. Each released a spill of pale brown barley and black weevils.

The merchants were standing huddled together in the doorway, daylight behind them, but Annoura's light cast their faces in sharp relief. Worried faces. Despairing faces.

"We would be most happy to winnow each sack we sell," Mistress Arnon said unsteadily. "For only a slight additional—"

"For half the last price I offered," Berelain cut in sharply. Wrinkling her nose in disgust, she moved her skirts clear of the weevils scuttling among the grain on the floor. "You will never get all of them."

"And no millet," Perrin said grimly. His men needed

food, and so did the soldiers, but the millet grains were hardly bigger than the weevils. Winnow as they would, he would bring back weevils and millet in equal weight. "We'll take extra beans instead. But they get winnowed, too."

Suddenly someone shrieked outside in the street. Not a cat or a rat, but a man in terror. Perrin did not even realize he had drawn his axe until he found the haft in his hand as he pushed through the merchants in the doorway. They huddled closer together, licking their lips and not even trying to see who had screamed.

Kireyin was backed up against the wall of a warehouse across the way, his shining helmet with the white plume lying on the pavement beside his winecup. The man's sword was half out of the scabbard, but he seemed frozen, staring with bulging eyes at the wall of the building Perrin had just come out of. Perrin touched his arm, and he jumped.

"There was a man," the Ghealdanin said uncertainly. "He was just there. He looked at me, and . . ." Kireyin scrubbed a hand over his face. Despite the cold, sweat glistened on his forehead. "He walked through the wall. He did. You must believe me." Someone moaned; one of the merchants, Perrin thought.

"I saw the man, too," Seonid said behind him, and it was his turn to give a start. His nose was useless in this place!

Giving the wall Kireyin had indicated a last glance, the Aes Sedai stepped away from it with a palpable unwillingness. Her Warders were tall men, towering over her, but they stayed only far enough away to gain room to draw their swords. Though what the grim-eyed Warders were to fight if Seonid was serious, Perrin could not imagine.

"I find it difficult to lie, Lord Perrin," Seonid said dryly when he expressed doubt, but her tone quickly became as serious as her face, and her eyes were so intent that they alone began to make Perrin feel uneasy. "The dead are walking in So Habor. Lord Cowlin fled the town for fear of his wife's spirit. It seems there was doubt as to how she died. Hardly a man or woman in the town has not seen someone dead, and a good many have seen more than one. Some say people have died from the touch of someone dead. I cannot verify that, but people have died of fright, and others because of it. No one goes out at night in So Habor, or walks into a room unannounced. People strike out at shadows and surprises with whatever is to hand, and sometimes they have found a husband, wife or neighbor dead at their feet. This is not hysteria or a tale to frighten children, Lord Perrin. I have never heard of the like, but it is real. You must leave one of us here to do what we can."

Perrin shook his head slowly. He could not afford to lose an Aes Sedai if he was to free Faile. Mistress Arnon began to weep even before he said, "So Habor will have to face its dead alone."

But fear of the dead only explained so much. Maybe people were too frightened to think of washing, but it seemed unlikely that fear would take everyone that way. They just did not seem to care anymore. And weevils thriving in winter, in freezing cold? There was worse wrong in So Habor than spirits walking, and every instinct told him to leave at a dead run, without looking back. He purely wished that he could.

CHAPTER
27

What Must Be Done

The winnowing took place on the snowy eastern riverbank, where there was nothing to cut the sharp north wind. Men and women from the town hauled sacks across the bridges in four-horse wagons and one-horse carts even barrows pushed by hand. Normally buyers brought their own wagons to the warehouses, or at worst the grain and dried beans only had to be carried as far as the wharf, but Perrin had no intention of sending his cart drivers into So Habor. Or anyone else, for that matter. Whatever was wrong in that town might be catching. Anyway, the drivers were uneasy enough as it was, frowning at the dirty townsfolk, people who never spoke, but laughed nervously when they accidentally met someone's eye. The grimy-faced merchants overseeing the work were no better. In the drivers' native Cairhien, merchants were clean, respectable people, at least outwardly, who very seldom twitched just because someone moved at the corner of their vision. Between merchants with a tendency to peer suspiciously at anyone they did not know, and townsfolk who dragged their feet recrossing the bridges, clearly reluctant to go back inside their own walls, the cart drivers were right on edge. They gathered in little clusters, pale, dark-clad men and women, gripping the hilts of their belt knives and peering at the taller locals as if at murderous madmen.

Perrin rode about slowly, watching the winnowing, examining the row of carts that stretched up the rise and out of sight waiting to be loaded, or the town's wagons and carts and barrows rolling across the bridges. He made sure he was in plain view. He was not sure why the sight of him pretending to be unconcerned should settle anyone else's nerves, yet it seemed to. Enough that no one started running, at least, though they continued to look askance at the people of So Habor. They kept their distance, too, and just as well. Let the notion that some of those folk might not be alive get into the Cairhienin's heads, and half would whip up their cart horses to flee then and there. Most of the rest might not wait much past dark. That sort of tale could twist anyone's head, come night. The wan sun, nearly hidden by gray overcast, still sat less than halfway to its noonday peak, yet increasingly it was obvious they would have to be there through the night. Maybe more than one. His jaw knotted with the effort of not grinding his teeth, and even Neald began to avoid his scowls. He did not snap at anyone. He just wanted to.

It was an arduous process, the winnowing. Every last sack had to be opened and emptied onto large flat wicker baskets, each of which took two people to toss the grain or beans. The cold wind carried away weevils in a shower of black flecks, and men and women with woven two-handed fans added to the gusts. A swift current swept away everything that was blown into the river, but soon the snow on the riverbank was trampled underfoot and the gray slush layered with insects dead or dying from the cold, and a liberal coating of oats and barley speckled with red beans. There was always a new layer to replace what feet mashed into the snow. What was left on the baskets seemed cleaner, though, if not entirely clean when it was poured back into the coarse jute bags, which had been turned inside out and beaten fiercely with sticks by children to shake out vermin. The refilled sacks went into the Cairhienin's carts as soon as the tops were tied, but the piles of empty bags grew at a prodigious rate.

He was leaning on the pommel of Stayer's saddle, trying to calculate whether it was taking two whole cart loads from the warehouses to fill one of his carts with grain, when Berelain brought her white mare up beside him, holding her scarlet cloak close against the wind with one red-gloved hand. Annoura reined in a few paces away, her ageless face smooth and unreadable. The Aes Sedai appeared to be giving them privacy, yet she was close enough to hear anything above whispers even without any tricks of the Power.

Smooth face or no, her beak of a nose gave her a predatory look today. Her beaded braids seemed some strange eagle's lowered crest.

"You cannot save everyone," Berelain said calmly. Away from the stink of the town, her scent was sharp with urgency, and razor-edged with anger. "Sometimes, you must choose. So Habor is Lord Cowlin's duty. He had no right to abandon his people." Not angry with him, then.

Perrin frowned. Did she think he felt guilty? Balanced against Faile's life, the troubles of So Habor could not budge the scales a hair. But he turned his bay so he was looking at the gray town walls across the river, not the hollow-eyed children piling up empty sacks. A man did what he could. What he had to. "Does Annoura have an opinion on what's happening here?" he growled. Quietly, but somehow he had no doubt the Aes Sedai heard.

"I've little idea what Annoura thinks," Berelain replied, making no effort to lower her voice. She not only did not care who overheard, she wanted to be heard. "She is not as forthcoming as she once was. As I once thought she was. It is up to her to mend what she has torn." Without looking at the Aes Sedai, she turned and rode away.

Annoura remained behind, eyes unblinking on Perrin's face. "You are *ta'veren*, yes, but you are still only a thread in the Pattern, as am I. In the end, even the Dragon Reborn is just a thread to be woven into the Pattern. Not even a *ta'veren* thread chooses how it will be woven."

"Those threads are people," Perrin said wearily. "Sometimes maybe people don't want to be woven into the Pattern without any say."

"And you think this makes a difference?" Not waiting on an answer, she lifted her reins and heeled her fine-ankled brown mare after Berelain in a gallop that fanned her cloak behind her.

She was not the only Aes Sedai who wanted words with Perrin.

"No," he told Seonid firmly after listening to her, patting Stayer's neck. It was the rider wanted soothing, though. He wanted to be away from So Habor. "I said no, and I mean no."

She sat her saddle stiffly, a pale little woman carved of ice. Except that her eyes were dark coals burning, and she reeked of affronted fury barely in check. Seonid was mild

as milk-water with the Wise Ones, but he was not a Wise
One. Behind her, Alharra's dark face was a stone, gray
streaking his curly black hair like frost. Wynter's face was
red above his curled mustaches. They had to accept what
passed between their Aes Sedai and the Wise Ones, but
Perrin was not . . . The wind whipped their Warder cloaks
about, leaving their hands free for swords if need be. Rip-
pling in the wind, the cloaks shifted in shades of gray and
brown, blue and white. It was easier on the stomach than
seeing them make parts of a man disappear. Some easier.

"If I have to, I'll send Edarra to bring you back," he
warned.

Her face stayed cold, her eyes hot, yet a quiver ran
through her, swaying the small white gem hanging on her
forehead. Not from fear of what the Wise Ones would do
to her if she had to be brought back, just from the same offense at Perrin that made her scent a hooked thorn. He was
growing accustomed to offending Aes Sedai. Not a habit a
wise man got into, but there seemed no way out of it.

"What about you?" he asked Masuri. "Do you want to
stay in So Habor as well?"

The slim woman was known for speaking straight to the
point, direct as a Green for all she was Brown, but she said
calmly, "Would you not send Edarra after me, too? There
are many ways to serve, and we cannot always pick the
ways we would wish." Which, come to think, might be to
the point, in a way. He still had no idea why she visited
Masema in secret. Did she suspect that he knew? Masuri's
face was a bland mask. Kirklin wore a bored expression,
now they were out of So Habor. He managed to seem
slumped while sitting his horse erect, without a worry in
the world or a thought in his head. A man who believed that
of Kirklin would return the next day to buy a second pig in
a poke.

The townsfolk worked mechanically as the sun rose
higher, like people who wanted to lose themselves in the
task at hand and feared the return of memories when they
stopped. Perrin decided So Habor was making him fanciful. Still, he thought he was right. The air beyond the walls
still looked too dim, as though a shading cloud hung over
the town.

At noon, the cart drivers cleared patches of snow on the

slope rising from the river to make small fires and brew weak tea with leaves brewing their third pot, or maybe fourth. There had been no tea to be had in the town. Some of the drivers looked at the bridges as if thinking to enter So Habor and see what they could find to eat. A glance at the dirt-caked people working the winnowing baskets sent them back to dig out their small bags of oatmeal and ground acorn. At least they knew that mix was clean. A few eyed the sacks already loaded on the carts, but the beans needed to be soaked and the grain run through the large handmills that had been left back in the camp, and that was after the cooks picked out as many more weevils as they thought men could not stomach eating.

Perrin had no appetite, not for the cleanest bread, but he was drinking what passed for tea from a battered tin cup when Latian found him. The Cairhienin did not actually come to him. Instead, the short man in the striped dark coat rode slowly past the small fire where Perrin was standing, then reined in with a frown a little upslope. Dismounting, Latian lifted his gelding's near forehoof and frowned at it. Of course, he did look up twice to see whether Perrin was coming.

With a sigh, Perrin returned the dented cup to the blocky little woman he had borrowed it from, a graying cart driver who spread her dark skirts in a curtsy. And grinned and shook her head at Latian. Likely, she could sneak ten times as well as the fellow. Neald, squatting by the fire with his hands wrapped around another tin cup, laughed out loud so hard he had to wipe a tear from his eye. Maybe he was beginning to go crazy. Light, but this place gave a man cheerful thoughts.

Latian straightened long enough to make Perrin a leg and say, "I see you, my Lord," then ducked back down to snatch up the foreleg again like a fool. You did not grab at a horse's legs that way unless you wanted kicking. But then, Perrin expected nothing but foolishness, really. First there was Latian's playing at being Aiel, with his shoulder-long hair tied off in a tail at the nape of his neck in weak imitation of how Aiel cut theirs, and now the man was playing at being a spy. Perrin rested a hand on the gelding's neck to soothe the animal after all that snatching and put an interested look

on his face as he peered at a hoof that had absolutely nothing wrong with it. Except for a nick in the shoe where the
iron might break in a few days if it was not replaced. His
hands itched for farrier's tools. It seemed years since he had
changed a horse's shoes, or worked a forge.

"Master Balwer sends word, my Lord," Latian said
softly, head down. "His friend is traveling to sell his wares,
but is expected back tomorrow or the next day. He said to
ask whether it will be all right if we catch up to you then."
Peering under the horse's belly at the winnowers down by
the river, he added, "Though it hardly looks as if you will
be away before."

Perrin scowled down at the winnowing. He scowled at
the line of carts waiting their turn to be loaded, at the half
dozen or so that already had their canvas covers lashed
down. One of those held the first of the leather for patching boots and candles and such. No oil, though. The lamp
oil in So Habor smelled as rancid as the cooking oil. What
if Gaul and the Maidens brought word of Faile? An actual
sighting, perhaps? He would give anything to talk to someone who had seen her, could tell him she was unharmed.
What if the Shaido began to move suddenly? "Tell Balwer
not to wait too long," he growled. "As for me, I'll be away
inside the hour."

He was as good as his word. Most of the carts and drivers had to be left behind to make the one-day journey back
to camp on their own, and Kireyin and his green-helmeted
soldiers to guard them, with orders that no one was to cross
the bridges. Cold-eyed, appearing completely recovered
from his breakdown, the Ghealdanin assured him that he
was fit and ready. Very likely, orders or not, he would be
going back into So Habor just to convince himself he was
not afraid. Perrin did not waste time trying to talk him out
of it. For one thing, Seonid had to be found. She was not
precisely hiding, yet she had learned of his departure, and,
leaving her Warders to hold her horse quite openly, she
dodged about on foot trying to keep carts between herself and
him. The pale Aes Sedai could not hide her scent, though,
or if she could, she did not know it was necessary. She was
surprised when he tracked her down quickly, and indignant
when he marched her to her horse ahead of Stayer. Even

so, he was well under the hour riding away from So Habor, with the Winged Guards making their ring of red armor around Berelain, the Two Rivers men surrounding the eight loaded carts that trundled along behind the three remaining banners, and Neald grinning for all he was worth. Not to mention trying to chat up the Aes Sedai. Perrin did not know what to do if the fellow really was going mad. As soon as the rise hid So Habor behind them, he felt the loosening of a knot he had not realized was riding between his shoulders. That left only ten others, and a knot of impatience twisting his belly. Berelain's obvious sympathy could not loosen those.

Neald's gateway took them from the snow-covered field to the small clearing of the Traveling ground amid the towering trees, four leagues in a step, but Perrin did not wait for the handful of carts to come through. He thought he heard Berelain make a vexed sound when he booted Stayer to a quick trot, back toward the camp. Or maybe it was one of the Aes Sedai. Much more likely.

There was a sense of stillness when he rode in among the Two Rivers men's tents and huts. The sun still hung not too far off overhead in the gray sky, but there were no cookpots on the fires and very few of the men gathered around the campfires, holding their cloaks close and peering intently into the flames. A handful were sitting on the rough stools that Ban Crawe knew how to make; the rest stood or squatted. No one so much as looked up. Certainly no one came running to take his horse. Not stillness, he realized. Tension. The smell somehow minded him of a bow drawn to the point of breaking. He could almost hear the creak.

As he dismounted in front of the red-striped tent, Dannil appeared from the direction of the low Aiel tents, walking fast. Sulin and Edarra, one of the Wise Ones, were following him, and keeping up easily though neither appeared to hurry. Sulin's face was a sun-dark leather mask. Edarra's, barely revealed by the dark shawl wrapped around her head, was an image of calm. Despite her bulky skirts, she made as little sound as the white-haired Maiden, not so much as a faint clink from her gold and ivory bracelets and necklaces. Dannil was chewing the edge of one thick mustache, absently pulling his sword an inch out of its rough leather scabbard and shoving it back hard. Pull and shove. He drew a deep breath before speaking.

"The Maidens brought in five Shaido, Lord Perrin. Arganda took them over to the Ghealdanin tents to put them to the question. Masema's with them."

Perrin brushed aside Masema's presence inside the camp. "Why did you let Arganda take them?" he asked Edarra. Dannil could not have stopped it, but the Wise Ones were a different proposition.

Edarra appeared not much older than Perrin, yet her cool blue eyes seemed to have seen far more than he ever would. She folded her arms beneath her breasts in a rattle of bracelets. And with a touch of impatience. "Even Shaido know how to embrace pain, Perrin Aybara. It will take days to bring any of them to talk, and there seemed no reason to wait."

If Edarra's eyes were cool, Sulin's were blue ice. "My spear-sisters and I could have done it faster ourselves, a little, but Dannil Lewin said you wanted no blows struck. Gerard Arganda is an impatient man, and he mistrusts us." She sounded as though she would have spat if she were not Aiel. "You may not learn much, in any case. They are Stone Dogs. They will yield slowly, and as little as possible. In this, it is always necessary to put together a little from one with a little from another to make a picture."

Embrace pain. There had to be pain, when you put a man to the question. He had not let that thought form in his head before this. But to get Faile back . . .

"Have somebody rub Stayer down," he said roughly, thrusting the reins at Dannil.

The Ghealdanin portion of the camp could not have been more different from the rude shelters and haphazardly placed tents of the Two Rivers men. Here, the peaked canvas tents stood in precise rows, most with a steel-tipped cone of lances standing at the entry flaps and saddled horses tethered at the side, ready to mount. The flicking of the horses' tails and the long streamers on the lances, lifting on a cold breeze, were the only disordered things to be seen. The paths between the tents were all the same width, and a straight line could have been drawn through the rows of cookfires. Even the creases in the canvas, from where the

tents had been folded away at the bottom of carts until the
snows came, made straight lines. All orderly and neat.

A smell of oatmeal porridge and boiled acorn hung in
the air, and some green-coated men were scraping the last
of the midday meal from their tin plates with their fingers. Others were already scouring out the cookpots. None
showed any sign of tension. They were just eating and doing chores, with about equal pleasure. It was something that
had to be done.

A large knot of men stood gathered in a ring near the
sharpened stakes that marked the outer edge of the camp.
No more than half wore the green coats and burnished
breastplates of Ghealdanin lancers. Some of the others carried lances or had swords belted over their rumpled coats.
Those ranged from fine silk or good wool to the pickings of
a ragbag, but none could be called clean except in comparison to So Habor. You could always tell Masema's men, even
from the back.

Another smell came to him as he approached the circle of
men. The smell of meat roasting. And there was a muffled
sound that he tried not to hear. When he began pushing his
way through, the soldiers looked around at him and gave
way grudgingly. Masema's men started back, muttering
about yellow eyes and Shadowspawn. Either way, he gained
passage to the front.

Four tall men, red-haired or pale in the gray-and-brown
cadin'sor, lay bound with their wrists lashed to their ankles
in the small of their backs and stout lengths of branch tied
behind their knees and elbows. Their faces were battered
and bruised, and they had wadded rags tied between their
teeth. The fifth man was naked, staked out between four
stout pegs driven into the ground and stretched so tight his
sinews stood out. He thrashed as much as his binding allowed, though, and howled into the rags stuffing his mouth,
a muffled bellow of agony. Hot coals made a small cluster on his belly, giving off a faint smoke. It was the smell
of blistering flesh that Perrin's nose had caught. The coals
clung to the stretched man's skin, and every time his writhing managed to throw one off, a grinning fellow in a filthy
green silk coat, squatting beside him, used a pair of tongs
to replace it with another from a potful melting a circle of
mud in the ground. Perrin knew him. His name was Hari,

and he liked to collect ears strung on a leather cord. Men's ears, women's ears, children's ears; it never minded to Hari.

Without thinking, Perrin strode forward and kicked the little pile of coals off the bound man. Some of them struck Hari, who jumped back with a startled squeal that turned to a shriek when his hand came down in the pot. He toppled over sideways, cradling his burned hand and glaring at Perrin, a weasel in a human skin.

"The savage makes a sham, Aybara," Masema said. Perrin had not even noticed the man standing there, face like a scowling stone beneath his shaved scalp. His dark fevered eyes held a measure of contempt. The scent of madness skittered through the stink of burned flesh. "I know them. They pretend to feel pain, but they do not; not the way other men do. You must be willing and able to hurt a stone to make one of them talk."

Arganda, rigid beside Masema, was gripping his sword hilt so hard that his hand shook. "Perhaps you are willing to lose your wife, Aybara," he grated, "but I will not lose my queen!"

"It has to be done," Aram said, half pleading, half demanding. He was on Masema's other side, clutching the edges of his green cloak as if to keep his hands from the sword on his back. His eyes were almost as hot as Masema's. "You taught me that a man does what he must."

Perrin forced his fists to unknot. What had to be done, for Faile.

Berelain and the Aes Sedai came pushing through the crowd, Berelain wrinkling her nose slightly at the sight of the man stretched out between the pegs. The three Aes Sedai might have been looking at a piece of wood for all their expression. Edarra and Sulin were with them, neither more affected. Some of the Ghealdanin soldiers frowned at the two Aiel women and muttered under their breath. Masema's rumpled, dirty-faced men glared at Aiel and Aes Sedai alike, but most edged away from the three Warders, and those who did not were pulled away by their companions. Some fools knew the limits of stupidity. Masema glared at Berelain with burning eyes before deciding to pretend she did not exist. Some fools knew no limits.

Bending, Perrin untied the rag around the pegged man's mouth and tugged the wad from between his teeth. He just managed to snatch his hand back from a snap as vicious as any Stayer could have given.

Immediately, the Aielman threw back his head and began to sing in a deep, clear voice:

> Wash the spears; while the sun climbs high.
> Wash the spears; while the sun falls low.
> Wash the spears; who fears to die?
> Wash the spears; no one I know!

Masema's laughter rose in the middle of the singing. Perrin's hackles rose, too. He had never heard Masema laugh before. It was not a pleasant sound.

He did not want to lose a finger, so he pulled his axe out of its belt loop and carefully used the top of the axe head against the man's chin to push his mouth shut. Eyes the color of the sky looked up at him out of a sun-dark face, unafraid. The man smiled.

"I don't ask you to betray your people," Perrin said. His throat hurt with the effort of keeping his voice steady. "You Shaido captured some women. All I want to know is how to get them back. One is named Faile. She's as tall as one of your women, with dark tilted eyes, a strong nose and a bold mouth. A beautiful woman. You'd remember her, if you had seen her. Have you?" Pulling the axe away, he straightened.

The Shaido stared at him for a moment, then raised his head and began to sing again, never taking his eyes from Perrin. It was a jolly song, with the rollicking sound of a dance:

> I once met a man who was far from home.
> His eyes were yellow and his wits were stone.
> He asked me to hold smoke in my hand,
> and said he could show me a watery land.
> He put his head in the ground and his feet in the air,
> and said he could dance like a woman fair.
> He said he could stand till he turned to stone.
> When I blinked my eyes, he was gone.

Letting his head fall back, the Shaido chuckled, deep and rich. He could have been lounging at ease on a feather bed.

"If . . . If you can't do this," Aram said desperately, "then go away. I'll help see to it."

What had to be done. Perrin looked at the faces around him. Arganda, scowling with hatred, at him as much as the Shaido, now. Masema, stinking of madness and filled with a scornful hate. You must be willing and able to hurt a stone. Edarra, her face as unreadable as the Aes Sedai's, arms folded calmly beneath her breasts. Even Shaido know how to embrace pain. It will take days. Sulin, the scar across her cheek still pale on her leathery skin, her gaze level and her scent implacable. They will yield slowly and as little as possible. Berelain, smelling of judgment, a ruler who had sentenced men to death and never lost a night's sleep. What had to be done. Willing and able to hurt a stone. Embrace pain. Oh, Light, Faile.

The axe was as light as a feather rising in his hand, and came down like a hammer on the anvil, the heavy blade shearing through the Shaido's left wrist.

The man grunted in pain, then reared up convulsively with a snarl, deliberately spraying the blood that gouted from his wrist across Perrin's face.

"Heal him," Perrin said to the Aes Sedai, stepping back. He did not try to wipe his face. The blood was seeping into his beard. He felt hollow. He could not have lifted the axe again if he had to for his life.

"Are you mad?" Masuri said angrily. "We cannot give the man back his hand!"

"I said, Heal him!" he growled.

Seonid was already moving, though, lifting her skirts to glide across the ground and kneel at the man's head. He was biting at his severed wrist, trying futilely to stem the flow of blood with the pressure of his teeth. But there was no fear in his eyes. Or in his smell. None.

Seonid gripped the Shaido's head, and suddenly he convulsed again, flinging his arm out wildly. The spray of blood dwindled as he jerked, and was gone before he slumped back to the ground, gray-faced. Unsteadily, he raised the stump of his left arm to look at the smooth skin that now covered the end. If there was a scar, Perrin could not see it. The man bared teeth at him. He still did not smell afraid. Seonid slumped, too, as if she had strained to her limit.

Alharra and Wynter took a step forward, and she waved them away, rising by herself with a heavy sigh.

"I've been told you can hold out for days and still say next to nothing," Perrin said. His voice sounded too loud in his ears. "I don't have time for you to show how tough you are, or how brave. I know you're brave and tough. But my wife's been a prisoner too long. You'll be separated and asked about some women. Whether you've seen them and where. That's all I want to know. There'll be no hot coals or anything else; just questions. But if anybody refuses to answer, or if your answers are too different, then everybody loses something." He was surprised to find that he could lift the axe after all. The blade was smeared with red.

"Two hands and two feet," he said coldly. Light, he sounded like ice. He felt like ice to his bones. "That means you get four chances to answer the same. And if you all hold out, I still won't kill you. I'll find a village to leave you in, some place that will let you beg, somewhere the boys will toss a coin to the fierce Aielmen with no hands or feet. You think on it and decide whether it's worth keeping my wife from me."

Even Masema was staring at him as if he had never before seen the man standing there with an axe. When he turned to go, Masema's men and the Ghealdanin alike parted in front of him as though to let a whole fist of Trollocs through.

He found the hedge of sharpened stakes in front of him, and the forest a hundred paces or so beyond, but he did not change direction. Carrying the axe, he walked until huge trees surrounded him and the smell of the camp was left behind. The smell of blood he carried with him, sharp and metallic. There was no running from that.

He could not have said how long he walked through the snow. He barely noticed the sharpening slant of the bars of light that sliced the shadows beneath the forest canopy. The blood was thick on his face, in his beard. Beginning to dry. How many times had he said he would do anything to get Faile back? A man did what he had to. For Faile, anything.

Abruptly, he raised the axe behind his head in both hands and hurled it as hard as he could. It spun end over end, and slammed into the thick trunk of an oak with a solid *thcunk*.

Letting out a breath that seemed locked in his lungs, he

sank down on a rough stone outcrop that stuck up as high and broad as a bench, and put his elbows on his knees. "You can show yourself now, Elyas," he said wearily. "I can smell you there."

The other man stepped lightly out of the shadows, yellow eyes glowing faintly beneath the wide brim of his hat. The Aiel were noisy, compared to him. Adjusting his long knife, he took a seat beside Perrin on the outcrop, but for a time he merely sat combing his fingers through the gray-streaked beard that fanned across his chest. He nodded toward the axe stuck in the side of the oak. "I told you once to keep that till you got to like using it too much. Did you start liking it? Back there?"

Perrin shook his head hard. "No! Not that! But . . ."

"But what, boy? I think you almost have Masema scared. Only, you smell scared, too."

"About time he was scared of something," Perrin muttered, shrugging uncomfortably. Some things were hard to give voice. Maybe it was time to, though. "The axe. I didn't notice it, the first time; only looking back. That was the night I met Gaul, and the Whitecloaks tried to kill us. Later, fighting Trollocs in the Two Rivers, I wasn't sure. But then, at Dumai's Wells, I was. I'm afraid in a battle, Elyas, afraid and sad, because maybe I'll never see Faile again." His heart clenched till his chest hurt. Faile. "Only . . . I've heard Grady and Neald talk about how it is, holding the One Power. They say they feel more *alive*. I'm too frightened to spit, in a battle, but I feel more alive than any time except when I'm holding Faile. I don't think I could stand it if I came to feel that way about what I just did back there. I don't think Faile would have me back if I came to that."

Elyas snorted. "I don't think you have that in you, boy. Listen, danger takes different men in different ways. Some are cold as clockwork, but you never struck me as the cold sort. When your heart starts pounding, it heats your blood. Stands to reason it heightens your senses, too. Makes you aware. Maybe you'll die in a few minutes, maybe in a heart-beat, but you're not dead now, and you know it from your teeth to your toenails. Just the way things are. Doesn't mean you like it."

"I would like to believe that," Perrin said simply.

"Live as long as I have," Elyas replied in a dry voice, "and you'll believe. Till then, just take it that I've lived longer than you have, and I've been there before you."

The two of them sat looking at the axe. Perrin wanted to believe. The blood on his axe looked black, now. Blood had never looked so black before. How long had it been? From the angle of the light sifting through the trees, the sun was falling.

His ears caught the crunch of hooves in the snow, slowly coming toward him. Minutes later, Neald and Aram appeared, the one-time Tinker pointing out tracks and the Asha'man shaking his head impatiently. It was a clear trail, but in truth, Perrin would not have bet on Neald being able to follow it. He was a city man.

"Arganda thought we ought to wait till your blood cooled," Neald said, leaning on his saddle and studying Perrin. "Me, I think it can't get any cooler." He nodded, a touch of satisfaction around his mouth. He was accustomed to people being afraid of him, because of his black coat and what it represented.

"They talked," Aram said, "and they all gave the same answers." His scowl said he did not like the answers. "I think the threat of leaving them to beg frightened them more than your axe. But they say they've never seen the Lady Faile. Or any of the others. We could try the coals again. They might remember then." Did he sound eager? To find Faile, or to use the coals?

Elyas grimaced. "They'll just give you back the answers you've already given them, now. Tell you what you want to hear. It was a small chance, anyway. There's thousands of Shaido and thousands of prisoners. A man could live his whole life among that many people and never meet more than a few hundred to remember."

"Then we have to kill them," Aram said grimly. "Sulin said the Maidens made sure to take them when they had no weapons, so they could be questioned. They won't just settle down to be *gai'shain*. If even one escapes, he can let the Shaido know we're here. Then they'll be coming after us."

Perrin's joints felt rusted, aching as he stood up. He could not just let the Shaido go. "They can be guarded, Aram." Haste had almost lost him Faile completely, and he had been hasty again. Hasty. Such a mild word for cutting off a man's hand. And to no purpose. He had always tried to think carefully and move carefully. He had to think now, but every thought hurt. Faile was lost in a sea of white-clad prisoners. "Maybe other *gai'shain* would know where she is," he muttered, turning back toward the camp. But how to put his hands on any of the Shaido's *gai'shain*? They were never allowed outside the camp except under guard.

"What about that, boy?" Elyas asked.

Perrin knew what he meant without looking. The axe. "Leave it for whoever finds it." His voice turned harsh. "Maybe some fool gleeman will make a story out of it." He strode away toward the camp, never looking back. With its empty loop, the thick belt around his waist was too light. All to no purpose.

Three days later the carts returned from So Habor, heavy laden, and Balwer entered Perrin's tent with a tall unshaven man, wearing a dirty woolen coat and a sword that looked much better cared for. At first, Perrin did not recognize him behind an untrimmed month's growth of beard. Then he caught the man's scent.

"I never expected to see you again," he said. Balwer blinked, as much as a gasp of startlement from anyone else. Doubtless the bird-like little man had been looking forward to presenting a surprise.

"I've been searching for . . . for Maighdin," Tallanvor said roughly, "but the Shaido moved faster than I could. Master Balwer says you know where she is."

Balwer gave the younger man a sharp look, but his voice remained as dry and emotionless as his scent. "Master Tallanvor reached So Habor just before I left, my Lord. It was the merest chance that I encountered him. But perhaps a fortunate chance. He may have some allies for you. I will let him tell it."

Tallanvor frowned at his boots and said nothing.

"Allies?" Perrin prompted. "Nothing less than an army will be much use, but I'll take any aid you can bring."

Tallanvor looked at Balwer, who returned a half bow and a blandly encouraging smile. The unshaven man drew a deep breath. "Fifteen thousand Seanchan, near enough. Most are Taraboners, actually, but they ride under Seanchan

banners. And . . . And they have at least a dozen *damane*."
His voice quickened with urgency, a need to finish before
Perrin could cut him off. "I know it's like taking help from
the Dark One, but they're hunting the Shaido, too, and I'd
take the Dark One's help to free Maighdin."

For a moment, Perrin stared at the two men, Tallanvor
nervously thumbing his sword hilt, Balwer like a sparrow
waiting to see which way a cricket would hop. Seanchan.
And *damane*. Yes, that *would* be like taking the Dark
One's help. "Sit down and tell me about these Seanchan,"
he said.

CHAPTER
28

A Cluster of Rosebuds

From the day they left Ebou Dar, traveling with Valan Luca's Grand Traveling Show and Magnificent Display of Marvels and Wonders was every bit as bad as Mat's darkest thoughts had made it. For one thing, it rained almost every day for a few hours and once for three days running, cold winter rain in downpours little short of snow and icy drizzles that slowly soaked a coat through and left you shivering before you knew it. Water ran off the hard-packed road as if it had been paved in stone, leaving at worst a thin slick of mud, but that long train of wagons and horses and people covered little enough ground when the sun shone. In the beginning, the showfolk had been all eagerness to leave the city where lightning sank ships in the night and strange murders had everyone looking over their shoulders, to be away from a jealous Seanchan nobleman who would be hunting his wife furiously and might take out his anger on anyone associated with spiriting her out of his clutches. In the beginning, they pressed ahead as fast as the horses could pull the wagons, urging the animals for a quicker step, another mile. But every mile seemed to make them feel that much farther from danger, that much safer, and by the first afternoon . . .

"Have to take care of the horses," Luca explained, watching the team unhitched from his ridiculously painted wagon and led away to the horselines through a light drizzle. The sun still sat little more than halfway down to the horizon, but already gray tendrils were rising from the smoke holes of tents and the metal chimneys of the box-like living wagons. "Nobody's chasing us, and it's a long way to

Lugard. Good horses are hard to come by, and expensive."
Luca gave a sour frown and shook his head. Mention of
expense always soured him. He was tight with a penny,
except where his wife was concerned. "Not many places
between here and there worth stopping more than a day.
Most villages won't provide a full crowd even if the whole
population turns out, and you can never tell how a town
will be until you set up. You're not paying me enough to
give up what I can earn, though." Hitching his embroidered
crimson cloak closer against the damp, he glanced over his
shoulder toward his wagon. The smell of something bitter
drifted through the light rain. Mat was not sure he would
want to eat anything Luca's wife cooked. "You're certain
nobody is chasing us, right, Cauthon?"

Irritably tugging his woolen cap lower, Mat stalked away
through the brightly colored sprawl of tents and wagons
grinding his teeth. Not paying enough? For what he had offered, Luca should have been willing to *run* his animals all
the way to Lugard. Well, not exactly run—he did not want
to kill horses, after all—but that puffed-up popinjay should
have been willing to bloody push hard.

Not far from Luca's wagon, Chel Vanin was seated on a
three-legged stool that he overlapped, stirring some sort of
dark stew in a small kettle that hung over a small fire. Rain
dripped into the kettle from the drooping brim of his hat,
but the fat man did not seem to notice, or care. Gorderan
and Fergin, two of the Redarms, grumbled curses as they
drove pegs into the muddy ground for the guy ropes of
the dirty-brown canvas tent they shared with Harnan and
Metwyn. And with Vanin, too, but Vanin possessed skills
that he considered put him above raising tents, and the Redarms agreed with only a little reluctance. Vanin was an
experienced farrier, but more importantly, he was the best
tracker and the best horsethief in the country, unlikely as
that seemed to look at him, and you could name the country
you chose.

Fergin caught sight of Mat, and bit off an oath as his
hammer missed the tent peg and hit his thumb. Dropping
the hammer, he stuck the thumb in his mouth and squatted
there complaining shrilly around it. "We're going to be out
in this all night guarding those women, my Lord. Can't you

hire some of those horse handlers to do this so we can at least stay dry till we have to get wet?"

Gorderan poked Fergin's shoulder with a thick finger. He was as wide as Fergin was skinny, and a Tairen despite his gray eyes. "Horse handlers'll put up the tent and steal everything in it that's loose, Fergin." Another poke. "You want one of those lightfingers walking off with my crossbow, or my saddle? That's a good saddle." A third poke nearly pushed Fergin over sideways. "We don't get this tent up, and Harnan'll have us standing guard all night."

Fergin glowered and grumbled, but he picked up his hammer, wiping the mud off on his coat. He was a good enough soldier, but not very bright.

Vanin spat through the gap in his teeth, just missing the kettle. The stew smelled wonderful after whatever Latelle was making, but Mat decided he was not going to eat here, either. Tapping his wooden spoon on the rim of the kettle to clean it, the fat man looked up at Mat through heavy-lidded eyes. His round face often looked half-asleep, but only a fool believed it. "At this rate, we'll reach Lugard about the end of summer. If we ever do."

"We will, Vanin," Mat said, more confidently than he felt at the moment. The rough woolen coat he had donned dry a few hours ago only shed rain in spots, and water was trickling down his back. It was hard to feel confident with icy rain sliding down your backbone. "Winter's almost done. We'll move faster once spring comes. You'll see. Come the middle of spring, and we'll be in Lugard."

He was not so sure of that, either. They covered no more than two leagues that first day, and after that, two and a half made a good day. Not many places could be called towns along the Great North Road, a name that began to change very quickly as the show crept north. People called it "the Ebou Dar Road," or "the Ferry Road," or sometimes just "the road," as if there were only one. But Luca stopped at every last town, real or so-called, walled or jumped-up village with six streets and a rough-paved excuse for a town square. Near half a day went into just getting the show set up and the canvas wall erected around it with that huge red-lettered blue banner hung across the entrance. Valan Luca's Grand Traveling Show. It was just not in Luca to pass up the chance of a crowd. Or the coins in their purses. Or the chance to flourish one of his bright red cloaks and bask in their adulation. Luca liked that almost as much as the coin. Almost.

The strangeness of the performers and the caged animals from far-off lands were sufficient to pull people. The animals from not so far were enough, for that matter; few had been far enough into the countryside to see a bear much less a lion. Only heavy rain lessened the crowd, and when the rain was too stiff, the jugglers and acrobats refused to perform anyway without some sort of covering overhead. Which made Luca stalk about in a sullen snit and talk wildly of finding enough canvas tarps to shelter every act, or having a tent made large enough to hold the entire show. One tent! The man was nothing if not grandiose in his ambitions. Why not a palace on wheels while he was about it?

If Luca and the slow way the show moved had been all Mat had to worry about, though, he would have been a happy man. Sometimes, two or three slow-moving trains of Seanchan settlers who had gotten an early start passed with their strangely shaped, peaked wagons and odd-looking cattle or sheep or goats before the first wagon from the show began to move. Sometimes columns of Seanchan soldiers overtook them as they ambled along at a slow walk, ranks of men wearing helmets like huge insects' heads, stepping out smartly, and columns of horsemen with their armor of overlapping plates painted in stripes. Once, the riders were on *torm,* bronze-scaled creatures like horse-sized cats. Except for having three eyes, anyway. Twenty or so of them snaking along in a sinuous lope faster than a horse could trot. Neither the riders nor their mounts gave the show a second glance, but the show's horses went wild as the *torm* passed, screaming and rearing in the traces. The lions and leopards and bears roared in their cages, and the peculiar deer flung themselves against the bars trying to flee. It took hours to quiet everything down enough for the wagons to move again, and Luca insisted on having the caged animals' scrapes seen to first. His animals were a large investment. Twice, officers in thin-plumed helmets decided to check the warrant for Luca's horses, and Mat oozed cold sweat the size of grapes until they moved on again, satisfied. As the show crept north, the numbers of Seanchan on the road dwindled, yet he still sweated when he saw another party, soldiers or settlers either one. Maybe Suroth really was keeping Tuon's disappearance a secret, but the Seanchan would be searching for her. All it would take was one meddlesome officer who actually compared the numbers on the warrant with the number of horses. He would search the wagons with a fine-tooth comb after that, for certain. Just one officious *sul'dam* who thought there might be a woman who could channel among the jugglers and tumblers and contortionists. He sweated plums! Unfortunately, not everyone had a proper regard for their own skins.

Outside a flyspeck village called Weesin, a thatch-roofed little cluster of houses where not even Luca thought two coppers could be shaken loose, Mat stood with a heavy woolen cloak pulled around him in a driving rain and watched the three Aes Sedai steal back into the show as the sun set. Thunder boomed in the distance. They were swathed in dark cloaks with the hoods well up, yet he had no doubts who they were. In the downpour, they passed within ten feet without seeing him, but the silver medallion hanging beneath his shirt went cold against his chest. At least one of them was channeling, or holding the Power, anyway. Burn him, they were all three mad as loons.

No sooner did the Aes Sedai vanish among the wagons and tents than three more cloaked shapes appeared, hurrying after them. One of these women had a sharper eye, raising a hand to point at him, but the others only paused, and then they scurried after the Aes Sedai together. He started to curse, then left it unuttered. He was beyond that. If he named the people he wanted wandering around where a Seanchan patrol might see them, the Aes Sedai and the *sul'dam* would come about even with Tuon and Selucia.

"I wonder what they want?" Noal said behind him, and Mat gave a jump that let a torrent of rain into his cowl and down his neck. He wished the knobbly old man would quit sneaking up on him.

"I intend to find out," he muttered, jerking his cloak straight. He hardly knew why he bothered. His coat was only a little damp, but his linen shirt was already soaked.

Oddly enough, Noal was no longer with him when he reached the gray-streaked wagon with its fading whitewash where the Aes Sedai and *sul'dam* slept. The man liked sticking his nose in everywhere. Maybe he had decided he was wet enough. Blaeric and Fen were already wrapped in their blankets beneath the wagon, apparently oblivious to rain or mud, but he would not have wagered on either being asleep. Indeed, one sat up as he squelched up to the wagon. Whichever it was, he said nothing, yet Mat could feel the man's eyes. He did not hesitate, though, and he did not bother with knocking.

The interior was crowded with all six women on their feet, dripping cloaks still in hand. Two lamps mounted in gimbals on the walls gave a good light, better than he could have wished for, in a way. Six faces swiveled toward him with those frozen looks women gave a man when he put a foot where they did not want it. The air in the wagon smelled of damp wool and felt as if lightning had just struck, or might at any moment. Rain drummed on the roof, and thunder rolled, but the foxhead medallion felt no cooler than any other piece of silver. Maybe Blaeric and Fen had let him come inside thinking he would get his head snapped off. Maybe they just wanted to stay out of this themselves. But then, a Warder was ready to die if his Aes Sedai decided it was necessary. Not Mat Cauthon. He pushed the door shut with his hip. It hardly gave him a twinge anymore. Seldom, anyway.

When he challenged them, Edesina fiercely, shaking out the black hair that spilled down her back. "I am grateful to you for rescuing me from the Seanchan, Master Cauthon, and I will show my gratitude, but there are limits. I am not your servant to be ordered about. There were no Seanchan in the village, and we kept our faces hidden. There was no need to send your . . . watchdogs . . . after us." The look she shot at the three Seanchan women could have fried eggs. Edesina was over being nervous about anyone with a Seanchan accent. She wanted some of her own back, and the *sul'dam* were close to hand. Mat was counting on that fabled Aes Sedai self-control to keep matters short of violence. He hoped it was not already stretched too far to hold. Those old memories recalled Aes Sedai going up like an Illuminator's wares.

Bethamin's dark face showed no sign of alarm. She had finished shaking out her cloak and hanging it on a peg while Edesina was speaking, then smoothed her dress over her hips. Tonight, she wore faded green petticoats. She complained that the Ebou Dari garment was indecent, and he supposed that he would have to find her something else now they were away from the coast, but she did fill out that very low narrow neckline nicely. She sounded too much like a mother for his taste, though. "They *did* keep their faces hidden, my Lord," she drawled, "and they stayed together. No one tried to sneak off. Very well behaved, all in all." A mother praising her children. Or maybe a dog trainer praising the dogs. Yellow-haired Seta nodded approvingly. Definitely a dog trainer.

"If my Lord wishes to keep them confined," Renna said fulsomely, "we can always use the *a'dam*. They really shouldn't be trusted loose." She even offered him a bow, in the Seanchan way, bending herself at a sharp right angle. Her big brown eyes looked hopeful. Teslyn gasped and clutched her wet cloak to her bosom. She certainly was not over her fear of the *sul'dam*, for all she looked as though she could eat nails. Joline, haughty as ever, drew herself up, eyes flashing. Aes Sedai serenity or no, lightning might as well strike when Joline's eyes started flashing. It was often so with pretty women.

"No," Mat said hastily. "There's no need for that. You give those things to me, and I'll get rid of them." Light, why had he ever saddled himself with these women? What seemed the best idea at the time could look pure quill stupid in hindsight. "All of you just have to be careful. We're not thirty miles from Ebou Dar yet. The roads are full of bloody Seanchan." He gave an apologetic look to the three Seanchan women. They *were* on his side, after all. In a manner of speaking. They had nowhere else to go except Egeanin, and they had realized who had the money. Bethamin's eyebrows twitched upward in surprise. Seanchan nobles did not apologize, even with a glance.

"Seanchan soldiers did pass through the village yesterday," Teslyn said, her Illianer accent particularly strong. Joline's flashing eyes shifted to her, but she took no notice beyond turning away to hang up her own cloak. "They did ask questions about strangers on the road. And some did complain about being sent north." Teslyn glanced over her shoulder at the *sul'dam,* then jerked her eyes away and took a deep breath. "It does seem the Return be aimed east. The soldiers did believe the Ever Victorious Army will present Illian to their empress before the end of spring. The City itself, and all the rest." Supposedly Aes Sedai gave up the lands of their birth when they went to the White Tower, but to any Illianer, the city of Illian was 'the City,' and you could hear the capital.

"That's good," Mat said half to himself, thinking. Soldiers talked out of turn all the time; that was one reason you did not tell your plans to every trooper until the last minute. Teslyn's thin eyebrows rose, and he added, "It means the road to Lugard will be clear most of the way." Teslyn's nod was curt and not very pleased. What Aes Sedai were supposed to do and what they did were often widely different.

"We didn't speak to anyone, my Lord, only watched the girls," Bethamin said, even more slowly than usual, and Seanchan usually talked like honey pouring in a snowstorm. She was clearly in charge among the three *sul'dam,* but she looked at each of the others before going on. "In Ebou Dar, all the talk in the *sul'dam* quarters was of Illian. A fat land and a fat city, where many would earn new names. And wealth." She tossed that in as if wealth hardly counted alongside a new name. "We should have realized you'd want to know about such things." Another deep breath almost popped her out of that dress. "If you have any questions, my Lord, we'll tell you what we know."

Renna made him another bow, her face eager, and Seta piped up with, "We could listen in the towns and villages where we stop, too, my Lord. The girls can be shifty, but you can trust us."

Why, when a woman offered to help you, did she always start by sticking you in a pot of hot water and stoking up the fire? Joline's face became a disdainful mask of ice. The Seanchan women were beneath her notice; she made that clear with a glance. It was Mat bloody Cauthon who received her freezing gaze. Edesina's mouth thinned, and she tried to stare holes in him and the *sul'dam* both. Even Teslyn managed indignation. She was grateful for rescue, too, but she was Aes Sedai. And she directed her frown at him. He suspected she would jump like a startled frog if one of the *sul'dam* clapped her hands.

"What I want," he explained patiently, "is for all of you to stay with the wagons." You had to be patient with women, including Aes Sedai. He was bloody well learning that by heart. "One whisper there's an Aes Sedai with this show, and we'll be hip-deep in Seanchan hunting for her. Rumors of Seanchan with the show won't serve us any better. Either way, somebody will come to find out what's behind it sooner or later, and we'll all be in the pickling kettle. Don't flaunt yourselves. You need to stay low till we get closer to Lugard. That isn't so much to ask, now is it?" Lightning lit up the wagon's windows with a blue flash, and thunder crashed overhead, so close it rattled the wagon.

It was too much to ask, apparently, as the days wore on. Oh, the Aes Sedai kept their hoods well up when they went outside—the rain gave enough excuse for that; the rain and the cold—but one or another rode on the wagon seat as often as not, and they made no real effort to pass as servants around the showfolk. Not that they admitted who they were, of course, or ordered anyone about or even spoke to anyone much besides each other, but what servant clearly expected people to move out of her way? They went into the villages, too, and sometimes the towns, if they were sure there were no Seanchan there. When an Aes Sedai was sure of something, it had to be true. Twice they came scurrying back when they found a town half-full of settlers on their way north. They told him what they learned on their visits. He thought they did. Teslyn did seem grateful, after an Aes Sedai fashion. And Edesina. After a fashion.

Despite their differences, Joline, Teslyn and Edesina stuck together like herded geese. If you saw one, you saw all three. Likely that was because when you saw them taking a stroll, all neatly cloaked and hidden as they were, a minute later Bethamin and Renna and Seta appeared trailing after them. Oh so casually, but never letting "the girls" out of sight. The goose-herds. A blind man could see there was tension between the two groups of women. A blind man could see none of them were servants. The *sul'dam* had held respected positions, positions of authority, and they moved almost as arrogantly as the Aes Sedai. He was stuck with the story, though.

Bethamin and the other two were as leery of other Seanchan as the Aes Sedai were, yet they also followed the Aes Sedai when they went into a village or town, and Bethamin always reported the tidbits they had picked up by eavesdropping, with Renna wearing an ingratiating smile and Seta chirping in that 'the girls' had missed this or that, or claimed not to have heard; you could never be sure with someone who had the audacity to call herself Aes Sedai; maybe he should reconsider having them leashed, just till everything was safe.

Their tales really were not that different from what the sisters told him. Townsfolk's talk of what they had overheard from Seanchan passing through. Many of the settlers were nervous, their heads full of tales about savage Aiel ravaging through Altara, though the local people all said that was up north somewhere. It seemed someone higher might be thinking the same, though, because many settlers had been diverted east, toward Illian. An alliance had been concluded with someone powerful who was expected to give the High Lady Suroth access to many lands. The women refused to be convinced that they need not listen for rumors. They never quite got around to handing over the *a'dam,* either. In truth, those silvery leashes and the three *sul'dam* were the only real lever he had with the Aes Sedai. Gratitude. From an Aes Sedai! Ha! Not that he really thought about putting those collars on the sisters again. Not often, anyway. He was well and truly stuck.

He truly did have no need of what the *sul'dam* and Aes Sedai learned. He had better sources, people he trusted. Well, he trusted Thom, when the white-haired gleeman could be routed out from playing Snakes and Foxes with Olver or mooning over a much-creased letter he carried tucked in the breast of his coat. Thom could walk into a common room, tell a story, maybe juggle a bit, and walk out knowing what was in the head of every man there. Mat trusted Juilin, too—he did almost as well as Thom, without juggling or storytelling—but Juilin always insisted on taking Thera with him, demurely clutching his arm as they strolled into a town. To get her used to freedom again, the man said. She smiled up at Juilin, those big eyes shining darkly, that full little mouth asking to be kissed. Maybe she had been Panarch of Tarabon, the way Juilin and Thom claimed, but Mat was beginning to doubt it. He had heard some of the contortionists joking about how the Taraboner serving girl was wearing the Tairen thief-catcher out till he could barely walk. Panarch or serving girl, though, Thera still started to kneel any time she heard a drawling accent.

Mat figured that any Seanchan who asked her a question would get everything she knew, beginning with Juilin Sandar and ending with which wagon the Aes Sedai were in, all answers delivered from her knees. Thera was a bigger danger than Aes Sedai and *sul'dam* put together, in his book. Juilin bridled at the slightest suggestion his woman might be unreliable, though, and spun his bamboo staff as if he was considering cracking Mat's head for him. There was no solution, but Mat found a stopgap, a way to get a little warning if the worst occurred.

"Of course I can follow them," Noal said, with a gap-toothed grin that said it would be child's play. Laying a gnarled finger alongside his bent nose, he slipped the other knobbly hand beneath his coat, where he kept his knives. "Are you sure it wouldn't be better just to make sure she can't talk to anyone? Just a suggestion, lad. If you say not, then not." Mat most emphatically said not. He had killed one woman in his life, and left another to be butchered. He was not going to add a third to his soul.

"It seems Suroth might have made an alliance with some king," Juilin reported with a smile over a cup of mulled wine. At least Thera seemed to be making him smile more. She huddled beside Juilin's stool in their cramped tent, her head lying on his lap, and he stroked her hair softly with his free hand. "At least, there's considerable talk of some powerful new ally. And those settlers are all frightened out of their wits by Aiel."

"Most of the settlers seem to have been sent east," Thom said, peering sadly into his cup. As Juilin grew happier day by day, he seemed to grow sadder. Noal was out shadowing Juilin and Thera, and Lopin and Nerim were sitting cross-legged at the back of the tent, but the two Cairhienin serving men had their mending baskets out and were examining Mat's good coats from Ebou Dar for any repairs they thought necessary, so the small tent still seemed crowded. "And a great many soldiers, too," Thom went on. "Everything says they're going to fall on Illian like a hammer."

Well, at least he knew he was hearing the unvarnished truth when he heard it from them. No Aes Sedai spinning words on their heads or *sul'dam* trying to smarm their way into his good graces. Bethamin and Seta had even learned to curtsy. Somehow, he felt more comfortable with Renna bending herself double. It seemed honest. Strange, but honest.

For himself, town or village, Mat took no more than a quick look around, with his collar turned up and his cap pulled down, before heading back to the show. He seldom wore a cloak. A cloak could make it difficult to use the knives he carried tucked about his person. Not that he expected to need them. It was just a prudent precaution. There was no drinking, no dancing, and no gambling. Especially no gambling. The sound of dice rattling on a table in an inn's common room pulled at him, but his sort of luck with dice was bound to be remarked, even if it did not lead to somebody pulling a knife, and in this part of Altara both men and women carried knives tucked behind their belts and were ready to use them. He wanted to pass through unnoticed, so he walked by the dice games, nodded coolly to the tavern maids who smiled at him, and never drank more than a cup of wine and usually not that. After all, he had work to do back at the show. Work of a sort. He had begun it the very first night after leaving Ebou Dar, and a rough job it was.

"I need you to go with me," he had said then, pulling open the cupboard built into the side of the wagon beneath his bed. He kept his chest of gold in there, all honestly come by through gambling. As honestly as he could, anyway. The greater part came from one horse race, and his luck was no better than any other man's with horses. For the rest . . . If a man wanted to toss dice or play at cards or pitch coins, he had to be ready to lose. Domon, seated on the other bed rubbing a hand over the bristle on his shaved scalp, had learned that lesson. The fellow should have been willing to sleep on the floor like a good *so'jhin,* but in the beginning he had insisted on flipping a coin with Mat each night for the second bed. Egeanin got the first, of course. Tossing coins was as easy as dice. As long as the coin did not land on edge, the way it sometimes did for him. But Domon had made the offer, not him. Until Mat had won four times straight, and then the fifth night the coin did land on edge, three times in a row. They took turn and turn about, now. But it was still Domon's turn for the floor, tonight.

Finding the smallish washleather bag he was after, he stuffed it into his coat pocket and straightened, pushing the cupboard shut with his foot. "You have to face her some time," he said. "And I need you to smooth things over." He needed someone to attract Tuon's ire, someone to make him seem acceptable by comparison, but he could not say that, could he? "You're a Seanchan noble, and you can keep me from putting my boot in my mouth."

"Why do you need to smooth things over?" Egeanin's drawl was hard as a saw. She stood against the wagon's door with her fists on her hips, blue eyes augering out from beneath her long black wig. "Why do *you* need to see her? Haven't you done enough?"

"Don't tell me you're afraid of her," Mat scoffed, dodging the question. What answer could he give that did not sound insane? "You could tuck her under your arm almost as easily as I could. But I promise not to let her cut your head off or beat you up."

"Egeanin do no be afraid of anything, boy," Domon growled protectively. "If she does no want to go, then you trot off to court the girl by yourself. Stay the night, if you choose."

Egeanin continued to glare at Mat. Or through him. Then she glanced at Domon, her shoulders slumped a little, and she snatched her cloak from its peg on the wall. "Get a move on, Cauthon," she growled. "If it has to be done, best it's done and over with." She was out of the wagon in a flash, and Mat had to hurry to catch her up. You could almost think she did not want to be alone with Domon, as little sense as that made.

Outside the windowless purple wagon, black in the night, a shadow shifted in the deeper shadows. The sickle moon came out from behind the clouds long enough for Mat to recognize Harnan's lantern jaw.

"All quiet, my Lord," the file-leader said.

Mat nodded and took a deep breath, feeling for the washleather bag in his pocket. The air was clean, washed by the rain and away from the horselines. Tuon must be relieved to be away from the dung smell, and the rank odor of the animal cages. The performers' wagons to his left were as dark as the canvas-topped storage wagons to his right. No use waiting any longer. He pushed Egeanin up the purple wagon's steps ahead of him.

There were more people inside than he expected. Setalle

was seated on one of the beds, working her embroidery hoop again, and Selucia stood at the far end scowling beneath her head scarf, but Noal was sitting on the other bed, apparently lost in thought, and Tuon sat cross-legged on the floor playing Snakes and Foxes with Olver.

The boy twisted around with a wide-mouthed grin that almost split his face when Mat came in. "Noal has been telling us about Co'dansin, Mat," he exclaimed. "That's another name for Shara. Did you know the Ayyad tattoo their faces? That's what they call women who can channel, in Shara."

"No, I didn't," Mat said, settling a grim eye on Noal. It was bad enough that Vanin and the Redarms were teaching the boy bad habits, not to mention what he was picking up from Juilin and Thom, without Noal filling his head with made-up nonsense.

Suddenly Noal slapped his thigh and sat up straight. "I remember now," he said, and then the fool began to recite.

> Fortune rides like the sun on high
> with the fox that makes the ravens fly.
> Luck his soul, the lightning his eye,
> He snatches the moons from out of the sky.

The broken-nosed old man looked around as if just realizing anyone else was there. "I've been trying to remember that. It's from the Prophecies of the Dragon."

"Very interesting, Noal," Mat muttered. Those colors whirled in his head just the way they had that morning, when the Aes Sedai were panicking. They flashed away without making a picture this time, but he felt as cold as if he had spent a night sleeping under a bush in his skin. The last thing on earth he needed was anybody else linking him to the Prophecies. "Maybe some time you can recite the whole thing for us. But not tonight, eh?"

Tuon looked up at him through her eyelashes, a black porcelain doll in a dress that was too big for her. Light, but she had long lashes. She ignored Egeanin as if the other woman did not exist, and in truth, Egeanin was doing her best to appear part of a cabinet built into the wall. So much for hoping for a diversion.

"Toy doesn't mean to be rude," Tuon murmured in that

slow honey drawl. "He just has never been trained in manners. But it is late, Master Charin; time for Olver to be in bed. Perhaps you will escort him to his tent? We'll play again another time, Olver. Would you like me to teach you to play stones?"

Olver most emphatically would. He almost wriggled, saying so. The boy liked anything that gave him a chance to smile at a woman, not to mention a chance to say things that should have gotten him slapped till his ears swelled up bigger than they already were. If Mat ever found out which of his "uncles" was teaching him that . . . But the lad gathered the pieces of his game and carefully rolled up the line-marked cloth without a second urging. He even made a very good leg, thanking the High Lady, before letting Noal lead him from the wagon. Mat nodded approvingly. He had taught the boy how to make a leg, but the boy usually added a leer for a pretty woman. If he ever found out who . . .

"You have a reason for interrupting me, Toy?" Tuon said in cool tones. "It *is* late, and I was thinking of going to sleep."

He made a leg and gave her his best smile. He could be polite even if she was not. "I just wanted to make sure you were all right. These wagons are uncomfortable, on the road. And I know you aren't happy with the clothes I could find you. I thought this might make you feel a little better." Fishing the leather bag from his pocket, he presented it with a flourish. Women always liked that little extra flourish.

Selucia tensed, blue eyes sharpening, but Tuon waggled her slim fingers and the bosomy maid subsided. A little. Mat liked feisty women, by and large, but if she ruined this, he was going to paddle her bottom. He hung on to his smile with an effort, and even managed to ratchet it up a notch.

Tuon turned the bag over her hands several times before untying the drawstrings and spilling what it contained into her lap, a heavy necklace of gold and carved amber. An expensive piece, and Seanchan work to boot. He was proud of finding the thing. It had been the property of an acrobat, who had it from a Seanchan officer whose fancy she caught, but she had been willing to sell now that her officer was left behind. It did not suit her skin, whatever that meant. He smiled and waited. Jewels always softened a woman's heart.

No one's reaction was quite what he expected, though. Tuon lifted the necklace in front of her face with both hands, studying it as if she had never seen such a thing before. Selucia's lip curled in a sneer. Setalle set her embroidery down on her knees and looked at him, the large golden hoops in her ears swaying as she shook her head.

Abruptly, Tuon thrust the necklace back over her shoulder toward Selucia. "It does not suit me," she said. "Would you like it, Selucia?" Mat's smile slipped a little.

The cream-skinned woman took the necklace between thumb and forefinger, as if holding a dead rat by the tail. "A piece for a shea dancer to wear with her veil," she said wryly. With a twist of her wrist, she hurled the necklace at Egeanin, snapping, "Put it on!" Egeanin caught the thing just before it hit her face. Mat's smile slid the rest of the way off his.

He expected an explosion, but Egeanin immediately fumbled open the clasp and pushed her heavy wig back to fasten it behind her neck. Her face might have been molded from snow for all the expression on it.

"Turn," Selucia commanded, and it was a command, without any doubt. "Let me see."

Egeanin turned. Stiff as a fence post, but she turned.

Setalle looked at her intently, with a puzzled shake of her head, then gave Mat a different head shake before returning to her embroidery. Women had as many ways of shaking their heads as they had looks. This one said he was a fool, and if he did not catch the finer nuances, he was just as glad. He did not think he would have liked them. Burn him, he bought a necklace for Tuon, who gave it to Selucia right in front of him, and now it was *Egeanin's*?

"She came for a new name," Tuon said musingly. "What does she call herself?"

"Leilwin," Selucia replied. "A fitting name for a shea dancer. Leilwin Shipless, perhaps?"

Tuon nodded. "Leilwin Shipless."

Egeanin jerked as though every word was a slap. "May I withdraw?" she asked stiffly, bending in a sharp bow.

"If you want to go, then go," Mat growled. Bringing her in the first place had not been the best notion he ever had, but maybe he could recover a little without her.

Eyes locked on the floorboards, Egeanin sank to her knees. "Please, may I withdraw?"

Tuon sat there straight-backed on the floor staring through the taller woman, clearly not seeing her at all. Selucia eyed Egeanin up and down, pursing her lips. Setalle pushed her needle through the cloth stretched on her hoop. No one so much as glanced at Mat.

Egeanin dropped to her face, and Mat bit back a startled oath when she kissed the floor. "Please," she said hoarsely, "I beg leave to withdraw."

"You will go, Leilwin," Selucia said, cold as a queen speaking to a chickenthief, "and you will not let me see your face again unless it is covered by a shea dancer's veil."

Egeanin scrambled backward on hands and knees and all but tumbled out the door, so fast that Mat was left gaping.

With an effort, he managed to regain his smile. There seemed little point in staying, but a man could make a graceful exit. "Well, I suppose—"

Tuon wriggled her fingers again, still not looking at him, and Selucia cut him short. "The High Lady is weary, Toy. You have her permission to go."

"Look, my name is Mat," he said. "An easy name. A simple name. Mat." Tuon might as well have been a porcelain doll in truth for all the response she made.

Setalle set down her embroidery, though, and rose with one hand resting lightly on the hilt of the curved dagger stuck behind her belt. "Young man, if you think you're going to lounge about till you get to see us readying for bed, you're sadly mistaken." She smiled saying it, but she did have her hand on her knife, and she was Ebou Dari enough to stick a man on a whim. Tuon remained an unmoving doll, a queen on her throne somehow mistakenly dressed in ill-fitting clothes. Mat left.

Egeanin was leaning on one hand against the side of the wagon, her head hanging. Her other hand was gripping the necklace around her throat. Harnan moved, a little way off in the darkness, just to show he was still there. A wise man, to keep clear of Egeanin just then. Mat was too irritated for wisdom.

"What was that about?" he demanded. "You don't have to go on your knees to Tuon anymore. And Selucia? She's a bloody lady's maid! I don't know anybody who'd jump for his queen the way you jumped for her."

Egeanin's hard face was shadowed, but her voice was haggard. "The High Lady is . . . who she is. Selucia is her *so'jhin*. No one of the low Blood would dare meet her *so'jhin*'s eyes, and maybe not the High Blood, either." The clasp broke with a metallic snap as she jerked the necklace free. "But then, I'm not of any Blood, now." Rearing back, she put her whole body into throwing the necklace as far into the night as she could.

Mat opened his mouth. He could have bought a dozen prime horses with what he paid for that thing and had coin left. He closed it again without saying a word. He might not always be wise, but he was wise enough to know when a woman really might try to stick a knife in him. He knew another thing, as well. If Egeanin behaved this way around Tuon and Selucia, then he had better make sure the *sul'dam* were kept clear. The Light only knew what *they* would do if Tuon started wiggling her fingers.

That left him with a job of work to do. Well, he hated work, but those old memories had his head stuffed full of battles. He hated battle, too—a man could get killed dead!—but it was better than work. Strategy and tactics. Learn the ground, learn your enemy, and if you could not win one way, you found another.

The next night he returned to the purple wagon, alone, and once Olver had finished his lesson in stones from Tuon, Mat inveigled his way into a game. At first, sitting on the floor across the board from the dark little woman, he was not sure whether to win or lose. Some women liked to win every time, but the man had to make her work for it. Some liked the man to win, or at least more often than he lost. Neither made any sense to him—he liked to win, and the easier, the better—but that was how it was. While he was dithering, Tuon took matters out of his hands. Halfway through the game, he realized she had him in a trap he could not get out of. Her white stones were cutting off his black everywhere. It was a clean and resounding win for her.

"You don't play very well, Toy," she said mockingly. Despite the tone, her big, liquid eyes considered him coolly, weighing and measuring. A man could drown in eyes like that.

He smiled and made his goodbyes before there could be any thought of kicking him out. Strategy. Think to the future. Do the unexpected. The next night, he brought a small red paper flower made by one of the show's seamstresses. And presented it to a startled Selucia. Setalle's eyebrows rose, and even Tuon seemed taken aback. Tactics. Put your opponent off balance. Come to think, women and battles were not that different. Both wrapped a man in fog and could kill him without trying. If he was careless.

Every night he visited the purple wagon for a game of stones under Setalle and Selucia's watchful eyes, and he concentrated on the crosshatched board. Tuon was very good, and it was all too easy to find himself watching the way she placed her stones, with her fingers bent back in a curiously graceful way. She was used to having fingernails an inch long and taking care not to break them. Her eyes were a danger, too. You needed a clear head in stones or battle, and her gaze seemed to reach inside his skull. He buckled down to the game, though, and managed to win four of the next seven, with one draw. Tuon was satisfied when she won and determined when she lost, with none of the temper tantrums he had feared, no scathing comments aside from insisting on calling him Toy, not very much of that icy regal hauteur, as long as they were playing anyway. She purely enjoyed the game, laughing exultantly when she pulled him into a trap, laughing in delight when he managed a clever placement to escape. She seemed a different woman once she lost herself in the stones board.

A flower sewn from blue linen followed the paper blossom, and two days later, a pink silk bloom that spread out as wide as a woman's palm. Both handed to Selucia. Her blue eyes increasingly set in a suspicious frown when they rested on him, but Tuon told her she could keep the flowers, and she stored them away carefully, folded in a linen cloth. He let three days pass without a present, then brought a little cluster of red silk rosebuds, complete with short stems and glistening leaves that looked as real as nature, only more perfect. He had asked the seamstress to make it on the day he bought that first paper flower.

Selucia took a step, reaching to accept the rosebuds with a curl to her lip, but he sat down and put the flowers beside the board, a little toward Tuon. He said nothing, just left it lying there. She never so much as glanced at it. Dipping into the small leather bags that held the stones, he plucked one from each and shuffled them between his hands till even he was unsure which was where, then offered his closed fists. Tuon hesitated a moment, studying his face with no expression, then tapped his left hand. He opened it to display the glistening white stone.

"I've changed my mind, Toy," she murmured, placing the white stone carefully on the intersection of two lines near the center of the board. "You play very well."

Mat blinked. Could she know what he was up to? Selucia was standing at Tuon's back, seemingly absorbed in the almost empty board. Setalle turned a page in her book and shifted a little to get a better light. Of course not. She was talking about stones. If she even suspected his real game, she would toss him out on his ear. Any woman would. It had to be the stones.

That was the night they played to a draw, with each of them controlling half the board in irregular pools and patches. In truth, she won a victory.

"I have kept my word, Toy," she drawled as he was replacing the stones in the bags. "No attempts to escape, no attempts at betrayal. This is confining." She gestured around at the interior of the wagon. "I wish to take walks. After dark will do. You may accompany me." Her eyes touched the cluster of rosebuds, then rose to his face. "To make sure I don't run away."

Setalle marked her place with a slim finger and looked at him. Selucia stood behind Tuon and looked at him. The woman *had* kept her word, mad as that seemed. Walks after dark, with most of the showfolk already in their beds, would do no harm, not with him there to make sure. So why did he feel that he was losing control of the situation?

Tuon agreed to go cloaked and hooded, which was something of a relief. The black hair was growing back in on her shaved scalp, but so far it was little more than long fuzz, and unlike Selucia, who very likely slept in her head scarf, Tuon had shown no inclination to cover her head. A child-sized woman with hair shorter than any man not going bald would have been remarked even in the night. Setalle and Selucia always followed at a little distance in the darkness, the lady's maid to keep a protective eye on her mistress and Setalle to keep an eye on the maid. At least, he thought that was how it was. Sometimes it seemed they were both watching him. The two of them were awfully friendly for guard and prisoner. He had overheard Setalle cautioning Selucia that he was a rogue with women, a fine thing for her to be saying! And Selucia had calmly replied that her lady would break his arms if he showed any disrespect, just as if they were not prisoners at all.

He thought to use these walks to learn a little more about Tuon—she did not talk much over a stones board—but she had a way of ignoring what he asked or deflecting the subject, usually to him.

"The Two Rivers is all forests and farms," he said as they strolled along the main street of the show. Clouds hid the moon, and the colorful wagons were indistinguishable dark shapes, the performers' platforms lining the street merely shadows. "Everybody grows tabac and raises sheep. My father breeds cows, too, and trades horses, but mostly, it's tabac and sheep from one end to the other."

"Your father trades horses," Tuon murmured. "And what do you do, Toy?"

He glanced over his shoulder at the two women ghosting along ten paces back. Setalle might not be close enough to hear, if he kept his voice down, but he decided to be honest. Besides, the show was dead quiet in the darkness. She might hear, and she knew what he had been doing in Ebou Dar. "I'm a gambler," he said.

"My father called himself a gambler," Tuon said softly. "He died of a bad wager."

And how were you supposed to find out what *that* meant?

Another night, walking along a row of animal cages, each one built to fill an entire wagon, he said, "What do you do for fun, Tuon? Just because you enjoy it. Aside from playing stones." He could almost feel Selucia bristling at his use of her name from thirty feet away, but Tuon did not seem to mind. He thought she did not.

"I train horses and *damane*," she said, peering into a cage that held a sleeping lion. The animal was only a large shadow lying on the straw behind the thick bars. "Does he really have a black mane? There are no lions with black manes in all of Seanchan."

She trained *damane?* For fun? Light! "Horses? What kind of horses?" It might be warhorses, if she trained bloody *damane.* For fun.

"Mistress Anan tells me you're a scoundrel, Toy." Her voice was cool, not cold. Composed. She turned toward him, face hidden in the shadows of her cowl. "How many women have you kissed?" The lion woke up and coughed, a deep sound guaranteed to raise the hair on anyone's head. Tuon did not even flinch.

"Looks like rain's coming again," he said weakly. "Selucia will have my hide if I get you back soaked." He heard her laugh softly. What had he said that was funny?

There was a price to pay, of course. Maybe things were going his way and maybe not, but when you thought they were, there was always a price.

"Bunch of chattering magpies," he complained to Egeanin. The afternoon sat on the horizon, a red-gold ball half hidden by clouds, casting the show in long shadows. There was no rain, for once, and in spite of the cold they were sitting hunched beneath the green wagon they shared, playing stones in plain sight of anyone who walked by. A good many did, men hurrying about some last-minute chore, children snatching the final chance to roll hoops through the mud puddles and toss balls before night fell. Women holding their skirts up glanced at the wagon in passing, and even when they were hooded, Mat knew what their expressions were. Hardly a woman in the show would speak to Mat Cauthon. Irritably, he rattled the black stones he held gathered in his left hand. "They'll get their gold when we reach Lugard. That's all they ought to care about. They shouldn't be poking their noses into my business."

"You can hardly blame them," Egeanin drawled, studying the board. "You and I are supposed to be fleeing lovers, but you spend more time with . . . her . . . than with me." She still had trouble not calling Tuon High Lady. "You behave like a man courting." She reached to place her stone, then stopped with her hand above the board. "You can't think she'll complete the ceremony, can you? You can't be that big a fool."

"What ceremony? What are you talking about?"

"You named her your wife three times that night in Ebou Dar," she said slowly. "You really don't know? A woman says three times that a man is her husband, and he says three times she's his wife, and they're married. There are blessings involved, usually, but it's saying it in front of witnesses that makes it a marriage. You *really* didn't know?"

Mat laughed, and shrugged his shoulders, feeling the knife hanging behind his neck. A good knife gave a man a feeling of comfort. But his laugh was hoarse. "But she didn't say anything." He had bloody well been stuffing a gag in her mouth at the time! "So whatever I said, it doesn't mean anything." But he knew what Egeanin was going to say. Sure as water was wet, he knew. He had been told who he was going to marry.

"With the Blood, it's a little different. Sometimes a noble from one end of the Empire marries a noble from the other. An arranged marriage. The Imperial family never has any other kind. They may not want to wait until they can be together, so one acknowledges the marriage where she is, and the other where he is. As long as they both speak in front of witnesses, inside a year and a day, the marriage is legal. You truly didn't *know*?"

Sure was sure, but the stones still spilled from his hand onto the board, bouncing everywhere. The bloody *girl* knew. Maybe she thought this whole thing was an adventure, or a game. Maybe she thought being kidnapped was as much fun as training horses or bloody *damane*! But he knew he was a trout waiting for her to set the hook.

He stayed away from the purple wagon for two days. There was no use running—he already had the bloody hook in his mouth, and he had put it there himself—but he did not have to swallow the flaming thing. Only, he knew it was just a matter of when she decided to jerk the line tight.

As slowly as the show moved, eventually they reached the ferry across the Eldar, running from Alkindar on the west bank to Coramen on the east, tidy little walled towns of tile-roofed stone buildings with half a dozen stone docks each. The sun was climbing high, hardly a cloud crossed the sky, and those white as new-washed wool. No rain today, maybe. It was an important crossing, with trading ships from upriver tied to some of the docks and big barge-like ferries crawling from one town to the other on long sweeps. The Seanchan apparently thought so, too. They had military camps outside both towns, and from the stone walls beginning to rise around the camps and the stone structures going up inside, they had no intention of leaving soon.

Mat crossed over with the first wagons, riding Pips. The brown gelding looked ordinary enough to an undiscerning eye; it would not seem out of place for him to be ridden by a fellow in a rough woolen coat with a woolen cap pulled down over his ears against the cold. He was not actually considering making a run for the hilly wooded ridge country behind Coramen. Thinking about it, but not really considering. She was going to set the hook whether he ran or not. So he sat Pips at the end of one of the stone ferry landings, watching the show cross over and trundle away through the town. There were Seanchan on the landings, a squad of beefy men in segmented armor painted blue and burnt gold under a lean young officer with one thin blue plume on his odd-looking helmet. They seemed to be there just to keep order, but the officer checked Luca's horse warrant, and Luca inquired whether the noble lord might know of ground outside the town suitable for his show to perform. Mat could have wept. He could see soldiers wearing striped armor in the street behind him, wandering in and out of shops and taverns. A *raken* swooped down out of the sky on long, ribbed wings, alighting outside one of the camps across the river. Three or four of the snake-necked creatures were already on the ground. There had to be hundreds of soldiers in those camps. Maybe a thousand. And Luca was going to put on his show.

Then one of the ferries hit the rope-padded bumpers at the end of the landing, and the ramp came down to let the windowless purple wagon rumble off onto the stones. Setalle was driving. Selucia sat on one side of her, peering out from the hood of a faded red cloak. On the other side, swathed in a dark cloak so not an inch of her showed, was Tuon.

Mat thought his eyes were going to fall out of his head. If his heart did not pound its way out of his chest first. The dice had started up in his head, that rattling feel of dice rolling across a table. They were going to come up the Dark One's eyes, this time; he just knew it.

There was nothing to do except fall in beside the purple wagon, though, riding along as though life were wonderful, riding along the wide main street through criers for shops and hawkers selling things from trays. And Seanchan soldiers. They were not marching in formation now, and they eyed the brightly painted wagons with interest. Riding along and waiting for Tuon to shout. She had given her word, but a prisoner would say anything to get the shackles loosened. All she had to do was raise her voice, and summon a thousand Seanchan soldiers for rescue. The dice bounced and spun in Mat's head. Riding along, waiting for the Dark One's eyes.

Tuon never spoke a word. She peeked curiously past the edge of her deep cowl, curiously and cautiously, but she kept her face hidden, and even her hands, all wrapped in that dark cloak and even huddling against Setalle like a child seeking the protection of her mother in a strange crowd. Never a word until they had passed the gates of Coramen and were rumbling toward the base of the ridge that rose behind the town, where Luca was already gathering the show's wagons. That was when Mat really knew there was no escape for him. She was going to set the hook all right. She was just biding her bloody time.

He made sure all the Seanchan stayed in their wagons that night, and the Aes Sedai, too. Nobody had seen any *sul'dam* or *damane* that Mat knew, but the Aes Sedai did not argue for once. Tuon did not argue, either. She made a demand that sent Setalle's eyebrows almost to her hairline. It was phrased as a request, in a way, a reminder of a promise he had made, but he knew a demand when a woman made one. Well, a man had to trust the woman he was going to marry. He told her he had to think on it, just so she would not start imagining she could have anything she wanted out of him. He thought on it all the day that Luca put on his show, thinking and sweating while as many Seanchan as not came to gape at the performers. He thought on it while the wagons wound eastward through the hills, moving slower than ever, but he knew what answer he had to give.

On the third day after leaving the river, they reached the salt town of Jurador, and he told Tuon that he would. She smiled at him, and the dice in his head stopped dead. He would always remember that. She smiled, and *then* the dice stopped. A man could weep!

CHAPTER
29

Something Flickers

This do be madness," Domon rumbled from where he stood with his arms folded as if blocking the way out of the wagon. Maybe he was. His jaw was thrust forward belligerently, sticking out a beard that was trimmed short but still longer than the hair on his head, and he was working his hands like a man thinking of making fists, or grappling with something. A wide man, Domon, and not as fat as he looked on first glance. Mat wanted to avoid fists or grappling, if he could.

He finished tying the black silk scarf around his neck, hiding his scar, and tucked the long ends into his coat. The chance that there was anyone in Jurador who knew about a man in Ebou Dar wearing a black scarf . . . Well, the odds seemed good even discounting his luck. Of course, there was always his being *ta'veren* to be factored in, but if that was going to bring him face-to-face with Suroth or a fistful of servants from the Tarasin Palace, he could stay in bed with a blanket wrapped around his head, and it still would happen. Sometimes, you just had to trust to luck. The trouble was, when he woke this morning, the dice had again been tumbling in his head. They were bouncing off the inside of his skull still.

"I promised," he said. It was good to be back in decent clothes. The coat was a fine green wool, well cut and hanging almost to his knees and the turned-down tops of his boots. There was no embroidery—maybe it could do with a little—but he had a touch of lace at his cuffs. And a good silk shirt. He wished he had a mirror. A man needed to look his best on a day like this. Picking up his cloak from the bed, he swung it across his shoulders. Not a gaudy thing like Luca's. Dark gray, nearly as dark as night. Only the lining was red. His cloak pin was simple silver knots no larger than his thumbs.

"She gave her word, Bayle," Egeanin said. "Her word. She will not break that, ever." Egeanin sounded absolutely convinced. More convinced than Mat was, anyway. But sometimes a man had to take a chance. Even if he was wagering his neck. He *had* promised. And he did have his luck.

"It still be madness," Domon grumbled. But he moved grudgingly away from the door when Mat settled his broad-brimmed black hat on his head. Well, when Egeanin motioned him aside with a quick jerk of her head, anyway. He kept his glower, though.

She followed Mat out of the wagon, scowling herself and fiddling with her long black wig. Maybe she still felt uneasy with it, or maybe it fit differently now that she had close to a month's growth of her own hair underneath. Not enough to go about bare-headed yet, in any case. Not till there was at least another hundred miles between them and Ebou Dar. Maybe it would not be safe until they crossed the Damona Mountains into Murandy.

The sky was clear, the sun just cresting the horizon, invisible yet behind the show's canvas wall, and the morning was warm only compared to a snowstorm. Not the crispness of a late-winter morning in the Two Rivers, but a chill that slowly bored deep and put a faint mist in your breath. The showfolk were scurrying about like ants in a kicked anthill, filling the air with shouted demands to know who had moved those juggling rings or borrowed that pair of red-spangled breeches or shifted this performing platform. It looked and sounded like the start of a riot, yet there was no real anger in any of the voices. They shouted and waved arms all the time, but it never came to blows when there was a show in the offing, and somehow every performer would be in place and ready before the first patrons were let in. They might be slow packing up for the road, but performing meant money, and they could move fast enough for that.

"You really *do* think you can marry her," Egeanin muttered, striding along at his side, kicking her worn brown

woolen skirts. There was nothing dainty about Egeanin.
She had a long stride, and she kept up easily. Dress or no
dress, she seemed to need a sword on her hip. "There's no
other explanation for this. Bayle is right. You *are* mad!"

Mat grinned. "The question is, does she mean to marry
me? The strangest people marry, sometimes." When you
knew you were going to hang, the only thing to do was
grin at the noose. So he grinned and left her standing there
with a scowl on her hard face. He thought she was growling curses under her breath, though he did not understand
why. She was not the one who had to marry the last person on earth she wanted to. A noblewoman, all cool reserve
and her nose in the air, when he liked barmaids with ready
smiles and willing eyes. The heir to a throne, and not just
any throne; the Crystal Throne, the Imperial Throne of
Seanchan. A woman who spun his head like a top and left
him wondering whether he held her captive or she held him.
When fate gripped you by the throat, there was nothing to
do but grin.

He kept a jaunty pace till he was in sight of the windowless purple wagon, and then he missed a step. A cluster of
acrobats, four limber men who called themselves the Chavana brothers though it was plain as their noses they came
from different countries, not just different mothers, rushed
out of a green wagon nearby, shouting and gesturing wildly
at one another. They spared a glance for the purple wagon
and another for Mat, but they were too engrossed in their
argument, and trotting too fast, for more. Gorderan was
leaning against one of the purple wheels, scratching his
head and frowning at the two women who stood at the foot
of the wagon's wooden steps. Two women. Both swathed in
dark cloaks, faces concealed, yet there was no mistaking
the flowered head scarf hanging out of the taller woman's
cowl. Well. He should have know Tuon would want her maid
along. Noblewomen never went anywhere without a maid.
Bet a penny or bet a crown, in the end it all came down to
a toss of the dice just the same. They had had their chance
to betray him. Still, he was betting on a woman making the
same choice twice running. On two women doing it. What
fool would make odds on that? But he had to toss the dice.
Except, they were already rolling.

He met Selucia's cold blue stare with a smile and swept

off his hat to make an elegant leg to Tuon. Not too showy, with just a small flourish of his cloak. "Are you ready to go shopping?" He very nearly called her "my Lady," but until she was willing to say his name . . .

"I have been ready for an hour, Toy," Tuon drawled coolly. Casually lifting an edge of his cloak, she glanced at the red silk lining and eyed his coat before letting the cloak fall. "Lace suits you. Perhaps I will have lace added to your robes if I make you a cupbearer."

His smile slipped for an instant. Could she still make him *da'covale* if she married him? He would have to ask Egeanin. Light, why did women never make it easy?

"Do you want me to come along, my Lord?" Gorderan asked slowly, not quite looking at the women now. He tucked his thumbs behind his belt and did not quite look at Mat, either. "Just to carry, maybe?"

Tuon did not say a word. She just stood there looking up at Mat, waiting, big eyes getting cooler by the second. The dice bounced and rattled in his head. Well, he only hesitated a heartbeat before jerking his head to send the Redarm away. Maybe two heartbeats. He had to trust his luck. Trust her word. *Trust is the sound of death.* He stepped on that thought hard. This was no song, and no old memory could guide him. The dice inside his skull kept spinning.

With a slight bow, he offered his arm, which Tuon examined as if she had never seen an arm before, pursing those full lips. Then she gathered her cloak and set off with Selucia gliding at her heels, leaving him to hurry after them. No, women never did make it easy.

Despite the early hour, two burly fellows with cudgels were already guarding the entrance, and a third with a clear glass pitcher to take the coins and dump them through a slot in the iron-strapped box on the ground. Each of the three looked too clumsy to palm a copper without falling on his face, but Luca took no chances. Twenty or thirty people were already waiting inside the heavy ropes that led to the big blue banner naming Luca's show, and unfortunately, Latelle was there, too, stern-faced in a dress sewn with crimson spangles and a cloak sewn with blue. Luca's wife trained bears. Mat thought the bears did their tricks for fear she might bite them.

"I have everything in hand," he told her. "Believe me, there's nothing to worry about." He might as well have spared his breath.

Latelle ignored him, frowning worriedly at Tuon and Selucia. She and her husband were the only two showfolk who knew who they were. There had seemed no reason to tell either about this morning's jaunt. Luca, at least, would have had kittens. The stare Latelle shifted to Mat was not worried, just stone hard. "Remember," she said quietly, "if you send us to the gallows, you send yourself." Then she sniffed and went back to studying the people waiting to get in. Latelle was even better than Luca at judging the weight of a purse before the drawstrings were undone. She was also ten times tougher than her husband. The dice tumbled on. Whatever had set them spinning, he had not yet reached the fateful point. The deciding point.

"She is a good wife for Master Luca," Tuon murmured when they had gone a little way.

Mat looked at her sideways, and resettled his hat on his head. There had been no mockery in her tone. Did she hate Luca *that* much? Or was she saying what sort of wife *she* would be? Or . . . ? Burn him, he could go as crazy as Domon thought he was, trying to puzzle this woman out. She had to be the reason for the feel of dice in his head. What was she going to do?

It was a short walk away from the rising sun to the town, along a hard-packed road through hills that were treeless here, but people dotted the road the way windmills and salt pans dotted the hills. Staring straight ahead, they moved so purposefully they seemed not to see anyone in front of them. Mat dodged a round-faced man who nearly walked right into him, which made him have to jump away from a white-haired old fellow making a good speed on spindly legs. That put him in front of a plump girl who would have run up the front of him if he had not jumped again.

"Are you practicing a dance, Toy?" Tuon said, peering up at him over a slim shoulder. Her breath made a faint white mist in front of her cowl. "It isn't very graceful."

He opened his mouth, just to point out how crowded the road was, and suddenly he realized he could no longer see anyone beyond her and Selucia. The people who had been there were just gone, the road empty as far as he could see before it made a bend. Slowly, he turned his head. There was no one between him and the show, either, just the folk waiting in line, and that looked no longer than before. Beyond the show, the road wound into the hills toward a distant forest, empty. Not a soul in sight. He pressed fingers against his chest, feeling the foxhead medallion through his coat. Just a piece of silver on a rawhide cord. He wished it felt cold as ice. Tuon arched an eyebrow. Selucia's stare named him fool.

"I can't buy you a dress standing here," he said. That was the point of this expedition, his promise to find Tuon something better than dresses that hung on her and made her look a child in a grownup's clothing. At least, he was pretty sure he had promised that, and she was perfectly certain. The needlework of the show's seamstresses met with Tuon's approval, but not the cloth they had available. Performers' costumes glittered with spangles and beads and bright colors, but the cloth was usually whatever could be found cheaply. Those who had better kept it and used it till it wore out. Jurador made its money from salt, though, and salt made a great deal of money. The town's shops should offer any sort of material a woman could wish.

There was no finger-wiggling, this time. Tuon shared a look with Selucia. The taller woman shook her head, a wry, rueful twist to her mouth. Tuon shook *her* head. And they gathered their cloaks and started toward the town's iron-studded gates. Women! He hurried to catch up again. They were his prisoners, after all. They were. Their shadows stretched out long in front of them. Had any of those people cast shadows before they vanished? He could not recall any of them breathing a mist, either. It hardly seemed to matter. They were gone, and he was not going to think about where they had come from or where they had gone. Probably something to do with being *ta'veren*. He was going to put it out of his head. He was. The dice rattling away left room for nothing else.

The gate guards seemed incurious about strangers, or at least about a man and two women afoot. Hard-faced fellows in white-painted breastplates and conical helmets with what looked like horsetails for crests, they ran impassive eyes over the cloaked women, lingering suspiciously a moment on Mat for some reason, and then returned to leaning on their halberds and staring blankly at the road. They were local men, most likely, in any case not Seanchan. The salt merchants and the local lady, Aethelaine, who apparently said whatever the salt merchants told her to, had sworn the Oaths of Return without hesitation and offered to pay a salt tax before they were asked. No doubt the Seanchan would get around to installing some sort of official here eventually, just to keep an eye on everything, but for the moment, they had more important uses for their soldiers. Mat had sent Thom and Juilin both to make sure there were no Seanchan in Jurador before agreeing to this excursion. A fool could trip over his own luck if he was not careful.

It was a prosperous, busy town, Jurador, with stone-paved streets, most of them wide and all lined with stone buildings roofed in reddish tiles. Houses and inns rubbed shoulders with stables and taverns, in a noisy jumble with a blacksmith's clanging hammer on an anvil here and the racketing of a rugweaver's looms there, and everywhere, it seemed, coopers hammering bands on tight barrels for transporting salt. Hawkers cried pins and ribbons, meat pies and roasted nuts from trays, or winter-wrinkled turnips and sorry plums from barrows. On every street men and women stood guard over the display goods on narrow tables in front of their shops and bellowed lists of what was offered within.

Picking out the salt merchants' houses was easy, though, three stories of stone rather than two, covering eight times as much ground as any others, each with a columned walk overlooking the street and shielded by white wrought-iron screens between the columns. The lower windows on most houses had those screens, though not always painted. That much was reminiscent of Ebou Dar, but little else was, beyond the olive complexions of the people. There were no deep necklines exposing cleavage here, no skirts sewn up to display colored petticoats. The women wore embroidered dresses with high necks right up to their chins, a little embroidery for the common folk, a great deal for the richer, who wore cloaks embroidered top to bottom and sheer veils hanging over their faces from combs of gold-work or carved ivory stuck into dark, coiled braids. The men's short coats were worked almost as thickly, in colors just as bright, and rich or poor, most men wore a long belt knife with a blade a little less curved than those in Ebou Dar. Rich or poor, the fellows did have a tendency to fondle their knife hilts as if expecting a fight, so maybe that was the same.

The Lady Aethelaine's palace appeared no different from the outside than the salt merchants' mansions, but it was located on the town's main square, a wide expanse of polished stone where a broad round marble fountain sprayed water into the air. People filled their buckets and big pottery water jars from pipes spilling into stone basins at the corners of other squares, though. The big fountain put out a smell of brine. It was a symbol of Jurador's wealth, pumped from the same source as the salt wells in the surrounding hills. Mat got to see a good deal of the town before the sun climbed even halfway to its noon peak.

Every time Tuon and Selucia spotted a shop with silks displayed out front, they stopped at the long narrow table to feel bolts of cloth and whisper with their heads together, waving off the attentions of the watchful shopkeeper. Those kept a *very* watchful eye, until they realized Mat was with the two women. In their stout woolens, well worn and badly fitting, they did not look customers for silk. Mat, with one side of his cloak thrown back to expose the lining, did. Whenever he tried to show an interest, though—women said they wanted you to show an interest!—whenever he got close enough to hear what they were saying, the women fell silent and looked at him, cool dark eyes and cool blue staring out of their deep cowls, until he fell back a step or two. Then Selucia would bend her head to Tuon's, and they would go back to murmuring and fingering silk, red silk, blue silk, green silk, smooth shimmering silk and brocaded silk. Jurador was a very wealthy town. Luckily, he had tucked a fat purse of gold into his coat pocket. None of it seemed to be right, though. Inevitably, Tuon shook her head, and the pair of them glided away into the crowd with Mat hurrying to keep up as far as the next shop showing silks. The dice continued to bounce off the inside of his skull.

They were not the only ones from the show who had come into the town. He spotted Aludra, her face framed by beaded braids, walking through the crowd with a gray-haired man who had to be a salt merchant from the amount of bright embroidery covering his silk coat in flowers and hummingbirds. What would the Illuminator want with a salt merchant? Whatever she was saying to him, his pleased smile had added a few creases to his face, and he was nodding.

Tuon shook her head, and the two women glided toward the next shop, ignoring the shopkeeper's deep bows. Well, most of those were directed at Mat. Maybe the skinny fool thought he wanted to buy silk for himself. Not that he would have passed up a new silk coat or three, but who could think about coats when he was waiting for those bloody dice to stop? Just a little embroidery, on the sleeves and shoulders.

Thom went by clutching his bronze-colored cloak around him, knuckling his long white mustaches and yawning as if he had spent the night awake. He might have. The gleeman had not taken to drink again, but Lopin and Nerim complained about him remaining awake till all hours, burning a lamp so he could read and re-read his precious letter. What could be so fascinating in a letter from a dead woman? A dead woman. Light, maybe those people on the road . . . ! No; he was not going to think about that at all.

Tuon plucked one fold of silk and let it drop as she turned away without trying another. Selucia gave the stout shopkeeper such a stare before following that the woman started back in affront. Mat offered her a smile. Affronted shopkeepers could lead to town guards asking questions, and who could say where that might lead? He knew he could smile most women into feeling soothed. The round-faced woman sniffed at him and bent to smoothing the bolt of silk as tenderly as tucking in a babe. Most women, he thought sourly.

Down the street, a woman in a plain cloak let her hood fall back, and Mat's breath caught in his throat. Edesina lifted her cowl again, but she took no hurry with it, and the damage was done anyway, an Aes Sedai's ageless face displayed for anyone who knew what they were seeing. No one in the street gave a sign that they had noticed anything, but he could not see every face. Was anyone thinking of a reward? There might be no Seanchan in Jurador at the moment, but they did pass through.

Edesina glided around a corner, and two dark-cloaked shapes followed her. Two. Had the *sul'dam* left only one of their number in the camp to watch two Aes Sedai? Or maybe Joline or Teslyn was somewhere close by, and he had missed seeing her. He craned his neck, searching the throng for another plain cloak, but every one he saw had at least a little embroidery.

Abruptly, it hit him like a stone between the eyes. Every cloak he could see had at least a little embroidery. Where were bloody Tuon and bloody Selucia? Were the dice spinning faster?

Breathing hard, he went up on his toes, but the street was a river of embroidered cloaks, embroidered coats and dresses. It did not mean they were trying to escape. Tuon *had* given her word; she had passed up a perfect chance for betrayal. But all either woman had to do was say three words, and anyone who heard them likely would recognize a Seanchan accent. That might be sufficient to set the hounds on his trail. There were two shops ahead that seemed to be offering cloth, one on either side of the street. Neither with a pair of dark-cloaked women at the tables out front. They could have turned a corner easily enough, but he had to trust to luck. His luck was especially good when the game was random. Bloody women probably thought it *was* a bloody game. Burn him, let his luck run good.

Closing his eyes, he spun in a circle in the middle of the street and took a step. At random. He bumped into someone solid, hard enough to make them both grunt. A bulky fellow with a small mouth and a little poorly done scrollwork on the shoulders of his rough coat stood glaring at him when he opened his eyes, glaring and fingering the hilt of his curved knife. Mat did not care. He was facing straight at one of the two shops. Pulling his hat down tight, he ran. The dice *were* rolling faster.

Divided shelves stuffed with bolts of cloth lined the walls of the shop from floor to ceiling, and more stood stacked on long tables out in the floor. The shopkeeper was a scrawny woman with a large mole on her chin, her assistant slim and pretty and angry-eyed. He dashed inside just in time to hear the shopkeeper say, "For the last time, if you won't tell me what you're here for, I'm going to send Nelsa for the guards." Tuon and Selucia, faces still hidden in their hoods, were walking slowly along one wall full of cloth, stopping to touch a bolt but neither paying the shopkeeper any heed.

"They're with me," Mat said breathlessly. Tugging the purse from his pocket, he tossed it on the nearest clear table. The heavy clink it made landing put a wide smile on the shopkeeper's narrow face. "Give them whatever they want," he told her. And to Tuon, he added firmly, "If you're going to buy anything, it's going to be here. I've had all the exercise I care for this morning."

He would have had the words back as soon as they left his mouth, if he could. Speak to a woman that way, and she flared in your face like one of Aludra's firesticks, every time. But Tuon's big eyes looked up at him from the shelter of her hood. And her full mouth curved slightly in a smile. It was a secret smile, for herself, not him. The Light only knew what it meant. He hated it when women did that. At least the dice had not stopped. That had to be a good sign, right?

Tuon had no need of words to make her choices, silently pointing out bolt after bolt and measuring with her small dark hands how much the shopkeeper was to cut off with her shears. The woman did the work herself instead of delegating it to her assistant, and well she might, considering. Red silk in several shades went under those long sharp scissors, and green silk in a few shades, and more varieties of blue silk than Mat knew existed. Tuon chose out some fine linen in several thicknesses, and lengths of bright wool—she consulted Selucia over those in muffled whispers—but mostly it was silk. He got back much less of his purse than he had expected.

Once all that cloth had been folded and neatly tied, then bundled into a larger length of coarse linen—at no extra charge, thank you very much—it made a mound as fat as a peddler's pack. It did not surprise him at all to learn that he was expected to carry the thing across his shoulders, with his hat dangling in one hand. Dress your best, buy a woman silk, and she still found a way to make you work! Maybe she was making him pay for speaking firmly.

He earned plenty of stares from gaping fools as he made his way out of the town behind the two women. They glided along smug as cats full of cream. Even cloaked and hooded, their backs said it all. The sun was still well short of midday, but the line of people waiting to get into the show stretched down the road almost to the town. Most gaped and pointed as if he were a painted fool. One of the big horse handlers guarding the coin box gave a gap-toothed smirk and opened his mouth, but Mat returned him a level look, and the fellow decided to put his eyes back on the coins going from towns-folk to glass pitcher to box. Mat thought he had never been so relieved to be inside Luca's show.

Before he and the two women had gotten three steps inside the entrance, Juilin came running up, for a wonder without Thera or his red cap. The thief-catcher's face could have been carved from ancient oak. Eyeing the people flowing past them into the show, he pitched his voice low. Low and urgent. "I was coming to find you. It's Egeanin; she's been . . . hurt. Come quickly."

The man's tone said enough, but worse, Mat realized the dice in his head were drumming, now. He flung the pack of cloth at the horse handlers with a hasty injunction to guard it as close as the coin-box or he would set the women on them, but he did not wait to see whether they took him seriously. Juilin darted back the way he had come at a run, and Mat ran after him, along the wide main street of the show where noisy gawking crowds were watching the four bare-chested Chavana brothers stand on one another's shoulders, and contortionists in filmy trousers and glittering vests sit on their own heads, and a slack-rope walker in spangled blue breeches climbing a long wooden ladder to begin her performance. Short of the slack-rope walker, Juilin dodged into one of the narrower streets, where laundry hung from lines between the tents and wagons, performers sat on stools and wagon steps waiting to go on, and show children ran playing with balls and hoops. Mat knew where they were headed, now, but the thief-catcher ran too fast to overtake.

Ahead, he saw his green wagon. Latelle was peering underneath, and Luca, in one of his bright red cloaks, was waving a pair of jugglers to move along. The two women, in baggy trousers and with faces painted white like a noble's fools, took a good look under the wagon before they obeyed. As he came closer, he could see what they had they been staring at. Coatless, Domon was sitting on the ground under the edge of the wagon, cradling a limp Egeanin in his arms. Her eyes were closed, and a trickle of blood ran from the corner her mouth. Her wig hung askew. That stood out, for some reason. She always fussed so to keep that wig straight. The dice beat like thunder.

"This could be disaster," Luca growled, splitting his glower between Mat and Juilin. It was an angry glower, though, not frightened. "You may have brought me to disaster!" He shooed away a gaggle of wide-eyed children, and growled at a plump woman in skirts that glittered with silvery spangles. Miyora made leopards do tricks that even Latelle would not try, but she merely tossed her head before gliding off. No one took Luca as seriously as he took himself.

The man gave a start when Tuon and Selucia hurried up, and looked on the point of telling them to go, too, before he thought better of it. In fact, he began to frown thoughtfully. And worriedly. It seemed his wife had not told him about Mat and the women leaving the show, and it was clear they had been somewhere. The blue-eyed woman had the huge bundle of cloth on her back now, with her arms doubled behind her, though she stood straight despite the bulk. You would think a lady's maid was used to carrying things, but her face was a picture of frustrated irritation. Latelle eyed her up and down, then sneered at Mat as if he were the reason the woman was thrusting her considerable bosom out. Luca's wife was very good at sneering, yet Tuon's stern expression made Latelle nearly look mild. A judge peered out of her cowl, a judge ready to pass sentence.

For the moment, Mat did not care what the women thought. Those *bloody* dice. Tossing his cloak back, he went to one knee and touched fingers to Egeanin's throat. Her pulse beat weakly, thin and fluttering.

"What happened?" he asked. "Have you sent for one of the sisters?" Moving Egeanin might be enough to kill her, but there might be time for Healing, if the Aes Sedai were quick. He was not about to say that name aloud, though, with people walking by, pausing for curious stares before

Luca or Latelle hurried them on. Everyone moved quicker for her than for him. Latelle herself was the only one who really jumped for Luca.

"Renna!" Domon spat the name. Despite his short cap of hair and that Illianer beard that left his upper lip bare, he did not look ridiculous, now. He looked afraid and murderous, a dangerous combination. "I did see her stab Egeanin in the back and run. If I could have reached her, I would have broken her neck, but my hand be all that's holding Egeanin's blood in. Where be that bloody Aes Sedai?" he snarled. So much for being careful with his tongue.

"I be right here, Bayle Domon," Teslyn announced coldly, rushing up with Thera, who took one horrified look at Tuon and Selucia and latched on to Juilin's arm with a squeak, eyes on the ground. The way she began trembling, she might be there herself in a minute.

The hard-eyed Aes Sedai made a face as if she had a mouthful of briars when she saw what lay in front of her, or maybe where it lay, but she swiftly crouched underneath the wagon beside Domon and clasped Egeanin's head in her bony hands. "Joline do be better at this than I," she muttered, half under her breath, "but I may be able—"

The silver foxhead went cold against Mat's chest, and Egeanin jerked so violently that her wig fell off, nearly pulling herself out of Domon's grasp as her eyes popped open wide. The convulsion lasted only long enough for her to sit halfway up with a frozen gasp; then she slumped back against Domon's chest, panting, and the medallion became just a piece of worked silver again. He was almost accustomed to that. He hated being accustomed to that.

Teslyn slumped, too, on the point of falling over until Domon shifted his grip on Egeanin to steady the Aes Sedai with one hand. "Thank you," Teslyn said after a moment, the words sounding dragged from her. "But I need no help." She used the side of the wagon to help her rise, though, her cold Aes Sedai gaze daring anyone to comment. "The blade did slide on a rib and so did miss her heart. All she does need now be rest and food."

She had not delayed to grab a cloak, Mat realized. In one direction along the narrow street, a clutch of women in spangled cloaks was watching from in front of a green-striped tent, their gazes intent and focused. In the other, half a dozen men and women in white-striped coats and tight breeches, acrobats who performed on horseback, darted looks toward Teslyn between putting their heads together to whisper. Too late to worry about someone recognizing an Aes Sedai's face. Too late to worry that one of them knew Healing when he saw it done. The dice battered at the inside of Mat's head. They had not stopped; the game was not played out, yet.

"Who's looking for her, Juilin?" he asked. "Juilin?"

The thief-catcher gave over glaring at Tuon and Selucia and murmuring to Thera, though he continued to pat the trembling woman. "Vanin and the Redarms, Lopin and Nerim. Olver, too. He was away before I could catch him. But in this . . ." He stopped soothing Thera long enough to gesture toward the main street. The babble of voices was clearly audible even at this distance. "All she needs is to lay hands on one of those fancy cloaks, and she can slip out with the first folk to leave. If we try stopping every woman with her hood up, or even try looking inside, we'll have a riot on our hands. These people are touchy."

"Disaster," Luca moaned, wrapping his cloak around himself tightly. Latelle put an arm around him. It must have been like being comforted by a leopard, but in any case, Luca did not look much comforted.

"Burn me, why?" Mat growled. "Renna was always ready to lick my bloody wrist! I thought if anybody went over the edge . . . !" He did not even glance at Thera, but Juilin still scowled at him darkly.

Domon had stood up with Egeanin in his arms. She struggled feebly at first—Egeanin was not a woman to let herself be carried about like a doll—but eventually she seemed to realize that if she did make her own feet, she would fall over. She sagged against the Illianer's chest with a resentful glower. Domon would learn; even when a woman needed help, if she did not want it, she made you pay for giving it. "I'm the only one who knew her secret," she drawled in a weak voice. "The only one who might give it away, at least. She may have thought it would be safe to go home, with me dead."

"What secret?" Mat asked.

The woman hesitated, for some reason, frowning at Domon's chest. Finally she sighed. "Renna was leashed, once. So were Bethamin and Seta. They can channel. Or maybe learn to; I don't know. But the *a'dam* worked on those three. Maybe it works on any *sul'dam*." Mat whistled through his teeth. Now, that would be a kick in the head for the Seanchan.

Luca and his wife exchanged puzzled glances, plainly not understanding a word. Teslyn's mouth hung open, Aes Sedai serenity washed away in shock. Selucia made an angry sound, though, blue eyes blazing, and dropped the bundle of cloth from her back as she took a step toward Domon. A quick flash of Tuon's fingers stopped her in her tracks, though it was a quivering halt. Tuon's face was a dark mask, unreadable. She did not like what she had heard, though. Come to think, she had said *she* trained *damane*. Oh, burn him, on top of everything else, he was going to marry a woman who could channel?

The sound of horses' hooves announced Harnan and the other three Redarms coming along the narrow way between the tents and wagons at a quick trot. Their swords were belted on under their cloaks, Metwyn with a dagger almost as long as a short-sword to boot, and Gorderan had his heavy crossbow hanging at his saddle, already drawn and latched. The crank at his belt would take a full minute to pull back the thick cord, but this way, all he need do was place a bolt. Harnan carried a double-curve horsebow, with a bristling quiver at his hip. Fergin was leading Pips.

Harnan did not bother dismounting. Eyeing Tuon and Selucia suspiciously, and Luca and Latelle with almost as much doubt, he leaned down from his saddle, the crude hawk tattoo sharp on his cheek. "Renna stole a horse, my Lord," he said quietly. "Rode down one of the horse handlers at the entrance getting out. Vanin's following her. He says she could reach Coramen some time tonight. That's the way she headed. She's moving a lot faster than the wagons did. But she's riding bareback; we can catch her, with luck." He sounded as if that luck were a matter of fact. The men of the Band trusted Mat Cauthon's luck more than he did himself.

There did not seem to be any choices, really. The dice were still pounding in his head. There was still a chance they might fall his way. A small chance. Mat Cauthon's luck. "Get your people on the road as fast as they can pack up, Luca," he said, stepping up onto Pips. "Leave the wall and anything else you can't get onto the wagons fast. Just go."

"Are you crazy?" Luca spluttered. "If I try to chase those people out, I *will* have a riot! And they'll want their coin back!" Light, the man would think of money with his neck stretched on the headsman's block.

"Think what you'll have if a thousand Seanchan find you here tomorrow." Mat's voice was as cold as he could make it. If he failed, the Seanchan would run Luca's show down in short order however fast they flogged their horses. Luca knew it, too, from the twist of his mouth, as if he had just bitten a rotting plum. Mat made himself ignore the man. The dice were drumming hard, but they had not stopped yet. "Juilin, leave all the gold for Luca except one good purse." Maybe the man could bribe his way clear, once the Seanchan saw he did not have their Daughter of the Nine bloody Moons. "Gather everybody and ride out as soon as you can. Once you're out of sight of the town, take to the forest. I'll find you."

"Everybody?" Sheltering Thera with his body, Juilin jerked his head toward Tuon and Selucia. "Leave those two in Jurador, and the Seanchan might stop with getting them back. It might slow them down, at least. You keep saying you're going to turn them loose sooner or later."

Mat met Tuon's eyes. Big dark liquid eyes, in a smooth expressionless face. She had pushed her hood back a little, so he could see her face clearly. If he left her behind, then she could not say the words, or if she did, he would be too far way for the words to matter. If he left her behind, he would never learn why she smiled those mysterious smiles, or what lay behind the mystery. Light, he *was* a fool! Pips danced a few impatient steps.

"Everybody," he said. Did Tuon nod slightly, as if to herself? Why would she nod? "Let's ride," he told Harnan.

They had to walk their horses through the crowds to get out of the show, but as soon as they reached the road, Mat put Pips to a gallop, cloak streaming behind and head down to keep his hat from blowing off. It was not a pace you could keep a horse at for long. The road wound around hills and crossed ridges, occasionally cutting through where the rise was not too high. They splashed across ankle-deep streams and thundered over low wooden bridges crossing deeper water. Trees began to appear on the slopes again, pine and leatherleaf showing green among the winter-bare branches of the others. Farms clung to some of the hills, low tile-roofed stone houses and taller barns, and now and then a hamlet of eight or ten houses.

A few miles from the show, Mat spotted a wide man ahead of them, sitting his saddle like a sack of suet. The horse was a leggy dun, eating ground at a steady trot. It figured that a horse thief had an eye for a good animal. Catching the sound of their hooves, Vanin looked back, but he only slowed to a walk. That was bad.

When Mat slowed Pips beside the dun, Vanin spat. "Best wager we got is we find her horse run to death, so I can track her afoot from there," he muttered. "She's pushing harder than I figured, with her bareback. If we push, we can maybe catch her by sunset. If her horse don't founder or die, that's about the time she'll make Coramen."

Mat tipped back his head to glance at the sun, almost straight overhead. It was a long way to cover in less than half a day. If he turned back, he could be a good distance the other side of Jurador by sunset, in company with Thom and Juilin and the others. With Tuon. With the Seanchan knowing to hunt Mat Cauthon. The man who had kidnapped the Daughter of the Nine Moons could not own enough luck to get off with being made *da'covale*. And sometime tomorrow or the next day, they would plant Luca on an impaling stake. Luca and Latelle, Petra and Clarine and the rest. A thicket of impaling stakes. The dice rattled and bounced in his head.

"We can make it," he said. There was no other choice.

Vanin spat.

There was only one way to cover a great deal of ground quickly on a horse, if you meant to be on a live horse at the end. They walked the animals for half a mile, then trotted half a mile. The same at a canter, then a run, and it was back to a walk. The sun began to slide downward, and the dice spun. Around sparsely forested hills and over tree-topped ridges. Streams that could be crossed in three strides, barely wetting the horses' hooves, and streams thirty paces across with flat bridges of wood or sometimes stone. The sun sank lower and lower, and the dice spun faster and faster. Almost back to the Eldar, and no sign of Renna except scuffs on the hard dirt of the road that Vanin pointed to as if they were painted signs.

"Getting close, now," the fat man muttered. He did not sound happy, though.

Then they rounded a hill, and there was another low bridge ahead. Beyond, the road twisted north to cross the next ridge through a saddle. The sun, sitting atop the ridge, blazed in their eyes. Coramen lay on the other side of that ridge. Pulling his hat low for shade, Mat searched the road for a woman, for anyone, mounted or afoot, and his heart sank.

Vanin cursed and pointed.

A lathered bay was laboring its way up the slope on the other side of the river, a woman frantically kicking its flanks, urging it to climb. Renna had been too anxious to reach the Seanchan to stick with the road. She was maybe two hundred paces from them, and she might as well have been miles. Her mount was on the point of collapsing, but she could get down and run within sight of the garrisons before they could reach her. All she had to do was reach the crest, another fifty feet.

"My Lord?" Harnan said. He had an arrow nocked and his bow half raised. Gorderan held the heavy crossbow to his shoulder, a thick pointed bolt in place.

Mat felt something flicker and die inside him. He did not know what. Something. The dice rolled like thunder. "Shoot," he said.

He wanted to close his eyes. The crossbow snapped; the bolt made a black streak through the air. Renna slammed forward when it hit her back. She had almost managed to push herself erect against the bay's neck when Harnan's arrow took her.

Slowly, she toppled from the horse, sliding down the slope, rolling, bouncing off saplings, tumbling faster and faster until she splashed into the stream. For a moment, she floated facedown against the bank, and then the current caught her and pulled her away, skirts billowing up on the water. Slowly she drifted toward the Eldar. Maybe, eventually, she would reach the sea. And that made three.

It hardly seemed to matter that the dice had stopped. That made three. *Never again,* he thought as Renna floated out of sight around a bend. *If I die for it, never again.*

They did not press, riding back eastward. There was no point, and Mat felt too bone-weary. They did not stop, though, except to breathe and water the horses. No one wanted to talk.

It was the small hours of the night when they reached Jurador, the town a dark mass with the gates shut tight. Clouds covered the moon. Surprisingly, the canvas walls of Luca's show were still in place just beyond the town. With a pair of bulky men wrapped in blankets snoring beneath the big banner as they guarded the entrance. Even from the road, in the dark, it was plain that wagons and tents filled the space behind the wall.

"At least I can tell Luca he doesn't have to run after all," Mat said wearily, turning Pips toward the banner. "Maybe he'll give us a place to sleep a few hours." For all the gold he had left, Luca should give them his own wagon, but knowing the man, Mat had hopes for clean straw somewhere. Tomorrow, he would set out to find Thom and the others. And Tuon. Tomorrow, when he had rested.

A greater shock waited inside Luca's huge wagon. It truly was roomy inside, at least for a wagon, with a narrow table sitting in the middle and space to walk around it. Table, cupboards and shelves all were polished till they glowed. Tuon was sitting in a gilded chair—Luca would have a chair, and gilded, when everybody else made do with stools!—with Selucia standing at her back. A beaming Luca was watching Latelle offer Tuon a plate of steaming pastries, which the dark little woman was examining as if she would actually eat something that Luca's wife had cooked.

Tuon showed no surprise at all at Mat walking into the wagon. "Is she captured, or dead?" she said, picking up a pastry with her fingers curved in that curiously graceful way.

"Dead," he said flatly. "Luca, what in the Light—"

"I forbid it, Toy!" Tuon snapped, pointing a finger at him sharply. "I forbid you to mourn a traitor!" Her voice softened, slightly, but it remained firm. "She earned death by betraying the Empire, and she would have betrayed you as easily. She was trying to betray you. What you did was justice, and I name it so." Her tone said that if she named a thing, then it was well and truly named.

Mat squeezed his eyes shut for a moment. "Is everyone else still here, too?" he demanded.

"Of course," Luca said, still smiling like a bullgoose fool. "The Lady—the High Lady; forgive me, High Lady." He bowed deeply. "She talked to Merrilin and Sandar, and. . . . Well, you see how it was. A very persuasive woman, the Lady. The High Lady. Cauthon, about my gold. You *said* they were to hand it over, but Merrilin said he'd slit my throat first, and Sandar threatened to crack my head, and . . ." He trailed off under Mat's stare, then suddenly brightened again. "Look what the Lady gave me!" Snatching open one of the cupboards, he pulled out a folded paper that he held reverently in both hands. It was thick paper, and white as snow; expensive. "A warrant. Not sealed, of course, but signed. Valan Luca's Grand Traveling Show and Magnificent Display of Marvels and Wonders is now under the personal protection of the High Lady Tuon Athaem Kore Paendrag. Everyone will know who that is, of course. I could go to Seanchan. I could put on my show for the Empress! May she live forever," he added hastily, with another bow to Tuon.

For nothing, Mat thought bleakly. He sank down on one of the beds with his elbows on his knees, earning a very pointed look from Latelle. Likely only Tuon's presence kept her from clouting him!

Tuon raised a peremptory hand, a black porcelain doll but every inch a queen despite the shabby too-large dress. "You are not to use that except at need, Master Luca. *Great* need!"

"Of course, High Lady; of course." Luca bobbed bows as if he might be kissing the floorboards any minute.

All for bloody nothing!

"I did make specific mention of who is not under my protection, Toy." Tuon took a bite of pastry and delicately brushed a crumb from her lip with a finger. "Can you guess whose name heads that list?" She smiled. Not a malicious smile. Another of those smiles for herself, amusement or delight in something he could not see. Suddenly, he noticed something. That little cluster of silk rosebuds he had given her was pinned to her shoulder.

Despite himself, Mat began to laugh. He threw his hat down on the floor and laughed. With everything, all his efforts, he did not know this woman at all! Not a bit! He laughed until his ribs hurt.

CHAPTER
30

What the Oath Rod Can Do

The sun sat on the horizon, perfectly silhouetting the White Tower in the distance, but the cold of the previous night seemed to be deepening, and dark gray clouds marching across the sky threatened a snowfall. Winter was diminishing, yet it had clung past when spring should have begun, loosening its hold fitfully. The noises of morning penetrated Egwene's tent, isolated as it was from everything around it. The camp seemed to vibrate. Laborers would be bringing in water from the wells, and extra measures of firewood and charcoal in carts. Serving women would be fetching sisters' breakfasts, and novices in the second sitting scurrying to theirs, those in the first and third to classes. It was a momentous day, though none of them knew it. Likely, today would see an end to the spurious negotiations that were going on in Darein, at a table under a pavilion at the foot of the bridge to Tar Valon. Spurious on both sides. Elaida's raiders continued to strike with impunity on the other side of the river. In any case, today would be the last meeting for some time.

Peering at her own breakfast, Egwene sighed and picked a tiny black fleck out of the steaming porridge, wiping it from her fingers on a linen napkin without looking closely enough to be sure that it was a weevil. If you could not be sure, then you worried less about what remained in the bowl. She put a spoonful into her mouth and tried to concentrate on the sweet slivers of dried apricot that Chesa had blended in. *Did* something crack under her teeth?

"It all feeds the belly, my mother used to say, so pay it no mind," Chesa murmured as if talking to herself. That was how she gave Egwene advice, without straying across the line between mistress and maid. At least, she gave advice when Halima was not present, and the other woman had left early this morning. Chesa was sitting on one of the clothing chests, in case Egwene wanted something or needed an errand run, but now and then her eyes strayed to the pile of garments that were to go the washwomen today. She never minded darning or mending in front of Egwene, but in her book, sorting laundry would have been stepping over that line.

Smoothing the grimace from her face, Egwene was about to tell the woman to go get her own breakfast—Chesa considered eating before Egwene finished another transgression—but before she could open her mouth, Nisao pushed into the tent, surrounded by the glow of *saidar*. As the entry flaps fell, Egwene caught a glimpse of Sarin, Nisao's bald, black-bearded stump of a Warder, waiting outside. The small sister's cowl was down, carefully arranged on her shoulders so the yellow velvet lining showed, yet she was clutching her cloak as though she felt the cold intensely. She said nothing, just gave Chesa a sharp look. Chesa waited for Egwene's nod, gathered her own cloak and scurried out. She might not be able to see the light of the Power, but she knew when Egwene wanted privacy.

"Kairen Stang is dead," Nisao said without preamble. Her face was smooth, her voice steady, and chill. Short enough to make Egwene feel tall, she stood as though straining for an extra inch. Nisao did not usually do that. "Seven sisters had already tested for resonance before I got there. There is no doubt she was killed using *saidin*. Her neck was broken. Shattered. As if her head had been wrenched around full circle. At least it was quick." Nisao drew a deep, unsteady breath, then realized what she had done and pulled herself up even straighter. "Her Warder is primed for murder. Someone gave him an herbal concoction to put him to sleep, but he will be trouble to handle once he wakes." She did not put the usual dismissive Yellow twist on the mention of herbs, a measure of her upset no matter how calm her face was.

Egwene set her spoon down on the tiny table and leaned back. Suddenly, her chair did not feel comfortable anymore. Now the next best after Leane was Bode Cauthon. A novice. She tried not to think of what else Bode was. With the extra days of practice, Bode could do the work almost as well as Kairen could have. Almost. She did not mention that, though. Nisao knew some secrets, but not all. "Anaiya, and now Kairen. Both Blue Ajah. Do you know of any other link between them?"

Nisao shook her head. "Anaiya had been Aes Sedai fifty or sixty years when Kairen came to the Tower, as I recall. Perhaps they had mutual acquaintances. I just don't know, Mother." Now she sounded tired, and her shoulders slumped a little. Her quiet investigation into Anaiya's death had gotten nowhere, and she had to be aware Egwene was going to add Kairen.

"Find out," Egwene ordered. "Discreetly." This second murder would cause enough ruction without her adding to it. For a moment, she studied the other woman. Nisao might make excuses after the fact, or claim she had been doubtful from the start, but until then, she was always a model of Yellow Ajah self-assurance and absolute certainty. Not now, however. "Are many sisters walking about holding *saidar*?"

"I've noticed several, Mother," Nisao said stiffly. Her chin rose within a fraction of defiance. After a moment, though, the glow around her winked out. She pulled her cloak tighter, as if she had suddenly lost warmth. "I doubt it would have done Kairen any good. Her death was too sudden. But it makes a person feel . . . safer."

After the small woman left, Egwene sat stirring her porridge with her spoon. She did not see any more dark flecks, but her appetite was gone. Finally, she rose and settled the seven-striped stole around her neck, then swung her cloak onto her shoulders. Today of all days, she would not sit mired in gloom. Today of all days, she must follow her routine exactly.

Outside, high-wheeled carts trundled along the frozen ruts of the camp streets, filled with big water barrels or piles of split firewood and sacks of charcoal, the drivers and the fellows riding behind alike enveloped in their cloaks against the cold. As usual, families of novices hurried along the wooden walkways, usually managing to make their courtesies to passing Aes Sedai without slowing. Failure in the proper respects to a sister could earn a switching, but so could tardiness, and teachers were generally less tolerant than Aes Sedai encountered in passing, who at least might make allowances for why a novice went rushing by.

The white-clad women still leapt out of the way at sight of the striped stole hanging from Egwene's cowl, of course, but she refused to let her mood be soured, any more than it already was, by novices curtsying in the street, slipping and sliding on the ice-hard ground and sometimes almost falling on their faces before their cousins could grab them. "Cousin" was what members of the same family had taken to calling one another, and somehow that seemed to tie them closer together, as if they really were related, and close cousins at that. What did sour her mood were the few Aes Sedai she saw out and about, gliding along the walkways through ripples of curtsies. There were no more than a dozen or so between her tent and the Amyrlin's study, but three out of every four were wrapped in the light of the Power as well as cloaks. They walked in pairs more often than not, followed by any Warders they had. They seemed watchful, too, enveloped in *saidar* or not, cowls swiveling constantly as they scanned everyone in sight.

It minded her of the time spotted fever had struck Emond's Field, and everyone walked around clutching brandy-soaked handkerchiefs to their noses—Doral Barran, the Wisdom then, had said that would help stave it off—clutching their handkerchiefs and watching one another to see who would be the next to break out in spots and fall over. Eleven people died before the fever ran its course, but it was a month after the last person fell sick before everyone was willing to put those handkerchiefs away. For a long time, she had associated the smell of brandy with fear. She could almost smell it now. Two sisters had been murdered in their midst, by a man who could channel, not to mention apparently being able to come and go as he chose. Fear was running through the Aes Sedai faster than spotted fever ever could.

The tent she used as a study was already warm when she arrived, the brazier giving off a scent of roses. The mirrored stand-lamps and table-lamp were lit. Her routine was well known. Hanging her cloak on the cloak rack in the corner, she took her seat behind the writing table, automatically catching the unsteady chair leg that always tried to fold. All she had to do was follow routine. Tomorrow, she could announce what had been done.

Her first visitor was a shock, perhaps the last woman she expected to walk into the tent. Theodrin was a willowy, apple-cheeked Brown, a copper-skinned Domani with a stubborn set to her mouth. Once, she had always looked ready to smile. She glided across the worn carpets, close enough for the fringe of her shawl to brush the writing table. As she made a very formal curtsy, Egwene extended her left hand so the woman could kiss her Great Serpent ring. Formality must be met with formality.

"Romanda wishes to know if she can meet with you today, Mother," the slender Brown said. Softly, but there was a stubbornness buried in her tone, too.

"Tell her, at any time she chooses, Daughter," Egwene replied carefully. Theodrin offered another curtsy without changing expression.

As the Brown moved to leave, one of the Accepted brushed by her into the tent, pushing back her banded white hood. Emara was a thin woman, and as small as Nisao. It seemed a strong wind might blow her away, yet she had a very firm hand with the novices given into her care, firmer than many sisters. But then, she was hard on herself, and a novice's life was supposed to be hard. Emara's gray eyes rolled to the fringe on Theodrin's shawl, and her mouth twisted into a scornful grin before she smoothed it away to spread her snowy, banded skirts for Egwene. Bright spots of color flamed on Theodrin's cheeks.

Egwene slapped a hand down on the table hard enough to rattle the stone inkwell and the sand jar. "Have your forgotten how to be courteous to an Aes Sedai, child?" she said sharply.

Emara went pale—the Amyrlin did have a reputation, after all—and hastily made an even deeper curtsy for Theodrin, who acknowledged it with a wooden nod before gliding from the tent a good deal more swiftly than she had entered.

What Emara stammered out, in an Illianer accent made thicker by nerves, was a request from Lelaine to meet with the Amyrlin. Romanda and Lelaine had been much less formal, once, appearing unannounced and whenever they wished, but the declaration of war on Elaida had changed a great deal. Not everything, but enough to go on with. Egwene returned the same reply to Lelaine that she had to Romanda, though in a more clipped tone, and Emara almost fell over making her curtsy and practically ran out of the tent. One more nail fastening together the legend of Egwene al'Vere, the Amyrlin Seat who made Sereille Bagand look like a goose-down pillow.

As soon as the Accepted was gone, Egwene raised her hand and frowned at what it had covered. The folded square of paper that Theodrin had deposited on the table while kissing her ring. Her frown deepened when she opened it. The script that covered the small page managed to flow while being precise, but there was an inkblot on one edge. Theodrin was very neat. Perhaps she was trying to conform to the general view of Browns.

Romanda has sent two sisters to Travel to Cairhien and investigate some tale that has the Yellow Sitters buzzing. I don't know what the rumor is, Mother, but I will find out. I heard one of them mention Nynaeve, not as if she were in Cairhien, but as if the rumor was somehow connected to her.

The fool woman had even signed her name!

"What is that, Mother?"

Egwene gave a start of surprise, and barely caught the folding chair leg before it dropped her onto the carpets. She refocused her scowl on Siuan, who stood just inside the entry flaps with her blue-fringed shawl on her arms and her leather folders pressed to her breasts. The blue-eyed woman's eyebrows raised slightly at Egwene's startlement.

"Here," Egwene said irritably, thrusting the paper at her. This was no time to be jumping and twitching! "You know about Kairen?" Of course, she must, but Egwene still said, "Have you made the necessary changes?" Necessary changes. Light, she sounded as pompous as Romanda. She *was* on edge. Only at the last did she think to embrace *saidar* and weave a ward against eavesdropping; only after the ward was in place did she think that today might not be the best time for anyone to think she had private matters to discuss with Siuan.

Siuan was not on edge. She had weathered storms. And

managed to recover from drowning, some might say. Today was only a little windy, to her. "No need until we know for sure about the boats, Mother," she replied calmly, setting her folders on the table and neatly squaring them between the inkwell and the sand jar. "The less time Bode has to think about it, the less chance she'll panic." Calm as a pond. Even two murdered sisters could not ruffle Siuan. Or sending a novice of only a few months to replace one of them.

A frown creased her forehead as she read the note, though. "First Faolain goes into hiding," she growled at the paper, "and now Theodrin brings this to you instead of to me. That fool girl has less brains than a fisher-bird! You'd think she wants someone to find out she's keeping an eye on Romanda for you." Keeping an eye. A polite way of saying "spy." They were both practiced in euphemisms. That went with being Aes Sedai. Today, euphemisms grated on Egwene.

"Perhaps she does want to be discovered. Perhaps she's tired of Romanda telling her what to do, what to say, what to think. I had an Accepted in here who *sneered* at Theodrin's shawl, Siuan."

The other woman made a dismissive gesture. "Romanda tries to tell everyone what to do. And what to think. As for the rest, things will change once Theodrin and Faolain can swear on the Oath Rod. I don't suppose anyone will actually insist they be tested for the shawl now. Until then, they must take what comes."

"That isn't good enough, Siuan." Egwene managed to keep her tone level, but it took an effort. She had at least suspected what she was letting those two in for when she told them to attach themselves to Romanda and Lelaine. She had needed to know what the Sitters were scheming at, and still needed to know, yet she had a duty to them. They had been the first to swear fealty to her, and of their own free will. Besides which . . . "Much of what's said about Theodrin and Faolain can be said of me, too. If *Accepted* can show them disrespect . . ." Well, she had no fear of *that*. The sisters were another matter. Especially the Sitters. "Siuan, I have no hope at all of uniting the Tower if Aes Sedai doubt me."

Siuan snorted forcefully. "Mother, by now even Lelaine and Romanda know you're the Amyrlin Seat in truth,

whether or not they'll admit it. That pair wouldn't have
fallen in line with Deane Aryman. I think they're beginning to see you as another Edarna Noregovna."

"That's as may be," Egwene said dryly. Deane was considered the White Tower's savior, after Bonwhin's disaster
with Artur Hawkwing. Edarna was believed to have been
the most politically skilled woman ever to hold the staff and
stole. Both had been very strong Amyrlins. "But as you've
reminded me, I have to make sure I don't end up like Shein
Chunla." Shein had begun as a strong Amyrlin, firmly in
charge of the Tower and the Hall, and ended as a puppet
doing exactly as she was told.

Siuan nodded, in approval and agreement. She really was
teaching Egwene the Tower's history, and she often brought
up Amyrlins who had misstepped fatally. Including herself.
"This is another matter, though," she muttered, tapping the
note against her fingers. "When I lay my hands on Theodrin, I'll make her wish she was a novice. And Faolain! If
they think they can shirk off now, I swear, I'll gut the pair
of them like grunters on the dock!"

"You'll gut who?" Sheriam asked as she walked in
through the ward in a gust of cold air.

Egwene's chair almost dropped her onto the carpets
again. She needed to get a chair that did not try to fold up
every time she moved. She was willing to bet Edarna never
jumped as if she had itchoak down her back.

"No one who concerns you," Siuan said calmly, putting the paper to one of the table-lamp's flames. It burned
quickly, right to her fingertips, and then she mashed it out
between her hands and brushed the ash away. Only Egwene,
Siuan and Leane knew the truth of Faolain and Theodrin.
And the two sisters themselves, of course. Though there
was a great deal neither of them knew, either.

Sheriam accepted the rebuff with equanimity. The fire-
haired woman seemed to have recovered completely from
her collapse in the Hall. At least, she had recovered her
outer dignity, for the most part. Watching Siuan burn the
note, her tilted green eyes might have tightened a little, and
she did touch the narrow blue stole hanging from her shoulders as if to remind herself that it was there. She did not
have to accept Siuan's orders—putting her Keeper in that
position had seemed too harsh to Egwene, in the end—but

Sheriam knew very well that Siuan had no need to accept her orders either, which had to gall her now that Siuan stood so far beneath her in the Power. Knowing there were secrets she was not privy to had to gall her, as well. Sheriam would have to live with it though.

She also had brought a paper, which she laid on the table in front of Egwene. "I met Tiana on the way here, Mother, and told her I'd give this to you."

"This" was the day's report on runaways, though those no longer came every day, or even every week, since the novices had been organized into families. Cousins supported one another through frustrations and tears, and managed to talk one another out of the worst mistakes, like running away. There was only one name on the page. Nicola Treehill.

Egwene sighed and set the paper down. She would have thought Nicola's greed for learning would have kept her feet still no matter how frustrated the woman grew. And yet, she could not say she was sorry to see the end of her. Nicola was conniving and unscrupulous, willing to try blackmail or whatever else she thought would advance her. Very likely she had had help. Areina would not have balked at stealing horses for the pair of them to flee.

Abruptly, the date beside the name caught her eye. Two dates, actually, marked as questions. Months were seldom named, much less days numbered, except in official documents and treaties. Signed, sealed and witnessed in the city of Illian on the twelfth day of Saven, this Year of Grace. . . . And for reports of this nature, and entering a woman's name in the novice book. For common use, so many days before this feastday or after that sufficed. Written out, dates always looked a little strange to her. She had to count on her fingers to be sure of what she saw.

"Nicola ran away three or four days ago, Sheriam, and Tiana is just reporting it? She isn't even sure whether it *was* three days or four?"

"Nicola's cousins covered for her, Mother." Sheriam shook her head ruefully. Strangely, her small smile seemed amused, though. Or even admiring. "Not from love; apparently, they were glad to see the child go and afraid she'd be brought back. She was quite overbearing about her Talent at Foretelling. I'm afraid Tiana is very upset with them. None will be sitting comfortably in their classes today, or for days to come, I fear. Tiana says she intends to give them each a dose of the strap instead of breakfast every day till Nicola is found. I think she might relent, though. With Nicola gone so long before her flight was discovered, it may be some time before she's located."

Egwene winced slightly. She could recall her own visits to the study of the Mistress of Novices, then occupied by the very woman in front of her. Sheriam had a strong arm. A daily dose would be fierce. But hiding a runaway's flight was more serious than sneaking out after hours or pulling a prank. She pushed the report to one side.

"Tiana will handle it as she sees fit," she said. "Sheriam, has there been any change in how the sisters talk about my dream?" She had revealed the dream about a Seanchan attack the very morning after dreaming it, and the women she told stared at her apathetically, apparently because of the freshness of Anaiya's death. That had stunned everyone.

Instead of answering, Sheriam cleared her throat and smoothed her blue-slashed skirts. "You may not be aware, Mother, but one of Nicola's cousins is Larine Ayellin. From Emond's Field," she added, as if Egwene did not know that. "No one would think you were playing favorites if you pardoned the whole family. Whether or not she relents, Tiana does mean to be very sharp with them in the meantime. They will suffer."

Leaning back, carefully because of the wobbly chair leg, Egwene frowned up at the other woman. Larine was almost the same age as she, and a close friend growing up. They had spent hours together, gossiping and practicing putting their hair in braids for when the Women's Circle said they were old enough. Despite that, Larine had been one of the few Emond's Field girls who seemed to accept that Egwene might really be the Amyrlin Seat, though she showed it mainly by keeping her distance. But did Sheriam think Egwene would play *favorites*? Even Siuan looked taken aback. "You should know better than anyone, Sheriam, novice discipline is the province of the Mistress of Novices. Unless a girl is being abused, anyway, and you haven't suggested that. Besides, if Larine thinks she can get away with helping a runaway today—helping a runaway, Sheriam!— what will she think she can get away with tomorrow? She can reach the shawl, if she has the gumption to stick with it. I won't lead her down a path that ends with her being sent away for misbehavior. Now. What are they saying about my dream?"

Sheriam's tilted green eyes blinked, and she glanced at Siuan. Light, the woman thought Egwene was being hard because Siuan was present? Because Siuan might carry tales? She should know better; she *had* been the Mistress of Novices. "The attitude among the sisters, Mother," Sheriam said finally, "is still that the Seanchan are a thousand miles away, they don't know how to Travel, and if they start marching on Tar Valon, we'll learn of it before they're within two hundred leagues."

Siuan muttered something under her breath that sounded vile, but not surprised. Egwene wanted to curse, too. Worries over Anaiya's murder had had nothing to do with the sisters' apathy. They did not believe that Egwene was a Dreamer. Anaiya had been sure, but Anaiya was dead. Siuan and Leane believed, yet neither stood high enough now to be listened to with more than impatient politeness, if that. And it was quite clear that Sheriam did not believe. She obeyed her oath of fealty as scrupulously as Egwene could have wished for, but you could not order someone to believe. They only mouthed what you told them, and nothing changed.

When Sheriam left, Egwene found herself wondering what had brought the woman in the first place. Could it have been just to point out that Larine was going to be punished? Surely not. But she had said nothing else, apart from answering Egwene's questions.

Shortly, Myrelle arrived, followed closely by Morvrin. Egwene could feel each of them release the Source before she entered the tent, and they left their Warders waiting outside. Even in brief glimpses as the entry flaps were pushed aside, the men looked wary, even for Warders.

Myrelle's big dark eyes flashed at the sight of Siuan, and her nostrils flared. Morvrin's round face remained smooth as polished stone, but she brushed her dark brown skirts with both hands as if wiping something off. Perhaps it was unconscious. Unlike Sheriam, they did have to accept Siuan's orders, and neither liked that at all. It was not that Egwene wanted to grind their noses, but she trusted Siuan, and oaths or no oaths, she did not entirely trust them. Not to the degree she did Siuan. Besides, there were times it was inconvenient if not impossible for her to tell the sisters sworn to her what she wanted done. Siuan could carry messages, and this way, Egwene could be sure they were obeyed.

She asked about talk of her dream straightaway, but unsurprisingly, their stories were the same as Sheriam's. The Seanchan were far off. There would be plenty of warning should that change. The story had been the same for a good week and a half. Worse. . . .

"It might be different if Anaiya were alive," Morvrin said, balancing atop one of the rickety stools in front of the writing table. In spite of her bulk, she did it easily and gracefully. "Anaiya had a reputation for arcane knowledge. I always thought she should have chosen Brown, myself. If she said you were a Dreamer—" Her teeth clicked shut at a sharp look from Egwene. Myrelle suddenly took an interest in warming her hands at the brazier.

Neither of them believed, either. Except for Siuan and Leane, no one in the whole camp believed that Egwene had had a true dream. Varilin had taken over the talks in Darein, deftly pushing Beonin into a lesser role, and she offered constant excuses as to why she could not pass on a warning at just this moment. Perhaps in a few days, when the talks were going more smoothly. As if they were ever anything other than sisters talking in circles without saying a word that might send the other side away offended. No one at all but Siuan and Leane. She thought they believed.

Myrelle turned from the brazier as if steeling herself to put a hand on the coals. "Mother, I have been thinking about the day Shadar Logoth was destroyed—" She broke off and turned back to the brazier as a long-faced woman in deep blue entered the tent carrying a three-legged stool painted in bright spirals.

Maigan was beautiful, with large eyes and full lips, but she seemed elongated somehow. She was not that tall, but even her hands seemed long. She gave Morvrin a cool nod, and pointedly ignored Myrelle. "I brought my own seat today, Mother," she said, making as much of a curtsy as she could with the stool in one hand. "Yours are rather unsteady, if I may say so."

It had come as no surprise that Anaiya's death meant the

Blue Ajah would name someone else to Egwene's "advisory council," but she had hoped for the best when she learned who it was to be. Maigan had been one of Siuan's allies when Siuan was Amyrlin.

"Do you mind if I send Siuan for tea, Mother?" Maigan said as she settled onto her stool. "You really should have a novice or Accepted to run errands, but Siuan will do."

"The novices have their classes, Daughter," Egwene replied, "and even with the arrangement of families, the Accepted hardly have time for their own studies." Besides which, she would have to send a novice or Accepted to stand in the cold any time she wanted to speak to someone in privacy. Hard on one who would not yet have been taught how to ignore heat or cold, and a flag planted outside the tent telling everyone there might be something worth eavesdropping on. "Siuan, will you please bring us some tea? I'm sure we could all do with a hot cup."

Maigan raised a long-fingered hand as Siuan started for the entrance. "I have a jar of mint honey in my tent," she said imperiously. "Fetch that. And mind you don't filch any. I remember you used to have a sweet tooth. Hurry, now." Maigan had been an ally. Now she was one of many sisters who blamed Siuan for breaking the White Tower.

"As you say, Maigan," Siuan replied in a meek voice, and even bent her knee slightly before she hurried out. And she did hurry. Maigan stood as high as Myrelle or Morvrin, and there were no orders or oaths of fealty to protect her here. The long-faced woman gave a small, satisfied nod. Siuan had had to beg to be accepted back into the Blue Ajah, and rumor had it that Maigan had been the most insistent on the begging.

Morvrin made her excuses to leave behind Siuan, perhaps meaning to catch her up for some reason, but Myrelle took one of the stools and engaged in a competition with Maigan: who could ignore the other most completely. Egwene did not understand the animosity between the two women. Sometimes, people just disliked one another. In any case, it did not make for conversation. Egwene took the opportunity to leaf through the pages in Siuan's folders, but she could not concentrate on rumors out of Illian and innuendoes out of Cairhien. There seemed nothing to account for Theodrin's claim of a tale that had set the

Yellow Sitters buzzing. Siuan would have said something, if she had known.

Maigan and Myrelle stared at her as if watching her turn over sheets of paper was the most interesting activity in the world. She would have sent them both away, but she wanted to find out what Myrelle had been thinking about the day Shadar Logoth had been scooped out of the earth. She could not send one away without sending both. Drat the pair of them!

When Siuan returned, with a wooden tray holding a silver teapot and porcelain cups—and Maigan's white-glazed honey jar—she was followed into the tent by a soldier in plate-and-mail armor, a young Shienaran with his hair shaved off except for a topknot. Young, but not young. Ragan's dark cheek carried a puckered white scar from an arrow, and his face was hard in the way only the face of a man who lived with death every hour could be hard. As Siuan distributed teacups, he bowed, one hand holding a moon-crested helmet on his hip, the other on his sword hilt. Nothing in his expression said he had ever met her before.

"Honor to serve, Mother," he said formally. "Lord Bryne sent me. He said to tell you that it seems the raiders may have crossed to this side of the river last night. With Aes Sedai. Lord Bryne is doubling the patrols. He advises that sisters stay close to the camp. To avoid incidents."

"May I be excused, Mother?" Siuan said suddenly, with the slightly abashed sound of a woman who found herself with an urgent need for the jakes.

"Yes, yes," Egwene said, as impatiently as she could manage, and barely waited for the other woman to dash out of the tent before going on. "Tell Lord Bryne that Aes Sedai go where they wish, when they wish." She snapped her mouth shut before she could call him "Ragan," but that only served to make her seem severe. She hoped it did.

"I will tell him, Mother," he replied, making another bow. "Heart and soul to serve."

Maigan smiled faintly as he departed. She deprecated soldiers—Warders were good and necessary; soldiers made messes for others to clean up, in her opinion—but she did favor anything that seemed to indicate a wedge between Egwene and Gareth Bryne. Or perhaps better to say that

Lelaine favored. In this, Maigan was Lelaine's woman to her toenails. Myrelle merely looked puzzled. She knew that Egwene got on well with Lord Gareth.

Egwene got up and poured herself a cup of tea. And took a touch of Maigan's honey. Her hands were quite steady. The boats were in place. In a few hours, Leane would gather Bode and ride well away from the camp before explaining what they were going to do. Larine must take the punishment she had earned, and Bode must do what needed doing. Egwene had been younger than Bode when she was set to hunt Black sisters. Shienarans served their war against the Shadow in the Blight, heart and soul. Aes Sedai, and those who would become Aes Sedai, served the Tower. A stronger weapon against the Shadow than any sword, and no less sharp to an unwary hand.

When Romanda arrived, with Theodrin to hold open the entry flap for her, the gray-haired Yellow made a very exact curtsy, neither a fraction more nor less than propriety required from Sitter to Amyrlin. They were not in the Hall, now. If the Amyrlin was only first among equals there, she was a little more in her own study, even for Romanda. She did not offer to kiss Egwene's ring, though. There were limits. She eyed Myrelle and Maigan as if thinking of asking them to leave. Or perhaps telling them. It was a prickly point. Sitters expected obedience, but neither was of her Ajah. And this was the Amyrlin's study.

In the end, she did neither, merely allowed Theodrin to take her cloak, embroidered with borders of yellow flowers, and pour her a cup of tea. Theodrin did not have to be asked to do either, and she retreated to a corner, twitching her shawl and her mouth set sullenly, as Romanda took the empty stool. Despite the stool's uneven legs, Romanda managed to make it seem a seat in the Hall of the Tower, or maybe a throne, as she adjusted the yellow-fringed shawl she had worn beneath her cloak.

"The talks are going badly," she said in that high, musical voice. She still made it sound a proclamation. "Varilin is chewing her lips in frustration. Magla is frustrated, too, for that matter, and even Saroiya. When Saroiya starts grinding her teeth, most sisters would be shouting." Excepting Janya, every Sitter who had held a chair before the Tower divided had insinuated herself into the negotiations. They were talking with women they had known in the Hall back then, after all. Beonin was nearly reduced to running errands.

Romanda touched the tea to her lips, then held the cup out to one side on its dish without saying a word. Theodrin darted from the corner to take the cup over to the tray, adding honey before she returned the cup to the Sitter and herself to the corner. Romanda tasted the tea again and nodded in approval. Theodrin's face colored.

"The talks will go as they go," Egwene said carefully. Romanda had opposed any sort of negotiations, spurious or not. And she knew what was to happen tonight. Keeping the Hall in the dark about that had seemed a needless slap in the face.

The tight bun on the back of Romanda's head bobbed as she nodded. "They have shown us one thing already. Elaida won't allow the Sitters speaking for her to budge an inch. She is dug into the Tower like a rat in a wall. The only way to flush her is to send ferrets in after her." Myrelle made a sound in her throat, earning a surprised glance from Maigan. Romanda's eyes remained steady on Egwene's.

"Elaida will be removed one way or another," Egwene said calmly, setting her teacup down on its dish. Her hand did not shake. What had the women learned? How?

Romanda grimaced faintly at her tea as if after all it lacked sufficient honey. Or in disappointment that Egwene had not said more. The woman shifted on her stool with the air of a swordswoman setting herself for another attack, blade coming up. "The things you've said about the Kin, Mother. That there are over a thousand of them rather than a few dozen. That some are five or six hundred years old." She shook her head over the impossibility. "How could all of that have escaped the Tower?" She was challenging, not asking a question.

"We only recently learned how many wilders there are among the Sea Folk," Egwene replied gently. "And we still aren't sure how many there really are." Romanda's grimace was not so small, this time. It had been the Yellow that first confirmed hundreds of Sea Folk wilders in Illian alone. First blow to Egwene.

One blow was not enough to finish Romanda, though. Or

even to wound her very badly. "We will have to hunt them down, once our business is done here," she said in grim tones. "Letting a few dozen remain in Ebou Dar and Tar Valon, just to help us trace runaways, was one thing, but we cannot allow a thousand wilders to remain . . . organized." She put even more contempt into the word, into the idea of wilders organizing, than she did into the rest. Myrelle and Maigan were watching closely, listening. Maigan was even leaning forward, she was so intent. Neither knew more than the stories Egwene had spread, which everyone assumed came through Siuan's eyes-and-ears.

"Well over a thousand," Egwene corrected, "and not one a wilder. All women sent away from the Tower, except for a few runaways who evaded capture." She did not raise her voice, but she made each point firmly, meeting Romanda's gaze. "In any case, how do you propose to hunt them down? They are spread through every country, in every sort of occupation. Ebou Dar was the only place they ever gathered or met other than by chance, and all those fled when the Seanchan came. Since the Trolloc Wars, the Kin have allowed the Tower to know only what they wanted known. Two thousand years, hiding under the White Tower's nose. Their numbers have grown while the Tower's numbers dwindled. How do you propose to find them now, among all the wilders out there that the Tower has always ignored because they were 'too old' to become novices? Kinswomen don't stand out in any way, Romanda. They use the Power almost as often as Aes Sedai, but they show age like anyone else, if more slowly. If they want to remain hidden, we will never be able to find them." And that was several more blows for Egwene, with none taken. Romanda wore a faint sheen of sweat on her forehead, a sure sign of desperation in an Aes Sedai. Myrelle was sitting very still, but Maigan seemed about to fall off her stool onto her nose no matter how steady it was.

Romanda licked her lips. "If they channel, they would achieve the look. If they age, they cannot be channeling very often if at all. And neither way could they live five or six hundred years!" No more dissimulation, it seemed.

"There is only one real difference between Aes Sedai and the Kin," Egwene said quietly. The words still seemed loud. Even Romanda appeared to be holding her breath. "They left the White Tower before they could swear on the Oath Rod." There; it was in the open finally.

Romanda jerked as if she had taken a mortal blow. "You've not taken the Oaths yet," she said hoarsely. "Do you mean to abandon them? To ask sisters to abandon them?" Myrelle or Maigan gasped. Perhaps both.

"No!" Egwene said sharply. "The Three Oaths are what make us Aes Sedai, and I will swear on the Oath Rod as soon as it is ours!" Drawing a deep breath, she modulated her tone. But she leaned toward the other woman, too, trying to draw her in, to include her. To convince her. She almost stretched out a hand. "As it is, sisters retire to spend their last years in quiet, Romanda. Wouldn't it be better if those were *not* their last years? If sisters retired into the Kin, they could tie the Kin to the Tower. There would be no need for a futile hunt, then." She had gone this far; she might as well go the last step. "The Oath Rod can unbind as well as bind."

Maigan thudded to the carpets on her knees and scrambled up, brushing at her skirts as indignantly as if she had been pushed. Myrelle's olive face looked a little pale.

Moving slowly, Romanda set her teacup on the edge of the writing table and stood, drawing her shawl around her. Expressionless, she stood staring down at Egwene while Theodrin settled her yellow-embroidered cloak on her shoulders, fastened the golden pin and arranged the folds as carefully as any lady's maid. Only then did Romanda speak, in a voice like stone. "When I was a little girl, I dreamed of becoming Aes Sedai. From the day I reached the White Tower, I tried to live as an Aes Sedai. I have lived as Aes Sedai, and I will die as Aes Sedai. This cannot be allowed!"

She turned smoothly to go, but she knocked over the stool she had been sitting on, apparently without noticing. Theodrin hurried out after her. With concern on her face, oddly enough.

"Mother?" Myrelle drew a deep breath, fingers plucking at her deep green skirts. "Mother, are you really suggesting . . . ?" She trailed off, apparently unable to say it. Maigan sat on her stool as though forcing herself not to lean forward again.

"I have laid out the facts," Egwene said calmly. "Any

decision will be the Hall's. Tell me, Daughter. Would you choose to die, when you could live and continue to serve the Tower?"

The Green sister and the Blue exchanged glances, then realized what they had done and snapped back to ignoring one another. Neither answered, but Egwene could almost see the thoughts churning behind their eyes. After a few moments, she got up and set the stool back upright. Even that failed to rouse them further than perfunctory apologies for making her see to that herself. Then they lapsed into silent reflection.

She tried to return to the pages in Siuan's folders—the stalemate at the Stone of Tear was dragging on, and no one admitted to any idea of how it would end—but not long after Romanda's departure, Lelaine arrived.

Unlike Romanda, the slender Blue Sitter was alone, and poured her own tea. Settling onto the empty stool, she tossed her fur-lined cloak back over both shoulders and let it hang from a silver cloak pin set with large sapphires. She wore her shawl, too; Sitters usually did. Lelaine was more direct than Romanda. Or so it might have seemed, on the surface. Her eyes held a sharp glitter.

"Kairen's death put another crimp in the chances of making any sort of agreement with the Black Tower," she murmured over her teacup, inhaling the fumes. "And there's poor Llyw to deal with. Perhaps Myrelle will take him. Two of her three belonged to someone else first. No one else has ever saved two Warders whose Aes Sedai died."

Egwene was not the only one to hear special emphasis in that. Myrelle's face definitely paled. She had two secrets to hide, and one was that she had four Warders. The passing of Lan Mandragoran's bond from Moiraine to her had been something not done in hundreds of years. Today, it was looked upon like bonding a man against his will. Something not done in even more hundreds of years. "Three is enough for me," she said breathlessly. "If you will excuse me, Mother?"

Maigan laughed softly as Myrelle left the tent walking fast. Not so fast that she failed to embrace *saidar* before the entry flaps fell, though.

"Of course," Lelaine said, exchanging amused looks with the other Blue, "they say she marries her Warders. All of them. Perhaps poor Llyw won't do for a husband."

"He *is* as wide as a horse," Maigan put in. Despite her amusement over Myrelle's flight, there was no maliciousness in her voice. She was simply stating a fact. Llyw was a very large man. "I think I know a young Blue who might take him. She isn't interested in men that way."

Lelaine nodded in a way that said the young Blue had found her Warder. "Greens can be very odd. Take Elayne Trakand, for example. Actually, I never thought Elayne would choose Green. I had her marked out for the Blue. The girl has a deft feel for the currents in politics. Though she also has a tendency to wander into deeper water than might be safe. Wouldn't you say so, Mother?" Smiling, she sipped at her tea.

This was not at all like Romanda's subtle feeling-out. This was slash and slash, with the blade appearing out of nowhere. Did Lelaine know about Myrelle and Lan? Had she sent someone to Caemlyn, and if so, how much had she learned? Egwene wondered whether Romanda had also felt off-balance and dazed.

"Do you think Kairen's murder is enough to stop an agreement?" she said. "For all anyone knows, this could be Logain returning for some mad revenge." Why in the Light had she said that? She needed to put a rein on her tongue and keep her wits. "Or more likely, some poor fool from a farm around here, or one of the bridge towns." Lelaine's smile deepened, and it was mocking, not amused. Light, the woman had not shown this much disrespect in months.

"If Logain wanted revenge, Mother, I suspect he would be in the White Tower trying to kill Reds." Despite her smile, her voice was smooth and level. A disturbing contrast. Perhaps that was her intention. "Perhaps it's a pity he isn't doing that. He might remove Elaida. But that would be easier than she deserves. No, Kairen won't stop an agreement any more than Anaiya did, but the two combined will make sisters worry even harder about safeguards and strictures. We may need these men, but we *must* be certain *we* are in control. Complete control."

Egwene nodded. A small nod. She agreed, but . . . "There might be difficulties bringing them to accept that," she said. Difficulties. She was displaying a positive talent for understatement today.

"The Warder bond could be modified slightly," Maigan said. "As it is, you can make the man do as you wish with a little tweaking, but the need to tweak could be removed quite easily."

"That sounds too much like Compulsion," Egwene said firmly. She had learned that weave from Moghedien, but only to work on how to counter it. The thing was filth, the theft of another person's will, of their whole being. Someone who was Compelled did anything you ordered. Anything. And believed it was their own choice. Just thinking about it made her feel dirty.

Maigan met her gaze almost as levelly as Lelaine had, though, and her voice was as smooth as her face. She had no thoughts of filth. "Compulsion was used on sisters in Cairhien. That seems certain, now. But I was talking about the bond, a different thing entirely."

"You think you can talk the Asha'man into accepting the bond?" Egwene could not keep the incredulity out of her voice. "Aside from that, who is going to do this bonding? Even if every sister who doesn't have a Warder took an Asha'man, and every Green took two or three, there aren't enough sisters. That's if you can find one who doesn't mind being bonded to a man who is going to go mad."

Maigan nodded at each point as if accepting it. And adjusted her skirts as if not really listening. "If the bond can be changed in one way," she said once Egwene finished, "it should be possible to change it in others. There might be a way to remove the sharing, perhaps some of the awareness. Then perhaps the madness would not be a problem. It would be a different sort of bond, not like the Warder bond at all. I'm certain everyone will agree it wouldn't be like having a Warder, really. Any sister could bond whatever number of Asha'man was necessary."

Abruptly, Egwene realized what was happening. Lelaine sat apparently peering into her teacup, but she was studying Egwene through her eyelashes. And using Maigan as a stalking horse. Smothering anger, Egwene did not have to make her voice cold. It was ice.

"That sounds *exactly* like Compulsion, Lelaine. It *is* Compulsion, and no twisting of words will make it anything else. I *will* point that out to anyone else who suggests this. And I will order the birch for anyone who does more than suggest. Compulsion is banned, and it will remain banned."

"As you say," Lelaine replied, which might have meant anything at all. What came next was more pointed. "The White Tower makes mistakes upon occasion. It is impossible to live or move without making mistakes. But we live, and we go on. And if we sometimes need to conceal our mistakes, whenever possible, we rectify them. Even when it is painful." Putting her cup back on the tray, she left with Maigan at her heels. Maigan embraced the Source before she left the tent. Lelaine did not.

For a time, Egwene concentrated on keeping her breathing steady. She performed the river contained by the bank. Lelaine had not quite said that Egwene al'Vere as Amyrlin was a mistake that might have to be rectified, but she had come very close.

At midday, Chesa brought Egwene's meal on another wooden tray, warm crusty bread with only one or two suspiciously dark flecks and lentil stew with slivers of tough turnip and woody carrot and bits of something that might have been goat. One spoonful was all Egwene could get down. It was not Lelaine that troubled her. Lelaine had threatened her before, if not since she made it clear that she *was* the Amyrlin and not a puppet. Instead of eating, she stared at Tiana's report lying to the side of the table. Nicola might not have gained the shawl in spite of her potential, but the Tower had long experience in taking muleheaded, fault-riddled women and turning them into confident Aes Sedai. Larine had a bright future ahead of her, but she had to learn to obey the rules before she could begin learning which could be broken and when. The White Tower was good at teaching both things, but the first always came first. Bode's future would be brilliant. Her potential almost equaled Egwene's. But Aes Sedai, Accepted or novice, the Tower required you to do what was needed *for* the Tower. Aes Sedai, Accepted, novice or Amyrlin.

Chesa was voluble in her disappointment when she returned to find the tray almost untouched, especially after she had found a practically untouched breakfast. Egwene considered claiming an upset stomach and rejected it. After

Chesa's tea worked on her headaches—at least for a few days, until they returned fiercer than ever and every night—the plump woman had turned out to have a collection of herbal remedies for every ill, purchased from every peddler with a glib tongue and each viler-tasting than the last. She had a way of looking so downhearted when you would not drink the awful mixtures that you found yourself swallowing them just to keep her from worrying. Sometimes, surprisingly, they worked, but they were never anything Egwene wanted to put in her mouth. She sent Chesa away with the tray and a promise to eat later. No doubt Chesa would present a supper big enough to stuff a goose.

She felt like smiling at the thought—Chesa would stand over her, wringing her hands, till she ate every bite—but her eyes fell back on Tiana's report. Nicola, Larine and Bode. The White Tower was a strict taskmistress. Unless the Tower is at war by consensus of the Hall, the Amyrlin shall not . . . But the Tower was at war.

She did not know how long she sat staring at that piece of paper with one name on it, but when Siuan returned, she had made up her mind. A strict taskmistress who never played favorites.

"Have Leane and Bode gone?" she asked.

"At least two hours ago, Mother. Leane had to deliver Bode, and then ride downriver."

Egwene nodded. "Please have Daishar saddled. . . ." No. Some people recognized the Amyrlin's horse by this time. Too many. There was no time for arguments and explanations. No time to assert her authority and make it stick. "Saddle Bela, and meet me on the corner two streets north." Almost everyone knew Bela, too. Siuan's horse, everybody knew.

"What do you mean to do, Mother?" Siuan asked worriedly.

"I mean to take a ride. And Siuan, tell no one." She caught the other woman's eyes, held them with her own. Siuan had been Amyrlin, and able to stare down a stone. Egwene was Amyrlin, now. "Not anyone, Siuan. Now go on. Go. And hurry." Forehead still creased, Siuan hurried.

As soon as she was alone, Egwene slid the stole from her neck, folded it carefully, and tucked it into her belt pouch.

Her cloak was good wool, and stout, but quite plain. Without the stole dangling from her cowl, she could have been anyone.

The walkway in front of her study was empty, of course, but once she crossed the frozen street, she made her way through the usual white river of novices speckled with Accepted and the occasional Aes Sedai. The novices bent knees to her without slowing, the Accepted offered curtsies as she passed, once they saw that the skirts beneath her cloak were not banded white, and the Aes Sedai glided along with their own faces hidden by their cowls. If any noticed that she was not followed by a Warder, well, a number of sisters lacked Warders. And not everyone was surrounded by the glowing nimbus of *saidar*. Just most.

Two streets from her study, she stopped at the edge of the wooden walkway facing away from the stream of hurrying women. She tried not to fret. The sun sat halfway down toward the horizon in the west, a golden ball stabbed by the broken peak of Dragonmount. The mountain's shadow already stretched across the camp, casting the tents in evening dimness.

At last Siuan appeared, mounted on Bela. The shaggy little mare walked surefooted on the slick street, but Siuan clung to reins and saddle as if she were afraid of falling off. Maybe she was. Siuan was one of the worst riders Egwene had ever seen. When she scrambled down from the saddle in a flurry of skirts and muttered curses, she looked relieved to have escaped with her life. Bela whickered at Egwene in recognition. Tugging her disarrayed cowl back into place, Siuan opened her mouth too, but Egwene held up a warning hand before the other woman could speak. She could see the word "Mother" forming on Siuan's lips. And likely it would have been loud enough to be heard fifty paces off.

"Tell no one," Egwene said softly. "And no notes or hints, either." That should cover everything. "Keep Chesa company till I get back. I don't want her worried."

Siuan gave a reluctant nod. Her mouth almost looked sullen. Egwene suspected she had been wise to add "notes" and "hints." Leaving the onetime Amyrlin Seat looking like a sulky girl, she climbed smoothly into Bela's saddle.

She had to walk the stout mare, at first, because of the frozen ruts in the camp's streets. And because everyone would wonder if they saw Siuan riding Bela at anything faster than a walk. She tried to ride like Siuan, swaying uncertainly, clinging to the saddle's tall pommel with one hand and sometimes both. It made her feel as if she were about to fall off, too. Bela twisted her head around to look at her. She knew who was on her back, and she knew Egwene rode better than this. Egwene continued to imitate Siuan and tried not to think about where the sun stood. All the way out of the camp, beyond the rows of wagons, until the first trees hid her from tents and wagons.

Then she bent over the pommel to press her face into Bela's mane. "You carried me away from the Two Rivers," she whispered. "Can you run as fast now?" Straightening, she dug in her heels.

Bela could not gallop like Daishar, but her sturdy legs churned through the snow. She had been a carthorse, once, not a racer or warhorse, but she gave what she had, stretching out her neck as bravely as Daishar ever could. Bela raced, and the sun slid lower as if the sky had suddenly become greased. Egwene lay low in the saddle and urged the mare on. A race with the sun that Egwene knew she could not win. But even if she could not beat the sun, there was still time. She thumped her heels in time with Bela's hooves, and Bela ran.

Twilight rolled over them, and then darkness, before Egwene saw the moon glinting on the water of the Erinin. Still time. It was almost the spot where she had sat Daishar with Gareth, watching the riverships slide toward Tar Valon. Reining Bela in, she listened.

Stillness. And then a muffled curse. The quiet grunts and scrapes of men dragging a heavy burden across the snow and trying for silence. She turned Bela through the trees toward the sounds. Shadows stirred, and she heard the soft whisper of steel sliding from scabbards.

Then a man muttered, not far enough under his breath, "I know that pony. It's one of the sisters. The one they say used to be Amyrlin. She doesn't look it to me. No older'n the one they say's Amyrlin now."

"Bela is not a pony," Egwene said crisply. "Take me to Bode Cauthon."

A dozen men coalesced out of the night shadows among the trees, surrounding her and Bela. They all seemed to think she was Siuan, but that was all right. To them, Aes Sedai was Aes Sedai, and they guided her to where Bode was sitting a horse not much taller than Bela and holding a dark cloak around her. Her dress was dark, too. White would have stood out, tonight.

Bode recognized Bela, too, and reached out to scratch the mare's ear fondly when Egwene rode up beside her.

"You're staying ashore," Egwene said quietly. "You can go back with me when it's done."

Bode jerked her hand back as if stung at the sound of Egwene's voice. "Why?" she said, not quite a demand. She had learned that much, at least. "I can do this. Leane Sedai explained to me, and I can do it."

"I know you can. But not as well as I can. Not yet." That seemed too much like a criticism that the other woman had not earned. "I am the Amyrlin Seat, Bode. Some decisions, only I can make. And some things, I shouldn't ask a novice to do when I can do them better." Perhaps that was not a great deal milder, but she could not explain about Larine and Nicola, or the price the White Tower demanded of all its daughters. The Amyrlin could not explain the one to a novice, and a novice was not ready to learn about the other.

Even in the night, the set of Bode's shoulders said she did not understand, but she had learned not to argue with Aes Sedai, too. Just as she had learned that Egwene *was* Aes Sedai. The rest, she would learn eventually. The Tower could take all the time it needed to teach her.

Dismounting, Egwene handed Bela's reins to one of the soldiers and raised her skirts to tramp through the snow toward the labored sounds of dragging. It was a large rowboat, being pushed and pulled across the snow like a sled. A bulky sled that had to be maneuvered between trees, though with fewer curses once the men doing the pushing and pulling realized that she was following them closely. Most men guarded their tongues around Aes Sedai, and if they could not see her face between the darkness and her cowl, who else would be down here by the river? If they knew she was not the same woman intended at first to accompany them, who questioned Aes Sedai?

They eased the boat into the river, careful of splashes, and six men scrambled aboard to set oars in rag-padded oarlocks. The men were barefoot, to avoid the noise of a boot scraping on the hull planks. Smaller boats plied these waters, but tonight, they had to master the currents. One of the men on the bank gave her a hand to steady herself climbing in, and she settled on a seat in the bow, holding her cloak close. The boat slid way from the bank, silent except for the faint swirl of the oars in the water.

Egwene looked ahead, south toward Tar Valon. The white walls gleamed in the light of a fat, waning moon, and lamp-lit windows gave the city a muted glow, almost as if the island was embracing *saidar*. The White Tower stood out even in the darkness, windows alight, the great mass shining beneath the moon. Something flashed across the moon, and her breath caught. For an instant, she thought it had been a Draghkar, an evil sight on this of all nights. Only a bat, she decided. Spring might be near enough for bats to be venturing out. Pulling her cloak tighter, she peered toward the city drawing nearer. Nearer.

As the tall wall of Northharbor loomed in front of the boat, the oarsmen backed water so the bow just missed kissing the wall beside the harbor entrance. Egwene almost put out a hand to fend off from the pale stone before the boat could bump into the wall. That thump would surely have been heard by the soldiers on guard. The oars made only a small gurgling noise as they swept back, though, and the boat stopped where she could have touched the massive iron chain across the harbor, its huge links giving off their own faint gleam from the grease coating them.

There was no need for touching, though. No need for waiting, either. Embracing *saidar,* she was barely aware of the thrill of life filling her before she had the weaves in place. Earth, Fire and Air surrounding the chain; Earth and Fire touching it. The black iron flashed to white across the whole width of the harbor mouth.

She had just time to realize that someone had embraced the Source not far away, above her on the wall, then something struck the boat, struck her, and she was aware of cold water enveloping her, filling her nose, her mouth. Darkness.

Egwene felt hardness beneath her. She heard women's voices. Excited voices.

"Do you know who this is?"

"Well, well. We certainly got better than we bargained for tonight."

Something was pressed to her mouth, and warmth trickled in, tasting faintly of mint. She swallowed convulsively, suddenly aware of how cold she was, shivering. Her eyes flickered open. And fastened on the face of the woman holding her head and the cup. Lanterns held by soldiers crowding around gave light enough for her to make out the face clearly. An ageless face. She was inside Northharbor.

"That's it, girl," the Aes Sedai said encouragingly. "Drink it all down. A strong dose, for now."

Egwene tried to push the cup away, tried to embrace *saidar*, but she could feel herself sliding back down into darkness. They had been waiting for her. She had been betrayed. But by whom?

EPILOGUE

An Answer

Rand stared out of the window at the steady rain falling out of a gray sky. Another storm down out of the Spine of the World. The Dragonwall. He thought spring must be coming soon. Spring always came, eventually. Earlier here in Tear than back home, it should be, though there seemed little sign of it. Lightning forked silver-blue across the sky, and long moments passed before the peal of thunder. Distant lightning. The wounds in his side ached. Light, the herons branded into his palms ached, after all this time.

Sometimes, pain is all that lets you know you're alive, Lews Therin whispered, but Rand ignored the voice in his head.

The door creaked open behind him, and he looked over his shoulder at the man who came into the sitting room. Bashere was wearing a short, gray silk coat, a rich shimmering coat, and he had the baton of the Marshal-General of Saldaea, an ivory rod tipped with a golden wolf's head, tucked behind his belt next to his scabbarded sword. His turned-down boots had been waxed till they shone. Rand tried not to let his relief show. They had been gone long enough.

"Well?" he said.

"The Seanchan are amenable," Bashere replied. "Crazy as loons, but amenable. They require a meeting with you in person, though. The Marshal-General of Saldaea isn't the Dragon Reborn."

"With this Lady Suroth?"

Bashere shook his head. "Apparently a member of their royal family has arrived. Suroth wants you to meet someone called the Daughter of the Nine Moons."

Thunder rolled again for distant lightning.

We rode on the winds of the rising storm,
We ran to the sounds of the thunder.
We danced among the lightning bolts,
and tore the world asunder.

—Anonymous fragment of a poem believed
written near the end of the previous Age,
known by some as the Third Age.
Sometimes attributed to the
Dragon Reborn.

The End

of the Tenth Book of

The Wheel of Time

Glossary

A Note on Dates in This Glossary. The Toman Calendar (devised by Toma dur Ahmid) was adopted approximately two centuries after the death of the last male Aes Sedai, recording years After the Breaking of the World (AB). So many records were destroyed in the Trolloc Wars that at their end there was argument about the exact year under the old system. A new calendar, proposed by Tiam of Gazar, celebrated freedom from the Trolloc threat and recorded each year as a Free Year (FY). The Gazaran Calendar gained wide acceptance within twenty years after the Wars' end. Artur Hawkwing attempted to establish a new calendar based on the founding of his empire (FF, From the Founding), but only historians now refer to it. After the death and destruction of the War of the Hundred Years, a third calendar was devised by Uren din Jubai Soaring Gull, a scholar of the Sea Folk, and promulgated by the Panarch Farede of Tarabon. The Farede Calendar, dating from the arbitrarily decided end of the War of the Hundred Years and recording years of the New Era (NE), is currently in use.

Arad Doman: A nation on the Aryth Ocean, currently racked by civil war and by wars against those who have declared for the Dragon Reborn. Its capital is Bandar Eban. In Arad Doman, the ruler (king or queen) is elected by a council of the heads of merchant guilds (the Council of Merchants), who are almost always women. He or she must be from the noble class, not the merchant, and is elected for life. Legally the king or queen has absolute authority, except that he or she can be deposed by three-quarter vote of the Council. The current ruler is King Alsalam Saeed Almadar, Lord of Almadar, High Seat of House Almadar. His present whereabouts are much shrouded in mystery.

armsmen: Soldiers who owe allegiance or fealty to a particular lord or lady.

Asha'man: (1) In the Old Tongue, "Guardian" or "Guardians," but the word always meant a guardian of justice and truth. (2) The name given, both collectively and as a rank, to the men who have come to the Black Tower, near Caemlyn in Andor, in order to learn to channel. Their training concentrates largely on the ways in which the One Power can be used as a weapon, and in another departure from the usages of the White Tower, once they learn to seize *saidin*, the male half of the Power, they are required to perform all chores and labors with the Power. When newly enrolled, a man is termed a Soldier; he wears a plain black coat with a high collar, in the Andoran fashion. Being raised to Dedicated brings the right to wear a silver pin, called the Sword, on the collar of his coat. Promotion to Asha'man brings the right to wear a Dragon pin, in gold and red enamel, on the collar opposite the Sword. Although many women, including wives, flee when they learn that their men actually can channel, a fair number of men at the Black Tower are married, and they use a version of the Warder bond to create a link with their wives. This same bond, altered to compel obedience, has recently been used to bond captured Aes Sedai as well.

Balwer, Sebban: Formerly secretary to Pedron Niall (the Lord Captain Commander of the Children of the Light) in public, and secretly Niall's spymaster. After Niall's death, Balwer aided the escape of Morgase (once Queen of Andor) from the Seanchan in Amador for his own reasons, and now is employed as secretary to Perrin t'Bashere Aybara and Faile ni Bashere t'Aybara. Perrin is beginning to suspect that there is more to Balwer than at first appeared.

Band of the Red Hand: *see Shen an Calhar.*

Blood, the: Term used by the Seanchan to designate the nobility. There are degrees of nobility. The High Blood shave

the sides of their heads and paint multiple fingernails—
the higher the rank, the more nails painted—but a member of the lesser Blood, the low Blood, may have only
the nails of the little fingers painted. One can be raised
to the Blood as well as born to it, and this is frequently a
reward for outstanding accomplishment or service to the
Empire.

calendar: There are 10 days to the week, 28 days to the
month, and 13 months to the year. Several feastdays are
not part of any month; these include Sunday (the longest
day of the year), the Feast of Thanksgiving (once every
four years at the spring equinox), and the Feast of All
Souls Salvation, also called All Souls Day (once every
ten years at the autumn equinox). While the months have
names—Taisham, Jumara, Saban, Aine, Adar, Saven,
Amadaine, Tammaz, Maigdhal, Choren, Shaldine, Nesan,
and Danu—these are seldom used except in official documents and by officials. For most people, using the seasons
is good enough.

Captain-General: (1) The military rank of the leader of
the Queen's Guard, in Andor. This position is currently
held by Lady Birgitte Trahelion. (2) The title given to the
head of the Green Ajah, though known only to members
of the Green. This position is currently held by Adelorna
Bastine in the Tower, and Myrelle Berengari among the
rebel Aes Sedai contingent under Egwene al'Vere.

Cha Faile: (1) In the Old Tongue, "the Falcon's Talon."
(2) Name taken by the young Cairhienin and Tairens,
attempted followers of *ji'e'toh*, who have sworn fealty to
Faile ni Bashere t'Aybara. In secret, they act as her personal
scouts and spies. Since her capture by the Shaido, they
continue their activities under the guidance of Sebban
Balwer.

Children of the Light: Society of strict ascetic beliefs,
owing allegiance to no nation and dedicated to the defeat
of the Dark One and the destruction of all Darkfriends.
Founded during the War of the Hundred Years by Lothair
Mantelar to proselytize against an increase in Darkfriends, they evolved during the war into a completely
military society. They are extremely rigid in their beliefs,
and certain that only they know the truth and the right.

They consider Aes Sedai and any who support them to be Darkfriends. Known disparagingly as Whitecloaks, they were formerly headquartered in Amador, Amadicia, but were forced out when the Seanchan conquered the city. Their sign is a golden sunburst on a field of white. *See also* Questioners.

Companions, the: The elite military formation of Illian, currently commanded by First Captain Demetre Marcolin. The Companions provide a bodyguard for the King of Illian and guard key points around the nation. Additionally, the Companions have traditionally been used in battle to assault the enemy's strongest positions, to exploit weaknesses, and, if necessary, to cover the retreat of the King. Unlike most other such elite formations, foreigners (excepting Tairens, Altarans and Murandians) are not only welcome, they can rise even to the highest rank, as can commoners, which also is unusual. The uniform of the Companions consists of a green coat, a breastplate worked with the Nine Bees of Illian, and a conical helmet with a faceguard of steel bars. The First Captain wears four rings of golden braid on the cuffs of his coat, and three thin golden plumes on his helmet. The Second Captain wears three rings of golden braid on each cuff, and three golden plumes tipped with green. Lieutenants wear two yellow rings on their cuffs, and two thin green plumes, under-lieutenants one yellow ring and a single green plume. Bannermen are designated by two broken rings of yellow on the cuffs and a single yellow plume, squadmen by a single broken ring of yellow.

Consolidation, the: When the armies sent by Artur Hawkwing under his son Luthair landed in Seanchan, they discovered a shifting quilt of nations often at war with one another, where Aes Sedai often reigned. Without any equivalent of the White Tower, Aes Sedai worked for their own individual goals, using the Power. Forming small groups, they schemed against one another constantly. In large part it was this constant scheming for personal advantage and the resulting wars among the myriad nations that allowed the armies from east of the Aryth Ocean to begin the conquest of an entire continent, and for their descendants to complete it. This conquest, during which the descendants of the original armies became Seanchan as much as they conquered Seanchan, took more than nine hundred years and is called the Consolidation.

Corenne: In the Old Tongue, "the Return." The name given by the Seanchan both to the fleet of thousands of ships and to the hundreds of thousands of soldiers, craftsmen and others carried by those ships, who will come behind the Forerunners to reclaim the lands stolen from Artur Hawkwing's descendants. *See also Hailene.*

cuendillar: A supposedly indestructible substance created during the Age of Legends. Any known force used in an attempt to break it is absorbed, making *cuendillar* stronger. Although the making of *cuendillar* has been thought lost forever, rumors of new objects made from it have surfaced. It is also known as heartstone.

currency: After many centuries of trade, the standard terms for coins are the same in every land: crowns (the largest coin in size), marks and pennies. Crowns and marks can be minted of gold or silver, while pennies can be silver or copper, the last often called simply a copper. In different lands, however, these coins can be of different sizes and weights. Even in one nation, coins of different sizes and weights have been minted by different rulers. Because of trade, the coins of many nations can be found almost anywhere. For that reason, bankers, moneylenders and merchants all use scales to determine the value of any given coin. Even large numbers of coins are weighed for this reason. The only paper currency is "letters-of-rights," which are issued by bankers, guaranteeing to present a certain amount of gold or silver when the letter-of-rights is presented. Because of the long distances between cities, the length of time needed to travel from one to another, and the difficulties of transactions at long distance, a letter-of-rights may be accepted at full value in a city near to the bank that issued it, but it may be accepted only at a lower value in a city farther away. Generally, someone of means intending a long journey will carry one or more letters-of-rights to exchange for coin when needed. Letters-of-rights are usually accepted only by bankers or merchants, and would never be used in shops.

da'covale: (1) In the Old Tongue, this would be translated literally as "one who is owned," or "person who is property." (2) Among the Seanchan, the term often used, along with "property," for slaves. Slavery has a long and unusual history among the Seanchan, with slaves having the ability to rise to positions of great power and open authority, including over those who are free. *See also so'jhin.*

Darkhounds: Shadowspawn created from lupine stock corrupted by the Dark One. While they resemble hounds in their basic shape, they are blacker than night and the size of ponies, weighing several hundred pounds each. They usually run in packs of ten or twelve, although the tracks of a larger pack have been sighted. They make no mark on soft ground, but leave prints in stone, and are frequently accompanied by the smell of burned sulphur. They will not usually venture out into the rain, but once running rain fails to stop them. Once they are on the trail, they must be confronted and defeated or the victim's death is inevitable. The only exception to this is when the victim can reach the other side of a river or stream, since Darkhounds will not cross flowing water. Or supposedly not. Their blood and saliva are poison, and if either touches the skin, the victim will die slowly and in great pain. *See also* Wild Hunt.

Daughters of Silence, the: During the history of the White Tower (over three thousand years), various women who have been put out have been unwilling to accept their fates and have tried to band together. Such groups—most of them by far, at least—have been dispersed by the White Tower as soon as found and punished severely and publicly to make sure that the lesson is carried to everyone. The last group to be dispersed called themselves the Daughters of Silence (794–798 NE). The Daughters consisted of two Accepted who had been put out of the Tower and twenty-three women they had gathered and trained. All were carried back to Tar Valon and punished, and the twenty-three were enrolled in the novice book. Only one of those, Saerin Asnobar, managed to reach the shawl. *See also* Kin, the.

Deathwatch Guards, the: The elite military formation of the Seanchan Empire, including both humans and Ogier.

The human members of the Deathwatch Guard are all *da'covale,* born as property and chosen while young to serve the Empress, whose personal property they are. Fanatically loyal and fiercely proud, they often display the ravens tattooed on their shoulders, the mark of a *da'covale* of the Empress. The Ogier members are known as Gardeners, and they are not *da'covale.* The Gardeners are as fiercely loyal as the human Deathwatch Guards, though, and are even more feared. Human or Ogier, the Deathwatch Guards not only are ready to die for the Empress and the Imperial family, but believe that their lives are the property of the Empress, to be disposed of as she wishes. Their helmets and armor are lacquered in dark green and blood-red, their shields are lacquered black, and their spears and swords carry black tassels. *See also da'covale.*

Defenders of the Stone, the: The elite military formation of Tear. The current Captain of the Stone (commander of the Defenders) is Rodrivar Tihera. Only Tairens are accepted into the Defenders, and officers are usually of noble birth, though often from minor Houses or minor branches of strong Houses. The Defenders are tasked to hold the great fortress called the Stone of Tear, in the city of Tear, to defend the city, and to provide police services in place of any City Watch or the like. Except in times of war, their duties seldom take them far from the city. Then, as with other elite formations, they are the core around which the army is formed. The uniform of the Defenders consists of a black coat with padded sleeves striped black-and-gold with black cuffs, a burnished breastplate, and a rimmed helmet with a faceguard of steel bars. The Captain of the Stone wears three short white plumes on his helmet, and on the cuffs of his coat three intertwined golden braids on a white band. Captains wear two white plumes and a single line of golden braid on white cuffs, lieutenants one white plume and a single line of black braid on white cuffs and under-lieutenants one short black plume and plain white cuffs. Bannermen have gold-colored cuffs on their coats, and squadmen have cuffs striped black and gold.

Delving: (1) Using the One Power to diagnose physical condition and illness. (2) Finding deposits of metal ores with the One Power. That this has long been a lost ability among Aes Sedai may account for the name becoming attached to another ability.

Depository: A division of the Tower Library. There are twelve publicly known Depositories, each having books and records pertaining to a particular subject, or to related subjects. A Thirteenth Depository, known only to Aes Sedai, contains secret documents, records and histories which may be accessed only by the Amyrlin Seat, the Keeper of the Chronicles, and the Sitters in the Hall of the Tower. And, of course, by the handful of librarians who maintain the Depository.

***der'morat-*:** (1) In the Old Tongue, "master handler." (2) Among the Seanchan, the prefix applied to indicate a senior and highly skilled handler of one of the exotics, one who trains others, as in *der'morat'raken*. *Der'morat* can have a fairly high social status, the highest of all held by *der'sul'dam*, the trainers of *sul'dam*, who rank with fairly high military officers. *See also morat-*.

Erith: Daughter of Iva daughter of Alar. An attractive young Ogier woman whom Loial intends to marry, although at present he is on the run from her.

Fain, Padan: Former Darkfriend, now more and worse than a Darkfriend, and an enemy of the Forsaken as much as he is of Rand al'Thor, whom he hates with a passion. Last seen in Far Madding with Toram Riatin.

Fel, Herid: The author of *Reason and Unreason* and other books. Fel was a student (and teacher) of history and philosophy at the Academy of Cairhien. He was discovered in his study torn limb from limb.

First Reasoner: The title given to the head of the White Ajah. This position is currently held by Ferane Neheran in the White Tower. Ferane Sedai is one of only two Ajah heads to sit in the Hall of the Tower at present.

First Weaver: The title given to the head of the Yellow Ajah. This position is currently held by Suana Dragand in the White Tower. Suana Sedai is one of only two Ajah heads to sit in the Hall of the Tower at present.

Fists of Heaven, the: Lightly armed and lightly armored Seanchan infantry carried into battle on the backs of the flying creatures called *to'raken*. All are small men, or women, largely because of limits as to how much weight a *to'raken* can carry for any distance. Considered to be among the toughest of soldiers, they are used primarily for raids, surprise assaults on positions at an enemy's rear, and where speed in getting soldiers into place is of the essence.

Forerunners, the: *See Hailene.*

Forsaken, the: The name given to thirteen powerful Aes Sedai, men and women both, who went over to the Shadow during the Age of Legends and were trapped in the sealing of the Bore into the Dark One's prison. While it has long been believed that they alone abandoned the Light during the War of the Shadow, in fact others did as well; these thirteen were only the highest-ranking among them. The Forsaken (who call themselves the Chosen) are somewhat reduced in number since their awakening in the present day. Those thought to have survived are Demandred, Semirhage, Graendal, Mesaana, Moghedien, and two who were reincarnated in new bodies and given new names, Osan'gar and Aran'gar, although it seems possible that Osan'gar may also be dead. The life of a Forsaken is always uncertain. Recently, a man calling himself Moridin has appeared, and seems to be yet another of the dead Forsaken brought back from the grave by the Dark One. The same may be possible regarding the woman calling herself Cyndane, but since Aran'gar was a man brought back as a woman, speculation as to the original identities of Moridin and Cyndane may prove futile until more is learned.

Gregorin: Full name Gregorin Panar de Lushenos. A member of the Council of Nine in Illian who presently serves as the Steward for the Dragon Reborn in Illian.

Hailene: In the Old Tongue, "Forerunners," or "Those Who Come Before." The term applied by the Seanchan to the massive expeditionary force sent across the Aryth Ocean to scout out the lands where Artur Hawkwing once ruled. Now under the command of the High Lady Suroth, its numbers swollen by recruits from conquered lands, the *Hailene* has gone far beyond its original goals, and has in fact been succeeded by the Return. *See* Return.

Hanlon, Daved: A Darkfriend, formerly commander of the White Lions in service to the Forsaken Rahvin while he held Caemlyn using the name Lord Gaebril. From there, Hanlon took the White Lions to Cairhien under orders to further the rebellion against the Dragon Reborn. The White Lions were destroyed by a "bubble of evil," and Hanlon has been ordered back to Caemlyn and, under the name Doilin Mellar, has ingratiated himself with Elayne, the Daughter-Heir. According to rumor, he has done considerably more than ingratiate himself.

Head Clerk: The title given to the head of the Gray Ajah. This position is currently held by Serancha Colvine, a woman of reputedly fastidious behavior, in the Tower.

heart: The basic unit of organization in the Black Ajah. In effect, a cell. A heart consists of three sisters who know each other; each member of the heart knows one additional sister of the Black.

Illuminators, Guild of: A society that held the secret of making fireworks. It guarded this secret very closely, even to the extent of murder. The Guild gained its name from the grand displays, called Illuminations, that it provided for rulers and sometimes for greater lords. Lesser fireworks were sold for use by others, but with dire warnings of the disaster that could result from attempting to learn what was inside them. The Guild once had chapter houses in Cairhien and Tanchico, but both are now destroyed. In addition, the members of the Guild in Tanchico resisted the invasion by the Seanchan and the survivors were made *da'covale*, and the Guild as such no longer exists. However, individual Illuminators have escaped Seanchan rule, and perhaps more grand displays will be seen in the not-too-distant future. *See also da'covale.*

Ishara: The first Queen of Andor (*circa* FY 994–1020). At the death of Artur Hawkwing, Ishara convinced her husband, one of Hawkwing's foremost generals, to raise the siege of Tar Valon and accompany her to Caemlyn with as many soldiers as he could break away from the army. Where others tried to seize the whole of Hawkwing's empire and failed, Ishara took a firm hold on a small part and succeeded. Today, nearly every noble House in Andor contains some of Ishara's blood, and the right to claim the Lion Throne depends both on direct descent from her and on the number of lines of connection to her that can be established.

Kaensada: An area of Seanchan that is populated by less-than-civilized hill tribes. These tribes fight a great deal among themselves, as do individual families within the tribes. Each tribe has its own customs and taboos, the latter of which often make no sense to anyone outside that tribe. Most of the tribesmen avoid the more civilized residents of Seanchan.

Katar: A city in Arad Doman known for its mines and forges. Katar is wealthy enough that its Lords occasionally need reminding that they are part of Arad Doman.

Kin, the: Even during the Trolloc Wars, more than two thousand years ago (circa 1000–1350 AB), the White Tower continued to maintain its standards, putting out women who failed to measure up. One group of these women, fearing to return home in the midst of the wars, fled to Barashta (near the present-day site of Ebou Dar), as far from the fighting as was possible to go at that time. Calling themselves the Kin, and Kinswomen, they kept in hiding and offered a safe haven for others who had been put out. In time, their approaches to women told to leave the Tower led to contacts with runaways, and while the exact reasons may never be known, the Kin began to accept runaways, as well. They made great efforts to keep these girls from learning anything about the Kin until they were sure that Aes Sedai would not swoop down and retake them. After all, everyone knew that runaways were always caught sooner or later, and the Kin knew that unless they held themselves secret, they themselves would be punished severely.

Unknown to the Kin, Aes Sedai in the Tower were aware of their existence almost from the very first, but prosecution of the wars left no time for dealing with them. By the end of the wars, the Tower realized that it might not be in their best interests to snuff out the Kin. Prior to that time, a majority of runaways actually had managed to escape, whatever the Tower's propaganda, but once the Kin began helping them, the Tower knew exactly where any runaway was heading, and they began retaking nine out of ten. Since Kinswomen moved in and out of Barashta (and later Ebou Dar) in an effort to hide their existence and their numbers, never staying more than ten years lest someone notice that they did not age at a normal speed, the Tower believed they were few, and they certainly were keeping themselves low. In order to use the Kin as a trap for runaways, the Tower decided to leave them alone, unlike any other similar group in history, and to keep the very existence of the Kin a secret known only to full Aes Sedai.

The Kin do not have laws, but rather rules (called "the Rule") based in part on the rules for novices and Accepted in the White Tower, and in part on the necessity of maintaining secrecy. As might be expected given the origins of the Kin, they maintain the Rule very firmly on all of their members.

Recent open contacts between Aes Sedai and Kinswomen, while known only to a handful of sisters, have produced a number of shocks, including the facts that there are twice as many Kinswomen as Aes Sedai and that some have lived more than a hundred years longer than any Aes Sedai who has lived since before the Trolloc Wars. The effect of these revelations, both on Aes Sedai and on Kinswomen, is as yet a matter for speculation. *See also* Daughters of Silence, the; Knitting Circle, the.

Knitting Circle, the: The leaders of the Kin. Since no member of the Kin has ever known how Aes Sedai arrange their own hierarchy—knowledge passed on only when an Accepted has passed her test for the shawl—they put no store in strength in the Power but give great weight to age, with the older woman always standing above the younger. The Knitting Circle (a title chosen, like the Kin, because it is innocuous) thus consists of the thirteen oldest Kinswomen resident in Ebou Dar, with the oldest given the title of Eldest. By the rules, all will have to step down when it is time for them to move on, but so long as they are resident in Ebou Dar, they have supreme authority over the Kin, to a degree that any Amyrlin Seat would envy. *See also* Kin, the.

Lady of the Shadows: A Seanchan term for death.

Lance-Captain: In most lands, noblewomen do not personally lead their armsmen into battle under normal circumstances. Instead, they hire a professional soldier, almost always a commoner, who is responsible for both training and leading their armsmen. Depending on the land, this man can be called a Lance-Captain, Sword-Captain, Master of the Horse, or Master of the Lances. Rumors of closer relationships than lady and servant often spring up, perhaps inevitably. Sometimes they are true.

Legion of the Dragon, the: A large military formation, all infantry, giving allegiance to the Dragon Reborn, trained by Davram Bashere along lines worked out by himself and Mat Cauthon, lines which depart sharply from the usual employment of foot. While many men simply walk in to volunteer, large numbers of the Legion are scooped up by recruiting parties from the Black Tower, who first gather all of the men in an area who are willing to follow the Dragon Reborn, and only after taking them through gateways near Caemlyn winnow out those who can be taught to channel. The remainder, by far the greater number, are sent to Bashere's training camps.

length, units of: 10 inches = 1 foot; 3 feet = 1 pace; 2 paces = 1 span; 1000 spans = 1 mile; 4 miles = 1 league.

marath'damane: In the Old Tongue, "those who must be leashed," and also "one who must be leashed." The term applied by the Seanchan to any woman capable of channeling who has not been collared as a *damane*.

Master of the Lances: *See* Lance-Captain.

Master of the Horse: *See* Lance-Captain.

Mera'din: In the Old Tongue, "the Brotherless." The name adopted, as a society, by those Aiel who abandoned clan and sept and went to the Shaido because they could not accept Rand al'Thor, a wetlander, as the *Car'a'carn,* or because they refused to accept his revelations concerning the history and origins of the Aiel. Deserting clan and sept for any reason is anathema among the Aiel, therefore their own warrior societies among the Shaido were unwilling to take them in, and they formed this society, the Brotherless.

morat-: In the Old Tongue, "handler." Among the Seanchan, it is used for those who handle exotics, such as *morat'raken*, a *raken* handler or rider, also informally called a flier. *See also der'morat-.*

Prophet, the: More formally, the Prophet of the Lord Dragon. Once known as Masema Dagar, a Shienaran soldier, he underwent a revelation and decided that he had been called to spread the word of the Dragon's Rebirth. He believes that nothing—nothing!—is more important than acknowledging the Dragon Reborn as the Light made flesh and being ready when the Dragon Reborn calls, and he and his followers will use any means to force others to sing the glories of the Dragon Reborn. Forsaking any name but "the Prophet," he has brought chaos to much of Ghealdan and Amadicia, large parts of which he controls. He joined with Perrin Aybara, who was sent to bring him to Rand, and has, for reasons unknown, stayed with him even though this delays his going to the Dragon Reborn.

Queen's Guards, the: The elite military formation in Andor. In peacetime the Guard is responsible for upholding the Queen's law and keeping the peace. The uniform of the Queen's Guard includes a red undercoat, gleaming mail and plate armor, a brilliant red cloak, and a conical helmet with a barred visor. High-ranking officers wear knots of rank on their shoulder, and may wear golden lion-head spurs. A recent addition to the Queen's Guard is the Daughter-Heir's personal bodyguard, which is composed entirely of women with the sole exception of its captain, Doilin Mellar.

Questioners, the: An order within the Children of the Light. They refer to themselves as the Hand of the Light, and their avowed purposes are to discover the truth in disputations and uncover Darkfriends. In the search for truth and the Light, their normal method of inquiry is torture, their normal manner that they know the truth already and must only make their victim confess to it. At times they act as if they are entirely separate from the Children and the Council of the Anointed, which commands the Children. The head of the Questioners is the High Inquisitor, at present Rhadam Asunawa, who sits on the Council of the Anointed. Their sign is a blood-red shepherd's crook.

Redarms: Soldiers of the Band of the Red Hand, who have been chosen out for temproary police duty to make sure that other soldiers of the Band cause no trouble or damage in a town or village. So named because, while on duty, they wear very broad red armbands that almost cover their entire sleeves. Usually chosen from among the most experienced and reliable men. Since any damages must be paid for by the men serving as Redarms, they work hard to make sure all is quiet and peaceful. A number of former Redarms were chosen to accompany Mat Cauthon to Ebou Dar. *See also* Band of the Red Hand.

Return, the: *See Corenne.*

Sea Folk hierarchy: The Atha'an Miere, the Sea Folk, are ruled by the Mistress of the Ships to the Atha'an Miere. She is assisted by the Windfinder to the Mistress of the Ships, and by the Master of the Blades. Below this come the clan Wavemistresses, each assisted by her Windfinder and her Swordmaster. Below her are the Sailmistresses (ship captains) of her clan, each assisted by her Windfinder and her Cargomaster. The Windfinder to the Mistress of the Ships has authority over all Windfinders to clan Wavemistresses, who in turn have authority over all the Windfinders of her clan. Likewise, the Master of the Blades has authority over all Swordmasters, and they in turn over the Cargomasters of their clans. Rank is not hereditary among the Sea Folk. The Mistress of the Ships is chosen, for life, by the First Twelve of the Atha'an Miere, the twelve most senior clan Wavemistresses. A clan Wavemistress is elected by the twelve most senior Sailmistresses of her clan, called simply the First Twelve, a term which is also used to designate the senior Sailmistresses present anywhere. She can also be removed by a vote of her clan's First Twelve. In fact, anyone other than the Mistress of the Ships can be demoted, even all the way down to deckhand, for malfeasance, cowardice or other crimes. Also, the Windfinder to a Wavemistress or Mistress of the Ship who dies will, of necessity, have to serve a lower ranking woman, and her own rank thus decreases.

Seandar: The Imperial capital of Seanchan, located in the northeast of the Seanchan continent. It is also the largest city in the Empire.

Seekers: More formally, Seekers for Truth, they are a police/spy organization of the Seanchan Imperial Throne. Although most Seekers are *da'covale* and the property of the Imperial family, they have wide-ranging powers. Even one of the Blood can be arrested for failure to answer any question put by a Seeker, or for failure to cooperate fully with a Seeker, this last defined by the Seekers themselves, subject only to review by the Empress. Those Seekers who are *da'covale* are marked on either shoulder with a raven and a tower. Unlike the Deathwatch Guards, Seekers are seldom eager to show their ravens, in part because it necessitates revealing who and what they are.

sei'mosiev: In the Old Tongue, "lowered eyes," or "downcast eyes." Among the Seanchan, to say that one has "become *sei'mosiev*" means that one has "lost face." *See also sei'taer.*

sei'taer: In the Old Tongue, "straight eyes," or "level eyes." Among the Seanchan, it refers to honor or face, to the ability to meet someone's eyes. It is possible to "be" or "have" *sei'taer*, meaning that one has honor and face, and also to "gain" or "lose" *sei'taer. See also sei'mosiev.*

Shara: A mysterious land that lies to the east of the Aiel Waste. The land is protected both by inhospitable natural features and by man-made walls. Little is known about Shara, as the people of that land appear to work to keep their culture secret. The Sharans deny that the Trolloc Wars touched them, despite Aiel statements to the contrary. They deny knowledge of Artur Hawkwing's attempted invasion, despite the accounts of eyewitnesses from the Sea Folk. The little information that has leaked out reveals that the Sharans are ruled by a single absolute monarch, a Sh'boan if a woman and a Sh'botay if a man. That monarch rules for exactly seven years, then dies. The rule then passes to the mate of that ruler, who rules for seven years and then dies. This pattern has repeated itself since the time of the Breaking of the World. The

Sharans believe that the deaths are the "Will of the Pattern."

There are channelers in Shara, known as the Ayyad, who are tattooed on their faces at birth. The women of the Ayyad enforce the laws regarding the Ayyad stringently. A sexual relationship between Ayyad and non-Ayyad is punishable by death for the non-Ayyad, and the Ayyad is also executed if force on his or her part can be proven. If a child is born of the union, it is left exposed to the elements, and dies. Male Ayyad are used as breeding stock only. When they reach their twenty-first year or begin to channel, whichever comes first, they are killed by Ayyad women and the body cremated. Supposedly, the Ayyad channel the One Power only at the command of the Sh'boan or Sh'botay, who is always surrounded by Ayyad women.

Even the name of the land is in doubt. The natives have been known to call it many different names, including Shamara, Co'dansin, Tomaka, Kigali, and Shibouya.

Shen an Calhar: In the Old Tongue, "the Band of the Red Hand." (1) A legendary group of heroes who had many exploits, finally dying in the defense of Manetheren when that land was destroyed during the Trolloc Wars. (2) A military formation put together almost by accident by Mat Cauthon and organized along the lines of military forces during what is considered the height of the military arts, the days of Artur Hawkwing and the centuries immediately preceding. *See also* Redarms.

Sisnera, Darlin: A High Lord in Tear, he was formerly in rebellion against the Dragon Reborn, but now serves as Steward for the Dragon Reborn in Tear.

so'jhin: The closest translation from the Old Tongue would be "a height among lowness," though some translate it as meaning "both sky and valley" among several other possibilities. *So'jhin* is the term applied by the Seanchan to hereditary upper servants. They are *da'covale*, property, yet occupy positions of considerable authority and often power. Even the Blood step carefully around *so'jhin* of the Imperial family, and speak to *so'jhin* of the Empress herself as to equals. *See also* Blood, the; *da'covale*.

Stump: A public meeting among the Ogier. The meeting can be within or between *stedding*. It is presided over by the Council of Elders of a *stedding*, but any adult Ogier may speak, or may choose an advocate to speak for him. A Stump is often held at the largest tree stump in a *stedding,* and may last for several years. When a question arises that affects all Ogier, a Great Stump is held, and Ogier from all *stedding* meet to address the question. The various *stedding* take turns hosting a Great Stump.

Sword-Captain: *See* Lance-Captain.

Taborwin, Breane: Once a bored noblewoman in Cairhien, she lost her wealth and status and is now not only a servant, but in a serious romantic relationship with a man whom she once would have scorned.

Taborwin, Dobraine: A lord in Cairhien. He currently serves as Steward for the Dragon Reborn in Cairhien.

Tarabon: A nation on the Aryth Ocean. Once a great trading nation, a source of rugs, dyes and the Guild of Illuminators' fireworks among other things, Tarabon has fallen on hard times. Racked by anarchy and civil war compounded by simultaneous wars against Arad Doman and the Dragonsworn, it was ripe for the picking when the Seanchan arrived. It is now firmly under Seanchan control; the chapter house of the Guild of Illuminators has been destroyed and most Illuminators themselves made *da'covale*. Most Taraboners appear grateful that the Seanchan have restored order, and since the Seanchan allow them to continue living their lives with minimal interference, they have no desire to bring on more warfare by trying to chase the Seanchan out. There are, however, some lords and soldiers who remain outside the Seanchan sphere of influence and hope to reclaim their land.

wasp-jelly: A small aquatic creature that appears to be made of jelly but stings severely when touched.

weight, units of: 10 ounces = 1 pound; 10 pounds = 1 stone; 10 stone = 1 hundredweight; 10 hundredweight = 1 ton.

Wild Hunt, the: It is believed by many that the Dark One (often called Grim, or Old Grim, in Tear, Illian, Murandy, Altara and Ghealdan) rides out in the night with the "black dogs," or the Darkhounds, hunting souls. This is the Wild Hunt. It is believed by many that merely seeing the Wild Hunt pass means imminent death, either for the viewer or for someone dear to the viewer. It is held to be especially dangerous to meet the Wild Hunt at a crossroads, just before sunrise or just after sunset. *See also* Darkhounds.

Winged Guards, the: The personal bodyguards of the First of Mayene, and the elite military formation of Mayene. Members of the Winged Guards wear red-painted breastplates and red helmets shaped like rimmed pots that come down to the napes of their necks in the back, and carry red-streamered lances. Officers have wings worked on the sides of their helmets, and rank is denoted by slender plumes.

Wise Woman: Honorific used in Ebou Dar for women famed for their incredible abilities at healing almost any injury. A Wise Woman is traditionally marked by a red belt. While some have noted that many, indeed most, Ebou Dari Wise Women were not even from Altara, much less Ebou Dar, what was not known until recently, and still is known only to a few, is that all Wise Women are in fact Kinswomen and use various versions of Healing, giving out herbs and poultices only as a cover. With the flight of the Kin from Ebou Dar after the Seanchan took the city, no Wise Women remain there. *See also* Kin, the.

Younglings, the: The first Younglings were young men studying under the Warders at the White Tower. They fought against their teachers who attempted to free Siuan Sanche after she was deposed from the Amyrlin Seat. Led by Gawyn Trakand, the Younglings remained loyal to the White Tower, and fought skirmishes against Whitecloaks under Eamon Valda. They accompanied Elaida's embassy to the Dragon Reborn in Cairhien and saw action against the Aiel and Asha'man at Dumai's Wells. On their return to Tar Valon, they found themselves barred from the city.

The Younglings wear green cloaks with Gawyn's White Boar; those who fought against their teachers in Tar Valon wear a small silver tower on their collars. They accept recruits wherever they go, but they do not take veterans or older men. One requirement is that the recruit must be willing to put aside all loyalties except to the Younglings. Older members teach the new recruits Warder techniques since they have given over accepting instruction from Warders, and several have refused offers of bonding from Aes Sedai. In many ways they hardly seem attached to the Tower and Aes Sedai at all. This is a result in part of their suspicion that they were not meant to survive the expedition to Cairhien.

PROLOGUE

A preview of
Knife of Dreams

Book Eleven of
The Wheel of Time

Embers Falling on Dry Grass

The sun, climbing toward midmorning, stretched Galad's shadow and those of his three armored companions ahead of them as they trotted their mounts down the road that ran straight through the forest, dense with oak and leatherleaf, pine and sourgum, most showing the red of spring growth. He tried to keep his mind empty, still, but small things kept intruding. The day was silent save for the thud of their horses' hooves. No bird sang on a branch, no squirrel chittered. Too quiet for the time of year, as though the forest held its breath. This had been a major trade route once, long before Amadicia and Tarabon came into being, and bits of ancient paving stone sometimes studded the hard-packed surface of yellowish clay. A single farm cart far ahead behind a plodding ox was the only sign of human life now besides themselves. Trade had shifted far north, farms and villages in the region dwindled, and the fabled lost mines of Aelgar remained lost in the tangled mountain ranges that began only a few miles to the south. Dark clouds massing in that direction promised rain by afternoon if their slow advance continued. A red-winged hawk quartered back and forth along the border of the trees, hunting the fringes. As he himself was hunting. But at the heart, not on the fringes.

The manor house that the Seanchan had given Eamon Valda came into view, and he drew rein, wishing he had a helmet strap to tighten for excuse. Instead he had to be content with re-buckling his sword belt, pretending that it had been sitting wrong. There had been no point to wearing armor. If the morning went as he hoped, he would have had to remove breastplate and mail in any case, and if it went badly, armor would have provided little more protection than his white coat.

Formerly a deep-country lodge of the King of Amadicia, the building was a huge, blue-roofed structure studded with red-painted balconies, a wooden palace with wooden spires at the corners atop a stone foundation like a low, steep-sided hill. The outbuildings, stables and barns, workmen's small houses and craftsfolks' workshops, all hugged the ground in the wide clearing that surrounded the main house, but they were nearly as resplendent in their blue-and-red paint. A handful of men and women moved around them, tiny figures yet at this distance, and children were playing under their elders' eyes. An image of normality where nothing was normal. His companions sat their saddles in their burnished helmets and breastplates, watching him without expression. Their mounts stamped impatiently, the animals' morning freshness not yet worn off by the short ride from the camp.

"It's understandable if you're having second thoughts, Damodred," Trom said after a time. "It's a harsh accusation, bitter as gall, but—"

"No second thoughts for me," Galad broke in. His intentions had been fixed since yesterday. He was grateful, though. Trom had given him the opening he needed. They had simply appeared as he rode out, falling in with him without a word spoken. There had seemed no place for words, then. "But what about you three? You're taking a risk coming here with me. A risk you have no need to take. However the day runs, there will be marks against you. This is my business, and I give you leave to go about yours." Too stiffly said, but he could not find words this morning, or loosen his throat.

The stocky man shook his head. "The law is the law. And I might as well make use of my new rank." The three golden star-shaped knots of a captain sat beneath the flaring sunburst on the breast of his white cloak. There had been more than a few dead at Jeramel, including no fewer than three of the Lords Captain. They had been fighting the Seanchan then, not allied with them.

"I've done dark things in service to the Light," gaunt-faced Byar said grimly, his deep-set eyes glittering as though at a personal insult, "dark as moonless midnight, and likely I will again, but some things are too dark to be allowed." He looked as if he might spit.

"That's right," young Bornhald muttered, scrubbing a gauntleted hand across his mouth. Galad always thought of him as young, though the man lacked only a few years on him. Dain's eyes were bloodshot; he had been at the brandy again last night. "If you've done what's wrong, even in service to the Light, then you have to do what's right to balance it." Byar grunted sourly. Likely that was not the point he had been making.

"Very well," Galad said, "but there's no fault to any man who turns back. My business here is mine alone."

Still, when he heeled his bay gelding to a canter, he was pleased to have them gallop to catch him and fall in alongside, white cloaks billowing behind. He would have gone on alone, of course, yet their presence might keep him from being arrested and hanged out of hand. Not that he expected to survive in any case. What had to be done, had to be done, no matter the price.

The horses' hooves clattered loudly on the stone ramp that climbed to the manor house, so every man in the broad central courtyard turned to watch as they rode in: fifty of the Children in gleaming plate-and-mail and conical helmets, most mounted, with cringing, dark-coated Amadician grooms holding animals for the rest. The inner balconies were empty except for a few servants who appeared to be watching while pretending to sweep. Six Questioners, big men with the scarlet shepherd's crook upright behind the sunflare on their cloaks, stood close around Rhadam Asunawa like a bodyguard, away from the others. The Hand of the Light always stood apart from the rest of the Children, a choice the rest of the Children approved. Gray-haired Asunawa, his sorrowful face making Byar look fully fleshed, was the only Child present not in armor, and his snowy cloak carried just the brilliant red crook, another way of standing apart. But aside from marking who was present, Galad had eyes for only one man in the courtyard. Asunawa might have been involved in some way—that remained unclear—yet only the Lord Captain Commander could call the High Inquisitor to account.

Eamon Valda was not a large man, but his dark, hard face had the look of one who expected obedience as his due. As the very least he was due. Standing with his booted feet apart and his head high, command in every inch of him, he wore the white-and-gold tabard of the Lord Captain Commander over his gilded breast- and backplates, a silk tabard more richly embroidered than any Pedron Niall had worn. His white cloak, the flaring sun large on either breast in thread-of-gold, was silk as well, and his gold-embroidered white coat. The helmet beneath his arm was gilded and worked with the flaring sun on the brow, and a heavy gold ring on his left hand, worn outside his steel-backed gauntlet, held a large yellow sapphire carved with the sunburst. Another mark of favor received from the Seanchan.

Valda frowned slightly as Galad and his companions dismounted and offered their salutes, arm across the chest. Obsequious grooms came running to take their reins.

"Why aren't you on your way to Nassad, Trom?" Disapproval colored Valda's words. "The other Lords Captain will be halfway there by now." He himself always arrived late when meeting the Seanchan, perhaps to assert that some shred of independence remained to the Children—finding him already preparing to depart was a surprise; this meeting must be very important—but he always made sure the other high-ranking officers arrived on time even when that required setting out before dawn. Apparently it was best not to press their new masters too far. Distrust of the Children was always strong in the Seanchan.

Trom displayed none of the uncertainty that might have been expected from a man who had held his present rank barely a month. "An urgent matter, my Lord Captain Commander," he said smoothly, making a very precise bow, neither a hair deeper nor higher than protocol demanded. "A Child of my command charges another of the Children with abusing a female relative of his, and claims the right of Trial Beneath the Light, which by law you must grant or deny."

"A strange request, my son," Asunawa said, tilting his head quizzically above clasped hands, before Valda could speak. Even the High Inquisitor's voice was doleful; he sounded pained at Trom's ignorance. His eyes seemed dark hot coals in a brazier. "It was usually the accused who asked to give the judgment to swords, and I believe usually when he knew the evidence would convict him. In any case, Trial Beneath the Light has not been invoked for nearly four hundred years. Give me the accused's name, and I will deal with the matter quietly." His tone turned chill as a sunless cavern in winter, though his eyes still burned. "We are among strangers, and we cannot allow them to know that one of the Children is capable of such a thing."

"The request was directed to me, Asunawa," Valda snapped. His glare might as well have been open hatred. Perhaps it was just dislike of the other man's breaking in. Flipping one side of his cloak over his shoulder to bare his ring-quilloned sword, he rested his hand on the long hilt and drew himself up. Always one for the grand gesture, Valda raised his voice so that even people inside probably heard him, and declaimed rather than merely spoke.

"I believe many of our old ways should be revived, and that law still stands. It will always stand, as written of old. The Light grants justice because the Light is justice. Inform your man he may issue his challenge, Trom, and face the one he accuses sword-to-sword. If that one tries to refuse, I declare that he has acknowledged his guilt and order him hanged on the spot, his belongings and rank forfeit to his accuser as the law states. I have spoken." That with another scowl for the High Inquisitor. Maybe there really was hatred there.

Trom bowed formally once more. "You have informed him yourself, my Lord Captain Commander. Damodred?"

Galad felt cold. Not the cold of fear, but of emptiness. When Dain drunkenly let slip the confused rumors that had come to his ears, when Byar reluctantly confirmed they were more than rumors, rage had filled Galad, a bone-burning fire that nearly drove him insane. He had been sure his head would explode if his heart did not burst first. Now he was ice, drained of any emotion. He also bowed formally. Much of what he had to say was set in the law, yet he chose the rest with care, to spare as much shame as possible to a memory he held dear.

"Eamon Valda, Child of the Light, I call you to Trial Beneath the Light for unlawful assault on the person of Morgase Trakand, Queen of Andor, and for her murder." No one had been able to confirm that the woman he regarded as his mother was dead, yet it must be so. A dozen men were certain she had vanished from the Fortress of the Light before it fell to the Seanchan, and as many testified she had not been free to leave of her own will.

Valda displayed no shock at the charge. His smile might have been intended to show regret over Galad's folly in making such a claim, yet contempt was mingled in it. He opened his mouth, but Asunawa cut in once more.

"This is ridiculous," he said in tones more of sorrow than of anger. "Take the fool, and we'll find out what Darkfriend plot to discredit the Children he is part of." He motioned, and two of the hulking Questioners took a step toward Galad, one with a cruel grin, the other blank-faced, a workman about his work.

Only one step, though. A soft rasp repeated around the courtyard as Children eased their swords in their scabbards. At least a dozen men drew entirely, letting their blades hang by their sides. The Amadician grooms hunched in on themselves, trying to become invisible. Likely they would have run, had they dared. Asunawa stared around him, thick eyebrows climbing up his forehead in disbelief, knotted fists gripping his cloak. Strangely, even Valda appeared startled for an instant. Surely he had not expected the Children to allow an arrest after his own proclamation. If he had, he recovered quickly.

"You see, Asunawa," he said almost cheerfully, "the Children follow my orders, and the law, not a Questioner's whims." He held out his helmet to one side for someone to take. "I deny your preposterous charge, young Galad, and throw your foul lie in your teeth. For it is a lie, or at best a mad acceptance of some malignant rumor started by Darkfriends or others who wish the Children ill. Either way, you have defamed me in the vilest manner, so I accept your challenge to Trial Beneath the Light, where I will kill you." That barely squeezed into the ritual, but he had denied the charge and accepted the challenge; it would suffice.

Realizing that he still held the helmet in an outstretched hand, Valda frowned at one of the dismounted Children, a lean Saldaean named Kashgar, until the man stepped forward to relieve him of it. Kashgar was only an under-lieutenant, almost boyish despite a great hooked nose and thick mustaches like inverted horns, yet he moved with open reluctance, and Valda's voice was darker and acrid as he went on, unbuckling his sword belt and handing that over, too.

"Take a care with that, Kashgar. It's a heron-mark blade." Unpinning his silk cloak, he let it fall to the paving stones, followed by his tabard, and his hands moved to the buckles of his armor. It seemed that he was unwilling to see if others would be reluctant to help him. His face was calm enough, except that angry eyes promised retribution to more than Galad. "Your sister wants to become Aes Sedai, I understand, Damodred. Perhaps I understand precisely where this originated. There was a time I would have regretted your death, but not today. I may send your head to the White Tower so the witches can see the fruit of their scheme."

Worry creasing his face, Dain took Galad's cloak and sword belt, and stood shifting his feet as though uncertain he was doing the right thing. Well, he had been given his chance, and it was too late to change his mind, now. Byar put a gauntleted hand on Galad's shoulder and leaned close.

"He likes to strike at the arms and legs," he said in a low voice, casting glances over his shoulder at Valda. From the way he glared, some matter stood between them. Of course, that scowl differed little from his normal expression. "He likes to bleed an opponent until the man can't take a step or raise his sword before he moves for the kill. He's quicker than a viper, too, but he'll strike at your left most often and expect it from you."

Galad nodded. Many right-handed men found it easier to strike so, but it seemed an odd weakness in a blademaster. Gareth Bryne and Henre Haslin had made him practice alternating which hand was uppermost on the hilt so he would not fall into that. Strange that Valda wanted to prolong a fight, too. He himself had been taught to end matters as quickly and cleanly as possible.

"My thanks," he said, and the hollow-cheeked man made a dour grimace. Byar was far from likable, and he himself seemed to like no one save young Bornhald. Of the three, his presence was the biggest surprise, but he was there, and that counted in his favor.

Standing in the middle of the courtyard in his gold-worked white coat with his fists on his hips, Valda turned in a tight circle. "Everyone move back against the walls," he commanded loudly. Horseshoes rang on the paving stones as the Children and the grooms obeyed. Asunawa and his Questioners snatched their animals' reins, the High Inquisitor wearing a face of cold fury. "Keep the middle clear. Young Damodred and I will meet here—"

"Forgive me, my Lord Captain Commander," Trom said with a slight bow, "but since you are a participant in the Trial, you cannot be Arbiter. Aside from the High Inquisitor, who by law may not take part, I hold the highest rank here after you, so with your permission . . . ?" Valda glared at him, then stalked over to stand beside Kashgar, arms folded across his chest. Ostentatiously he tapped his foot, impatient for matters to proceed.

Galad sighed. If the day went against him, as seemed all but certain, his friend would have the most powerful man in the Children as his enemy. Likely Trom would have had in any event, but more so now. "Keep an eye on them," he told Bornhald, nodding toward the Questioners clustered on their horses near the gate. Asunawa's underlings still ringed him like bodyguards, every man with a hand on his sword hilt.

"Why? Even Asunawa can't interfere now. That would be against the law."

It was very hard not to sigh again. Young Dain had been a Child far longer than he, and his father had served his entire life, but the man seemed to know less of the Children than he himself had learned. To Questioners, the law was what they said it was. "Just watch them."

Trom stood in the center of the courtyard with his bared sword raised overhead, blade parallel to the ground, and unlike Valda, he spoke the words exactly as they were written. "Under the Light, we are gathered to witness Trial Beneath the Light, a sacred right of any Child of the Light. The Light shines on truth, and here the Light shall illuminate justice. Let no man speak save he who has legal right, and let any who seek to intervene be cut down summarily. Here, justice will be found under the Light by a man who pledges his life beneath the Light, by the force of his arm and the will of the Light. The combatants will meet unarmed where I now stand," he continued, lowering the sword to his side, "and speak privately, for their own ears alone. May the Light help them find words to end this short of bloodshed, for if they do not, one of the Children must die this day, his name stricken from our rolls and anathema declared on his memory. Under the Light, it will be so."

As Trom strode to the side of the courtyard, Valda moved toward the center in the walking stance called Cat Crosses the Courtyard, an arrogant saunter. He knew there were no words to stop blood being shed. To him, the fight had already begun. Galad merely walked out to meet him. He was nearly a head taller than Valda, but the other man held himself as though he were the larger, and confident of victory.

His smile was all contempt, this time. "Nothing to say, boy? Small wonder, considering that a blademaster is going to cut your head off in about one minute. I want one thing straight in your mind before I kill you, though. The wench was hale the last I saw her, and if she's dead now, I'll regret it." That smile deepened, both in humor and disdain. "She was the best ride I ever had, and I hope to ride her again one day."

Red-hot searing fury fountained inside Galad, but with an effort he managed to turn his back on Valda and walk away, already feeding his rage into an imagined flame as his two teachers had taught him. A man who fought in a rage, died in a rage. By the time he reached young Bornhald, he had achieved what Gareth and Henre had called the oneness. Floating in emptiness, he drew his sword from the scabbard Bornhald proffered, and the slightly curved blade became a part of him.

"What did he say?" Dain asked. "For a moment there, your face was murderous."

Byar gripped Dain's arm. "Don't distract him," he muttered.

Galad was not distracted. Every creak of saddle leather was clear and distinct, every ringing stamp of hoof on paving stone. He could hear flies buzzing ten feet away as though they were at his ear. He almost thought he could see the movements of their wings. He was one with the flies, with the courtyard, with the two men. They were all part of him, and he could not be distracted by himself.

Valda waited until he turned before drawing his own weapon on the other side of the courtyard, a flashy move, the sword blurring as it spun in his left hand, leaping to his right hand to make another blurred wheel in the air before settling, upright and rock steady before him, in both hands. He started forward, once more in Cat Crosses the Court-yard.

Raising his own sword, Galad moved to meet him, without thought assuming a walking stance perhaps influenced by his state of mind. Emptiness, it was called, and only a trained eye would know that he was not simply walking. Only a trained eye would see that he was in perfect balance every heartbeat. Valda had not gained that heron-mark sword by favoritism. Five blademasters had sat in judgment of his skills and voted unanimously to grant him the title. The vote always had to be unanimous. The only other way was to kill the bearer of a heron-mark blade in fair combat, one on one. Valda had been younger then than Galad was now. It did not matter. He was not focused on Valda's death. He focused on nothing. But he intended Valda's death if he had to Sheathe the Sword, will-ingly welcoming that heron-mark blade in his flesh, to achieve it. He accepted that it might come to that.

Valda wasted no time with maneuvering. The instant he was within range, Plucking the Low-hanging Apple flashed toward Galad's neck like lightning, as though the man truly did intend to have his head in the first minute. There were several possible responses, all made instinct by hard training, but Byar's warnings floated in the dim recesses of his mind, and also the fact that Valda had warned him of this very thing. Warned him twice. Without conscious thought, he chose another way, stepping sideways and for-ward just as Plucking the Low-hanging Apple became the Leopard's Caress. Valda's eyes widened in surprise as his stroke missed Galad's left thigh by inches, widened more as Parting the Silk laid a gash down his right forearm, but he immediately launched into the Dove Takes Flight, so fast that Galad had to dance back before his blade could bite deeply, barely fending off the attack with Kingfisher Circles the Pond.

Back and forth they danced the forms, gliding this way then that across the stone paving. Lizard in the Thornbush met Lightning of Three Prongs. Leaf on the Breeze coun-tered Eel Among the Lily Pads, and Two Hares Leaping met the Hummingbird Kisses the Honeyrose. Back and forth as smoothly as a demonstration of the forms. Galad tried attack after attack, but Valda *was* as fast as a viper. The Wood Grouse Dances cost him a shallow gash on his left shoulder, and the Red Hawk Takes a Dove another on the left arm, slightly deeper. River of Light might have taken the arm completely had he not met the draw-cut with a desperately quick Rain in High Wind. Back and forth, blades flashing continuously, filling the air with the clash of steel on steel.

How long they fought, he could not have said. There was no time, only the moment. It seemed that he and Valda moved like men under water, their motions slowed by the drag of the sea. Sweat appeared on Valda's face, but he smiled with self-assurance, seemingly untroubled by the slash on his forearm, still the only injury he had taken. Galad could feel the sweat rolling down his own face, too, stinging his eyes. And the blood trickling down his arm. Those wounds would slow him eventually, perhaps already had, but he had taken two on his left thigh, and both were more serious. His foot was wet in his boot from those, and he could not avoid a slight limp that would grow worse with time. If Valda was to die, it must be soon.

Deliberately, he drew a deep breath, then another, through his mouth, another. Let Valda think him becoming winded. His blade lanced out in Threading the Needle, aimed at Valda's left shoulder and not quite as fast as it could have been. The other man countered easily with the Swallow Takes Flight, sliding immediately into the Lion Springs. That took a third bite in his thigh; he dared not be faster in defense than in attack.

Again he launched Threading the Needle at Valda's shoulder, and again, again, all the while gulping air through his mouth. Only luck kept him from taking more wounds in those exchanges. Or perhaps the Light really did shine on this fight.

Valda's smile widened; the man believed him on the edge of his strength, exhausted and fixated. As Galad began Threading the Needle, too slowly, for the fifth time, the other man's sword started the Swallow Takes Flight in an almost perfunctory manner. Summoning all the quickness that remained to him, Galad altered his stroke, and Reaping the Barley sliced across Valda just beneath his rib cage.

For a moment it seemed that the man was unaware he had been hit. He took a step, began what might have been Stones Falling from the Cliff. Then his eyes widened, and he staggered, the sword falling from his grip to clatter on the paving stones as he sank to his knees. His hands went to the huge gash across his body as though trying to hold his insides within him, and his mouth opened, glassy eyes fixed on Galad's face. Whatever he intended to say, it was blood that poured out over his chin. He toppled onto his face and lay still.

Automatically, Galad gave his blade a rapid twist to shake off the blood staining its final inch, then bent slowly to wipe the last drops onto Valda's white coat. The pain he had ignored now flared. His left shoulder and arm burned; his thigh seemed to be on fire. Straightening took effort. Perhaps he was nearer exhaustion than he had thought. How long *had* they fought? He had thought he would feel satisfaction that his mother had been avenged, but all he felt was emptiness. Valda's death was not enough. Nothing except Morgase Trakand alive again could be enough.

Suddenly he became aware of a rhythmic clapping and looked up to see the Children, each man slapping his own armored shoulder in approval. Every man. Except Asunawa and the Questioners. They were nowhere to be seen.

Byar hurried up carrying a small leather sack and carefully parted the slashes in Galad's coatsleeve. "Those will need sewing," he muttered, "but they can wait." Kneeling beside Galad, he took rolled bandages from the sack and began winding them around the gashes in his thigh. "These need sewing, too, but this will keep you from bleeding to death before you can get it." Others began gathering around, offering congratulations, men afoot in front, those still mounted behind. None gave the corpse a glance except for Kashgar, who cleaned Valda's sword on that already bloodstained coat before sheathing it.

"Where did Asunawa go?" Galad asked.

"He left as soon as you cut Valda the last time," Dain replied uneasily. "He'll be heading for the camp to bring back Questioners."

"He rode the other way, toward the border," someone put in. Nassad lay just over the border.

"The Lords Captain," Galad said, and Trom nodded.

"No Child would let the Questioners arrest you for what

happened here, Damodred. Unless his captain ordered it. Some of them would order it, I think." Angry muttering began, men denying they would stand for such a thing, but Trom quieted them, somewhat, with raised hands. "You know it's true," he said loudly. "Anything else would be mutiny." That brought dead silence. There had never been a mutiny in the Children. It was possible that nothing before had come as close as their own earlier display. "I'll write out your release from the Children, Galad. Someone may still order your arrest, but they'll have to find you, and you'll have a good start. It will take half the day for Asunawa to catch the other Lords Captain, and whoever falls in with him can't be back before nightfall."

Galad shook his head angrily. Trom was right, but it was all wrong. Too much was wrong. "Will you write releases for these other men? You know Asunawa will find a way to accuse them, too. Will you write releases for the Children who don't want to help the Seanchan take our lands in the name of a man dead more than a thousand years?" Several Taraboners exchanged glances and nodded, and so did other men, not all of them Amadician. "What about the men who defended the Fortress of the Light? Will any release get their chains struck off or make the Seanchan stop working them like animals?" More angry growls; those prisoners were a sore point to all of the Children.

Arms folded across his chest, Trom studied him as though seeing him for the first time. "What would you do, then?"

"Have the Children find someone, anyone, who is fighting the Seanchan and ally with them. Make sure that the Children of the Light ride in the Last Battle instead of helping the Seanchan hunt Aiel and steal our nations."

"Anyone?" a Cairhienin named Doirellin said in a high-pitched voice. No one ever made fun of Doirellin's voice. Though short, he was nearly as wide as he was tall, there was barely an ounce of fat on him, and he could put walnuts between all of his fingers and crack them by clenching his fists. "That could mean Aes Sedai."

"If you intend to be at Tarmon Gai'don, then you will have to fight alongside Aes Sedai," Galad said quietly. Young Bornhald grimaced in strong distaste, and he was not the only one. Byar half-straightened before bending back to his task.

But no one voiced dissent. Doirellin nodded slowly, as if he had never before considered the matter.

"I don't hold with the witches any more than any other man," Byar said finally, without raising his head from his work. Blood was seeping through the bandages even as he wrapped. "But the Precepts say, to fight the raven, you may make alliance with the serpent until the battle is done." A ripple of nods ran through the men. The raven meant the Shadow, but everyone knew it was also the Seanchan Imperial sigil.

"I'll fight beside the witches," a lanky Taraboner said, "or even these Asha'man we keep hearing about, if they fight the Seanchan. Or at the Last Battle. And I'll fight any man who says I'm wrong." He glared as though ready to begin then and there.

"It seems matters will play out as you wish, my Lord Captain Commander," Trom said, making a much deeper bow than he had for Valda. "To a degree, at least. Who can say what the next hour will bring, much less tomorrow?"

Galad surprised himself by laughing. Since yesterday, he had been sure he would never laugh again. "That's a poor joke, Trom."

"It is how the law is written. And Valda did make his proclamation. Besides, you had the courage to say what many have thought while holding their tongues, myself among them. Yours is a better plan for the Children than any I've heard since Pedron Niall died."

"It's still a poor joke." Whatever the law said, that part had been ignored since the end of the War of the Hundred Years.

"We'll see what the Children have to say on the matter," Trom replied, grinning widely, "when you ask them to follow us to Tarmon Gai'don to fight alongside the witches."

Men began slapping their shoulders again, harder than they had for his victory. At first it was only a few, then more joined in, until every man including Trom was signaling approval. Every man but Kashgar, that was. Making a deep bow, the Saldaean held out the scabbarded heron-mark blade with both hands.

"This is yours, now, my Lord Captain Commander."

Galad sighed. He hoped this nonsense would fade away

before they reached the camp. Returning there was foolish enough without adding in a claim of that sort. Most likely they would be pulled down and thrown in chains if not beaten to death even without it. But he had to go. It was the right thing to do.